利用不同感官之間的協作來高效學習吧！

Memorize 7000 Vocabularies Once and for All !

五感 學+練

7000 英單

過腦不忘強記術

張翔 / 著

USER'S GUIDE

通通看過來，強記術的秘密在這裡～

強記秘密 1

隨掃隨聽，單詞例句音檔連結

單字，如果知道怎麼唸，很容易就背得起來！每個單元附音檔 QR Code，讓您能隨時隨地用耳朵「聽」單字，強化記憶。

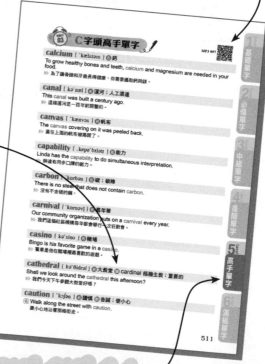

強記秘密 2

不只標明詞性，還提供關聯詞與同反義詞

整理單字之間的結構或意義，能減輕背誦的負擔。在詞性說明的旁邊，會適時附有「**關聯詞**」、「**同義詞**」、「**反義詞**」，讓您掌握詞彙間的關聯性，背誦省時，不再痛苦。

強記秘密 3

精選 7000 英單，完全命中

依據教育部公布的 7000 單字，按照**難易程度適當劃分等級**，讓您按部就班學習，不再有挫折感！

文法句型補充，單字靈活運用

強記秘密 4

單字，不只要會認，也要會用！例句下方的「**文法解析**」，提點搭配的介係詞或某些動詞的不規則三態變化；「**焦點句型**」，說明應用該單詞的句型架構，使您精準表達和運用。

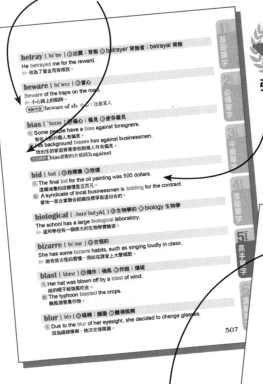

依照詞性提供例句，用法一目瞭然

強記秘密 5

例句可以幫助記憶單字。若一個單字具有多種詞性，本書則**會依照詞性列舉不同的例句**。了解不同的用法，能夠使您的英文表達豐富多樣，不呆板！

精選試題，驗收成效

強記秘密 6

本書後面的練習題，讓您檢測實力！題目亦附解析和補充，使您的**詞彙量進一步增加**，練習同時也在學習！

利用不同感官之間的協作來高效學習吧！

　　字彙量對於學習任何語言來說，都是最重要的基礎。單字在英文中就像是要進行烹飪時，食材所扮演的角色——即使廚藝再怎麼高超，若是沒有食材，也會面臨「巧婦難為無米之炊」的窘境。文法或其他較高階的能力如同廚藝一般，固然重要，但若沒有足夠的詞彙作為基礎，也沒有施展空間。然而背誦單字總令人望而生畏，一翻開單字書就是密密麻麻的複雜單字，過程又是枯燥乏味，讓背單字如同折磨一般，而單字背不好又會影響到英文整體表現，讓人對學習英文生出滿滿的挫敗感。

　　這些問題我也曾深有體會，因此更希望廣大學生們能不受背誦單字所困擾。我個人的學習經驗是，單字的拼法與視覺記憶是最表層也是最單純的一步，若想進一步加深印象，讓短期記憶轉化為長期記憶，一方面可以透過聲音記憶，如多聽單字發音來達成，一方面則是要能看到這個單字在文章句子中是如何使用的，而這些過程重複多次後就會很難忘記了。

　　而語言習得有一個很重要的理論，那就是輸出與輸入都很重要。因此在上述的聽與讀之外，也要記得同時說與寫，因為在輸出的過程中，會進一步去消化輸入學到的內容並重新組織，這對於學習單字的幫助也非常顯著。而本書強調同時運用不同感官，同時兼顧輸入與輸出來深化背誦記憶，除了讓學生能以更高的效率學習單字，也希望讀者能在學習之餘，找到學習的樂趣。

張 翔

目 CONTENTS 錄

7000 Essential
Vocabulary for
High School Students

Basic Vocabulary

LEVEL
1

基礎單字

單字難易度 ★☆☆☆☆
文法難易度 ★★★☆☆
生活出現頻率 ★★★★★
考題出題頻率 ★★☆☆☆

名 名詞　動 動詞　形 形容詞　副 副詞　介 介係詞　連 連接詞
代 代名詞　助 助動詞　嘆 感嘆詞　關 相關單字 / 片語
同 同義詞　反 反義詞

ability [ə`bɪlətɪ] 名 能力；能耐

She has an extraordinary ability to whistle and sing at the same time.
▶▶ 她有同時吹口哨和唱歌的特別才能。

able [`ebḷ] 形 能幹的；有能力的

I will be able to solve the problem soon.
▶▶ 我很快就能解決掉這個問題。
焦點句型 **be able to V.** 能夠⋯

about [ə`baʊt] 介 大約；關於

Let's talk about something else.
▶▶ 讓我們談談別的事吧。

above [ə`bʌv] 副 在上面 介 在⋯上面

副 There are snowy peaks above.
上面是白雪皚皚的群峰。
介 There is a mirror above the washbasin.
在洗臉盆上方有一面鏡子。

abroad [ə`brɔd] 副 在國外；到國外

Diana decided to study abroad after graduating from college.
▶▶ 黛安娜決定大學畢業後就出國念書。

across [ə`krɔs] 介 橫越；穿過

We walked across the street.
▶▶ 我們穿越了馬路。

act [ækt] 名 行為；行動 動 行動；做事

名 My first act was to run into the classroom.
我做的第一件事便是跑進教室。
動 We should act immediately.
我們應該立即行動。

action [`ækʃən] 名 行動；活動

Now is the time for action.
▶▶ 現在是採取行動的時候了。

actor / actress [`æktə] / [`æktrɪs] 名演員 / 女演員

He was considered the best actor in America.
▶▶ 他被認為是全美國最出色的演員。

add [æd] 動增加；添加

The noise of the crowd added to the excitement of the race.
▶▶ 人群的嘈雜聲為賽事增添了興奮的氣氛。

afraid [ə`fred] 形害怕的

Are you afraid of dogs?
▶▶ 你怕狗嗎？
焦點句型 be afraid of +名詞，be afraid 之後亦可接 that 子句。

after [`æftə] 介在…以後 連在…之後

介 I hope to arrive sometime after lunch.
我希望午飯後可以到達。
連 After he reached the age of 68, his health got worse.
在年齡過了六十八歲後，他的健康每況愈下。

afternoon [`æftə`nun] 名下午

I'll leave for New York this afternoon.
▶▶ 我今天下午將前往紐約。
文法解析 leave 的意思為「離開」，leave for 則表示「前往」，例：leave Taipei（離開臺北）、leave for Taipei（前往臺北）。

again [ə`gɛn] 副再一次

She's out at the moment, so I'll phone again later.
▶▶ 她現在不在，我稍後再打電話給她。

age [edʒ] 名年齡 動使變老

名 What's the age of that old building?
那棟古老的建築有多少年的歷史了呢？
動 I could see her illness had aged her.
我看得出來，她生病以後老了很多。

ago [ə`go] 副在…以前

We toured France about three years ago.
▶▶ 我們大約三年前去法國遊玩過。

agree [əˋgri] 動 同意 關 agreement 同意；一致

This bill does not agree with your original estimate.
▶▶ 這張帳單與你當初的估計不符。

(焦點句型) agree with sb./sth. 同意…；和…一致

air [ɛr] 名 空氣；天空

The air in the city is severely polluted.
▶▶ 這座城市的空氣汙染程度非常嚴重。

airplane / plane [ˋɛrˏplen] / [plen] 名 飛機

The airplane cleaved the clouds.
▶▶ 那架飛機鑽入雲中。

airport [ˋɛrˏport] 名 機場；航空站

I'm waiting for Mr. Brown in the airport lounge.
▶▶ 我在機場的候機室等候布朗先生。

all [ɔl] 形 所有的；全部的 副 完全地；全然地 名 全部

形 Our aim is that all children complete secondary education.
　　我們的宗旨是讓所有孩童完成中等教育。
副 The water went all over her skirt.
　　水全灑在她的裙子上。
名 Tom had lost all of his things.
　　湯姆失去了他所有的東西。

allow [əˋlau] 動 允許；准許

My boss allows us to smoke here.
▶▶ 老闆允許我們在這裡抽菸。

almost [ˋɔlˏmost] 副 幾乎；差不多

It was almost dark when they got there.
▶▶ 他們抵達那裡時，天幾乎都要黑了。

along [əˋlɔŋ] 副 向前 介 沿著

副 He sang loudly as he walked along.
　　他邊向前走邊大聲唱歌。
介 He drives a car along the river.
　　他沿著河開車。

already [ɔlˋrɛdɪ] 副 已經

He had already gone when I arrived.
▶▶ 當我抵達時，他已經走了。

also [ˋɔlso] 副 也；還

Since you've accepted the invitation, I'll also accept it.
▶▶ 既然你已接受邀請，那我也會接受。

although [ɔlˋðo] 連 雖然；儘管

Although Dan is very poor, he works hard to earn a living.
▶▶ 雖然丹很窮，但他努力工作、賺錢維生。

always [ˋɔlwez] 副 總是 關 all the time 一直；向來

The boys always make fun of Mr. Smith.
▶▶ 那群男孩總是嘲弄史密斯先生。
文法解析 make fun of sb. 表示「嘲笑、嘲弄某人」，帶有負面含意。

and [ænd] 連 和；及；與

My mother and father have never agreed on this matter.
▶▶ 我父母在這件事情上的意見從未一致過。

angry [ˋæŋgrɪ] 形 生氣的 關 angrily 生氣地 / anger 憤怒

The professor was angry at John for cheating on the exam.
▶▶ 教授對約翰在考試中作弊感到十分生氣。
焦點句型 be angry at sb. 對某人生氣

animal [ˋænəml̩] 名 動物 關 predator 掠食者

Animals obey their instincts.
▶▶ 動物是依循著本能行動的。

another [əˋnʌðɚ] 形 另一的；再一的 代 另一個；再一個

形 He drank another cup of coffee.
他又喝了一杯咖啡。
代 I don't like this one. Please show me another.
我不喜歡這個，請給我看另一個。

Level 1 基礎單字
Level 2 必備單字
Level 3 中級單字
Level 4 進階單字
Level 5 高手單字
Level 6 滿級單字

answer [ˈænsɚ] 名 答案 動 回答

名 This answer is correct.
這個答案是正確的。

動 I asked her what the matter was, but she didn't answer.
我問她發生了什麼事，但她沒有回答。

ant [ænt] 名 螞蟻

He flicked an ant off the table.
▶▶ 他把桌上的螞蟻彈掉。

any [ˈɛnɪ] 形 任何的；任一的 代 任何人；任何一個

形 I don't have any money.
我沒有任何錢了。

代 Richard is taller than any of us.
理查比我們當中任何人都高。

anybody / anyone [ˈɛnɪˌbɑdɪ] / [ˈɛnɪˌwʌn] 代 任何人

Luke doesn't believe anybody.
▶▶ 路克不相信任何人。

anything [ˈɛnɪˌθɪŋ] 名 任何事（物）

I don't know anything.
▶▶ 我什麼都不知道。

apartment [əˈpɑrtmənt] 名 公寓

Sam lives alone in an apartment.
▶▶ 山姆獨自住在公寓裡。

appear [əˈpɪr] 動 出現；顯露

The defendant failed to appear in court.
▶▶ 被告未出庭。

apple [ˈæpḷ] 名 蘋果

Throw away the apple because it is rotten.
▶▶ 丟掉那顆蘋果吧，它都已經爛掉了。

area [`ɛrɪə] 名 地區；區域

There were over two inches of rain in coastal areas.

▶▶ 沿海地區的降雨量超過了兩英寸。

arm [ɑrm] 名 手臂

There must be something wrong with my left arm because it is numb.

▶▶ 我的左手臂一定出了什麼問題，因為它現在發麻。

around [ə`raʊnd] 副 在周圍；到處 介 在…周圍；圍繞

副 I heard laughter all around.
我聽到周圍的笑聲。

介 The sunshine is all around us.
陽光圍繞著我們。

arrive [ə`raɪv] 動 到達 關 pickup 接送；搭車地點

The ceremony did not begin until the host arrived.

▶▶ 主持人抵達之後，典禮才開始。

art [ɑrt] 名 藝術

Art lies in concealing the fact that it is art.

▶▶ 藝術妙在含蓄而不顯露。

as [æz] 連 當…的時候 副 像…一樣地 介 作為；以…的身分

連 The phone rang just as I was leaving the house.
我正要出門時，電話就響起來了。

副 Tony is as tall as his father.
東尼和他的爸爸一樣高。

介 She works as an interpreter in that company.
她在那間公司擔任口譯員。

ask [æsk] 動 詢問；要求

She asked me to drive her home.

▶▶ 她要求我開車載她回家。

(焦點句型) ask sb. to V. 要求某人做某事

at [æt] 介 在…地點或時刻

A red bus is stopping at the bus stop.

▶▶ 一輛紅色的公車正停在公車站。

attack [əˋtæk] 動攻擊 名攻擊 關 media 媒體

動 The governor was attacked by the media for lying.
　州長因為說謊而受到媒體抨擊。
名 How can we stop their attack?
　我們該如何阻止他們的攻擊呢？

aunt [ænt] 名伯母；姑姑；阿姨；嬸嬸

I inherited this car from my aunt.
▶▶ 我從我阿姨那裡繼承了這台車。

away [əˋwe] 副遠離；離開

An apple a day keeps the doctor away.
▶▶ 一天一蘋果，醫生遠離我。

UNIT 02　B字頭基礎單字

MP3 002

baby [ˋbebɪ] 名嬰兒

Some babies cry during the night.
▶▶ 有些嬰兒夜裡會哭鬧不休。

back [bæk] 副後退地 名背部 動使後退 形後面的

副 Please go back three steps.
　請退後三步。
名 A camel has a hump on its back.
　駱駝的背上有個駝峰。

bad [bæd] 形壞的；不好的；不健全的

I'm afraid I've got some bad news for you.
▶▶ 我恐怕要告訴你一些壞消息。

bag [bæg] 名袋子 關 hermetically 密封地 / seal 封

This bag is hermetically sealed.
▶▶ 這個袋子封得死死的。

ball [bɔl] 名球；球狀體 動使成球形

The two boys are kicking a ball on the grass.
▶▶ 兩個男孩正在草地上踢球。

banana [bəˋnænə] 名 香蕉

There are two bunches of bananas on the table.
▶▶ 桌子上放著兩串香蕉。

band [bænd] 名 樂隊 關 drown out 壓過…的聲音

The band drowned out our conversation.
▶▶ 樂隊的演奏聲蓋過了我們的談話聲。

bank [bæŋk] 名 銀行；河堤

My salary is paid directly into my bank account.
▶▶ 我的薪水直接存入我的銀行帳戶。

baseball [ˋbesˌbɔl] 名 棒球 關 inning（棒球的）一局

Baseball is very popular in America.
▶▶ 棒球在美國很受歡迎。

basket [ˋbæskɪt] 名 籃子

Mary came up to me, carrying a basket of apples.
▶▶ 瑪莉提著一籃蘋果向我走來。

basketball [ˋbæskɪtˌbɔl] 名 籃球

The boys always play basketball in the afternoon.
▶▶ 這些男孩總是在下午打籃球。

bat [bæt] 名 蝙蝠；球棒

A bat can fly in the dark.
▶▶ 蝙蝠能在暗處飛。

bath [bæθ] 名 洗澡；浴缸

I like to take a bath or shower to relieve my pain.
▶▶ 我喜歡透過泡澡和淋浴忘卻討厭的事物。

bathroom [ˋbæθˌrum] 名 浴室

Lucy is taking a shower in the bathroom.
▶▶ 露西正在浴室淋浴。

Level 1 基礎單字
Level 2 必備單字
Level 3 中級單字
Level 4 進階單字
Level 5 高手單字
Level 6 滿級單字

beach [bitʃ] 名海灘 關 pleasant 舒適的 / ambiance 氣氛

The little beach hotel has a pleasant ambiance.
▶▶ 這家濱海小旅館的氛圍舒適宜人。

bean [bin] 名豆子

Does she like beans or peas?
▶▶ 她喜歡吃蠶豆還是豌豆呢？

bear [bɛr] 名熊 動忍受

名 I like that Teddy Bear a lot.
　　我非常喜歡那隻泰迪熊。
動 He could not bear that his friends should laugh at him.
　　他受不了朋友們竟然嘲笑他。

beautiful [`bjutəfəl] 形美麗的；漂亮的

The view from the top of the hill is really beautiful.
▶▶ 從山頂往下看，風景真美。

because [bɪ`kɔz] 連因為

They didn't go for a walk because it was raining.
▶▶ 因為下著雨，所以他們沒有去散步。

become [bɪ`kʌm] 動變得；變成

They have become good friends.
▶▶ 他們變成了好朋友。
文法解析 become 動詞三態變化為 become / became / become。

bed [bɛd] 名床 關 go to bed 睡覺

What time do you usually go to bed?
▶▶ 你通常幾點會上床睡覺呢？

bedroom [`bɛdˌrum] 名臥房；寢室

You are not allowed to enter Amy's bedroom.
▶▶ 你沒被允許進入艾咪的臥房。

bee [bi] 名蜜蜂

Mr. Anderson is as busy as a bee.
▶▶ 安德森先生像蜜蜂般忙碌。

beef [bif] 名牛肉

Many farmers avoid eating beef.
▶▶ 很多農夫不吃牛肉。

before [brˋfor] 介在…之前 連在…以前 副以前；曾經

介 Only two days remained before the examination.
距離考試只剩下兩天的時間了。

連 Check it carefully before you hand it in.
繳交上來之前，要仔細核對一下。

副 I think we've met somewhere before.
我覺得我們以前似乎在哪裡見過面。

begin [brˋgɪn] 動開始；著手

He is about to begin his term as president.
▶▶ 他的總統任期即將開始。

文法解析 begin 動詞三態變化為 begin / began / begun。

behind [brˋhaɪnd] 介在…的後面；在…的背後 副在後面

介 There's a small garden behind the house.
這棟房子後面有一座小花園。

副 Danny drove, and his son sat behind.
丹尼開車，而他的兒子坐在後座。

believe [brˋliv] 動相信；信任

I know you don't believe me, but please hear me out.
▶▶ 我知道你不相信我，但請聽我把話說完。

焦點句型 hear sb. out 聽某人把話說完

bell [bɛl] 名鈴；鐘

He awoke to the ringing bell of an alarm.
▶▶ 他被鬧鐘的鈴聲喚醒。

belong [bəˋlɔŋ] 動屬於 片belong to 屬於；是…的成員

They belong to a younger generation.
▶▶ 他們屬於較年輕的一代。

below [bəˋlo] 介在…下面；在…以下 副在下方；到下面

介 Their language development is below average.
他們的語言發展低於一般水準。

Level 1 基礎單字
Level 2 必備單字
Level 3 中級單字
Level 4 進階單字
Level 5 高手單字
Level 6 滿級單字

belt [bɛlt] 名 皮帶；腰帶 動 用帶子束緊

I need a belt to keep up my trousers.
▶▶ 我需要一條腰帶繫緊褲子。

bench [bɛntʃ] 名 長凳；長椅

The old couple sat on the bench chatting.
▶▶ 這對老夫婦坐在長椅上聊天。

beside [bɪ`saɪd] 介 在⋯旁邊

Come and sit beside me.
▶▶ 過來坐在我旁邊。

best [bɛst] 形 最好的 副 最好地 名 最好

形 I think Suzy's plan is the best.
我認為蘇西的方案最好。
副 Tony works best in the morning.
東尼早上的工作效率最好。

between [bɪ`twin] 介 （時間、空間等）在⋯之間 副 在中間

There was a break between our meeting and the lecture.
▶▶ 我們的會議和講座之間有休息時間。

bicycle / bike [`baɪsɪkḷ] / [baɪk] 名 腳踏車

He lost control of his bicycle and fell down.
▶▶ 他因控制不住他的腳踏車而跌倒。
焦點句型 lose control of sth. 失去對某物的控制

big [bɪg] 形 大的；巨大的；主要的 關 margin 差數；邊緣

The bill was approved by a big margin.
▶▶ 議案以絕對性優勢獲得多數人的贊同通過。

bird [bɝd] 名 鳥

Lucy keeps a pair of little birds.
▶▶ 露西養著一對小鳥。

bite [baɪt] 名咬；一口之量 動咬；啃

名 The dog gave the postal worker a nasty bite.
那隻狗猛咬了郵局人員一口。
動 The dog bit him and made his hand bleed.
那隻狗把他的手咬得鮮血直流。
文法解析 bite動詞三態變化為 bite / bit / bitten。

black [blæk] 形黑色的 名黑色

▶▶ Coal is black.
煤炭是黑的。

blind [blaɪnd] 形瞎的 動使看不見

I turn a blind eye to her behavior.
▶▶ 我假裝沒看到她的行為。
焦點句型 turn a blind eye to sth. 對…視而不見

block [blɑk] 名街區 動阻塞；封鎖

名 The store is three blocks away.
那家商店離這裡有三條街遠。
動 The police blocked off the street after the accident.
意外發生之後，警方封鎖了那條街。

blow [blo] 動吹動；颳（風）

A breeze blew over the garden.
▶▶ 一陣微風吹過花園。
文法解析 blow動詞三態變化為 blow / blew / blown。

blue [blu] 形藍色的 名藍色

He is wearing a white T-shirt and blue jeans.
▶▶ 他穿了一件白色 T 恤和藍色牛仔褲。
文法解析 名詞用法如 be dressed in blue，表示「穿藍色衣服」。

boat [bot] 名小船

We crossed the river in a boat.
▶▶ 我們搭乘一艘小船過河。

body [`bɑdɪ] 名 身體；主體

You can imprison my body but not my soul.
▶▶ 你可以禁錮我的身體，卻束縛不了我的心靈。

book [buk] 名 書本 動 預訂；預約 關 paperback 平裝本

名 She has written several books on the subject.
她已經寫了好幾本有關這方面的書了。
動 I want to book this traveling group.
我想要預約這個旅行團。

bore [bor] 動 使厭煩 關 bored 感到無聊的 / boring 令人覺得無聊的

I don't have any interest in government class; it bores me a lot.
▶▶ 我對政府管理學沒什麼興趣，它令我感到無聊。

born [bɔrn] 形 天生的；出生的

Jenny was considered a born movie star.
▶▶ 珍妮被視為天生的電影明星。

borrow [`bɑro] 動 借入

I borrowed the magazine from my classmate.
▶▶ 我的這本雜誌是跟同學借的。
(焦點句型) borrow sth. from sb. 從某人那裡借東西

boss [bɔs] 名 老闆 動 指揮

名 The boss made his employees work hard.
那名老闆讓他底下的員工都努力工作。
動 Jack usually bosses around others.
傑克經常對他人頤指氣使。
(焦點句型) boss around sb. 指揮某人（動詞片語）

both [boθ] 代 兩者；兩個 副 兩者皆 形 兩個都

代 Both of them are dead.
他們雙方都死了。
副 We like Nancy and Tom both.
南西和湯姆兩個我們都喜歡。
形 Both his parents are living.
他的雙親都健在。

Level 1 基礎單字

Level 2 必備單字

Level 3 中級單字

Level 4 進階單字

Level 5 高手單字

Level 6 滿級單字

bottle [ˋbɑtl̩] 名 瓶子 動 用瓶裝

名 The drunk man used a bottle as a pillow and fell asleep.
醉漢拿了一個瓶子充當枕頭，並睡著了。

動 I don't know when this wine was bottled.
我不知道這酒是何時裝瓶的。

bottom [ˋbɑtəm] 名 底部 形 底部的

名 There is some tea left in the bottom of your cup.
你的杯底剩下一些茶。

形 The bottom layer is a mixture of sand and clay.
最下面的一層是沙和泥的混合物。

bow [baʊ] 動 向下彎 名 彎腰；鞠躬

動 He bowed to show respect.
他彎下身來，以示尊敬。

名 He felt great pain in his back with a mere bow.
只要一彎腰，他的背部就一陣劇痛。

bowl [bol] 名 碗

Would you like another bowl of soup?
▸▸ 你想要再喝一碗湯嗎？

box [bɑks] 名 盒子；箱 動 裝箱

名 Mother brought home a box of chocolates.
媽媽帶了一盒巧克力回家。

動 Strawberries are usually boxed before being shipped to market.
在運往市場前，通常會先將草莓裝箱。

boy [bɔɪ] 名 男孩

I used to play here when I was a little boy.
▸▸ 小時候我經常在這裡玩耍。

文法解析 **sb. used to + V** 用以表示「以前的習慣」，**to** 為不定詞，後接原形動詞；**sb. be used to + Ving** 則為「現在習慣」，此時 **to** 為介係詞，後接名詞或動名詞。

brave [brev] 形 勇敢的

Larry is a brave boy.
▸▸ 賴瑞是個勇敢的男孩。

bread [brɛd] 名麵包

Would you like a piece of bread?
▶▶ 你想來一片麵包嗎？

break [brek] 名休息；裂口 動打破

名 Take a break and have a cup of tea.
休息一下，喝杯茶。
動 If you break that vase, you'll have to pay for it.
假如你打破了那個花瓶，就得賠償。
文法解析 break 的動詞三態變化為 break / broke / broken。

breakfast [`brɛkfəst] 名早餐 動吃早餐

What do you usually have for breakfast?
▶▶ 你早餐通常都吃些什麼呢？

bridge [brɪdʒ] 名橋；橋梁 動架橋於

名 Do you know any famous bridges?
你知道任何有名的橋嗎？
動 They chopped down a tree to bridge the stream.
為了在溪流上架橋，他們砍下了一棵樹。

bright [braɪt] 形明亮的；（顏色）鮮亮的

It's a bright, sunny day.
▶▶ 今天陽光普照。

bring [brɪŋ] 動帶來；拿來 同 incur 招致

I hope Chris hasn't brought his brother with him.
▶▶ 我希望克里斯沒有帶著他的弟弟。
文法解析 bring 動詞三態變化為 bring / brought / brought。

brother [`brʌðɚ] 名兄弟

It is your little brother on the phone.
▶▶ 你的弟弟打電話找你。

brown [braʊn] 形褐色的；棕色的 名褐色

Tom often wears a pair of brown shoes.
▶▶ 湯姆經常穿一雙棕色的鞋子。

bug [bʌg] 名 小蟲 關 on the fly 在飛行

The bird caught a bug on the fly.
▶▶ 那鳥在飛行中捉住了一隻昆蟲。

build [bɪld] 動 建立；建築

His ambition is to build his own house.
▶▶ 他的雄心是建造一棟屬於自己的房子。
文法解析 build 動詞三態變化為 build / built / built。

bus [bʌs] 名 公車

I met Johnny on the bus last night.
▶▶ 我昨晚在公車上碰見強尼。

business [`bɪznɪs] 名 商業；生意；職業

The business plan was made by the government.
▶▶ 這個商業計畫是由政府制定的。

busy [`bɪzɪ] 形 繁忙的；忙碌的

I was busy all day today.
▶▶ 我今天一整天都很忙。

but [bʌt] 連 但是 介 除了…以外 副【俚】僅僅；只

連 I was going to write, but I lost your address.
　 我本來要寫信的，可是我把你的地址弄丟了。
介 No one knows the secret but me.
　 除了我以外，沒人知道這個祕密。

butter [`bʌtɚ] 名 奶油

Don't eat too much butter.
▶▶ 別吃太多奶油。

butterfly [`bʌtɚˌflaɪ] 名 蝴蝶

The caterpillar turned into a butterfly.
▶▶ 毛毛蟲變成了蝴蝶。

buy [baɪ] 動 買；購買 名 購買

I bought this book for you in London.
▶▶ 我在倫敦買了這本書給你。

Level 1 基礎單字
Level 2 必備單字
Level 3 中級單字
Level 4 進階單字
Level 5 高手單字
Level 6 滿級單字

by [baɪ] 介 經由；在…之前

He had finished the work by ten o'clock this morning.
▶▶ 今天上午十點鐘前，他已完成了這項工作。

UNIT 03 **C字頭基礎單字** MP3 003

cake [kek] 名 蛋糕

Would you like some more cake?
▶▶ 你還要再來點蛋糕嗎？

call [kɔl] 動 打電話；呼叫 名 通話；呼叫

動 Call me at my office this afternoon.
今天下午打電話到我辦公室來。
名 I'll give you a phone call tomorrow morning.
我明天早上會打電話給你。
焦點句型 give sb. a phone call 打電話給某人

camera [`kæmərə] 名 照相機

Does anyone use a film camera anymore?
▶▶ 還有人在用膠捲照相機嗎？

camp [kæmp] 名 露營 動 露營

名 The boys were looking forward to summer camp.
男孩們之前很期待夏令營的到來。
動 We camped next to a river last Sunday.
我們上週日在河邊露營。

can [kæn] 助 能；可以 名 罐頭 動 把（食品等）裝罐

助 Can I borrow ten books at the same time?
我能一次借十本書嗎？
名 I want to buy two cans of corn.
我想買兩罐玉米。
動 Cindy doesn't like canned fruit.
辛蒂不喜歡水果罐頭。

cap [kæp] 名 帽子 動 加蓋於

The little boy is wearing a baseball cap.
▶▶ 那名小男孩戴著一頂棒球帽。

car [kɑr] 名 汽車 同 vehicle / automobile

Henry bought his wife a new car.
▶▶ 亨利買了一輛新車給他太太。

card [kɑrd] 名 卡片

A banker's card states that a bank will pay the owner's checks to a stated amount.
▶▶ 支票保付卡註明說銀行將會按客戶支票上的指定金額做支付。

care [kɛr] 名 看護；照料 動 關心；在乎

名 The baby needs a lot of care.
這名嬰兒需要精心照料。
動 The only thing he seems to care about is money.
他似乎只關心錢。

careful [`kɛrfəl] 形 小心的；仔細的

Be careful! The car is coming.
▶▶ 小心！有車開過來了。

carrot [`kærət] 名 胡蘿蔔

Rabbits like eating carrots.
▶▶ 兔子喜歡吃胡蘿蔔。

carry [`kærɪ] 動 攜帶；搬運

Could you carry this bag for me?
▶▶ 你能幫我拿一下這個袋子嗎？

case [kes] 名 情形；情況

Here is a case in point.
▶▶ 這是一個很好的例子。

cat [kæt] 名 貓

When the cat is away, the mice will play.
▶▶ 貓一離開，老鼠就鬧翻天。

Level 1 基礎單字
Level 2 必備單字
Level 3 中級單字
Level 4 進階單字
Level 5 高手單字
Level 6 滿級單字

catch [kætʃ] 動抓住；接住 名捕捉；接球

動 The policeman caught the thief who was stealing a purse.
警察逮住了正在偷皮包的小偷。
名 Tony made a fine catch.
東尼接了一次漂亮的球。

celebrate [`sɛlə‚bret] 動慶祝 關 festival 節日

The festival was held at night to celebrate a historical event.
▶▶ 這節慶於晚上舉行，以慶祝一樁歷史事件。

文法解析 a historical event的意思為「（過去發生的）歷史事件」，指任何過去發生的事；
而 a historic event 指的是「具歷史意義的重要事件」。

cellphone [`sɛlfon] 名行動電話；手機 同 mobile phone

Cellphones technology is advancing all the time.
▶▶ 手機的科技總是不斷在創新。

cent [sɛnt] 名美分

A hundred cents make a dollar.
▶▶ 一百美分就是一美元。

center [`sɛntɚ] 名中心；中央

I work in the center of London.
▶▶ 我在倫敦的市中心工作。

certain [`sɝtən] 形確定的；一定會的 代某幾個；某些

形 The doctor was certain that the young man had gone mad.
醫生確信那個年輕人已經發瘋。
代 Certain of them are responsible.
他們當中的某幾個人很有責任感。

chair [tʃɛr] 名椅子

Mary sat in a chair reading a novel.
▶▶ 瑪莉坐在椅子上看小說。

chance [tʃæns] 名機會

I have a chance to study abroad.
▶▶ 我獲得一個去國外深造的機會。

change [tʃendʒ] 動 改變 名 變化 關 conversion 改變；轉換

動 You have changed a lot since we met.
自我們相遇之後你變了好多。

名 You should adapt yourself to the change of environment.
你必須適應環境的變化。

(焦點句型) adapt oneself to... 使自己適應…

cheap [tʃip] 形 便宜的；廉價品的

The clothes sold in that shop are always cheap.
▶▶ 那家店賣的衣服都很便宜。

check [tʃɛk] 動 檢查；核對 名 支票

動 I have checked your answers and none of them are correct.
我確認過你的答案，沒有一個是正確的。

名 In the past, people often got checks as a form of payment.
在過去，人們的薪水經常以支票支付。

cheese [tʃiz] 名 乳酪；起司

Milk, butter and cheese are brought here from dairy farms.
▶▶ 牛奶、奶油和起司是從好幾間酪農場運到這裡的。

chicken [ˋtʃɪkən] 名 雞；雞肉

Mr. Brown built a house for chicken.
▶▶ 布朗先生建造了一間雞舍。

child [tʃaɪld] 名 小孩 關 children 小孩（複數形）

A child is playing in the park.
▶▶ 一個孩子正在公園裡玩耍。

chocolate [ˋtʃɑkəlɪt] 名 巧克力

Chocolate is a popular gift on Valentine's Day.
▶▶ 巧克力在情人節是很熱門的禮物。

choice [tʃɔɪs] 名 選擇；抉擇 形 精選的；上等的

I have no choice but to give up.
▶▶ 我不得不放棄。

(焦點句型) have no choice but + to V（別無選擇）只好…；不得不

Level 1 基礎單字
Level 2 必備單字
Level 3 中級單字
Level 4 進階單字
Level 5 高手單字
Level 6 滿級單字

choose [tʃuz] 動選擇 關 opt for sth. 選擇某物、某事

Billy chose me as his partner.
▶▶ 比利選擇我當夥伴。

文法解析 choose 動詞三態變化為 choose / chose / chosen。

church [tʃɜtʃ] 名教堂

The church stands on the hill.
▶▶ 那座教堂佇立於山丘上。

circle [`sɜkl] 名圓形 動畫圓圈；圍著 關 loop 環

名 These girls and boys are sitting in a circle on the floor.
這群男孩和女孩在地板上坐成一圈。

動 The teachers are used to circling the pupils' spelling mistakes in red ink.
教師們習慣用紅筆圈出學生的拼寫錯誤。

city [`sɪtɪ] 名城市 關 citizenship 公民身分

Venice is one of the most beautiful cities in the world.
▶▶ 威尼斯是世界上最美麗的城市之一。

class [klæs] 名班級；階級

Jane and I are in the same class.
▶▶ 我和珍同班。

clean [klin] 形乾淨的；清潔的 動打掃；把⋯弄乾淨

形 Be careful to keep yourself clean.
注意保持自身清潔。

動 Don't forget to clean your room!
別忘了清理你的房間！

clear [klɪr] 形清楚的；清澈的 副清晰地 動清除

形 In seriously polluted cities, clear sky is seldom seen.
在汙染嚴重的城市，很少能看見晴朗的天空。

副 I can hear you loud and clear.
你的聲音很宏亮，我聽得很清楚。

clerk [klɜk] 名職員

He works the hardest among all those clerks.
▶▶ 在那群職員當中，他工作得最努力。

climb [klaɪm] 動 攀登；上升；爬

The sun climbed steadily in the sky.
▶▶ 太陽在空中緩緩升起。

clock [klɑk] 名 時鐘；計時器

The clock shows just 6 o'clock.
▶▶ 時鐘指著六點整。

close [klos] / [kloz] 形（距離）接近的；親密的 動 關閉

形 The two buildings are close together.
　　這兩座建築物緊鄰著。
動 Close the door, please!
　　請關上門！

clothes [kloz] 名 衣服 關 lining 內襯

She wears different clothes every day.
▶▶ 她每天都穿不一樣的衣服。
文法解析 every day（每天）為副詞片語；everyday（日常的）則為形容詞。

cloud [klaʊd] 名 雲 動 以雲遮蔽

The sky suddenly became covered with dark clouds.
▶▶ 天空突然變得烏雲密布。

club [klʌb] 名 俱樂部

My father joined the golf club.
▶▶ 我的父親加入了高爾夫俱樂部。

coat [kot] 名 外套；大衣 關 put on 穿上（衣服）

It's cold outside. Put your coat on.
▶▶ 外面很冷，把外套穿上吧。

coffee [`kɔfɪ] 名 咖啡

How about having some coffee?
▶▶ 要不要喝點咖啡？

cold [kold] 形 冷的；寒冷的 名 感冒 關 catch a cold 感冒

形 It was bitterly cold that night.
　　那天晚上的天氣非常寒冷。

1 Level 基礎單字
2 Level 必備單字
3 Level 中級單字
4 Level 進階單字
5 Level 高手單字
6 Level 滿級單字

名 I caught a cold last night.
我昨晚感冒了。

collect [kə`lɛkt] 動蒐集

I collect many foreign stamps.
▶▶ 我蒐集了許多外國郵票。

color [`kʌlɚ] 名顏色 動把…塗上顏色

名 The color of leaves is green in summer.
夏天樹葉的顏色是綠的。
動 The children colored the Easter eggs.
孩子們替復活節的蛋塗上顏色。

come [kʌm] 動來；來到

Come and look at the picture.
▶▶ 過來看看這幅畫。

comfortable [`kʌmfətəbl̩] 形 舒適的

I feel comfortable talking with Gina.
▶▶ 和吉娜聊天讓我覺得很舒服。

common [`kɑmən] 形 常見的；普通的 名公共用地

Smith is a very common last name in England.
▶▶ 在英國，史密斯是很常見的姓氏。

computer [kəm`pjutɚ] 名電腦

Daniel loves to play computer games.
▶▶ 丹尼爾愛玩電腦遊戲。

convenient [kən`vinjənt] 形方便的

It is very convenient to live near the school.
▶▶ 住在學校附近非常方便。

cook [kʊk] 動烹調；煮 名廚師

動 My mother cooked dinner for me.
我母親幫我煮晚餐。
名 They dismissed the cook.
他們把廚師解僱了。

cookie [ˋkʊki] 名 餅乾 關 gulp 一（大）口

She ate the cookie in one gulp.
▶▶ 她一口就將那塊餅乾吃掉了。

cool [kul] 形 涼快的 動 （使）冷卻

形 What I'd like is a cool drink.
　　我想要一杯清涼的飲料。
動 Let the hot milk cool off before drinking it.
　　等熱牛奶涼一點再喝。
（焦點句型）cool off 冷卻；冷靜

copy [ˋkɑpɪ] 名 副本；複製品 動 複製 關 certificate 證明書

Send me the copy of your certificate.
▶▶ 把你證書的副本寄給我。

corner [ˋkɔrnɚ] 名 角落

I hit my knee on the corner of the table.
▶▶ 我的膝蓋撞到了桌角。

correct [kəˋrɛkt] 形 正確的 動 改正；糾正 關 amend 修訂；修改

形 Well done! All your answers are correct.
　　做得好！你的答案全對了。
動 Would you help me correct my pronunciation?
　　你能幫忙糾正我的發音嗎？

cost [kɔst] 名 價值；代價 動 花費；值

名 The cost of this book was fifteen dollars.
　　這本書的售價是十五美元。
動 We'll take a bus, because it won't cost much.
　　我們會搭公車前往，因為花費會比較少。

couch [kaʊtʃ] 名 長沙發 關 owing to 由於（後接名詞）

My husband slept on the couch last night owing to the conflict with me.
▶▶ 由於和我吵架，所以我先生昨晚睡沙發。

count [kaʊnt] 動 計算；計數 名 計數；總計

動 Close your eyes and count up to twenty.
　　閉上眼睛數到二十。

Level 1 基礎單字
Level 2 必備單字
Level 3 中級單字
Level 4 進階單字
Level 5 高手單字
Level 6 滿級單字

名 The count is one strike and three balls.
球數是一好球、三壞球。

country [`kʌntrɪ] 名國家

Joan loves her country very much.
▶▶ 瓊安十分熱愛她的國家。

course [kors] 名課程

John has finished his middle school course.
▶▶ 約翰完成了中學學業。

cousin [`kʌzn̩] 名堂（或表）兄弟姐妹 關 sibling 手足

I have one cousin who is the same age as me.
▶▶ 我有一個年齡相仿的表姐。

cover [`kʌvɚ] 名封面 動覆蓋；掩蓋

名 On the front cover of the magazine is a picture of a boy.
雜誌的封面是一個男孩的照片。
動 The ground was covered with snow.
地面上覆蓋著一層雪。

cow [kaʊ] 名乳牛

There is a herd of cows on the grass.
▶▶ 草地上有一群乳牛。

crazy [`krezɪ] 形瘋狂的

The crazy man shouted at everyone.
▶▶ 那名瘋狂的男人對著每個人咆哮。

cross [krɔs] 名十字形 動使交叉

名 Her earrings are in the shape of a cross.
她的耳環是十字形。
動 I'll keep my fingers crossed for you.
我會為你祈禱。
焦點句型 keep one's fingers crossed 祈禱；祈求好運

cry [kraɪ] 動哭；叫；喊 名（一陣）哭聲

動 The baby never stops crying.
這名嬰兒不停地哭泣。

Level 1 基礎單字

Level 2 必備單字

Level 3 中級單字

Level 4 進階單字

Level 5 高手單字

Level 6 滿級單字

名 A baby usually has a cry after waking.
嬰兒醒後通常會哭一陣。

cup [kʌp] 名 杯子

I'd like to have a cup of coffee.
>> 我想喝一杯咖啡。

cut [kʌt] 動 切；割；剪 名 切口；傷口

動 Please cut the cake into ten pieces.
請把蛋糕切成十塊。

名 The cut on my finger is healing well.
我手指上的傷口癒合得很好。

文法解析 本單字的動詞三態同形，皆為 cut。

cute [kjut] 形 可愛的 關 outrageously 不尋常地；驚人地

Leila keeps her outrageously cute smile.
>> 萊拉臉上始終掛著非常可愛的笑容。

UNIT 04 D 字頭基礎單字

MP3 004

dance [dæns] 名 舞蹈 動 跳舞 關 dancer 舞者

名 She is interested in modern dance.
她對現代舞十分感興趣。

動 I can't dance very well.
我舞跳得不太好。

dangerous [`dendʒərəs] 形 危險的 同 risky

It is dangerous to make the dog angry.
>> 激怒這隻狗很危險。

dark [dɑrk] 形 黑暗的 名 黑暗；暗處 關 hurry 趕緊；匆忙

形 It was getting dark, so we hurried home.
天暗下來了，所以我們急忙趕回家。

名 My younger sister is afraid of the dark.
我妹妹怕黑。

date [det] 名 日期；約會 動 約會；註明日期

名 We already set the date for the wedding.
我們已經訂好了結婚日期。

動 I'll date Lucy on Friday.
我星期五要和露西約會。

daughter [`dɔtɚ] 名 女兒

Paul's daughter is a doctor.
▶▶ 保羅的女兒是一名醫生。

day [de] 名 白天；日 關 every day 每天；天天（為片語）

We work eight hours every day.
▶▶ 我們每天工作八小時。

dead [dɛd] 形 死的；失效的

Amanda's grandfather is dead.
▶▶ 亞曼達的祖父過世了。

deal [dil] 名 交易；協議 動 交易；處理 同 transaction

名 I have just closed a deal.
我剛結束一筆交易。

動 Tom doesn't know how to deal with the difficult problem.
湯姆不知道該如何處理這個難題。

(焦點句型) deal with sth. 處理某事

dear [dɪr] 形 親愛的 名 親愛的（人）

形 He lost everything that was dear to him.
他所珍視的一切都失去了。

名 Be a good girl, dear.
親愛的，做個好女孩。

death [dɛθ] 名 死；死亡 關 sudden 突然的；意外的

The death of her mother was sudden.
▶▶ 她母親的死很突然。

decide [dɪ`saɪd] 動 決定 關 decision 決心；果斷

We can't decide anything yet.
▶▶ 我們還不能做任何決定。

Level 1 基礎單字

Level 2 必備單字

Level 3 中級單字

Level 4 進階單字

Level 5 高手單字

Level 6 滿級單字

deep [dip] 形深的 副深深地

形 Her love for the child was very deep.
她對孩子的愛是很深的。
副 The ship sank deep into the sea.
這艘船深深地沉入了海底。

define [dɪˋfaɪn] 動下定義 關 definition 定義

Who is entitled to define normality and abnormality?
▶▶ 誰有權力定義正常與異常呢？
焦點句型 be entitled to 有權做某事

desk [dɛsk] 名書桌 關 drawer 抽屜

The students took their books out of their desk drawers.
▶▶ 學生們從書桌的抽屜中拿出書本。

dictionary [ˋdɪkʃənˏɛrɪ] 名字典

Sophia is a walking dictionary because she knows almost everything.
▶▶ 蘇菲亞是部活字典，所有的事情她幾乎都知道。

die [daɪ] 動死；（草木）凋謝

His uncle died in battle.
▶▶ 他伯伯戰死沙場。

different [ˋdɪfərənt] 形不同的

The two houses are very different in style.
▶▶ 這兩棟房子的風格很不一樣。
文法解析 比較兩物的不同，通常用 be different from；表達在某方面不同，則用 in，例如 be different in the tastes（在品味方面各有所好）。

difficult [ˋdɪfəˏkəlt] 形困難的

I find it difficult to get up early in the morning.
▶▶ 我覺得早起很困難。

dig [dɪg] 動挖；挖掘

The children are busy digging in the sand.
▶▶ 這群孩子們忙於在沙子上挖洞。

dinner [`dɪnɚ] 名晚餐

Would you like to go out to dinner with me?

▶▶ 你願意和我一起外出共進晚餐嗎？

dirty [`dɜtɪ] 形髒的；汙穢的 動弄髒 反 clean

Your hands are dirty. Go and wash them.

▶▶ 你的手好髒，快去洗手。

dish [dɪʃ] 名（盛食物的）盤、碟

Mary put the apples in a dish.

▶▶ 瑪莉把蘋果放在一個盤子裡。

do [du] 助構成疑問句或否定句 動做；製作

助 Do you drink a cup of coffee every day?
你每天都會喝一杯咖啡嗎？

動 Ivy does a lot of household chores every day, but her sister doesn't.
艾薇每天做很多家事，可是她妹妹卻不做。

焦點句型 do household chores 做家事

doctor / doc [`dɑktɚ] 名醫生；博士

You must see a doctor right now.

▶▶ 你現在必須去看醫生。

dog [dɔg] 名狗 關 guard 保衛；守衛

He keeps a dog to guard the house.

▶▶ 他養了一條狗來看家。

doll [dɑl] 名玩偶；洋娃娃

The little girl is playing with a doll.

▶▶ 小女孩正在玩洋娃娃。

dollar [`dɑlɚ] 名美元；錢

They spent over one million dollars on the campaign.

▶▶ 他們花了一百多萬美元參加競選。

door [dor] 名門；門口

My mother asked me to lock the door.

▶▶ 我母親要我把門鎖上。

down [daʊn] 副向下 介往…下方 形向下的

副 The sun is going down and it will be dark soon.
太陽正下沉，天色很快就會變暗了。

介 Walk down the street, and you will see the bookstore.
沿著這條街走，你就會看到書店。

dozen [`dʌzn̩] 名（一）打；十二個

A dozen eggs, please.
▶▶ 請給我一打雞蛋。

draw [drɔ] 動畫；繪製；拖；拉

Eric drew a picture of his father.
▶▶ 艾瑞克畫了一張他爸爸的畫像。

文法解析 draw 動詞三態變化為 draw / drew / drawn。

dream [drim] 名夢 動做夢；夢到

名 The girl had a strange dream last night.
那女孩昨晚做了一個奇怪的夢。

動 I had never dreamed that I could get this job.
我做夢也沒有想到我能得到這份工作。

dress [drɛs] 名洋裝 動穿衣服 關 banquet 宴會

名 I wore an evening dress to the banquet.
我穿了一件晚禮服出席宴會。

動 The man dressed himself fashionably.
那名男子打扮得很時髦。

drink [drɪŋk] 動喝；喝酒 名飲料；酒

動 We sat drinking coffee and chatting for hours.
我們坐了好幾個小時，一邊喝咖啡一邊聊天。

名 The store sells soft drinks only.
這間店只賣不含酒精的飲料。

drive [draɪv] 動開車；駕駛 名駕車旅行

動 I drive to work every day.
我每天開車去上班。

名 We went for a drive in the afternoon.
我們下午開車出去兜風。

文法解析 drive 動詞三態變化為 drive / drove / driven。

Level 1 基礎單字
Level 2 必備單字
Level 3 中級單字
Level 4 進階單字
Level 5 高手單字
Level 6 滿級單字

driver [`draɪvɚ] 名 駕駛員；司機

May's father is a taxi driver.
▶▶ 梅的父親是一位計程車司機。

drop [drɑp] 動 滴落；掉落

I dropped some lemon juice on the fish.
▶▶ 我在魚肉上滴了幾滴檸檬汁。

drum [drʌm] 名 鼓 動 打鼓

I hear someone beating a drum.
▶▶ 我聽到有人在打鼓。

dry [draɪ] 形 乾燥的 動 把…弄乾

形 The paint is dry now.
油漆現在乾了。
動 She dried her tears with a handkerchief.
她用手帕擦乾眼淚。

duck [dʌk] 名 鴨子

The ducks are swimming around the pond.
▶▶ 鴨子在池塘裡游泳。

during [`djʊrɪŋ] 介 在…期間

They swim during the holidays.
▶▶ 他們在休假期間去游泳。

MP3 005

each [itʃ] 代 各個；每個 形 每個的 副 各自；每一個

代 The lady gave two candies to each of them.
那名女士給他們每人兩顆糖果。
形 You may find that each child gives a different answer to the question.
你也許會發現每個孩子對問題的回答都不相同。
副 The pencils are three dollars each.
鉛筆一支賣三美元。

ear [ɪr] 名耳朵 關 pleasant 令人愉快的

The sound of music is pleasant to the ear.
▶▶ 音樂聲很悅耳。
焦點句型 I'm all my ears. 我洗耳恭聽。

early [`ɜlɪ] 形早的；提早的 副提早；在初期

形 We had an early dinner today.
我們今天很早就吃晚餐。
副 Please come early.
請提早一點來。

earth [ɜθ] 名地球；地面

Earth goes round the sun.
▶▶ 地球繞著太陽轉。
文法解析 earth 一般小寫即可，除非當作「行星、星體」，例如 Mars, Venus and Earth（火星、金星與地球）。此外，Earth = the earth 都指「地球」。

east [ist] 名東方 形東方的 副向東方

名 China faces the Pacific on the east.
中國大陸東邊面向太平洋。
形 He has returned from east Africa.
他剛從東非回來。

easy [`izɪ] 形容易的

The new dance looks easy.
▶▶ 這種新式舞蹈看起來很容易。

eat [it] 動吃；進食

People who are vegetarians don't eat meat.
▶▶ 素食者不吃肉。

egg [ɛg] 名蛋

We have boiled eggs for breakfast every day.
▶▶ 我們每天早餐都吃水煮蛋。

either [`iðə] 副也不 代（兩者中）任何一個 形（兩者中）任一的 連或者

副 I don't like the movie, either.
我也不喜歡那部電影。

Level 1 基礎單字
Level 2 必備單字
Level 3 中級單字
Level 4 進階單字
Level 5 高手單字
Level 6 滿級單字

代 Either of us is willing to help you.
我們倆都願意向你伸出援手。

形 There are flowers on either side of the road.
道路的兩旁都有花。

elephant [`ɛləfənt] 名 大象 關 a herd of 一群

There are a herd of elephants in the zoo.
▶▶ 動物園裡有一群大象。

else [ɛls] 副 其他；另外

What else would you like?
▶▶ 你還需要什麼別的嗎？

email [`imel] 名 電子郵件 動 發電子郵件 關 contact 聯繫

名 We contact with friends through email.
我們用電子郵件與朋友聯繫。

動 My sister emailed me many jokes.
姐姐用電子郵件寄了很多笑話給我。

end [ɛnd] 名 末端；盡頭 動 結束

名 I'm going on holiday at the end of October.
十月底我要去渡假。

動 They have ended the game.
他們已經結束了這場比賽。

engineer [ˌɛndʒə`nɪr] 名 工程師；技師

A computer engineer can get high pay but little time to be with his family.
▶▶ 電腦工程師享有高薪，卻少有時間陪伴家人。

enjoy [ɪn`dʒɔɪ] 動 享受；享有（權利等）關 enjoyment 樂趣

We enjoy free medical care.
▶▶ 我們享有免費的醫療服務。

enough [ə`nʌf] 副 足夠地；十分 形 足夠的；充足的 名 足夠

副 I have played enough tonight.
我今晚已經玩夠了。

形 We have enough chairs for everyone.
我們有足夠的椅子讓大家坐。

enter [`ɛntɚ] 動 進入；加入

Don't enter the office without knocking.
▶▶ 別不敲門就進辦公室。

envelope [`ɛnvə,lop] 名 信封

You forgot to attach a stamp to the envelope.
▶▶ 你忘了在信封上貼郵票。

eraser [ɪ`resɚ] 名 橡皮擦

May I borrow your eraser?
▶▶ 我可以借用你的橡皮擦嗎？

error [`ɛrɚ] 名 錯誤

There is an error in the report.
▶▶ 這份報告裡面有錯誤。

even [`ivən] 副 甚至 形 相等的；平坦的

副 It isn't very warm here even in summer.
即使是夏天，這裡也不怎麼暖和。
形 The score is even now.
目前雙方是同分。

evening [`ivnɪŋ] 名 傍晚；晚上

I'll do my homework in the evening.
▶▶ 我會在傍晚時做功課。

ever [`ɛvɚ] 副 從來；至今

Nobody ever comes to see my mother.
▶▶ 至今沒有人來看過我母親。

every [`ɛvrɪ] 形 每一；每個

He was given every chance to complete the job.
▶▶ 上頭給予他完成這項工作的一切機會。

everyone / everybody [`ɛvrɪ,wʌn ] / [ `ɛvrɪ,badɪ] 代 每個人

Everyone should conform to the rules.
▶▶ 每個人應當遵守規則。
(焦點句型) conform to 遵照；遵守

Level 1 基礎單字
Level 2 必備單字
Level 3 中級單字
Level 4 進階單字
Level 5 高手單字
Level 6 滿級單字

everything [`ɛvrɪ.θɪŋ] 代每件事；一切事物

The boy was curious about everything he heard.
▶▶ 那男孩對他聽見的一切都感到好奇。

example [ɪg`zæmpḷ] 名例子 關 prototype 原型

I can't understand. Can you give me an example?
▶▶ 我不太了解，可以舉個例子說明嗎？

excellent [`ɛksḷnt] 形出色的；傑出的

Your performance in the play was excellent.
▶▶ 你在這齣劇中的表現非常傑出。

except [ɪk`sɛpt] 介除了⋯之外 連除了

The museum is open every day except Mondays.
▶▶ 除了星期一之外，博物館每天都開放。

excite [ɪk`saɪt] 動刺激 關 excited 感到興奮的 / exciting 令人興奮的

The news of the actor's arrival excited the crowd.
▶▶ 那名演員抵達的消息使人歡呼雀躍。

exercise [`ɛksɚ.saɪz] 動運動 名運動；習題 同 workout（名詞）

動 I think you should exercise more.
　　我認為你應該多運動。
名 I don't get much exercise because I sit in the office all day.
　　我很少運動，因為我整天坐在辦公室。

expect [ɪk`spɛkt] 動期望；預期

I expect you will win the game.
▶▶ 我期待你贏得比賽。

expensive [ɪk`spɛnsɪv] 形昂貴的

The trip was expensive and uncomfortable.
▶▶ 這次的旅行既昂貴又受罪。

experience [ɪk`spɪrɪəns] 名經驗 動體驗

名 It was a really terrible experience to go out with Dick.
　　和迪克出門真是個可怕的經驗。
動 I want to experience country life.
　　我想要體驗鄉村生活。

Level 1 基礎單字

Level 2 必備單字

Level 3 中級單字

Level 4 進階單字

Level 5 高手單字

Level 6 滿級單字

explain [ɪkˋsplen] 動解釋

I asked him to explain where he was last night.
▶▶ 我要他解釋他昨晚人在何處。

eye [aɪ] 名眼睛

David has blue eyes.
▶▶ 大衛有一雙碧眼。

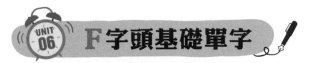 **UNIT 06 F字頭基礎單字**

 MP3 006

face [fes] 名臉；面孔 動面對

名 Tracy has a very pretty face.
　崔西有張漂亮的臉蛋。
動 The garden faces south.
　這座花園面向南方。

fact [fækt] 名事實；真相 關 alter 改變；修改

Nothing can alter the facts.
▶▶ 任何事情都改變不了事實。

factory [ˋfæktərɪ] 名工廠 關 debate 辯論；爭論

They debated whether to close the factory.
▶▶ 對於是否關閉工廠，他們爭論不休。

fail [fel] 動失敗；不及格

He failed to win the game.
▶▶ 他輸了比賽。

fall [fɔl] 動落下；下降 名秋天；落下；跌落

Leaves are falling from the trees.
▶▶ 葉子從樹上落下。
文法解析 fall 動詞三態變化為 fall / fell / fallen。

family [ˋfæməlɪ] 名家庭；家族

Mary has a quite large family.
▶▶ 瑪莉的家族相當龐大。

famous [`femǝs] 形 有名的

Switzerland is famous for its mountains.
▶▶ 瑞士以其山岳聞名。

fan [fæn] 名 扇子；風扇；狂熱者

She cooled herself with a fan.
▶▶ 她搧扇子讓自己涼快一些。

far [fɑr] 副 遙遠地 形 遙遠的

副 How far did John go?
　約翰走了多遠呢？
形 He lives on the far bank of the river.
　他住在老遠的河對岸。

farm [fɑrm] 名 農場；農田

My brother works on a farm.
▶▶ 我弟弟在一個農場工作。

farmer [`fɑrmɚ] 名 農人

Laura is both a farmer and a housewife.
▶▶ 蘿拉既是農婦又是家庭主婦。

fast [fæst] 副 很快地 形 快速的

副 Don't drive so fast.
　別開得這麼快。
形 Danny is a fast reader.
　丹尼讀書的速度很快。

fat [fæt] 形 胖的；多脂肪的 名 脂肪

My sister's boyfriend is very fat.
▶▶ 我姐姐的男友很胖。

father [`fɑðɚ] 名 父親 關 miserly 吝嗇的

The miserly father refused to spend money on his kids.
▶▶ 那名吝嗇的父親拒絕把錢花在自己的孩子身上。

feed [fid] 動 餵養；飼養 名 一餐；飼料

We should feed the baby every hour.
▶▶ 我們必須每小時餵小孩一次。

feel [fil] 動 感覺 名 氣氛;觸感 關 feeling 感覺

I can't feel where the handle is in the dark.

▶▶ 黑暗中我摸不出把手在哪裡。

文法解析 feel 動詞三態變化為 feel / felt / felt。

festival [`fɛstəvl] 名 節慶 關 eagerly 熱切地 / annual 一年的

I am eagerly looking forward to the annual film festival.

▶▶ 我非常期待年度影展。

few [fju] 形 很少數的 名 少數 關 a few 有些;幾個（後接可數名詞）

形 There were few people in the streets yesterday.
昨天街上的人很少。

名 A few of my classmates are doctors.
我有幾個同學是醫生。

fight [faɪt] 動 打架 名 戰鬥;爭吵

動 Two men are fighting in the office.
兩個男人正在辦公室打架。

名 There were many fights between the two countries.
這兩個國家有過很多次的戰爭。

文法解析 fight 動詞三態變化為 fight / fought / fought。

file [faɪl] 名 檔案 動 存檔;歸檔

I have a huge pile of files to deal with at present.

▶▶ 我目前有一大堆檔案要處理。

焦點句型 deal with 處理 / at present 目前

fill [fɪl] 動 填空;填滿

He filled my glass with beer.

▶▶ 他將我的杯子斟滿了啤酒。

焦點句型 fill A with B 用 B 裝滿 A

finally [`faɪnḷɪ] 副 終於;最後

He finally decided to buy a new LCD screen.

▶▶ 他終於決定買一台新的液晶螢幕。

find [faɪnd] 動 找到;發現 名 發現（物）

After six months, Ann finally found a job.

▶▶ 六個月後，安終於找到了工作。

Level 1 基礎單字
Level 2 必備單字
Level 3 中級單字
Level 4 進階單字
Level 5 高手單字
Level 6 滿級單字

文法解析 find動詞三態變化為 find / found / found。

fine [faɪn] 形美好的 副很好地 動處以罰金 名罰款

形 It's turned out fine again.
天氣轉晴了。

動 The judge fined him heavily.
法官重罰了他。

名 The driver paid a fifty-dollar fine for speeding.
司機因超速而被罰款五十美元。

finger [`fɪŋɚ] 名手指

Luke burnt his finger when he lit a cigar.
▶▶ 路克點雪茄時燙到了手指。

finish [`fɪnɪʃ] 動完成；結束 名結束；終結

動 I haven't finished reading the book yet.
我還沒讀完這本書。

名 The soldiers fought to the finish.
士兵們堅持戰鬥到底。

fire [faɪr] 名火；火災 動解僱；開（槍、砲）

名 Did you know horses are afraid of fire?
你知道馬怕火嗎？

動 The man was fired on the spot.
那名男子被當場解僱。

焦點句型 on the spot 立即；當場

first [fɝst] 形第一的 副首先 名第一個

形 Sunday is the first day of the week.
星期日是每週的第一天。

副 In this instance, you should call the police first.
在這種情況下，你應該先報警。

fish [fɪʃ] 名魚 動捕魚；釣魚 關 go fishing 去釣魚

名 How many fish did you get?
你捕到多少條魚？

動 They often go fishing on weekends.
他們經常在週末去釣魚。

Level 1 基礎單字

Level 2 必備單字

Level 3 中級單字

Level 4 進階單字

Level 5 高手單字

Level 6 滿級單字

floor [flor] 名地板；（樓房的）層

There's broken glass on the floor.
▶▶ 地上有玻璃碎片。

flower [`flaʊɚ] 名花；花卉

The little girl loves the beautiful flowers in the park.
▶▶ 小女孩喜愛公園裡的漂亮花朵。

fly [flaɪ] 動飛行 名蒼蠅

動 Several seagulls flew across the sky.
幾隻海鷗飛過天空。
名 Flies buzzed around the dead cow.
一群蒼蠅圍繞著那隻牛的屍體嗡嗡地叫。
文法解析 fly 動詞三態變化為 fly / flew / flown。

follow [`falo] 動跟隨；接在…之後

The dog followed her wherever she went.
▶▶ 她走到哪，那條狗就跟到哪。

food [fud] 名食物

Milk is the natural food for babies.
▶▶ 牛奶是嬰兒的天然食物。

fool 名傻瓜 動愚弄 關 imitation 模仿

名 You are such a fool to believe him.
妳真是個傻子，居然相信他。
動 Your poor imitation can not fool me.
你那愚拙的模仿騙不了我。

foot [fʊt] 名腳；足 關 feet 腳；足（複數形）

I usually go to school on foot.
▶▶ 我通常走路去上學。
文法解析 搭乘交通工具通常用介係詞 by，例如 by bus（搭公車）、by train（坐火車）等；
唯獨「走路」的慣用說法為 on foot。

for [fɔr] 介為了；向；往 連因為；由於

Lisa did it for her husband.
▶▶ 麗莎為了丈夫做這件事。

foreign [`fɔrɪn] 形外國的 關 foreigner 外國人

He likes to collect stamps from foreign countries.
▶▶ 他喜歡蒐集國外的郵票。

forget [fɚ`gɛt] 動忘記

I'll never forget meeting my husband at the first time.
▶▶ 我永遠忘不了和我丈夫第一次見面的情景。
文法解析 forget 動詞三態變化為 forget / forgot / forgotten。

fork [fɔrk] 名叉子；岔路 關 chopstick 筷子 / knife 刀子

We usually use chopsticks instead of knives and forks.
▶▶ 我們通常會用筷子，而非刀叉。
焦點句型 instead of 代替

free [fri] 形自由的；免費的 動解放；使自由

He felt himself absolutely free at last.
▶▶ 最後，他覺得自己完全自由了。

fresh [frɛʃ] 形新鮮的

These vegetables are fresh. I picked them this morning.
▶▶ 這些蔬菜是我今天早上摘的，很新鮮。

friend [frɛnd] 名朋友 關 friendly 友善的

He is a close friend of mine.
▶▶ 他是我的摯友。

frog [frɑg] 名蛙；青蛙

A frog jumped into the water.
▶▶ 一隻青蛙跳下水。

front [frʌnt] 形前面的 名前面 關 slip 滑跤 / stair 樓梯

形 This is our front garden.
　這是我們的前院。
名 She slipped on the stairs and spilt coffee all down her front.
　她在樓梯上滑了一跤，咖啡全灑在了她面前。

fruit [frut] 名 水果

I like fruit and vegetables because they are good for health.
▶▶ 我喜歡水果和蔬菜，因為它們對健康有益。

full [fʊl] 形 滿的；充滿的

The bus is full, so we have to wait for the next one.
▶▶ 那班公車擠滿了人，我們只好等下一班。

fun [fʌn] 名 樂趣；玩笑

We had a lot of fun at the party last night.
▶▶ 昨晚的舞會我們玩得很開心。

funny [`fʌnɪ] 形 有趣的；滑稽可笑的

That's a funny joke.
▶▶ 那是則有趣的笑話。

future [`fjutʃɚ] 名 未來

Little Bobby made up his mind to be a policeman in the future.
▶▶ 小鮑比下定決心將來要成為一名警察。
(焦點句型) make up one's mind 下定決心

 G字頭基礎單字

MP3 007

game [gem] 名 遊戲；比賽

Football is a game which interests me a lot.
▶▶ 橄欖球是我很感興趣的一種運動。

garden [`gɑrdṇ] 名 花園 關 botanical 植物的

There is a botanical garden in Paris.
▶▶ 巴黎有個植物園。

gate [get] 名 大門；柵欄門

Please keep the garden gate closed.
▶▶ 請把花園的大門關上。

Level 1 基礎單字
Level 2 必備單字
Level 3 中級單字
Level 4 進階單字
Level 5 高手單字
Level 6 滿級單字

get [gɛt] 動獲得；得到
I got a letter from my sister.
▶▶ 我收到了我妹妹的一封信。

ghost [gost] 名鬼；靈魂 關 exist 存在
Ghosts do not exist.
▶▶ 鬼魂是不存在的。

giant [`dʒaɪənt] 形巨大的 名巨人 關 lift 舉起；抬起
形 I cannot lift such a giant stone.
　 我無法舉起這塊巨石。
名 In the famous novel, Gulliver was a giant.
　 在這篇著名的小說裡，格列佛是個巨人。

gift [gɪft] 名禮物；天賦
This watch is a gift from my mother.
▶▶ 這支手錶是母親送我的禮物。

girl [gɝl] 名女孩
The girl at the cash desk was very warm-hearted in helping people.
▶▶ 櫃檯的那個女收銀員非常熱心助人。

give [gɪv] 動給予；送給
I gave Jack a book for his birthday.
▶▶ 我送傑克一本書當作他的生日禮物。
文法解析 give 動詞三態變化為 give / gave / given。

glad [glæd] 形高興的；樂意的
The man was glad to hear the news.
▶▶ 聽到那則消息，男子感到很高興。

glass [glæs] 名玻璃；玻璃杯
We have a set of table glass.
▶▶ 我們有一組玻璃餐具。

glasses [`glæsɪz] 名眼鏡 關 steam 蒸氣 / fog（因蒙上霧）變模糊
The steam fogged my glasses.
▶▶ 蒸氣讓我的眼鏡蒙上一層霧。

glove [glʌv] 名 手套

I wear gloves in the winter.
▶▶ 我在冬天會戴手套。

go [go] 動 去；離去；行走

We went to London last summer.
▶▶ 我們去年夏天去了倫敦。

<u>文法解析</u> go動詞三態變化為go / went / gone。

god / God [gɑd] 名 神；上帝 關 goddess 女神

Thank God you've arrived.
▶▶ 謝天謝地，你終於到了。

good [gʊd] 形 好的 名 善；好事

Exercise is good for your health.
▶▶ 運動有益於健康。

goodbye [gʊd`baɪ] 名 再見

She kissed her husband goodbye.
▶▶ 她與丈夫吻別。

grade [gred] 名 年級；等級

I am a third-grade student in high school.
▶▶ 我是高中三年級的學生。

grandfather [`grænd͵fɑðɚ] 名 （外）祖父

My grandfather arrived in New York after the Civil War.
▶▶ 我祖父在南北戰爭之後來到紐約。

grandmother [`grænd͵mʌðɚ] 名 （外）祖母 關 darn 縫補

My grandmother used to darn her own stockings.
▶▶ 祖母過去總是自己縫補襪子。

grass [græs] 名 草；草地 關 field 原野

The sheep were eating the grass in a field.
▶▶ 羊群在原野上吃青草。

Level 1 基礎單字
Level 2 必備單字
Level 3 中級單字
Level 4 進階單字
Level 5 高手單字
Level 6 滿級單字

gray [gre] 形灰色的 名灰色

My father has gray hair.
▶▶ 我父親有白頭髮。

great [gret] 形大的；偉大的

There is a great tree in front of our house.
▶▶ 我們家前面有棵大樹。

green [grin] 形綠色的 名綠色 關 leaf 葉子 / spring 春天

形 Green tomatoes are sour.
未成熟的番茄是酸的。
名 Leaves are in green in the spring.
葉子在春天是綠色的。

ground [graʊnd] 名地面；土地

Snow covers the ground.
▶▶ 雪覆蓋著地面。

group [grup] 名團體；群 動聚合；成群

A group of airplanes appeared in the sky.
▶▶ 飛機群出現在天空中。

grow [gro] 動種植；成長

The village is growing into a town.
▶▶ 這座村莊正逐漸發展成一個城鎮。
文法解析 grow 動詞三態變化為 grow / grew / grown。

guess [gɛs] 動猜測；推測 名猜測；猜想

動 I can guess what will happen next.
我能推測出接下來會發生什麼事。
名 I'd said that there would be 100 people there, but it's just a guess.
我想說那裡會有一百人，但這也只是猜測而已。

guitar [gɪˋtɑr] 名吉他

Everyone watched Brian playing guitar.
▶▶ 每個人都看著布萊恩彈奏吉他。

guy [gaɪ] 名傢伙

Hey, guys, how about going fishing this afternoon?
▶▶ 嗨夥伴們，下午去釣魚怎麼樣？

MP3 008

UNIT 08 H字頭基礎單字

habit [`hæbɪt] 名 習慣

He wishes he could break the habit of smoking.
▶▶ 他希望他可以戒掉抽菸的習慣。

hair [hɛr] 名 頭髮 關 haircut 髮型

There are a few hairs in the book.
▶▶ 書裡面有幾根頭髮。

half [hæf] 名 一半 形 一半的 副 一半地

名 Two halves make a whole.
半個加半個，合起來就是完整的一個。
形 We run half a mile every day.
我們每天跑半英里。

ham [hæm] 名 火腿

I had ham and eggs for breakfast.
▶▶ 我早餐吃了火腿和蛋。

hand [hænd] 名 手 動 遞交

名 She prepared him a meal with her own hands.
她親手為他做了一頓飯。
動 He handed the old lady a letter.
他交給那位上了年紀的女士一封信。

hang [hæŋ] 動 吊；掛

He hung the wet raincoat on the line.
▶▶ 他把溼雨衣掛在曬衣繩上。
文法解析 hang 三態變化為 hang / hung / hung。

happen [`hæpən] 動 發生；碰巧

A terrible traffic accident happened there yesterday.
▶▶ 昨天那裡發生了一起嚴重的交通事故。

Level 1 基礎單字
Level 2 必備單字
Level 3 中級單字
Level 4 進階單字
Level 5 高手單字
Level 6 滿級單字

happy [`hæpɪ] 形快樂的 關 accept 接受 / invitation 邀請

I am happy to accept your invitation.
▶▶ 我很高興接受你的邀請。

hard [hɑrd] 形硬的 副努力地

形 The ice is as hard as rock.
那塊冰像石頭一樣硬。
副 She tried hard, but she failed.
她努力嘗試過，卻未能成功。

hat [hæt] 名帽子

She was wearing a white hat.
▶▶ 她戴著一頂白色的帽子。

hate [het] 動仇恨；不喜歡 名仇恨；厭惡 關 kind-hearted 好心腸的

動 The kind-hearted people hate violence.
仁慈的人討厭暴力。
名 He looked at me with hate in his eyes.
他看我的眼神透露出厭惡感。

have [hæv] 助已經；曾經 動有；擁有

助 John and David haven't finished the job yet.
約翰與大衛尚未完成那項工作。
動 This coat has no pockets.
這件衣服沒有口袋。
文法解析 have 當助動詞時，須與動詞的完成式搭配，「have + 完成式」表示一個到現在已完成的動作，例如 have eaten（已吃）。

head [hɛd] 名頭；首領 動率領 關 headache 頭痛

名 She laid her head upon my shoulder.
她把頭靠在我的肩膀上。
動 A car headed the procession.
一輛汽車為遊行隊伍開路。

health [hɛlθ] 名健康 關 healthy 健康的

Health is more important to most people than money.
▶▶ 對大多數人來說，健康比金錢更重要。

hear [hɪr] 動 聽到;聽見 關 opinion 意見

We must hear opinions contrary to ours.
▶▶ 我們必須聽取反對的意見。
(焦點句型) be contrary to + N 與…相反

heart [hɑrt] 名 內心;心臟

Paulina gave her heart to her boyfriend.
▶▶ 寶琳娜真心愛著她的男朋友。

heat [hit] 名 熱度 動 加熱

名 The sun gives off heat.
太陽散發出熱能。
動 The stove heats the room.
暖爐使房間溫暖起來。
(焦點句型) give off 發出（例：give off heat and light 發出熱和光）

heavy [`hɛvɪ] 形 重的;大量的 關 heavily 沉重地

The box is too heavy for me.
▶▶ 這個箱子對我來說太重了。

height [haɪt] 名 高度

She is the same height as her sister.
▶▶ 她和她姐姐一樣高。

hello [hə`lo] 嘆 哈囉（問候語）;喂（電話應答語）

Hello, who's speaking, please?
▶▶ 喂你好，請問你是哪一位呢？

help [hɛlp] 動 幫助;促進 名 有幫助的人或事物

She helped Tony choose some new clothes.
▶▶ 她幫東尼挑了一些新衣服。

helpful [`hɛlpfəl] 形 有用的;有幫助的 關 advice 建議

My teacher always gives me helpful advice.
▶▶ 老師總會給我有用的建議。

Level 1 基礎單字
Level 2 必備單字
Level 3 中級單字
Level 4 進階單字
Level 5 高手單字
Level 6 滿級單字

hen [hɛn] 名 母雞 關 hatch 孵化

The hen is hatching its eggs.
▶▶ 母雞正在孵蛋。

here [hɪr] 副 在這裡;到這裡

We live here during summer vacations.
▶▶ 我們暑假都住在這裡。

hide [haɪd] 動 隱藏;隱瞞

I think you are hiding something from me.
▶▶ 我覺得你有事情瞞著我。

文法解析 hide動詞三態變化為 hide / hid / hidden。

high [haɪ] 形 高的 副 在高處

形 Yushan is the highest mountain in Taiwan.
玉山是臺灣最高的山。
副 An eagle circled high overhead.
一隻老鷹在高空中盤旋。

hill [hɪl] 名 小山 關 stand 站立;坐落

His red house stands on a hill.
▶▶ 他的紅色房子位於山丘上。

history [`hɪstərɪ] 名 歷史 關 archaeology 考古學

History is my favorite subject at school.
▶▶ 歷史是我在學校中最喜愛的科目。

hit [hɪt] 動 打擊;擊中 名 打擊;擊中 關 bullet 子彈

動 A bullet hit him in the leg.
一顆子彈擊中了他的腿。
名 Roy got ten hits and didn't make any mistakes.
羅伊擊中十次,毫無遺漏。

hobby [`hɑbɪ] 名 嗜好

One of my hobbies is writing novels.
▶▶ 我的興趣之一是寫小說。

1 Level 基礎單字

2 Level 必備單字

3 Level 中級單字

4 Level 進階單字

5 Level 高手單字

6 Level 滿級單字

hold [hold] 動 握住；持有；舉行 名 握住

動 The meeting will be held at the Town Hall.
這次的會議將在市政廳舉行。

名 Jack lost hold of the rope and fell to the ground.
傑克沒有抓住繩子，因而摔到地上。

文法解析 hold動詞三態變化為hold / held / held。

holiday [`hɑlə‚de] 名 假日；假期

We are going to America for our holiday.
▶▶ 我們將去美國渡假。

home [hom] 名 家；住家 副 在家 形 家庭的

名 Richard's home is on the right side of the street.
理查的家在這條街的右手邊。

副 Has Mary come home yet?
瑪莉到家了嗎？

homework [`homwɜk] 名 回家作業

I'll watch TV after I finish my homework.
▶▶ 我做完功課後要去看電視。

honest [`ɑnɪst] 形 誠實的

It was honest of her to turn in the money that she found on the road.
▶▶ 她很誠實，將路上拾獲的金錢交給警察。

焦點句型 turn in 呈交；撿到東西交給警察

honey [`hʌnɪ] 名 蜂蜜

It tastes good if you add some honey to the black tea.
▶▶ 在紅茶裡加些蜂蜜嚐起來很棒。

hope [hop] 動 希望；期待 名 希望；期望

動 I hope to see you and your family soon.
我期待不久後能見到你和你的家人。

名 You mustn't give up hope.
你絕對不能放棄希望。

horse [hɔrs] 名 馬 關 jockey 職業賽馬騎師

Riding a horse is very difficult for me.
▶▶ 對我來說，騎馬很困難。

hospital [`hɑspɪtḷ] 名 醫院 關 injure 傷害

The injured rider was sent to the hospital.
▶▶ 受傷的騎士被送至醫院。

hot [hɑt] 形 熱的

The weather has been very hot.
▶▶ 天氣一直很熱。

hotel [ho`tɛl] 名 旅館；飯店 關 recommend 推薦

Please recommend a good hotel for us.
▶▶ 請為我們推薦一間好旅館。

hour [aʊ♂] 名 小時

It took us five hours to finish the job.
▶▶ 我們花了五個小時的時間完成這項工作。

house [haʊs] 名 房子 關 housewife 家庭主婦

They built a house by the roadside.
▶▶ 他們在路邊蓋了一棟房子。

how [haʊ] 副 怎樣；如何

How did you climb to the top of that building?
▶▶ 你是如何爬上那棟建築物的頂樓的呢？

however [haʊ`ɛv♂] 副 無論如何

I thought the data were correct; however, some of them are wrong.
▶▶ 我以為資料是正確的，但其中有誤。

hundred [`hʌndrəd] 名 一百 形 一百的；許多的

名 The child can count from one to a hundred.
這孩子能從一數到一百。
形 I have got a hundred things to do.
我有許多事情要做。

hungry [`hʌŋgrɪ] 形 飢餓的

The hungry child asked for a piece of bread.
▶▶ 那名飢餓的孩子要了一塊麵包吃。

hurt [hɜt] 動 傷害 名 傷；痛；創傷

動 Danny kicked the machine hard and hurt his toes.
丹尼用力踢了這台機器，傷了他的腳趾。

名 The massage made the hurt go away.
按摩使疼痛消失了。

(焦點句型) hurt one's feelings 傷到某人的感情

husband [`hʌzbənd] 名 丈夫 關 wife 妻子（複數形為wives）

Husbands and wives have different roles.
▶▶ 丈夫和妻子的角色各有不同。

 I 字頭基礎單字

MP3 009

ice [aɪs] 名 冰

I would like some ice in my soda.
▶▶ 我的汽水要加點冰塊。

idea [aɪ`diə] 名 主意；概念 關 ideology 意識形態

I have a new idea.
▶▶ 我想到新的主意了。

if [ɪf] 連 如果；是否

If I were you, I would never do that.
▶▶ 如果我是你，我絕對不會那麼做。

文法解析 本句為「與現在事實相反」的假設語氣，此時if子句中的動詞須使用過去式（例如：If I studied hard、If I were you等）。

important [ɪm`pɔrtn̩t] 形 重要的

It is important to see that everything goes well.
▶▶ 確保一切順利是很重要的。

inch [ɪntʃ] 名 英寸 關 foot 呎；英尺

There are twelve inches in a foot.
▶▶ 一呎有十二吋。

Level 1 基礎單字
Level 2 必備單字
Level 3 中級單字
Level 4 進階單字
Level 5 高手單字
Level 6 滿級單字

insect [ˋɪnsɛkt] 名昆蟲

Insects have six legs.
▶▶ 昆蟲有六隻腳。

inside [ɪnˋsaɪd] 介在…裡面 副在裡面 名裡面；內部 形裡面的

介 He parked his car inside the gate.
他把車停在大門裡面。
副 There was nothing inside.
裡面什麼也沒有。

interest [ˋɪntərɪst] 名興趣 動使有興趣 關interested 感興趣的 / interesting 有趣的

名 I have lost my interest in chemistry.
我對化學已不感興趣。
動 The activity interested him very much.
這個活動引起他的興趣。

文法解析 與本單字相關的衍生詞彙（形容詞）有兩個：interested（人）感興趣的、
interesting（事物）有趣的。

焦點句型 have interest in sth. / be interested in sth. 對某物感興趣

interview [ˋɪntɚ͵vju] 名面談 動會面

I have an interview tomorrow, and I'm very nervous now.
▶▶ 我明天有場面試，我現在很緊張。

invite [ɪnˋvaɪt] 動邀請

He invited several of his friends to the show.
▶▶ 他邀請了幾個朋友去看表演。

island [ˋaɪlənd] 名島嶼 關continent 大陸；陸地

Australia is an island and an continent.
▶▶ 澳洲的幅員包括一座島跟一塊陸地。

item [ˋaɪtəm] 名項目；條款

Ivy listed the items she wanted to buy.
▶▶ 艾薇列出了自己想要買的清單項目。

jacket [`dʒækɪt] 名夾克 關 sunburn 曬傷

She put on a jacket for fear of sunburn.
▶▶ 她穿上夾克以防曬傷。

(焦點句型) for fear of + N/Ving 以免;唯恐

jeans [dʒinz] 名牛仔褲

The pair of jeans is too tight for me.
▶▶ 這條牛仔褲對我來說太緊了。

job [dʒɑb] 名工作

I'm looking for a new job.
▶▶ 我正在找一份新工作。

join [dʒɔɪn] 動參加;連接

He never joined the other boys in his class to play games.
▶▶ 他從不加入班上男生的團體運動。

joke [dʒok] 名笑話;玩笑 動開玩笑

A joke never gains an enemy but often loses a friend.
▶▶ 玩笑話往往不會樹立敵人,但卻會讓你因此失去朋友。

joy [dʒɔɪ] 名歡樂;喜悅 關 joyful 喜悅的

We'd like to wish you joy and success in your life together.
▶▶ 我們祝你們倆一起生活愉快,萬事如意。

juice [dʒus] 名果汁

We have many kinds of juice: orange juice, strawberry juice, and so on.
▶▶ 我們的果汁種類很多,有柳橙汁、草莓汁等等。

jump [dʒʌmp] 動跳躍 名跳躍 關 warm 溫暖的;暖和的

Jumping up and down keeps you warm.
▶▶ 上下跳一跳吧,可以保暖。

just [dʒʌst] 副正好;恰好 形公正的;正義的

副 The mother was just about to call her son when he phoned her.
那名母親準備打給兒子時,對方恰好就打給她了。

形 Mr. Donaldson is a just man who would never cheat.
唐納森先生充滿正義感，絕不會騙人。

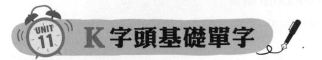 **K 字頭基礎單字**

MP3 011

keep [kip] 動 維持；持有

The model always keeps in good shape.
▶▶ 這個模特兒總是維持著優美的體態。
(焦點句型) in good shape（人或東西）狀態良好

key [ki] 形 主要的；關鍵的 名 鑰匙 動 用鍵盤輸入

形 We found some key evidence to prove his crime.
我們找到證實他犯罪的關鍵證據。
名 I lost my keys yesterday.
我昨晚遺失了我的鑰匙。
動 Please key in your name in the form.
請在這個表格內輸入你的名字。
(焦點句型) key in 用鍵盤輸入

kick [kɪk] 動 踢 名 踢 關 violent 暴力的

動 He kicked the ball to his partner.
他把球踢給他的同伴。
名 The dog got a kick by his violent master.
這隻狗被牠殘暴的主人踢了一腳。

kid [kɪd] 名 小孩 動 戲弄；取笑

名 The kid was crying loudly to find his mother.
這個孩子大聲哭著要找媽媽。
動 I was just kidding. Never mind!
我只是在開玩笑，不要介意！

kill [kɪl] 動 殺死；消磨時間 關 kill time 打發、消磨時間

The murderer killed four people in that house.
▶▶ 那名殺人兇手在那棟屋子裡殺害了四個人。

kind [kaɪnd] 形 仁慈的 名 種類 關 goodwill 善意；好心

形 The kind woman fed the stray dogs.
那位仁慈的婦人餵食流浪狗。

Level 1 基礎單字

Level 2 必備單字

Level 3 中級單字

Level 4 進階單字

Level 5 高手單字

Level 6 滿級單字

名 There are many kinds of clothes in the department store.
百貨公司裡有許多種類的衣服。

king [kɪŋ] 名國王 關 pardon 赦免 / criminal 罪犯

The King pardoned the criminals.
▶▶ 國王赦免了罪犯們。

kiss [kɪs] 動親吻 名吻

動 He kissed me on the cheek before leaving.
他離開前在我臉頰上吻了一下。
名 She gave me a kiss and a hug.
她給了我一個吻和擁抱。

kitchen [`kɪtʃɪn] 名廚房

My mother is busy cooking in the kitchen.
▶▶ 我媽媽在廚房裡忙著煮飯。

kite [kaɪt] 名風箏 關 dangle 吊；掛 / wire 金屬線；電線

A kite dangles on a telephone wire.
▶▶ 一只風箏懸掛在電話線上。

knee [ni] 名膝蓋

The basketball player hurt her knee in the game.
▶▶ 那名籃球員在比賽中傷了膝蓋。

knife [naɪf] 名刀子 關 steak 牛排

I use the knife to cut the steak.
▶▶ 我用刀切牛排。
文法解析 本單字的複數形為 knives。

knock [nɑk] 動敲；擊；打 名敲

動 Someone is knocking on the door.
有人在敲門。
名 He jokingly gave me a knock on the head.
他開玩笑地敲了一下我的頭。

know [no] 動知道；認識

I dare not let my father know the truth.
▶▶ 我不敢讓父親知道事實。

文法解析 know動詞三態變化為 know / knew / known。

knowledge [`nɑlɪdʒ] 名知識；學問

We go to school to gain knowledge about many different things.
▶▶ 我們上學是為了得到各種事物的知識。

MP3 012

lake [lek] 名湖；池

The old man fishes by the lake.
▶▶ 那位老人家在湖邊釣魚。

lamp [læmp] 名燈；燈火 關 ultraviolet 紫外線的 / pest 害蟲

They use ultraviolet lamps to kill pests.
▶▶ 他們使用紫外線燈殺死害蟲。

land [lænd] 名陸地；土地 動登陸

名 Mr. Hill owns 300 acres of land.
希爾先生擁有三百英畝的土地。
動 She landed the top job in the company.
她在公司謀得了最高階的職位。

language [`læŋgwɪdʒ] 名語言 關 convey 傳達 / verbal 言語的

Body language can convey more information than verbal language.
▶▶ 肢體語言可以傳達的訊息比口語還多。

large [lɑrdʒ] 形大的；多的 關 gather 使聚集

A large number of people gathered to see the star.
▶▶ 大量的人潮聚集著要一睹那位明星的風采。

last [læst] 動持續 副最後；在最後 形最後的 名最後的人或事物

動 The heavy rain will last for a long time.
大雨還會持續很長一段時間。
副 The one who leaves last should turn off the light.
最後一位離開的人要關燈。
形 The last game will take place tomorrow.
最後一場比賽將於明日舉行。

(焦點句型) turn off 關掉 / take place 舉行；發生

late [let] 形遲的 副遲到地 關 later 之後；較晚地

形 I was late for the train.
我沒趕上火車。
副 He went to school late yesterday.
他昨天上學遲到。

laugh [læf] 動笑；嘲笑 名笑；笑聲 關 hairstyle 髮型 / hearty 衷心的；熱誠的

動 They laughed at my new hairstyle.
他們嘲笑我的新髮型。
名 The girl gave a hearty laugh.
女孩發自內心地笑了。
(焦點句型) laugh at sb./sth. 嘲笑某人或某事

lawyer [`lɔjɚ] 名律師 同 attorney 關 law 法律 / innocent 無罪的

The lawyer said her client was innocent.
▶ 律師說她的客戶是無罪的。

lazy [`lezɪ] 形懶惰的 關 laziness 懶散；怠惰

The lazy boy does almost nothing every day.
▶ 那個懶惰的男孩每天都無所事事。

lead [lid] 動領導；引領 名榜樣；指導

動 After the first half of the race, I was leading.
跑了一半賽程後，我領先了。
名 All the children followed Daniel's lead.
所有孩子都服從丹尼爾的領導。
(文法解析) lead 動詞三態變化為 lead / led / led。

leader [`lidɚ] 名領導者

The leader encouraged her team to work hard.
▶ 那名領導者鼓勵她的團隊努力工作。

learn [lɜn] 動學習；認識到

You are never too old to learn.
▶ 學習不嫌老。

least [list] 副至少（at least）形最少的 代最少（the least）

副 At least, he apologized for his mistake.
至少，他為他犯的錯道歉了。

形 He has the least money of all of us.
在我們所有人當中，他的錢最少。

代 Ann helps the least in the project.
在這個專案中，安出的力是最少的。

leave [liv] 動離開；離去 名休假 關 annual leave 年假 / unpaid leave 無薪假

動 Mr. Watson left without saying goodbye.
華森先生不告而別。

名 She asked for a leave because her father was in the hospital.
她因父親住院而請假。

文法解析 leave 的動詞三態變化為 leave / left / left。

焦點句型 ask for a leave 請假 / take a day off 請一天假

left [lɛft] 形左邊的 名左邊

My left hand has less strength than my right hand.
▶▶ 我左手的力氣比右手小。

leg [lɛg] 名腿；足

The runner injured himself in the leg.
▶▶ 那名跑者的腿部受傷。

lemon [`lɛmən] 名檸檬 關 pot 鍋子；罐子

You can use a slice of lemon to clean the pot.
▶▶ 你可以用一片檸檬把鍋子清得很乾淨。

文法解析 a slice of 一片。slice 指的是（切下來的）食物薄片，常見用法如：a slice of bread（一片麵包）、a slice of ham（一片火腿）等。

less [lɛs] 副更少；更小 形更少的；更小的

Laura eats less than before.
▶▶ 蘿拉吃得比以前少。

文法解析 less 作為形容詞時，為 little 的比較級，常修飾不可數名詞，例如：less time（較少時間）、less importance（次要）等；less 當副詞可修飾形容詞、副詞或動詞，表示「程度」，例如 eat less（吃得較少）。

lesson [`lɛsn̩] 名課業；一節課

Lesson ten is about business English.
▶▶ 第十課是商用英語的內容。

let [lɛt] 動讓；允許

His question let me confused.
▶▶ 他的問題令我感到困惑。

letter [`lɛtɚ] 名字母；信 關 depressing 令人沮喪的

The letter was depressing to read.
▶▶ 這封信閱讀起來真令人沮喪。

level [`lɛvl̩] 名水準；水平線 形水平的 關 locate 坐落於

The castle is located 800 meters above sea level.
▶▶ 這座城堡位於海拔八百公尺高的地方。

library [`laɪˌbrɛrɪ] 名圖書館

You can get a book from the library.
▶▶ 你可以從圖書館借書。

lie [laɪ] 動說謊 名謊言

動 You can see that she is lying from her shaking hands.
看到她發抖的手，就知道她在說謊。
名 Do not tell a lie.
不要說謊。

文法解析 除了「說謊」之外，lie 還有「躺；臥」的意思，其三態變化須看字義。表示「說謊」時，三態變化為 lie / lied / lied；當「躺；臥」時，則為 lie / lay / lain。

life [laɪf] 名生活；生命 關 ambition 抱負；野心

My ambition is to become the author of my own life.
▶▶ 我的志願是成為自己人生當中的作者。

light [laɪt] 名燈；光 形明亮的；淺色的 動點燃；照亮

名 Passion without knowledge is like fire without light.
空有熱情卻無知識，猶如毫無光芒的火焰。
形 I was attracted by her light blue eyes.
我被她淺藍色的眼珠吸引住了。
動 He lit up the room with a flashlight.
他用手電筒照亮房間。

Level 1 基礎單字
Level 2 必備單字
Level 3 中級單字
Level 4 進階單字
Level 5 高手單字
Level 6 滿級單字

文法解析 light 動詞三態變化為 light / lit / lit。

like [laɪk] 動 喜歡 介 像；如

動 Barbara likes classical music.
芭芭拉喜歡古典音樂。

介 She looks like an angel in that white dress.
她穿著那件白色洋裝，看起來猶如天使。

line [laɪn] 名 線條 動 排隊 關 align 使成一直線

名 Do you know how long the line is?
你知道這條線有多長嗎？

動 A lot of people lined up to see the star.
為了一睹那位明星的風采，許多人排隊等候著。

焦點句型 line up = get in line 排隊 / cut in line 插隊

lion [`laɪən] 名 獅子 關 wild 野生的；粗野的 / animal 動物

The lion is a wild animal.
▶ 獅子是充滿野性的動物。

lip [lɪp] 名 嘴唇

The woman closed her lips and said nothing.
▶ 那個女人緊閉雙唇，什麼也不說。

list [lɪst] 名 清單；列表 動 列表；編目

名 This is the list of the guests who will come to our party.
這是要來參加我們宴會的賓客名單。

動 Please list what you have done on the paper.
請在這張紙上列出你已經完成的項目。

listen [`lɪsn̩] 動 聽 關 listen to 聽；聽從

They listened to the speech with great interest.
▶ 他們饒有興致地聽演講。

little [`lɪtl̩] 形 小的 副 很少地 名 沒有多少 關 a little 有點

形 He looked after the little child.
他照顧那個小孩。

副 Nancy took a nap because she was a little tired.
南西有點累了，所以去小憩。

名 The man had little to tell us.
那名男子沒有什麼好告訴我們。

文法解析 little的比較級為less（較少的），最高級則為least（最少的）。

焦點句型 look after 照顧 / take a nap 打盹；午睡

live [lɪv] / [laɪv] 動生存；居住 形有生命的；活的

動 They have lived here for over twenty years.
他們住在這裡超過二十年。
形 We sell live fish at the market.
我們在市場販賣活魚。

lonely [`lonlɪ] 形孤單的；寂寞的 關 unfamiliar 不熟悉的

I feel lonely in the unfamiliar environment.
▶ 在不熟悉的環境裡我感到孤單。

long [lɔŋ] 形長的；長久的 副長期地 動渴望 關 distance 距離

形 There is a long distance between our homes.
我們家之間距離很遠。
副 Ben waited for me all day long.
班等了我一整天。

焦點句型 long for 渴望；嚮往（動詞片語）。例如：I long for change.（我渴望改變。）

look [luk] 動看；注意 名看；表情 關 confusion 困惑 / reflection 反射

動 Elliot looked at me in confusion.
艾略特困惑地看著我。
名 I took a look at the reflection in the mirror.
我看了一眼鏡中的影像。

lose [luz] 動遺失；喪失 反 gain / win

I tried hard not to lose my cellphone.
▶ 我努力不要弄丟了手機。

文法解析 lose三態變化為lose / lost / lost。

lot [lɑt] 名很多；大量 關 warehouse 倉庫

A lot of books were kept in the warehouse.
▶ 倉庫裡堆著一大堆書。

文法解析 a lot of = lots of 許多（lots of較為口語），後面接可數或不可數名詞。

Level 1 基礎單字

Level 2 必備單字

Level 3 中級單字

Level 4 進階單字

Level 5 高手單字

Level 6 滿級單字

loud [laʊd] 形 大聲的；響亮的 關 loudly 大聲地

His loud voice woke me up.
▶▶ 他響亮的聲音把我吵醒了。

(焦點句型) wake sb. up 把某人叫醒 / sb. wake up 某人醒來

love [lʌv] 動 愛；熱愛 名 愛；愛情 關 sincere 真誠的；忠實的

動 It is difficult to remember how much you love me.
現在很難想起你有多愛我。
名 My love for you is sincere and strong.
我對你的愛是認真且堅定不移的。

lovely [`lʌvlɪ] 形 動人的；可愛的

My younger sister grew into a lovely lady.
▶▶ 我的妹妹長成一位充滿魅力的小姐。

low [lo] 形 低的 副 向下；低低地 關 bend 彎曲（過去式為bent）

形 She doesn't like low dresses, but she likes low shoes.
她不喜歡低胸洋裝，但喜歡低筒鞋。
副 His head bent low, as if he were seeking something.
他的頭彎得低低的，像是在找什麼似的。

(文法解析) as if/as though（彷彿；好像）可以引導子句，表示說話者認為極有可能、或看上去為真相的事情。

lucky [`lʌkɪ] 形 幸運的 關 luckily 幸運地

I was very lucky to get this bag so cheaply.
▶▶ 能以這麼便宜的價格買到這個包包，我真是幸運極了。

lunch [lʌntʃ] 名 午餐

We went for lunch together.
▶▶ 我們一起去吃午餐。

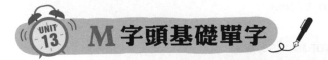

UNIT 13 **M 字頭基礎單字**　　MP3 013

machine [məˋʃin] 名 機器；機械 關 efficient 效率高的

This machine is more efficient than that one.
▶▶ 這台機器的工作效率比那台好。

Level 1 基礎單字
Level 2 必備單字
Level 3 中級單字
Level 4 進階單字
Level 5 高手單字
Level 6 滿級單字

mad [mæd] 形 瘋狂的 同 insane 關 madly 瘋狂地

The loud noise drove me mad.
▶▶ 持續不斷的噪音要把我逼瘋了。

(焦點句型) **drive sb. mad/crazy** 使某人發瘋；把某人逼瘋

magic [`mædʒɪk] 形 魔術的 名 魔術 關 magician 魔術師

形 Harry Potter is a boy with magic power.
哈利波特是個有魔法的男孩。
名 Kevin performed magic in the TV program.
凱文在電視節目裡表演魔術。

mail [mel] 名 郵件 動 郵寄 關 postcard 明信片

名 I got a mail from my mother.
我收到母親的來信。
動 David mailed a postcard to his friend.
大衛寄了一張明信片給他的朋友。

main [men] 形 主要的；最重要的

You did not answer my main question.
▶▶ 你沒有回答我主要的問題。

make [mek] 動 做；製造

The teacher taught us how to make a cake.
▶▶ 老師教我們做蛋糕。

man [mæn] 名 成年男人；人類 關 men 男人（複數形）

The man proposed to his girlfriend.
▶▶ 那名男性向女友求婚。

(焦點句型) **propose to sb.** 向某人求婚

many [`mɛnɪ] 形 許多的；多的 代 許多人；許多

How many cars does your father have?
▶▶ 你父親有幾台車呢？

(文法解析) **How many** 用來詢問某人擁有或需要的「數量」（須為可數名詞），助動詞必須與主詞一致（例如：本句主詞為 **your father**，因此搭配助動詞 **does**）。

map [mæp] 名 地圖 動 繪製…的地圖

There are maps of towns, countries, and the world in the library.
▶▶ 圖書館裡存放著各城市、國家和世界的地圖。

mark [mɑrk] 名 記號 動 標記 關 sticker 貼紙;標籤紙

名 Did you notice the mark on the wall?
你有注意到牆上的記號嗎?
動 He marked the page he read with a sticker.
他用標籤紙標記他讀到哪一頁。

market [`mɑrkɪt] 名 市場

The product will find a good market in Brazil.
▶▶ 這項產品在巴西會有好的銷路。

mathematics / math [ˌmæθə`mætɪks] / [mæθ] 名 數學

Brian is good at mathematics.
▶▶ 布萊恩擅長數學。
(焦點句型) be good at + N/Ving 擅長於…

matter [`mætɚ] 名 事情 動 要緊

名 Please let me have your thoughts on the matter.
請讓我知道你對此事的看法。
動 Nothing matters now.
所有的事情現在都不重要了。

may [me] 助 也許;可以 關 punish 懲罰

You may be punished if you don't follow the rules.
▶▶ 你如果不遵守規則,很可能會被罰。
(文法解析) 相關詞為 might,有兩種用法:其一為 may 的過去式;其二表示更加遲疑、不確定的「可能、也許」。

maybe [`mebɪ] 副 或許;大概

It's clouding up. Maybe it'll rain this afternoon.
▶▶ 天空轉陰了,今天下午也許會下雨。
(焦點句型) cloud up/over 天氣轉陰;烏雲密布(動詞片語)

meal [mil] 名 一餐 關 lose weight 減重

She eats only two meals a day in order to lose weight.
▶▶ 為了減肥,她每天只吃兩餐。

mean [min] 動意指 形惡劣的

動 Do you mean we have to hire an extra worker?
你的意思是我們得再額外僱用一名工人嗎？

形 Her mean trick was discovered by her friend.
她惡劣的詭計被朋友發現。

文法解析 mean 動詞三態變化為 mean / meant / meant。

meat [mit] 名肉

It is better to eat more vegetables than meat every day.
▶▶ 和肉相比，每天最好多吃一點蔬菜。

media [`midɪə] 名媒體 關 coverage 新聞報導 / issue 事件

The singer cares about the mass media coverage of the issue.
▶▶ 這名歌手關心大眾媒體對這項議題的報導。

文法解析 media 的單數形為 medium，但當「媒體」時習慣採用複數形。句中的 the mass media 指「大眾傳播媒介」，包含網路、電視、報紙、廣播等。

medicine [`mɛdəsn̩] 名藥 關 instruction 指示

You should take medicine according to the doctor's instructions.
▶▶ 你應該要按照醫生的指示用藥。

焦點句型 take medicine 服藥 / according to 根據

medium [`midɪəm] 形中間的；中等的

Lucy is a girl of medium height.
▶▶ 露西的身高中等。

meet [mit] 動碰見；遇到 關 meeting 會議；會面

I am eager to meet her family.
▶▶ 我迫不及待要和她的家人碰面。

焦點句型 be eager to + V / be eager for + N 渴望做某事；渴望某物

member [`mɛmbɚ] 名成員；會員

The meeting is only open to our club members.
▶▶ 這場討論會只開放給我們社團的成員。

menu [`mɛnju] 名菜單

The waiter showed us the menu.
▶▶ 服務生出示菜單給我們。

Level 1 基礎單字
Level 2 必備單字
Level 3 中級單字
Level 4 進階單字
Level 5 高手單字
Level 6 滿級單字

middle [`mɪdl̩] 形 中間的；中等的 名 中間

形 The woman in her middle age is her mother.
那名中年婦女是她的媽媽。
名 Put the sofa in the middle of the living room.
把沙發放在客廳中間。

焦點句型 in the middle of 在…中間；在…中途

milk [mɪlk] 名 牛奶 關 spill 溢出；濺出（過去分詞為spilt）

It's no use crying over spilt milk.
▶▶ 覆水難收。

million [`mɪljən] 名 百萬

The population of the city is over one million.
▶▶ 那座城市的人口超過一百萬。

mind [maɪnd] 名 頭腦；思想 動 介意

名 My friend has a brilliant mind.
我朋友的智力超群。
動 Would you mind if I opened the window?
你介意我開窗戶嗎？

mine [maɪn] 名 礦坑 代 我的（東西）關 discovery 發現

The discovery of the new mine excited everybody.
▶▶ 發現新礦坑的消息讓所有人都為之振奮。

minute [`mɪnɪt] 名 分鐘；片刻

Please wait a minute. Our manager is busy now.
▶▶ 請稍待一會兒，我們經理正在忙。

miss [mɪs] 動 想念；未擊中 名 失誤 關 target 靶子；目標

動 I miss my old friends from my high school days.
我想念高中時期的老朋友。
名 He hit the target three times without a miss.
他三次都命中目標，毫無失誤。

mistake [mɪ`stek] 名 錯誤；過失 關 blame 責備

Do not blame others for small mistakes.
▶▶ 不要為了小錯而去責備他人。

焦點句型 blame sb. for sth. = blame sth. on sb. 把某事怪罪到某人身上

modern [`mɑdən] 形現代的 關 ballet 芭蕾舞

Modern dance comes from ballet.
>> 現代舞由芭蕾衍生而來。

moment [`momənt] 名時刻；瞬間 關 cherish 珍愛

I cherish every moment I spend with you.
>> 我珍惜與你共處的每一刻。

money [`mʌnɪ] 名錢

Money is important to everyone.
>> 錢財對所有人而言都很重要。

monkey [`mʌŋkɪ] 名猴子；猿

When the tree fell, the monkeys ran away.
>> 樹倒猢猻散。

(焦點句型) **run away** 逃跑；出走

month [mʌnθ] 名月

Which month is the nicest month of the year?
>> 一年中最美好的月份是哪個月呢？

moon [mun] 名月亮 關 shine 發光；照耀

The moon is still the moon, whether it shines or not.
>> 不管皎潔與否，月亮終究是月亮。

more [mor] 形更多的；另外的 關 earn 賺得；掙得

He works hard in order to earn more money.
>> 為了賺更多錢，他努力工作。

morning [`mɔrnɪŋ] 名早晨；上午 關 go jogging 去慢跑

I went jogging this morning.
>> 我今天早上去慢跑。

most [most] 形最多的；大部分的 代最多數 副最多；最大程度地

形 Most people take their holidays in the summer.
大多數人在夏季休假。
代 I finally persuaded most of them.
我終於說服他們之中大多數的人。

1 Level 基礎單字
2 Level 必備單字
3 Level 中級單字
4 Level 進階單字
5 Level 高手單字
6 Level 滿級單字

副 I like summer the most.
我最喜歡夏天。

mother [`mʌðɚ] 名 母親

My mother gave birth to me and brought me up on her own.
▶▶ 我媽媽獨力生養我。

(焦點句型) give birth to 生產 / bring up 養育 / on one's own 獨自

mountain [`maʊntn̩] 名 山

Many animals live in the mountains.
▶▶ 許多動物棲息於山林中。

mouse [maʊs] 名 老鼠

The cat is chasing a mouse.
▶▶ 貓正在追老鼠。

mouth [maʊθ] 名 嘴；口

You should cover your mouth when you sneeze.
▶▶ 打噴嚏時應該遮住嘴巴。

move [muv] 動 移動；感動 關 movement 運動；移動

The couple will move in the apartment next month.
▶▶ 這對夫妻下個月會搬進這棟公寓。

movie / film [`muvɪ] / [fɪlm] 名 （一部）電影

Ivan invited me to see a movie with him.
▶▶ 艾文邀我和他去看電影。

much [mʌtʃ] 形 大量的 代 許多 副 非常

形 How much rent do you pay?
你付多少租金呢？
代 Much of the time was wasted yesterday.
昨天浪費了很多時間。
副 Katie hasn't changed much since she was in high school.
高中以後的凱蒂並沒有多大的變化。

文法解析 與名詞連用時，much 只能搭配「不可數名詞」；many 則會與「可數名詞的複數形」
連用。

mud [mʌd] 名爛泥

My coat is covered with mud.
▶▶ 我的外套沾上了汙泥。

museum [mju`zɪəm] 名博物館 關 famous 出名的 / exhibit 展示

The famous paintings of Da Vinci will be exhibited in the museum.
▶▶ 達文西的名畫即將在博物館展出。

music [`mjuzɪk] 名音樂 關 musician 音樂家 / pastime 消遣

Listening to music is one of my pastimes.
▶▶ 聽音樂是我的消遣之一。

must [mʌst] 助必須 關 soldier 士兵 / obey 服從

Soldiers must obey orders.
▶▶ 軍人必須服從命令。

UNIT 14 **N 字頭基礎單字**

MP3 014

name [nem] 名名字 動給…取名 關 surname 姓氏

I am not good at remembering others' names.
▶▶ 我不擅長記別人的名字。

national [`næʃənl̩] 形國家的；全國性的

Scott played basketball for the national team.
▶▶ 史考特為國家隊打籃球。

nature [`netʃɚ] 名自然 關 generous 慷慨的

It is his nature to be generous.
▶▶ 慷慨大方是他的天性。

near [nɪr] 介在…附近 形近的；接近的 副接近

介 Molly lives near the school, but she is still late for school every day.
莫莉就住在學校附近，但她還是天天遲到。
形 Where is the nearest supermarket?
最近的超市在哪裡呢？

Level 1 基礎單字
Level 2 必備單字
Level 3 中級單字
Level 4 進階單字
Level 5 高手單字
Level 6 滿級單字

neck [nɛk] 名脖子 關 scarf 圍巾

My mother threw a scarf over her neck.
▶▶ 母親隨手把一條圍巾披在脖子上。

need [nid] 動 需要 名 需要；需求

動 I will come here whenever you need my help.
無論何時，只要你需要我幫忙，我都會過來。
名 He donated money to the people in need.
他捐款給有需要的人。

net [nɛt] 名網 動 編網

The fishermen caught fish in their nets.
▶▶ 漁夫們用網捕魚。

never [`nɛvɚ] 副 從未；永不

He said that he has never told a lie.
▶▶ 他聲稱他從來沒說過謊。

new [nju] 形 新的 關 replace 取代

I bought a new table to replace the old one.
▶▶ 我買了一張新桌子取代舊的。

news [njuz] 名 新聞

The news really surprised us.
▶▶ 這則新聞令我們感到震驚。

newspaper [`njuz͵pepɚ] 名 報紙 關 article 文章

Lisa writes articles for the newspaper.
▶▶ 麗莎替報紙撰寫文章。

next [nɛkst] 形 其次的；居後的 副 其次；然後 關 patient 病患

形 The nurse called the next patient.
護士呼叫下一位病患。
副 What are you going to do next?
你下一步要怎麼做？

nice [naɪs] 形 善良的；好的

She is such a nice person that everyone likes her.
▶▶ 她是個很棒的人，大家都喜歡她。

night [naɪt] 名 晚上；夜晚 關 owl 貓頭鷹 / active 在活動中的

Owls are only active at night.
▶▶ 貓頭鷹只在夜間活動。

no / nope [no] / [nop] 形 沒有 副 不是 名 沒有；否定

形 No two men think alike.
　 沒有人的想法是相同的。
副 Jack is no better than a liar.
　 傑克和騙子沒什麼兩樣。

nobody [`no͵bɑdɪ] 代 沒有人 名 無名小卒

代 Nobody called you yesterday.
　 昨天沒人打電話找你。
名 Although I am a nobody today, I will become a somebody in the future.
　 雖然我今天還只是個無名小卒，但我將來必定要成為大人物。

noise [nɔɪz] 名 噪音；聲響

There was a noise downstairs.
▶▶ 樓下傳來一陣很吵的聲音。

noisy [`nɔɪzɪ] 形 吵鬧的；喧鬧的 關 annoying 惱人的

The noisy traffic is annoying to the people in the area.
▶▶ 這區的居民都覺得嘈雜的交通聲令人心煩。

noon [nun] 名 正午；中午

At noon, the sun is high in the sky.
▶▶ 正午，烈日當空。

north [nɔrθ] 名 北方 形 北方的 副 向北方

名 He drove toward the north.
　 他開車向北方行駛。
形 Mexico is in the southern part of North America.
　 墨西哥位於北美大陸的南邊。

nose [noz] 名 鼻子

Dogs have good noses.
▶▶ 狗的嗅覺很靈敏。

Level 1 基礎單字
Level 2 必備單字
Level 3 中級單字
Level 4 進階單字
Level 5 高手單字
Level 6 滿級單字

note [not] 名筆記 動注意

名 I took notes during the class.
我上課時把老師講的內容都做了筆記。
動 He noted the girl with beautiful earrings.
他注意到那個戴著美麗耳環的女孩。
(焦點句型) take a note 記下 / take note of sth. 關注

nothing [`nʌθɪŋ] 代無事;無物 名微不足道的人或事

I found nothing in the bag.
▶▶ 我發現背包裡什麼也沒有。

notice [`notɪs] 動注意 名布告 關 presence 出席 / hardly 幾乎不

動 She was so quiet that her presence was hardly noticed.
她一聲不響,幾乎沒有人留意到她在場。
名 The notice says that Sally will be our new manager.
布告上說莎莉是我們的新任經理。

now [naʊ] 副現在;馬上 名現在;目前

副 You must clean up your room right now.
你必須現在就清理你的房間。
名 Now is the best time to go shopping.
現在是購物的最佳時機。

number [`nʌmbɚ] 名數字 動編號 關 conference room 會議室

A number of people left the conference room.
▶▶ 一些人離開了會議室。
文法解析 a number of 為形容詞片語,修飾後面的複數名詞。

nurse [nɝs] 名護士 關 measure 測量 / blood pressure 血壓

The nurse measured my blood pressure.
▶▶ 護士替我量血壓。

MP3 015

O.K. / OK / okay [o`ke] 形可以的;很好的

Is it O.K. for you to complete the report?
▶▶ 你可以完成這份報告嗎?

Level 1 基礎單字

Level 2 必備單字

Level 3 中級單字

Level 4 進階單字

Level 5 高手單字

Level 6 滿級單字

o'clock [ə`klɑk] 副 ⋯點鐘

I came here at eight o'clock.
▶▶ 我八點時來到這裡。

office [`ɔfɪs] 名 辦公室

They are chatting in the office.
▶▶ 他們在辦公室裡聊天。

officer [`ɔfɪsɚ] 名 官員

The officer kept saying I did something wrong.
▶▶ 這名官員不斷重申我做錯了事。

often [`ɔfən] 副 常常；經常

Do you go to the movies often?
▶▶ 你常常去看電影嗎？
焦點句型 go to the movies 看電影

oil [ɔɪl] 名 油 關 well 井；水井

There are many oil wells in the oil field.
▶▶ 油田裡有許多油井。

old [old] 形 年老的；舊的 關 support 支撐 / cane 拐杖

The old man supported himself with a cane.
▶▶ 這個老人用一根手杖作為支撐。

once [wʌns] 副 曾經；一次 連 一旦 名 一次；一回

副 I have been here once before.
我以前曾經來過這裡。
連 Once you give up, you will lose.
一旦放棄，你就會輸。

online [`ɑn,laɪn] 形 線上的 關 bill 法案 / prohibit 禁止 / alcohol 酒

The bill that prohibits online alcohol advertising finally passed.
▶▶ 禁止線上酒類廣告的法案終於通過了。

only [`onlɪ] 形 唯一的 副 只；僅僅 關 ingredient 原料

形 She is the only female in her department.
她是她部門裡唯一的女生。

副 We use only the best ingredients.
我們只使用最好的原料。

open [`opən] 動打開 形打開的；開放的

動 He opened the door to see who rang the bell.
他開門看是誰按的電鈴。
形 People all over the world can take the open course through the Internet.
全世界的人都可以透過網路上這堂公開課程。
(焦點句型) ring the bell 按電鈴 / all over the world 世界各地

or [ɔr] 連或者；否則 關 apologize 道歉 / sincerely 誠懇地

Apologize sincerely or she will not forgive you.
▶ 你得誠心道歉，不然她不會原諒你。

orange [`ɔrɪndʒ] 名柳丁 形橘色的

名 I ate some oranges after dinner.
我晚餐後吃了一些柳丁。
形 Cathy wore an orange T-shirt.
凱西穿了一件橘色 T 恤。

order [`ɔrdɚ] 名次序；有條理 動下命令

名 She kept her room in the best order.
她把房間維持得井井有條。
動 My father ordered me to buy a newspaper.
爸爸命令我去買份報紙。
(焦點句型) in order 按照順序；情況良好

other [`ʌðɚ] 形其他的 代另一方；其餘的人或物

I don't want this book; I want the other one.
▶ 我不想要這本書，我想要的是另外一本。
(文法解析) 當代名詞的 other 等於「other（形）+ 名詞」，例如：若句子開頭出現 some kids，後面的 other kids 就可以寫成 others。

outside [`aut`saɪd] 介在…外面 副在外面 形外面的 名外面；外部

介 I saw a man outside the classroom.
我看到教室外有一個男人。
副 It's such a nice day. Let's go outside.
天氣這麼好，我們出門走走吧。

Level 1 基礎單字

Level 2 必備單字

Level 3 中級單字

Level 4 進階單字

Level 5 高手單字

Level 6 滿級單字

形 He enjoyed the outside scenery through the window.
他透過窗戶欣賞外面的風景。

over [`ovɚ] 介 在…上方；超過 副 越過；超過 形 結束的

介 I jumped over the stream.
我躍過溪流。

副 The soup spilled over.
湯溢出來了。

形 We felt excited when the examination was over.
考試結束時，我們感到很興奮。

own [on] 形 自己的 動 擁有

形 We made our own sandwiches for the picnic.
我們自己做野餐的三明治。

動 The gentleman owns the villa.
這名紳士擁有那棟別墅。

UNIT 16 P 字頭基礎單字

MP3 016

pack [pæk] 名 一包 動 打包

名 My mother asked me to buy a pack of paper.
媽媽叫我去買一包紙。

動 We will leave tomorrow, but I haven't begun to pack yet.
我們明天動身，但我還沒有開始收拾行李呢。

package [`pækɪdʒ] 名 包裹；包

There were only three pieces of clothing in the package.
▶▶ 包裹裡只有三件衣服。

page [pedʒ] 名 書頁

Please turn to page eight and read the text.
▶▶ 請翻到第八頁，並閱讀課文。

paint [pent] 名 油漆；顏料 動 繪畫；油漆 關 portrait 肖像畫

名 My mother bought me a box of paints.
媽媽替我買了一盒顏料。

動 Linda painted my portrait.
琳達畫了一張我的肖像。

pair [pɛr] 名一對；一雙 關 sock(s) 短襪

The boy lost one of the pair of socks.
▶▶ 男孩弄丟了其中一隻襪子。

pants [pænts] 名褲子 關 stain 變髒 / mud 泥

My pants were stained with mud.
▶▶ 我的褲子被爛泥弄髒了。

paper [`pepɚ] 名紙；報紙；試卷

The English paper was quite difficult.
▶▶ 這次的英文試題很難。

parent [`pɛrənt] 名雙親；家長 關 single mother/father 單親媽媽/爸爸

I grew up in a single-parent family.
▶▶ 我在單親家庭長大。

park [park] 名公園 動停放 關 basement 地下室

名 We exercise in the park every morning.
我們每天早晨都去公園運動。
動 Denny parked his car in the basement.
丹尼把車停在地下室。

part [part] 名部分 動分開

名 I only read this part of the chapter.
我只讀了這個章節的這一部分內容。
動 Nina doesn't want to part from her family.
妮娜捨不得與家人分開。

party [`partɪ] 名派對；黨派

They held a birthday party for Bob.
▶▶ 他們為鮑伯舉辦了一場生日派對。

pass [pæs] 動通過；經過 名及格 關 mature 成熟的

動 As time passes by, we become more mature.
隨著時間流逝，我們變得更為成熟。
名 I only got a pass in English.
我的英文剛好及格而已。

past [pæst] 形 過去的 名 過去 介 經過；通過

形 In the past few years, they have been dealing with quite a few companies.
在過去幾年當中，他們與滿多公司做生意，一直都很成功。

名 My husband used to smoke in the past.
我老公以前會抽菸。

介 My colleague went past my house.
我同事經過我家。

pay [pe] 動 付錢 關 payment 支付；支付的款項

Larry forgot to pay the phone bill.
▶▶ 賴瑞忘了繳電話費。

pen [pɛn] 名 原子筆

My roommate used my pen without asking me.
▶▶ 我室友沒先問過我，就拿我的筆去用。

pencil [`pɛnsl̩] 名 鉛筆 關 sharpen 削尖

The boy sharpened his pencils.
▶▶ 那位男孩把鉛筆削尖。

people [`pipl̩] 名 人（複數）

I saw many people at the dance party.
▶▶ 我在舞會上見到了許多人。

perhaps [pɚ`hæps] 副 也許；可能 關 decide 決定

Perhaps he decided to quit his job.
▶▶ 也許他決定辭去工作了。

（焦點句型）quit one's job（某人）辭職

person [`pɝsn̩] 名 人（單數） 關 everyone 每個人 / everything 每件事或物

Sarah is a nice person who always treats everyone well.
▶▶ 莎拉是個好人，總是待人和善。

pet [pɛt] 名 寵物

Mr. Watson keeps a dog as a pet.
▶▶ 華森先生養了一隻狗當寵物。

Level 1 基礎單字
Level 2 必備單字
Level 3 中級單字
Level 4 進階單字
Level 5 高手單字
Level 6 滿級單字

photograph / photo [`fotə‚græf ] / [ `foto] 名照片 動照相

I was so ugly in this photograph.
▶▶ 我在這張照片裡真難看。

piano [pɪ`æno] 名鋼琴

George plays piano very well.
▶▶ 喬治的鋼琴彈得非常好。

pick [pɪk] 動選擇 名選擇

She picked the best piece of cake for herself.
▶▶ 她為自己挑了一塊最好的蛋糕。

picnic [`pɪknɪk] 名野餐 動野餐

名 My family went on a picnic on Sunday.
我的家人星期天去野餐。
動 They decided to go picnicking in the park.
他們決定去公園裡野餐。

文法解析 picnic 過去式與過去分詞為 picnicked，現在分詞為 picnicking。

焦點句型 go on a picnic 去野餐

picture [`pɪktʃɚ] 名圖片；相片 動想像；描繪 關 castle 城堡

He took some pictures of the castle.
▶▶ 他拍了幾張城堡的相片。

焦點句型 take a picture 拍照

pie [paɪ] 名派

My mother made some apple pie for the picnic.
▶▶ 我媽媽為野餐烤了一些蘋果派。

piece [pis] 名一塊；一片

He tore a piece of paper from the notebook.
▶▶ 他從筆記本上撕了一張紙。

文法解析 paper（紙張）為不可數名詞，紙張數目須使用 piece，如：a piece of paper（一張紙）、two pieces of paper（兩張紙），複數形必須用 piece 呈現。

pig [pɪg] 名豬

A pig is a domestic animal.
▶▶ 豬是一種家畜。

Level 1 基礎單字
Level 2 必備單字
Level 3 中級單字
Level 4 進階單字
Level 5 高手單字
Level 6 滿級單字

pin [pɪn] 名針 動釘住 關 stab 刺入；戳

My finger was stabbed with a pin.
▶▶ 我的手指被大頭針刺傷。

pink [pɪŋk] 形粉紅色的 名粉紅色

形 She tied up her hair with a pink ribbon.
她用一條粉紅色緞帶將頭髮紮起來。
名 Pink is the color I dislike most.
粉紅色是我最不喜歡的顏色。

pipe [paɪp] 名管子 動以管傳送

Copper pipes are sold in lengths.
▶▶ 銅管按長度出售。

place [ples] 名地方 動放置 關 venue 發生地

名 It is a good place to play badminton.
這裡是打羽毛球的好地方。
動 I placed some dishes on the dining table.
我放了幾道菜在餐桌上。

plan [plæn] 動計畫；打算 名計畫

動 He planned a trip around the island.
他計畫環島旅行。
名 The boss seems satisfied with his plan.
老闆看起來對他的計畫很滿意。
焦點句型 be satisfied with 對…感到滿意

planet [`plænɪt] 名行星

The Solar System is made up of all the planets that orbit the Sun.
▶▶ 太陽系是由所有環繞太陽運行的行星所組成。

plant [plænt] 名工廠；植物 動栽種

These plants grow in many areas of China.
▶▶ 這些植物在中國許多地方皆有生長。

plate [plet] 名盤子

The waiter accidentally broke the plate.
▶▶ 侍者不小心把盤子打破了。

play [ple] 動玩耍 名玩耍；遊戲；戲劇

動 The children are playing with a ball.
孩子們正在玩球。
名 Work and play are important for everyone.
工作和娛樂對每個人而言都很重要。

player [`pleə] 名運動員；玩家

The players are warming up beside the swimming pool.
▶▶ 運動員們在游泳池邊暖身。
焦點句型 warm up 暖身

please [pliz] 動使高興 嘆請

動 Pamela was pleased by his compliment.
潘蜜拉被他的恭維取悅了。
嘆 Wait for a while, please.
請稍待一會兒。

pleasure [`plɛʒə] 名愉悅；滿意；樂趣

Are you here on business or for pleasure?
▶▶ 你是來這裡工作還是來玩的？

pocket [`pɑkɪt] 名口袋 形袖珍的 關 change 零錢

名 He took out some change from his pocket.
他從口袋掏出一些零錢。
形 Pocket books are easy to carry around.
袖珍書便於攜帶。

point [pɔɪnt] 名點；要點 動瞄準；指向

名 I totally agree with your points.
我完全同意你的論點。
動 He pointed in the right direction for me.
他向我指出正確的方向。

police [pə`lis] 名警方；警察

There were over 200 police officers on duty.
▶▶ 有超過二百名員警值勤。

polite [pəˋlaɪt] 形 有禮貌的

A polite person is welcomed everywhere.
▶▶ 有禮貌的人到哪裡都受歡迎。

pond [pɑnd] 名 池塘

Most farms have a pond from which cattle can drink.
▶▶ 大多數農場都有水槽讓牛群飲水。

pool [pul] 名 水池

Her earring dropped into the pool.
▶▶ 她的耳環掉進水池中。

poor [pʊr] 形 貧窮的

Although I am poor, I am rich in spirit.
▶▶ 雖然我很窮，但是我的心靈很富足。

popcorn [ˋpɑpˏkɔrn] 名 爆米花

Many people watch movies while eating popcorn.
▶▶ 很多人一邊吃爆米花，一邊看電影。

popular [ˋpɑpjələ] 形 流行的；受歡迎的

Eager fans lined up to see the popular singer.
▶▶ 熱切的歌迷們排隊去見這位流行歌手。
(焦點句型) be popular with sb. 受…歡迎

possible [ˋpɑsəbḷ] 形 可能的

I don't think it is possible to persuade him.
▶▶ 我不認為有可能說服他。

pot [pɑt] 名 鍋；壺

They drank a pot of coffee.
▶▶ 他們喝了一壺咖啡。

potato [pəˋteto] 名 馬鈴薯 關 sprout 發芽

A sprouted potato is not good to eat.
▶▶ 發芽的馬鈴薯不能吃。

Level 1 基礎單字
Level 2 必備單字
Level 3 中級單字
Level 4 進階單字
Level 5 高手單字
Level 6 滿級單字

power [`pauɚ] 名 力量；權力

Francis Bacon said: "Knowledge is power."
▶▶ 法蘭西斯‧培根說：「知識就是力量。」

practice [`præktɪs] 名 練習 動 實踐 關 practitioner 實踐者

名 Practice makes perfect.
熟能生巧。
動 She never practices what she says.
她從不實踐她說過的話。

prepare [prɪ`per] 動 準備

Peggy stayed up late to prepare for the test.
▶▶ 佩姬熬夜準備考試。

present [`prɛznt ] / [ prɪ`zɛnt] 名 禮物 形 目前的 動 呈現

形 I was very anxious about the present crisis.
我對目前的危機感到焦慮。
動 Remember to present smiles no matter how nervous you are.
無論你多緊張，都要記得展現笑容。

pretty [`prɪtɪ] 形 漂亮的；美好的

The blonde is very pretty.
▶▶ 那位金髮女孩非常漂亮。

price [praɪs] 名 價格

He thought the price of the computer was high.
▶▶ 他認為那台電腦的價格很貴。

probably [`prabəblɪ] 副 可能地 同 supposedly

This year's budget for education probably will be cut down .
▶▶ 今年的教育預算可能會有縮減。

problem [`prabləm] 名 問題

They have found no solution to the problem so far.
▶▶ 他們目前還沒找到問題的解決方法。

program [`progræm] 名 節目；計畫

The last item on the program was a grand display of fireworks.
▶▶ 活動的最後一項節目是大型煙火表演。

Level 1 基礎單字
Level 2 必備單字
Level 3 中級單字
Level 4 進階單字
Level 5 高手單字
Level 6 滿級單字

proud [praʊd] 形 驕傲的

He is too proud to ask questions.
▶▶ 他傲慢到不屑於發問。

public [`pʌblɪk] 形 公共的；公開的 名 公眾；民眾

形 The park in town is public, but some gardens are private.
城市裡的公園是對大眾開放的，但有些花園是私人的。
名 The public is angry at the president.
民眾對總統十分憤怒。

pull [pʊl] 動 拉；拖

Don't pull so hard or the handle will come off.
▶▶ 別太使勁拉，不然把手會脫落。

push [pʊʃ] 動 推 名 推

Tom tried to push the door open but it was stuck.
▶▶ 湯姆試著把門推開，但門卡住了。

put [pʊt] 動 放置

Never put off until tomorrow what you can do today.
▶▶ 今日事，今日畢。

文法解析 put 動詞三態同形，皆為 put。

焦點句型 put off 拖延

 Q 字頭基礎單字

MP3 017

quarter [`kwɔrtɚ] 名 四分之一 動 分成四等分

It's a quarter to six.
▶▶ 現在是五點四十五分。

queen [kwin] 名 女王；皇后

The royal family consists of the king, queen and their relations.
▶▶ 皇室由國王、王后以及他們的親屬組成。

question [`kwɛstʃən] 名問題 動質疑

The teacher did not answer my question.
▶▶ 老師沒有回答我的問題。

quick [kwɪk] 形快的；迅速的

What you need to do is just to give your suit a quick brush.
▶▶ 你只需要把你的西裝很快地刷一刷就行了。

quiet [`kwaɪət] 形安靜的 名安靜 動使安靜

形 Keep quiet. The baby is sleeping.
　　安靜，嬰兒正在睡覺。
名 He enjoys the quiet of country life.
　　他享受鄉村生活的安靜。

quite [kwaɪt] 副相當地

She looks quite pale.
▶▶ 她的臉色很蒼白。

 R字頭基礎單字

MP3 018

rabbit [`ræbɪt] 名兔子

A rabbit hopped across the path.
▶▶ 一隻兔子蹦蹦跳跳地穿過小徑。

race [res] 動賽跑 名種族

動 He raced with me.
　　他和我賽跑。
名 There are various races in the country.
　　這個國家有很多民族。

radio [`redɪˏo] 名收音機

We can listen to music on the radio.
▶▶ 我們能用收音機聽音樂。

rain [ren] 名雨 動下雨

名 We had better stay home because of the heavy rain.
　　外面正下著大雨，我們最好待在家裡。

MEMORIZE 7000 VOCABULARIES ONCE AND FOR ALL！

動 It rains cats and dogs every winter.
每逢冬天都會下大雨。

(焦點句型) it rains cats and dogs 下大雨

rainbow [`ren,bo] **名**彩虹

Sophia was so excited to see the rainbow that she almost forgot to take a picture.
▶▶ 蘇菲亞看到彩虹時太過興奮，以至於差點忘記拍照。

rainy [`renɪ] **形**多雨的

This visitor finds the rainy weather of the United Kingdom annoying.
▶▶ 這位遊客覺得英國多雨的氣候很討厭。

raise [rez] **動**舉起；提高；提出

That is why he raised the question.
▶▶ 這就是他之所以提出問題的原因。

reach [ritʃ] **動**到達；伸手拿

He finally reached his goal.
▶▶ 他終於達成目標。

read [rid] **動**閱讀；讀懂

I can read French, but I can't speak it.
▶▶ 我看得懂法文，但卻不會說。

文法解析 read的動詞三態同形，皆為read，僅發音不同。

ready [`rɛdɪ] **形**準備好的

Are you ready for the game?
▶▶ 你準備好要比賽了嗎？

real [`riəl] **形**真的；真實的 **副** really 真正地

We didn't believe their threats were for real.
▶▶ 我們不相信他們的威脅是真的。

reason [`rizn̩] **名**理由

Give me a specific reason for your action.
▶▶ 針對你的行為，給我一個具體的理由。

Level 1 基礎單字
Level 2 必備單字
Level 3 中級單字
Level 4 進階單字
Level 5 高手單字
Level 6 滿級單字

red [rɛd] 名紅色 形紅色的

名 Red means good luck in Chinese culture.
在中華文化裡，紅色是吉利的象徵。
形 She had her hair dyed red.
她把頭髮染紅了。

relative [`rɛlətɪv] 形相對的；有關係的 名親戚

形 Nothing is fixed in this world; everything is relative.
世上沒有什麼是固定不變的，一切都是相對的。
名 His relatives are always curious about when he will marry.
親戚們對他何時結婚總是感到好奇。

remember [rɪ`mɛmbɚ] 動記得

I remembered suddenly that I had an appointment.
▶▶ 我突然想起我有個約會。

repeat [rɪ`pit] 動覆誦；重複

If you repeat what you learn, it helps you remember it.
▶▶ 覆誦你所學的東西，會幫助你記憶。

report [rɪ`port] 動報告；舉報 名報告

動 He reported the details of the incident.
他報告事件的細節。
名 Turn in your report by Friday.
在禮拜五前繳交你的報告。

reporter [rɪ`portɚ] 名記者

The minister was surrounded by reporters in no time.
▶▶ 部長很快被記者圍住。

rest [rɛst] 名休息 動依賴

名 Let's take a rest.
讓我們休息一下。
動 The whole plan rests on everything going right.
整個計畫都建立在事情順利進行的前提下。

restaurant [`rɛstərɑnt] 名餐廳

This restaurant serves Tibetan food.
▶▶ 這家餐廳供應藏式料理。

rice [raɪs] 名稻米；米飯

Rice is the staple of the area.
▶▶ 稻米是這個地區的主食。

rich [rɪtʃ] 形富裕的；豐富的

The rich man looked down on the beggars.
▶▶ 那位富翁瞧不起乞丐。

ride [raɪd] 動騎；乘 名騎乘；兜風

動 He rides a bike to school.
他騎腳踏車去學校。
名 We went for a ride in the car.
我們開車兜風。
文法解析 ride動詞三態變化為 ride / rode / ridden。

right [raɪt] 形右邊的；正確的 名右邊

形 "England" is the right answer to the question.
「英格蘭」是這題的正確答案。
名 The person standing on my right is my best friend.
站在我右邊的人是我最好的朋友。

ring [rɪŋ] 動按鈴 名戒指

動 Ring the bell to inform me of your coming.
按電鈴告訴我你到了。
名 He proposed to her with a diamond ring.
他用鑽石戒指向她求婚。
文法解析 ring動詞三態變化為 ring / rang / rung。

rise [raɪz] 動上升 名升起

動 It seems that every year the prices for everything rise.
每年的物價似乎都會上漲。
名 The rise in the unemployment rate is continuing.
失業率仍持續上升。
文法解析 rise動詞三態變化為 rise / rose / risen。

river [`rɪvɚ] 名小河

My mother is fishing by the river.
▶▶ 我媽媽在河邊釣魚。

Level 1 基礎單字
Level 2 必備單字
Level 3 中級單字
Level 4 進階單字
Level 5 高手單字
Level 6 滿級單字

road [rod] 名道路

Hard work is the road to success.
▶▶ 努力工作是通往成功之路。

robot [`robɑt] 名機器人

The robot can help you do the housework.
▶▶ 這個機器人可以幫你做家事。

rock [rɑk] 名石頭

Mountains are made of rocks.
▶▶ 山是由岩石構成的。

roll [rol] 動捲；滾動 名名冊

動 Let's roll up our sleeves!
　　準備動手吧！
名 Vicky is not in the roll of the class.
　　薇琪不在班級名冊中。

room [rum] 名房間

He booked a room in the hotel.
▶▶ 他在飯店訂了一間房。

rose [roz] 名玫瑰花 形玫瑰色的

名 No rose is without a thorn.
　　沒有不帶刺的玫瑰。
形 The young girl has rose cheeks.
　　這個年輕少女有著玫瑰色的雙頰。

round [raʊnd] 形圓的 名巡迴；巡視 介在…四周 動環繞而行

形 In ancient times, few people believed that the Earth is round.
　　在古代，很少有人相信地球是圓的。
名 The doctor is on his round of visits.
　　醫生在視察病房。
介 They sat round the table.
　　他們圍桌而坐。

row [ro] 名列；排 動划船

名 The sum of the three rows is 85.
　　這三列的總和是八十五。

Level
1
基礎單字

Level
2
必備單字

Level
3
中級單字

Level
4
進階單字

Level
5
高手單字

Level
6
滿級單字

(動) They rowed across the lake.
他們划船過湖。

rule [rul] (名)規則 (動)統治

(名) He does everything by rules.
他事事墨守成規。

(動) Every four years, we choose a government to rule us.
每隔四年,我們就得選出一個政府來治理國家。

ruler [`rulɚ] (名)統治者;直尺

The new nation needs a modern ruler.
▶▶ 這個新興的國家需要具有現代思想的統治者。

run [rʌn] (動)奔跑

The dog is running after the truck.
▶▶ 狗正在追逐卡車。

文法解析 run動詞三態變化為 run / ran / run。

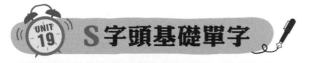 **S 字頭基礎單字**

 MP3 019

sad [sæd] (形)難過的 (關) sadness 悲傷

I feel sad because the activity was canceled.
▶▶ 我很難過,因為活動取消了。

safe [sef] (形)安全的

It is not safe to take so much money with you.
▶▶ 你帶著那麼多錢並不安全。

salad [`sæləd] (名)沙拉

I ordered fruit salad and a cup of coffee.
▶▶ 我點了水果沙拉和一杯咖啡。

sale [sel] (名)出售

The sale of alcohol to people under 18 is not allowed.
▶▶ 法律禁止向十八歲以下的人出售含有酒精的飲料。

salt [sɑlt] 名 鹽 形 含鹽的 關 salty 鹹的

名 My father forgot to put salt in the soup.
我爸爸忘記在湯裡放鹽。
形 Tom brushes teeth with salt water.
湯姆用鹽水刷牙。

same [sem] 形 同樣的 副 同樣地 名 同樣的事；一模一樣

形 He is the same person I met yesterday.
他就是我昨天遇到的那個人。
副 "High" and "hi" are pronounced the same.
「high」和「hi」發音相同。
名 My sister thinks the same as I do.
我妹妹跟我想的一模一樣。

save [sev] 動 儲蓄；拯救 關 salvage 救助

He saves one hundred dollars every day.
▶▶ 他每天存一百元。

say [se] 動 說；講

They say our company is losing a lot of money.
▶▶ 他們說我們公司賠了許多錢。

school [skul] 名 學校

I think my school days were the most memorable in my life.
▶▶ 我認為學校生活是我一生中最難忘的日子。

science [`saɪəns] 名 科學

Science and technology are related to each other.
▶▶ 科學和技術是相輔相成的。

sea [si] 名 海洋

There are lots of secrets under the sea.
▶▶ 深海裡藏著許多秘密。

season [`sizn̩] 名 季節

Fall is the season I like the best.
▶▶ 秋天是我最喜歡的季節。

seat [sit] 名座位 動給…安排座位；使坐下

名 Go back to your seat.
回到你的座位上。
動 He seated himself on a rock.
他坐在一塊石頭上。
文法解析 做動詞用時為及物動詞，受詞多是人，且常會在受詞後用副詞片語或介係詞片語補充說明坐下的位置。

second [`sɛkənd] 形第二的 名（時間）秒

形 Andy got second prize in the cooking contest.
安迪在這次烹飪比賽中獲得第二名。
名 Every second counts.
爭分奪秒。

secretary [`sɛkrə,tɛrɪ] 名祕書

As a secretary, Isabella reminds her boss of every meeting.
▶ 身為祕書，伊莎貝拉要提醒老闆每一個會議。

see [si] 動看；理解

I saw him going out of his home with a lady.
▶ 我看見他和一位女士一起從家裡出來。
文法解析 see動詞三態變化為 see / saw / seen。

seed [sid] 名種子 動播種

Bananas have small seeds.
▶ 香蕉的種子很小。

sell [sɛl] 動賣；銷售

He sells handmade cookies.
▶ 他販售手工餅乾。

send [sɛnd] 動寄出

He sent off his resume over a month ago but got no response.
▶ 他在一個多月前就寄出履歷了，但一直沒有下文。

sentence [`sɛntəns] 名句子 動判決

名 A sentence usually contains a subject and a verb.
句子通常包括主語和動詞。

Level 1 基礎單字
Level 2 必備單字
Level 3 中級單字
Level 4 進階單字
Level 5 高手單字
Level 6 滿級單字

(動) The murderer was sentenced to death.
那個殺人犯被判死刑。

serious [`sɪrɪəs] (形) 嚴肅的

He told me the bad news with a serious expression.
▶▶ 他神色肅穆地告訴我這個壞消息。

service [`sɜvɪs] (名) 服務

I tipped the waiter for his good service.
▶▶ 我給了那個服務生小費，因為他的服務品質很棒。

set [sɛt] (名) 一套 (動) 設置

(名) She bought a dinner set that was made in China.
她買了一套中國製的餐具。
(動) I always set the alarm clock for 6 a.m.
我總是把鬧鐘設在早上六點。
文法解析 set 的動詞三態同形，皆為 set。

several [`sɛvərəl] (形) 幾個的 (代) 幾個

He felt hungry and ate several buns.
▶▶ 他很餓，就吃了幾個小圓麵包。

shake [ʃek] (動) 搖動 (名) 搖動；握手

(動) The whole house shakes when a train goes past.
火車駛過時，整座房子都搖動起來。
(名) Give the bottle a good shake before opening it.
打開瓶子前，先使勁搖一搖。
文法解析 shake 動詞三態變化為 shake / shook / shaken。

shall [ʃæl] (助) 將；會

Shall we call the police?
▶▶ 我們該叫警察嗎？
文法解析 shall 的過去式為 should。

shape [ʃep] (名) 形狀 (動) 使成形

A huge shape could be seen in the distance.
▶▶ 從遠處就能看見一個巨大的形體。

share [ʃɛr] 動 分享 名 份；股份

動 Thomas and I share a room.
湯瑪斯和我共用一間房。

名 I have had my share of dessert.
我已經吃完我那一份點心。

sharp [ʃɑrp] 形 尖銳的

A sharp knife makes a clean cut.
▶▶ 尖銳的刀子切得乾淨俐落。

sheep [ʃip] 名 綿羊

There are a flock of sheep in this area.
▶▶ 這個區域有一群羊。

文法解析 sheep 單複數同形，複數形式也是 sheep。

ship [ʃɪp] 名 船；艦

A big ship needs deep water.
▶▶ 大船走深水。

shirt [ʃɜt] 名 襯衫

His father looks handsome in that blue shirt.
▶▶ 他父親穿那件藍色襯衫看起來很英俊。

shoe [ʃu] 名 鞋子

I prefer comfortable shoes to famous brand shoes.
▶▶ 我偏好舒適的鞋子勝於名牌鞋。

shop [ʃɑp] 名 商店 關 salon 沙龍；美容院

I bought some snacks in the shop.
▶▶ 我在商店裡買了些點心。

short [ʃɔrt] 形 短的

Selina's uncle thinks her skirt is too short.
▶▶ 賽琳娜的叔叔覺得她的裙子太短了。

shorts [ʃɔrts] 名 短褲

He always wears those shorts no matter how cold it is.
▶▶ 不管天氣多冷，他總是穿著那件短褲。

Level 1 基礎單字
Level 2 必備單字
Level 3 中級單字
Level 4 進階單字
Level 5 高手單字
Level 6 滿級單字

shoulder [`ʃoldə] 名肩膀

The manager tapped me on the shoulder.
▶▶ 主管拍了拍我的肩。

shout [ʃaut] 動呼喊 名叫喊

The man in black shouted that his daughter was missing.
▶▶ 那個黑衣男人大叫他的女兒不見了。

show [ʃo] 名展覽；表演 動出示

名 The superstar will attend the fashion show.
　　那位巨星將出席這場時尚秀。
動 Show me your identity card, please.
　　請給我看身分證。

shower [`ʃauə] 名淋浴 動淋浴

I took a shower after exercising.
▶▶ 我運動後沖了個澡。

sick [sɪk] 形生病的

When she got up, she felt a little sick and took some medicine.
▶▶ 她起來時感到有點不舒服，於是吃了些藥。

side [saɪd] 名旁邊

He let me stand by his side.
▶▶ 他讓我站在他身邊。

sight [saɪt] 名情景

At the sight of her, I became completely stiff.
▶▶ 一看到她，我就全身僵硬。

sign [saɪn] 名記號 動簽署 關 marker 標記

名 Silence is not always a sign of wisdom.
　　沉默並不一定是智慧的表現。
動 Sign the contract after careful thinking.
　　經過審慎的思考後再簽署合約。

simple [`sɪmpl̩] 形簡單的

Writing a check is quite a simple procedure to him.
▶▶ 對他來說開張支票是個十分簡單的手續。

since [sɪns] 副 此後 介 自…以來 連 因為；由於

副 She left school three years ago and has worked as a nurse ever since.
她三年前畢業後便一直在當護士。

介 He has been blind since the accident.
意外發生後他就成了盲人。

連 Since I have no friends, I feel lonely sometimes.
因為我沒有朋友，有時候會覺得孤單。

sing [sɪŋ] 動 唱；唱歌

The boy sings a song for his mother.
▶▶ 那個男孩唱了首歌獻給母親。

singer [`sɪŋɚ] 名 歌手

Maria Carey is a world-famous singer.
▶▶ 瑪麗亞・凱莉是聞名世界的歌手。

sir [sɜ] 名 先生

Here is your package, sir.
▶▶ 先生，這是你的包裹。

sister [`sɪstɚ] 名 姐妹

I have three sisters: Anna, Gina and Mandy.
▶▶ 我有三個姊妹，安娜、吉娜和曼蒂。

sit [sɪt] 動 坐

I'd rather sit on a chair than on the floor.
▶▶ 和坐地板相比，我倒不如坐在椅子上。

size [saɪz] 名 大小；尺寸

The size of the clothe does not fit me.
▶▶ 這件衣服的大小不適合我。

skirt [skɜt] 名 裙子

Not all girls like to wear skirts.
▶▶ 並非所有女孩都喜歡穿裙子。

sky [skaɪ] 名 天空

There were no clouds in the sky.
▶▶ 天空萬里無雲。

Level 1 基礎單字
Level 2 必備單字
Level 3 中級單字
Level 4 進階單字
Level 5 高手單字
Level 6 滿級單字

sleep [slip] 動睡；睡覺 名睡眠

動 He did not sleep well last night.
他昨晚沒睡好。

名 My mother doesn't get enough sleep.
我媽媽睡眠不足。

slim [slɪm] 形苗條的 動減重；瘦身

Some girls take every measure to keep slim.
▶▶ 有些女孩想盡辦法要保持苗條。

slow [slo] 形緩慢的 副緩慢地 動使慢下來

形 Einstein was said to be a rather slow learner in his childhood.
據說愛因斯坦小時候學習遲緩。

副 The old man runs slow.
那個老人跑得很慢。

small [smɔl] 形小的

Jack is very small for his age.
▶▶ 按他的年齡來說，傑克的個子顯得太小了。

smart [smɑrt] 形聰明的

Mark is smart but lazy.
▶▶ 馬克雖然聰明，卻很懶惰。

smell [smɛl] 動聞到 名氣味

動 I smell the flowers in the garden.
我聞到庭院中的花香。

名 The smell of the rotten fish is terrible.
魚類腐敗的氣味令人作嘔。

smile [smaɪl] 動微笑 名微笑

動 He made the baby smile.
他讓嬰兒笑了。

名 Her sweet smile made me feel good.
她甜美的笑容使我覺得舒暢。

smoke [smok] 名煙；煙霧 動抽菸

名 Smoke is coming from the chimney.
煙從煙囪裡冒出來。

動 Smoking is not allowed in the library.
圖書館禁止吸菸。

snake [snek] 名蛇

The child was frightened by the snake.
▶▶ 這小孩被蛇嚇了一跳。

snow [sno] 名雪 動下雪

名 The snow surprised the tourists.
雪帶給旅客驚喜。
動 It's snowing outside.
現在外面正在下雪。

so [so] 副如此地；很 連所以

副 Tommy is so kind.
湯米是個很仁慈的人。
連 I lost the keys, so I could not enter my house.
我把鑰匙弄丟了，所以無法進家門。

sofa [`sofə] 名沙發

This sofa gives comfort.
▶▶ 這沙發坐起來很舒服。

soldier [`soldʒɚ] 名軍人

My brother became a soldier two years ago.
▶▶ 我哥哥兩年前去當兵。

some [sʌm] 形一些的 代若干；一些

形 He lent some books to me.
他借我一些書。
代 The cake tastes good. Would you like some?
這個蛋糕嘗起來不錯，你要來一點嗎？
文法解析 lend sth. to sb. 將（某物）借給（某人）

someone / somebody [`sʌm͵wʌn ] / [ `sʌm͵bɑdɪ] 代某一個人

Are you expecting someone?
▶▶ 你在期盼某人來嗎？

Level 1 基礎單字
Level 2 必備單字
Level 3 中級單字
Level 4 進階單字
Level 5 高手單字
Level 6 滿級單字

something [`sʌmθɪŋ] 代某事

He thought of something and then ran out.
▶▶ 他想到某事就跑出去了。

sometimes [`sʌm͵taɪmz] 副有時

Sometimes I help my mother do housework.
▶▶ 有時候我幫忙媽媽做家事。

somewhere [`sʌm͵hwɛr] 副在某處

I must have lost my earring somewhere.
▶▶ 我一定在什麼地方弄丟了耳環。

son [sʌn] 名兒子

Like father, like son.
▶▶ 虎父無犬子。

song [sɔŋ] 名歌曲

This song is very touching.
▶▶ 這首歌曲很感人。

soon [sun] 副很快地

Soon learned, soon forgotten.
▶▶ 學得快，忘得快。

sorry [`sɔrɪ] 形難過的；抱歉的

I'm sorry to remind you of the experience.
▶▶ 我很抱歉讓你想起那次經歷。

sound [saʊnd] 名聲音 動聽起來 形徹底的

名 I heard the sound from next door.
　　我聽見隔壁的聲音。
動 Your proposal sounds great.
　　你的提議聽起來很棒。

soup [sup] 名湯

I had a bowl of chicken soup.
▶▶ 我喝了一碗雞湯。

south [sauθ] 名南方 形南方的

名 The man faces to the south.
男子面向南方。
形 A south wind is blowing.
正在刮南風。

space [spes] 名空間 動隔開

There is no space for you here.
▶▶ 這裡的空間容不下你了。

speak [spik] 動說話

She always speaks to her colleagues at lunchtime.
▶▶ 她總在午休時間和同事講話。
文法解析 speak動詞三態變化為speak / spoke / spoken。

special [`spɛʃəl] 形特別的

Her special hairstyle impressed me.
▶▶ 她特殊的髮型讓我印象深刻。

spell [spɛl] 動用字母拼

How do you spell the word "terrific?"
▶▶ 「terrific」這個單字怎麼拼？

spend [spɛnd] 動花費（時間或金錢）

He spends little on entertainment.
▶▶ 他的娛樂花費很少。

spring [sprɪŋ] 名春天；源泉 動跳；彈開

Spring is coming.
▶▶ 春天快到了。

square [skwɛr] 形公正的；方正的 名廣場

形 His dealing is not quite square.
他行事不甚公正。
名 We had a weekly assembly on the square.
我們在廣場舉行週會。

Level 1 基礎單字
Level 2 必備單字
Level 3 中級單字
Level 4 進階單字
Level 5 高手單字
Level 6 滿級單字

stair [stɛr] 名 樓梯

The master's room is upstairs, but to get to the library you must go down stairs.
▶▶ 院長的房間在樓上，但是你需要下樓才能到圖書館。

stand [stænd] 動 站起；立起

Stand still, I am trying to draw you.
▶▶ 站著別動，我想把你畫下來。

star [stɑr] 名 星星 動 主演

名 Many stars are shining in the sky.
無數的星星在天空閃爍。
動 She has starred in thirty films.
她主演過三十部電影。

start [stɑrt] 動 開始 名 開始

動 I started to do my homework in the evening.
我傍晚開始做作業。
名 He didn't like the idea from the start.
他從一開始就不喜歡這個主意。

station [`steʃən] 名 車站

I get off at the next station.
▶▶ 我在下一站下車。

stay [ste] 動 停留；暫住 名 停留；逗留

動 She stayed at the hotel tonight.
她今晚在旅館留宿。
名 My stay in the village was a wonderful experience.
我這次在村裡暫住，是個很棒的體驗。

still [stɪl] 副 仍然 形 靜止的；寂靜的

Mary still disapproved their marriage.
▶▶ 瑪莉仍然反對他們的婚事。

stop [stɑp] 動 停止 名 停止

動 He tried hard to stop smoking.
他努力嘗試戒菸。
名 The stop of the construction broke the contract.
建設的停擺造成違約。

MEMORIZE 7000 VOCABULARIES ONCE AND FOR ALL！

store [stor] 名 商店 動 儲存

The guy openly shoplifted from the convenience store.

▶▶ 一個傢伙公然在便利商店順手牽羊。

story [`storɪ] 名 故事

She told stories to the children.

▶▶ 她說故事給小孩聽。

straight [stret] 形 正直的；筆直的

He drew a straight line on the paper.

▶▶ 他在紙上畫了一條直線。

strange [strendʒ] 形 陌生的；奇怪的

It's strange that we've never met before.

▶▶ 奇怪的是我們以前從未見過面。

street [strit] 名 街道

Leaves made the street look messy.

▶▶ 落葉讓街道看起來很髒亂。

string [strɪŋ] 名 繩子

He wrapped the package in brown paper and tied it with string.

▶▶ 他用棕色包裝紙把包裹包好，又用細繩捆上。

strong [strɔŋ] 形 強壯的；強烈的

The strong coach caught the robber.

▶▶ 強壯的教練抓住了搶匪。

student [`stjudn̩t] 名 學生

The students gathered quickly.

▶▶ 學生們很快到齊了。

study [`stʌdɪ] 動 學習 名 學習；研究

動 I study Korean on my own.
我自學韓語。

名 Emma concentrated on her studies.
艾瑪專注學習。

stupid [ˋstjupɪd] 形 笨的

You are not stupid but careless.
▶▶ 你不是笨，而是不用心。

subject [ˋsʌbdʒɪkt] 名 主題；科目 形 服從的；易受⋯的

History is my favorite subject.
▶▶ 歷史是我最喜歡的科目。

successful [səkˋsɛsfəl] 形 成功的

The man turned out to be a successful businessman.
▶▶ 這個男人最後成為一位成功的企業家。

sugar [ˋʃʊgɚ] 名 糖

Sugar-free beverages are popular.
▶▶ 無糖飲料很受歡迎。

sun [sʌn] 名 太陽 動 曬

The sun rose at six o'clock.
▶▶ 太陽在六點升起。

sunny [ˋsʌnɪ] 形 充滿陽光的；晴朗的

It is a pity to stay home in such a sunny day.
▶▶ 在這樣晴朗的天氣待在家裡很可惜。

supermarket [ˋsupɚ͵mɑrkɪt] 名 超級市場

Bread is cheap in this supermarket because they bake it themselves.
▶▶ 這家超市的麵包很便宜，因為是他們自己烤的。

sure [ʃʊr] 形 確信的

Are you sure the information is correct?
▶▶ 你確定消息是正確的嗎？

surprise [səˋpraɪz] 動 使驚喜 名 驚喜 關 surprised 感到驚訝的 / surprising 令人驚訝的

動 Joe's appearance surprised me.
喬的出現使我驚喜。
名 My mother gave me a new bicycle as a surprise.
媽媽送我一台腳踏車作為驚喜。

Level 1 基礎單字

Level 2 必備單字

Level 3 中級單字

Level 4 進階單字

Level 5 高手單字

Level 6 滿級單字

sweet [swit] 形甜的 名糖果；甜食

形 Charley has sweet teeth.
查理愛吃甜食。

名 You should not eat too many sweets.
你不該吃太多糖果。

T 字頭基礎單字

MP3 020

table [`tebḷ] 名桌子

He put a vase on the table.
▶▶ 他在桌子上放了一個花瓶。

tail [tel] 名尾巴

A fox cannot hide its tail.
▶▶ 狐狸尾巴是藏不住的。

take [tek] 動拿走；取走

He took a sweater out of the drawer.
▶▶ 他從抽屜中拿出一件毛衣。

文法解析 take動詞三態變化為 take / took / taken。

talk [tɔk] 動談話 名談話

動 What are you talking about?
你們在談些什麼？

名 A phone call interrupted their talk.
一通電話打斷了他們的談話。

tall [tɔl] 形高的

The tall boy next to the principal is my brother.
▶▶ 校長身邊的高個兒男孩是我的哥哥。

tape [tep] 名錄音帶 動用錄音帶錄

名 Before CDs and MP3s, people listened to tapes to learn English.
在 CD 和 MP3 出現前，人們聽錄音帶學英文。

動 I have taped what you just said.
我已經把你剛才說的話錄下來了。

taste [test] 名味覺；體驗；品味 動品嚐

名 Their trip to America gave them a taste for western goods.
美國之行讓他們見識到了西方的商品。

動 How does the steak taste?
這牛排嚐起來如何？

taxi / taxicab / cab [`tæksɪ ] / [ `tæksɪ͵kæb] / [kæb] 名計程車

He took a taxi to school.
▶▶ 他搭計程車去學校。

tea [ti] 名茶

How about a cup of tea?
▶▶ 來一杯茶如何？

teach [titʃ] 動教；講授

Mr. Smith teaches me guitar.
▶▶ 史密斯先生教我吉他。

teacher [`titʃɚ] 名老師 關 mentor 導師

Teachers are not always right.
▶▶ 老師並非總是對的。

team [tim] 名隊

A team without a leader will fail.
▶▶ 沒有領導者的團隊終將失敗。

teenager [`tin͵edʒɚ] 名青少年

Teenagers spend most of their time with their friends.
▶▶ 青少年大部分的時間都和朋友在一起。

telephone / phone [`tɛlə͵fon] / [fon] 名電話 動打電話

He picked up the telephone and called his friend.
▶▶ 他拿起電話，打給朋友。

television / TV [`tɛləvɪʒən] 名電視

What's on television tonight?
▶▶ 今晚電視有什麼節目？

tell [tɛl] 動 告訴

She told me that she had to leave.
▶▶ 她告訴我她必須離開。

temple [`tɛmpl̩] 名 廟宇；寺院

Sarah went to the temple to worship.
▶▶ 莎拉到廟裡拜拜。

tennis [`tɛnɪs] 名 網球

Jack and I played tennis in the park after school.
▶▶ 傑克和我放學後在公園裡打網球。

terrible [`tɛrəbl̩] 形 嚇人的

I cannot forget the terrible nightmare.
▶▶ 我無法忘卻那可怕的惡夢。

test [tɛst] 名 考試 動 測驗

名 He did not prepare for the test, but he passed with flying colors.
他沒有準備，卻高分通過考試。
動 I think he made these proposals mainly to test public opinion.
我想他提出這些建議，主要是為了試探輿論的反應。

than [ðæn] 連 比；比較

Ted is older than I.
▶▶ 泰德比我年長。

thank [θæŋk] 動 感謝

Thanks for your company.
▶▶ 謝謝你的陪伴。

that [ðæt] 代 那個 連 引導子句 關 impossible 不可能的 / incredible 不可置信的

代 That is my favorite novel.
那是我最喜歡的小說。
連 His hope that she will accept the invitation is impossible.
他希望她能接受邀約是異想天開。

theater [`θɪətɚ] 名 戲院

My roommate invited me to the theater tonight.
▶▶ 我室友約我今晚去看戲。

then [ðɛn] 副 當時；那時

I was so naïve then that I believed his lies.
▶▶ 我當時太過天真，竟然聽信他的謊言。

there [ðɛr] 副 在那裡；到那裡

Kelly's house is over there.
▶▶ 凱莉的房子在那裡。

these [ðiz] 形 這些的

I decided to throw away these books.
▶▶ 我決定把這些書丟掉。

thick [θɪk] 形 厚的

The thick dictionary contains more than sixty thousand words.
▶▶ 這本很厚的字典收錄有超過六萬個單字。

thin [θɪn] 形 薄的；瘦的

The thin girl looks very pale.
▶▶ 這個很瘦的女孩看起來臉色蒼白。

thing [θɪŋ] 名 事物；東西

There is another thing I want to ask you about.
▶▶ 我還有一件事想問你。

think [θɪŋk] 動 思考 關 obsess 迷住；使煩擾

Think how much you can earn if you open a restaurant in such a good location.
▶▶ 試想，要是在這樣的黃金地段開一家餐館，會賺多少錢。

third [θɝd] 形 第三的 名 第三

The third team member is not here yet.
▶▶ 第三位團員還沒有到。

this [ðɪs] 形 這；這個 代 這個（人、事、物）

形 This movie is very boring.
這部電影相當乏味。
代 No one cares about this.
沒人會關心這個。

those [ðoz] 形 那些的

She is fed up with those admirers.
▶▶ 她受夠那些愛慕者了。

though [ðo] 連 但是；雖然；儘管

Though his job was hard, Terry enjoyed it.
▶▶ 泰瑞的工作很辛苦，但他樂在其中。

thousand [`θauzn̩d] 名 一千

I won one thousand dollars in the game.
▶▶ 我在比賽中獲得一千元。

throat [θrot] 名 喉嚨

I have a sore throat. Maybe I caught a cold.
▶▶ 我喉嚨很痛，也許我感冒了。

through [θru] 介 通過

He searched through his pockets for a cigarette.
▶▶ 他摸遍口袋想找支菸。

throw [θro] 動 投；擲；拋

Someone threw a stone at my car.
▶▶ 有人向我的車扔了一塊石頭。

ticket [`tɪkɪt] 名 票；券

Buy the tickets before entering the theater.
▶▶ 進戲院前先買票。

tidy [`taɪdɪ] 形 整潔的 動 整頓

形 Mother is used to making the house tidy and clean.
媽媽習慣把房子打掃乾淨。
動 Tidy up your room before playing.
玩耍前先把房間整理好。

tie [taɪ] 名 領帶 動 打結

名 Diana gave her father a tie as a birthday present.
黛安娜送父親一條領帶作為生日禮物。
動 She tied the old newspapers for recycling.
她把舊報紙捆好回收。

Level 1 基礎單字
Level 2 必備單字
Level 3 中級單字
Level 4 進階單字
Level 5 高手單字
Level 6 滿級單字

tiger [`taɪgɚ] 名老虎

A tiger was lying on the grass.
▶▶ 一隻老虎躺在草地上。

time [taɪm] 名時間

Time waits for no man.
▶▶ 時間不等人。

tip [tɪp] 名小費 動付小費

名 Should I give him some tips?
我該給他一些小費嗎？
動 I tipped the waiter two dollars.
我給服務生兩塊錢小費。

tire [`taɪɚ] 名輪胎 動使疲倦 開 tired 疲倦的

名 Which tire went flat?
哪個輪胎漏氣了？
動 I'm tired of my mother's nagging.
我受夠媽媽的嘮叨了。

today [tə`de] 名今天 副在今天

名 Today is my birthday.
今天是我生日。
副 I must finish my homework today.
我今天必須完成作業。

toe [to] 名腳趾

Ben felt great pain in his toes after the long walk.
▶▶ 長途跋涉過後班覺得腳趾很痛。

together [tə`gɛðɚ] 副一起地

I stuck the two pieces of paper together.
▶▶ 我把這兩張紙黏在一起。

toilet [`tɔɪlɪt] 名洗手間

The passenger left without flushing the toilet.
▶▶ 那位旅客沒沖水就離開洗手間。

tomato [tə`meto] 名 番茄

Cut the tomatoes and mushrooms into quarters.
▶▶ 將番茄和蘑菇切成四分之一大小。

tomorrow [tə`mɔro] 名 明天 副 在明天

名 What day is tomorrow?
明天星期幾？
副 The employee will set off tomorrow.
那名員工明天啟程。
(焦點句型) set off 出發；啟程

tonight [tə`naɪt] 副 在今晚

Will you come to the party tonight?
▶▶ 今晚你會來參加派對嗎？

too [tu] 副 也；太

He likes rabbits. I like rabbits, too.
▶▶ 他喜歡兔子，我也喜歡。

tool [tul] 名 工具 關 shed （通常是木製的、存放工具的）小屋

The gardener's tools are kept in the shed.
▶▶ 園丁的工具放在小屋裡。

tooth [tuθ] 名 牙齒

My dentist took out my loose tooth.
▶▶ 我的牙醫把我鬆動的牙齒拔掉了。

top [tɑp] 形 頂端的 名 頂端 動 勝過

形 This mission is top priority.
以這份任務為第一優先。
名 The tower is on the top of the hill.
這座塔位於山頂上。

topic [`tɑpɪk] 名 主題

The weather is a common topic to talk about with strangers.
▶▶ 天氣是和陌生人聊天時的常見話題。

Level 1 基礎單字
Level 2 必備單字
Level 3 中級單字
Level 4 進階單字
Level 5 高手單字
Level 6 滿級單字

total [`totḷ] 形全部的 名全部 動總計

形 The total number of students on the playground was 250.
在操場上的學生共兩百五十位。

名 The total is three hundred articles.
全部共有三百件。

touch [tʌtʃ] 動碰；觸摸 名接觸；聯繫

動 Lisa touched my arm to get my attention.
麗莎碰我的手臂，以引起我的注意。

名 Wherever you are, remember to keep in touch with me.
無論你在哪裡，記得和我保持聯絡。

towel [`tauəl] 名毛巾

Help yourself to a clean towel.
▶▶ 請隨便拿一條乾淨毛巾用。

town [taun] 名小鎮

The whole town knows of the news.
▶▶ 全城鎮都知道這件新聞。

toy [tɔɪ] 名玩具

The baby was pleased with the toys.
▶▶ 嬰兒被玩具逗樂了。

traffic [`træfɪk] 名交通；交易

The illegal traffic in protected animals is quite common there.
▶▶ 非法買賣保育類動物在那裡是司空見慣的事。

train [tren] 名火車 動訓練

名 I take the train to school every day.
我每天搭火車去上學。

動 She was trained as a singer by a famous professor of music.
她受到一位知名音樂教授的指導，接受歌手的訓練。

treat [trit] 動處理；對待 關 treatment 對待；待遇

My stepmother treats me as her own child.
▶▶ 我的繼母對我視如己出。

tree [tri] 名樹

The children are listening to their teacher telling stories under the tree.
▶▶ 孩子們在樹下聽老師說故事。

trip [trɪp] 名旅行

They went on a trip to South Korea.
▶▶ 他們去南韓旅遊。

trouble [`trʌbḷ] 名麻煩

His request really caused a lot of trouble for her.
▶▶ 他的要求造成她很大的麻煩。

truck [trʌk] 名卡車

The driver of the truck got into an accident.
▶▶ 這位卡車司機捲入了一場意外。

try [traɪ] 動試圖 名嘗試

動 I tried again and again to open the box.
我反覆試著打開盒子。
名 Let's give it a try.
我們就試試看吧！

T-shirt [`tiʃɜt] 名 T 恤

This sport T-shirt doesn't fit.
▶▶ 這件運動 T 恤不合身。

turn [tɜn] 動轉動；旋轉 名轉向；轉動

動 Billy heard her voice and turned back.
比利聽到她的聲音便回頭。
名 The car made a left turn.
汽車朝向左轉。

twice [twaɪs] 副兩次；兩回

I go to the gym twice a week.
▶▶ 我一個禮拜上兩次健身房。

type [taɪp] 名類型 動打字 關 genre （藝術作品）類型

名 She is the type of girl I like.
她是我喜歡的那型女孩。

Level 1 基礎單字
Level 2 必備單字
Level 3 中級單字
Level 4 進階單字
Level 5 高手單字
Level 6 滿級單字

動 He typed a letter on his computer to his sister in Japan.
他打了封信給在日本的姊姊。

 **U 字頭基礎單字**

MP3 021

uncle [`ʌŋkḷ] 名 叔叔；伯伯；舅舅；姑父；姨父

I met my uncle on the street yesterday.
▶▶ 我昨天在街上遇到我叔叔。

understand [ˌʌndɚˋstænd] 動 瞭解

This theory is hard to understand.
▶▶ 這個理論很難理解。

uniform [`junəˌfɔrm] 名 制服 動 使穿制服

I have to wear a uniform when I work.
▶▶ 我工作時要穿制服。

until / till [ənˋtɪl] / [tɪl] 連 直到…時 介 到…為止

連 He kept asking her on a date until she turned him down firmly.
他不斷追求她，直到她堅定地拒絕他為止。
介 Jane did not sleep until midnight.
珍直到半夜才睡覺。

up [ʌp] 副 向上地 介 沿著；向…上游

副 The boy picked up a stone and threw it over the fence.
男孩撿起一塊石子扔過柵欄。
介 She walked up the path.
她沿著小路向上走。

use [juz] 動 使用 名 使用；利用 同 deploy

動 Mary used a ribbon to tie up her hair.
瑪莉用緞帶綁頭髮。
名 We should make the best use of the resources in the library.
我們應該善用圖書館的資源。

useful [`jusfəl] 形 有用的

The dictionary you gave me is very useful.
▶▶ 你送我的字典非常有用。

Level 1 基礎單字

Level 2 必備單字

Level 3 中級單字

Level 4 進階單字

Level 5 高手單字

Level 6 滿級單字

usually [`juʒʊəlɪ] 副 通常

Swans are usually considered graceful.

▶▶ 人們通常認為天鵝很優雅。

 **UNIT 22 V 字頭基礎單字**

 MP3 022

vegetable [`vɛdʒətəbļ] 名 蔬菜

She likes all kinds of vegetables, but eggplant is the exception.

▶▶ 她喜歡各種蔬菜，但是茄子例外。

very [`vɛrɪ] 副 非常

My son likes collecting butterfly specimens very much.

▶▶ 我兒子非常喜歡收藏蝴蝶標本。

video [`vɪdɪˏo] 名 電視；錄影

I've seen the video several times.

▶▶ 我看過這個影片好幾次了。

violin [ˏvaɪə`lɪn] 名 小提琴

The young girl practices the violin every day.

▶▶ 這小女孩每天練習拉小提琴。

visit [`vɪzɪt] 動 拜訪；探望 名 訪問；參觀

動 This afternoon we're going to visit a friend in the hospital.
今天下午我們將去探望一位住院的朋友。

名 I paid a visit to my Chinese teacher.
我去拜訪國文老師。

visitor [`vɪzɪtɚ] 名 訪客；觀光客

We saw the comings and goings of the visitors to the factory.

▶▶ 我們看到來廠訪問的客人進進出出。

voice [vɔɪs] 名 聲音

I've got a bad cold, and I've lost my voice.

▶▶ 我得了重感冒，已經無法說話了。

wait [wet] 動等待

I am sorry to keep you waiting.
▶▶ 很抱歉讓你等待。

wake [wek] 動醒

I woke up early this morning.
▶▶ 我今天早上很早醒來。

文法解析 wake動詞三態變化為 wake / woke / woken。

walk [wɔk] 動走;散步 名步行

動 She walks to school every day.
她每天走路上學。

名 Would you like to take a walk with me?
你想和我一起散步嗎?

wall [wɔl] 名牆壁

There was a wall around the park.
▶▶ 公園四周曾經有圍牆圍住。

want [wɑnt] 動想要

He wants to travel in Europe but he lacks money.
▶▶ 他想去歐洲旅遊,但是沒有錢。

warm [wɔrm] 形暖和的 動使暖和

形 The day was warm and cloudless.
天氣溫暖而晴朗。

動 The fire soon warmed the room.
爐火使房間迅速暖和起來。

watch [wɑtʃ] 動觀看;注視 名手錶

動 They watched TV together in the living room.
他們在客廳一起看電視。

名 Steven showed us his new watch.
史蒂芬把新手錶展示給我們看。

water [`wɑtə] 名水 動澆水

名 His gloves dropped into the water.
他的手套掉進水裡。

動 Can you water the flowers for me?
你可以幫我澆花嗎？

wave [wev] 名波浪 動搖動

名 In a small bay, big waves will never build up.
在小的港灣裡，永遠也不會形成大的波濤。

動 The officer waved his men on.
軍官揮手示意士兵前進。

way [we] 名路；道路

I witnessed a car accident on my way home.
▶▶ 我在回家途中目擊一場車禍。

weak [wik] 形虛弱的

The baby cat looks very weak, so we must help it.
▶▶ 這隻小貓看起來非常虛弱，所以我們必須幫助牠。

wear [wεr] 動穿；戴

Arthur wore a yellow T-shirt yesterday.
▶▶ 亞瑟昨天穿了一件黃色 T 恤。

文法解析 wear動詞三態變化為 wear / wore /worn。

weather [`wεðə] 名天氣

The weather today is nice.
▶▶ 今天天氣很好。

week [wik] 名星期

She goes to the cinema once a week.
▶▶ 她每星期會去看一次電影。

weekend [`wiˌkεnd] 名週末

Lanny came home for the weekend.
▶▶ 蘭尼回家過週末。

Level 1 基礎單字
Level 2 必備單字
Level 3 中級單字
Level 4 進階單字
Level 5 高手單字
Level 6 滿級單字

welcome [`wɛlkəm] 動 歡迎 名 歡迎 形 受歡迎的

動 We welcomed her return with a banquet.
我們舉辦盛宴歡迎她回來。

名 I was moved to receive such a welcome here.
我很感動在這裡受到如此歡迎。

well [wɛl] 形 健康的 副 良好地

形 Lucy doesn't seem well. What's wrong?
露西看起來不太好，怎麼了嗎？

副 Little John acts well.
小約翰表現得很好。

文法解析 比較級 better；最高級 best。

west [wɛst] 名 西方 形 西方的

名 The sun sets in the west.
太陽西下。

形 He has been to most of the west part of Europe.
西歐大部分的地方他都去過。

wet [wɛt] 形 潮濕的 動 弄濕

形 Her hair got wet from the sudden rain.
突如其來的雨淋濕了她的頭髮。

動 I wetted the towel and covered my nose and mouth.
我把毛巾弄濕摀住口鼻。

what [hwɑt] 形 什麼（表示疑問） 代 什麼

形 What time is it, please?
請問現在幾點？

代 I do not know what they are talking about.
我不知道他們在說什麼。

when [hwɛn] 副 當…時；何時 連 當…時

副 It was a time when cars were rare.
那是汽車很罕見的時代。

連 When he was a child, his parents divorced.
當他還是個孩子時，父母就離婚了。

where [hwɛr] 副 在哪裡；往哪裡 連 …的地方

副 Where were you born and raised?
你在哪裡出生與長大的呢？

(連) I'll meet her where I first met you.
我將在初次見你的地方與她碰面。

whether [`hwɛðɚ] (連) 是否

I have no idea whether to go or stay.
▶▶ 我不知道該離開還是留下。

which [hwɪtʃ] (形) 哪一個 (代) 哪一個

(形) Which color do you like?
你喜歡哪個顏色？
(代) Which is my seat?
哪一個是我的座位？

while [hwaɪl] (連) 當…的時候

Strike the iron while it is hot.
▶▶ 打鐵趁熱。

white [hwaɪt] (名) 白色 (形) 白色的

(名) The color of the lilies is white.
百合花是白色的。
(形) White clothes get dirty easily.
白色衣服容易弄髒。

who [hu] (代) 誰；…的人

That's the man who came to our house yesterday.
▶▶ 那就是昨天來過我們家的人。

whose [huz] (代) 誰的

Whose bag was missing?
▶▶ 誰的背包弄丟了？

why [hwaɪ] (副) 為什麼

Why does he always boss me around?
▶▶ 他為什麼總是對我頤指氣使？

wide [waɪd] (形) 寬廣的 (副) 張得很大地

(形) The road was just wide enough for two vehicles to pass.
這條路的寬度剛好能容兩輛車通過。

副 She opened the window wide to let air come into the room.
她把窗戶開大一些，好讓房間通風。

wife [waɪf] 名妻子

Frank's wife is a professor at Harvard University.
▶▶ 弗蘭克的妻子是哈佛大學的教授。

will [wɪl] 助將；會 名意志

助 I will go on an errand tomorrow.
我明天要出差。
名 He has a strong will.
他的意志堅強。

win [wɪn] 動獲勝

Hemingway once won the Nobel Prize for literature.
▶▶ 海明威曾獲得諾貝爾文學獎。

wind [wɪnd] 名風

A cold wind blew from the northwest.
▶▶ 冷風從西北方向吹來。

window [`wɪndo] 名窗戶

He broke the window accidentally.
▶▶ 他不小心打破了窗戶。

wise [waɪz] 形聰明的

The wise man taught his son many important lessons.
▶▶ 這位聰明的男人教了他兒子許多重要的課題。

wish [wɪʃ] 動希望；但願 名願望

動 I wish you Happy Birthday.
祝你生日快樂。
名 She made a wish that her mother would recover as soon as possible.
她許了個心願，希望她母親早日康復。

with [wɪð] 介帶有；與…一起

Benson looked at me with anger.
▶▶ 班森憤怒地看著我。

without [wɪˋðaʊt] 介 沒有

He agreed with my suggestion without hesitation.
▶▶ 他毫不猶豫地同意了我的建議。

woman [ˋwʊmən] 名 女性;婦女

That little girl has grown into a pretty woman.
▶▶ 小女孩已長成一個漂亮的女人。

wonderful [ˋwʌndəfəl] 形 令人驚奇的;很棒的

The trip to Australia was a wonderful experience.
▶▶ 那趟澳洲行十分美妙。

word [wɜd] 名 文字;話

Rita was frustrated by her father's words.
▶▶ 芮塔因她父親的話而感到挫折。

work [wɜk] 名 工作;勞動 動 工作

名 I have to take my work home today.
今天我得把工作帶回家做。
動 My father started working when he was just 14.
我父親十四歲就開始工作了。

worker [ˋwɜkə] 名 工人

Lisa's uncle shared his story as a rubber worker.
▶▶ 麗莎的叔叔分享他作為橡膠工人的故事。

world [wɜld] 名 世界

Blind people live in a dark world.
▶▶ 盲人生活在黑暗的世界裡。

worry [ˋwɜɪ] 動 擔心 名 煩惱

動 She worried about the interview the next day.
她擔憂著隔天的面試。
名 I have a great worry for his condition.
我非常擔心他的狀況。

write [raɪt] 動 書寫

He wrote a letter to his aunt.
▶▶ 他寫了封信給他的阿姨。

Level 1 基礎單字
Level 2 必備單字
Level 3 中級單字
Level 4 進階單字
Level 5 高手單字
Level 6 滿級單字

writer [ˋraɪtɚ] 名作者；作家

My favorite writer is J.K. Rowling.
▶▶ J.K. 羅琳是我最愛的作家。

wrong [rɑŋ] 形錯誤的 副錯誤地

形 Although his answer was wrong, he provided a new viewpoint.
雖然他的答案是錯的，但也提供了一個新觀點。
副 The salesman spelled my name wrong.
推銷員把我的名字拼錯了。

 Y、Z 字頭基礎單字

MP3 024

yard [jɑrd] 名院子

The yard was overgrown with weeds.
▶▶ 這座庭院雜草叢生。

year [jɪr] 名年；一年

I have not seen him in over ten years.
▶▶ 我超過十年沒見到他了。

yellow [ˋjɛlo] 名黃色 形黃色的

名 Yellow and blue are colors that go well together.
黃與藍是很搭的顏色。
形 The cover of the book is yellow.
這本書的封面是黃色。

yes / yeah [jɛs] / [jɛə] 副是；是的 名同意；贊成票

副 Oh, yes. It's delicious.
喔，是的，味道很鮮美。
名 It is not a "yes or no" question.
這不是一個是非題。

yesterday [ˋjɛstɚde] 副昨天

I called you three times yesterday.
▶▶ 我昨天打了三次電話給你。

yet [jɛt] 副 還沒

He hasn't eaten anything yet.
▶▶ 他還沒吃東西。

young [jʌŋ] 形 年輕的

Young people and old people do not always agree.
▶▶ 年輕人和長者的想法經常有所不同。

zero [`zɪro] 名 零；零度；零號

The temperature has fallen to zero.
▶▶ 氣溫降到零度。

zoo [zu] 名 動物園

The grandfather took his grandson to the zoo.
▶▶ 爺爺帶著他孫子去動物園。

Level 1 基礎單字
Level 2 必備單字
Level 3 中級單字
Level 4 進階單字
Level 5 高手單字
Level 6 滿級單字

7000 Essential
Vocabulary for
High School Students

Novice Vocabulary

LEVEL 2
必備單字

單字難易度 ★☆☆☆☆
文法難易度 ★★☆☆☆
生活出現頻率 ★★★★★
考題出題頻率 ★★☆☆☆

名 名詞　動 動詞　形 形容詞　副 副詞　介 介係詞　連 連接詞
代 代名詞　關 相關單字／片語　同 同義詞　反 反義詞

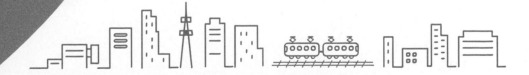

absence [`æbsn̩s] 名缺席

His frequent absence annoyed the teacher.
▶▶ 他時常曠課，讓老師很生氣。

absent [`æbsn̩t] 形缺席的

Michelle was absent from the class this morning.
▶▶ 蜜雪兒早上缺課。

accept [ək`sɛpt] 動接受 關 acceptance 接受

He finally accepted my advice.
▶▶ 他終於接受我的建議。

accident [`æksədənt] 名事故；偶發事件

This road is well known for the frequent accidents that happen on it.
▶▶ 這條路因交通事故頻生而惡名昭彰。

account [ə`kaʊnt] 名帳目；描述 動視為；負責 關 audit 審計

名 She gave a highly descriptive account of the journey.
她十分生動地敘述了那次的旅程。
動 You should account for your mistake.
你必須為你的過失負責。

active [`æktɪv] 形活躍的

Mandy is an active leader.
▶▶ 曼蒂是個活躍的領導人。

activity [æk`tɪvətɪ] 名活動

Cooperative activity is essential to effective community work.
▶▶ 要把社區工作做好，合作活動勢必不可少。

actual [`æktʃuəl] 形實際的

What were his actual words?
▶▶ 他實際上說了什麼？

addition [əˋdɪʃən] 名增加

In addition to sausages, I prepared fried chicken and cake.
▶▶ 除了香腸，我還準備了炸雞和蛋糕。

address [əˋdrɛs] 名地址；致詞 動對…說話

名 What's your address?
你的住址是什麼？
動 President George W. Bush addressed the Senate on the issue of Iraq.
美國總統布希就伊拉克問題向參議院發表了演說。

admit [ədˋmɪt] 動容許…進入；承認

You will not be admitted without a ticket.
▶▶ 沒有票的話禁止入場。

adult [əˋdʌlt] 名成年人 形成人的

名 This film is suitable for both adults and children.
這部電影老少皆宜。
形 He'd spent all his adult life in the army.
他的成年生活全是在軍隊裡度過的。

advance [ədˋvæns] 名前方 動使前進

名 Would you please do me a favor? Thanks in advance.
你可以幫我一個忙嗎？先謝謝你了。
動 The date of the meeting was advanced from June 20 to June 7.
會議日期由六月二十日提前到了六月七日。
焦點句型 in advance 提前；事先

advice [ədˋvaɪs] 名忠告；建議 關 regret 後悔

I regretted that I didn't take his advice.
▶▶ 我很後悔沒有接受他的忠告。

affair [əˋfɛr] 名事件

Our president has not said anything about the affair so far.
▶▶ 至今，我們的總統還沒有對這次事件發表任何聲明。

affect [əˋfɛkt] 動影響

The quarrel with my mother in the morning affected my mood greatly.
▶▶ 早上和媽媽的爭吵嚴重影響我的心情。

Level 1 基礎單字
Level 2 必備單字
Level 3 中級單字
Level 4 進階單字
Level 5 高手單字
Level 6 滿級單字

against [əˋgɛnst] 介 反對

Sixty people voted against the new project.
▶▶ 六十個人對新計畫投反對票。

ahead [əˋhɛd] 副 在前方；向前

The hills ahead are not wooded.
▶▶ 前面的山上沒有樹木。

aid [ed] 動 援助 名 援助

動 Ray aided Joyce with her homework.
雷協助喬艾絲做作業。
名 I am willing to come to your aid.
我很樂意幫忙你。

aim [em] 名 目標 動 瞄準

名 Have an aim in life, or your energies will all be wasted.
設立一個人生目標，否則你的精力將會白白浪費掉。
動 He did not aim his words at you.
他的話不是針對你說的。

aircraft [ˋɛr͵kræft] 名 飛機

The aircraft is designed to withstand difficult conditions.
▶▶ 這架飛機是為應對惡劣環境而設計的。

alarm [əˋlɑrm] 名 警報器 動 使驚慌

名 The thief touched the alarm accidentally and soon got arrested.
小偷誤觸警報器，很快就被抓起來了。
動 She was alarmed by the loud noise.
她被那聲巨響嚇壞了。

album [ˋælbəm] 名 相簿

The album contains photographs from my childhood.
▶▶ 這本相簿有著我童年的照片。

alike [əˋlaɪk] 形 相似的 副 相似地

形 The twin brothers seem alike.
這對雙胞胎兄弟長得很像。
副 The boss treats everyone alike.
老闆對大家一視同仁。

alive [ə`laɪv] 形 活的

In the evening, the town really comes alive.
▶▶ 到了晚上，城裡變得相當生氣勃勃。

alone [ə`lon] 形 單獨的 副 單獨地

形 She watches TV when she is alone.
獨自一人時，她便看電視。
副 For years, Mary lived alone in New York.
瑪莉孤身一人在紐約住了好幾年。

aloud [ə`laʊd] 副 高聲地

The baby cried aloud.
▶▶ 嬰兒放聲大哭。

altogether [ˌɔltə`gɛðɚ] 副 總共

I am not altogether happy about the decision.
▶▶ 我對這個決定並不十分滿意。

among [ə`mʌŋ] 介 在…之中

Tom has always been popular among his classmates.
▶▶ 湯姆在同學中一直很受歡迎。

amount [ə`maʊnt] 名 總數；合計 動 總計

名 The amount of this company's investment in Czechia is about 10 billion dollars.
這家公司在捷克的投資總額約為十億美金。
動 The bill amounts to 1,000 dollars.
帳單的金額總共是一千元。

ancient [`enʃənt] 形 古老的 關 antique 古物；古玩

I like Chinese ancient culture, so I collect a lot of chinese antiques.
▶▶ 我喜愛中國古代文化，所以我收集很多中國古玩。

anger [`æŋgɚ] 名 憤怒

He was filled with anger at the way he had been treated.
▶▶ 他因遭受如此待遇而滿腔怒火。

Level 1 基礎單字
Level 2 必備單字
Level 3 中級單字
Level 4 進階單字
Level 5 高手單字
Level 6 滿級單字

angle [`æŋgl̩] 名角度

Looking at it now from a different angle, I see that I was wrong.
▶▶ 現在從不同的角度來看，我發現我錯了。

ankle [`æŋkl̩] 名腳踝

My right ankle hurts.
▶▶ 我的右腳踝很痛。

anytime [`ɛnɪ͵taɪm] 副任何時候 關 accompany 陪伴

Anytime you feel sad, I will accompany you.
▶▶ 無論何時你感到沮喪，我都會陪伴著你。

anyway [`ɛnɪ͵we] 副無論如何

I have to go to see him anyway.
▶▶ 無論如何我必須去見他。

anywhere / anyplace [`ɛnɪ͵hwɛr] / [`ɛnɪ͵ples] 副任何地方

Did you go anywhere last night?
▶▶ 你昨天晚上有沒有到什麼地方去？

ape [ep] 名猿；猴子 動模仿

名 Have you ever seen an ape?
你曾經看過猿猴嗎？
動 He apes his elder brother in everything he does.
他一切都模仿他的哥哥。

appearance [ə`pɪrəns] 名外表；出現

All the fans are looking forward to the appearance of the singer.
▶▶ 歌迷們都期待著歌手的出現。

appetite [`æpə͵taɪt] 名胃口；食慾

Don't spoil your appetite by eating between meals.
▶▶ 不要在兩餐之間吃東西，以免影響胃口。

apply [ə`plaɪ] 動申請

She applied for the position but was turned down.
▶▶ 她申請這個職位，但遭到拒絕。

文法解析 apply to 後面接「申請的單位或機構」；apply for 後面接「申請的東西、職位」

appreciate [ə`priʃɪ,et] 動欣賞

I appreciate Mr. Chuang for his humor and optimism very much.
>> 我非常欣賞莊先生的幽默和樂觀。

approach [ə`protʃ] 動接近

As the stranger approached, the dog started to bark loudly.
>> 當陌生人接近，那隻狗就開始大聲吠叫。

argue [`ɑrgju] 動爭吵 關 argument 爭論；論點 / contention 爭論 / refute 反駁

They argued about who was responsible for the housework.
>> 他們為誰該做家事而爭吵。

army [`ɑrmɪ] 名軍隊；陸軍

They formed a small army of about 2,000 men.
>> 他們組建了一支約兩千人的小規模軍隊。

arrange [ə`rendʒ] 動安排 關 arrangement 布置；準備 / placement 布置

The party was arranged quickly.
>> 派會很快就安排好了。

arrival [ə`raɪvl̩] 名到達；到達的人 (物)

Toni Morrison is a recent arrival on the contemporary fiction scene.
>> 托尼 • 莫里森是當代小說界的一個新面孔。

arrow [`æro] 名箭

Time flies like an arrow.
>> 光陰似箭。

article [`ɑrtɪkl̩] 名文章；論文

I read the writer's articles every day.
>> 我每天都讀這位作者的文章。

artist [`ɑrtɪst] 名藝術家

Whoever made this cake is a real artist.
>> 做出這個蛋糕的人真是個藝術家。

Level 1 基礎單字
Level 2 必備單字
Level 3 中級單字
Level 4 進階單字
Level 5 高手單字
Level 6 滿級單字

asleep [ə`slip] 副 睡著的

He fell asleep quickly because he was so tired.
▶▶ 因為很疲倦，所以他很快就睡著了。

attempt [ə`tɛmpt] 動 嘗試 名 企圖

動 They attempted to discover the truth.
他們試圖找出真相。
名 The government is making policies in an attempt to decrease the unemployment rate.
政府正在制定政策，試圖降低失業率。

attend [ə`tɛnd] 動 出席

I hope my dear parents can attend my graduation ceremony.
▶▶ 我希望我親愛的父母可以出席我的畢業典禮。

attention [ə`tɛnʃən] 名 注意

I paid great attention to the lecture.
▶▶ 我聽課非常專心。

(焦點句型) pay attention to sth./sb. 專注於…

author [`ɔθɚ] 名 作者

I wonder who the author of this masterpiece is.
▶▶ 我想知道誰是這件傑出作品的作者。

available [ə`veləbḷ] 形 可取得的

These kinds of suits are available at any department stores.
▶▶ 這些款式的套裝可以在任一家百貨公司買到。

average [`ævərɪdʒ] 形 平均的

The average score of the class is eighty.
▶▶ 這個班級的平均分數是八十分。

avoid [ə`vɔɪd] 動 避免 關 bypass 繞過

She braked suddenly and avoided an accident.
▶▶ 她緊急剎車，成功避免事故發生。

B字頭必備單字

MP3 026

backpack [`bæk͵pæk] 名 背包 動 把⋯放入背包

名 Don't let the backpack out of your sight.
別讓背包離開你的視線。

動 He backpacked all the books when the bell rang.
鐘響時他將所有書都放入背包。

backward / backwards [`bækwəd ] / [ `bækwədz] 副 向後方地；向後地

On hearing someone calling him from behind, he went backward.
▶▶ 他聽到背後有人叫他，於是往回走。

badminton [`bædmɪntən] 名 羽毛球

The Lins always play badminton together on Sundays.
▶▶ 林家總在星期天一起打羽毛球。

bake [bek] 動 烘；烤

We bake bread and cake in an oven.
▶▶ 我們用烤箱烘焙麵包與糕點。

bakery [`bekərɪ] 名 麵包店

A nice smell came from the bakery.
▶▶ 麵包店裡飄出了誘人的香味。

balance [`bæləns] 名 平衡 動 使平衡

名 The child couldn't keep his balance on his new bicycle.
那個孩子騎著他的新自行車，難以保持平衡。

動 The judge balanced the arguments from both sides.
法官權衡了雙方的論點。

balcony [`bælkənɪ] 名 陽台

My mother is watering the plants in the balcony.
▶▶ 我媽媽在陽台澆花。

balloon [bə`lun] 名 氣球 動 膨脹 同 explode 爆炸

名 The girl was startled when the balloon exploded.
女孩在氣球爆炸時嚇了一跳。

動 He balloons his cheeks when he is hesitant.
他猶豫不決時會鼓起雙頰。

Level 1 基礎單字

Level 2 必備單字

Level 3 中級單字

Level 4 進階單字

Level 5 高手單字

Level 6 滿級單字

bar [bɑr] 名棒；條 動禁止

名 Wendy bought a bar of soap from the store.
溫蒂從店裡買了一條肥皂。

動 He has been barred from practicing medicine.
他被禁止行醫。

barbecue [`bɑrbɪkju] 名烤肉

My college classmates and I are going to have a barbecue this Friday.
▶▶ 我和大學同學將於禮拜五舉行烤肉野餐。

barber [`bɑrbə] 名理髮師

The barber is busy with his work now.
▶▶ 理髮師正忙於工作。

bark [bɑrk] 動吠

A dog keeps barking at me.
▶▶ 一隻狗不斷對我狂吠。

base [bes] 名基底；疊 動以…為基礎

名 The machine rests on a wide base of steel.
這台機器由一個很大的鋼製底座支撐。

動 The novel is based on historical facts.
這本小說以史實為基礎。

焦點句型 be based on sth. 以…為基礎

basic [`besɪk] 形基本的 名基本；要素（通常用複數形）

These poor people lack the basic necessities of life.
▶▶ 這些窮人缺乏生活的基本必需品。

basics [`besɪks] 名基本因素

If you want to be an architect, taking classes for basics of design is essential.
▶▶ 如果你想成為建築師，必須修習基本設計。

basis [`besɪs] 名基礎

On the basis of our sales forecasts, we may begin to make a profit next year.
▶▶ 根據我們的銷售預測，我們明年將開始獲利。

焦點句型 on the basis of sth. 根據…

bathe [beð] 動沐浴；用水洗

Will you help me bathe the baby?
▶▶ 你能幫我替嬰兒洗澡嗎？

battle [`bætl] 名戰役 動作戰

名 His cousin died in the battle.
他表哥喪生於那次戰役。
動 She has battled against cancer for a long time.
她和癌症長期鬥爭。

beard [bɪrd] 名鬍子 關 mustache / moustache 髭；八字鬍

He has decided to grow a beard and a moustache.
▶▶ 他已經決定要蓄鬍。

beat [bit] 名拍子；節奏 動打；敲

名 The song has a good beat.
這首歌的節奏很強。
動 Little children like to beat drums.
小孩子喜歡打鼓。

beauty [`bjutɪ] 名美女

Beauty and the Beast is a well-known fairy tale.
▶▶〈美女與野獸〉是一篇知名的童話故事。

beer [bɪr] 名啤酒

The two brothers drank beer in the yard.
▶▶ 兩兄弟在院子裡喝啤酒。

beg [bɛg] 動乞求

Terry begged me to keep the secret.
▶▶ 泰瑞懇求我保守祕密。

beginner [bɪ`gɪnɚ] 名初學者

He performs very well as a beginner.
▶▶ 作為初學者，他表演得很棒了。

behave [bɪ`hev] 動行動；舉止 關 behavior 行為

We behave according to the customs of our culture.
▶▶ 我們依據文化規範行事。

Level 1 基礎單字
Level 2 必備單字
Level 3 中級單字
Level 4 進階單字
Level 5 高手單字
Level 6 滿級單字

being [`biɪŋ] 名生命；存在 同 entity

Wars would claim thousands of living beings.
▶▶ 戰爭會奪走數以千計的生命。

belief [bɪ`lif] 名相信；信仰；信念

She has lost her belief in God.
▶▶ 她不再信上帝了。

bend [bɛnd] 動使彎曲 名彎曲

動 Larry bent down and kissed the child.
賴瑞彎腰親吻小孩。
名 There is a sharp bend in the road here.
這段路上有一處急轉彎。
文法解析 bend 動詞三態變化為 bend / bent / bent。

better [`bɛtɚ] 形較好的；更好的 副更；較大程度地

形 She changed her seat to get a better view.
為了看得更清楚，她換了位子。
副 I like spring better than autumn.
比起秋天，我更喜歡春天。

beyond [bɪ`jɑnd] 介超過

Helen's beauty is beyond description.
▶▶ 海倫的美貌難以用筆墨形容。

bill [bɪl] 名帳單

They are arguing about who has to pay the bill.
▶▶ 他們為了誰該付帳而爭執。

billion [`bɪljən] 名十億 關 trillion 兆

Andy hit the jackpot and won one billion.
▶▶ 安迪中了十億大獎。

birth [bɝθ] 名出生；血統

The exact date of his birth is not known.
▶▶ 沒人知道他確切的出生日期。

biscuit [`bɪskɪt] 名餅乾

Do you want to try some biscuits I made yesterday?
▶▶ 你想嘗嘗我昨天做的餅乾嗎？

bit [bɪt] 名一點；小片

Would you like a bit of chocolate?
▶▶ 你要來一點巧克力嗎？

blackboard [`blæk͵bord] 名黑板 關 chalk 粉筆

The teacher wrote on the blackboard with chalk.
▶▶ 老師在黑板上用粉筆寫字。

blame [blem] 動責備

Sarah felt depressed after being blamed for the mistake by her father.
▶▶ 莎拉因犯錯被父親責罵後感到很沮喪。

blank [blæŋk] 名空白 形空白的

名 Please fill out the blanks on the form.
　　請填寫問卷的空格處。
形 He gave me a blank check.
　　他給我一張空白支票。

blanket [`blæŋkɪt] 名毛毯

The shivering dog curled up in a blanket.
▶▶ 那隻狗蜷縮在毯子裡不停顫抖。

blood [blʌd] 名血

George's face is covered with blood.
▶▶ 喬治血流滿面。

board [bord] 名布告欄

Did you read the latest announcement on the board?
▶▶ 你看過布告欄上的最新公告了嗎？

boil [bɔɪl] 動烹煮；煮沸 名煮沸

動 We have boiled eggs for breakfast every day.
　　我們每天早餐都吃水煮蛋。
名 The water is coming to a boil.
　　水快煮開了。

Level 1 基礎單字
Level 2 必備單字
Level 3 中級單字
Level 4 進階單字
Level 5 高手單字
Level 6 滿級單字

bone [bon] 名骨頭

Doris suffered a broken bone in her foot.
▶▶ 桃莉絲的一隻腳骨折了。

bookstore [`buk͵stor] 名書店

Jenny went to the bookstore by bus.
▶▶ 珍妮坐公車去書店。

border [`bɔrdɚ] 名邊境

The army was deployed along the border.
▶▶ 軍隊沿著邊境部署。

bother [`baðɚ] 動打擾

She is studying; we had better not bother her.
▶▶ 她在念書，我們最好別打擾她。

brain [bren] 名腦

It is said that eating fish is beneficial to your brain.
▶▶ 據說吃魚肉對大腦有益。

branch [bræntʃ] 名樹枝；分枝 動長出新枝；分岔

名 A sparrow stopped on a branch.
一隻麻雀停在樹枝上。
動 The tree branches over the roof.
樹的分枝越過了屋頂。

brand [brænd] 名品牌 動打下烙印；加汙名於

名 Jennifer only buys famous brands.
珍妮佛只買名牌物品。
動 The criminals are all branded as devils.
所有罪犯都和惡魔畫上等號。

brief [brif] 形短暫的 名摘要；短文

形 He made a brief speech in the class.
他在課堂上做了一段簡短的演講。
名 The boss asked her secretary to make a brief about this meeting.
老闆要求祕書做一個關於這次會議的摘要。

brilliant [`brɪljənt] 形 有才氣的；出色的

William is truly a brilliant programmer.
▶▶ 威廉實在是個出色的程式設計師。

broad [brɔd] 形 寬闊的

Vivian has a broad mind.
▶▶ 薇薇安心胸開闊。

brush [brʌʃ] 名 刷子 動 刷

名 I paint with a brush.
　我用筆刷作畫。
動 He brushed his teeth quickly.
　他刷牙速度很快。

building [`bɪldɪŋ] 名 建築物

The new hospital is a big building.
▶▶ 這所新開的醫院是一座很大的建築物。

bun [bʌn] 名 小圓麵包

She gave buns to her coworkers as snacks.
▶▶ 她送小圓麵包給同事當點心。

burden [`bɝdən] 名 負荷

I don't want to be a burden to my children when I become older.
▶▶ 我年邁時不想成為孩子們的負擔。

burn [bɝn] 動 燃燒 名 燒傷 關 campfire 營火；篝火

動 I feel warm with the campfire burning.
　燃燒的篝火使我感到溫暖。
名 He got burns from the fire accident.
　他在火災中被燒傷。

burst [bɝst] 動 爆炸 名 爆炸

動 He burst into tears when thinking of his ex-girlfriend.
　他一想起前女友就大哭了起來。
名 A burst of hand-clapping followed Cathy's performance.
　凱西表演完後響起一陣掌聲。

Level 1 基礎單字
Level 2 必備單字
Level 3 中級單字
Level 4 進階單字
Level 5 高手單字
Level 6 滿級單字

businessman [`bɪznɪsmən] 名 商人

That businessman tried to bribe the government officers.
▶▶ 那位商人試著賄賂政府官員。

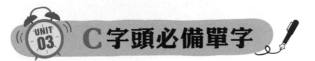 **C字頭必備單字**

cabbage [`kæbɪdʒ] 名 包心菜

Cabbage is easy to grow.
▶▶ 包心菜很容易栽培。

cafe [kə`fe] 名 咖啡館

I am on my way to the cafe.
▶▶ 我在前往咖啡館的路上。

cage [kedʒ] 名 籠子 動 把…關入籠中 關 canary 金絲雀

名 The canary is singing sweetly in a cage.
　金絲雀在籠中甜美地歌唱。
動 I felt terribly caged in that office.
　待在那間辦公室讓我感覺很像被關在籠子裡，非常難受。

calendar [`kæləndɚ] 名 日曆

She took a look at the calendar to make sure what day it was.
▶▶ 她瞄了一眼日曆，以確認那天是星期幾。

calm [kɑm] 形 平靜的 動 使平靜

形 The sea was calm after the storm.
　經過這場風暴，大海平靜下來了。
動 We calmed the old lady down.
　我們讓那位老太太冷靜了下來。

camel [`kæml̩] 名 駱駝

A camel is called the ship of the desert.
▶▶ 駱駝被稱為沙漠之舟。

cancel [`kænsl̩] 動 取消

I am sorry to cancel our date because I feel uncomfortable and dizzy.
▶▶ 很抱歉因為我頭暈不適而取消約會。

MEMORIZE 7000 VOCABULARIES ONCE AND FOR ALL！

cancer [ˋkænsɚ] 名 癌

Helen died of breast cancer.
▶▶ 海倫死於乳癌。

candle [ˋkændl̩] 名 蠟燭

The candle burned for a long time.
▶▶ 蠟燭燃燒了很久。

capital [ˋkæpətl̩] 名 首都；資本 形 主要的

名 The capital of Australia is Canberra.
　　澳洲首都是坎培拉。
形 The capital character in the play has not come yet.
　　這齣劇的主要角色還未出現。

cartoon [kɑrˋtun] 名 卡通

The boy is fond of Disney cartoons.
▶▶ 這個男孩喜歡迪士尼卡通。
焦點句型 be fond of sb./sth. 喜愛…

cash [kæʃ] 名 現金 動 兌現

名 I have no cash with me. Can I pay you later?
　　我沒帶現金，能否晚點付給你？
動 Can you cash the check for me?
　　你可以幫我兌現這張支票嗎？

castle [ˋkæsl̩] 名 城堡

A young and beautiful princess lives in the castle.
▶▶ 一位年輕貌美的公主住在城堡裡。

cause [kɔz] 動 引起 名 原因

動 What caused John to quit his job?
　　是什麼原因使約翰辭職的？
名 The cause of this accident is still unclear.
　　這一事故的起因仍有待釐清。

ceiling [ˋsilɪŋ] 名 天花板

Curtains go from the ceiling to the floor.
▶▶ 窗簾從天花板垂到地板上。

Level 1 基礎單字
Level 2 必備單字
Level 3 中級單字
Level 4 進階單字
Level 5 高手單字
Level 6 滿級單字

cell [sɛl] 名 細胞 關 cellular 細胞組成的

Our body is made up of cells.
▶▶ 無數的細胞構成我們的身體。

centimeter [`sɛntə,mitə] 名 公分

Human brains have more than 100 million cells per cubic centimeter.
▶▶ 人腦每立方公分有一億多個細胞。

central [`sɛntrəl] 形 中央的

The shops are in a central position in the city.
▶▶ 商店開設在城市的中心位置。

century [`sɛntʃərɪ] 名 世紀

The 17th century is said to be "a century of geniuses".
▶▶ 十七世紀被稱為「天才的世紀」。

cereal [`sɪrɪəl] 名 穀類作物

Eating food made from cereals is good for one's health.
▶▶ 吃穀類食物對人的健康有益。

chain [tʃen] 名 鏈子 動 鏈住；拴住

名 The dog was fastened to a post by a chain to prevent it from running away.
那隻狗被鏈子拴在柱子上，以免牠跑掉。
動 Lydia finds it cruel to chain the horse all the time.
莉迪亞覺得一直把一匹馬拴著十分殘忍。

chalk [tʃɔk] 名 粉筆

The teacher dropped a piece of chalk on the floor.
▶▶ 老師掉了一支粉筆在地上。

challenge [`tʃælɪndʒ] 名 挑戰 動 向⋯挑戰

名 I always face challenges.
我總是面對挑戰。
動 He challenged me to play another tennis game.
他向我挑戰再打一場網球。

channel [`tʃænḷ] 名 通道；頻道 動 傳輸

名 A little puppy was stuck in the channel.
一隻小狗被困在管道內。

(動) Mary channeled information to her mother.
瑪莉把消息傳給了她的母親。

chapter [`tʃæptɚ] (名)章節

The main arguments were compressed into one chapter.
▶▶ 主要的論證被壓縮成一個章節。

character [`kærɪktɚ] (名)個性

He has a changeable character.
▶▶ 他的性格多變。

charge [tʃɑrdʒ] (動)索價 (名)費用

(動) The store charges a fee to deliver items.
這間店會收運費。
(名) The charge for drinks at this restaurant is low.
這間餐廳只收取少量茶點費。

chart [tʃɑrt] (名)圖表

This is a weather chart.
▶▶ 這是一張氣象圖。

chase [tʃes] (名)追求；追逐 (動)驅逐；追趕

(名) For some, the chase to fulfill their dreams never ends.
對某些人來說,他們永遠都在追求夢想成真。
(動) Chase that dog out of the house.
把那隻狗趕出房子。

cheat [tʃit] (動)欺騙；作弊 (名)騙子

(動) He cheated me into lending him money.
他哄騙我借錢給他。
(名) I will never forgive that cheat.
我不會原諒那個騙子。

cheer [tʃɪr] (名)歡呼 (動)喝采

(名) The crowd burst into cheers.
人群中爆發出一片歡呼聲。
(動) We cheered excitedly when she walked on the stage.
當她走上舞台時,我們激動地喝采。

Level 1 基礎單字
Level 2 必備單字
Level 3 中級單字
Level 4 進階單字
Level 5 高手單字
Level 6 滿級單字

chemical [`kɛmɪkl̩] 形化學的 名化學藥品

形 He is a chemical engineer in the corporation.
他是那間公司的化學工程師。
名 Keep the baby away from the chemicals.
讓嬰兒遠離化學製品。

chess [tʃɛs] 名西洋棋

The game of chess is a battle of wits.
▶▶ 下棋是鬥智的遊戲。

chief [tʃif] 形主要的 名首領

形 The chief reason for going to school is to learn.
上學的主要原因是為了學習。
名 My father is the chief of police.
我父親是一位警長。

childhood [`tʃaɪld͵hʊd] 名童年 關 spin a story 編造故事

I remember that I loved listening to my father spinning stories in my childhood.
▶▶ 我記得我小時候很喜歡聽爸爸編的故事。

childish [`tʃaɪldɪʃ] 形孩子氣的

Although he is over thirty, his behavior is very childish.
▶▶ 雖然他已年過三十，行為還是很幼稚。

China [tʃaɪnə] 名中國

Mr. Lin is an emigrant from China.
▶▶ 林先生是中國來的移民。

chopstick [`tʃɑp͵stɪk] 名筷子

Indians eat with their hands instead of using chopsticks.
▶▶ 印度人用手吃東西，而不用筷子。

claim [klem] 動主張 名要求 關 proclaim 宣告 / allege 宣稱

動 He claimed that he was rich.
他聲稱自己很有錢。
名 She made a claim to be the owner of the land.
她要求成為這塊地的主人。

clap [klæp] 名鼓掌 動拍擊

名 Please give a clap to our guest.
請為來賓鼓掌。

動 The audience cheered and clapped.
觀眾又是喝彩又是鼓掌。

classic [`klæsɪk] 形經典的；典型的 名經典 關 classical 古典的

形 He wore a classic suit to the wedding.
他穿著一身傳統套裝去參加婚禮。

名 He collected over 100 classic books.
他收藏超過一百本經典著作。

文法解析 classic 的意思是「經典的；品質優秀的」，而 classical 的意思是「古典的；傳統的」，著重形容歷史悠久的事物，常用於藝術作品。

classmate [`klæs met] 名同學 關 junior 較年輕的

My classmate is junior to me by two years.
▶▶ 我的同學小我兩歲。

clever [`klɛvɚ] 形聰明伶俐的

The boss works faster with his clever assistant.
▶▶ 老闆的聰慧助理讓他能以更快的速度辦公。

click [klɪk] 名喀嚓聲

I heard a click when the lock opened.
▶▶ 當鎖打開時，我聽見一陣喀嚓聲。

climate [`klaɪmɪt] 名氣候 關 celsius 攝氏

He could not stand the terrible English climate.
▶▶ 他忍受不了英國糟糕的氣候。

cloth [klɔθ] 名布料

This gown is made of silk cloth.
▶▶ 這件禮服是由絲綢料子做成。

clothing [`kloðɪŋ] 名衣服

Food, clothing, and a place to live are important things in life.
▶▶ 食、衣、住是生活中必不可少的。

1 Level 基礎單字
2 Level 必備單字
3 Level 中級單字
4 Level 進階單字
5 Level 高手單字
6 Level 滿級單字

cloudy [ˋklaʊdɪ] 形 多雲的

I take an umbrella with me on such cloudy days.

▶▶ 像這樣的多雲天氣，我都會帶著雨傘。

coal [kol] 名 煤

Coal was replaced by oil as the main fuel around the world.

▶▶ 石油取代了煤成為這世界上的主要燃料。

coast [kost] 名 海岸；沿岸 關 offshore 近岸的

The land is barren on the east coast.

▶▶ 東海岸的土地貧瘠。

cockroach / roach [ˋkɑkrotʃ] / [rotʃ] 名 蟑螂

The woman found a cockroach in the kitchen.

▶▶ 女子在廚房發現一隻蟑螂。

cocoa [ˋkoko] 名 可可粉

Cocoa is used in making chocolate.

▶▶ 可可粉能用來做巧克力。

coin [kɔɪn] 名 硬幣

He put a coin into the machine.

▶▶ 他投了一塊硬幣到機器裡。

cola / Coke [ˋkolə] / [kok] 名 可樂

Two hot dogs and one cola, please.

▶▶ 請給我兩份熱狗和一瓶可樂。

college [ˋkɑlɪdʒ] 名 學院

The outstanding manager graduated from the best college in the nation.

▶▶ 那位傑出的經理畢業於他們國家最優秀的大學。

comb [kom] 動 梳 名 梳子

動 The mother combed the child's hair.
母親梳理孩子的頭髮。

名 That is not my comb.
那不是我的梳子。

combine [kəmˋbaɪn] 動 合併；聯合

Anna decided to combine the two departments together.
▶▶ 安娜決定合併這兩個部門。

comic [ˋkɑmɪk] 形 滑稽的；喜劇的 名 漫畫

形 Robin Williams had a good career as a comic actor.
羅賓 · 威廉斯有個成功的喜劇演員生涯。
名 He reads the comics in the paper every day.
他每天都看報上的漫畫。

command [kəˋmænd] 動 指揮 名 命令 同 mandate

動 The captain commanded everyone to retreat.
上校指揮全員開始撤退。
名 I will not follow his unreasonable command.
我不會服從他不合理的命令。

commercial [kəˋmɝʃəl] 形 商業的 名 商業廣告

形 The area was opened to commercial development.
這個地區已開放供商業發展使用。
名 The TV show was cut short due to many commercials.
由於廣告太多，這個電視節目長度有所刪減。

company [ˋkʌmpənɪ] 名 公司

Mr. Wu is the owner of our company.
▶▶ 吳先生是我們公司的持有人。

compare [kəmˋpɛr] 動 比較

It is interesting to compare their situation with ours.
▶▶ 把他們的狀況與我們的相比很有意思。

complete [kəmˋplit] 動 完成 形 完整的

動 If you complete your work, you can leave earlier.
如果你完成了工作，就可以提早離開。
形 We need a complete examination of the situation.
我們必須完整檢視整個情形。

complex [ˋkɑmplɛks] 形 複雜的 名 複合物

形 The equation is too complex to remember.
這個方程式太複雜難記了。

Level 1 基礎單字
Level 2 必備單字
Level 3 中級單字
Level 4 進階單字
Level 5 高手單字
Level 6 滿級單字

名 A petrochemical complex is to be built here.
一個石油化學聯合企業將於此設立。

concern [kən`sən] 動 關心

David was concerned about me so much.
▶▶ 大衛非常關心我。

conclude [kən`klud] 動 結束 關 conclusion 結論

The story concludes with the hero's death.
▶▶ 小說以主角的死亡而告終。

condition [kən`dɪʃən] 名 條件；情況 動 以…為條件

名 Foggy weather has made driving conditions very dangerous.
霧天開車很危險。
動 Ability and effort condition success.
才能和努力是成功的條件。

confident [`kɑnfədənt] 形 有信心的

She is quite confident of winning his heart.
▶▶ 她很有自信贏得他的心。

conflict [`kɑnflɪkt ] / [ kən`flɪkt] 名 衝突 動 鬥爭

名 This conflict is difficult to solve.
這場衝突難以解決。
動 The two parties conflict with each other.
兩個政黨相互鬥爭。

congratulation [kən͵grætʃə`leʃən] 名 祝賀

Congratulations on your exam results!
▶▶ 恭喜你考出了好成績！

connection [kə`nɛkʃən] 名 連結 同 correlation

He has no connection to that prank.
▶▶ 他與那個惡作劇無關。

consider [kən`sɪdə] 動 仔細考慮 關 consideration 考慮

I try to consider every possible result.
▶▶ 我試著仔細考量所有可能的結果。

contact [`kɑntækt ] / [ kən`tækt] 名聯絡 動接觸

名 I still keep in contact with my old friends.
我仍然和老朋友保持聯絡。
動 You have to contact the new client.
你必須和新客戶接觸。

contain [kən`ten] 動包含

This dictionary contains the definition of many words.
▶▶ 這本辭典含有許多單字的定義。

continue [kən`tɪnju] 動繼續;連續 關 ongoing 進行的

They continued their work.
▶▶ 他們繼續他們的工作。

contract [`kɑntrækt ] / [ kən`trækt] 名契約 動定契約

名 Please sign your name here after reading the contract.
看完契約後請在此處簽名。
動 We contracted with a Japanese firm for the purchase of their products.
我們和一間日本廠商簽約,購買他們的產品。

control [kən`trol] 動管理;控制 名管理;控制

動 Tony could not control his tears.
東尼忍不住流下眼淚來。
名 He always keeps things under control.
他總是讓事情處於他的控制之下。

conversation [ˌkɑnvɚ`seʃən] 名交談 同 discourse

I heard their secret conversation.
▶▶ 我聽到他們的祕密對話。

corn [kɔrn] 名玉米

That cookie is made from corn.
▶▶ 那個餅乾是用玉米作的。

countryside [`kʌntrɪˌsaɪd] 名鄉間

From the hill, there is a great view of the countryside.
▶▶ 從山上望去,可以看到附近鄉間的壯麗景色。

1 Level 基礎單字
2 Level 必備單字
3 Level 中級單字
4 Level 進階單字
5 Level 高手單字
6 Level 滿級單字

couple [ˋkʌpḷ] 名配偶；夫妻 動結合

名 The young couple decided to start their tour immediately.
那對年輕夫婦決定立即開始旅遊。

動 Andrew is going to couple with Yvonne.
安德魯即將和伊娃結婚。

courage [ˋkɝɪdʒ] 名勇氣

He showed great courage and determination.
▶▶ 他表現得十分勇敢和果斷。

court [kort] 名法院

The suspect was not in court.
▶▶ 被告沒有出庭。

cowboy [ˋkaʊˌbɔɪ] 名牛仔

My father loves to watch cowboy movies.
▶▶ 我爸爸很愛看牛仔片。

crayon [ˋkreˌɑn] 名蠟筆

The picture was drawn with crayons.
▶▶ 這幅畫是用蠟筆畫的。

cream [krim] 名乳酪；軟膏

The cream is for use on the face only.
▶▶ 此軟膏只供臉部使用。

create [krɪˋet] 動創造 關 creation 創造

The main purpose of industry is to create wealth.
▶▶ 工業的主要宗旨是創造財富。

crime [kraɪm] 名罪行

It is a crime to steal from another person.
▶▶ 偷竊他人的東西是一種罪行。

crisis [ˋkraɪsɪs] 名危機

Our president tried hard to deal with the economic crisis.
▶▶ 我們的總統努力試著解決經濟危機。

crow [kro] 名烏鴉

They view crows as inauspicious symbols.
▶▶ 他們把烏鴉當成不吉利的象徵。

crowd [kraʊd] 名人群 動擠

名 Security guards watched the crowd.
　　保全人員監視人群。
動 They crowded onto the bus.
　　他們擠上公車。

culture [`kʌltʃə] 名文化 關 cultural 文化的

I want to know more about Japanese culture.
▶▶ 我希望更了解日本文化。

cure [kjʊr] 動治癒 名治癒

動 It is still not possible to cure his disease.
　　他的疾病仍無法治癒。
名 There is no cure for cancer currently.
　　目前沒有治癒癌症的方法。

curious [`kjʊrɪəs] 形好奇的

I am curious about the cause of his anger.
▶▶ 我很好奇他生氣的原因。

current [`kɝənt] 形目前的 名電流；水流

形 What are the current headlines?
　　目前的新聞頭條是什麼？
名 The block becomes magnetic when the current is switched on.
　　一通上電流，這塊板子就會產生磁性。

curtain [`kɝtṇ] 名窗簾 動裝上簾子

名 I closed the curtain since the sunlight hurt my eyes.
　　我把窗簾拉上，因為陽光太刺眼了。
動 They curtained the stage before their performance.
　　他們表演前在舞台裝上布幕。

custom [`kʌstəm] 名習俗

I think these interesting old customs should be saved.
▶▶ 我認為這些有趣的古老習俗應該保存下去。

Level 1 基礎單字
Level 2 必備單字
Level 3 中級單字
Level 4 進階單字
Level 5 高手單字
Level 6 滿級單字

customer [`kʌstəmə] 名 客戶

The customer seems unhappy with her service.
▶▶ 顧客似乎不滿意她的服務。

cycle [`saɪkl̩] 名 周期；循環

The seasons of the year make a cycle.
▶▶ 一年四季構成一個循環。

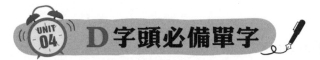

daily [`delɪ] 形 每日的 副 每日地

形 What I should do first is my daily homework.
　　我該做的第一件事就是做每日的回家作業。
副 Exercise daily benefits your health.
　　每日運動有益健康。

damage [`dæmɪdʒ] 名 損害 動 損害

名 The typhoon caused a great damage to our transportation system.
　　颱風對我們的交通系統造成巨大破壞。
動 Such a chemical will damage your health.
　　這種化學物質會損害你的健康。

dancer [`dænsə] 名 舞者

The dancer moves very gracefully.
▶▶ 舞蹈家非常優雅地移動著步伐。

danger [`dændʒə] 名 危險

The boat is in danger of sinking.
▶▶ 這艘船正陷入沉船危機。

data [`detə] 名 資料；數據 關 database 資料庫

According to our data, women's income is increasing.
▶▶ 我們的資料顯示，女性收入正在提高。

deaf [dɛf] 形 耳聾的

The deaf woman cannot hear what you say.
▶▶ 那個耳聾的女人無法聽到你說什麼。

debate [dɪˋbet] 動辯論 名辯論

動 The subject was hotly debated.
這個題目曾有過熱烈的辯論。

名 A fierce debate is going on.
一場辯論正在激烈進行中。

debt [dɛt] 名債

He promised to pay the debt.
▸▸ 他承諾會還債。

decision [dɪˋsɪʒən] 名決定

She made a final decision on the case.
▸▸ 她對這件案子做了最終決斷。

deer [dɪr] 名鹿

Hunters chased the deer silently.
▸▸ 獵人們悄悄地追捕那隻鹿。

degree [dɪˋgri] 名學位；程度

Linda got her degree in Japan.
▸▸ 琳達在日本拿到學位。

delay [dɪˋle] 動延緩 名耽擱

動 Kevin has no choice but to delay the honeymoon.
凱文別無選擇，只好延後蜜月旅行。

名 His delay made the boss mad.
他的耽擱惹得老闆發怒。

delicious [dɪˋlɪʃəs] 形美味的

The delicious desserts were provided by Maggie.
▸▸ 這些美味的點心是瑪姬提供的。

deliver [dɪˋlɪvɚ] 動運送；遞送 關 delivery 運送

Will you deliver, or do I have to come to the shop to collect the goods?
▸▸ 是由你們送貨，還是我需要到店裡取貨呢？

dentist [ˋdɛntɪst] 名牙醫 關 toothache 牙痛 / toothbrush 牙刷

The girl asked the dentist whether the bad tooth should be pulled out.
▸▸ 那女孩問牙醫是否要拔掉蛀牙。

Level 1 基礎單字
Level 2 必備單字
Level 3 中級單字
Level 4 進階單字
Level 5 高手單字
Level 6 滿級單字

deny [dɪ`naɪ] 動拒絕;否認

I denied that I stole the money.
▶▶ 我否認我偷了錢。

department [dɪ`pɑrtmənt] 名部門

She is the most important person in our department.
▶▶ 她是我們部門最重要的人才。

depend [dɪ`pɛnd] 動依賴

Do not depend on others to give you answers.
▶▶ 別依賴別人給你答案。

(焦點句型) depend on sb./sth. 取決於…;依賴…

depth [dɛpθ] 名深度

Nobody knew the depth of her love for the child.
▶▶ 誰也不知道她對這孩子的愛有多深。

describe [dɪ`skraɪb] 動描述

It is hard to describe his appearance.
▶▶ 他的外貌很難形容。

description [dɪ`skrɪpʃən] 名敘述

Can you give me a description in detail of the incident?
▶▶ 你可以把那件事詳細地解釋給我聽嗎?

desert [`dɛzət ] / [ dɪ`zɜt] 名沙漠;甜點 動拋棄

名 I saw only a camel in the desert.
沙漠裡我只看見一隻駱駝。
動 A homeless person occupied the deserted house.
一位街友佔用了那棟廢棄的屋子。

design [dɪ`zaɪn] 名設計 動設計

名 Her latest design is very good.
她最新的設計非常棒。
動 My sister designed a website to promote the new product.
我姐姐設計了一個網站推廣新產品。

detail [`ditel] 名 細節

If you want to know all the details, Ms. Chen will tell you later.
▶▶ 若你想了解詳情，等會兒陳小姐會來向你說明。

develop [dɪ`vɛləp] 動 發展 關 development 發展

Plants develop from seeds.
▶▶ 植物由種子發育而成。

dial [`daɪəl] 動 撥

He dialed the number to find out who called him yesterday.
▶▶ 他撥打這個號碼，以找出昨天誰打電話給他。

dialogue [`daɪə,lɔg] 名 對話

This movie is all action with very little dialogue.
▶▶ 這部電影裡盡是動作，對話極少。

diamond [`daɪmənd] 名 鑽石

I need your promise instead of a diamond.
▶▶ 我需要的是你的承諾，而不是鑽石。

diary [`daɪərɪ] 名 日記；日誌

Do you have the habit of keeping a diary?
▶▶ 你有寫日記的習慣嗎？
(焦點句型) keep a diary 寫日記

diet [`daɪət] 名 飲食

There is an obvious connection between diet and health.
▶▶ 飲食與健康之間有著明顯的關聯。

difference [`dɪfərəns] 名 差異

Did you notice any difference in John today?
▶▶ 你有注意到約翰今天哪裡不一樣嗎？

difficulty [`dɪfə,kʌltɪ] 名 困難

I will do my best in spite of the difficulty.
▶▶ 無論有多困難，我都會盡我所能。

Level 1 基礎單字
Level 2 必備單字
Level 3 中級單字
Level 4 進階單字
Level 5 高手單字
Level 6 滿級單字

direct [dəˋrɛkt] 形直達的；直接的 動指示；命令

形 He took a direct flight to New York.
他搭乘直航班機到紐約。

動 My boss directed me to cancel the meeting.
我的老闆指示我取消這次會議。

direction [dəˋrɛkʃən] 名方向

I have no sense of direction, so I always lose my way.
▶ 我沒有方向感，所以常常迷路。

director [dəˋrɛktɚ] 名導演 關 directive 指導的

The director taught the actor how to perform the role.
▶ 導演指導演員如何演出這個角色。

disagree [ˌdɪsəˋgri] 動不同意 同 dissent 關 disagreement 不同意

I disagree with you, but I know you have the right to express your own opinion.
▶ 我不同意你，但是我明白你有提出意見的權利。

disappear [ˌdɪsəˋpɪr] 動消失

He walked away and disappeared into a crowd of people.
▶ 他離開後消失在人群中。

discover [dɪsˋkʌvɚ] 動發現；發覺

Columbus discovered America in 1492.
▶ 哥倫布於一四九二年發現美洲新大陸。

discovery [dɪsˋkʌvərɪ] 名發現

Due to the discovery of the fossil, the village became renowned worldwide.
▶ 由於發現化石，這個村莊變得舉世聞名。

discuss [dɪˋskʌs] 名討論

We discussed how to deal with the affair.
▶ 我們討論如何處理這件事。

discussion [dɪˋskʌʃən] 名討論

They had a discussion about whether to permit her resignation.
▶ 他們討論是否允許她離職。

disease [dɪˋziz] 名 疾病

The old man died of a severe disease.
▶▶ 那個老人死於重病。

display [dɪˋsple] 動 展出 名 展示

動 Her writing displays natural talent.
她寫的作品顯示出她天賦極高。
名 On New Year's Eve, the display of fireworks is excellent.
除夕夜的煙火很吸引人。

distance [ˋdɪstəns] 名 距離

There is a long distance between the two stops.
▶▶ 這兩站之間距離很長。

distant [ˋdɪstənt] 形 有距離的；疏遠的

After the argument, my aunt has become distant with me.
▶▶ 爭吵過後，我和阿姨變得疏遠了。

divide [dəˋvaɪd] 動 分開 關 dividend 被除數

We were divided into four groups.
▶▶ 我們被分為四個小組。

division [dəˋvɪʒən] 名 分割

The road forms the division between the two cities.
▶▶ 這條路成了這兩座城市的分界線。

domestic [dəˋmɛstɪk] 形 國內的；家務的

The summit concerns both foreign and domestic policies.
▶▶ 這場高峰會關乎國內外政策。

dot [dɑt] 名 圓點 動 以點表示；分散

名 He watched until the airplane was just a dot in the sky.
他望著那飛機，直到飛機變成天空中的一顆小圓點為止。
動 The dotted dress is suitable for her.
這件圓點洋裝很適合她。

double [ˋdʌbḷ] 形 雙倍的 副 加倍地 名 二倍 動 加倍

副 You have to double-check this document.
這份文件你要再次確認。

Level 1 基礎單字
Level 2 必備單字
Level 3 中級單字
Level 4 進階單字
Level 5 高手單字
Level 6 滿級單字

名 His income is the double of mine.
他的收入是我的兩倍。
動 I will double the pay if you complete the work.
如果你完成這份工作，我會加倍給薪。

doubt [daʊt] 動懷疑 名懷疑

動 He doubted his classmate stole his money.
他懷疑同學偷了他的錢。
名 There is no doubt about his loyalty.
他的忠誠無庸置疑。

dove [dʌv] 名鴿子

The dove is a symbol of peace.
▶▶ 鴿子是和平的象徵。

download [`daʊnlod] 動下載

Tommy downloaded many movies from the website, ignoring the copyrights.
▶▶ 湯米在網站上下載很多電影，忽視了著作權。

downstairs [ˌdaʊn`stɛrz] 副向下；往樓下 形 樓下的 名樓下

副 Anna is coming downstairs.
安娜正下樓來。
形 The children are downstairs, playing toys and laughing out loud.
孩子們在樓下玩著玩具，並大聲嬉笑。
名 The whole downstairs needs repainting.
樓下全部都需要重新粉刷。

dragon [`drægən] 名龍

Dragons symbolize emperors in ancient China.
▶▶ 在中國古代，龍象徵著君王。

drama [`drɑmə] 名戲劇

She feels sorry for the tragic actress in the drama.
▶▶ 她同情戲裡苦命的女演員。

drawer [`drɔɚ] 名抽屜

Anthony took his digital camera from the drawer.
▶▶ 安東尼從抽屜裡拿出數位相機。

drawing [`drɔɪŋ] 名繪圖

He made a drawing of the old farmhouse.
▶▶ 他畫了一幅古老農舍的畫。

drug [drʌg] 名藥 關 abuse 濫用

The officials discussed how to stop drug abuse.
▶▶ 官員們討論如何防止藥物濫用。

dryer [`draɪə] 名烘衣機；吹風機

Don't put that sweater in the dryer.
▶▶ 別把那件毛衣放到烘乾機裡。

due [dju] 形預定的 名應付款

形 We are due to leave tomorrow.
　　我們預定明天啟程。
名 Have you paid your membership dues?
　　你已經繳交會員費了嗎？

dull [dʌl] 形單調乏味的

It is dull to talk with such a strict man.
▶▶ 和這麼嚴肅的人說話很無趣。

duty [`djutɪ] 名責任；義務

It is not my duty to wake you up every morning.
▶▶ 我沒有義務每天早上叫你起床。

UNIT 05 E 字頭必備單字

MP3 029

eagle [`igḷ] 名鷹

Eagles fly alone, but sheep flock together.
▶▶ 老鷹獨自翱翔，而綿羊成群行動。

earn [ɝn] 動賺取

His achievements earned him respect and admiration.
▶▶ 他的成就為他贏來了他人的尊敬和仰慕。

Level 1 基礎單字
Level 2 必備單字
Level 3 中級單字
Level 4 進階單字
Level 5 高手單字
Level 6 滿級單字

earring(s) [`ɪr,rɪŋ] 名耳環

Do you have the earrings in particular design?
▶▶ 你有那款特殊設計的耳環嗎？

earthquake [`ɜθ,kwek] 名地震

He stays calm during earthquakes.
▶▶ 他在地震時鎮定自若。

ease [iz] 動緩和；減輕 名容易；不費力；舒適

動 The medicine eased Gina's pain.
藥物減輕了吉娜的痛苦。
名 Our volleyball team won the game with ease.
我們的排球隊輕鬆贏下了那場比賽。

eastern [`istən] 形東方的 名東方人

形 The foreigner is very interested in eastern art.
這位外國人對東方藝術非常有興趣。
名 The Easterns have a rich cultural heritage that spans thousands of years.
東方人擁有跨越數千年的豐富文化遺產。

edge [ɛdʒ] 名邊緣

Mother put a pen by the edge of the table.
▶▶ 母親把一隻筆放在桌邊。

edition [ɪ`dɪʃən] 名版本

The second edition is slightly different in content from the first one.
▶▶ 第二版和第一版之間的內容有點差異。

education [,ɛdʒə`keʃən] 名教育

Some parents let their children receive formal education at a very early age.
▶▶ 有些父母很早就讓孩子接受正規教育。

effect [ɪ`fɛkt] 名影響

Modern farming methods can have a harmful effect on the environment.
▶▶ 現代農業的耕作方法可能對環境造成負面影響。
(焦點句型) have an effect on sb./sth. 對…造成影響

effective [ɪˋfɛktɪv] 形 有效果的

Punishment is not always effective against bad behavior.
▶▶ 懲罰對不良行為並非總是有效。

effort [ˋɛfət] 名 努力

He spares no effort to live up to his mother's expectations.
▶▶ 他不遺餘力地完成母親的期待。

elder [ˋɛldə] 形 年長的 名 長輩

形 Her elder daughter is the same age as me.
　　她的長女和我一樣大。
名 The well-behaved girl is welcomed among elders.
　　那位應對得體的女孩很受長輩歡迎。

electric [ɪˋlɛktrɪk] 形 電的

Brian plays the electric guitar like a professional.
▶▶ 布萊恩彈電吉他已達專業人士的水準。

electrical [ɪˋlɛktrɪk!] 形 電的

Henry is a merchandiser who sells electrical appliances.
▶▶ 亨利是個販售電器的商人。

emotion [ɪˋmoʃən] 名 情感；情緒

He is not good at expressing emotions.
▶▶ 他不擅長表達情感。

emphasize [ˋɛmfə͵saɪz] 動 強調

The mayor's speech emphasized the importance of attracting industry to the town.
▶▶ 市長的發言強調了吸引工業進駐城鎮的重要性。

employ [ɪmˋplɔɪ] 動 雇用 關 employment 雇用

His parents employed a tutor to teach him mathematics.
▶▶ 他的父母雇了一位家庭教師教他數學。

employee [͵ɛmplɔɪˋi] 名 職員；受雇者 關 workforce 勞動力

The employees should unite to fight for more money.
▶▶ 員工們應該為了賺更多錢而團結努力。

Level 1 基礎單字
Level 2 必備單字
Level 3 中級單字
Level 4 進階單字
Level 5 高手單字
Level 6 滿級單字

employer [ɪmˋplɔɪɚ] 名 雇主

Our employer is so considerate that we all respect her very much.
▶▶ 我們的雇主非常體貼，我們都非常敬重她。

empty [ˋɛmptɪ] 形 空的 動 倒空

形 The house had been standing empty for some time.
這房子已經有一段時間沒人住了。
動 Please empty the bottle and give it back to me.
請把瓶子清空後還給我。

encourage [ɪnˋkɝɪdʒ] 動 鼓勵 關 encouragement 鼓勵

I write a mail to encourage him every time he feels depressed.
▶▶ 每當他感到沮喪時，我就會寫封信鼓勵他。

ending [ˋɛndɪŋ] 名 結局

The drama has a strange ending.
▶▶ 這部戲的結局很奇怪。

enemy [ˋɛnəmɪ] 名 敵人

Don't make an enemy of him.
▶▶ 不要與他為敵。

energy [ˋɛnɚdʒɪ] 名 精力；能量；能源

She always works with lots of energy.
▶▶ 她工作時總是精力充沛。

engine [ˋɛndʒən] 名 引擎 關 diesel 柴油引擎

The engine of the six-year-old car is still powerful.
▶▶ 這輛車有六年了，引擎仍舊非常強而有力。

entire [ɪnˋtaɪr] 形 全部的

Read the entire text aloud.
▶▶ 大聲念出整段課文。

entrance [ˋɛntrəns] 名 入口

I will meet you at the entrance of the hospital.
▶▶ 我在醫院的入口處等你。

environment [ɪn`vaɪrənmənt] 名環境 關 environmental 環境的

Studies show that the home environment has a great influence on children's growth.
▶▶ 研究顯示家庭環境對孩子的成長影響深遠。

equal [`ikwəl] 形平等的 動等於；比得上 名對手 關 equalize 使相等

形 All men are equal.
人人都是平等的。
動 Nobody can equal Tony in swimming.
在游泳方面，沒有人比得上東尼。
名 She has no equal in cooking.
她在烹飪方面無人匹敵。

escape [əs`kep] 動逃走 名漏出

動 The dog escaped from his master.
這隻狗從他主人那裡逃脫。
名 Can you smell an escape of gas?
你有聞到瓦斯漏氣嗎？

especially [əs`pɛʃəlɪ] 副特別地

I like the country, especially in spring.
▶▶ 我尤其喜歡春天時的鄉村。

essay [`ɛse] 名短文；隨筆

Ken wrote an essay as his contribution to the magazine.
▶▶ 肯恩寫了一篇短文投稿雜誌。

eve [iv] 名前夕

They broke up on the eve of Valentine's Day.
▶▶ 他們在情人節前夕分手。

event [ɪ`vɛnt] 名事件

She was involved in the strange event.
▶▶ 她被捲入奇怪的事件裡。

evil [`ivl̩] 形邪惡的 名邪惡

形 The old lady gazed at me with the evil eye.
那位老婦人用惡毒的眼神瞪著我。

1 Level 基礎單字
2 Level 必備單字
3 Level 中級單字
4 Level 進階單字
5 Level 高手單字
6 Level 滿級單字

名 Some people return good for evil.
有些人以德報怨。

exact [ɪɡˋzækt] 形 正確的

No one knows his exact name.
▶▶ 沒人知道他真正的名字。

examination / exam [ɪɡ͵zæməˋneʃən] 名 考試 同 scrutiny

We will have an examination in mathematics tomorrow.
▶▶ 明天我們將有一個數學考試。

examine [ɪɡˋzæmɪn] 動 檢查；測驗 同 probe

The captain examined the ship last night.
▶▶ 船長昨晚檢查了船。

excitement [ɪkˋsaɪtmənt] 名 興奮 關 excite 使興奮

There was a lot of excitement over the team's victory.
▶▶ 團隊的勝利讓眾人感到興奮。

excuse [ɪkˋskjuz] 名 藉口 動 原諒

名 He gave an excuse to avoid being blamed.
他找藉口以免挨罵。
動 Excuse me, do you know where the bus stop is?
不好意思，你知道公車站牌在哪裡嗎？

焦點句型 excuse me 不好意思；打擾一下（用於禮貌地引起他人注意）

exist [ɪɡˋzɪst] 動 存在

Do you believe aliens exist?
▶▶ 你相信外星人存在嗎？

expense [ɪkˋspɛns] 名 費用 關 expenditure 支出

The engineers went through with the highway project, even though the expenses had risen.
▶▶ 儘管費用增加了，工程師們仍把他們的高速公路專案做完。

expert [ˋɛkspɝt] 名 專家 形 熟練的；有經驗的

名 The expert says the plan is impossible.
專家說這個計畫無法實行。

Level 1 基礎單字
Level 2 必備單字
Level 3 中級單字
Level 4 進階單字
Level 5 高手單字
Level 6 滿級單字

形 My sister is an expert pianist and performs all over the world.
我姐姐是個經驗豐富的鋼琴家，她在全世界都有表演。

express [ɪk`sprɛs] 動表達 關 expression 表達；表情

It's hard for me to express my thoughts.
▶▶ 我很難表達我的想法。

extra [`ɛkstrə] 形額外的 副特別地

形 We can get extra money if we succeed.
如果我們成功，可以獲得額外的獎金。

副 They were paid extra for working late.
他們拿到了加班費。

eyebrow / brow [`aɪ͵braʊ] / [braʊ] 名眉毛

He had his eyebrows trimmed.
▶▶ 他修剪了他的眉毛。

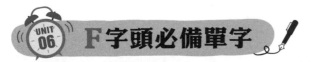

UNIT 06 F字頭必備單字

MP3 030

factor [`fæktɚ] 名因素

Waiting is one of the necessary factors for winning this game.
▶▶ 等待是贏得這場比賽必不可少的條件之一。

failure [`feljɚ] 名失敗

His failure made him sad.
▶▶ 他因失敗而難過。

fair [fɛr] 形公平的

They all agree that the decision was fair.
▶▶ 他們一致同意這個決定是公平的。

false [fɔls] 形錯誤的；虛假的

I don't want to give you a false impression.
▶▶ 我不想給你一個錯誤的印象。

fashion [`fæʃən] 名 流行

Her hairstyle is out of fashion.
▶▶ 她的髮型過時了。

fate [fet] 名 命運

It's said that people's fate is related to their character.
▶▶ 據說人的命運與性格相關。

fault [fɔlt] 名 錯誤 關 default 違約

He said the mistake was not his fault.
▶▶ 他說會出現這個錯誤，並非他的問題。

favor [`fevɚ] 動 喜好 名 喜好

動 I favor coffee, especially in the morning.
我偏愛咖啡，尤其是早上的時候。
名 They will look with favor on your proposal.
他們將會贊同你的提議。
焦點句型 in favor of sb./sth. 贊成⋯；支持⋯

favorite [`fevərɪt] 形 最喜歡的

Chanel is my favorite brand of perfume.
▶▶ 香奈兒是我最喜愛的香水品牌。

fear [fɪr] 名 害怕；恐懼 動 害怕；擔心 關 fearful 嚇人的

名 The little boy cried with fear.
這個小男孩害怕得大哭。
動 I fear that you'll be late if you don't go now.
如果你現在不出發的話，我擔心你會遲到。

feature [`fitʃɚ] 名 特色 同 attribute

The new car design incorporates all the latest safety features.
▶▶ 這款新車的設計具備最新安全措施的一切特點。

fee [fi] 名 費用

If you want to join, there's a fee of $50.
▶▶ 如果你要入會，需繳入會費五十美元。

feeling [`filɪŋ] 名 感受

Nina neglected her brother's feeling.
▶▶ 妮娜忽略了她弟弟的感受。

fellow [`fɛlo] 名 同事；夥伴

Henry knows some fine fellows.
▶▶ 亨利認識一些好夥伴。

female [`fimel] 形 女性的 名 女性

形 Female perfume smells differently from male's.
女性香水聞起來和男性香水不一樣。
名 The staff in our company is all female.
我們公司的職員都是女性。

fever [`fivɚ] 名 熱

I had a slight fever and headache.
▶▶ 我有點發燒和頭痛。

field [fild] 名 田野

We camped in a field near the village.
▶▶ 我們在靠近村莊的田地裡露營。

figure [`fɪgjɚ] 名 數字 動 找出；指出

名 Experts put the real figure at closer to 75%.
專家們估計真實的數字較接近於百分之七十五。
動 I finally figured out the main points of this essay.
我終於釐清這篇文章的重點了。
(焦點句型) figure out 理解；釐清

final [`faɪn̩] 形 最後的；最終的 關 finally 終於

The headmaster has the final say.
▶▶ 校長有最終決定權。

fireman / firewoman [`faɪrmən ] / [ `faɪrˌwʊmən] 名 消防員

The fireman rushed into the burning house to rescue the children.
▶▶ 消防員衝進著火的房子搶救小孩。

Level 1 基礎單字
Level 2 必備單字
Level 3 中級單字
Level 4 進階單字
Level 5 高手單字
Level 6 滿級單字

firm [fɜm] 形 堅定的 名 公司

形 Bella has a firm belief in God.
貝拉對上帝的信仰很堅定。

名 He set up a firm on his own after graduation.
他畢業後就創了自己的公司。

fisherman [`fɪʃəmən] 名 漁夫

The water pollution has a strong impact on fishermen.
▶▶ 水汙染對漁夫們造成很大的衝擊。

fit [fɪt] 形 適合的 動 適合；勝任

形 She is so introverted that she is not fit to be a salesperson.
她非常內向，不適合當業務員。

動 I do not fit the miniskirt well.
我不適合穿迷你裙。

fix [fɪks] 動 修理

I tried to fix my broken bicycle.
▶▶ 我試著修理壞掉的腳踏車。

flag [flæg] 名 旗子

The hotel flies the American flag when it has guests from the US.
▶▶ 這家旅館有美國客人時就掛起美國國旗。

flat [flæt] 形 平坦的

I got a flat tire on my way home.
▶▶ 我的車子在回家途中爆胎了。

flight [flaɪt] 名 飛行

They met on a flight to Australia.
▶▶ 他們在飛往澳大利亞的航班上相遇。

flow [flo] 動 流出 名 流量

動 The river flows toward the north.
這條河流向北邊。

名 She tried to stop the flow of blood from the wound.
她試圖為傷口止血。

flu [flu] 名 流行性感冒

I was infected with flu.
▶▶ 我染上流行性感冒。

focus [`fokəs] 動 集中焦點 名 焦點 關 binoculars 雙筒望遠鏡

動 I focused on the shortest dancer on the stage.
　我專注看著舞台上那名最矮的舞者。
名 He took out the binoculars and adjusted the focus.
　他取出雙筒望遠鏡並調整了焦距。

(焦點句型) focus on sb./sth. 專注於…

fog [fɑg] 名 霧；霧氣 關 foggy 有霧的

Heavy fog is common in November.
▶▶ 濃霧在十一月是很常見的。

folk [fok] 名 人們 形 民間的 關 folklore 民間傳說

名 They are just simple country folk.
　他們只不過是普通的鄉下人。
形 Let's see the folk dance performance.
　一起去看民俗舞蹈表演吧。

following [`fɑləwɪŋ] 名 下列人物或事物 形 接著的

名 The nurse called the following to come to the cabin: Steve, Debbie, and Ben.
　護士喊了下面幾個人：史帝夫、黛比與班，請他們進診間。
形 They were married in 1978 and had a daughter the following year.
　他們於一九七八年結婚，第二年就生了個女兒。

foolish [`fulɪʃ] 形 愚笨的

The foolish thief left his fingerprints on the window.
▶▶ 愚蠢的小偷把指紋留在窗戶上。

football [`fut͵bɔl] 名 足球

Willy informed me of the football practice after class.
▶▶ 威利通知我放學後練習足球。

force [fors] 名 力量 動 強制 關 compulsory 強迫的

名 The moral force is on our side.
　道義的力量站在我們這邊。

Level 1 基礎單字
Level 2 必備單字
Level 3 中級單字
Level 4 進階單字
Level 5 高手單字
Level 6 滿級單字

(動) The policemen forced the criminals to hand over their arms.
警方迫使罪犯交出武器。

forest [`fɔrɪst] (名)森林

Thousands of old trees were lost in the forest fire.
▶▶ 成千上萬棵老樹在森林大火中被燒毀。

forgive [fə`gɪv] (動)原諒

A mother will always forgive her children.
▶▶ 母親總是會原諒孩子。

文法解析 forgive 動詞三態變化為 forgive / forgave / forgiven。

form [fɔrm] (名)形式；表格 (動)形成

(名) It was a form of blackmail.
那是一種勒索。
(動) These tracks were formed by rabbits.
這些腳印是兔子留下的。

formal [`fɔrml̩] (形)正式的

We are requested to wear formal clothing to the meeting.
▶▶ 我們被要求穿著正式套裝出席會議。

former [`fɔrmɚ] (形)以前的

In former days, there was a farm here.
▶▶ 從前這兒有個農場。

forth [forθ] (副)向前

They went forth into the desert.
▶▶ 他們向前走進了沙漠。

forward [`fɔrwəd] (副)向前 (動)發送

(副) She moved forward to see the sign clearer.
她往前移動，好把招牌看得更清楚。
(動) Please forward this letter to the following address.
請將這封信轉送至下面的地址。

fox [fɑks] (名)狐狸

A fox came onto the land to look for food.
▶▶ 一隻狐狸到這片土地來找食物。

freedom [`fridəm] 名自由

The criminal in the jail desired freedom.
▶▶ 監獄裡的囚犯嚮往著自由。

friendship [`frɛndʃɪp] 名友誼

I cherish the friendship with all of you.
▶▶ 我珍惜和你們所有人的友誼。

fries [fraɪz] 名薯條

I had two double cheese burgers and three packets of French fries.
▶▶ 我吃了兩個雙層吉事漢堡和三包薯條。

fry [fraɪ] 動油炸；煎；炒

I could smell bacon frying in the kitchen.
▶▶ 我能聞到廚房裡煎培根的味道。

function [`fʌŋkʃən] 名功能

What is his function on the committee?
▶▶ 他在委員會的職務是什麼？

furniture [`fɜnɪtʃɚ] 名家具

Plastic furniture is commonly used outside.
▶▶ 塑膠家具通常在戶外使用。

further [`fɜðɚ] 副更遠地 形更進一步的

副 We had walked further than I realized.
　　在我不知不覺中我們已走得很遠。
形 The other questions are worth further discussion.
　　其他問題值得更進一步的討論。

G字頭必備單字

MP3 031

gain [gen] 動獲得 名獲得

動 They gained ground in the battle.
　　他們在那場戰役中獲得了土地。
名 No pain, no gain.
　　一分耕耘，一分收穫。

garbage [`gɑrbɪdʒ] 名垃圾 關 bin 垃圾桶

He threw away the garbage.
▶▶ 他把垃圾丟了。

gardener [`gɑrdənɚ] 名園丁

The gardener is watering the flowers.
▶▶ 園丁正在澆花。

garlic [`gɑrlɪk] 名蒜

I like to eat everything with garlic.
▶▶ 我喜歡所有加大蒜的食物。

gather [`gæðɚ] 動集合

I can't start writing my report until I gather enough materials.
▶▶ 我要蒐集了足夠的材料才能開始寫報告。

general [`dʒɛnərəl] 名將軍 形一般的

名 No one dares to disobey the general's command.
　沒人敢違抗將軍的命令。
形 In general, we do not enter from that door.
　一般情況下，我們不從那個門進入。

generous [`dʒɛnərəs] 形慷慨的

The generous woman adopted the orphan.
▶▶ 那個慷慨的女人收養了這個孤兒。

gentle [`dʒɛntl̩] 形溫柔的

Jessie comforted me with her gentle tone.
▶▶ 潔西用溫柔的語調安慰我。

gentleman [`dʒɛntl̩mən] 名紳士

Be careful with Tom. He's not a gentleman!
▶▶ 小心湯姆，他可不是正人君子！

giraffe [dʒəˋræf] 名長頸鹿

A giraffe may eat up to 75 pounds of leaves per day.
▶▶ 一隻長頸鹿一天可以吃超過七十五磅的樹葉。

glue [glu] 名膠水 動黏

名 She attached the label to the notebook with glue.
她用膠水把標籤黏在筆記本上。
動 The boy's eyes were glued to the screen.
男孩目不轉睛地盯著螢幕。

goal [gol] 名目標

The company has achieved all its goals this year.
▶▶ 這家公司已經達成今年所有的目標。

goat [got] 名山羊

The tiger pounced on the goat.
▶▶ 那隻老虎撲向那隻山羊。

gold [gold] 形金的 名金子；黃金

形 My father has a gold watch.
我父親有一隻金錶。
名 Gold is widely associated with wealth.
人們廣泛地將黃金與財富聯想在一起。

golden [`goldn] 形金色的；黃金的

Wearing a golden ring is old-fashioned for youngsters.
▶▶ 戴黃金戒指對年輕人來說很老氣。

goose [gus] 名鵝

We saw a flock of geese swimming in the lake.
▶▶ 我們看見一群鵝在湖裡游水。
文法解析 goose的複數形為geese。

govern [`gʌvən] 動統治

The president promised to govern the country with fairness.
▶▶ 總統承諾將以公平的方式治理國家。

government [`gʌvənmənt] 名政府

People lost their faith in the government.
▶▶ 人民對政府失去了信心。

Level 1 基礎單字
Level 2 必備單字
Level 3 中級單字
Level 4 進階單字
Level 5 高手單字
Level 6 滿級單字

gradual [`grædʒʊəl] 形 逐漸的 關 gradually 逐漸地

The change was so gradual that we hardly noticed it.
▶▶ 這種變化很慢，我們幾乎難以察覺。

grain [gren] 名 穀類

Not a grain of rice was wasted.
▶▶ 一粒米也沒有浪費。

gram [græm] 名 公克

It weighs three hundred grams.
▶▶ 它有三百公克重。

grand [grænd] 形 壯麗的；堂皇的

My aunt lives in a grand house.
▶▶ 我姑姑住在一間富麗堂皇的房子裡。

grape [grep] 名 葡萄

I think it's just sour grapes of him.
▶▶ 我認為他不過是酸葡萄心態。

greet [grit] 動 迎接；問候

Henry greeted me with shining smile.
▶▶ 亨利帶著閃亮的微笑迎接我。

growth [groθ] 名 成長

Childhood is a period of rapid growth.
▶▶ 幼年是生長迅速的時期。

guard [gɑrd] 名 警衛 動 防衛

名 The guard pays more attention to strangers.
警衛對陌生人會加注意。
動 A helmet guards your head against injuries.
安全帽可以保護你的頭部免受傷害。

guava [`gwɑvə] 名 芭樂

She thinks guava is good for your health.
▶▶ 她認為芭樂有益你的健康。

Level 1 基礎單字
Level 2 必備單字
Level 3 中級單字
Level 4 進階單字
Level 5 高手單字
Level 6 滿級單字

guest [gɛst] 名客人

Our guests will arrive by noon.
▶▶ 我們的客人中午就會抵達。

guide [gaɪd] 名嚮導；引導者 動引導；指引

名 We should hire a guide.
我們應該要雇一位嚮導。
動 He used a flashlight to guide me.
他用手電筒為我引路。

gun [gʌn] 名槍；砲

Does your gun shoot straight?
▶▶ 你的槍打得準嗎？

gymnasium / gym [dʒɪm`nezɪəm] / [dʒɪm] 名體育館；健身房

You must have the memebership to enter this gym.
▶▶ 你必須有會員資格才可進入這間健身房。

UNIT 08 H字頭必備單字

MP3 032

haircut [`hɛr,kʌt] 名理髮

He looks younger after the haircut.
▶▶ 他理髮後顯得年輕些。

hall [hɔl] 名廳；堂

They are waiting for you in the hall.
▶▶ 他們在大廳等你。

hamburger / burger [`hæmbɝgɚ ] / [ `bɝgɚ] 名漢堡

Eating too many hamburgers will make you heavy.
▶▶ 吃太多漢堡會使你變胖。

handle [`hændl̩] 動處理 名把手

動 Our store doesn't handle that item.
我們店不處理那個品項。
名 The handle of the door doesn't work.
這門的把手不動了。

handsome [`hænsəm] 形 英俊的

The handsome boy received many chocolates on Valentine's Day.
▶▶ 那個帥氣的男孩在情人節收到許多巧克力。

hardly [`hɑrdlɪ] 副 勉強地；幾乎不

Alfred can hardly afford the rent.
▶▶ 阿爾弗雷德幾乎負擔不起租金。

heaven [`hɛvn̩] 名 天堂

May her soul rest in Heaven.
▶▶ 希望她的靈魂在天國安息。

hero / heroine [`hɪro ] / [ `hɛroɪn] 名 英雄/女英雄

Hua Mu-Lan was said to be a heroine since she replaced her father to join the army.
▶▶ 花木蘭因代父從軍被認為是名女英雄。

highly [`haɪlɪ] 副 大大地；高高地

The man is a highly respected figure.
▶▶ 那名男子是備受尊重的人物。

highway [`haɪwe] 名 高速公路

The car was found in the woods off the highway.
▶▶ 這輛車在公速公路旁的樹林中被人發現。

hike [haɪk] 名 健行

We went on a four-mile hike to the lake.
▶▶ 我們走了四英里路到湖邊。

hip [hɪp] 名 屁股

He was hit on the hip by a basketball.
▶▶ 他被一顆籃球打中了屁股。

hippopotamus / hippo [ˌhɪpə`pɑtəməs ] / [ `hɪpo] 名 河馬

The children enjoyed watching the hippopotamus rolling in the mud.
▶▶ 孩子們喜歡看河馬在泥中打滾。

historical [hɪsˋtɔrɪkl̩] 形 歷史的

The post-graduate student focused on historical research mainly.
▶▶ 那位研究生主要專注於歷史研究。

hole [hol] 名 孔；洞

We squeezed through a hole in the fence.
▶▶ 我們從籬笆的一個洞口硬擠進去。

hop [hɑp] 動 單腳跳 名 單腳跳

動 He had hurt his left foot and had to hop along.
他左腳受傷了，不得不單腳跳行。
名 You can step on the platform with a mere hop.
你一跳就可以站上講台。

host / hostess [host] / [hostɪs] 名 主人/女主人；主持人

Will was invited to be the host of the show.
▶▶ 威爾應邀擔任節目主持人。

huge [hjudʒ] 形 龐大的；巨大的

I have a huge pile of files to deal with at present.
▶▶ 目前我有一大堆檔案要處理。

human [ˋhjumən] 形 人類的 名 人

形 We should avoid human error.
我們應該避免人為錯誤。
名 Humans have done great damage to the environment of the planet.
人們對地球環境造成了嚴重的破壞。

humble [ˋhʌmbl̩] 形 謙虛的

Although he won the prize, he kept humble.
▶▶ 雖然他得了獎，他仍然非常謙虛。

hunt [hʌnt] 動 打獵 名 獵取

動 Smith hunted a deer and carried it home.
史密斯獵了一頭鹿回家。
名 The hunt of tigers is not allowed in this mountain.
這座山禁獵老虎。

Level 1 基礎單字
Level 2 必備單字
Level 3 中級單字
Level 4 進階單字
Level 5 高手單字
Level 6 滿級單字

hunter [`hʌntɚ] 名獵人

The hunter followed a boar for miles.
▶▶ 獵人跟蹤一頭野豬好幾英里。

hurry [`hɜrɪ] 動加快；催促 名倉促

動 She hurried home to see her baby.
　　她趕緊回家看她的孩子。
名 I packed my luggage in a hurry.
　　我匆匆打包行李。

I 字頭必備單字

MP3 033

ideal [aɪ`diəl] 形理想的

You have an ideal family.
▶▶ 你有個理想的家庭。

identity [aɪ`dɛntətɪ] 名身分

An identity card is necessary for opening a bank account.
▶▶ 銀行開戶需要身分證。

ignore [ɪg`nor] 動忽略

He ignored what I said deliberately.
▶▶ 他故意忽略我說的話。

ill [ɪl] 形生病的 副不友善地、惡劣地

形 I felt ill and dizzy this morning.
　　我今早感到暈眩不適。
副 Betty always speaks ill of others.
　　貝蒂常常說人壞話。

image [`ɪmɪdʒ] 名影像；形象

Randall couldn't get the image of the beautiful woman out of his mind.
▶▶ 朗多忘不了這位美麗女子的模樣。

imagine [ɪ`mædʒɪn] 動想像 同 envision

I cannot imagine what I would do if I had no money.
▶▶ 我不敢想像如果我沒錢會做出什麼事。

MEMORIZE 7000 VOCABULARIES ONCE AND FOR ALL !

importance [ɪm`pɔrtn̩s] 名 重要性

The case is of great importance to our company.
▶▶ 這件案子對我們公司來說非常重要。

impressive [ɪm`prɛsɪv] 形 令人印象深刻的

The words he told me were too impressive to forget.
▶▶ 他告訴我的那些話讓我印象深刻，難以忘懷。

improve [ɪm`pruv] 動 改善 關 improvement 改善

I want to improve my English writing skills by writing an essay every week.
▶▶ 我想藉由每個禮拜寫一篇短文，來加強英語寫作能力。

include [ɪn`klud] 動 包括 同 incorporate

The member list includes you and me.
▶▶ 成員名單包括你和我。

income [`ɪnkəm] 名 收入

My mother brought me up on her small income.
▶▶ 我媽媽靠著微薄的收入把我養大。

increase [ɪn`kris ] / [ `ɪnkris] 動 增加 名 增加

動 Travel increases one's knowledge of the world.
旅遊能增進對世界的瞭解。
名 Crimes are on the increase.
犯罪活動不斷地增加。

indeed [ɪn`did] 副 實在地

These problems are indeed difficult ones, but I am sure they can be solved.
▶▶ 這些問題固然是有些困難，但我相信都能解決。

independence [ˌɪndɪ`pɛndəns] 名 獨立

He gained complete independence after he got his first salary.
▶▶ 得到第一份薪水後他就徹底獨立了。

independent [ˌɪndɪ`pɛndənt] 形 獨立的

My sister has moved away from home and is independent.
▶▶ 妹妹已經從家裡搬出去，變得獨立了。

Level 1 基礎單字
Level 2 必備單字
Level 3 中級單字
Level 4 進階單字
Level 5 高手單字
Level 6 滿級單字

indicate [`ɪndəˌket] 動 指示

The light above the elevator indicated that it was at the tenth floor.
▶▶ 電梯上方的燈顯示為十樓。

individual [ˌɪndə`vɪdʒuəl] 形 個別的 名 個人

形 There are individual differences in the ability to learn a foreign language.
外語學習能力因人而異。
名 Exceptions cannot be made for individuals.
不能對個人有特殊對待。

industry [`ɪndəstrɪ] 名 工業

The development of this industry will take several years.
▶▶ 這項工業的發展要經過幾年的時間。

influence [`ɪnfluəns] 名 影響 動 影響

名 The price of oil has a considerable influence on people's lives.
油價對人們的生活有著相當的影響。
動 I was never influenced by him.
我從未被他影響。

(焦點句型) have an influence on sb./sth. 對…產生影響

ink [ɪŋk] 名 墨汁 動 塗上墨水

名 The ink stained the page.
墨水弄髒了書頁。
動 They inked the contract yesterday.
他們昨天簽了合約。

insist [ɪn`sɪst] 動 堅持

She insisted on my going with her.
▶▶ 她堅持要我和她一起去。

(焦點句型) insist on sth. 堅持…

instance [`ɪnstəns] 名 例子 動 舉例

名 Pets help people in many ways; for instance, they make people happy.
寵物能在各方面對人類起到幫助，比如說牠們能讓人感到快樂。
動 He instanced Ang Lee when it comes to Taiwan directors.
提到台灣導演時，他舉李安為例。

instant [`ɪnstənt] 形 即時的

Evelyn ate a bowl of instant noodles.
▶▶ 伊芙琳吃了一碗泡麵。

instead [ɪn`stɛd] 副 作為替代

What you need is a friend instead of a girlfriend now.
▶▶ 現在你需要的是朋友，而不是女朋友。
(焦點句型) instead of N. 代替…；而非…

instruction [ɪn`strʌkʃən] 名 教導；操作指南

The instruction manual completely defeated me.
▶▶ 這操作指南把我完全弄糊塗了。

instrument [`ɪnstrəmənt] 名 樂器；器具

This instrument is used to measure the wind speed.
▶▶ 這台儀器用來測量風速。

internal [ɪn`tɜnḷ] 形 國內的；內部的

We need to hold an internal inquiry to find out who is responsible.
▶▶ 我們應該進行內部調查，找出應對此事承擔責任的人。

international [,ɪntɚ`næʃənḷ] 形 國際的

English is an international language.
▶▶ 英文是國際語言。

Internet [`ɪntɚ,nɛt] 名 網際網路

You can find various types of information on the Internet.
▶▶ 你可以在網路上找到各式各樣的資訊。

introduce [,ɪntrə`djus] 動 介紹

Introduce yourself to your new colleagues.
▶▶ 介紹你自己給新同事認識。

introduction [,ɪntrə`dʌkʃən] 名 介紹

The salesperson gave me a basic introduction of their products.
▶▶ 推銷員向我大致介紹了他們的產品。

Level 1 基礎單字
Level 2 必備單字
Level 3 中級單字
Level 4 進階單字
Level 5 高手單字
Level 6 滿級單字

iron [`aɪən] 名鐵；熨斗 形堅強如鐵的 動熨衣；燙平

名 The door is made of iron.
這扇門是鐵做的。

形 My elder brother has an iron will.
我哥哥擁有鋼鐵般的意志。

動 Mother usually irons her shirt in the evening.
母親通常在晚上燙她的襯衫。

 **J 字頭必備單字**

 MP3 034

jam [dʒæm] 名果醬；堵塞；擁擠 動阻塞

名 She put the jam on the toast.
她把果醬塗在吐司上。

動 The crowds jammed the streets, and no cars could pass.
街上擠滿了人群，汽車都無法通行。

jog [dʒɑg] 動慢跑

Our mayor goes jogging with his family every morning.
▶▶ 我們市長每天早上都和家人一起慢跑。

joint [dʒɔɪnt] 名接合處；關節 形共同的

名 My mom suffers from pain in her leg joints.
我媽腿部關節疼痛。

形 We have opened a joint account at the bank.
我們在銀行開了一個共同的帳戶。

journal [`dʒɜnl] 名期刊

The quality of this journal is praised worldwide.
▶▶ 這本期刊的品質得到世界稱揚。

judge [dʒʌdʒ] 名法官 動裁決；評斷

名 The judge sentenced him ten years in prison.
法官判處他十年監禁。

動 Who has the right to judge others?
誰有權審判他人？

judgement / judgment [`dʒʌdʒ,mənt] 名審判；判斷 同 verdict

Anna infers a conclusion on her judgment.
▶▶ 安娜用自己的判斷力做出結論。

justice [`dʒʌstɪs] 名公正；正義 反 injustice

The justice of these remarks was clear to everyone.
▶▶ 人人都明白這些評論是公正的。

UNIT 11 K 字頭必備單字

MP3 035

keeper [`kipɚ] 名看守人 關 trustee 受託管理人

She was employed as the keeper of the records for the organization.
▶▶ 她受該機構聘請，擔任資料紀錄的管理者。

ketchup [`kɛtʃəp] 名番茄醬

He eats fried potatoes with ketchup.
▶▶ 他吃油炸馬鈴薯配番茄醬。

kilogram [`kɪlə,græm] 名公斤

One kilogram equals 1,000 grams.
▶▶ 一公斤等於一千公克。

UNIT 12 L 字頭必備單字

MP3 036

lack [læk] 名缺少；缺乏 動缺少；沒有

名 Due to lack of money, he decided to do part-time work.
　　因為缺錢，他決定做兼職工作。
動 The rich man lacks for nothing.
　　這個富人什麼都不缺。

(焦點句型) lack of sth. 缺少…

lady [`ledɪ] 名女士；淑女

The gorgeous lady made me fall under her spell.
▶▶ 那位美麗的淑女讓我臣服於她的魅力之下。

Level 1 基礎單字
Level 2 必備單字
Level 3 中級單字
Level 4 進階單字
Level 5 高手單字
Level 6 滿級單字

ladybug [`ledɪˌbʌg] 名 瓢蟲

There is a red ladybug with a black spot on each wing.
▶▶ 有隻紅色瓢蟲，雙翅各有一個黑點。

lamb [læm] 名 小羊；羊肉

The shepherd gathered his lambs.
▶▶ 牧羊人將小羊趕到一起。

lane [len] 名 巷

I live in the tallest building in the lane.
▶▶ 我住在巷內最高的那棟建築裡。

lantern [`læntən] 名 燈籠

The lanterns were hung in the streets.
▶▶ 大街上掛著燈籠。

lap [læp] 名 膝部 動 輕拍

名 She holds her cat in her lap.
她把貓抱在膝上。
動 The waves lapped the bottom of the cliff.
海浪輕拍著崖壁。

latest [`letɪst] 名 最新的

Julie always wears the latest styles.
▶▶ 茱莉總是穿著最新風格的衣服。

latter [`lætə] 形 後者的

The latter point is the most important.
▶▶ 後面提及的那一點是最重要的。

law [lɔ] 名 法律 同 statute

You should do nothing against the law.
▶▶ 你不該做違法的事。

lay [le] 動 放置；產卵

He was told to never lay a finger on the antiques.
▶▶ 他被告知不能碰觸這些古董。

leadership [`lidɚʃɪp] 名領導力

The party grew under his leadership.
>> 這個政黨在他的領導下興旺起來。

leaf [lif] 名葉子

The trees are thick with leaves.
>> 這些樹長滿了茂密的樹葉。

legal [`liɡḷ] 形合法的 同judicial

The driver was more than three times over the legal limit for alcohol.
>> 那位駕駛者體內的酒精含量超過了法律允許限度的三倍。

lend [lɛnd] 動借出

Can you lend me that book for a few days?
>> 你能把那本書借給我幾天嗎？

文法解析 lend動詞三態變化為 lend / lent / lent。

length [lɛŋθ] 名長度

This room is twice the length of the kitchen.
>> 這間屋子的長度是廚房的兩倍。

lens [lɛnz] 名透鏡；鏡片

Have you got your lenses in?
>> 你戴了隱形眼鏡嗎？

liberal [`lɪbərəl] 形自由主義的；開明的 衍liberty 自由

He's always considered himself a liberal person.
>> 他總認為自己是個開明的人。

lid [lɪd] 名蓋子

Put the lid on the pot.
>> 把壺蓋蓋上。

lift [lɪft] 名舉起 動舉起

名 With a lift of my hand, I suggested he should go.
我揮揮手，暗示他該走了。

動 The plane will take off once the fog has lifted.
只要霧氣散去，飛機就會起飛。

Level 1 基礎單字

Level 2 必備單字

Level 3 中級單字

Level 4 進階單字

Level 5 高手單字

Level 6 滿級單字

likely [`laɪklɪ] 形 很可能的 副 很可能

形 She is likely to sign the contract.
她可能會簽署那份合約。
副 We will most likely be late.
我們很有可能會遲到。
(焦點句型) be likely to V. 可能會…

limit [`lɪmɪt] 動 限制 名 限制

動 Linda was limited to staying out until ten o'clock at night.
琳達被限制要十點以前到家。
名 Hans was fined heavily for breaking the speed limit.
漢斯因為超速而遭到重罰。

link [lɪŋk] 動 連結 名 連結

動 By linking directly to our bodies, computers can pick up what we feel.
藉由直接和我們的身體相連，電腦就能夠知道我們的感覺。
名 That is the only weak link in his reasoning.
那是他推理中唯一薄弱的環節。

liquid [`lɪkwɪd] 名 液體

The liquid will freeze at zero degrees.
▶▶ 這種液體會在零度時凝固。

listener [`lɪsn̩ɚ] 名 聽眾

This singer has a lot of listeners and fans.
▶▶ 這位歌手有許多聽眾和粉絲。

liver [`lɪvɚ] 名 肝

Staying up late harms the liver.
▶▶ 熬夜傷肝。

local [`lokl̩] 形 當地的 名 當地居民

形 Many of the local people attended his grandfather's funeral.
許多當地人都參加了他祖父的葬禮。
名 Even the locals do not know the location of the monument.
連本地人都不知道紀念館的位置。

Level 1 基礎單字

Level 2 必備單字

Level 3 中級單字

Level 4 進階單字

Level 5 高手單字

Level 6 滿級單字

lone [lon] 形孤單的

The lone person in the room was Mr. Davidson.
▶▶ 房間裡只有戴維森先生一個人。

loss [lɔs] 名損失

Her departure is a great loss to the orchestra.
▶▶ 她的離開是管弦樂隊的一大損失。

lower [`loɚ] 動降低

The company lowered its prices to get more business.
▶▶ 公司降價以得到更多生意。

luck [lʌk] 名運氣

I wish you good luck on the exam.
▶▶ 祝你考試順利。

UNIT 13 M 字頭必備單字

MP3 037

magazine [ˌmæɡəˋzin] 名雜誌

The magazine published a story written by a high school student.
▶▶ 這家雜誌刊登了一篇由高中生寫的故事。

maintain [menˋten] 動維持

I wonder how Camilla maintains her slender figure.
▶▶ 我想知道卡蜜拉如何維持苗條的身材。

major [`medʒɚ] 形較大的；主要的 動主修

形 You must ask approval for all major expenditures.
　　一切重大開支均須報請批准。
動 I majored in Sociology.
　　我主修社會學。

(焦點句型) major in 主修…（科系）

male [mel] 形男性的 名男性

形 A male nurse took my temperature.
　　一位男護士幫我量了體溫。

㈎ Presidents used to all be males.
過去總統都是男性。

manage [`mænɪdʒ] ㈧管理 ㈾ management 管理

She has her own style in managing the staff.
▸▸ 她自有一套管理員工的方法。

manager [`mænɪdʒɚ] ㈎經理

Rita was promoted to be the manager of human resources department.
▸▸ 芮塔晉升為人力資源部門經理。

mango [`mæŋgo] ㈎芒果

Both sides of the road were planted with fresh green mango trees.
▸▸ 道路兩旁都種上了翠綠的芒果樹。

manner [`mænɚ] ㈎禮貌

His bad manners suggest that he got drunk.
▸▸ 從他的無禮態度可以看出他已經醉了。

marriage [`mærɪdʒ] ㈎婚姻

Their marriage ended in divorce.
▸▸ 他們的婚姻以離婚收場。

marry [`mærɪ] ㈧結婚 ㈾ married 已婚的

My sister is going to marry next month.
▸▸ 我姐姐下個月要結婚了。

mask [mæsk] ㈎面具 ㈧遮蓋

㈎ The clown wore a comical mask to please people.
小丑戴上滑稽的面具取悅大眾。
㈧ Klein masked his real feelings by smiling.
克萊恩用微笑掩飾他真正的感受。

mass [mæs] ㈎大量

The mass of public opinion is in favor of the decision.
▸▸ 公眾輿論支持該決策。

master [`mæstɚ] 名大師；主人 動精通

名 The dog is running to its master.
那隻狗跑向牠的主人。
動 Russian is a difficult language to master.
俄語是門難以精通的語言。

mat [mæt] 名墊子

Please wipe your feet on the mat before leaving the bathroom.
▶▶ 離開浴室前請先在地墊上擦擦腳。

match [mætʃ] 名火柴 動相配、配對

名 He struck a match to light the candle.
他劃了一根火柴點燃蠟燭。
動 Judy will match against me in the final.
茱蒂將在總決賽中和我較量。

mate [met] 名配偶；比賽 動配對

名 She is not single; her mate is not here.
她並非單身，只是配偶沒來。
動 They mated a boy with another for the game.
他們將男生兩兩配成一對參加比賽。

material [mə`tɪrɪəl] 名材料；原料

Enough materials should be collected before writing.
▶▶ 寫作之前要收集足夠的資料。

mature [mə`tjʊr] 形成熟的

Mark has grown more mature.
▶▶ 馬克變得更成熟了。

meaning [`minɪŋ] 名意義

Her real meaning was that she did not want to go.
▶▶ 她真正的意思是她並不想去。

means [minz] 名方法

I must obtain the scholarship by all means.
▶▶ 我一定要想方設法得到獎學金。

Level 1 基礎單字
Level 2 必備單字
Level 3 中級單字
Level 4 進階單字
Level 5 高手單字
Level 6 滿級單字

measure [`mɛʒɚ] 動測量 名措施；手段 關 measurement 測量

動 The experts are trying to measure the depth of this part of the ocean.
專家們試著測量海洋這部分的深度。

名 The government took measures to solve the problem.
政府採取措施以解決問題。

medical [`mɛdɪkl̩] 形醫學的

The hospital has a commitment to provide the best possible medical care.
▶▶ 這家醫院承諾要盡可能提供最好的醫療服務。

melody [`mɛlədɪ] 名旋律

The melody sounds familiar.
▶▶ 這個旋律聽起來很耳熟。

membership [`mɛmbɚˌʃɪp] 名會員

You have to pay 3,000 dollars a year for your membership.
▶▶ 您必須每年支付三千元的會員費。

memory [`mɛmərɪ] 名記憶

The memory of their conversation still bothered him.
▶▶ 回憶起他們的談話，他仍心有餘悸。

mention [`mɛnʃən] 動提起 名提及

動 As mentioned above, breakfast is crucial for us.
正如上述所言，早餐對我們非常重要。

名 The boy gave a mention of the secret.
男孩提到了這個秘密。

message [`mɛsɪdʒ] 名訊息

He left a message for you that he would come home late tonight.
▶▶ 他給你留言說今晚會晚點回家。

metal [`mɛtl̩] 名金屬

The frame is made of metal.
▶▶ 邊框是金屬製成的。

meter [`mitɚ] 名公尺

Are you running in the 100-meter race?
▶▶ 你有參加百米賽跑嗎？

method [`mɛθəd] 名方法

Those methods of studying are not suitable for everyone.
▶▶ 那些讀書方法並非人人適用。

midnight [`mɪd͵naɪt] 名午夜 關 curfew 宵禁

Three men robbed the gas station at midnight.
▶▶ 三名男子半夜搶劫加油站。

mile [maɪl] 名英里

The nearest village was miles away.
▶▶ 最近的村莊也在數英里之外。

military [`mɪlə͵tɛrɪ] 形軍事的 名軍事

形 The military force of this nation is very strong.
這個國家的軍事力量非常強大。
名 He joined the military three months ago.
他三個月前從軍去了。

minor [`maɪnɚ] 形較小的；次要的 名未成年者

形 The birth of her son was a minor interruption to her career.
兒子的出生只是她職業生涯的一個小插曲。
名 At just 14 years old, Ronny was still a minor.
榮尼年僅 14 歲,還未成年。

minority [maɪ`nɔrətɪ] 名少數

Only a small minority of students are interested in politics these days.
▶▶ 現在只有極少數學生對政治感興趣。

mirror [`mɪrɚ] 名鏡子 動反映

名 The witch saw her reflection in the mirror.
女巫看見她鏡中的倒影。
動 The surface of the lake mirrored the blue sky.
湖面映照著蔚藍的天空。

mix [mɪks] 名混合 動混合

名 The town offers a fascinating mix of old and new.
這個小鎮新舊結合,很有魅力。
動 Oil does not mix with water.
油不溶於水。

Level 1 基礎單字
Level 2 必備單字
Level 3 中級單字
Level 4 進階單字
Level 5 高手單字
Level 6 滿級單字

mixture [`mɪkstʃɚ] 名混合物 同 hybrid

Air is a mixture of gases.
▶▶ 空氣是各種氣體的混合物。

model [`mɑdl] 名模特兒 動模仿

名 Her tallness and slenderness qualifies her as a model.
她高挑纖細的身材讓她足以當模特兒。
動 Bill modeled himself on his policeman father.
比爾將他的警察父親視為榜樣。

mood [mud] 名心情

I can't go out with a dreary mood.
▶▶ 我不能帶著陰鬱的心情出門。

mop [mɑp] 動拖地

My cousin helped me to mop the floor.
▶▶ 我表姐幫我拖地。

motion [`moʃən] 名動作

Never get on or off a bus while it is in motion.
▶▶ 車未停穩時，切勿上下公車。

motorcycle [`motɚˌsaɪkl] 名摩托車

My uncle picked me up by a motorcycle.
▶▶ 叔叔騎摩托車來接我。

mug [mʌg] 名馬克杯

I drank all of the water in my mug.
▶▶ 我喝光了馬克杯裡的水。

musical [`mjuzɪkl] 形音樂的；有音樂天賦的 名音樂劇

形 Her family is very musical; they all play instruments.
她家人極具音樂天賦，他們都會演奏樂器。
名 Michael is fond of all kinds of musicals.
麥可對什麼類型的音樂劇都有興趣。

musician [mju`zɪʃən] 名音樂家

The conductor of the orchestra is a musician.
▶▶ 管弦樂隊的指揮是個音樂家。

nail [nel] 名指甲；釘子 動釘

名 Zoe had her nails cut.
佐伊剪了指甲。
動 I nailed the bookshelf to the wall.
我把書架釘在牆上。

narrow [`næro] 形窄的 動變窄

形 The taxi is too narrow to contain all of us.
這台計程車太窄了，擠不下我們所有人。
動 The river narrows from the point.
這條河從這裡開始就變窄了。

nation [`neʃən] 名國家

In 1790, the new nation had fewer than four million people.
▶▶ 一七九〇年時，這個新建立的國家人口不到四百萬。

natural [`nætʃərəl] 形天然的；自然的

Her curly hair is natural.
▶▶ 她的頭髮是自然捲。

naughty [`nɔtɪ] 形淘氣的

Naughty Johnny did not obey his parents.
▶▶ 頑皮的強尼不聽父母的話。

nearby [`nɪr͵baɪ] 形附近的 副不遠地

形 It is convenient to go to the nearby theater.
去附近那間戲院非常方便。
副 We can invite Frank to join us. He lives nearby.
我們可以邀請弗蘭克加入，他就住在附近。

nearly [`nɪrlɪ] 副幾乎 關 classmate 同學

He nearly forgot his elementary school classmates.
▶▶ 他幾乎忘了他的小學同學。

necessary [`nɛsə͵sɛrɪ] 形必要的 反 unnecessary

Throw the objects away if they are not necessary.
▶▶ 扔掉不需要的東西。

Level 1 基礎單字

Level 2 必備單字

Level 3 中級單字

Level 4 進階單字

Level 5 高手單字

Level 6 滿級單字

necklace [`nɛklɪs] 名 項鍊

Yvonne received a necklace from her husband on their wedding anniversary.
▶▶ 伊娃在結婚紀念日時收到丈夫送的項鍊。

needle [`nidḷ] 名 針 動 用針縫

名 She used a needle to sew the button onto the shirt.
她用針把鈕子縫到襯衫上。
動 My father needled the hole in my pants.
爸爸縫合我褲子上的裂縫。

negative [`nɛgətɪv] 形 否定的 名 否定語 同 adverse

形 There can be negative results from getting too much sun.
曬太多太陽會造成負面影響。
名 If you don't respond tomorrow, I'll take it as a negative.
如果你明天沒有回應，我就當作你否決了。

neighbor [`nebɚ] 名 鄰居 動 與…為鄰

名 My new neighbor is a young university student.
我的新鄰居是名年輕的大學生。
動 Linda's apartment neighbors a park.
琳達的公寓與一個公園相鄰。

neither [`niðɚ] 代 （兩者之中）沒有一個 連 既不…也不…

代 Neither of my parents attended my graduation ceremony.
爸媽都沒有來我的畢業典禮。
連 He likes neither romance movies nor animated movies.
他不喜歡愛情電影，也不愛動畫電影。

nephew [`nɛfju] 名 侄子；外甥

My nephew is older than me.
▶▶ 我的侄子年紀比我大。

nerve [nɝv] 名 神經

I am always in a state of nerves on the eve of an examination.
▶▶ 考試前夕我總是非常緊張。

nervous [`nɝvəs] 形 擔心的；緊張的；神經的

I feel a little nervous during interviews.
▶▶ 面試過程我有點緊張。

network [`nɛt‚wɝk] 名網路

Marketing strategies nowadays are often highly associated with social networks.
▶▶ 如今的行銷策略往往和社群網路密不可分。

niece [nis] 名姪女

My sister's daughter is my niece.
▶▶ 姐姐的女兒是我的姪女。

nod [nɑd] 動點頭 名點頭

動 My mother nodded silently in agreement.
我媽媽默默點頭表示同意。
名 My colleague gave me a nod of recognition on the bus.
同事在公車上向我點頭致意。

none [nʌn] 代沒有人

None of us have been to Japan.
▶▶ 我們都沒有去過日本。

noodle [`nudl̩] 名麵條

Chinese food is often served with noodles or rice.
▶▶ 中式餐常常有麵條或米飯。

nor [nɔr] 連（用在neither後）也不

There is neither a river nor a stream nearby.
▶▶ 附近既無河流也沒有小溪。

northern [`nɔrðən] 形北方的

The white-haired lady has traveled in northern countries.
▶▶ 那位白髮女士曾遊歷北方諸國。

notebook [`not‚bʊk] 名筆記本

She wrote her diary in a notebook.
▶▶ 她把日記寫在筆記本裡。

novel [`nɑvl̩] 形新奇的 名長篇小說

形 When a novel idea appears, people should write it down.
有新點子出現時，應該把它寫下來。

Level 1 基礎單字
Level 2 必備單字
Level 3 中級單字
Level 4 進階單字
Level 5 高手單字
Level 6 滿級單字

名 The latest published novel sells well.
新出版的小說賣得很好。

nut [nʌt] 名堅果

We can crack nuts with nutcrackers.
▶▶ 我們可以用胡桃鉗把堅果夾碎。

 **O 字頭必備單字**

MP3 039

obey [əˋbe] 動服從 同 comply

The driver was fined for not obeying the traffic rules.
▶▶ 司機因不遵守交通規則遭到罰鍰。

object [ˋɑbdʒɪkt] / [əbˋdʒɛkt] 名物品 動抗議

名 There were many unknown objects in the lab.
實驗室裡有許多不明物體。
動 Do you object to smoking?
你反對吸菸嗎？

obvious [ˋɑbvɪəs] 形明顯的

It is obvious that they are having an affair with each other.
▶▶ 顯然他們兩個正在交往。

occur [əˋkɜ] 動發生

It occurred to me that I left my umbrella in the classroom.
▶▶ 我突然想到我把雨傘忘在教室。

ocean [ˋoʃən] 名海洋

Ireland borders the Atlantic Ocean.
▶▶ 愛爾蘭與大西洋相鄰。

offer [ˋɔfɚ] 名提供 動提供

名 He was so excited to get the offer from the company.
他非常興奮得到那間公司的聘用。
動 The hosts offered a variety of snacks for the seminar.
主辦方為研討會提供了各種點心。

official [ə`fɪʃəl] 形 官方的 名 官員

形 The official documents concerning the sale of this land were made public.
賣出這片土地相關的官方文件是公開的。
名 My uncle is a government official.
我叔叔是個政府官員。

operate [`ɑpə͵ret] 動 操作；運轉 關 operative 操作的

The washing machine does not operate properly.
▶▶ 洗衣機無法正常運行。

operator [`ɑpə͵retɚ] 名 操作者

You have to consult the machine operator.
▶▶ 你必須去請教操作機器的人。

opinion [ə`pɪnjən] 名 意見

We were invited to give our opinions about how the work should be done.
▶▶ 我們應邀對於如何完成工作發表意見。

ordinary [`ɔrdn͵ɛrɪ] 形 普通的

One who is different from ordinary people is called abnormal.
▶▶ 和常人不同者會被稱為不正常。

organ [`ɔrgən] 名 器官 關 organic 有機的

The heart is a vital organ of the body.
▶▶ 心臟是人體的重要器官。

organization [͵ɔrgənə`zeʃən] 名 機構 關 organize 組織

He is a member of the organization.
▶▶ 他是這個組織的成員之一。

origin [`ɔrɪdʒɪn] 名 起源；血統

Many Americans are African by origin.
▶▶ 許多美國人都是非洲裔。

owner [`onɚ] 名 持有者

Mr. Brown is the owner of the villa.
▶▶ 布朗先生是這間別墅的所有人。

基礎單字 Level 1
必備單字 Level 2
中級單字 Level 3
進階單字 Level 4
高手單字 Level 5
滿級單字 Level 6

MEMORIZE 7000 VOCABULARIES ONCE AND FOR ALL !

pain [pen] 名 疼痛；痛苦 動 傷害 關 stomachache 肚子痛

名 I got a severe pain in my stomach.
我的胃很痛。

動 His cruel words really pained me.
他殘酷的話語讓我很心痛。

painful [`penfəl] 形 痛苦的

The dog's bite on my leg is very painful.
▶▶ 我腿上被狗咬到的傷口非常疼痛。

painting [`pentɪŋ] 名 繪畫

The thief tried to steal the famous painting in the gallery.
▶▶ 竊賊試圖盜取美術館裡那幅知名畫作。

pajamas [pə`dʒæməz] 名 睡衣

Annie wore pajamas to bed.
▶▶ 安妮穿著睡衣去睡覺。

pale [pel] 形 蒼白的 關 complexion 膚色

Vampires are said to have an extremely pale complexion.
▶▶ 聽說吸血鬼有著極度蒼白的膚色。

pan [pæn] 名 平底鍋

Put the butter into the pan.
▶▶ 把奶油放進平底鍋裡。

panda [`pændə] 名 貓熊

The panda is now a rare animal for it is almost extinct.
▶▶ 貓熊因為瀕臨絕種，現在是稀有動物。

papaya [pə`paɪə] 名 木瓜

Papaya is a tropical fruit.
▶▶ 木瓜是熱帶水果。

pardon [`pɑrdn̩] 名原諒 動寬恕

名 I beg your pardon. Could you help me?
不好意思，可以請你幫忙嗎？
動 Pardon me for my delay.
請原諒我的遲到。

participate [pəˋtɪsəˏpet] 動參與

I participate in this forum every year.
▶▶ 我每年都參加這個論壇。
(焦點句型) participate in sth. 參加…

particular [pəˋtɪkjələ] 形特別的

There is one particular patient I'd like you to see.
▶▶ 我想讓你見一個特別的病人。

partner [`pɑrtnə] 名夥伴

My partners and I have to cooperate to get the work done.
▶▶ 我和我的夥伴們必須合作把工作完成。

password [`pæsˏwɜd] 名密碼

I forget the password to log in.
▶▶ 我忘記登入密碼了。

paste [pest] 動貼上；黏貼 名漿糊

動 He pasted the scraps to the notebook.
他把剪報資料貼在筆記本上。
名 I stuck the sheets together with paste.
我用漿糊把這些紙黏起來。

path [pæθ] 名路徑

I walked along the path to the post office.
▶▶ 我沿著這條小路前往郵局。

patient [`peʃənt] 名病人 形有耐心的 關 patience 耐心

名 The doctor made a diagnosis of the patient's disease.
醫生對病人的病做出診斷。
形 Be patient with your sister. She's just a three-year old kid.
對你妹妹有耐心一點，她只是個三歲小孩。
(焦點句型) be patient with sb./sth. 對…有耐心

Level 1 基礎單字
Level 2 必備單字
Level 3 中級單字
Level 4 進階單字
Level 5 高手單字
Level 6 滿級單字

pattern [`pætən] 名 形式；模式；花紋

The murders all seem to follow a pattern.
>> 這些兇殺案似乎都有規律可循。

peace [pis] 名 和平

We hope for peace between our country and our neighbors.
>> 我們希望我國和鄰國之間維持和平。

peaceful [`pisfəl] 形 和平的；寧靜的

The hillsides looked very peaceful.
>> 山坡顯得非常安靜。

peach [pitʃ] 名 桃子

He has eaten just a peach all day.
>> 他整天只吃了一顆桃子。

peak [pik] 名 最高點；高峰；山頂 動 達到最高點

名 Traffic reaches its peak between 8 and 9 in the morning.
上午八、九點鐘之間是交通的尖峰時刻。
動 Unemployment peaked at 7% in July.
七月份的失業率達到百分之七的高峰。

pear [pɛr] 名 梨子

The pear tastes sour.
>> 這顆梨子很酸。

per [pə] 介 每

The typhoon is moving at the speed of twenty kilometers per hour.
>> 颱風以時速二十公里的速度移動。

perfect [`pɜfɪkt] 形 完美的

The professional actress is perfect.
>> 這名職業女演員非常完美。

period [`pɪrɪəd] 名 期間

She was taken on for a three-month trial period and became a permanent member of staff.
>> 她經過了三個月的試用期，並成為正式員工。

personal [`pɝsənl] 形 個人的 關 personality 人格特質

Carol left her current job for personal reasons.
▶▶ 凱洛因私人因素而離開現在的工作。

phrase [frez] 名 片語 動 用言詞表達

名 A verb and a preposition form a phrase.
一個動詞和一個介系詞形成一個片語。
動 I prefer to phrase my apology in a different way.
我偏好以不同的方式表示歉意。

pillow [`pɪlo] 名 枕頭 動 以…為枕

名 He became sleepless without a pillow.
沒有枕頭他就會失眠。
動 I pillowed my head on his arm and fell asleep.
我把頭枕在他手臂上睡著了。

pizza [`pɪzɑ] 名 披薩

Martha divided the pizza into eight pieces.
▶▶ 瑪莎把披薩分成八塊。

plain [plen] 形 平坦的；明白的 名 平原

形 The manager made it plain that we should leave.
經理明確表示要我們離開。
名 Our old house was situated on the plain.
我們的舊房子坐落在平原上。

platform [`plæt͵fɔrm] 名 月台

Passengers are waiting for the train on the platform.
▶▶ 乘客在月台上等火車。

playground [`ple͵graʊnd] 名 操場；遊樂場

A few students are running in the playground.
▶▶ 一些學生在操場上跑步。

pleasant [`plɛznt] 形 愉快的

It is so pleasant to talk with you.
▶▶ 和你聊天非常愉快。

Level 1 基礎單字
Level 2 必備單字
Level 3 中級單字
Level 4 進階單字
Level 5 高手單字
Level 6 滿級單字

plus [plʌs] 介加 形優勢；正的 名加號；正數

介 One plus one equals two.
一加一等於二。

形 It is a plus factor to know a foreign language.
懂外語是一種優勢。

名 You can get a plus if you multiply two minuses.
將兩個負數相乘可以得到正數。

poem [`poɪm] 名詩

Robert wrote a poem about war.
▶▶ 羅伯特寫了一首關於戰爭的詩。

poet [`poɪt] 名詩人

Li He was a talented but short-lived poet.
▶▶ 李賀是個富有才情卻早夭的詩人。

poetry [`poɪtrɪ] 名詩；詩集

Richard doesn't think he could ever like that kind of poetry.
▶▶ 理查認為他永遠都不會喜歡那種詩。

poison [`pɔɪzn̩] 名毒藥 動下毒

名 They added poison to the milk powder.
他們在奶粉裡下毒。

動 The soil here was poisoned by industrial waste.
這裡的土壤遭到工業廢棄物的毒害。

policeman / cop [pə`lismən] / [kɑp] 名警察

I asked the policeman how to get to the station.
▶▶ 我問警察要如何到達車站。

policy [`pɑləsɪ] 名政策

The changeable policies have made the public mad.
▶▶ 反覆不定的政策引起了公憤。

pop [pɑp] 名流行樂

Modanna is the most influential pop singer in 80s.
▶▶ 瑪丹娜是八零年代最具影響力的歌手。

population [ˌpɑpjəˈleʃən] 名人口 關 census 人口普查

Do you agree the government should control population sizes?
▶▶ 你同意政府應該控制人口嗎？

pork [pork] 名豬肉

Muslims do not eat pork.
▶▶ 穆斯林不吃豬肉。

port [port] 名港口

The ship made port.
▶▶ 船抵達港口。

pose [poz] 動擺姿勢 名姿勢

動 The photographer asked the model to pose naturally.
攝影師要模特兒自然地擺姿勢。
名 He held a pose like the Statue of Liberty.
他擺出自由女神像的姿勢。

position [pəˈzɪʃən] 名位置

Hugh is the only possible person for this position.
▶▶ 休是唯一可能擔任此職的人。

positive [ˈpɑzətɪv] 形正面的

I appreciate his positive attitude toward everything.
▶▶ 我欣賞他對每件事都抱持正向態度。

possibility [ˌpɑsəˈbɪlətɪ] 名可能性

The general would not accept that defeat was a possibility.
▶▶ 那位將軍不願意承認有失敗的可能。

post [post] 名郵件 動郵寄；公布

名 The last post has arrived and there was no letter for you.
最後一批郵件已到，但是沒有你的信。
動 I asked my mother to post a letter.
我請媽媽幫我寄了封信。

postcard [ˈpostˌkɑrd] 名明信片

My friend sent me a postcard from New Zealand.
▶▶ 我的朋友從紐西蘭寄明信片給我。

Level 1 基礎單字
Level 2 必備單字
Level 3 中級單字
Level 4 進階單字
Level 5 高手單字
Level 6 滿級單字

pound [paʊnd] 名磅 動重擊

名 The package weighs two pounds.
這個包裹有兩磅重。

動 Louis pounded the wall with anger.
路易斯憤怒地捶牆。

powerful [`paʊəfəl] 形有力的 同 potent

Powerful nations sometimes try to control weaker ones.
▶▶ 有時候強國會試圖控制弱國。

praise [prez] 動稱讚 名榮耀 關 acclaim 歡呼；稱讚

動 My teacher praised me all the time.
我的老師總是稱讚我。

名 Too much praise is a burden.
過多的讚美是一種負擔。

pray [pre] 動祈禱 關 prayer 禱告

I pray my mother will recover soon.
▶▶ 我祈禱母親能很快恢復健康。

prefer [prɪ`fɝ] 動偏愛

I prefer staying home all day to going out with him.
▶▶ 我寧願待在家一整天也不要跟他出去。

(焦點句型) prefer A to B 比起B更喜歡A；寧願A也不要B（A和B都是名詞）

president [`prɛzədənt] 名總統

The president was elected last year.
▶▶ 這位總統去年當選。

press [prɛs] 動壓下 名新聞界 關 pressure 壓力

動 Press the button and it will work.
按下這個按鈕它就會運轉。

名 The press is responsible for reporting on events.
新聞媒體負責對事件進行報導。

pride [praɪd] 名自豪；驕傲 動自豪

名 Catherine took pride in her wealth.
凱瑟琳以財富自豪。

Level 1 基礎單字

Level 2 必備單字

Level 3 中級單字

Level 4 進階單字

Level 5 高手單字

Level 6 滿級單字

動 He prides himself on knowing five languages.
他以會五種語言而自豪。

(焦點句型) take pride in sth./sb. 以⋯自豪

priest [prist] 名神父

The priest conducts the church service.
▶▶ 神父負責主持教堂儀式。

primary [`praɪ͵mɛrɪ] 形主要的

The primary problem is your laziness.
▶▶ 主要的問題在於你很懶惰。

prince / princess [prɪns] / [`prɪnsɛs] 名王子 / 公主

The prince fell in love with the daughter of a fisherman.
▶▶ 王子愛上了漁家女。

principal [`prɪnsəpḷ] 形首要的 名校長

形 The principal reason for this problem is lack of time.
這個問題的主要原因是時間不足。
名 The speech of the principal encouraged everyone.
校長的演講激勵了所有人。

principle [`prɪnsəpḷ] 名原則

Their principles are honesty and hard work.
▶▶ 他們的原則是誠實與勤奮工作。

print [prɪnt] 名印記；印刷的字 動印刷

名 The prints of his feet were left in the soil.
他的足跡留在泥土上。
動 The accident printed itself on his memory.
那次事故深深印在了他的記憶中。

printer [`prɪntɚ] 名印表機

Alice printed the documents by using a printer.
▶▶ 艾莉絲用印表機列印文件。

prison [`prɪzn̩] 名監獄

The man was finally sent to prison.
▶ 這名男子終於入獄了。

prisoner [`prɪzn̩ɚ] 名囚犯

The number of prisoners serving life sentences has fallen.
▶ 被判無期徒刑的囚犯數目下降了。

private [`praɪvɪt] 形私密的 關 privatize 使私有化

You have no right to look at my private letters.
▶ 你無權看我的私人信件。

prize [praɪz] 名獎品 動重視 關 premium 獎金；獎品

名 His writing won the first prize.
他的文章得了第一名。
動 I prize my family above everything.
我重視我的家庭勝過一切。

produce [prə`djus ] / [ `pradjus] 動生產 名農產品

動 These shrubs produce bright red berries.
這些灌木能長出鮮紅的漿果。
名 The family sold their produce online.
這家人線上販售農產品。

production [prə`dʌkʃən] 名製造

Thousands of men were employed in the production of cars.
▶ 成千上萬的人受雇生產汽車。

progress [prə`grɛs ] / [ `pragrɛs] 動進步 名進展

動 The course allows students to progress at their own speed.
本課程允許學生按各自的速度學習。
名 We have made great progress in controlling inflation.
我們在抑制通貨膨脹方面取得了巨大進展。

project [`pradʒɛkt ] / [ prə`dʒɛkt] 名計畫 動投射

名 They are budgeting for the new project.
他們在為新計畫編列預算。
動 The pictures they took were projected onto the screen.
他們拍攝的照片投影在螢幕上。

promise [`prɑmɪs] 名諾言 動約定

名 I believe he will keep his promise.
我相信他會遵守諾言。
動 James promised me to help celebrate my birthday.
詹姆斯承諾要幫我慶祝生日。

proper [`prɑpɚ] 形適當的

Talking about hobbies is a proper topic for new acquaintances.
▶▶ 對剛認識的人而言，興趣是個適宜的話題。

propose [prə`poz] 動提議；求婚

Man proposes but God disposes.
▶▶ 謀事在人，成事在天。

protect [prə`tɛkt] 動保護

Troops have been sent to protect aid workers against attack.
▶▶ 已經派出部隊保護援助人員免遭襲擊。

protective [prə`tɛktɪv] 形保護的

Workers should wear full protective clothing.
▶▶ 工人應該穿著全套防護服。

prove [pruv] 動證實

Cindy was proven to be innocent.
▶▶ 辛蒂被證實是無辜的。

provide [prə`vaɪd] 動提供

They provided the service of charging batteries.
▶▶ 他們提供電池充電的服務。

pudding [`pʊdɪŋ] 名布丁

The proof of the pudding is in the eating.
▶▶ 空談不如實踐。

pumpkin [`pʌmpkɪn] 名南瓜

Pumpkin pie is a traditional American dish served on Thanksgiving.
▶▶ 南瓜派是美國傳統的感恩節菜餚。

Level 1 基礎單字
Level 2 必備單字
Level 3 中級單字
Level 4 進階單字
Level 5 高手單字
Level 6 滿級單字

punish [`pʌnɪʃ] 動 處罰 兼 punishment 處罰

Ralph was punished for brawling with others.
▶▶ 拉爾夫因和別人打架而受罰。

pupil [`pjupḷ] 名 學生

To our surprise, the introverted pupil got an excellent grade in physical education.
▶▶ 出乎我們意料的是，那個內向的學生在體育課取得了優異的成績。

puppy [`pʌpɪ] 名 小狗

Isabelle fed the puppy some milk.
▶▶ 伊莎貝爾餵小狗喝牛奶。

purple [`pɝpḷ] 名 紫色 形 紫色的

名 Purple is her favorite color.
紫色是她最喜歡的顏色。
形 Which one do you like, the purple dress or the white dress?
你喜歡紫色還是白色的洋裝？

purpose [`pɝpəs] 名 目的

Our strength is in our unity of purpose.
▶▶ 我們的力量就在於我們的目標一致。

puzzle [`pʌzḷ] 名 難題 動 迷惑

名 What to choose is really a puzzle to me.
如何選擇對我而言是個難題。
動 The questions have puzzled me for a long time, and I still don't know how to answer them.
這些問題讓我困惑許久，而我仍不知道要如何回答。

UNIT 17 Q 字頭必備單字　　　MP3 041

quality [`kwɑlətɪ] 名 品質

When costs are cut, product quality suffers.
▶▶ 一降低成本，產品品質就會受到影響。

quantity [`kwɑntətɪ] 名數量

You can get a discount if you buy in large quantity.
>> 大量購買可享有折扣。

quiz [kwɪz] 名測驗 動對…進行測驗

名 We had a quiz at the beginning of the class.
課堂一開始我們舉行測驗。
動 They were quizzed on math.
他們進行數學測驗。

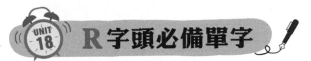 R 字頭必備單字

MP3 042

railroad / railway [`rel,rod ] / [ `rel,weɪ] 名鐵路

The railroad runs across the plain.
>> 鐵道穿過平原。

raincoat [`ren,kot] 名雨衣

It's bizarre to wear a raincoat on a sunny day.
>> 晴天時穿雨衣很奇怪。

range [rendʒ] 名範圍 動涉及

名 Do you know the range of questions on the final?
你知道期末考的範圍嗎？
動 Our conversation ranged over many topics.
我們的談話涉及很多話題。

rapid [`ræpɪd] 形迅速的

She made a rapid reply to the question.
>> 她迅速回答了問題。

rare [rɛr] 形稀有的

Environmentalists were able to preserve the rare turtle.
>> 環保人士能夠保護這種稀有烏龜。

rat [ræt] 名老鼠

These rats snuggle together to keep warm in the cold weather.
>> 這些老鼠天冷時會依偎在一起取暖。

Level 1 基礎單字
Level 2 必備單字
Level 3 中級單字
Level 4 進階單字
Level 5 高手單字
Level 6 滿級單字

rather [`ræðɚ] 副寧願

I would rather study than work.
▶▶ 我寧願念書也不要工作。

焦點句型 would rather A (than B) 寧願A（也不要B）（其中A、B皆為原形動詞）

reality [rɪ`ælətɪ] 名真實

His dream has become a reality.
▶▶ 他的夢想已經實現。

realize [`rɪəlaɪz] 動領悟；提解

Roger realized that he was wrong.
▶▶ 羅傑發現他錯了。

receive [rɪ`siv] 動收到；受到

Hamilton received a warm welcome at Cambridge.
▶▶ 漢米爾頓在劍橋受到熱烈的歡迎。

recent [`risn̩t] 形最近的

In recent years, Dorothy has become more and more slender.
▶▶ 近年來，多蘿西變得越來越苗條。

record [`rɛkɚd ] / [ rɪ`kɔrd] 名紀錄 動記錄 同 archive 檔案館

名 The movie broke a record for earning the most amount of money.
這部電影的票房破紀錄。
動 The nurse recorded my heartbeat and pulse.
護士記錄我的心跳和脈搏。

recover [rɪ`kʌvɚ] 動恢復；重新獲得

We hope you recover as soon as possible.
▶▶ 我們祝你早日康復。

refrigerator / fridge [rɪ`frɪdʒɚ,retɚ] / [frɪdʒ] 名冰箱

Put the fruit into the refrigerator, or it will go rotten.
▶▶ 把水果放進冰箱，不然它會腐爛。

refuse [rɪ`fjuz] 動拒絕 同 withhold 阻擋；抑制

Our proposal was refused by the board of directors.
▶▶ 我們的提案遭到董事會的拒絕。

regard [rɪˋgɑrd] 動認為 名注意

動 He is regarded as the best doctor in the village.
他被認為是村裡最好的醫生。
名 Jessica was driving without regard to speed limits.
潔西卡無視速限高速駕駛。

region [ˋridʒən] 名區域

There is only one KTV in this region.
▶▶ 這個地區裡只有一家KTV。

regular [ˋrɛgjələ] 形平常的；定期的

She pays regular visits to her grandparents.
▶▶ 她定期去看祖父母。

reject [rɪˋdʒɛkt] 動拒絕

The salesman was rejected by his customer again.
▶▶ 這個銷售員再度遭到顧客拒絕。

relate [rɪˋlet] 動敘述；有關係

The woman related her miserable experience.
▶▶ 那女人陳述她悲慘的經歷。

relation [rɪˋleʃən] 名關係；關聯

Sharon's interpersonal relations were not good.
▶▶ 雪倫的人際關係並不好。

relationship [rɪˋleʃənˏʃɪp] 名關係；感情關係

Their relationship is beginning to have problems.
▶▶ 他們的關係開始有問題。

religion [rɪˋlɪdʒən] 名宗教

There are many religions in the world, including Christianity.
▶▶ 世上有許多宗教，包含基督教。

remove [rɪˋmuv] 動移開；去除

He removed his hand from her shoulder.
▶▶ 他將手從她肩膀上拿開。

Level 1 基礎單字
Level 2 必備單字
Level 3 中級單字
Level 4 進階單字
Level 5 高手單字
Level 6 滿級單字

rent [rɛnt] 名租金 動租借 同 lease

名 Ms. Wu can't afford the rent.
吳小姐付不起租金。
動 Renting a bike for one day costs one hundred dollars.
租一台腳踏車一天要一百元。

repair [rɪ`pɛr] 動修理 名修理

動 Repairing your car will cost a minimum of $100.
修理你的汽車最少要一百美元。
名 The cell phone is badly in need of repair.
這支手機急需送修。

reply [rɪ`plaɪ] 名回答 動答覆；回應

My boss gave me a brief reply.
▶▶ 老闆給我一個簡短的回答。

require [rɪ`kwaɪr] 動要求 衍 requirement 需要

A large office requires the employment of many people.
▶▶ 一個大事務所需要雇用很多人。

respect [rɪ`spɛkt] 名尊重 動尊重

名 The students showed little respect to their teacher.
這群學生相當不尊重老師。
動 Respect others and you will be respected.
尊重別人，你也將得到尊敬。

respond [rɪ`spɑnd] 動回答 衍 respondent 回答的

Respond to me if you hear my voice.
▶▶ 如果你聽到我的聲音，請回答我。

responsible [rɪ`spɑnsəbl̩] 形負責任的 衍 responsibility 責任

The bus driver is responsible for the passenges' safety.
▶▶ 公車司機應對乘客的安全負責。

(焦點句型) be responsible for sth./sb. 對…負責

restroom [`rɛst͵rum] 名洗手間；廁所

Your father called you after you went to the restroom.
▶▶ 你去洗手間之後，你父親有打電話過來。

result [rɪˋzʌlt] 名 結果 動 導致

名 A careless mistake can lead to bad results.
一個粗心的錯誤可能導致糟糕的結果。

動 The car accident resulted from drunk driving.
這場車禍源於酒駕。

return [rɪˋtɜn] 動 返回；回報 名 返回

動 Lucas will return home after one week.
盧卡斯一個禮拜後會返家。

名 On his return, he reported his findings to the committee.
他一回來就向委員會報告調查結果。

review [rɪˋvju] 名 複習 動 複習

名 I did a thorough review before the examination.
我在考前做了一次徹底的複習。

動 We'll review the situation at the end of the month.
我們將於月底回顧形勢。

riches [ˋrɪtʃɪz] 名 財產

She gave away all her riches and ran away with her lover.
▶ 她放棄所有的財產和情人私奔。

rocky [ˋrɑkɪ] 形 岩石的 關 rock 搖動；岩石

Johnson walked along the rocky path.
▶ 強森沿著石頭小徑走去。

role [rol] 名 角色

Everyone plays an important role in society.
▶ 每個人都在社會中扮演重要的角色。

roof [ruf] 名 屋頂

A cat was lying on the roof.
▶ 一隻貓躺臥在屋頂上。

rooster [ˋrustɚ] 名 公雞；好鬥者

The rooster made a loud sound.
▶ 公雞大聲啼叫。

Level 1 基礎單字
Level 2 必備單字
Level 3 中級單字
Level 4 進階單字
Level 5 高手單字
Level 6 滿級單字

royal [`rɔɪəl] 形皇家的

The French Foreign Legion was founded by a royal order.
▶▶ 法國外籍兵團是按照皇家法令建立的。

rub [rʌb] 動摩擦

I rub my hands with lotion every night.
▶▶ 我每天晚上用乳液擦手。

rubber [`rʌbɚ] 名橡膠；橡皮 形橡膠的

名 This cable has a rubber casing.
　　這根電纜線外包有一層橡膠。
形 She works in a rubber factory.
　　她在橡膠工廠工作。

rude [rud] 形野蠻的；粗魯的

The man yelled at me with rude words.
▶▶ 那個男人用粗俗的話罵我。

runner [`rʌnɚ] 名跑者

The runner injured her ankle before the race.
▶▶ 這位跑者的腳踝在賽前受傷了。

UNIT 19　S字頭必備單字　　MP3 043

safety [`seftɪ] 名安全

Drive carefully. Nothing is more important than safety.
▶▶ 小心開車，安全至上。

sail [sel] 名乘船航行 動航行

名 It was only a short sail to the island.
　　乘船去那座島嶼，只需要短短的時間。
動 Gwen sailed the boat without any help.
　　格溫在沒有任何幫助的情況下駕船航行。

sailor [`selɚ] 名船員

They are the bravest sailors on this ship.
▶▶ 他們是這艘船上最勇敢的船員。

salesperson / salesman / saleswoman

[`selz͵pɝsn ] / [ `selzmən] / [`selz͵wumən] 名推銷員；店員 關 shopkeeper 店員

The salesperson recommended me some new clothes.
▶▶ 店員推薦我一些新款服飾。

salty [`sɔltɪ] 形鹹的

The salty cookies made me feel thirsty.
▶▶ 鹹餅乾讓我覺得口渴。

sample [`sæmpl̩] 名樣本

You can try the sample of the lotion.
▶▶ 你可以試用乳液的樣品。

sand [sænd] 名沙子

Sand is choking the river.
▶▶ 這條河正逐漸淤積。

sandwich [`sændwɪtʃ] 名三明治

Jimmy ate three sandwiches for breakfast.
▶▶ 吉米吃了三個三明治當早餐。

satisfy [`sætɪs͵faɪ] 動使滿足

The team's performance didn't satisfy the coach.
▶▶ 該隊的表現令教練很不滿意。

saw [sɔ] 名鋸子 動用鋸子鋸開

名 Bryan cut the board with a saw.
布萊恩用鋸子把木板切開。
動 The woodcutter sawed off the branches of tree.
樵夫把樹枝鋸掉。

scare [skɛr] 動驚嚇 名害怕 關 scared 嚇壞的

動 I was scared by the sudden thunder.
我被突如其來的雷聲嚇到。
名 She screamed with a scare.
她驚恐地尖叫。

Level 1 基礎單字
Level 2 必備單字
Level 3 中級單字
Level 4 進階單字
Level 5 高手單字
Level 6 滿級單字

scene [sin] 名 場景；鏡頭

In the first scene of the movie, the man falls in love.
▶ 那名男子在電影中的第一幕墜入愛河。

schedule [`skɛdʒʊl] 名 時刻表 動 將…列表 同 timetable

名 He looked at the schedule to make sure what time the train would come.
他望著時刻表，確認火車何時會來。
動 Andrew scheduled his appointments next week.
安德魯將他下禮拜的約會列成時間表。

scooter [`skutɚ] 名 （小型）機車

Charlie is too young to ride a scooter.
▶ 查理太年輕，還無法騎機車。

score [skor] 名 分數 動 得分

名 What was your final score?
你的期末考成績如何？
動 Nicole scored well on the English test.
妮可在英語測驗中獲得了高分。

screen [skrin] 名 螢幕

Take a rest after you have looked at the screen for over half an hour.
▶ 盯著螢幕半小時後就休息一下。

seafood [`si,fud] 名 海鮮

Local fishing fleets supply the market with all kinds of seafood.
▶ 當地的捕魚船隊供應市場各樣海鮮。

search [sɜtʃ] 動 搜尋 名 調查

動 The scientists searched for a more effective treatment for the disease.
科學家尋求這類疾病更有效的療法。
名 Brad made a long search for the references before writing the report.
撰寫報告前，布萊德花了很長一段時間找文獻。

secondary [`sɛkən,dɛrɪ] 形 第二的

This matter is of only secondary importance.
▶ 這件事是次要的。

secret [`sikrɪt] 名 祕密

The champion is still a secret.
▶▶ 冠軍人選仍然是個祕密。

section [`sɛkʃən] 名 部分

The fifth section of the examination is the writing test.
▶▶ 考試的第五部分是寫作測驗。

seek [sik] 動 尋找

The instant messaging software ICQ is named for the sound of "I seek you".
▶▶ 即時通訊軟體 ICQ 是以「我找你」的音命名。
文法解析 seek 動詞三態變化為 seek / sought / sought。

seem [sim] 動 似乎

You seem unhappy today. What's going on?
▶▶ 你今天看起來不太高興，發生什麼事了？

seesaw [`sisɔ] 名 蹺蹺板

The children are playing on the seesaw.
▶▶ 孩子們正在玩蹺蹺板。

seldom [`sɛldəm] 副 不常地；難得地

My relatives seldom visit me.
▶▶ 我的親戚很少來訪。

select [sə`lɛkt] 動 挑選

Audrey selected a diamond from the collection.
▶▶ 奧黛麗從收藏品中挑選了一枚鑽石。

selection [sə`lɛkʃən] 名 選擇

It is cruel to force her to make a selection.
▶▶ 逼她做抉擇非常殘忍。

self [sɛlf] 名 自我

An important idea in psychology is the concept of the self.
▶▶ 心理學所探討的一項重要概念就是自我。

Level 1 基礎單字
Level 2 必備單字
Level 3 中級單字
Level 4 進階單字
Level 5 高手單字
Level 6 滿級單字

selfish [`sɛlfɪʃ] 彤 自私的

A selfish person never thinks of anyone else.
▶▶ 自私的人從來不為他人著想。

sense [sɛns] 名 感覺；意識

William has no sense of humor.
▶▶ 威廉沒有幽默感。

sensitive [`sɛnsətɪv] 彤 敏感的

Mary is sensitive to strong smells.
▶▶ 瑪莉對強烈的氣味很敏感。

separate [`sɛpə,ret] 彤 分開的 動 分開

彤 She is separate from her mother because of war.
　　她因戰亂而與母親分開。
動 America separated from England in 1776.
　　美國在一七七六年脫離英國。

servant [`sɝvənt] 名 傭人

The rich man has many servants working for him.
▶▶ 富豪有許多傭人為他工作。

serve [sɝv] 動 服務

A single pipe serves all the houses with water.
▶▶ 一條導管供水給所有的房子。

settle [`sɛtl̩] 動 安排；解決　關 settlement 解決；安排

It's time for you to settle your differences with your father.
▶▶ 現在你該解決和你父親之間的分歧了。

sex [sɛks] 名 性；性別

Sex is natural-born but gender is learned.
▶▶ 生理性別是天生的，但社會性別是學習而來的。

shame [ʃem] 名 羞恥；羞愧 動 使羞愧

名 It was a shame that I did not live up to my parents' expectation.
　　沒有達到父母的期望使我羞愧。
動 Joseph was shamed by being blamed in the presence of his girlfriend.
　　在女友面前挨罵讓約瑟夫感到羞愧。

shark [ʃɑrk] 名鯊魚

Sharks eat meat.
▶▶ 鯊魚是肉食性的。

sheet [ʃit] 名床單

He slid under the sheets and closed his eyes.
▶▶ 他鑽進被子裡，閉上了眼睛。

shelf [ʃɛlf] 名架子

Bruce took the cup off the shelf.
▶▶ 布魯斯把杯子從架子上拿走。

shell [ʃɛl] 名貝殼 動剝

名 I found a delicate shell on the beach.
　　我在沙灘上發現一個精緻的貝殼。
動 She is shelling the peanuts.
　　她在剝花生。

shine [ʃaɪn] 動發光 名光亮

動 The sun is shining in the sky.
　　豔陽高照。
名 The clean tabletop had a good shine.
　　乾淨的桌面閃閃發光。

shock [ʃɑk] 名衝擊 動衝擊

名 My immediate reaction was shock.
　　我當下的反應是大吃一驚。
動 I was shocked by his sudden rage.
　　我被他突如其來的盛怒嚇到。

shoot [ʃut] 動射擊

Wayne shot a fox.
▶▶ 韋恩射中一隻狐狸。
文法解析 shoot 動詞三態變化為 shoot / shot / shot。

shore [ʃor] 名岸；濱

Waves wash the shore.
▶▶ 海浪拍打著海岸。

Level 1 基礎單字
Level 2 必備單字
Level 3 中級單字
Level 4 進階單字
Level 5 高手單字
Level 6 滿級單字

shot [ʃɑt] 名 開槍；射擊

Messi won the game with an incredible shot.
▶▶ 梅西用一記不可思議的射門贏得了比賽。

shut [ʃʌt] 動 閉上

The rude man told me to shut my mouth.
▶▶ 那名粗魯無禮的男人叫我閉嘴。
文法解析 shut 的動詞三態同形，皆為 shut。

shy [ʃaɪ] 形 害羞的

The shy girl stood still, not knowing what to say.
▶▶ 那個害羞的女孩靜靜站著，不知道該說什麼。

sidewalk [`saɪdwɔk] 名 人行道

They shoveled snow from the sidewalk.
▶▶ 他們鏟起人行道上的積雪。

silence [`saɪləns] 名 沉默

After the argument, there was a long silence.
▶▶ 爭吵過後是一段漫長的靜默。

silent [`saɪlənt] 形 沉默的

She seems silent sometimes, but she is easy to get along with.
▶▶ 她有時看起來很沉默，但她人很好相處。

silly [`sɪlɪ] 形 傻的

I'm not silly enough to believe you.
▶▶ 我還沒傻到會相信你。

silver [`sɪlvɚ] 名 銀 形 銀製的；銀色的

名 The lady looks gorgeous with the necklace made of silver.
那位女士戴著銀項鍊，十分美麗動人。
形 My mother has silver hair.
我母親一頭銀髮。

similar [`sɪmələ] 形 相似的；類似的

Their voices are so similar that it's hard to tell the difference between them.
▶▶ 他們的聲音如此相似，難以區別。

simply [`sɪmplɪ] 副 簡單地；僅僅地

I don't like driving. I do it simply because I have to get to work each day.
▶▶ 我不喜歡開車，開車只因為每天必須上班。

single [`sɪŋgḷ] 形 單一的；單身的 名 單一；單身者；單曲

形 My beautiful auntie remained single till the end of her days.
我美麗的姨媽終身未嫁。
名 Taylor released a new single.
泰勒釋出了新的單曲。

skill [skɪl] 名 技能；技巧 衍 skilled 熟練的

Reading and writing are different skills.
▶▶ 閱讀和寫作是不同的技能。

skin [skɪn] 名 皮膚

They make shoes from the skins of animals.
▶▶ 他們用動物的皮做鞋子。

sleepy [`slipɪ] 形 疲倦的；想睡的

Dave stays up late often, so he is always sleepy in class.
▶▶ 戴夫時常熬夜，所以課堂上總是想睡。

slide [slaɪd] 動 滑動 名 下滑

動 We slid down the grassy slope.
我們從草坡上滑了下來。
名 The economy is on the slide.
經濟日益衰退。
文法解析 slide 動詞三態變化為 slide / slid / slid。

slip [slɪp] 動 滑倒

Katarina slipped on the ice.
▶▶ 卡特琳娜在冰上滑倒了。

slipper [`slɪpɚ] 名 拖鞋

You had better not hit the cockroaches with your slippers.
▶▶ 你最好別拿拖鞋打蟑螂。

Level 1 基礎單字
Level 2 必備單字
Level 3 中級單字
Level 4 進階單字
Level 5 高手單字
Level 6 滿級單字

smooth [smuð] 形平滑的 動使平滑

形 Her skin is as smooth as silk.
她的皮膚如絲般平滑。
動 Jill smoothed her dress with an electric iron.
吉兒用電熨斗把洋裝燙平。

snack [snæk] 名小吃；點心 動吃點心

名 The snack was popular at one time.
這個點心曾流行一時。
動 I used to snack on French fries.
我過去常把薯條當點心吃。

snail [snel] 名蝸牛

Snails move very slowly.
▶▶ 蝸牛移動速度非常慢。

snowy [`snoɪ] 形積雪的；多雪的

Children are playing happily on the snowy ground.
▶▶ 孩子在雪地上玩得不亦樂乎。

soap [sop] 名肥皂

Laundry soap looks like cheese.
▶▶ 洗衣皂看起來像乳酪。

soccer [`sɑkɚ] 名足球 關 goalkeeper 守門員

Have you ever played indoor soccer?
▶▶ 你玩過室內足球嗎？

social [`soʃəl] 形社會的；社交的

Many college students have an active social life.
▶▶ 許多大學生都有豐富的社交生活。

society [sə`saɪətɪ] 名社會

His behavior is a danger to society.
▶▶ 他的行為對社會構成威脅。

sock [sɑk] 名 短襪；襪子

Not wearing socks saves me the trouble of washing them.
▶▶ 不穿襪子省了我洗襪子的麻煩。

soda [`sodə] 名 汽水

I drank a glass of soda.
▶▶ 我喝了一杯汽水。

soft [soft] 形 柔軟的

The silk cloth feels soft.
▶▶ 這塊絲綢摸起來很柔軟。

soil [sɔɪl] 名 土壤 動 弄髒

名 It was the first time I had been on African soil.
　　那是我第一次踏上非洲大地。
動 I don't want you to soil your hands with this sort of work.
　　我不希望你做這種事，免得弄髒了你的手。

solution [sə`luʃən] 名 解決

I am sure that the best solution to the problem was to do nothing about it.
▶▶ 我確定解決這個問題最好的辦法，就是什麼都不做。

solve [sɑlv] 動 解決

You should work hard to solve the problem.
▶▶ 你應該努力解決問題。

somewhat [`sʌm,hwɑt] 副 多少；幾分

It somewhat surprised me.
▶▶ 那多少讓我有點意外。

sort [sɔrt] 名 種 動 調和；排列

名 I didn't find the sort of ruler I wanted.
　　我沒找到我想要的那種尺。
動 The computer sorts the words into alphabetical order.
　　電腦按字母順序排列這些單字。

soul [sol] 名 靈魂

What happens to your soul after you die?
▶▶ 你去世後，你的靈魂會發生什麼事呢？

Level 1 基礎單字
Level 2 必備單字
Level 3 中級單字
Level 4 進階單字
Level 5 高手單字
Level 6 滿級單字

sour [saʊr] 形酸的 動變酸

形 George's mother prefers sour drinks.
喬治的母親喜歡喝酸酸的飲料。

動 The hot and humid weather soured the milk.
濕熱的天氣讓牛奶酸掉了。

source [sors] 名來源

The news comes from a reliable source.
▶▶ 這條消息來源可靠。

southern [`sʌðən] 形南方的

I find the southern climate to be too hot for me.
▶▶ 我發現南方的氣候對我而言太熱了。

soybean [`sɔɪbin] 名大豆

Soybeans are rich in protein.
▶▶ 大豆富含蛋白質。

speaker [`spikə] 名演說者

The speaker gave an interesting speech about whales.
▶▶ 講者就鯨魚為主題，發表了一場有趣的演講。

speech [`spitʃ] 名演講；言論

The professor gave a speech about global warming.
▶▶ 教授發表了一場關於全球暖化的演講。

speed [spid] 名速度 動加速

名 Liszt played piano with amazing speed.
李斯特以驚人的速度彈奏鋼琴。

動 The farmer speed the growth of the flowers by lighting up the garden at night.
農夫透過在夜裡照亮花園，增快花卉的成長速度。

spelling [`spɛlɪŋ] 名拼字；拼法

Your resume should not have any spelling errors.
▶▶ 你的履歷不該有拼錯字。

spider [`spaɪdə] 名 蜘蛛

Spiders have eight legs, so they are not a kind of insect.
▶▶ 蜘蛛有八隻腳，所以牠們不是昆蟲的一種。

spirit [`spɪrɪt] 名 精神

My spirits sank because I had to start all over again.
▶▶ 想到一切都得重新開始，我的心情就變得十分沉重。

spoon [spun] 名 湯匙

Use the spoon to eat the soup, please.
▶▶ 請用湯匙喝湯。

sport [sport] 名 運動

Baseball is my favorite sport.
▶▶ 棒球是我最喜愛的運動。

spot [spɑt] 動 看見；弄髒 名 點

動 The nobleman did not want to be spotted.
那名貴族不想被人發現。
名 This is the spot where we first met.
這裡就是我們首次相遇的地方。

spread [sprɛd] 動 傳開 名 擴散

動 Our leader spread the news that we had an important assignment today.
班長告訴我們今天有重要的作業。
名 The spread of fashion is often due to advertising.
時尚的傳播往往得益於廣告。

文法解析 spread 的動詞三態同形，皆為 spread。

stage [stedʒ] 名 舞台 動 上演

名 He performs magic on the stage.
他在台上表演魔術。
動 "Romeo & Juliet" will stage here next Friday.
「羅密歐與茱麗葉」將在下禮拜五於此上演。

stamp [stæmp] 名 郵票 動 壓印

名 Dan collects foreign stamps.
丹收集外國郵票。

(動) Martin stamped his name on the cover of notebook.
馬丁在筆記本的封面印上自己的名字。

standard [`stændəd] (名)標準 (形)標準的

(名) Standards often change over time.
標準往往隨著時間而改變。
(形) She has a standard figure for a girl at her age.
她擁有她那年齡的標準身材。

state [stet] (名)狀態 (動)陳述 (關) statement 陳述

(名) Guests complained about the state of the hotel.
客人們抱怨旅館的狀況。
(動) The facts are clearly stated in the report.
報導清楚說明了事實真相。

steak [stek] (名)牛排

Gordon was satisfied with the steak.
▶▶ 戈登對這份牛排很滿意。

steel [stil] (名)鋼；鋼鐵

Tin is damaged more easily than steel.
▶▶ 錫比鋼容易損壞。

step [stɛp] (名)腳步 (動)踏

(名) Lynn completed the task step by step.
琳恩一步一步地完成任務。
(動) He stepped out of the train and onto the platform.
他下火車踏上月臺。

stick [stɪk] (名)棍；棒 (動)黏

(名) Luke drove the stray dog away with a stick.
路克用棍子把流浪狗趕走。
(動) I always get stuck in a traffic jam.
我總是遇到塞車。
文法解析 動詞三態變化為 stick / stuck / stuck。

stone [ston] (名)石頭

A rolling stone gathers no moss.
▶▶ 滾石不生苔。

storm [stɔrm] 名風暴 動襲擊

名 The boats in the harbor were safe during the storm.
港口的船隻在暴風雨中安然無恙。
動 The enemy troops stormed the castle.
敵軍對城堡發動襲擊。

stranger [`strendʒɚ] 名陌生人

The baby starts crying on seeing strangers.
▶▶ 嬰兒一看到陌生人就開始哭。

strawberry [`strɔbɛrɪ] 名草莓 關 orchard 果園

The orchard produces strawberries in spring.
▶▶ 這座果園春天盛產草莓。

stream [strim] 名小溪 動流動

名 The stream doesn't have much water in it.
這條小溪的水不多。
動 Water streamed from the pipe.
水從水管流出。

stress [strɛs] 名壓力 動使緊張

名 Allen had too much stress from work.
艾倫的工作壓力太大了。
動 She felt stressed while speaking in front of the audience.
在觀眾面前演說令她感到緊張。

stretch [strɛtʃ] 動伸展 名伸展

動 The land stretched out as far as the eye could see.
遼闊的草原一望無際。
名 Laura had a stretch after getting up.
勞拉起床伸了個懶腰。

strict [strɪkt] 形嚴格的

Strict training brings him success.
▶▶ 嚴格的訓練造就了他的成功。

strike [straɪk] 動打擊 名罷工

動 Jeff was struck by his mother for doing poorly on the test.
傑夫因考試考差被媽媽打。

Level 1 基礎單字
Level 2 必備單字
Level 3 中級單字
Level 4 進階單字
Level 5 高手單字
Level 6 滿級單字

名 The workers went on strike because of the poor conditions.
由於工作條件太差，工人們都罷工。

文法解析 strike 動詞三態變化為 strike / struck / striken。

struggle [`strʌɡl̩] 動努力 名掙扎

動 Those students struggled to protect the old building from being torn down.
這些學生努力保護這棟舊房子免受拆除。

名 We usually don't know much about people's private struggles.
關於個人的掙扎，我們通常不會知道太多。

style [staɪl] 名風格；時尚

His style of working is out of tune with that of his colleagues.
▶▶ 他的行事風格與同事格格不入。

subway / underground / metro

[`sʌb͵we ] / [ `ʌndə͵ɡraʊnd] / [`mɛtro] 名地下鐵

Our subway trains run 18 hours a day.
▶▶ 我們的地鐵每天運作 18 小時。

succeed [sək`sid] 動成功

Your own wish to succeed is more important than anything else.
▶▶ 你想成功的決心比什麼都重要。

success [sək`sɛs] 名成功

Success comes with hard work.
▶▶ 成功來自勤奮。

such [sʌtʃ] 形這樣的

We are not such fools as to believe him.
▶▶ 我們才沒有傻到會去相信他。

sudden [`sʌdn̩] 形突然的 名突然

形 Morris gave me a sudden hug.
莫里斯突然抱住我。

名 She ran out of the door all of a sudden.
她突然奪門而出。

suggest [səˋdʒɛst] 動 提議；建議

The proposal is unsatisfactory. I hope someone will suggest a better one.
>> 這個提案讓人不滿意。我希望有人可以提出更好的建議。

suit [sut] 名 套裝 動 適合 關 suitable 合適的

名 Reynold sometimes wears a black suit.
雷諾有時穿著黑色套裝。

動 She suits light colors more than dark colors.
淺色比深色更適合她。

super [ˋsupɚ] 形 超級的

The price is reasonable because the quality is super.
>> 因為品質極佳，這個價格很合理。

supper [ˋsʌpɚ] 名 晚餐

I'll do my homework after supper.
>> 晚飯後我要做作業。

supply [səˋplaɪ] 動 供給 名 供應品 同 provision

動 His firm supplied all the furniture for the new building.
他的公司為新大廈提供所有家具。

名 Our supply of food is almost gone.
儲存的食物快吃完了。

support [səˋport] 動 支持 名 支持

動 My mother supported me in my choice of career.
媽媽支持我的職涯選擇。

名 I feel relieved with all of your support.
你們的支持使我感到安心。

surf [sɝf] 動 衝浪 名 海浪；浪花

動 If the waves are big enough, we'll go surfing.
如果浪夠大的話，我們就去衝浪。

名 The surf is very imposing.
浪花非常壯觀。

surface [ˋsɝfɪs] 名 表面 動 出現

名 Teeth have a hard surface layer called enamel.
牙齒有一層叫做琺瑯質的堅硬表層。

Level 1 基礎單字
Level 2 必備單字
Level 3 中級單字
Level 4 進階單字
Level 5 高手單字
Level 6 滿級單字

(動) The ducks dove and surfaced again several meters away.
鴨子潛入水中，然後在幾米外鑽出水面。

survive [səˋvaɪv] (動) 倖存 (關) survival 倖存者

No one survived the air crash.
▶▶ 無人倖存於那場空難。

swallow [ˋswɑlo] (動) 吞嚥 (名) 燕子

(動) He swallowed the pill without water.
他不用水就吞掉了藥丸。
(名) Swallows fly orderly.
燕子齊整地飛行。

sweater [ˋswɛtɚ] (名) 毛衣

Maggie wore two sweaters but still felt cold.
▶▶ 瑪姬穿了兩件毛衣，卻仍然覺得冷。

sweep [swip] (動) 掃 (名) 掃

(動) Ryan didn't want to sweep the restroom.
萊恩不想去掃廁所。
(名) They gave their living room a complete sweep.
他們把客廳徹底打掃了一次。
(文法解析) sweep 動詞三態變化為 sweep / swept / swept。

swim [swɪm] (動) 游泳 (名) 游泳 (關) swimsuit 泳裝

(動) They swim during the holidays.
他們在假日期間游泳。
(名) I go for a swim once a week.
我每個禮拜游一次泳。
(文法解析) swim 動詞三態變化為 swim / swam / swum。

swing [swɪŋ] (動) 搖動

His arms swung as he walked.
▶▶ 他邊走邊擺著雙臂。
(文法解析) swing 動詞三態變化為 swing / swung / swung。

switch [swɪtʃ] (名) 開關 (動) 轉換

(名) Where is the light switch?
電燈的開關在哪裡？

Level 1 基礎單字

Level 2 必備單字

Level 3 中級單字

Level 4 進階單字

Level 5 高手單字

Level 6 滿級單字

動 Ruth switched our plans without informing us.
露絲未告知我們就擅改了計劃。

symbol [`sɪmbl] 名象徵；標誌

A heart is a symbol of love.
▶▶ 心形是愛的象徵。

system [`sɪstəm] 名系統

The system designer made an incredible breakthrough.
▶▶ 系統設計師完成一個驚人的突破。

UNIT 20　**T**字頭必備單字　　　MP3 044

tale [tel] 名故事

Fairy tales are not real.
▶▶ 童話故事不是真的。

target [`tɑrgɪt] 名目標

Vanessa's questions were right on target.
▶▶ 凡妮莎所提出的問題個個擊中要害。

task [tæsk] 名任務

He would rather postpone the tasks than stay up late to complete them.
▶▶ 他寧願延緩工作，也不願熬夜完成。

tax [tæks] 名稅

The government's new higher taxes are really beginning to bite.
▶▶ 政府提高稅收的新措施真的開始引起不滿了。

tear [tɪr] / [tɛr] 名眼淚 動撕；撕破

名 The plot of the drama moved me to tears.
這齣戲的情節讓我感動落淚。

動 Ivan tore the letter with anger after reading it.
伊凡讀完信後憤怒地撕掉。

文法解析 tear動詞三態變化為 tear / tore / torn。

technology [tɛkˋnɑlədʒɪ] 名 科技

Science has contributed much to modern technology.
▶▶ 科學對現代技術作出了很大貢獻。

teens [tinz] 名 十多歲

She's not yet out of her teens yet.
▶▶ 她還不到二十歲。

temperature [ˋtɛmprətʃə] 名 溫度；氣溫

The temperature tomorrow will decrease owing to the cold front.
▶▶ 因為冷鋒面到來，明天的氣溫會下降。

term [tɝm] 名 術語 動 稱呼

名 The technical terms in their conversation confused me.
他們談話中的科技術語讓我困惑。
動 Peter termed his heavy brother a hippo.
彼得稱呼他的胖哥哥為河馬。

text [tɛkst] 名 課文；文本

The meanings of the texts may vary, according to interpretations.
▶▶ 根據詮釋的不同，文本的意義可能會有所差異。

textbook [ˋtɛkstˏbʊk] 名 教科書 關 workbook 練習簿

The textbook did not have many pages but was expensive.
▶▶ 教科書頁數不多，但很貴。

therefore [ˋðɛrˏfor] 連 因此；所以

He's only 17 and, therefore, can't vote yet.
▶▶ 他只有十七歲，因此沒有投票選舉的資格。

thief [θif] 名 小偷

The thief was arrested with the stolen goods.
▶▶ 竊賊連人帶贓物被警察逮個正著。

thirsty [ˋθɝstɪ] 形 口渴的

I always feel thirsty when I stay in an air-conditioned room.
▶▶ 當我待在冷氣房時，我時常感到口渴。

thought [θɔt] 名思維

Chelsea's first thought was to leave quickly.
▶▶ 切爾西的第一反應是迅速離開。

throughout [θru`aut] 介徹頭徹尾

Quincy stayed calm throughout the crisis.
▶▶ 昆西在整個危機期間保持冷靜。

thunder [`θʌndɚ] 名雷 動打雷

名 After the lightning came the thunder.
雷聲接著閃電而來。
動 It thundered and rained cats and dogs.
一邊打雷，一邊下著傾盆大雨。

thus [ðʌs] 動如此；因此

Does life on other planets exits? Many scientists have argued thus.
▶▶ 別的星球有生物存在嗎？許多科學家都因此爭論著。

tiny [`taɪnɪ] 形極小的

Fleas are tiny insects.
▶▶ 跳蚤是很小的昆蟲。

tire [taɪr] 動使疲倦 名輪胎

I really need a vacation! Heavy workload tires me.
▶▶ 我需要渡假！沉重的工作負擔使我疲備不堪。

tissue [`tɪʃu] 名面紙

The hotel provides tissue for every room.
▶▶ 這間飯店每間房間都提供面紙。

title [`taɪtl̩] 名標題 動加標題

名 Can you think of a title that exactly covers the whole idea?
你能想出一個概括整個主旨的標題嗎？
動 To title a book is difficult.
取書名很不容易。

toast [tost] 名吐司麵包 動烤麵包

名 Tom ate a piece of toast.
湯姆吃了一片吐司。

Level 1 基礎單字
Level 2 必備單字
Level 3 中級單字
Level 4 進階單字
Level 5 高手單字
Level 6 滿級單字

(動) I toasted bread for breakfast.
我烤麵包當早餐。

tofu [`tofu] (名)豆腐

Stinky tofu is a traditional side dish in Taiwan.
▶▶ 臭豆腐是台灣傳統小吃。

tone [ton] (名)音調

Eva told me the news in a cold tone.
▶▶ 伊娃冷冷地告訴我這個消息。

tongue [tʌŋ] (名)舌頭

He burned his tongue with red pepper.
▶▶ 他的舌頭被紅辣椒辣得很難受。

tour [tʊr] (名)旅行 (動)遊覽

(名) Mr. Adams made a tour around East Asia last year.
亞當斯先生去年到東亞旅行了一次。
(動) She toured Greece last summer.
她去年夏天到希臘觀光。

toward / towards [tə`wɔrd ] / [ tə`wɔrdz] (介)向；朝

I saw her walking toward the bank.
▶▶ 我看到她朝銀行走去。

track [træk] (名)蹤跡 (動)追蹤

(名) These tracks were formed by goats.
這些腳印是山羊留下的。
(動) We continued tracking the plane on our radar.
我們繼續用雷達追蹤那架飛機。

trade [tred] (名)商業；貿易 (動)交易；交換

(名) The two men worked in the same trade.
這兩人是同行。
(動) Jane traded her handkerchief for a loaf of bread.
珍用手帕換來一條麵包。

tradition [trə`dɪʃən] 名傳統

My parents did their best to keep up the family tradition.
▶▶ 我的父母為了維持家族傳統竭盡全力。

traditional [trə`dɪʃənl] 形傳統的 關 orthodox 傳統的；東正教的

The traditional concept of a woman's role is to stay home with the kids.
▶▶ 對於女性角色的傳統觀念就是在家育子。

trap [træp] 名圈套；陷阱 動誘捕

名 You almost fell into his trap!
你差點落入他的陷阱！
動 The bear was trapped.
那隻熊落入了陷阱。

trash [træʃ] 名垃圾

Joshua threw the garbage in the trash can.
▶▶ 約書亞把垃圾丟在垃圾桶裡。

travel [`trævḷ] 動旅行 名旅行

動 Scott has traveled over 20 countries around the world.
斯考特遊遍全世界二十個以上的國家。
名 In his travels, he learned a lot about different cultures.
在旅程中，他認識了許多不同的文化。

treasure [`trɛʒɚ] 名寶藏 動收藏

名 The pirates buried their treasure secretly.
海盜祕密地埋藏了他們的財寶。
動 The manager treasured his workers very much.
這位經理很愛惜人力。

trial [`traɪəl] 名試驗；審問；審判

They succeeded after many trials.
▶▶ 經過反覆試驗，他們終於成功了。

triangle [`traɪˌæŋgḷ] 名三角形

Two sides of a triangle must be longer than the third side.
▶▶ 三角形的兩邊長必大於第三邊。

1 Level 基礎單字
2 Level 必備單字
3 Level 中級單字
4 Level 進階單字
5 Level 高手單字
6 Level 滿級單字

trick [trɪk] 名詭計 動欺騙

名 He wants to play a trick on his old pal.
他想捉弄一下他的老朋友。

動 Kate tricked me that her purse had been stolen.
凱特騙我說她的錢包被偷了。

true [tru] 形真的；真實的

Is it true that they are getting married?
▶▶ 他們要結婚是真的嗎？

trust [trʌst] 名信任 動信任

名 I have strong trust in my father.
我絕對信賴我父親。

動 I trust you no matter how they say about you.
無論他們怎麼說你，我都相信你。

truth [truθ] 名真理；事實

Cliff told the truth that he had been in prison.
▶▶ 克里夫透露了他曾經坐牢的事實。

tube [tjub] 名管子

He squeezed out the last bit of toothpaste from the tube.
▶▶ 他將管子裡的最後一點牙膏擠了出來。

turtle [`tɝtl̩] 名海龜

The turtle is protected by its hard shell.
▶▶ 海龜受到它的硬殼保護。

typhoon [taɪ`fun] 名颱風

How many typhoons hit Taiwan this year so far?
▶▶ 今年到目前為止有多少颱風襲擊台灣？

typical [`tɪpɪkl̩] 形典型的

She is a typical teenage girl who likes music and movies.
▶▶ 她是個典型的青少年女孩，喜歡音樂和電影。

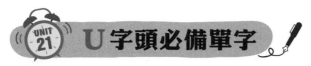
ugly [`ʌglɪ] 形 醜的

The ugly girl is nervous about her appearance.
▶▶ 醜女孩因外表感到自卑。

umbrella [ʌm`brɛlə] 名 雨傘

She got wet because she forgot her umbrella.
▶▶ 她因忘了帶傘而被雨淋濕。

unit [`junɪt] 名 單位；單元

The pound is the standard unit of money in Britain.
▶▶ 鎊是英國貨幣的標準單位。

universe [`junə‚vɝs] 名 宇宙

They thought the earth was the center of the universe.
▶▶ 他們認為地球是宇宙的中心。

university [‚junə`vɝsətɪ] 名 大學

How's your granddaughter getting along at university?
▶▶ 你的孫女大學過得怎樣？

unless [ʌn`lɛs] 連 除非

I will break up with you unless you explain who the girl is.
▶▶ 除非你解釋那個女孩是誰，不然我會跟你分手。

upload [`ʌp‚lod] 動 上傳（檔案）

The teacher uploaded his handouts for the students.
▶▶ 老師上傳了講義給學生。

upon [ə`pɑn] 介 在…上面

The village stands upon a hill.
▶▶ 這個村莊坐落在一座小山上。

upper [`ʌpɚ] 形 在上面的

The plates on the upper shelf were beyond my reach.
▶▶ 我拿不到上層架子上的盤子。

Level 1 基礎單字
Level 2 必備單字
Level 3 中級單字
Level 4 進階單字
Level 5 高手單字
Level 6 滿級單字

243

upset [ʌp`sɛt ] / [ `ʌpsɛt] 形苦惱的 動使心煩

形 Duncan was upset at not being invited.
沒有受到邀請讓鄧肯很不悅。

動 It really upsets him that she flirts with David.
她和大衛調情，實在讓他很不高興。

upstairs [`ʌp`stɛrz] 副在樓上；往樓上 形樓上的 名樓上

副 He went upstairs to see his father.
他上樓見他的父親。

形 Our upstairs neighbor is Ms. Hardcastle.
我們樓上的鄰居是哈凱絲女士。

名 The house has no upstairs.
這房子只有一層。

used [juzd] 形用過的；二手的

Students exchange used textbooks in order to save money.
▶▶ 學生們為了省錢互相交換二手教科書。

user [`juzɚ] 名使用者

The users can create their own accounts simply by filling out a form.
▶▶ 使用者只要填一張表格，就可以建立他們自己的帳號。

usual [`juʒʊəl] 形通常的；平常的

Today she seems quieter than usual.
▶▶ 今天她好像比平常安靜。

UNIT 22 **V字頭必備單字**

MP3 046

vacation [ve`keʃən] 名假期 動度假

名 The vacation period is coming, and I have an urge to travel.
假期快到了，我很想外出旅行。

動 I am planning where to vacation this summer.
我正在計劃這個夏天要去哪裡度假。

valley [`vælɪ] 名山谷

The house on the hill is near a valley.
▶▶ 山丘上的這座房子鄰近山谷。

Level 1 基礎單字
Level 2 必備單字
Level 3 中級單字
Level 4 進階單字
Level 5 高手單字
Level 6 滿級單字

valuable [`væljuəbl] 形 貴重的

This painting is very valuable because it is the masterpiece of a famous painter.
▶▶ 這幅繪畫非常名貴，因為它是一位知名畫家的傑作。

value [`vælju] 名 價值 動 重視；評價

名 The value of one thing differs from another.
不同事物的價值有所差異。
動 I cannot value the jewelry.
我無法估量珠寶的價值。

victory [`vɪktərɪ] 名 勝利

By working together well, they achieved victory.
▶▶ 團結讓他們獲勝。

view [vju] 名 景觀 動 觀看

名 There is a fine view from the window.
從這扇窗看到的景觀不錯。
動 Nancy views Anna as her younger sister.
南西把安娜當成妹妹。

village [`vɪlɪdʒ] 名 村莊

Lacking job opportunities, more and more people moved out the village.
▶▶ 因為缺乏工作機會，越來越多人搬出這個村莊。

vote [vot] 名 投票 動 投票 關 referendum 公投

名 We elected our new leader by vote.
我們投票選出新的領袖。
動 He was voted the worst dressed celebrity.
大家一致認為他是衣著最差的名人。

UNIT 23 **W 字頭必備單字**

MP3 047

waist [west] 名 腰部

Miriam is paralyzed from the waist down.
▶▶ 米莉亞姆下半身癱瘓。

waiter / waitress [`wetə ] / [ `wetrɪs] 名服務生；女服務生

The waitress gave me a cup of coffee.
▶▶ 女侍者遞給我一杯咖啡。

wallet [`wɑlɪt] 名錢包 相 purse （常指女用）錢包

The man grabbed his wallet and ran away.
▶▶ 扒手把他的錢包偷走，然後逃跑了。

war [wɔr] 名戰爭

The protesters demonstrated against the war.
▶▶ 抗議者舉行反戰示威。

wash [wɑʃ] 動洗；沖掉 名洗；洗滌

動 He washed off the dirt on his hands.
他把手上的泥土洗掉。
名 Olivia gave her muddy boots a good wash.
奧莉薇亞徹底清洗了她沾滿泥土的靴子。

waste [west] 動浪費 名廢棄物 形廢棄的

動 He wasted his time at university because he didn't work hard.
他浪費了他的大學時光，因為他不認真念書。
名 A lot of household waste can be recycled and reused.
許多家居廢棄物都可以回收再利用。
形 Throw out that waste paper.
把廢紙扔掉。

watermelon [`wɔtə͵mɛlən] 名西瓜

She patted the watermelon to make sure it was juicy.
▶▶ 她輕拍西瓜以確認它是否多汁。

wealth [wɛlθ] 名財富

Health is the most precious wealth.
▶▶ 健康是最珍貴的財富。

wedding [`wɛdɪŋ] 名婚禮 相 wed 結婚

The wedding will take place in September.
▶▶ 婚禮將於九月舉行。

weekday [`wik,de] 名平日；工作日

The office is open 9:00 a.m. to 5:00 p.m. on weekdays.
▶▶ 辦公室的開放時間是平日的早上九點到下午五點。

weigh [we] 動秤重

The vendor weighed the eggs and told me the price.
▶▶ 小販秤了蛋的重量，並告訴我價格。

weight [wet] 名重量

The weight of the desk is one kilogram.
▶▶ 這張書桌重一公斤。

western [`wɛstən] 形西方的

His western accent is thick.
▶▶ 他的西部口音很濃厚。

whale [hwel] 名鯨魚

The blue whale is the largest living animal in the world.
▶▶ 藍鯨是世界上最大的動物。

whatever [hwɑt`ɛvɚ] 形任何的 代任何

形 Whatever decision he made, I would support it.
無論他做出什麼決定我都會支持。
代 I will no longer care whatever you do.
你做任何事，我都不會在乎了。

wheel [hwil] 名輪子 動滾動

名 A boy was pushing the other along in a little box on wheels.
一個男孩用下面裝輪子的小箱子推著另一個男孩。
動 He wheeled his broken bike to get it fixed.
他獨自推著壞掉的腳踏車去修理。

whenever [hwɛn`ɛvɚ] 連無論何時；每當 副無論何時

Whenever I feel stressed, I go for a walk.
▶▶ 每當我感受到壓力時，我會去散步。

wherever [hwɛr`ɛvɚ] 副無論何處；無論何處 連無論在哪裡

Ashley promised to follow him wherever he went.
▶▶ 艾希莉發誓無論要到哪裡，都會跟著他。

1 Level 基礎單字
2 Level 必備單字
3 Level 中級單字
4 Level 進階單字
5 Level 高手單字
6 Level 滿級單字

whisper [`hwɪspɚ] 動 輕聲細語 名 輕聲細語

動 The girl whispered into the boy's ear.
女孩對著男孩的耳朵輕聲細語。
名 The patient said she heard whispers at night from the empty room.
病人說，她晚上會聽見空無一人的房間裡傳來竊竊私語。

whoever [hu`ɛvɚ] 代 任何人

I don't want to see them, whoever they are.
▶ 無論他們是誰，我都不想見。

whole [hol] 形 全部的 名 全部；全體

形 The newspapers exaggerated the whole affair wildly.
報章瘋狂誇大了整個事件。
名 The whole of our class feels unsatisfied with the teacher.
我們全班都對老師不滿。

whom [hum] 代 誰；…的人

The author whom you criticized in your review has written a reply.
▶ 你在評論中批評的那個作者寫了一則回覆。

width [wɪdθ] 名 寬度

The carpet is available in different widths.
▶ 這款地毯有各種寬度可供選擇。

wild [waɪld] 形 野生的；狂野的

Wild animals are mostly very fierce.
▶ 野生動物大多十分兇猛。

willing [`wɪlɪŋ] 形 願意，樂意（做某事）；積極的

The worker was willing to donate all his healthy organs after death.
▶ 這名工人願意心甘情願在死後捐出所有健全的器官。
(焦點句型) be willing to V. 願意…；樂意…

windy [`wɪndɪ] 形 多風的

Put on your jacket. The weather forecaster says today will be a windy day.
▶ 把夾克穿上。氣象播報員說今天風大。

wine [waɪn] 名葡萄酒

I drank a glass of wine before going to bed.
▶▶ 我睡前喝了一杯葡萄酒。

wing [wɪŋ] 名翅膀

This bird has a broken wing and cannot fly.
▶▶ 小鳥的一隻翅膀斷了，飛不起來了。

wire [waɪr] 名電線 關 plug 插頭 / socket 插座

The wire of the plug is not long enough for it to reach the socket.
▶▶ 這個插頭的電線不夠長，碰不到插座。

within [wɪˋðɪn] 介在…之內

They finished the house within half a year.
▶▶ 他們在半年內蓋好了這棟房屋。

wolf [wʊlf] 名狼

Wolves and dogs are canine animals.
▶▶ 狼和狗都是犬科動物。

wonder [ˋwʌndɚ] 名奇蹟 動想知道

名 The Pyramids were among the Seven Wonders of the World.
古埃及金字塔是世界七大奇觀之一。
動 I wonder why she quit her job.
我想知道她為何要辭職。

wood [wʊd] 名木材

All the furniture was made of wood.
▶▶ 所有傢俱都是用木頭製作的。

wooden [ˋwʊdn̩] 形木製的

The wooden furniture is unsuitable for such a humid environment.
▶▶ 木製家具不適合這樣的潮濕環境。

wool [wʊl] 名羊毛

Wool is one of the chief exports of Australia.
▶▶ 羊毛是澳洲的主要出口物資之一。

Level 1 基礎單字

Level 2 必備單字

Level 3 中級單字

Level 4 進階單字

Level 5 高手單字

Level 6 滿級單字

worm [wɜm] 名 蟲 動 蠕行

名 I found a worm on the leaf.
　我發現葉子上有隻蟲。
動 He wormed his small body through the bush.
　他蠕動他那瘦小的身體鑽過了樹籬。

worse [wɜs] 形 更壞的

The doctor said my uncle's condition has become worse.
▶▶ 醫師說我叔叔的狀況變得更糟了。
文法解析 worse 為 bad 的比較級，最高級為 worst。

worst [wɜst] 形 最差的 副 最差地

形 It was by far the worst speech she had ever made.
　這是她迄今發表過的最差的演講。
副 Hank played the worst during the basketball game.
　整場籃球比賽中，漢克打得最差。

worth [wɜθ] 名 價值

The mink coat is of amazing worth.
▶▶ 這件貂皮大衣價格不斐。

wound [wund] 名 傷口 動 傷害

名 The nurse washed the wound.
　護士清洗了傷口。
動 Kelly was wounded by the robber with knife.
　凱莉被搶匪持刀砍傷。

UNIT 24　Y、Z 字頭必備單字　　MP3 048

yam [jæm] 名 甘薯；山藥

It is good for one's health to eat yam.
▶▶ 吃番薯有益健康。

youth [juθ] 名 少年；少年時期

The youth wanted to drop out of school.
▶▶ 這位少年想輟學。

zebra [`zibrə] 名斑馬

Zebras have black and white stripes.
▶▶ 斑馬有著黑色和白色的條紋。

Level 1 基礎單字

Level 2 必備單字

Level 3 中級單字

Level 4 進階單字

Level 5 高手單字

Level 6 滿級單字

7000 Essential
Vocabulary for
High School Students

LEVEL 3

中級單字

單字難易度 ★★☆☆☆
文法難易度 ★★☆☆☆
生活出現頻率 ★★★★★
考題出題頻率 ★★★☆☆

名 名詞　動 動詞　形 形容詞　副 副詞　介 介係詞　連 連接詞
關 相關單字／片語　同 同義詞　反 反義詞

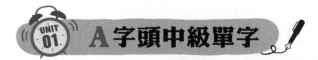

aboard [ə`bord] 副在船(飛機、火車)上 介在船(飛機、火車)上

副 We finally went aboard before it rained.
我們終於趕在下雨前登船。
介 He was already aboard the plane.
他已經登機了。

acceptable [ək`sɛptəbḷ] 形可接受的

Some of his ideas were not acceptable to me.
▶▶ 他的某些想法我無法接受。

accurate [`ækjərɪt] 形正確的；準確的 關 accurately 精準地

Do you know the accurate answer to the math question?
▶▶ 你知道那道數學問題的正確答案嗎？

ache [ek] 名疼痛

The patient suffers from the aches in his joints.
▶▶ 病人苦於關節疼痛。

achieve [ə`tʃiv] 動實現 關 achievement 成就

I hope you can achieve your goal as soon as possible.
▶▶ 我希望你儘早達成目標。

additional [ə`dɪʃənḷ] 形額外的；附加的

Additional remarks are printed in red.
▶▶ 附加記號是用紅色加印上去的。

admire [əd`maɪr] 動欽佩；讚賞

I admire my classmate for his perseverance in learning.
▶▶ 我對我同學的學習毅力相當敬佩。

advanced [əd`vænst] 形先進的；高等的

Ancient Greece was an advanced civilization.
▶▶ 古希臘是個先進的文明。

advantage [əd`væntɪdʒ] 名利益；優勢

Make the best use of your advantages.
▶▶ 善用你的優勢。

adventure [əd`vɛntʃə] 名冒險

I enjoy adventuring all over the world.
▶▶ 我喜愛在世界各地探險。

advertise [`ædvətaɪz] 動宣傳 關 advertisement / ad 廣告

If you want to attract more customers, try advertising in the local paper.
▶▶ 如果你要吸引更多顧客，試試在當地報紙刊登廣告。

advise [əd`vaɪz] 動勸告 關 advisory 諮詢的

My brother advised me not to take their words into consideration.
▶▶ 我哥哥建議我不要在意他們的話。

adviser / advisor [əd`vaɪsə] 名顧問

She has become our adviser.
▶▶ 她已經成為我們的顧問。

afford [ə`ford] 動能夠負擔

Everyone should contribute what he or she can afford.
▶▶ 人人都應該盡自己的能力作貢獻。

afterwards / afterward [`æftəwədz ] / [ `æftəwəd] 副以後

Afterwards, Judy was sorry for what she'd said.
▶▶ 後來茱蒂後悔說了那些話。

agriculture [`ægrɪˌkʌltʃə] 名農業

The strength of a country's economy is related to its agriculture and industry.
▶▶ 一個國家的經濟實力與其工農業息息相關。

airline [`ɛrˌlaɪn] 名航線；航空公司

Melissa's major is airline management.
▶▶ 梅麗莎的主修是航空管理。

Level 1 基礎單字
Level 2 必備單字
Level 3 中級單字
Level 4 進階單字
Level 5 高手單字
Level 6 滿級單字

alley [`ælɪ] 名巷；小徑

The alley was blocked by the crowd.
▶▶ 巷子被人群堵塞。

almond [`ɑmənd] 名杏仁

The pastry chef added some almonds to the cake.
▶▶ 甜點師加了一些杏仁在蛋糕上。

alphabet [`ælfə,bɛt] 名字母

There are 26 letters in the English alphabet.
▶▶ 英文字母有二十六個。

amaze [ə`mez] 動使…吃驚 關 amazement 驚奇

His desire to become a champion amazed me.
▶▶ 他對冠軍的執著使我吃驚。

ambassador [æm`bæsədə] 名大使；使節

An ambassador lives and works in an embassy.
▶▶ 大使在大使館中居住及工作。

ambition [æm`bɪʃən] 名志向

It has always been his ambition to become an engineer.
▶▶ 當工程師一直是他的理想。

ambulance [`æmbjələns] 名救護車

They helped the wounded into ambulances.
▶▶ 他們幫傷者上救護車。

angel [`endʒəl] 名天使

Mary's children are adorable as little angels.
▶▶ 瑪莉的孩子都像小天使一樣可愛。

announce [ə`nauns] 動宣告；公布 關 announcement 公告；聲明

The teacher announced the results of the test.
▶▶ 老師公布了考試的結果。

anxious [`æŋkʃəs] 形 擔憂的

I am anxious about my missing puppy.
▶▶ 我擔心失蹤的小狗。

anyhow [`ɛnɪˌhaʊ] 副 隨便；無論如何

It may snow, but I will go to town anyhow.
▶▶ 即使可能下雪，但我無論如何也要進城。

apart [ə`pɑrt] 副 分散地；遠離地

I don't want to live apart from my family.
▶▶ 我不想跟我的家人分開住。

apologize [ə`pɑləˌdʒaɪz] 動 道歉

I apologize for my bad attitude.
▶▶ 我為我糟糕的態度道歉。

appeal [ə`pil] 名 吸引力 動 呼籲；訴諸 同 petition

名 These subjects have lost their appeal for most students.
對多數的學生來說，這些學科已經失去了吸引力。
動 Politicians at all levels appealed for calm.
各級政治家們都在呼籲保持冷靜。

approve [ə`pruv] 動 批准；認可 同 endorse 衍 endorsement 支持

Maria's parents don't approve of her friends.
▶▶ 瑪麗亞的父母不喜歡她的朋友。

焦點句型 approve of sb./sth. 贊同…；喜歡…

apron [`eprən] 名 圍裙

She tied an apron around her waist.
▶▶ 她將圍裙繫在腰間。

armed [armd] 形 武裝的

The authorities decided to remain neutral in the armed conflict between the two countries.
▶▶ 當局決定在這兩個國家的武裝衝突裡維持中立。

Level 1 基礎單字
Level 2 必備單字
Level 3 中級單字
Level 4 進階單字
Level 5 高手單字
Level 6 滿級單字

arrest [əˋrɛst] 動逮捕 名逮捕

動 The robber was arrested by three policemen.
搶匪遭到三名警察逮捕。

名 The criminal was put under arrest outside the bank.
罪犯在銀行外遭到逮捕。

ash [æʃ] 名灰燼

The town was reduced to ashes in the war.
▶▶ 在戰爭中這座城鎮已化為灰燼。

aside [əˋsaɪd] 副在旁邊

The timid child stood aside looking at his mother closely.
▶▶ 那個怕羞的小孩站在一旁，緊盯著他的媽媽。

assist [əˋsɪst] 動援助 關 assistance 協助

Whenever you need my help, I will assist you.
▶▶ 無論何時你需要我的幫忙，我都會無條件協助你。

assistant [əˋsɪstənt] 名助理

Nancy is my good assistant.
▶▶ 南西是我稱職的助理。

assume [əˋsjum] 動假定

I assume that they are brother and sister.
▶▶ 我猜他們是兄妹。

athlete [ˋæθlit] 名運動員

She is a natural athlete.
▶▶ 她是個天生的運動健將。

attitude [ˋætətjud] 名態度 同 stance

The President's attitude toward the proposals were reflected in his New Year's address.
▶▶ 總統對那些建議的態度反映在他的新年獻詞中。

(焦點句型) attitude toward sb./sth. 對…的態度

attract [ə`trækt] 動 吸引

The handsome and easygoing boy really attracts me.
▶▶ 那個俊俏又隨和的男孩真的很吸引我。

attractive [ə`træktɪv] 形 迷人的

The meal looks attractive in photographs.
▶▶ 這餐點在照片上看起來很吸引人。

audience [`ɔdɪəns] 名 聽眾

His speech attracted a large audience.
▶▶ 他的演講吸引了廣大的聽眾。

automatic [ˌɔtə`mætɪk] 形 自動的

Harry is not used to driving a car without automatic gears.
▶▶ 哈利不習慣開沒有自動排檔的車。

automobile / auto [`ɔtəməˌbɪl ] / [ `ɔto] 名 汽車

The truck used a cable to tow the automobile.
▶▶ 卡車用纜索拖曳汽車。

avenue [`ævənju] 名 大道

Books are avenues to knowledge.
▶▶ 書籍是獲得知識的管道。

awake [ə`wek] 動 喚醒

Suddenly a loud noise awoke us.
▶▶ 突如其來的一聲巨響把我們吵醒了。

awaken [ə`wekən] 動 使⋯覺悟

My teacher's speech awakened us to the importance of a sense of duty.
▶▶ 老師的一席演講使我們認識責任感的重要。

award [ə`wɔrd] 名 獎賞 動 頒獎

名 The actor won an award for his performance.
　　這位演員因他的表演而獲獎。
動 Lisa was awarded the top prize.
　　麗莎榮獲頭獎。

Level 1 基礎單字
Level 2 必備單字
Level 3 中級單字
Level 4 進階單字
Level 5 高手單字
Level 6 滿級單字

aware [ə`wɛr] 形 意識到

He was not aware of the whole affair.
▶▶ 他對整件事情一無所知。

awful [`ɔfəl] 形 可怕的

We had an awful holiday. It rained every day.
▶▶ 我們的假期很糟糕，每天都在下雨。

awkward [`ɔkwəd] 形 笨拙的

The maid was awkward in serving the guests.
▶▶ 女僕對於服侍客人很笨拙。

 **B 字頭中級單字**

MP3 050

background [`bæk͵graʊnd] 名 背景

The choir chanted in the background.
▶▶ 唱詩班在後面唱著讚美詩。

bacon [`bekən] 名 培根；燻肉

I want a bacon cheeseburger.
▶▶ 我想要一個培根起司漢堡。

bacteria [bæk`tɪrɪə] 名 細菌

Bacteria can be harmful or helpful to humans.
▶▶ 細菌對人類有害或有益。
文法解析 bacteria 是 bacterium 的複數形，使用單數形的情況較為罕見。

badly [`bædlɪ] 副 非常地；惡劣地

This fireplace smoked badly.
▶▶ 這個壁爐煙冒得很厲害。

baggage [`bægɪdʒ] 名 行李

Please help me check my baggage before I board the plane.
▶▶ 請在我登機前幫我檢查行李。

bait [bet] 名誘餌 動誘惑

名 Free offers are often used as baits to attract customers.
贈品往往用作吸引顧客的誘餌。

動 He baited the little boy by giving him a lollipop.
他用一根棒棒糖誘惑那個小男孩。

bamboo [bæm`bu] 名竹子

Everything there is made of bamboo.
▶▶ 那裡每樣東西都是用竹子做的。

bang [bæŋ] 動重擊

Paul was banged on the head and injured severely.
▶▶ 保羅的頭部遭到重擊，受了重傷。

banker [`bæŋkə] 名銀行家

Eric became a banker after he got tired of being an engineer.
▶▶ 艾瑞克厭倦了當工程師之後，就成了一名銀行家。

bare [bɛr] 形赤裸的；光禿禿的

The landscape was bare except for some cactus.
▶▶ 除了幾株仙人掌外，周圍景色一片荒涼。

barely [`bɛrlɪ] 副簡直沒；幾乎不能

The food in the hotel was barely edible.
▶▶ 這家旅館的食物簡直不能入口。

barn [bɑrn] 名穀倉

Owing to a spark of a cigarette, the barn was reduced to ashes with its whole store of hay.
▶▶ 由於菸頭未熄，整個穀倉連同裡面存放的乾草全都燒成了灰燼。

barrel [`bærəl] 名大桶

You have eaten so much that your belly will be like a barrel.
▶▶ 你吃了那麼多東西，肚子要像水桶一樣了。

basement [`besmənt] 名地下室

The pipes froze in the basement.
▶▶ 地下室裡的水管結冰了。

Level 1 基礎單字
Level 2 必備單字
Level 3 中級單字
Level 4 進階單字
Level 5 高手單字
Level 6 滿級單字

bay [be] 名 海灣

The bay curved around to the south.
▶▶ 海灣呈弧形向南延伸。

bead [bid] 名 珠子 動 穿成一串

名 The girl is wearing a bead necklace.
女孩戴了一條串珠項鍊。
動 He beaded the pearls into a bracelet.
他把珍珠串成一條手鍊。

beam [bim] 動 放射；發光

Michelle sprang with a scare when the flashlight beamed her.
▶▶ 當手電筒照向米歇爾時，她驚恐地彈跳起來。

beast [bist] 名 野獸

Her husband was a real beast.
▶▶ 她丈夫真是個禽獸。

beetle [`bitl̩] 名 甲蟲

The student watched a beetle on the grass.
▶▶ 學生們在看草地上的一隻甲蟲。

beneath [bɪ`niθ] 介 在…之下

They found the body buried beneath a pile of leaves.
▶▶ 他們發現屍體埋在一堆樹葉下面。

benefit [`bɛnəfɪt] 名 利益

What kind of benefit will I get if I do you the favor?
▶▶ 如果我幫你這個忙，會得到什麼好處？

berry [`bɛrɪ] 名 莓果

Birds feed on nuts and berries in the winter.
▶▶ 鳥類靠堅果和莓果過冬。

besides [bɪ`saɪdz] 介 除了…之外還有 副 並且

介 Do you play any other instruments besides the piano?
除了鋼琴，你還會演奏其他樂器嗎？
副 She has left already. Besides, she doesn't want to see you again.
她早就離開了，況且，她也不想再見到你。

文法解析 besides 做介係詞使用時，是包含所接的名詞的，也就是「除了…還有」的意思；與之類似但不同的有 except（不包含）及 other than 與 apart from（兩者皆可為包含或不包含）

bet [bɛt] 名打賭 動下賭注

名 Let's have a bet on the results of the election.
來為選舉結果打個賭吧！

動 I bet he will win the game.
我打賭他會贏得比賽。

bind [baɪnd] 動綁；包紮

They bound the prisoner's hands behind his back.
▶▶ 他們把囚犯的手綁在背後。

文法解析 bind 動詞三態變化為 bind / bound / bound。

bitter [`bɪtɚ] 形苦的

Good medicine tastes bitter.
▶▶ 良藥苦口。

bleed [blid] 動流血

Susie was bleeding from a gash on her head.
▶▶ 蘇西頭上的傷口在出血。

文法解析 bleed 動詞三態變化為 bleed / bled / bled。

bless [blɛs] 動祝福

May God bless you!
▶▶ 願上帝保佑你！

bloody [`blʌdɪ] 形流血的

Jack came home with a bloody nose.
▶▶ 傑克流著鼻血回到家。

blouse [blauz] 名短衫

The blouse buttons up the back.
▶▶ 這件衣服是從背後扣鈕扣。

bold [bold] 形 大膽的

The woman made a bold comment to the mayor's face.
▶▶ 那位女士當著市長的面做出大膽的評論。

bomb [bɑm] 名 炸彈 動 轟炸

名 Hundreds of bombs were dropped on the city.
幾百枚炸彈投到了這座城市。
動 The enemy bombed the village twice a week.
敵軍一週轟炸那村落兩次。

bookcase [`buk,kes] 名 書架

She put her new book on the bookcase.
▶▶ 她把新書放到書架上。

boot [but] 名 長靴

I'll put my boots in the luggage.
▶▶ 我去把長靴放進行李箱裡。

bore [bor] 動 鑽孔 名 孔

動 They were boring for water.
他們鑿井取水。
名 What can you see through the little bore in the wall?
你能透過這牆上的小孔看到什麼嗎？

bowling [`bolɪŋ] 名 保齡球

Bowling is my favorite game.
▶▶ 保齡球是我最喜愛的運動。

brake [brek] 名 煞車 動 煞車

名 The car accident happened because the brakes weren't working.
車禍發生是因煞車失靈。
動 Hans braked suddenly because he saw a cat scurrying in front of him.
漢斯看見一隻貓從面前竄過，連忙緊急煞車。

brass [bræs] 名 黃銅；銅器

A brass band led the troops.
▶▶ 該團由一支銅管樂隊領導。

bravery [`brevərɪ] 名大膽；勇敢

He received an award for bravery from the police service.
▶▶ 他以其勇敢行為受到警務部門的嘉獎。

breast [brɛst] 名胸膛

They could tell the injured man was still alive because his breast was moving from breathing.
▶▶ 由於傷患胸口還有呼吸起伏，他們判斷他還活著。

breath [brɛθ] 名呼吸

The intensive sight really took our breath away.
▶▶ 那緊張的一幕讓我們屏住了呼吸。

breathe [brið] 動呼吸

Nick breathed deeply before speaking again.
▶▶ 尼克深吸一口氣，然後繼續說下去。

breeze [briz] 名微風

A warm breeze whispered through the trees.
▶▶ 一陣和煦的微風吹過樹林颯颯作響。

brick [brɪk] 名磚頭

This brick is two inches thick.
▶▶ 這磚塊有兩英寸厚。

bride [braɪd] 名新娘

A speech by the bride's father is one of the conventions of a wedding.
▶▶ 由新娘的父親致詞是婚禮的習俗之一。

broadcast [`brɔd͵kæst] 動廣播 名廣播節目

動 The President's speech was broadcast on a national television network.
總統的演說由全國電視聯播網播放。
名 He learned about the earthquake from the broadcast.
他經由廣播得知地震的消息。

brunch [brʌntʃ] 名早午餐

Tracy always gets up late, so she eats brunches.
▶▶ 翠西總是晚起，所以都吃早午餐。

bubble [`bʌbḷ] 名 泡沫

The little child blew soap bubbles with pleasure.
▶▶ 這個小孩興奮地吹著肥皂泡泡。

bucket [`bʌkɪt] 名 水桶

Max came down the hill carrying a bucket of water.
▶▶ 麥克斯提著一桶水下山。

bud [bʌd] 名 芽 動 萌芽

名 In the spring, tiny buds appear on all the trees.
所有樹木在春天都生出嫩芽。
動 The little trees are budding prosperously.
這些小樹正繁茂地萌芽。

budget [`bʌdʒɪt] 名 預算

It is essential for a company to balance its budget.
▶▶ 收支平衡對一間公司而言非常重要。

buffalo [`bʌfəˌlo] 名 水牛

In the past, native Americans hunted buffalo.
▶▶ 在過去，美國土著獵殺水牛。
文法解析 buffalo 單複數同形，複數形也是 buffalo。

buffet [bə`fe] 名 自助餐

Dinner will be a cold buffet, not a sit-down meal.
▶▶ 晚餐是自助冷餐會，不是坐著等服務生送來的那種。

bulb [bʌlb] 名 電燈泡

There's a light bulb missing in the bedroom.
▶▶ 臥室裡少一個電燈泡。

bull [bʊl] 名 公牛

The men ran away when the bull charged after them.
▶▶ 當公牛追在後頭時，人們四散奔逃。

bullet [`bʊlɪt] 名 子彈

A policeman shot a bullet in the robber's leg.
▶▶ 員警開槍射中搶匪腿部。

bump [bʌmp] 動 碰；撞

The two cars bumped into each other at the intersection.
▶▶ 這兩輛車於十字路口相撞。

bunch [bʌntʃ] 名 束；綑；串

On Vicky's birthday, she received a bunch of flowers from her admirer.
▶▶ 薇琪生日那天收到了愛慕者送來的一束花。

bundle [`bʌndl] 名 捆；包裹

I saw my uncle standing on the corner with a bundle of newspaper in his hands.
▶▶ 我看見叔叔提著一捆報紙站在街口。

bury [`bɛrɪ] 動 埋

She wants to be buried in the village graveyard.
▶▶ 她死後希望葬在村子的墓園裡。

bush [buʃ] 名 灌木叢

A bird in the hand is worth two in the bush.
▶▶ 雙鳥在林不如一鳥在手。

buzz [bʌz] 動 發出嗡嗡聲

The flies are buzzing around her annoyingly.
▶▶ 那群蒼蠅在她周圍發出惱人的嗡嗡聲。

 **C 字頭中級單字**

MP3 051

cabin [`kæbɪn] 名 小屋

I want a cabin for two.
▶▶ 我想要一個兩人的小木屋。

cable [`kebl] 名 電纜

The bridge was built with steel cables.
▶▶ 這座橋由鋼索建造而成。

cafeteria [ˌkæfə`tɪrɪə] 名 自助餐廳；自助食堂

I usually have lunch in a cafeteria.
▶▶ 我通常在食堂吃午餐。

1 Level 基礎單字
2 Level 必備單字
3 Level 中級單字
4 Level 進階單字
5 Level 高手單字
6 Level 滿級單字

267

campus [`kæmpəs] 名 校園

You can ride a bike on our campus.
▶▶ 在我們校園內你可以騎腳踏車。

canyon [`kænjən] 名 峽谷

Have you ever been to Grand Canyon National Park in America?
▶▶ 你有去過美國大峽谷國家公園嗎？

capable [`kepəbl] 形 有能力的

Nathan is capable of translating.
▶▶ 內森會翻譯。
(焦點句型) be capable of N./Ving 能夠…

captain [`kæptən] 名 船長；首領

She was captain of the hockey team at school.
▶▶ 她過去是曲棍球校隊的隊長。

capture [`kæptʃə] 動 俘獲；贏得 名 俘獲；採集

動 The gorgeous girl captured my heart.
那位亮麗的女孩攫住了我的心。
名 The soldier played dead to escape capture by the enemy.
那位士兵假死以免被敵人俘虜。

career [kə`rɪr] 名 職業

My aunt has a career in teaching high school English.
▶▶ 我阿姨的工作是高中英語教師。

carpenter [`kɑrpəntə] 名 木匠

The carpenter screwed the hinges to the door.
▶▶ 木匠把絞鏈用螺絲鎖在門上。

carpet [`kɑrpɪt] 名 地毯 動 鋪地毯

名 Turkish carpets are known for their high quality and beautiful patterns.
土耳其地毯以其優良品質與精美花紋而聞名。
動 The maid carpeted the stairs.
女僕在樓梯上鋪上地毯。

carriage [`kærɪdʒ] 名 車；馬車

Not everyone welcomed the horseless carriage.
▶▶ 並不是每一個人都喜歡這種不用馬拉的車。

cart [kɑrt] 名 手推車

She shopped in the supermarket with a cart.
▶▶ 她推著手推車逛超市。

cast [kæst] 動 擲；投 名 演員班底

動 Dorian cast a stone into the river.
多里安朝河裡擲石子。
名 The cast of the latest drama was very strong.
這齣新戲的演員陣容非常強大。

casual [`kæʒʊəl] 形 非正式的；隨意的；偶然的 副 casually 偶爾地

They had a casual meeting in the park.
▶▶ 他們在公園不期而遇。

cattle [`kætl̩] 名 牛群（恆為複數形）

We have put our cattle out to pasture.
▶▶ 我們已經把牛放到牧場上吃草去了。

cave [kev] 名 洞穴

Our ancestors once lived in caves.
▶▶ 我們的祖先曾居住在洞穴裡。

champion [`tʃæmpɪən] 名 冠軍

Kevin is the champion of the swimming competition.
▶▶ 凱文是游泳比賽的冠軍。

charm [tʃɑrm] 名 魅力

Her greatest charm is not her beauty but her personality.
▶▶ 她最大的魅力不在她的美麗，而在個性。

chat [tʃæt] 動 聊天

Stop chatting! The chairperson is starting her speech.
▶▶ 別閒聊了！主席開始演講了。

Level 1 基礎單字
Level 2 必備單字
Level 3 中級單字
Level 4 進階單字
Level 5 高手單字
Level 6 滿級單字

cheek [tʃik] 名臉頰

My boyfriend kissed me on the cheek before leaving.
▶▶ 我的男友在離開前吻了我的臉頰。

cheerful [`tʃɪrfəl] 形愉快的

He is a man of cheerful humor.
▶▶ 他是一個性格開朗幽默的人。

cherry [`tʃɛrɪ] 名櫻桃

Have you heard the story about Washington chopping down the cherry tree?
▶▶ 你聽過華盛頓砍倒櫻桃樹的故事嗎？

chest [tʃɛst] 名箱子

Chris put all his stationery in the delicate chest.
▶▶ 克里斯將所有的文具放入精緻的盒子裡。

chill [tʃɪl] 動使變冷 名寒冷；寒意

動 The night air chilled my bones.
夜裡的空氣寒冷刺骨。
名 Can you bear the chill? I can lend you my sweater.
你耐得住寒冷嗎？我可以借你毛衣。

chilly [`tʃɪlɪ] 形寒冷的；冷淡的

The visitors got a very chilly reception.
▶▶ 客人受到了非常冷淡的接待。

chimney [`tʃɪmnɪ] 名煙囪

The view, over roofs and chimneys, was rather gloomy.
▶▶ 從屋頂和煙囪上望去，景色相當陰暗。

chin [tʃɪn] 名下巴

Fasten the strap under the chin to keep the helmet in place.
▶▶ 把頭盔帶子繫在下巴上以固定頭盔。

chip [tʃɪp] 名碎片 動切

名 Eating fish and chips has become a British institution.
吃炸魚薯條已成為一種英國習俗。
動 The cook chipped the carrot quickly.
廚師迅速地將胡蘿蔔切片。

chop [tʃɑp] 動 砍；劈

I saw him chopping the giant tree.
▶▶ 我瞧見他在砍那棵巨樹。

cigarette [`sɪgəˌrɛt] 名 香菸

Exposure to cigarette smoke can be harmful to one's health.
▶▶ 吸二手菸有害健康。

cinema [`sɪnəmə] 名 電影；電影院

I can't remember last time we went to the cinema.
▶▶ 我不記得我們上次去電影院是什麼時候。

circus [`sɝkəs] 名 馬戲團

Steve is a performer in a circus.
▶▶ 史蒂夫是馬戲團的表演人員。

citizen [`sɪtəzn̩] 名 公民；市民

Citizens are dissatisfied with the new law.
▶▶ 市民們對新法律不滿。

civil [`sɪvl̩] 形 國家的；公民的

We must defend our civil liberties at all costs.
▶▶ 我們必須不惜一切代價捍衛公民自由。

clay [kle] 名 黏土

You can shape the clay into whatever you like.
▶▶ 你可以把黏土塑造成任何你喜歡的形狀。

cleaner [`klinɚ] 名 清潔劑

He washed the dishes with cleaner.
▶▶ 他用清潔劑洗碗。

client [`klaɪənt] 名 客戶

We should try our best to persuade our clients.
▶▶ 我們應該盡其所能說服客戶。

clinic [`klɪnɪk] 名 診所

We need to be at the clinic on Wednesday.
▶▶ 我們星期三必須去診所一趟。

Level 1 基礎單字
Level 2 必備單字
Level 3 中級單字
Level 4 進階單字
Level 5 高手單字
Level 6 滿級單字

clip [klɪp] 名夾子；別針；迴紋針 動剪輯；片段

名 Without a clip, the paper will separate into disorder.
沒有夾子，這些紙張會散得一團亂。

動 Here is a clip from her latest movie.
這是她最近一部電影的片段。

closet [`klɑzɪt] 名櫥櫃

The bartender took some glasses from the closet.
▶▶ 調酒師從櫥櫃裡拿出幾個杯子。

clothe [ˌkloð] 動給…穿衣

I clothed my dear dog on the cold days.
▶▶ 天冷的時候，我為我親愛的狗穿上衣服。

clown [klaʊn] 名小丑

The clown smiled at the children.
▶▶ 小丑對孩子們微笑。

clue [klu] 名線索

The prosecutors investigated the crime carefully by examining every clue.
▶▶ 檢察官檢視每條線索，認真調查這起案件。

coach [kotʃ] 名教練 動指導

名 My coach told me to try again.
教練讓我再試一次。

動 Joyce coaches students in German.
喬伊斯輔導學生學習德語。

cock [kɑk] 名公雞

When the cocks start to crow, it's time to wake up.
▶▶ 當公雞開始啼叫時，人們就該起床了。

cocktail [`kɑkˌtel] 名雞尾酒

What do you think of our special cocktail?
▶▶ 您覺得我們特製的雞尾酒怎麼樣？

coconut [`kokəˌnət] 名椰子

The coconut is particular to the tropics.
▶▶ 椰子是熱帶特有的東西。

collar [`kɑlɚ] 名衣領

Make sure the stain on the collar is removed, please.
▶▶ 請確認衣領上的汙漬都清理掉了。

collection [kə`lɛkʃən] 名收集

The old professor has a large collection of stamps.
▶▶ 那位老教授收藏許多郵票。

colony [`kɑlənɪ] 名殖民地

They created a colony there.
▶▶ 他們在那裡建立了殖民地。

colorful [`kʌləfəl] 形多彩的

I envy her colorful life so much.
▶▶ 我真羨慕她多采多姿的生活。

column [`kɑləm] 名圓柱；專欄

The dome was supported by nine columns.
▶▶ 這座圓頂由九根圓柱支撐。

comfort [`kʌmfət] 名舒適；安慰 動安慰

名 My husband was a great comfort to me when our son was ill.
兒子生病時，丈夫給了我莫大的安慰。
動 We want to comfort Mary, but we don't know what to say.
我們想安慰瑪莉，卻不知道說些什麼。

comma [`kɑmə] 名逗號

The comma between two independent clauses cannot be omitted.
▶▶ 兩個子句之間的逗號不可省略。

committee [kə`mɪtɪ] 名委員會

The committee is composed of five legislators.
▶▶ 這個委員會由五位立法委員組成。

communicate [kə`mjunə͵ket] 動溝通

I tried to communicate with him after the quarrel, but I failed.
▶▶ 我試著在吵架後與他溝通，但失敗了。

1 Level 基礎單字
2 Level 必備單字
3 Level 中級單字
4 Level 進階單字
5 Level 高手單字
6 Level 滿級單字

comparison [kəm`pærəsn̩] 名比較；對照

In comparison with Peter, you have well-proportioned features.
▶▶ 與彼得相比，你擁有勻稱的五官。

(焦點句型) in comparison with sth./sb. 和…相比

compete [kəm`pit] 動競爭

The two TV broadcasting companies have always competed with each other.
▶▶ 那兩家電視廣播公司長期以來互相競爭。

complaint [kəm`plent] 名抱怨 關 complain 抱怨

Our complaints fell on deaf ears.
▶▶ 我們的抱怨無人理會。

concert [`kɑnsət] 名音樂會；演唱會

She lingered after the concert, hoping to meet the star.
▶▶ 音樂會後她徘徊不去，希望能見到明星。

conclusion [kən`kluʒən] 名結論

What was the conclusion of the meeting?
▶▶ 這場會議的結論是什麼？

cone [kon] 名圓錐

Traffic cones were set up on the highway to warn other drivers.
▶▶ 高速公路上設置了交通錐，以警告其他駕駛。

confirm [kən`fɜm] 動證實

Recent court decisions have confirmed the rights of all children.
▶▶ 近來，法律確定了有關兒童的權利。

confuse [kən`fjuz] 動使迷惑

His strange behavior really confused me.
▶▶ 他不尋常的舉止讓我困惑。

connect [kə`nɛkt] 動連接

The towns are connected by train and bus services.
▶▶ 這些城鎮由火車和公車連接起來。

conscious [`kɑnʃəs] 形 意識到的；有意識的

I was conscious that someone was trailing me.
▶▶ 我察覺有人在跟蹤我。

considerable [kən`sɪdərəbḷ] 形 重大的；相當可觀的

There is considerable disagreement over the safety of the treatment.
▶▶ 這種療法的安全性有很大的爭議。

constant [`kɑnstənt] 形 不變的；持續的

Babies need constant attention.
▶▶ 嬰兒需要經常照顧。

continent [`kɑntənənt] 名 大陸

We're going to spend a weekend on the European continent.
▶▶ 我們要去歐洲大陸度過週末。

controller [kən`trolə] 名 管理員

His official job is Financial Controller.
▶▶ 他的職稱是財務管理師。

cooker [`kʊkə] 名 廚具；烹調器具

The cooker isn't working because a part in it is broken.
▶▶ 這個廚具因為零件毀損而無法使用。

costly [`kɔstlɪ] 形 高價的

Stan gave me a costly birthday gift.
▶▶ 斯坦送我一件昂貴的生日禮物。

cotton [`kɑtn̩] 名 棉花

Cotton is a very common type of material.
▶▶ 棉花是種十分常見的材質。

cough [kɔf] 動 咳 名 咳嗽

動 He could not stop coughing.
　 他咳個不停。
名 My father gave a cough as a signal to me.
　 爸爸對我咳嗽示意。

Level 1 基礎單字
Level 2 必備單字
Level 3 中級單字
Level 4 進階單字
Level 5 高手單字
Level 6 滿級單字

countable [`kaʊntəbļ] 形 可數的 反 uncountable

This word is a countable noun.
▶▶ 這個單字是可數名詞。

county [`kaʊntɪ] 名 縣

Sean is our new head of the county.
▶▶ 肖恩是我們的新縣長。

crab [kræb] 名 螃蟹

A crab pinched my finger yesterday.
▶▶ 昨天一隻螃蟹夾了我的手指。

cradle [`kredļ] 名 搖籃 動 輕托；輕抱

名 The mother rocked the baby to sleep in the cradle.
母親輕晃搖籃使嬰兒入睡。
動 The orphan cradled her teddy bear tenderly in her arms.
那孤兒把泰迪熊輕輕抱在懷裡。

crane [kren] 名 起重機

They will have to be moved by crane.
▶▶ 它們得用起重機吊運。

crash [kræʃ] 名 撞擊 動 撞毀

名 A girl was killed yesterday in a crash involving a stolen car.
昨天，一名女孩在一起涉及被盜汽車的車禍中喪生。
動 The truck crashed into the fence.
這輛卡車撞毀在籬笆上。

crawl [krɔl] 動 爬

The platform was crawling with gray-green uniforms.
▶▶ 月臺上擠滿了穿灰綠色制服的人。

creative [krɪ`etɪv] 形 有創造力的 關 create 創造

Mozart was such a creative musician that he composed so many masterpieces.
▶▶ 莫札特是個如此富有創造力的音樂家，譜出了這麼多傑作。

creator [krɪ`etɚ] 名 創造者

Christians believe that God is the creator of everything.
▶▶ 基督徒相信上帝是一切的創造者。

creature [`kritʃə] 名 生物

The dormouse is a shy nocturnal creature.
▶▶ 榛睡鼠是一種在夜間活動的膽小動物。

credit [`krɛdɪt] 名 信用;信賴 動 相信 關 credit card 信用卡

名 Your credit limit is now 200 dollars.
你的信用額度現在為二百美元。
動 No one credited the liar again.
沒有人再相信那個騙子的話。

crew [kru] 名 全體工作人員;全體船員

The passengers and crew were rescued by a lifeboat.
▶▶ 乘客及船員都被救生艇救出。

cricket [`krɪkɪt] 名 蟋蟀

Do you hear the crickets?
▶▶ 你聽到蟋蟀的鳴聲了嗎?

criminal [`krɪmənḷ] 形 犯罪的 名 罪犯

形 He specialized in criminal law.
他專攻刑法。
名 The villagers beat the criminal in anger.
村民們看到嫌犯時都憤怒地揍他。

crispy [`krɪspɪ] 形 脆的

I will suggest the crispy fried duck.
▶▶ 我建議你點香酥鴨。

crop [krɑp] 名 農作物

They get two crops of rice a year.
▶▶ 他們一年收穫兩季稻米。

crown [kraʊn] 名 王冠 動 加冕

名 The king wore a crown at official ceremonies.
國王出席官方儀式時頭戴王冠。
動 We saw the archbishop crowning the queen.
我們看見大主教替皇后加冕。

Level 1 基礎單字
Level 2 必備單字
Level 3 中級單字
Level 4 進階單字
Level 5 高手單字
Level 6 滿級單字

cruel [`kruəl] 形殘酷的 同 ruthless / relentless

The cruel man slapped his wife in the face.
▶▶ 那個殘忍的男人打了妻子一個耳光。

cupboard [`kʌbəd] 名櫥櫃；壁櫥

The naughty boy pushed over the cupboard.
▶▶ 頑皮的男孩弄倒了櫥櫃。

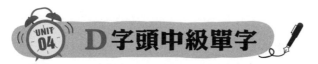

D 字頭中級單字

MP3 052

dairy [`dɛrɪ] 形乳製品的 名酪農場；乳製品

形 The company puts an emphasis on the dairy products.
公司將重心放在乳製品上。
名 The farmer went to his dairy at dawn.
農夫天剛亮便前往酪農場。

dam [dæm] 名水壩 動堵塞

名 Few creations of big technology capture people's attention like giant dams.
很少有重大的技術發明能像大型水壩這樣抓住人們的注意力。
動 The stream was dammed up.
這條溪被堵住了。

dare [dɛr] 動敢

I dare say that he will come.
▶▶ 我敢說他會來。

darling [`dɑrlɪŋ] 名親愛的人 形可愛的

名 Darling, this is my handmade present for you.
親愛的，這是我送你的手工禮物。
形 Teresa was amazed by the darling ornaments.
泰瑞莎對這些可愛的裝飾品感到驚奇。

dash [dæʃ] 動猛衝

All of his friends tried to block him, but he dashed through them excitedly.
▶▶ 他所有的朋友都來攔他，但他依然興奮地衝了過去。

dawn [dɔn] 名黎明 動變得明朗

名 I must get up at dawn.
我必須必須在黎明時分起床。
動 It dawned on me what he really meant.
我突然頓悟他真正的意思。

(焦點句型) it dawned on sb. + that 子句（某人）頓悟…

dealer [`dɪlə] 名商人 關 deal 交易

In the market, dealers were bargaining with growers over the price of coffee.
▶▶ 在市場上，商人正和種植者就咖啡的價格進行商談。

decade [`dɛked] 名十年

I finally saw him after a decade. We both had become old.
▶▶ 十年後我終於再見到他，我們倆都變老了。

deck [dɛk] 名甲板

As the storm began, everyone was below deck.
▶▶ 暴風雨來臨時，所有的人都躲到甲板下面去了。

decorate [`dɛkəˌret] 動裝飾 關 decoration 裝飾品

She decorated her dress with a brooch.
▶▶ 她用胸針裝飾洋裝。

decrease [dɪ`kris ] / [ `dikris] 動減少 名減少

動 The rate of inflation decreased to 3% last year.
去年通貨膨脹率降低為百分之三。
名 The decrease in clients made the company fall into bankruptcy.
客戶減少使公司破產了。

deed [did] 名行為；行動

I don't approve of his rude words and deeds.
▶▶ 我不認同他粗魯的言行。

deepen [`dipən] 動加深

The gloom deepened as the election results came in.
▶▶ 選舉結果陸續傳來，沮喪的心情越來越沉重。

Level 1 基礎單字
Level 2 必備單字
Level 3 中級單字
Level 4 進階單字
Level 5 高手單字
Level 6 滿級單字

definition [ˌdɛfəˋnɪʃən] 名定義

Can you give a more precise definition of the word?
▶▶ 你能給這個詞下個更確切的定義嗎？

democracy [dɪˋmɑkrəsɪ] 名民主制度

In a democracy, people elect their own leaders.
▶▶ 在民主制度下，人民可以自選領袖。

democratic [ˌdɛməˋkrætɪk] 形民主的

My friends share the same democratic ideals as me.
▶▶ 我的朋友們和我有一樣的民主理想。

deposit [dɪˋpɑzɪt] 名訂金；存款 動存入

名 You must pay a deposit if you want to reserve the room.
你要預訂房間，就必須先付訂金。
動 You should deposit your savings in the bank.
你應該把錢存到銀行裡。

designer [dɪˋzaɪnɚ] 名設計師

The No. 5 designer impressed me with her proficiency.
▶▶ 五號設計師純熟的技巧使我印象深刻。

desirable [dɪˋzaɪrəbl̩] 形合意的

Experience is desirable but not essential for this job.
▶▶ 做這份工作以有經驗為佳，但並非必要。

desire [dɪˋzaɪr] 名渴望 同aspire

I have no desire to see that movie.
▶▶ 我不想看那部電影。

dessert [dɪˋzɜt] 名甜點

My mother served my friends dessert.
▶▶ 媽媽用甜點招待我的朋友。

destroy [dɪˋstrɔɪ] 動摧毀

The typhoon destroyed the houses.
▶▶ 颱風毀了那些房子。

detect [dɪˋtɛkt] 動 發現

I detect a letter in the mailbox.
▶▶ 我發現信箱裡有封信。

determine [dɪˋtɜmɪn] 動 決定 關 determination 果斷；決心

When will you determine whether you will buy this book or not?
▶▶ 你什麼時候才能決定要不要買這本書？

devil [ˋdɛvḷ] 名 惡魔

They believed she was possessed by the devil.
▶▶ 他們認為她是被魔鬼附身。

dim [dɪm] 形 暗淡的；昏暗的 動（使）變暗

形 The dim room looked rather depressing.
昏暗的房間顯得相當壓抑。
動 The lights dimmed as the show was about to begin.
表演即將開始時，燈光暗了下來。

dime [daɪm] 名 一角硬幣

A dime is equivalent to ten cents.
▶▶ 一角等於十分。

dine [daɪn] 動 用餐

The manager's going to dine with us tonight.
▶▶ 今晚經理要和我們一起吃飯。

dinosaur [ˋdaɪnəˌsɔr] 名 恐龍

Do you know why all the dinosaurs died a long time ago?
▶▶ 你知道為什麼很久以前所有恐龍都滅絕了嗎？

dip [dɪp] 動 浸；浸泡

Julie dipped her toe into the pool to see how cold it was.
▶▶ 茱莉把腳趾伸進游泳池看水有多冷。

dirt [dɜt] 名 塵埃

Sweep away the dirt that is on the furniture.
▶▶ 把家具上的灰塵掃掉。

Level 1 基礎單字
Level 2 必備單字
Level 3 中級單字
Level 4 進階單字
Level 5 高手單字
Level 6 滿級單字

discount [`dɪskaʊnt] 名折扣 動減價

名 The customer asked the sales clerk for a discount.
客人要求店員打折。

動 That store discounts all its merchandise.
那間店所有的商品全部打折。

dishonest [dɪs`ɑnɪst] 形不誠實

I would rather remain poor than get money by dishonest means.
▶▶ 我寧可安於貧窮，也不願用不當手段賺錢。

disc / disk [dɪsk] 名唱片

Compact disc recordings give excellent sound reproduction.
▶▶ 雷射唱片播放的聲音保真度很高。

dislike [dɪs`laɪk] 動討厭 名反感

動 I dislike physical punishment.
我不喜歡體罰。

名 He has a dislike of vegetables.
他不喜歡吃蔬菜。

ditch [dɪtʃ] 名排水溝 動拋棄；丟棄

名 Megan drove into the ditch by accident.
梅根意外把車開進了水溝裡。

動 The government decided to ditch the plan.
政府決定放棄該計畫。

dive [daɪv] 動跳水；潛水 名跳水；潛水

動 Jacob dove into the river to retrieve his precious necklace.
雅各潛到河裡撿拾他珍貴的項鍊。

名 He prepared for the dive by checking his equipment thoroughly.
他透過仔細檢查裝備來為潛水做好準備。

文法解析 dive動詞三態變化為dive / dove / dove。

dizzy [`dɪzɪ] 形暈眩的

She felt too dizzy to stand.
▶▶ 她感到太暈而無法站直。

dock [dɑk] 名碼頭 動停泊

名 Meet me at 9 o'clock tonight at the dock.
今晚九點在碼頭等我。
動 The ship was docked at Seattle.
船停泊在西雅圖。

dolphin [`dɑlfɪn] 名海豚

Do you think it would be an idea to name the ship "Dolphin"?
▶▶ 你看把這艘船命名為「海豚號」怎麼樣？

donkey [`dɑŋkɪ] 名驢子

The merchant made the donkey carry his package on its back.
▶▶ 商人讓驢子馱著他的包裹。

dose [dos] 名一劑藥量 動給…開藥；給…用藥

名 Take a dose once after dinner.
晚餐後一次服一劑藥。
動 She dosed up the children with cough syrup.
她把止咳糖漿給孩子們吃。
(焦點句型) dose sb. (up) with sth. 給…服用（藥物）

doubtful [`dautfəl] 形懷疑的；有疑慮的

The interviewee is doubtful about telling all the truth.
▶▶ 受訪者對於是否交代所有實情心存疑慮。

doughnut [`do͵nʌt] 名甜甜圈

Elizabeth bought three doughnuts for breakfast.
▶▶ 伊莉莎白買了三個甜甜圈當早餐。

downtown [͵daun`taun] 副在市中心

His concert will take place downtown.
▶▶ 他的演唱會將於市中心舉行。

drag [dræg] 動拖、拉 同 shuffle

The box was so heavy that we had to drag it along the floor.
▶▶ 這箱子很重，我們不得不在地板上拖著走。

Level 1 基礎單字
Level 2 必備單字
Level 3 中級單字
Level 4 進階單字
Level 5 高手單字
Level 6 滿級單字

dragonfly [`drɑgən,flaɪ] 名蜻蜓

A dragonfly is flying high in the sky.
▶▶ 蜻蜓在空中飛舞。

drain [dren] 動排出 名排水管

動 The whole area will have to be drained before it can be used for farming.
整個地區都要排澇才能用來耕種。
名 Several mice rushed into the drain.
幾隻老鼠竄進排水管內。

dramatic [drə`mætɪk] 形戲劇性的

The incident turned out to be a dramatic result.
▶▶ 這件事最終以戲劇化的結局收尾。

drip [drɪp] 動滴下 名水滴

動 Water was dripping down through the roof.
水從屋頂上滴下來。
名 I found a drip on my face. Is it raining?
我發現臉上有水滴，下雨了嗎？

drown [draʊn] 動淹沒

A drowning man will catch at a straw.
▶▶ 溺水的人連一根稻草都會抓。

drugstore [`drʌg,stor] 名藥房 同 pharmacy

She bought some lipstick from the drugstore.
▶▶ 她在藥妝店買了一些口紅。

drunk [drʌŋk] 形酒醉的 名酒鬼；酗酒者

形 Sam was drunk on only two cans of beer.
山姆喝兩罐啤酒就醉了。
名 Cindy was scared by two drunks on the street.
辛迪在街上被兩個醉漢嚇到了。

dumb [dʌm] 形啞的

The dumb girl tried to convey something with her hands.
▶▶ 那個啞女孩試著用手勢傳達些什麼。

dump [dʌmp] 動 拋下 名 垃圾場

動 Nuclear waste should not be dumped in the sea.
核廢料不該倒入大海。

名 The poor cat lingered in the dump to find something to eat.
這隻可憐的貓在垃圾場徘徊覓食。

dumpling [`dʌmplɪŋ] 名 餃子

Ray ordered ten dumplings and a bowl of soup.
▶▶ 雷點了十個餃子和一碗湯。

dust [dʌst] 名 灰塵 動 擦去…的灰塵

名 A picky person hates dust.
吹毛求疵的人討厭灰塵。

動 He dusted the desk.
他掃去桌上的塵土。

 **E 字頭中級單字**

MP3 053

eager [`igə] 形 渴望的 關 eagerly 渴望地

Wendy listened to the story with eager attention.
▶▶ 溫蒂津津有味地聽著故事。

echo [`ɛko] 名 回音 動 發出回音

名 There was an echo on the line, and I couldn't hear clearly.
電話裡有回音，我聽不清楚。

動 The gunshot echoed through the forest.
槍炮聲在林中迴盪。

edit [`ɛdɪt] 動 編輯

I spent all week editing the magazine.
▶▶ 我花了一整個禮拜編寫這本雜誌。

editor [`ɛdɪtə] 名 編輯者

Emily is one of the editors of that well-known publisher.
▶▶ 愛蜜莉是那間知名出版社的編輯之一。

Level 1 基礎單字
Level 2 必備單字
Level 3 中級單字
Level 4 進階單字
Level 5 高手單字
Level 6 滿級單字

educate [ˋɛdʒʊˌket] 動 教育 關 education 教育

Their children were educated at a private school.
>> 他們的子女都上私立學校。

educational [ˌɛdʒʊˋkeʃənl] 形 教育性的

The documentary films broadcast on the channel are educational.
>> 這個頻道播映的紀錄片頗富教育性。

efficient [ɪˋfɪʃənt] 形 有效率的

This machine is more efficient than that one.
>> 這台機器工作效率比那台更高。

elbow [ˋɛlbo] 名 手肘

Be careful; don't touch the cut on my elbow.
>> 小心點，別碰到我手肘上的傷口。

elderly [ˋɛldəlɪ] 形 上了年紀的 關 elder 年長的

He was rather elderly with gray hair and blue eyes.
>> 他上了年紀，頭髮花白，眼眸湛藍。

elect [ɪˋlɛkt] 動 選擇

Elliot was elected as our class leader.
>> 艾略特被選為我們的班長。

election [ɪˋlɛkʃən] 名 選舉

The elections are scheduled for mid-June.
>> 選舉定於六月中旬舉行。

electricity [ɪˌlɛkˋtrɪsətɪ] 名 電

The electricity is off.
>> 停電了。

electronic [ɪlɛkˋtrɑnɪk] 形 電子的

Bob enjoys dancing to electronic music.
>> 鮑伯喜歡跟著電子音樂起舞。

element [ˋɛləmənt] 名 要素

There's always an element of risk in this sort of investment.
▶▶ 這種投資總帶有危險的成分。

elevator [ˋɛlə͵vetə] 名 電梯 關 escalator 電扶梯

The elevator is out of order. Let's take the escalator.
▶▶ 電梯故障了，我們搭電扶梯吧。

emergency [ɪˋmɝdʒənsɪ] 名 緊急情況

In case of emergency, please press the alarm bell.
▶▶ 遇到緊急情況時，請按下警鈴。

emotional [ɪˋmoʃənl] 形 情緒（上）的；情感強烈的

My friends always give me emotional support.
▶▶ 我的朋友總是給我精神上的支持。

emperor [ˋɛmpərə] 名 皇帝

Nero was an infamous emperor.
▶▶ 尼祿是個惡名昭彰的皇帝。

enable [ɪnˋebl] 動 使能夠

The conference will enable greater international cooperation.
▶▶ 這次會議能促進國際間的合作。

energetic [͵ɛnəˋdʒɛtɪk] 形 有精力的 關 energy 能源；能量

Tina was so energetic that no one believed she had stayed up so late last night.
▶▶ 蒂娜非常有活力，沒有人相信她前一天熬夜到很晚。

engage [ɪnˋgedʒ] 動 雇用；佔用；訂婚 關 engagement 預約；訂婚

My daughter is engaged to a nice young doctor.
▶▶ 我的女兒和一位不錯的年輕醫生訂了婚。

enjoyable [ɪnˋdʒɔɪəbl] 形 愉快的

We had a most enjoyable journey.
▶▶ 我們有一次非常愉快的旅行。

Level 1 基礎單字
Level 2 必備單字
Level 3 中級單字
Level 4 進階單字
Level 5 高手單字
Level 6 滿級單字

entry [`ɛntrɪ] 名入口

Excuse me. Do you know where the entry is?
▶▶ 不好意思，請問你知道入口在哪裡嗎？

envy [`ɛnvɪ] 名羨慕；嫉妒 動羨慕

名 He criticized her harshly out of envy.
出於嫉妒，他尖酸地批評她。
動 I envy you so much for traveling around the world.
我好羨慕你到全世界旅行。

erase [ɪ`res] 動擦掉

Don't erase the letters on blackboard!
▶▶ 別把黑板上的字擦掉！

excellence [`ɛksələns] 名優點；傑出

I appreciate his excellence in design.
▶▶ 我欣賞他的設計長才。
(焦點句型) excellence in sth. 有⋯的長才

exchange [ɪks`tʃendʒ] 動交換 名交換；交易所

動 Things on sale are not allowed to be exchanged.
特價品是不能退換的。
名 The activities of stock exchanges are regulated by law.
證券交易所的活動受到法律約束。

exhibition [ˌɛksə`bɪʃən] 名展覽

We went to the exhibition of Miller's paintings.
▶▶ 我們去參觀米勒畫展。

expectation [ˌɛkspɛk`teʃən] 名期望

We are confident in our expectation of a full recovery.
▶▶ 我們滿懷信心地期待著完全恢復。

experiment [ɪk`spɛrəmənt] 名實驗 動實驗

名 I wonder what the result of their long-term experiment will be.
我想知道他們長期實驗的結果。
動 Alice experiments on a large numbers of rats.
愛麗絲以大量的老鼠進行實驗。

explode [ɪk`splod] 動 爆炸 關 explosion 爆炸

Many boys explode firecrackers during the Lantern Festival.
>> 許多男孩在元宵節放鞭炮。

explore [ɪk`splor] 動 探查；探險

They went on an expedition to explore the Amazon River.
>> 他們遠赴亞馬遜河探險。

export [ɪks`port ] / [ `ɛksport] 動 輸出 名 出口

動 We export oil to the neighboring countries.
　我們出口石油到鄰國。
名 The government is planning to develop our export market.
　政府正在計劃拓展我們的出口市場。

expressive [ɪk`sprɛsɪv] 形 富有表情的；有表現力的

This opera is expressive of a mixture of despair and loneliness.
>> 這齣歌劇表現出一種絕望與孤獨交織的情感。

(焦點句型) be expressive of sth. 表現出（某種情感）

extreme [ɪk`strim] 形 極度的 名 極端的事 關 extremely 極度地

形 It is very unhealthy for you to be under extreme stress for a long time.
　長期處於極大的壓力之下，對你非常不健康。
名 This country has such extremes of wealth and poverty that I could not even imagine.
　這個國家的貧富差距之懸殊，簡直令我難以想像。

F字頭中級單字

MP3 054

fade [fed] 動 凋謝；褪色

Any memory of her childhood had faded from her mind.
>> 她童年的一切記憶都逐漸從腦海中消逝了。

faint [fent] 形 微弱的 動 昏厥

形 A faint blush came into her cheeks.
　她的臉色漸顯紅暈。
動 The father fainted when he heard of his son's death.
　聽到兒子的死訊時，父親昏了過去。

1 Level 基礎單字
2 Level 必備單字
3 Level 中級單字
4 Level 進階單字
5 Level 高手單字
6 Level 滿級單字

fairly [ˋfɛrlɪ] 副 公平地

Stuart told the facts fairly.
▶▶ 史都華實事求是地敘述這些事實。

fairy [ˋfɛrɪ] 名 小仙子；小精靈 形 仙女似的

名 Little Linda likes to read stories about fairies.
小琳達喜歡讀有關小仙子的故事。
形 The fairy princess captivated her admirers.
那位仙女般的公主擄獲了一眾愛慕者的心。

faith [feθ] 名 信任

I have faith in the future.
▶▶ 我對未來懷抱信心。

(焦點句型) have faith in sb./sth. 對⋯有信心

fake [fek] 形 冒充的 動 仿造

形 Fake designer watches are sold at a fraction of the price of the genuine articles.
名牌手錶贗品的售價僅為真品的幾分之一。
動 He faked his father's signature and signed the transcript.
他仿造爸爸的字跡在成績單上簽名。

familiar [fəˋmɪljɚ] 形 熟悉的

I'm pretty familiar with the scenery in my hometown.
▶▶ 我對家鄉的景色很熟悉。

fancy [ˋfænsɪ] 形 花俏的；豪華的 名 想像力；愛好

The decorations are too fancy for my taste.
▶▶ 以我的品味來說，那些裝飾太花俏了。

fare [fɛr] 名 費用

As the oil prices rise, bus fare is becoming more expensive.
▶▶ 隨著油價上漲，公車票價也變貴了。

farther [ˋfɑrðɚ] 副 更遠地 形 更遠的

副 We can't move farther with this out-of-date policy.
我們不能再繼續執行這項過時的政策了。
形 My home is farther from here than the station.
我家比車站離這裡更遠。

fashionable [`fæʃənəbḷ] 形 流行的

It's fashionable to go to Switzerland for the holidays.
▶▶ 去瑞士渡假現正風行。

faucet [`fɔsɪt] 名 水龍頭

Water is dripping from that leaky faucet.
▶▶ 水正從漏水的水龍頭滴下來。

fearful [`fɪrfəl] 形 嚇人的

Leslie is wearing a fearful mask.
▶▶ 萊斯利帶著一個可怕的面具。

feather [`fɛðɚ] 名 羽毛

Birds of a feather flock together.
▶▶ 物以類聚。

fence [fɛns] 名 圍牆 動 防衛

名 Roy built a fence around the garden.
　　羅伊在花園周圍築起了圍籬。
動 His property is fenced with wire.
　　他在房地四周圍有帶刺的鐵絲網。

fighter [`faɪtɚ] 名 戰士

Mona Rudao was a heroic fighter against Japan.
▶▶ 莫那魯道是個英勇的抗日戰士。

firework [`faɪr͵wɜk] 名 煙火

On New Year's Eve, the display of fireworks is amazing.
▶▶ 除夕夜的煙火很吸引人。

fist [fɪst] 名 拳頭 動 拳打；緊握 關 clench 握緊；捏緊；咬緊 / tremble 顫抖

名 Sandy clenched her fists to stop herself from trembling.
　　珊迪緊握拳頭，克制顫抖。
動 He fisted the post and then cried out.
　　他朝柱子上揮拳，然後放聲大哭。

flame [flem] 名 火焰 動 燃燒；（感情）爆發；（臉）泛紅

名 The flames were growing higher and higher.
　　火焰愈來愈大。

Level 1 基礎單字
Level 2 必備單字
Level 3 中級單字
Level 4 進階單字
Level 5 高手單字
Level 6 滿級單字

flash [flæʃ] 動閃亮 名閃光

動 I saw her diamond necklace flashing.
我看見她的鑽石項鍊閃亮著。
名 This camera has a built-in flash.
這種照相機有內置式閃光燈。

flashlight [`flæʃˌlaɪt] 名手電筒

They use flashlights at night.
▶▶ 他們在晚上使用手電筒。

flavor [`flevɚ] 名味道 動給⋯調味

名 Are there any choices of different flavors?
有不同口味的選擇嗎？
動 The cook flavored the sauce with salt and pepper.
廚師在醬汁裡加了鹽和胡椒以增添風味。

flesh [flɛʃ] 名肉；果肉

Tigers are flesh-eating animals.
▶▶ 虎是肉食性動物。

float [flot] 動漂浮

There is an empty boat floating on the river.
▶▶ 河裡漂浮著一艘空船。

flock [flɑk] 名禽群；人群

A flock of wild geese flew overhead.
▶▶ 一群野雁從頭頂飛過。

flood [flʌd] 名洪水 動淹沒

名 In 1975, the floods in that area made 200,000 people homeless.
一九七五年該地區的洪水使得二十萬人無家可歸。
動 The meadows were flooded when the storm came.
暴風雨一來，草地就被淹沒了。

flour [`flaʊr] 名麵粉

Flour is an important ingredient for cake and bread.
▶▶ 麵粉是蛋糕和麵包不可或缺的材料。

flute [flut] 名笛子

The child is playing his flute.
▶▶ 那孩子在吹著他的笛子。

foggy [`fɑgɪ] 形多霧的

It is very dangerous to drive on such foggy days.
▶▶ 在多霧的日子裡開車非常危險。

fold [fold] 動折疊

Ken is standing with his arms folded.
▶▶ 凱恩雙手交叉地站著。

follower [`fɑləwə] 名跟隨者

The old man is a faithful follower of his home football team.
▶▶ 那老翁是他家鄉足球隊的忠實擁護者。

fond [fɑnd] 形喜歡的

Jimmy is fond of cooking.
▶▶ 吉米喜歡烹飪。
(焦點句型) be fond of N./Ving 喜歡…

forever [fə`ɛvə] 副永遠

Will you love me forever?
▶▶ 你會永遠愛我嗎？

fortune [`fɔrtʃən] 名運氣；財富

The soothsayer told my fortune by reading my palm.
▶▶ 占卜師看手相幫我算命。

fountain [`faʊntṇ] 名噴泉

The fountain set in the middle of the garden is beautiful.
▶▶ 花園中央的噴泉很漂亮。

Level 1 基礎單字
Level 2 必備單字
Level 3 中級單字
Level 4 進階單字
Level 5 高手單字
Level 6 滿級單字

frank [fræŋk] 形 率直的；真誠的

Thank you for your frank apology.
▶▶ 謝謝你真誠的道歉。

freeze [friz] 動 凍結

It's so cold that even the river has frozen.
▶▶ 天氣冷得河水都結冰了。
文法解析 freeze動詞三態變化為 freeze / froze / frozen。

freezer [`frizɚ] 名 冷凍庫

We keep frozen food in a freezer.
▶▶ 我們在冷凍庫裡保存冷凍食品。

frequent [`frikwənt] 形 常有的

We have frequent meetings on weekends.
▶▶ 我們週末經常見面。

fright [fraɪt] 名 驚恐

The snake really created a fright.
▶▶ 這隻蛇引發恐慌。

frighten [`fraɪtn̩] 動 使震驚

I was totally frightened by his sudden death.
▶▶ 他突如其來的死訊令我震驚不已。

fuel [`fjuəl] 名 燃料 動 燃料補給

名 The most widely used car fuel is gasoline.
　最廣泛使用的汽車燃料是汽油。
動 The helicopter was already fueled and ready to go.
　直升機已加好油，準備起飛。

fund [fʌnd] 名 資金 動 資助 關 subsidize 補助

名 Where will the funds come from?
　資金會從哪來？
動 A man of wealth funds the private school.
　有富翁資助這間私立學校。

fur [fɝ] 名毛皮

That cat has soft white fur.
▶▶ 那隻貓有著柔軟的白色毛皮。

 G 字頭中級單字

MP3 055

gallon [`gælən] 名加侖

My car does forty miles to the gallon.
▶▶ 我的汽車每加侖汽油跑四十英里。

gamble [`gæmbl̩] 動賭博 名賭博

動 Many people visit Las Vegas to gamble their money.
許多人去拉斯維加斯賭博。
名 He took a gamble and lost a lot of money.
他孤注一擲，結果損失了一大筆錢。

gang [gæŋ] 名一隊；一群

A gang of workmen sat on the stairs relaxing.
▶▶ 一群工人坐在樓梯上休息。

gap [gæp] 名差距；缺口

There is no generation gap between my grandmother and me.
▶▶ 我和祖母之間沒有代溝。

garage [gə`rɑʒ] 名車庫

Dylan parked his car in the garage.
▶▶ 迪倫把車停在車庫。

gasoline / gas [`gæsl̩͵in] / [gæs] 名汽油 同 petrol

Gasoline powers the engines.
▶▶ 汽油帶給發動機動力。

geography [dʒi`ɑgrəfɪ] 名地理（學）關 geographical 地理的

The geography of Taiwan includes many mountains.
▶▶ 台灣的地理形勢有許多山脈。

gesture [`dʒɛstʃɚ] 名手勢；姿勢 動打手勢

名 A handshake is a gesture of friendship.
握手是友善的表示。
動 He gestured excitedly to encourage me to go more quickly.
他激動地打著手勢叫我快走。

glance [glæns] 動瞥視 名一瞥

動 Fiona glanced at the envelope and then tore it up.
費歐娜瞄了一下信封便把它撕掉。
名 Jason left without a glance at me.
傑森離開前一眼也沒看我。

(焦點句型) at first glance 乍看之下

global [`globl] 形全球的

The greenhouse effect is a global issue.
▶▶ 溫室效應是個全球議題。

glory [`glorɪ] 名光榮 動洋洋得意

名 The glory that goes with wealth doesn't last; virtue is a possession glorious and eternal.
錢財帶來的榮耀只是一時的，美德才是永恆的榮耀。
動 My family gloried in my success.
全家都為我的成功驕傲。

glow [glo] 動發光 名光輝

動 The moon glowed softly.
月亮散發柔和的光芒。
名 The glow in the dark guided me in the right direction.
黑暗中的亮光指引我正確的方向。

golf [gɑlf] 名高爾夫球 動打高爾夫球

名 My boss invited me to play golf on Sunday.
老闆約我星期天去打高爾夫球。
動 They go golfing every weekend.
他們每週末都打高爾夫球。

gossip [`gɑsəp] 動閒聊；說閒話

Hanna gossiped with her neighbors.
▶▶ 漢娜和鄰居閒聊了一會兒。

governor [`gʌvənə] 名統治者

We have to elect the best governor for our country.
▶▶ 我們必須為國家選出最好的統治者。

grab [græb] 動急抓

She tried to grab at the branch, but missed and fell.
▶▶ 她試著抓住樹枝，但沒抓著，就跌倒了。

graduate [`grædʒu,et] 名畢業生 動畢業

名 My cousin is a graduate of Harvard University.
　　我表姐是哈佛大學畢業生。
動 Mr. Lu graduated from high school three years ago.
　　盧先生三年前從高中畢業。

grasp [græsp] 動緊握

The salesman grasped my hand warmly.
▶▶ 銷售員熱情地跟我握手。

grasshopper [`græs,hɑpə] 名蚱蜢

I hadn't seen a grasshopper for years since I moved into the city.
▶▶ 搬進城裡後，我有好幾年沒見過蚱蜢了。

grassy [`græsɪ] 形多草的

We used to play around at the grassy hillside.
▶▶ 我們曾在那長滿青草的山坡上玩耍。

greedy [`gridɪ] 形貪婪的

They lured the greedy businessman with money.
▶▶ 他們用錢誘惑那個貪婪的商人。

greenhouse [`grin,haʊs] 名溫室

Carbon dioxide is one kind of greenhouse gas.
▶▶ 二氧化碳是一種溫室氣體。

grin [grɪn] 名露齒而笑 動露齒而笑

名 The infant gave me a grin of innocence.
　　這個嬰兒天真地朝我咧嘴一笑。
動 She grinned at me as she came into the room.
　　她走進房間的時候，朝我露齒一笑。

Level 1 基礎單字
Level 2 必備單字
Level 3 中級單字
Level 4 進階單字
Level 5 高手單字
Level 6 滿級單字

grocery [`grosərɪ] 名 雜貨；雜貨店

That grocery store is full of my childhood memories.
▶▶ 那間雜貨店滿是我的童年回憶。

guidance [`gaɪdn̩s] 名 引導；指導

Dennis did the work with his teacher's guidance.
▶▶ 丹尼斯在老師的指導下做這件工作。

gum [gʌm] 名 口香糖

Some students refresh themselves by chewing gum.
▶▶ 有些學生靠嚼口香糖振奮精神。

H 字頭中級單字　　MP3 056

hairdresser [`hɛr,drɛsɚ] 名 理髮師

I let that new hairdresser loose on my hair and look what she did!
▶▶ 我讓那個新來的理髮師大顯身手，看看她都做了什麼！

hallway [`hɔl,we] 名 門廳

Walking down the hallway, she headed to the front door.
▶▶ 她往下走去門廳，然後向前門走去。

hammer [`hæmɚ] 名 鐵鎚 動 （用鎚子）敲擊

名 The angry man attacked others with a hammer.
　　那個憤怒的人以鐵鎚攻擊人。
動 The craftsman hammered the nail into the board.
　　工匠把釘子釘進木板裡。

handful [`hændfəl] 名 少量；少數

We invited many people, but only a handful came.
▶▶ 我們邀了很多人，卻只有少數人前來。

handkerchief [`hæŋkɚ,tʃɪf] 名 手帕

She wiped the tears on her face with a handkerchief.
▶▶ 她用手帕把眼淚擦掉。

handy [ˋhændɪ] 形 有用的；方便的

There is a handy storage compartment beneath the oven.
▶▶ 在烤箱的下面有一個便利的櫥櫃。

hanger [ˋhæŋɚ] 名 衣架；掛鉤

I took my hat from the hanger before I left.
▶▶ 我離開前從掛鉤上取走帽子。

harbor [ˋhɑrbɚ] 名 港灣

There were many ships in the harbor.
▶▶ 港口內停泊著不少船隻。

harm [hɑrm] 動 傷害 名 傷害

動 Calm down, or you will harm those who love you most!
冷靜，不然你會傷了最愛你的人們。
名 Don't worry; I will prevent you from coming to harm.
別擔心，我不會讓你受到傷害的。

harmful [ˋhɑrmfəl] 形 有害的

Radiation is harmful to humans.
▶▶ 輻射對人體有害。

harvest [ˋhɑrvɪst] 名 收穫 動 收穫

名 The farmer was expecting a good harvest.
農人期待大豐收。
動 After so many years of hard work, Mel was finally harvesting the rewards.
過了多年的努力，梅爾最後收穫滿滿。

hasty [ˋhestɪ] 形 快速的

Be hasty, or you will miss the train.
▶▶ 快點，不然你要錯過火車了。

hatch [hætʃ] 動 孵化

The egg has already hatched.
▶▶ 這顆蛋已經孵化了。

hateful [ˋhetfəl] 形 可恨的；令人厭惡的

The villagers' hateful comments really upset him.
▶▶ 村民們充滿仇恨的言論讓他非常生氣。

Level 1 基礎單字
Level 2 必備單字
Level 3 中級單字
Level 4 進階單字
Level 5 高手單字
Level 6 滿級單字

hay [he] 名乾草

The warehouse is filled with nothing but hay.
▶▶ 倉庫裡除了乾草什麼都沒有。

headline [`hɛd͵laɪn] 名標題 動給…下標題

名 The headlines of these articles are sensational.
這些文章的標題都很聳動。
動 Please headline the essay properly.
請給這篇文章下個適當的標題。

headquarters [`hɛd͵kwɔrtəz] 名總部

Several companies have their headquarters in the area.
▶▶ 有幾家公司總部設在這個地方。

heal [hil] 動治癒

What the doctors should do is healing the sick.
▶▶ 醫生的職責就是治癒病人。

heap [hip] 名堆積 動堆積

名 Mother is sick of the heap of dirty clothes.
媽媽對那疊髒衣服很反感。
動 My sister heaped food onto my plate.
我姐在我的盤子裡堆了很多食物。

heater [`hitə] 名加熱器；暖氣機

Once installed, this heater operates automatically.
▶▶ 安裝完成後，加熱器就會自動運作。

heel [hil] 名腳後跟

There's a hole in the heel of my stocking.
▶▶ 我襪子後跟有一個洞。

hell [hɛl] 名地獄

Those who commit terrible crimes should go to hell.
▶▶ 那些罪大惡極的人都該下地獄。

helmet [`hɛlmɪt] 名安全帽

Martin paid a five-hundred dollar fine for not wearing a helmet.
▶▶ 馬丁因為沒戴安全帽而被罰五百元。

hesitate [`hɛzə,tet] 動 遲疑

She hesitated in momentary confusion.
▶▶ 她一時思想紊亂，猶豫不定。

hint [hɪnt] 名 暗示

There were subtle hints in his letter.
▶▶ 他的信中有些微妙的暗示。

hire [haɪr] 動 雇用；租用

They hired a room to stay overnight.
▶▶ 他們租了一間房間過夜。

historian [hɪs`torɪən] 名 歷史學家

Evans is a historian rather than a writer.
▶▶ 與其說伊文斯是個作家，不如說是個歷史學家。

historic [hɪs`tɔrɪk] 形 歷史性的

It was indeed a historic moment when the fossils were discovered.
▶▶ 發現這些化石真是歷史性的一刻。

holder [`holdə] 名 持有者

If you want to borrow the book, you have to ask the holder.
▶▶ 如果想借這本書，你必須詢問持有者。

hollow [`halo] 形 中空的

These eggs are all hollow.
▶▶ 這些蛋都是空心的。

holy [`holɪ] 形 神聖的

Christmas is a Christian holy day and usually celebrated on December 25th.
▶▶ 耶誕節是基督徒的一個神聖日子，人們常在十二月二十五日舉行慶祝。

homesick [`hom,sɪk] 形 思鄉的；想家的

The photographs of my family make me homesick.
▶▶ 家人的照片讓我很想家。

1 Level 基礎單字

2 Level 必備單字

3 Level 中級單字

4 Level 進階單字

5 Level 高手單字

6 Level 滿級單字

hometown [ˋhomˌtaʊn] 名 家鄉

She left her hometown to study overseas.
▶▶ 她離鄉到海外求學。

honesty [ˋɑnɪstɪ] 名 誠實

Honesty is the best policy.
▶▶ 誠實為上策。

honor [ˋɑnɚ] 名 榮耀

They celebrated in honor of Cathy's bravery.
▶▶ 他們大肆慶祝以表揚凱西的勇敢。

hopeful [ˋhopfəl] 形 有希望的

I promise you a hopeful future.
▶▶ 我承諾給你一個充滿希望的未來。

horn [hɔrn] 名 喇叭

Sounding a horn is not allowed at that school.
▶▶ 那間學校內禁鳴喇叭。

horrible [ˋhɔrəbḷ] 形 可怕的

The nightmare was truly horrible!
▶▶ 那場惡夢真可怕！

horror [ˋhɔrɚ] 名 恐怖

She screamed in horror.
▶▶ 她出於恐懼而驚聲尖叫。

hourly [ˋaʊɚlɪ] 形 每小時的 副 每小時地

形 There is an hourly train service to the suburbs.
郊外有一小時一班的火車。
副 This medicine is to be taken hourly.
這藥每小時吃一次。

housekeeper [ˋhaʊsˌkipɚ] 名 管家

Maria is a competent housekeeper.
▶▶ 瑪莉亞是個稱職的管家。

hug [hʌg] 動 抱 名 擁抱

動 They hugged each other passionately.
他們倆熱情地擁抱彼此。

名 Give me a hug before you go abroad.
你出國前給我一個擁抱吧。

hum [hʌm] 名 嗡嗡聲 動 嗡嗡作響；哼唱

名 The constant hum on the computer is annoying.
電腦不斷發出惱人的嗡嗡聲。

動 Do you hear the bees humming?
你聽到蜜蜂嗡嗡叫著嗎？

humid [`hjumɪd] 形 潮濕的

The island is hot and humid in the summer.
▶▶ 這個島在夏季又熱又潮濕。

humor [`hjumɚ] 名 幽默

Humor makes a person welcome.
▶▶ 幽默使人受歡迎。

humorous [`hjumərəs] 形 幽默的

He is such a humorous guy that he is popular among his friends.
▶▶ 他是個幽默的人，在朋友之間很受歡迎。

hunger [`hʌngɚ] 名 飢餓 關 famine 饑荒

The soldier started to feel faint from hunger.
▶▶ 士兵開始餓到有點頭暈。

hut [hʌt] 名 小屋

Regardless of the danger, my nephew climbed to the roof of the hut.
▶▶ 我外甥不顧危險地爬上了小屋的屋頂。

 I 字頭中級單字

MP3 057

icy [`aɪsɪ] 形 冰的

The waiter gave me a glass of icy water.
▶▶ 服務生給我一杯冰水。

Level 1 基礎單字
Level 2 必備單字
Level 3 中級單字
Level 4 進階單字
Level 5 高手單字
Level 6 滿級單字

imagination [ɪˌmædʒəˋneʃən] 名想像力

Christine is a girl of imagination.
▶▶ 克莉絲汀是個富有想像力的女孩。

immediate [ɪˋmidɪət] 形立即的 關 immediately 立刻

He made an immediate call when he saw the robber.
▶▶ 當他看到搶匪時立即撥打電話。

import [ɪmˋport] / [ˋɪmport] 動進口 名進口

動 Japan imports mostly natural resources from other countries.
日本由其它國家進口大部分的天然資源。
名 There is a large imbalance between our import and export trade.
我們的進出口貿易嚴重失衡。

impress [ɪmˋprɛs] 動留下深刻印象 關 impressive 令人印象深刻的

Peggy impressed me with her graceful dance.
▶▶ 佩姬優雅的舞步讓我印象深刻。

indoor [ˋɪnˌdor] 形屋內的

Oriana likes indoor activities because she doesn't want to get a suntan.
▶▶ 奧莉安娜喜歡室內運動，因為她不想曬黑。

indoors [ˋɪnˋdorz] 副在室內

Because of rain, we stayed indoors.
▶▶ 因為下雨，我們只好待在家裡。

industrial [ɪnˋdʌstrɪəl] 形工業的

The opportunities that the WTO brought has multiplied the quantity of industrial exports by 20 times.
▶▶ 世界貿易組織帶來的商機使工業產品出口量增加了二十倍。

inferior [ɪnˋfɪrɪə] 形較差的；下級的

The second applicant is inferior to the first one.
▶▶ 第二位應徵者不如第一位應徵者。

inform [ɪnˋfɔrm] 動通知

We will inform you if you are chosen.
▶▶ 如果錄取的話我們會通知你。

information [ˌɪnfə`meʃən] 名 知識；見聞；資訊

I read the newspaper every morning to get information about other countries.
▶▶ 我每天早上看報紙，了解國外的消息。

injury [`ɪndʒərɪ] 名 傷害

Excessive dosage of this drug can result in injury to the liver.
▶▶ 這種藥使用過量會損害肝臟。

inn [ɪn] 名 旅社；小酒館

They stayed in an inn after a long journey.
▶▶ 歷經長途跋涉，他們在旅社裡歇息。

inner [`ɪnə] 形 內部的

The inner rooms are decorated very creatively.
▶▶ 這些內部擺設頗具巧思。

innocent [`ɪnəsn̩t] 形 純潔的；無罪的；天真的

The jury pronounced the man innocent.
▶▶ 陪審團宣布此人無罪。

inspect [ɪn`spɛkt] 動 調查

The airport official inspected the shipment.
▶▶ 機場官員檢查了這批貨物。

inspector [ɪn`spɛktə] 名 檢查員

The smugglers ran away upon seeing two inspectors coming near.
▶▶ 一看到兩位檢查員走近，走私犯拔腿就跑。

intelligent [ɪn`tɛlədʒənt] 形 有智慧的

Mark's ideal spouse is intelligent.
▶▶ 馬克的理想對象必須要聰慧。

interrupt [ˌɪntə`rʌpt] 動 干擾 同 disrupt

The baby interrupted their sleep with his crying.
▶▶ 嬰兒的哭聲打斷了他們的睡眠。

Level 1 基礎單字
Level 2 必備單字
Level 3 中級單字
Level 4 進階單字
Level 5 高手單字
Level 6 滿級單字

invent [ɪn`vɛnt] 動 創造；發明

He invented a new type of machine.
▶▶ 他發明了一種新型機器。

inventor [ɪn`vɛntə] 名 發明家

Thomas Edison was a very famous inventor.
▶▶ 愛迪生是位有名的發明家。

investigate [ɪn`vɛstə,get] 動 研究；調查

The FBI has been called to investigate.
▶▶ 聯邦調查局奉命進行調查。

invitation [,ɪnvə`teʃən] 名 邀請

I received Sarah's invitation to her wedding.
▶▶ 我收到莎拉的結婚請帖。

ivory [`aɪvərɪ] 名 象牙 形 象牙製的

名 Ivory trading was once banned by the authority.
　　當局曾禁止象牙交易。
形 The ivory pendant cost more than fifty thousand dollars.
　　這個象牙製的垂飾要價超過五萬。

MP3 058

jail [dʒel] 名 監獄

He has been released from jail.
▶▶ 他出獄了。

jar [dʒɑr] 名 罐子；廣口瓶

We ate a whole jar of jam.
▶▶ 我們吃掉一整罐果醬。

jaw [dʒɔ] 名 下巴

A strong square jaw is a sign of firm character.
▶▶ 結實方正的下巴是性格堅強的標誌。

jazz [dʒæz] 名爵士樂

Chloe likes jazz and blues very much.
▶▶ 克洛伊非常喜歡爵士和藍調音樂。

jealous [`dʒɛləs] 形嫉妒的

Marilyn is jealous of her sister's popularity.
▶▶ 瑪莉蓮嫉妒她姐姐受人歡迎。

jeep [dʒip] 名吉普車

Traveling by jeep, we visited cities and farms.
▶▶ 我們坐吉普車拜訪了一些城市和農場。

jelly [`dʒɛlɪ] 名果凍

How about some jelly for dessert?
▶▶ 吃些果凍當點心如何？

jet [dʒɛt] 名噴射機 動噴出；搭飛機旅行

名 The accident happened as the jet was about to take off.
事故是在噴射機正要起飛時發生的。
動 The flamethrower jetted out flames.
噴火器噴出火焰。

jewel [`dʒuəl] 名寶石；珍貴的東西

A diamond is an expensive jewel.
▶▶ 鑽石是種昂貴的寶石。

jewelry [`dʒuəlrɪ] 名珠寶；首飾

Rebecca never wears jewelry.
▶▶ 瑞貝卡從不戴首飾。

journey [`dʒɜnɪ] 名旅程 動旅遊

名 How was your journey to Italy?
你的義大利之旅如何呢？
動 Jessica journeys frequently to Europe.
潔西卡常到歐洲旅遊。

joyful [`dʒɔɪfəl] 形愉快的

Thanks for inviting me to such a joyful party.
▶▶ 謝謝你邀請我來這麼愉快的派對。

1 Level 基礎單字
2 Level 必備單字
3 Level 中級單字
4 Level 進階單字
5 Level 高手單字
6 Level 滿級單字

juicy [`dʒusɪ] 形 多汁的

The watermelon I just ate was very juicy.
▶▶ 我剛吃的西瓜非常多汁。

jungle [`dʒʌŋgl] 名 叢林

The paper is a jungle of ads.
▶▶ 報上盡是雜七雜八的廣告。

junior [`dʒunjɚ] 名 晚輩；小學生；（四年制大學的）大三生 形 資淺的；初級的

名 Juniors in this major are usually under a great deal of academic pressure.
這個科系的大三生通常有很大的課業壓力。
形 Sophie attended a course to become a junior hotel manager.
蘇菲參加初階飯店經理課程。

junk [dʒʌŋk] 名 垃圾

Don't eat too much junk food.
▶▶ 不要吃太多垃圾食物。

 UNIT 11 K字頭中級單字 MP3 059

kangaroo [ˌkæŋgəˋru] 名 袋鼠

Australia is famous for its kangaroos.
▶▶ 澳洲以袋鼠聞名。

keyboard [`ki͵bord] 名 鍵盤

You have to clean your keyboard regularly.
▶▶ 你應該定期清潔你的鍵盤。

kidney [`kɪdnɪ] 名 腎臟

Surgeons have made a great breakthrough in kidney transplantation.
▶▶ 外科醫生們在腎臟移植領域取得了重大突破。

kilometer [`kɪlə͵mitɚ] 名 公里

I have walked over 10 kilometers since this morning.
▶▶ 我從早上走到現在已經超過十公里了。

kindergarten [`kɪndəˌgɑrtn̩] 名 幼稚園

Little Daisy learned how to write her name in kindergarten.
▶▶ 小黛西在幼稚園學會了怎麼寫她的名字。

kingdom [`kɪŋdəm] 名 王國

The kingdom increased in wealth and prosperity.
▶▶ 這個王國逐漸富足繁榮。

kit [kɪt] 名 工具箱

The plumber brought his kit to work.
▶▶ 水管工人帶著他的工具箱去工作。

knight [naɪt] 名 騎士；爵士 動 封…為爵士

名 The knights defeated their foes.
那些騎士戰勝了他們的敵人。
動 The king knighted the soldier for his bravery.
國王因這位軍人的英勇而封他為爵士。

knit [nɪt] 動 編織 名 編織物

動 I'm knitting my boyfriend a sweater.
我正在為我的男友織毛衣。
名 Don't put the knits here just anywhere.
別把織品隨意放在這裡。

knot [nɑt] 名 結 動 打結

名 He tied a knot to prevent leaking.
他打了個結以防外漏。
動 Sherry wore a scarf knotted around her neck.
雪莉在脖子上繫了一條圍巾。

koala [kəˋɑlə] 名 無尾熊

Koalas are great creatures.
▶▶ 無尾熊是很棒的生物。

Level 1 基礎單字
Level 2 必備單字
Level 3 中級單字
Level 4 進階單字
Level 5 高手單字
Level 6 滿級單字

label [`lebl̩] 名標籤 動貼標籤

名 Read the label on the merchandise carefully before you buy it.
買東西前仔細閱讀商品的標籤。
動 My English teacher has been labeled as the best in our school.
我的英文老師被稱為我們全校最好的。

lace [les] 名花邊；蕾絲；鞋帶 動繫鞋帶

名 Victoria rimmed the picture frame with lace.
維多利亞用緞帶為相框鑲邊。
動 He laced up his shoes.
他將鞋帶打結。

ladder [`lædɚ] 名梯子

The leader of our class climbed the ladder quickly.
▶▶ 班長敏捷地攀上了梯子。

lately [`letlɪ] 副最近

How have you been lately? We haven't seen each other for such a long time.
▶▶ 你近來如何？我們好久沒見了。

laughter [`læftɚ] 名笑聲

Our class filled with laughter.
▶▶ 我們班充滿了笑聲。

laundry [`lɔndrɪ] 名待洗衣物；洗衣店

Help me send it to the laundry to get it cleaned.
▶▶ 幫我把衣服送到洗衣店去洗。

lawn [lɔn] 名草地

We have to mow the lawn twice a week.
▶▶ 我們每週得修剪草坪兩次。

leak [lik] 動滲透；漏出 名漏洞

動 The rain was leaking in large drops through the roof.
雨水大滴大滴地從屋頂滲漏下來。
名 Check if there are any leaks in the pipe.
仔細檢查輸送管上是否有漏洞。

leap [lip] 動 跳躍 名 跳躍

動 Look before you leap.
三思而後行。
名 Wright made a leap to throw the ball.
懷特跳起來投球。

learning [`lɜnɪŋ] 名 學問

You can gain from book learning and travel experiences.
▶▶ 可以透過讀書學習和旅遊體驗來增進自我。

leather [`lɛðɚ] 名 皮革

Tom buys and sells leather goods.
▶▶ 湯姆買賣皮貨。

leisure [`liʒɚ] 名 空閒

What do you usually do in your leisure?
▶▶ 你空閒時通常做些什麼？

lemonade [ˌlɛmən`ed] 名 檸檬水

Drinking lemonade before meals will do harm to your stomach.
▶▶ 飯前喝檸檬水會傷胃。

leopard [`lɛpəd] 名 豹

Leopards run as fast as lightning.
▶▶ 豹跑起來快如閃電。

lettuce [`lɛtɪs] 名 萵苣

I'd like roast beef with Swiss cheese, tomato, and lettuce.
▶▶ 我要烤牛肉加瑞士乳酪、番茄與萵苣。

liberty [`lɪbətɪ] 名 自由

The liberty of minorities has gained through repetitive protests.
▶▶ 弱勢族群的自由是在反覆抗議中爭取而來的。

lick [lɪk] 動 舔 名 舔

動 The little cat licked my fingers.
小貓舔我的手指。
名 He gave the edge of the mug a lick.
他舔了舔杯緣。

Level 1 基礎單字
Level 2 必備單字
Level 3 中級單字
Level 4 進階單字
Level 5 高手單字
Level 6 滿級單字

lifetime [`laɪf,taɪm] 名一生

I swear that I will love you for my entire lifetime.
▶▶ 我發誓會愛你一生一世。

lighthouse [`laɪt,haʊs] 名燈塔

We could see the lighthouse in the distance.
▶▶ 我們看得見遠處的燈塔。

lightning [`laɪtnɪŋ] 名閃電

Lightning strikes caused many fires across the state.
▶▶ 雷擊在整個州造成了許多火災。

lily [`lɪlɪ] 名百合花

I can recognize the smell of lilies.
▶▶ 我可以認出百合花的香味。

limb [lɪm] 名枝幹；四肢

Edmund stood up and stretched his limbs.
▶▶ 艾德蒙起身伸展四肢。

litter [`lɪtɚ] 名小塊垃圾；廢棄物 動亂扔；亂丟垃圾

名 Why is litter everywhere on campus?
為什麼校園裡到處都是垃圾？
動 If you are caught littering on the platform, you must pay a fine.
如果你被逮到在月台上亂丟垃圾，將會遭到罰錢。

lively [`laɪvlɪ] 形有生氣的

The elderly people dancing in the park are so lively.
▶▶ 這些在公園跳舞的老人真有活力。

loaf [lof] 名一條（麵包）

Two white loaves, please.
▶▶ 請給我兩條白麵包。

lobby [`lɑbɪ] 名大廳

The guests are waiting in the lobby.
▶▶ 客人們正在大廳等待。

locate [`loket] 動 設立（建築）；位於

The new shopping mall will be located opposite the park.
▶▶ 新的購物中心將坐落在公園對面。

location [lo`keʃən] 名 位置

Excuse me. Do you know the exact location of the city government offices?
▶▶ 不好意思，請問你知道市政府的確切位置嗎？

lock [lɑk] 名 鎖 動 鎖上

名 She turned the key in the lock.
她轉動鎖裡的鑰匙。
動 Viola locked her passport and money in the safe.
維爾拉把自己的護照和錢鎖在保險櫃裡。

log [lɔg] 名 圓木；木材 動 伐木

名 The children hid something in the pile of logs.
孩子們在那堆木頭裡藏了點東西。
動 They have logged over one quarter of the forest so far.
到目前為止他們已經砍伐超過森林的四分之一。

lollipop [`lɑlɪpɑp] 名 棒棒糖

Ronaldo always come back home with a cake or lollipop in his hand.
▶▶ 羅納多回家時，手裡總拿著一塊蛋糕或棒棒糖。

loose [lus] 形 寬鬆的

I have got a loose tooth.
▶▶ 我有顆牙齒鬆掉了。

lord [lɔrd] 名 領主

Lions are lords of the jungle.
▶▶ 獅子是叢林之王。

loser [`luzɚ] 名 失敗者

You will never be a loser unless you give up trying.
▶▶ 除非你放棄嘗試，不然你永遠不會是個失敗者。

lover [`lʌvɚ] 名 愛人

Harold sacrificed himself to rescue his lover.
▶▶ 哈洛德為了救愛人犧牲自己。

Level 1 基礎單字
Level 2 必備單字
Level 3 中級單字
Level 4 進階單字
Level 5 高手單字
Level 6 滿級單字

luggage [`lʌgɪdʒ] 名行李

There's room for one more piece of luggage.
▶▶ 還有地方再放一件行李。

lung [lʌŋ] 名肺臟

One major cause of lung cancer is smoking.
▶▶ 引起肺癌的主要因素之一為抽菸。

UNIT 13 **M 字頭中級單字**

MP3 061

magical [`mædʒɪkl] 形有魔力的；神奇的

The TV commercial built up the drug pill to such a degree that it seemed to have magical effects.
▶▶ 這齣電視廣告如此吹捧這種藥丸，似乎它真有神效似的。

magician [mə`dʒɪʃən] 名魔術師

The magician changed the frog into a prince.
▶▶ 魔術師把青蛙變成了王子。

magnet [`mægnɪt] 名磁鐵

You can get a Hello Kitty magnet if you spend over 77 dollars.
▶▶ 消費滿七十七元可以獲得一個 Hello Kitty 磁鐵。

maid [med] 名女僕

Ask the maid to wipe the dirt off the floor.
▶▶ 叫女僕把地板上的污垢擦掉。

majority [mə`dʒɔrətɪ] 名多數

The majority oppose the proposal.
▶▶ 大多數人反對這個提議。

mall [mɔl] 名購物中心

I took my mother to the shopping mall's grand opening.
▶▶ 我帶媽媽去購物中心的開幕活動。

mankind / humankind [mæn`kaɪnd ] / [ `hjumən,kaind] 名人類

The outstanding scientist made a great contribution to mankind in 1983.
▶▶ 這位傑出的科學家在一九八三年為人類做出一項偉大的貢獻。

marble [`mɑrbḷ] 名大理石

The wall is made of marble.
▶▶ 這牆由大理石建造而成。

march [mɑrtʃ] 動前進 名行軍

動 Soldiers were marching up and down outside the government buildings.
士兵們在政府大樓外面來回練習佇列行進。
名 I have a bird's eye view of the march.
我鳥瞰行軍隊伍。

marvelous [`mɑrvələs] 形令人驚訝的

It is marvelous that he appeared at the event.
▶▶ 他出現在這場活動中真叫人驚訝。

mathematical [,mæθə`mætɪkḷ] 形數學的

He was lacking in mathematical training.
▶▶ 他數學方面訓練不夠。

mayor [`meɚ] 名市長

The mayor made few contributions to our city.
▶▶ 市長對我們的城市幾乎沒有貢獻。

meadow [`mɛdo] 名草地

I want to roll on the green meadow under the sun.
▶▶ 我想在太陽下於青草地上打滾。

meaningful [`minɪŋfəl] 形有意義的

What the professor told me was meaningful.
▶▶ 教授跟我說的話很有意義。

meanwhile [`min,hwaɪl] 連同時 名期間

連 I cleaned up the living room; meanwhile, mom vacuumed the floor.
我清理客廳，媽媽同時用吸塵器清理地板。
名 In the meanwhile, I will visit my grandmother.
在這期間我會去拜訪祖母。

基礎單字 Level 1

必備單字 Level 2

中級單字 Level 3

進階單字 Level 4

高手單字 Level 5

滿級單字 Level 6

medal [`mɛdḷ] 名獎章

His numerous medals hung on the entire wall.
▶▶ 整面牆掛著他眾多的獎章。

medium / media [`midiəm ] / [ `midiə] 名媒體

The singer cares about the mass media coverage of the issue.
▶▶ 這位歌手關心這項大眾傳播媒體報導的議題。

melon [`mɛlən] 名瓜；甜瓜

An waiter put some melons on the table.
▶▶ 服務員在桌上放了一些哈密瓜。

melt [mɛlt] 動融化；溶解

The salt melted in the hot soup quickly.
▶▶ 鹽在熱湯中迅速溶解。

mend [mɛnd] 動修補；修改

Darcy asked her to mend his socks.
▶▶ 達西叫她幫他補襪子。

mental [`mɛntḷ] 形心智的；心理的 關 cognitive 認知的

His mental age is greater than his physical one.
▶▶ 他的心理年齡比實際年齡大。

merry [`mɛrɪ] 形快樂的

It is common for people in Western countries to wish each other Merry
Christmas.
▶▶ 在西方國家，人們很常祝福彼此聖誕快樂。

mess [mɛs] 名雜亂；困境 動弄亂

名 Nancy always leaves her room in a mess.
南西總是把她的房間弄得一團亂。
動 Don't mess up the books. I just organized them.
別弄亂這些書，我才剛整理好。

microphone / mic [`maɪkrəˏfon] / [maik] 名麥克風

Johnny used a microphone so that everyone could hear him.
▶▶ 強尼使用麥克風，讓大家都能聽見他的聲音。

microwave [`maɪkro͵wev] 名微波爐 動微波加熱

名 She took the soup from the microwave.
她把湯從微波爐取出。
動 Can you help me microwave the spaghetti?
你可以幫我微波義大利麵嗎？

mighty [`maɪtɪ] 形巨大的；強大的

I can see the mighty iceberg without a telescope.
▶▶ 我不用望遠鏡就能看見那座大冰山。

minus [`maɪnəs] 介減去 形負的 名減號；缺點

介 Eight minus four is four.
八減四剩四。
形 Porter got an A minus on the test.
波特在這次考試得到 A-。
名 You made an error in the calculation since you replaced the minus by plus.
你的計算錯誤是因為把減號寫成加號。

miracle [`mɪrək]] 名奇蹟

It's a miracle nobody was killed in the crash.
▶▶ 車禍中無人喪生真是奇蹟。

misery [`mɪzərɪ] 名悲慘

I pity your misery.
▶▶ 我為你的悲慘際遇感到同情。

missile [`mɪs]] 名飛彈

The huge ship was sunk by a missile.
▶▶ 這個巨大的軍艦被一枚飛彈擊沉。

missing [`mɪsɪŋ] 形失蹤的

We noticed that Kelly was missing last night.
▶▶ 我們昨夜發現凱莉失蹤了。

mission [`mɪʃən] 名任務

There is no impossible mission for me.
▶▶ 對我而言沒有不可能的任務。

Level 1 基礎單字
Level 2 必備單字
Level 3 中級單字
Level 4 進階單字
Level 5 高手單字
Level 6 滿級單字

mist [mɪst] 名霧 動（使）濛上水汽

名 I can see nothing in the mist.
在霧中我什麼也看不見。

動 The steam of the hot spring misted up his glasses.
溫泉的熱氣讓他的眼鏡起霧了。

mob [mɑb] 名暴民 動圍住

名 The mob gathered outside the courthouse, demanding justice.
暴民聚集在法院外，要求伸張正義。

動 Eager fans mobbed the popular singer.
熱切的歌迷們團團圍住這位流行歌手。

mobile [`mobɪl] 形可動的

I use my mobile phone all day long.
▶▶ 我整天都在用手機。

moist [mɔɪst] 名潮濕的

Water the plants regularly to keep the soil moist.
▶▶ 定時灌溉植物以保持土壤濕潤。

moisture [`mɔɪstʃɚ] 名濕氣

This machine absorbs moisture from the air.
▶▶ 這台機器吸收空氣中的水分。

monk [mʌŋk] 名僧侶

The monks are vegetarians.
▶▶ 僧侶吃素。

monster [`mɑnstɚ] 名怪獸

Their huge dog is an absolute monster!
▶▶ 他們的大狗根本是隻怪獸！

monthly [`mʌnθlɪ] 形每月一次的 名月刊

形 I anticipated the monthly assembly would be interesting.
我期待這次月會將會很有趣。

名 I subscribed to three kinds of monthlies.
我訂了三種月刊。

moral [`mɔrəl] 形 道德的 名 寓意

形 Some readers tend to make moral judgements.
有些讀者傾向進行道德批判。

名 What is the moral of this story?
這個故事的寓意是什麼？

mosquito [mə`skito] 名 蚊子

He told me that female mosquitoes bite.
▶▶ 他告訴我母蚊子比較容易咬人。

mostly [`mostlɪ] 副 多半；主要地

Jewelry and lace are mostly feminine belongings.
▶▶ 珠寶和蕾絲大多是女性物品。

motel [mo`tɛl] 名 汽車旅館

The paparazzi took a photo when the two stars walked out the motel hand in hand.
▶▶ 狗仔隊拍到這兩個明星攜手走出汽車旅館。

moth [mɔθ] 名 蛾；蛀蟲

The dying moth lay on the floor.
▶▶ 垂死的蛾躺在地板上。

motor [`motɚ] 名 馬達

Rex started the motor.
▶▶ 雷克斯啟動了馬達。

multiply [`mʌltəplaɪ] 動 相乘

We've multiplied our profits over the last two years.
▶▶ 我們的利潤在過去兩年裡大大增加了。

murder [`mɝdɚ] 名 謀殺罪 動 謀殺

名 Tiffany is accused of murder.
蒂芬妮被指控謀殺。

動 They murdered the rich man for his fortune.
他們為了錢財謀殺那個富人。

Level 1 基礎單字
Level 2 必備單字
Level 3 中級單字
Level 4 進階單字
Level 5 高手單字
Level 6 滿級單字

muscle [`mʌsl̩] 名肌肉

Charles developed his muscles by going to the gym daily.
▶▶ 查爾斯每日上健身房鍛鍊肌肉。

mushroom [`mʌʃrʊm] 名蘑菇

The mushroom soup smells good.
▶▶ 蘑菇湯聞起來很棒。

mystery [`mɪstərɪ] 名神祕

The reason why Yvette did it remains a mystery.
▶▶ 伊薇特做那件事的原因仍是個謎。

UNIT 14 **N 字頭中級單字**

MP3 062

naked [`nekɪd] 形赤裸的

They are often naked, wandering around the house.
▶▶ 他們經常赤身裸體在房子周圍漫步。

nap [næp] 名小睡

I am used to taking a nap after lunch.
▶▶ 我午餐後習慣小睡一下。

(焦點句型) take a nap 小睡一下

napkin [`næpkɪn] 名餐巾紙

She wiped the fork with a napkin.
▶▶ 她用餐巾紙擦拭餐具。

native [`netɪv] 形天生的；本國的 同 indigenous

Are you a native speaker of English?
▶▶ 你的母語是英文嗎？

navy [`nevɪ] 名海軍；艦隊

The Navy is considering buying six new warships.
▶▶ 海軍正在考慮購買六艘新戰艦。

neat [nit] 彫整齊的

Lena always kept her room neat.
▶▶ 麗娜總是保持房間整潔。

necessity [nə`sɛsətɪ] 图必需品

Air and water are necessities for human beings.
▶▶ 空氣和水是人類的必需品。

necktie [`nɛktaɪ] 图領帶

I like the diamond pattern on your necktie.
▶▶ 我喜歡你領帶上的菱形花紋。

neighborhood [`nebɚ͵hʊd] 图鄰近的地方

I smell something burning in the neighborhood.
▶▶ 我聞到附近有燒焦味。

nest [nɛst] 图鳥巢 動築巢

图 A bird lays eggs in a nest.
　　鳥在巢裡下蛋。
動 Bees nested in the tree.
　　蜂群在樹上築巢。

nickname [`nɪk͵nem] 图綽號 動取綽號

图 He doesn't want to reveal his nickname.
　　他不想公開他的綽號。
動 Nicknaming others by their flaws is wicked.
　　用他人的缺點來取綽號很缺德。

normal [`nɔrml̩] 彫標準的；正常的

It's normal to feel tired after such a long trip.
▶▶ 這樣長途旅行之後感到疲勞是正常的。

novelist [`nɑvl̩ɪst] 图小說家

Most works of the novelist are about the life of the poor.
▶▶ 這個小說家大部分的作品是關於窮人的生活。

nun [nʌn] 图修女；尼姑

The nuns drew water from the well in the morning.
▶▶ 尼姑們在早上從井裡汲水。

Level 1 基礎單字
Level 2 必備單字
Level 3 中級單字
Level 4 進階單字
Level 5 高手單字
Level 6 滿級單字

oak [ok] 名 橡樹

This table is made of solid oak.
▶▶ 這張桌子是用實心橡木製作的。

observe [əb`zɜv] 動 觀察 關 observation 觀察

Leo observes keenly but says very little.
▶▶ 利奧觀察敏銳，卻很少發言。

occasion [ə`keʒən] 名 事件；場合 動 引起

名 What you wear depends on the occasion.
你應該視場合打扮。

動 His rude behavior occasioned a quarrel.
他粗魯的舉止引發爭執。

odd [ɑd] 形 單數的；奇怪的

It's no use keeping an odd earring.
▶▶ 只留一隻耳環沒有用。

omit [o`mɪt] 動 省略

You can omit this paragraph to make your report concise.
▶▶ 你可以省略這個段落，使你的報告更精簡。

onion [`ʌnjən] 名 洋蔥

Natalie shed tears while slicing the onion.
▶▶ 娜塔莉切洋蔥時掉下眼淚。

onto [`ɑntu] 介 在…之上

The tailor used a needle to sew the button onto the shirt.
▶▶ 裁縫用針把鈕子縫到襯衫上。

operation [ˌɑpə`reʃən] 名 操作；手術

Rick is at the hospital recovering from an operation on his leg.
▶▶ 瑞克正在醫院裡從腿部手術中恢復。

opportunity [ˌɑpəˋtjunətɪ] 名機會

Opportunity seldom knocks twice.
▶▶ 機不可失，失不再來。

opposite [ˋɑpəzɪt] 形相對的

Murphy's seat is opposite to mine.
▶▶ 墨菲坐在我對面。

optimistic [ˌɑptəˋmɪstɪk] 形樂觀的

He is an optimistic person fearing no difficulties.
▶▶ 他是個樂觀的人，不怕任何艱難。

oral [ˋorəl] 名口試 形口述的

名 After the written test, there will be an oral.
筆試過後，會有口試。
形 Oral agreements are not as strong as written ones.
口頭承諾的效力不如書面契約。

organic [ɔrˋgænɪk] 形器官的；有機的

The professor is a master of organic chemistry.
▶▶ 這名教授精通有機化學。

organize [ˋɔrgəˌnaɪz] 動組織

They organized the truckers into a union.
▶▶ 他們把卡車司機組成工會。

original [əˋrɪdʒənḷ] 形起初的 名原作

形 The original design is based on his own idea.
最初的設計是基於他自己的構想。
名 The originals were lost in the museum fire.
這位大師的原作已在博物館的火災中佚失了。

outdoor [ˋautˌdor] 形戶外的

The lively girl enjoys outdoor activities.
▶▶ 那個活潑的女孩喜歡戶外活動。

outdoors [autˋdorz] 副在戶外

The lovers went outdoors to avoid bothering others.
▶▶ 那對情侶跑到外面以免打擾他人。

Level 1 基礎單字
Level 2 必備單字
Level 3 中級單字
Level 4 進階單字
Level 5 高手單字
Level 6 滿級單字

outer [`autɚ] 形 外部的

The outer door was locked.
▸▸ 外面的門被鎖上了。

outline [`autlaɪn] 名 外形；輪廓；大綱 動 畫出輪廓

名 The outline of the tree looks like cotton candy.
　　那棵樹的輪廓宛如棉花糖。
動 The illustrator outlined before drawing.
　　這位插畫家畫畫前先描出輪廓。

oven [`ʌvən] 名 烤箱

She heated the dishes in the oven.
▸▸ 她用烤箱熱菜。

overseas [,ovɚ`siz] 形 國外的 副 在海外

形 International corporations sell their products to overseas market.
　　跨國企業將產品銷往海外市場。
副 The couple honeymooned overseas.
　　新婚夫妻到海外度蜜月。

owe [o] 動 虧欠

How much is owing to you?
▸▸ 欠你多少錢？

owl [aul] 名 貓頭鷹

Owls are active at night.
▸▸ 貓頭鷹是夜行性動物。

ownership [`onɚ,ʃɪp] 名 主權；所有權

The ownership of the land is uncertain.
▸▸ 那塊地的所有人尚未確定。

ox [ɑks] 名 公牛

Lennon is as strong as an ox.
▸▸ 藍儂像公牛一樣強壯。

pad [pæd] 图墊子；印章；便條紙簿 動填塞

图 Emma always kept a pad and a pencil by the phone.
艾瑪總在電話旁備有一本便條紙簿和一枝鉛筆。
動 All the sharp corners were padded with foam rubber.
所有尖的稜角都墊上了海綿橡膠。

painter [`pentə] 图畫家

Anderson's father didn't want him to be a painter.
▶▶ 安德森的爸爸不希望他當畫家。

pal [pæl] 图夥伴

I have no pals now.
▶▶ 我現在一個伴也沒有。

palace [`pælɪs] 图宮殿

The king and queen lived in the palace.
▶▶ 國王和王后住在宮殿裡。

palm [pɑm] 图手掌

I put a coin in his palm.
▶▶ 我把一枚硬幣放在他掌心裡。

pancake [`pæn͵kek] 图薄煎餅

I prepared several pancakes for breakfast.
▶▶ 我準備了幾片薄煎餅當早餐。

panic [`pænɪk] 图驚恐 動恐慌

图 He comforted her in her time of panic.
他在她驚慌時安撫她。
動 Don't panic when an earthquake happens.
地震發生時別慌。

parade [pə`red] 图遊行 動參加遊行

图 There is a Taiwan Gay Pride Parade annually.
每年都有一次台灣同志驕傲遊行。
動 The students paraded with a national flag in their hands.
學生們手持國旗遊行。

Level 1 基礎單字
Level 2 必備單字
Level 3 中級單字
Level 4 進階單字
Level 5 高手單字
Level 6 滿級單字

paradise [`pærə‚daɪs] 名 天堂；樂園

The toy department is a paradise for children.
▶▶ 玩具區對孩子而言是座天堂。

parcel [`pɑrsḷ] 名 包裹 動 捆成

名 There's a parcel and some letters for you.
有你的一個包裹和幾封信。
動 She parceled some food for the boys.
她給男孩包了些食物。

parrot [`pærət] 名 鸚鵡

The parrot can copy what you say.
▶▶ 鸚鵡會模仿你說的話。

passage [`pæsɪdʒ] 名 通道

They were stuck in the passage.
▶▶ 他們在通道裡被困住了。

passenger [`pæsṇdʒɚ] 名 乘客

A passenger asked the flight attendant for help.
▶▶ 一名乘客請求空姐幫忙。

passion [`pæʃən] 名 熱情；戀情

I have a passion for him, but he views me as his sister.
▶▶ 我對他懷抱愛慕之情，但他只將我當成妹妹。

passport [`pæspɔrt] 名 護照

You have to apply for a passport before going abroad.
▶▶ 你出國前必須申請護照。

pat [pæt] 動 輕拍 名 拍

動 My mother patted me to wake me up.
媽媽輕拍我叫我起床。
名 My brother gave me a pat on the shoulder.
我弟弟輕輕地拍了一下我的肩膀。

patience [`peʃəns] 名 耐心

Debby has amazing patience while taking care of her mother.
▶▶ 戴比照料母親時，有著驚人的耐心。

pause [pɔz] 動暫停

Derek paused his talk and started to cry.
▶▶ 德瑞克暫停談話，然後開始哭。

pave [pev] 動鋪設 關 pavement 路面；人行道

The road was paved with concrete.
▶▶ 路面由混凝土鋪成。

pea [pi] 名豌豆

He washed the peas and cooked them in the water.
▶▶ 他洗完豌豆後把它們放在水裡煮。

peanut [`pi,nʌt] 名花生

We drank beer with salted peanuts.
▶▶ 我們邊喝啤酒，邊配著吃鹹花生米。

pearl [pɝl] 名珍珠

The pearl necklace my father gave me is priceless.
▶▶ 爸爸送我的這條珍珠項鍊是無價之寶。

peel [pil] 名果皮 動剝皮；脫皮

名 Put the peel into the trash can.
把果皮丟到垃圾筒。
動 After sunbathing, my skin began to peel.
我曬了日光浴後，皮膚開始脫皮了。

penguin [`pɛngwɪn] 名企鵝

Global warming has a great impact on penguins.
▶▶ 全球暖化對企鵝影響甚大。

penny [`pɛnɪ] 名一分硬幣

The driver gave the beggar a penny.
▶▶ 司機給那個乞丐一分錢。

pepper [`pɛpɚ] 名胡椒

Neil added some pepper to the fried chicken.
▶▶ 尼爾在炸雞上灑了些胡椒粉。

Level 1 基礎單字
Level 2 必備單字
Level 3 中級單字
Level 4 進階單字
Level 5 高手單字
Level 6 滿級單字

perform [pɚˋfɔrm] 動 表演；表現

I performed in front of a large crowd.
▶▶ 我在一大群人面前表演。

performance [pɚˋfɔrməns] 名 演出 關 debut 首演 / premiere 初次上演

We applauded them for the perfect performance.
▶▶ 我們為他們完美的演出鼓掌。

permission [pɚˋmɪʃən] 名 允許

Without my permission, you can't enter my room.
▶▶ 沒有我的允許，你不許進我的房間。

permit [pɚˋmɪt] / [ˋpɝmɪt] 動 允許 名 許可證

動 They permitted her to leave.
他們允許她離開。
名 Have you got a permit to fish in this lake?
你有在這個湖裡釣魚的許可證嗎？

persuade [pɚˋswed] 動 說服

Don't try to persuade those who have prejudices. It's no use.
▶▶ 別試著說服有偏見的人，沒有用的。

photographer [fəˋtɑgrəfɚ] 名 攝影師

These photos were taken by an amateur photographer.
▶▶ 這些照片是一名業餘攝影師所拍攝的。

pigeon [ˋpɪdʒɪn] 名 鴿子

Do not feed the pigeons here.
▶▶ 不要在這裡餵鴿子。

pile [paɪl] 名 堆 動 堆積

名 She sighed on seeing the piles of documents on her desk.
看到桌上那疊文件時，她嘆了口氣。
動 We pile up used paper here for copying.
我們把廢紙堆在這裡用來影印。

pill [pɪl] 名 藥丸

Take a pill with warm water.
▶▶ 用溫水配藥吃。

pilot [`paɪlət] 名飛行員

The small airplane contains seats for the pilot, copilot, and several passengers.
▶▶ 小型飛機上有駕駛員、副駕駛員和幾名乘客的座位。

pine [paɪn] 名松樹

The grand master stood still under the pines.
▶▶ 宗師在松樹下佇立。

pineapple [`paɪn͵æpl̩] 名鳳梨

Cut some pineapple for your sister.
▶▶ 切一些鳳梨給你妹妹。

pint [paɪnt] 名品脫（液量單位，約等於半升）

We'd better get a couple of extra pints of milk tomorrow.
▶▶ 明天我們最好再多買幾品脫牛奶。

pit [pɪt] 名坑洞 動挖坑

名 The body had been dumped in a pit.
　屍體被扔進了深坑。
動 The hail pitted the roofs, hoods and trunk of cars.
　冰雹把車頂、引擎蓋和後車廂打得千瘡百孔。

pitch [pɪtʃ] 動投擲 名音高

動 Mr. Wang pitched the ball at high speed.
　王先生把球高速擲出。
名 Vitas is well-known for his high pitch.
　維塔斯以他的高音聞名。

pity [`pɪtɪ] 名同情；遺憾 動憐憫

名 It is a pity that you can't go.
　你不能去真可惜。
動 We pity the victims of the earthquake.
　我們同情地震受災戶。

plastic [`plæstɪk] 名塑膠 形塑膠的

名 The toy is made of plastic.
　這個玩具是塑膠製品。
形 The chairs were covered in some sort of plastic material.
　所有的椅子都包了一種塑膠膜。

Level 1 基礎單字
Level 2 必備單字
Level 3 中級單字
Level 4 進階單字
Level 5 高手單字
Level 6 滿級單字

playful [`plefəl] 形 愛玩的

His playful son always comes home late.
▶▶ 他愛玩的兒子常常晚回家。

plenty [`plɛntɪ] 名 豐富 形 充足的

名 We had plenty of food and drink.
　　我們的食物和飲料十分充足。
形 The resources in our nation are plenty.
　　我國資源豐富。

(焦點句型) plenty of sth. 充足的…；豐富的…

plug [plʌg] 名 插頭 動 塞住；插入

名 Pull the plug before you try to fix the vacuum.
　　修理吸塵器前，先拔掉插頭。
動 He plugged his ears with his fingers to block the noise.
　　他把手指插進耳朵，以擋住噪音。

pole [pol] 名 竿子；（南或北）極；（意見等）極端

Their opinions were at opposite poles of the debate.
▶▶ 他們的意見在辯論中截然相反。

political [pə`lɪtɪkl] 形 政治的

Donald is sensitive to political issues.
▶▶ 唐納德對政治議題很敏感。

politician [ˌpɑlə`tɪʃən] 名 政治家

Helen made up her mind to be a politician in the future.
▶▶ 海倫決定將來要當政治家。

politics [`pɑlətɪks] 名 政治學

What Joy majors in at college is politics.
▶▶ 喬伊大學主修的是政治學。

poll [pol] 名 投票 動 得票

名 The result of the poll won't be known until midnight.
　　投票結果要到半夜才能知道。
動 This candidate polled 56 percent of the votes.
　　這位候選人獲得百分之五十六的選票。

pollute [pə`lut] 動汙染

The lake was polluted greatly.
▸▸ 這片湖泊受到嚴重汙染。

pollution [pə`luʃən] 名汙染

The pollution in the river became more severe this year.
▸▸ 今年這條河的汙染更加嚴重。

porcelain [`pɔrslɪn] 名瓷器

I cherished the antique porcelain.
▸▸ 我很珍惜這個年代久遠的瓷器。

portion [`porʃən] 名部分 動分配

名 Your portion is twice as large as mine.
你的份是我的兩倍大。
動 She portioned the cake into eight pieces.
她把蛋糕分成八份。

portrait [`portret] 名肖像

The earl had his portrait painted and then hung it in the living room.
▸▸ 這位伯爵請人畫他的肖像畫，然後掛在客廳裡。

poster [`postə] 名海報

The posters on the wall were torn down immediately.
▸▸ 牆上的海報很快就被撕下。

postpone [post`pon] 動延緩 相 postponement 延後

The game has already been postponed three times.
▸▸ 這場比賽已經三度延期了。

pottery [`pɑtərɪ] 名陶器

My father bought me some pottery in China.
▸▸ 爸爸在中國買了些陶器給我。

pour [pɔr] 動倒

Pour out the sour milk.
▸▸ 把酸掉的牛奶倒掉。

poverty [`pɑvətɪ] 名 貧窮

These people once had fame and fortune; now all that is left to them is poverty.
▶▶ 這些人曾經名利雙收，現在則是一貧如洗。

powder [`paudə] 名 粉 動 灑粉

名 The mother put a powder on her baby's bottom.
媽媽在嬰兒的屁股上撲了粉。
動 The secretary is thinly powdered.
秘書擦了薄薄的粉底。

practical [`præktɪkḷ] 形 實用的

A book is a practical gift for her.
▶▶ 送她一本書是很實用的禮物。

precious [`prɛʃəs] 形 珍貴的

Clean water is a precious commodity in that part of the world.
▶▶ 在那裡，乾淨的水是珍貴的物資。

preparation [ˌprɛpə`reʃən] 名 準備

He went to the examination with his complete preparation.
▶▶ 他做好充足的預備去考試。

presence [`prɛzn̩s] 名 出席

Your presence is requested at the wedding.
▶▶ 你得出席婚禮。

pretend [prɪ`tɛnd] 動 假裝

I pretended that I had not fallen in love with him.
▶▶ 我假裝從沒愛過他。

prevent [prɪ`vɛnt] 動 預防

We must prevent crimes in the area.
▶▶ 我們必須預防這個地區的犯罪。

previous [`privɪəs] 形 先前的

Our previous teacher retired last week.
▶▶ 我們前一個老師上星期退休了。

probable [`prɑbəbḷ] 形 可能的

You have to list all probable solutions, and try each every day.
▶▶ 你必須把所有可能的解決方法列出，每天嘗試一個。

process [`prɑsɛs] 名 過程 動 處理

名 I'm afraid getting things changed will be a slow process.
要改變現狀，過程恐怕會很緩慢。
動 I sent three rolls of film away to be processed.
我送了三捲底片去沖洗。

producer [prə`djusɚ] 名 製造者 關 produce 生產

The police investigated the producer of the fakes.
▶▶ 警方調查贗品的製造商。

product [`prɑdʌkt] 名 產品

The plan was the product of careful thought of many days.
▶▶ 這個計畫是許多天仔細考慮的成果。

professor [prə`fɛsɚ] 名 教授

John is a professor with prestige of the university.
▶▶ 約翰是這所大學頗有聲望的教授。

profit [`prɑfɪt] 名 利潤 動 獲利 關 nonprofit 非營利的

名 The latest product is bound to make a profit.
這個最新產品一定會獲利。
動 Telling lies won't profit you.
說謊對你無益。

promote [prə`mot] 動 提倡

The major mission for salesmen is to promote products to their clients.
▶▶ 業務最主要的使命就是向顧客推銷產品。

pronounce [prə`naʊns] 動 發音

I think Korean is hard to pronounce.
▶▶ 我覺得韓文發音很困難。

proof [pruf] 名 證據

Do you have any proof that Miranda committed the crime?
▶▶ 你有能證明米蘭達犯罪的證據嗎？

Level 1 基礎單字
Level 2 必備單字
Level 3 中級單字
Level 4 進階單字
Level 5 高手單字
Level 6 滿級單字

property [`prɑpətɪ] 名財產

In general, the concept of private property embraces the ownership of productive resources.

▶▶ 一般而言，私有財產的概念包含生產資源的所有權。

protection [prə`tɛkʃən] 名保護 關 protect 保護

The citizen asked to be put under police protection.

▶▶ 市民請求警方保護。

pub [pʌb] 名酒館

My friends and I spent all night chatting in the pub.

▶▶ 我和朋友們整晚都在酒館裡聊天。

pump [pʌmp] 名抽水機 動抽水

名 After the flood, George used a pump to get the water out of his basement.
洪水過後，喬治用抽水機把地下室的水抽乾。

動 The well has been pumped dry.
井裡的水被抽乾了。

punch [pʌntʃ] 動以拳頭重擊 名打擊

動 She punched him on the nose.
她一拳打中了他的鼻子。

名 The gangster shot out his right arm and landed a punch on Lorrimer's nose.
那個流氓突然舉起右臂，一拳打在洛里莫的鼻子上。

puppet [`pʌpɪt] 名木偶；傀儡

The occupying forces set up a puppet government.

▶▶ 佔領軍建立了一個傀儡政府。

pure [pjʊr] 形純粹的

All I have for you is pure love

▶▶ 我能給你的只有純粹的愛。

purse [pɝs] 名錢包

Nora forgot to take her purse with her to the supermarket.

▶▶ 諾拉忘了帶錢包去超級市場。

Q字頭中級單字

MP3 065

queer [kwɪr] 形 奇怪的

A queer expression was on his face.
▶▶ 他臉上有一種奇怪的表情。

quit [kwɪt] 動 離去；放棄

He quit his job because of low pay.
▶▶ 他因低薪而辭去工作。

文法解析 quit的動詞三態同形，皆為quit。

quote [kwot] 動 引用

If you quote others' words, you have to note the origins.
▶▶ 引用他人論述時，必須註明出處。

R字頭中級單字

MP3 066

racial [`reʃəl] 形 種族的

As long as people still have prejudices, there will be racial conflict in the world.
▶▶ 只要人類仍持有偏見，世上的種族衝突將永不休止。

rag [ræg] 名 破布；碎片

The children were dressed in rags.
▶▶ 孩子們衣衫襤褸。

rank [ræŋk] 名 行列；社會地位 動 等級

名 Teachers are in a higher social rank than laborers.
老師比勞工享有更高的社會地位。
動 Our university is ranked 169th in the world.
我們學校的世界排名是一百六十九名。

rate [ret] 名 比率 動 估計

名 The unemployment rate is rising in Taiwan.
台灣的失業率正在上升。
動 How do you rate our chances of success?
你估計我們成功的機會多大？

Level 1 基礎單字
Level 2 必備單字
Level 3 中級單字
Level 4 進階單字
Level 5 高手單字
Level 6 滿級單字

raw [rɔ] 形生的；原始的

The Japanese are known for their love of raw fish.
▶▶ 日本人愛吃生魚片是出了名的。

ray [re] 名光線

The windows were shining in the reflected rays of the setting sun.
▶▶ 窗戶上閃耀著落日的餘暉。

razor [`rezɚ] 名剃刀；刮鬍刀

Leonard did not have a steady hand with the razor.
▶▶ 倫納德的手拿不穩剃刀。

react [rɪ`ækt] 動反應；反抗

How do acids react on metals?
▶▶ 酸對金屬會引起怎樣的化學反應？

reaction [rɪ`ækʃən] 名反應

His reaction to this news astonished me.
▶▶ 他對這則消息的反應使我震驚。

reasonable [`riznəbl̩] 形合理的

Give me a reasonable explanation.
▶▶ 給我個合理的解釋。

receipt [rɪ`sit] 名收據

File these receipts and then turn them in to the accountant.
▶▶ 把這些收據歸檔後交給會計師。

receiver [rɪ`sivɚ] 名收受者 關 receive 接受

Molly's more of a giver than a receiver.
▶▶ 與其說莫莉是個接受者，不如說她是個給予者。

recognize [`rɛkəɡˌnaɪz] 動認知

I can recognize his voice, but I don't remember his face.
▶▶ 我可以認出他的聲音，但不記得他的臉。

recorder [rɪ`kɔrdə] 名紀錄員

The recorder is absent today, so we have to find another one to take his place.
▶▶ 紀錄員今天請假，所以我們得找另一位代替。

rectangle [`rɛktæŋgḷ] 名長方形

Books are mostly made in rectangles.
▶▶ 書大部分都做成長方形。

reduce [rɪ`djus] 動減少

Costs have been reduced by 20% over the past year.
▶▶ 過去一年，費用已經減少了百分之二十。

regional [`ridʒənḷ] 形區域的

Most regional committees meet four times a year.
▶▶ 大部分的地區委員會都一年開四次會。

regret [rɪ`grɛt] 動後悔 名悔意

動 I regret that I didn't tell him the truth.
我很後悔沒有告訴他真相。
名 Her frown revealed her regret.
她緊蹙的眉頭透露出她的懊悔。

relax [rɪ`læks] 動放鬆

Relax by taking a hot bath.
▶▶ 洗個熱水澡放鬆一下吧。

release [rɪ`lis] 動解放 名釋放 同 liberate

動 Ian was released from prison after five years.
五年後伊恩出獄了。
名 We begged the gangsters for the release of our daughter.
我們懇求歹徒放了我們的女兒。

reliable [rɪ`laɪəbḷ] 形可靠的

Caroline is reliable and trustworthy. That's why everyone likes her.
▶▶ 凱洛琳既可靠又值得信賴。這就是為何大家都喜歡她。

relief [rɪ`lif] 名解除

The doctor's immediate aim is the relief of pain.
▶▶ 醫生第一步要做到的是解除痛苦。

1 Level 基礎單字
2 Level 必備單字
3 Level 中級單字
4 Level 進階單字
5 Level 高手單字
6 Level 滿級單字

religious [rɪˋlɪdʒəs] 形 宗教的

The religious rituals have been performed for centuries .
▶▶ 宗教儀式持續了好幾個世紀。

rely [rɪˋlaɪ] 動 依賴

Harvey is the only friend I can rely on.
▶▶ 哈維是我唯一能依靠的朋友。

remain [rɪˋmen] 動 殘留；仍然；繼續

Nothing remains after the thieves broke into our home.
▶▶ 小偷闖入過後，我們家裡被洗劫一空。

remind [rɪˋmaɪnd] 動 提醒

Please remind me of the schedule tomorrow.
▶▶ 請提醒我明天的行程。
(焦點句型) remind sb. of sth. 提醒（某人）…

remote [rɪˋmot] 形 遙遠的；偏僻的

She lived in a remote village.
▶▶ 她住在一個偏遠的小村落。

replace [rɪˋples] 動 代替 關 replacement 取代

They replaced her broken watch with a new one.
▶▶ 他們用新手錶取代她壞掉的那一隻。
(焦點句型) replace sth. with sth. 用…取代…

represent [ˌrɛprɪˋzɛnt] 動 代表；象徵

Doves represent peace.
▶▶ 鴿子象徵和平。

representative [rɛprɪˋzɛntətɪv] 形 典型的 名 典型；代表人員

形 This book is representative of the novels that the author is famous for.
這本書是作者出名的小說之代表作。
名 Tom is the representative of our school in the debate competition.
湯姆代表我們學校參加辯論比賽。

republic [rɪˋpʌblɪk] 名共和國 關 commonwealth 全體國民

I am a citizen of the Republic of China.
▶▶ 我是中華民國國民。

request [rɪˋkwɛst] 名要求 動請求

名 My ex refused my request to see him again.
我前任拒絕我再次見面的要求。
動 The dog looked at me as if to request some food.
那隻狗一直看著我，彷彿在跟我要食物吃似的。

reserve [rɪˋzɝv] 動保留 名貯藏；保留

動 In American universities, many jobs on campus are reserved for students.
美國的大學有許多工作崗位是留給學生的。
名 The reserve of food is sufficient for our need.
貯藏的食物足夠我們所需。

resist [rɪˋzɪst] 動抵抗 關 resistance 抵抗；反抗

She resisted following her father in her career.
▶▶ 她拒絕追隨父親的事業。
文法解析 resist 通常作及物動詞用，後面接名詞或動名詞，表示「抗拒、抵抗或拒絕某事物（的影響或誘惑）」。

resource [ˋrɪsors] 名資源

The small country lacks natural resources.
▶▶ 這個小國缺乏天然資源。

response [rɪˋspɑns] 名回應；答覆

I was heart-broken by his cold response.
▶▶ 我被他的冷淡回應傷透了心。

responsibility [rɪ͵spɑnsəˋbɪlətɪ] 名責任

They frankly admitted their responsibility.
▶▶ 他們坦率地承認了責任。

restrict [rɪˋstrɪkt] 動限制 關 restriction 限制

I try to restrict my smoking to five cigarettes a day.
▶▶ 我試著限制自己每天只抽五支菸。

Level 1 基礎單字
Level 2 必備單字
Level 3 中級單字
Level 4 進階單字
Level 5 高手單字
Level 6 滿級單字

reveal [rɪ`vil] 動 顯示

Her expression revealed panic.
▶▶ 她的表情顯得不安。

ribbon [`rɪbən] 名 絲帶；緞帶

The girl was wearing two blue silk ribbons in her hair.
▶▶ 女孩的頭髮上繫著兩條藍色絲帶。

rid [rɪd] 形 擺脫了的 動 使擺脫

I want to get rid of all my bad habits.
▶▶ 我想擺脫所有壞習慣。

(焦點句型) get rid of sth./sb. 擺脫…；除去…

ripe [raɪp] 形 成熟的

The fruits grew ripe and fell from the tree.
▶▶ 果子成熟後，從樹上落下。

risk [rɪsk] 名 危險 動 冒險

名 You have to analyze all risks before investing.
投資前你必須分析所有的風險。
動 He risked saving the drowning child.
他冒險搶救溺水兒童。

roar [ror] 名 吼叫 動 怒吼

名 The lion in the zoo let out a roar.
動物園裡的獅子吼了一聲。
動 Stop roaring at me! You're scaring me.
別吼了！你嚇到我了。

roast [rost] 動 烘烤 形 烘烤的 名 烘烤的肉

動 We roasted the meat in the oven.
我們用烤箱烤肉。
形 The roast duck smells great.
這隻烤鴨聞起來很棒。
名 We'll do a roast for dinner.
我們烤肉當晚餐。

rob [rɑb] 動 搶劫

They robbed the middle-aged woman and then ran away out of sight.
▶▶ 他們搶劫了那位中年婦女後，便跑得無影無蹤。

robbery [`rɑbərɪ] 名 搶劫

A four-man gang carried out the robbery.
▶▶ 這起搶劫是四人團夥所為。

robe [rob] 名 長袍 動 穿長袍

名 Andrea wore a robe after showering.
　安德莉亞洗澡後穿了件長袍。
動 The judge was robed in black.
　法官身著黑袍。

rocket [`rɑkɪt] 名 火箭 動 發射火箭

名 Onlookers applauded when the rocket finally reached orbit.
　火箭終於進入軌道時，旁觀者都拍手喝彩。
動 They succeeded in rocketing a satellite into orbit.
　他們成功把一顆衛星送入運行軌道。

romantic [ro`mæntɪk] 動 浪漫的 名 浪漫的人

形 He prepared a romantic dinner for his girlfriend on Valentine's Day.
　他在情人節為女友準備了浪漫晚餐。
名 It is said that men whose star sign is Pisces are romantics.
　大家都說雙魚座的男生很浪漫。

rot [rɑt] 動 腐敗 名 腐壞

動 The window frame had rotted away completely.
　窗框已經完全爛掉了。
名 The wooden beams showed signs of rot after the heavy rain.
　大雨過後，木梁顯出腐爛的跡象。

rotten [`rɑtn̩] 形 腐化的

The rotten apple had to be thrown out.
▶▶ 腐爛的蘋果得丟掉。

rough [rʌf] 形 粗糙的 名 粗暴的人

形 Her hands were rough because of hard work.
　她因勤奮工作使得雙手粗糙。

Level 1 基礎單字
Level 2 必備單字
Level 3 中級單字
Level 4 進階單字
Level 5 高手單字
Level 6 滿級單字

(名) Marcus is quite a rough in that he beats others without reason.
馬克斯無緣無故毆打他人，真是個粗暴的人。

roughly [`rʌflɪ] (副)粗略地；粗暴地

The number is roughly 20,000 according to the chart.
▶▶ 根據圖表，這個數字大約是兩萬。

routine [ru`tin] (名)慣例 (形)例行的

(名) I've gotten tired of the daily routine. What I do every day is the same.
我厭倦了每天的例行公事，每天都在做一樣的事情。
(形) Will you go to the routine meeting instead of me?
你可以代我去參加這次的例行會議嗎？

rug [rʌg] (名)地毯

He bought a shag rug to keep his feet warm in winter.
▶▶ 他買了一條粗毛毯子，以在冬天時溫暖雙腳。

rumor [`rumɚ] (名)謠言 (動)謠傳

(名) The rumor of his affair spread around the company.
他外遇的謠言傳遍了公司。
(動) Stop rumoring about her. I believe she is innocent.
別再散播她的謠言，我相信她的清白。

rush [rʌʃ] (動)倉促行事；猛衝 (形)緊急的；繁忙的

(動) The injured passengers were rushed to the hospital.
受傷的乘客被急忙送到醫院。
(形) I got caught in the rush hour traffic.
我遇上尖峰時刻的交通狀況，寸步難行。

rust [rʌst] (名)鐵鏽 (動)生鏽

(名) Amy tried hard to brush off the rust along the side.
艾咪試著把邊緣的鐵鏽刷掉。
(動) The knife is rusted; it is unusable.
刀子生鏽，不能再使用了。

sack [sæk] 名 大包；袋子

My sweater is in your sack.
▶▶ 我的毛衣在你的袋子裡。

sake [sek] 名 緣故；理由

For the sake of his health, he should stop smoking.
▶▶ 為了健康著想，他應該戒菸。

(焦點句型) for the sake of sth. 為了…

salary [`sælərɪ] 名 薪水 動 付薪水

名 Although the salary is unsatisfactory, I work with no complaints.
儘管薪水並不令人滿意，但我毫無怨言地工作。
動 Noel is a salaried man.
諾爾是受薪人士。

satisfactory [,sætɪs`fæktərɪ] 形 令人滿意的 關 satisfy 滿意

Elaine's working effectiveness is satisfactory.
▶▶ 伊蓮恩的工作成效令人滿意。

sauce [sɔs] 名 調味醬 動 加調味醬於

名 Owen added some chili sauce to his noodles.
歐文在麵裡加了些辣椒醬。
動 Gwendolyn never sauces her rice.
關德琳從來不在飯裡加醬。

saucer [`sɔsɚ] 名 托盤；茶碟

The waiter turned over the saucer.
▶▶ 服務生打翻了托盤。

sausage [`sɔsɪdʒ] 名 臘腸；香腸

I'm eager for a grilled sausage.
▶▶ 真想吃一根烤香腸。

saving [`sevɪŋ] 名 存款；救助

Paula has considerable savings in the bank.
▶▶ 寶拉在銀行有一筆可觀的積蓄。

Level 1 基礎單字
Level 2 必備單字
Level 3 中級單字
Level 4 進階單字
Level 5 高手單字
Level 6 滿級單字

scale [skel] 名刻度；規模；秤

Put a weight on the right side of the scale.
▶▶ 在磅秤右側放個砝碼。

scarce [skɛrs] 形稀少的 關 scarcely 幾乎不

The scarce food is insufficient for so many people.
▶▶ 稀缺的糧食無法滿足這麼多人的需求。

scarf [skɑrf] 名圍巾；領巾

I gave him a handmade scarf as his birthday gift.
▶▶ 我送他一條手織圍巾作為生日禮物。

scary [`skɛrɪ] 形駭人的

They sat in a circle and told scary ghost-stories.
▶▶ 他們圍成一圈講可怕的鬼故事。

scatter [`skætɚ] 動散布；消散 名散播物

動 When the tree fell, the monkeys scattered.
樹倒猢猻散。
名 The scatter of the flyers on the ground littered the street.
散落一地的傳單在街上隨處可見。

scholar [`skɑlɚ] 名有學問的人；學者

She is not only a scholar but an important politician.
▶▶ 她不只是個學者，還是個重要的政治家。

scholarship [`skɑlɚˏʃɪp] 名獎學金

Over 1,500 students applied for the scholarship.
▶▶ 超過一千五百名學生申請這項獎學金。

scientific [ˏsaɪən`tɪfɪk] 形科學的；有關科學的

The scientific terms are Greek to me.
▶▶ 這些科學術語我都不懂。

scientist [`saɪəntɪst] 名科學家

Scientists have found a cure for the disease.
▶▶ 科學家們已找出此疾病的治療方法。

scissors [`sɪzəz] 名剪刀

She cut the cloth using scissors.
▶▶ 她用剪刀把布剪開。

scout [skaʊt] 名斥候；偵查兵 動偵查

名 Both my brothers were scouts.
我的兩個哥哥都當過偵查兵。
動 They scouted the area for somewhere to stay the night.
他們四處查看，想找個過夜的地方。

scream [skrim] 動尖叫 名尖叫

動 Isabella screamed when she saw the cockroach.
伊莎貝拉看到蟑螂時大聲尖叫。
名 Did you hear the scream from the woods?
你聽到林子裡發出的尖叫聲嗎？

screw [skru] 名螺絲 動旋緊；轉動

名 One of the screws is loose.
有一顆螺絲鬆了。
動 You need to screw all the parts together.
你得用螺絲把所有的零件固定在一起。

scrub [skrʌb] 動擦拭；擦洗 名擦洗；灌木叢

動 The servant scrubbed the bathroom.
僕人刷洗浴室。
名 The teacher asked the students to give their hands a good scrub before eating.
老師要求學生在吃飯前把手洗乾淨。

seal [sil] 名海豹；印章 動密封

名 They are watching the seal show.
他們在看海豹表演。
動 Make sure you've signed the check before sealing the envelope.
一定要在支票上簽了名再封信封。

security [sɪ`kjʊrətɪ] 名安全

I'm responsible for your security.
▶▶ 我負責保護你的安全。

Level 1 基礎單字
Level 2 必備單字
Level 3 中級單字
Level 4 進階單字
Level 5 高手單字
Level 6 滿級單字

semester [səˋmɛstə] 名 半學年；一學期

She decided to transfer to another college this semester.
▶▶ 她決定在這個學期轉到另一所學校。

senior [ˋsinjə] 名 年長者 形 年長的

名 Seniors teach juniors.
　年長者教導年少者。
形 We should treat senior workers with respect.
　我們該尊重年長的工作者。

sensible [ˋsɛnsəbl̩] 形 可感覺的；理性的

Sophia kept sensible even if she met unreasonable customers.
▶▶ 蘇菲亞即使遇到無理的客人時還是保持理性。

separation [ˌsɛpəˋreʃən] 名 分離；隔離

They hugged each other in tears after a five-year separation.
▶▶ 經歷五年的分離，他們含淚相擁。

sexual [ˋsɛkʃuəl] 形 性的

There have been a lot of cases of sexual harassment in the American Navy.
▶▶ 美國海軍中已發生過多起性騷擾事件。

sexy [ˋsɛksɪ] 形 性感的

The girl is so sexy that she attracts everyone's attention.
▶▶ 那位女孩相當性感，攫住了所有人的目光。

shadow [ˋʃædo] 名 陰暗之處；影子 動 使有陰影

名 The willow's shadow falls on the lake.
　垂柳的影子倒映在湖面上。
動 A broad hat shadowed her face.
　一頂寬邊帽遮住了她的臉。

shallow [ˋʃælo] 形 淺的；淺薄的

The sea is shallow here.
▶▶ 這兒的海水很淺。

shampoo [ʃæmˋpu] 名 洗髮精 動 清洗

名 I'm used to this brand's shampoo.
　我習慣這種品牌的洗髮精。

Level 1 基礎單字
Level 2 必備單字
Level 3 中級單字
Level 4 進階單字
Level 5 高手單字
Level 6 滿級單字

動 Liz shampooed her hair and then dried it.
>> 麗茲洗了頭髮，然後吹乾。

shepherd [`ʃɛpəd] 名 牧羊人

The shepherd and his dog gathered the sheep.
>> 牧羊人和牧羊犬把羊群趕到一塊兒。

shiny [`ʃaɪnɪ] 形 發光的；晴朗的

The diamond ring looked shiny and expensive.
>> 那只鑽戒看起來閃閃發亮又昂貴。

shorten [`ʃɔrtn̩] 動 縮短；使變少

I've asked her to shorten my blue dress.
>> 我已經請她把我的藍色洋裝改短一點。

shortly [`ʃɔrtlɪ] 副 不久；馬上

Don't worry. He will come back shortly.
>> 別擔心，他很快就回來。

shovel [`ʃʌvl̩] 名 鏟子 動 剷除

名 James was working with a shovel.
　　詹姆斯用鏟子幹活。
動 They shoveled snow from the sidewalk.
　　他們鏟起人行道上的積雪。

shrimp [ʃrɪmp] 名 蝦子

Some people are allergic to shrimp.
>> 有些人對蝦子過敏。

shrink [ʃrɪŋk] 動 收縮；退縮

Will this soap shrink woolen clothes?
>> 這種肥皂會使羊毛衣物縮水嗎？
文法解析 shrink 動詞三態變化為 shrink / shrank / shrunk。

sigh [saɪ] 動 嘆息 名 嘆息

動 She just sighed without saying anything.
　　她只是嘆息，什麼也不說。

(名) On hearing my father's sigh, I knew he must be facing some difficulties.
聽見爸爸的嘆息聲，我知道他一定遇上了一些難題。

signal [`sɪgn̩] (名) 信號；號誌 (動) 打信號

(名) Obey the traffic signals, or you will get a fine.
注意交通號誌，不然會被罰款。
(動) I signaled to them with a flashlight.
我用手電筒向他們發信號。

significant [sɪgˋnɪfəkənt] (形) 有意義的

The principal gave a significant speech to the graduates.
▶ 校長向畢業生們發表了一場意義深遠的演講。

silk [sɪlk] (名) 絲；綢

Her skin is as smooth as silk.
▶ 她的皮膚像絲綢般柔滑。

similarity [ˏsɪməˋlærətɪ] (名) 類似；相似

The similarity of the twin brothers puzzled many people.
▶ 這對雙胞胎兄弟的相似度讓許多人困惑。

sin [sɪn] (名) 罪；罪惡 (動) 犯過失；犯罪

(名) It's a sin to curse others.
詛咒他人是種罪過。
(動) Allen had not only sinned but also committed a crime, so he was arrested.
艾倫不僅犯錯，還犯了罪，所以他被逮捕了。

sincere [sɪnˋsɪr] (形) 真實的；誠摯的

Please accept our sincere thanks.
▶ 請接受我們誠摯的謝意。

sink [sɪŋk] (動) 沉入 (名) 水槽

(動) The ship sank to the bottom of the sea.
船沉入海底。
(名) Don't just leave your dirty plates in the sink!
別把髒盤子往洗碗槽裡一放就不管了！

sip [sɪp] 動 啜飲；小口地喝

Grace sipped politely at her tea.
▶▶ 葛瑞絲彬彬有禮地小口喝著茶。

situation [ˌsɪtʃʊˋeʃən] 名 情勢 相 scenario 局面；情節

Her response is praiseworthy in that emergency situation.
▶▶ 在那種危急情況下，她的反應值得稱讚。

skate [sket] 動 溜冰；滑冰

It was so cold that we were able to go skating on the frozen lake.
▶▶ 天氣冷到我們能在湖上溜冰。

ski [ski] 名 滑雪板 動 滑雪

名 You can buy some skis in the store.
　　你可以在這間店買到滑雪板。
動 They go skiing in Switzerland every winter.
　　他們每年冬天都去瑞士滑雪。

skillful [ˋskɪlfəl] 形 熟練的；靈巧的

The worker is quite skillful in his work.
▶▶ 工人對他的工作相當熟練。

skinny [ˋskɪnɪ] 形 皮包骨的

You're skinny enough without going on a diet.
▶▶ 你不必節食就已經夠瘦了。

skip [skɪp] 動 略過 名 省略

動 You can skip the animation when you visit the website.
　　你造訪這個網站時可以略過動畫。
名 I read the splendid novel without a skip of any pages.
　　我把那本精彩的小說一頁不漏地讀完了。

slave [slev] 名 奴隸 動 做苦工

名 Slaves are deprived of their human rights.
　　奴隸的人權遭到剝奪。
動 They slaved away in order to earn money.
　　他們為了賺錢苦苦幹活。

Level 1 基礎單字
Level 2 必備單字
Level 3 中級單字
Level 4 進階單字
Level 5 高手單字
Level 6 滿級單字

sleeve [sliv] 名 衣袖

Clarence doesn't like long sleeves.
▶▶ 克拉倫斯不喜歡長袖衣服。

slender [`slɛndɚ] 形 苗條的

I envy Vicky's slender figure so much.
▶▶ 我好羨慕薇琪的苗條身材。

slice [slaɪs] 名 片；薄的切片 動 切成薄片

名 Cut the meat into thin slices.
把肉切成薄片。
動 I sliced the apple to make a salad.
我把蘋果切片用來做沙拉。

slippery [`slɪpərɪ] 形 滑溜的

In places, the path can be wet and slippery.
▶▶ 這條小徑有些路段又濕又滑。

slope [slop] 名 坡度；斜面

It is dangerous to ride a bike on a steep slope.
▶▶ 在陡坡上騎車很危險。

snap [snæp] 動 折斷；迅速抓住

He snapped the chopstick in two.
▶▶ 他把筷子折成兩半。

solid [`salɪd] 形 固體的

It was so cold that the stream had frozen solid.
▶▶ 天氣很冷，小河凍得凝結了。

someday [`sʌm,de] 副 將來有一天；來日

We will meet again someday.
▶▶ 我們來日會再重逢的。

somehow [`sʌm,haʊ] 副 不知何故

The details were supposed to be secret but were somehow leaked.
▶▶ 這些細節原屬秘密，可是不知怎麼給洩露出去了。

sometime [`sʌm,taɪm] 副某些時候；來日

The new product will be launched sometime next year.
▶▶ 新產品將會在明年某時發表。

sorrow [`sɑro] 名悲傷 動感到哀傷

名 Jeremy expressed his sorrow at the news of her death.
聽到她的死訊，傑瑞米表示哀傷。
動 They had sorrowed over his death.
他們對他的去世表示哀悼。

spaghetti [,spə`gɛtɪ] 名義大利麵

I am very keen on spaghetti.
▶▶ 我很愛義大利麵。

specific [spə`sɪfɪk] 形具體的；明確的；特殊的

Give me a specific example rather than abstract ones.
▶▶ 給我具體的例子而不要抽象的。

spice [spaɪs] 名香料

The island produces spice.
▶▶ 這座島嶼出產香料。

spill [spɪl] 動灑出；流出 名溢出

動 When spilled into the sea, oil can be toxic to marine plants and animals.
石油排入海洋就有可能危害海中的動植物。
名 The spill of the juice stained her dress.
濺出的果汁弄髒了她的洋裝。

spin [spɪn] 動旋轉；紡織 名旋轉

動 Stay away from the helicopter when its blades start to spin.
直升機的旋翼片開始轉動時，儘量離遠點兒。
名 The spin of the top is slowing down.
旋轉的陀螺慢了下來。
文法解析 spin動詞三態變化為 spin / spun / spun。

spinach [`spɪnɪtʃ] 名菠菜

I'll have the green peas instead of the spinach.
▶▶ 我想要份青豆而不是菠菜。

Level 1 基礎單字
Level 2 必備單字
Level 3 中級單字
Level 4 進階單字
Level 5 高手單字
Level 6 滿級單字

spit [spɪt] 動吐；吐口水 名唾液

動 Some rude drivers spit out the window.
有些粗魯無禮的駕駛會朝窗外吐口水。

名 Mary's spit flew as she talked.
瑪莉講話時口沫橫飛。

文法解析 spit 動詞三態變化為 spit / spat / spat。

spite [spaɪt] 名惡意

He pushed her out of spite.
▶▶ 他出於惡意推了她。

splash [splæʃ] 動濺起來 名飛濺聲

動 We splashed our way through the mud.
我們濺著泥漿前進。

名 The children jumped into the river with a splash.
孩子們撲通一聲跳進河裡。

spoil [spɔɪl] 動寵壞；損壞

Spare the rod, spoil the child.
▶▶ 不打不成器。

spray [spre] 名噴霧器 動噴；濺

名 The spray of pesticide benefits farmers.
這種殺蟲噴霧劑使農夫受益。

動 The waterfall sprayed water all around.
瀑布的水珠四處飛濺。

spy [spaɪ] 名間諜

We believe that she is a spy from our rival company.
▶▶ 我們懷疑她是競爭對手公司派來的間諜。

squeeze [skwiz] 動壓擠；擠 名緊抱；擁擠

動 Judith squeezed the lemon juice on the fish.
茱蒂絲把檸檬汁擠到魚肉上。

名 He gave my hand a squeeze to show his support.
他緊握我的手，表示他的支持。

squirrel [`skwɜəl] 名 松鼠

Squirrels feed on nuts.
▶▶ 松鼠以堅果為食。

stable [`stebḷ] 形 穩定的

Albert is satisfied with his stable job and high pay.
▶▶ 艾伯特相當滿意他的高薪又穩定的工作。

stadium [`stedɪəm] 名 室外運動場

The stadium is filled with a huge crowd today.
▶▶ 今天運動場擠滿了人。

staff [stæf] 名 棒；竿子；全體人員

The photo is of the staff of our company.
▶▶ 這張照片是我們公司的全體員工。

stale [stel] 形 不新鮮的；陳舊的

The stale bread tasted bad, but Kyle still ate it.
▶▶ 這不新鮮的麵包很難吃，但凱爾還是吃掉了。

stare [stɛr] 動 盯；凝視 名 盯；凝視

動 I saw a stranger staring at me in anger.
　　我看到那個陌生人憤怒地盯著我。
名 He gave her a rude stare.
　　他無禮地瞪了她一眼。

starve [stɑrv] 動 餓死；飢餓

The refugees starved to death for lack of food.
▶▶ 那些難民因缺乏食物餓死了。

statue [`stætʃʊ] 名 鑄像；雕像

Todd carved a beautiful statue out of marble.
▶▶ 陶德用大理石雕刻了一座美麗的雕像。

steady [`stɛdɪ] 形 穩固的

With the steady increase of China's national power, there is bound to be those who worry about this situation.
▶▶ 隨著中國國力穩定地持續增長，擔心此狀況的人增加許多。

Level 1 基礎單字
Level 2 必備單字
Level 3 中級單字
Level 4 進階單字
Level 5 高手單字
Level 6 滿級單字

steal [stil] 動偷

Rebecca stole money from her father so she could go to the movies.

▷▷ 麗貝卡從父親那裡偷了錢，所以她可以去看電影。

文法解析 steal 動詞三態變化為 steal / stole / stolen。

steam [stim] 名蒸汽 動蒸

名 The steam fogged my glasses.
蒸氣使我的眼鏡變模糊。
動 She is steaming fish.
她正在蒸魚。

steep [stip] 形險峻的

The hikers were determined to conquer the steep mountain path.

▷▷ 登山客下定決心克服這條嚴峻的山路。

sticky [`stɪkɪ] 形黏的；棘手的

The baby's hands were sticky with jam.

▷▷ 那嬰兒的雙手因沾滿了果醬而黏答答的。

stiff [stɪf] 形僵硬的

I've got a stiff neck.

▷▷ 我脖子僵硬了。

sting [stɪŋ] 動刺；叮

A bee stung me on the arm.

▷▷ 一隻蜜蜂螫了我的手臂。

stir [stɜ] 動攪拌

The yummy juice is done after some stirring.

▷▷ 稍加攪拌後，美味的果汁就完成了。

stitch [stɪtʃ] 名編織；一針 動縫；繡

名 You dropped a stitch here, so the button seems loose.
你這裡漏了一針，所以釦子看起來鬆鬆的。
動 The nurse cleansed the wound for the injured man before stitching it up.
護士先把傷患的傷口清洗乾淨後再縫合。

stomach [`stʌmək] 名 胃

When I start to talk in front of the class, I have butterflies in my stomach.
▶▶ 當我開始在全班面前講話時,我感到非常緊張。

stool [stul] 名 凳子

Victor pushed the stool under the table.
▶▶ 維克多把凳子推到桌子下面。

stormy [`stɔrmɪ] 形 暴風雨的;多風暴的

It is stormy outside; we should stay home.
▶▶ 外面狂風暴雨,我們應該待在家裡。

stove [stov] 名 爐子

She is heating the soup on the stove.
▶▶ 她在爐子上熱湯。

strategy [`strætədʒɪ] 名 戰略;策略 關 strategic 戰略(性)的;策略的

The strategy was designed to wear down the enemy's resistance.
▶▶ 這一策略旨在逐步削弱敵人的抵抗力。

straw [strɔ] 名 吸管;稻草

We don't use as many plastic straws these days.
▶▶ 如今,我們不再使用那麼多塑膠吸管了。

strength [strɛŋθ] 名 力量;強度

The strength of the typhoon had been underestimated.
▶▶ 颱風的強度被低估了。

strip [strɪp] 名 條 動 剝;剝除

名 A strip of path hides behind the woods.
樹林後藏著一條小徑。
動 They stripped off their clothes and jumped into water.
他們脫光衣服跳進水裡。

structure [`strʌktʃɚ] 名 構造;結構 動 建立組織

名 The structure of language has some connection with the process of thought.
語言結構與思維過程之間存在著某種聯繫。

動 The new manager structured the communication networks in our department.
新任經理在我們部門建立連絡系統。

stubborn [`stʌbən] 形 頑固的

Walker can be very stubborn when he wants to be!
▶▶ 沃克一倔強起來，簡直固執得要命！

studio [`stjudɪˌo] 名 工作室；播音室

He has his own studio for painting.
▶▶ 他有自己的繪畫工作室。

stuff [stʌf] 名 東西；材料 動 填塞；裝填

名 You need to prepare a lot of stuff if you want to go hiking.
如果你想去健行，必須準備許多東西。
動 The doll was stuffed with cotton.
這個洋娃娃裡頭塞著棉花。

substance [`sʌbstəns] 名 物質；物體；實質

Ice and snow are different forms of the same substance, water.
▶▶ 冰和雪都是水這一種物質的不同的形式。

subtract [səb`trækt] 動 扣除；移走 同 deduct

His beard subtracts from his good looks.
▶▶ 他的鬍子減弱了他的帥氣。

suburb [`sʌbɝb] 名 市郊；郊區

We live in the suburbs and drive downtown every day.
▶▶ 我們住在郊區，每天開車到市中心。

suck [sʌk] 動 吸；吸取 名 吸

動 Diana still sucks her thumb when she's worried.
黛安娜在憂慮時仍然會吸吮大拇指。
名 The baby took one suck of the milk.
嬰兒吸了一口牛奶。

suffer [`sʌfɚ] 動 受苦；遭受

Kevin suffers from the misery of a failed love.
▶▶ 凱文深受失戀所苦。

焦點句型 suffer from N./Ving 受…所苦

sufficient [sə`fɪʃənt] 形 充足的

Is it available in sufficient quantity?
▶ 這東西能不能足量供應？

suicide [`suə͵saɪd] 名 自殺；自滅

He committed suicide because of unemployment.
▶他因為失業而走上絕路。

sum [sʌm] 名 總計 動 合計

名 You will be fined the sum of 200 dollars.
你將被罰款二百美金。
動 To sum up, the essay is such a cliche.
總而言之，這篇文章都是陳腔濫調。

summary [`sʌmərɪ] 名 摘要

The summary of this thesis was written in half an hour.
▶ 這篇論文的摘要在半小時內寫成。

summit [`sʌmɪt] 名 頂點；高峰

Hannah is on the summit of her career.
▶ 漢娜正處於事業的顛峰。

superior [sə`pɪrɪɚ] 形 較優的 名 長官

形 Freshly brewed coffee is superior to instant coffee.
現煮的咖啡比即溶咖啡來得好。
名 My superior is the one who supervises me.
監督我的是我上司。

surround [sə`raund] 動 圍繞

Why do so many reporters surround us?
▶ 為什麼這麼多記者包圍我們？

survey [sə`ve] 動 檢查；測量 名 調查；勘測

動 You have to survey the references before you decide on your report's theme.
你必須在決定報告題目之前，先查閱過參考資料。
名 The professor asked for a three-week deadline for the survey.
教授要求在三週內完成調查。

survivor [səˋvaɪvə] 名 生還者 關 survive 倖存

Kelly was the only survivor of the accident.
▶▶ 凱莉是這場意外唯一的生還者。

suspect [səˋspɛkt] / [ˋsʌspɛkt] 動 懷疑 名 嫌疑犯

動 Suspecting nothing, he walked right into the trap.
　　他毫無覺察，直接走入陷阱。
名 The suspect listened to the witness.
　　嫌疑犯聽著目擊者說話。

suspicion [səˋspɪʃən] 名 懷疑；猜想

Mandy has a suspicion that her boyfriend is having an affair.
▶▶ 曼蒂懷疑她男友外遇。

swan [swɑn] 名 天鵝

The swan flapped its wings noisily.
▶▶ 天鵝大聲地拍打著翅膀。

swear [swɛr] 動 發誓；宣誓

I will not believe you unless you swear it is true.
▶▶ 除非你發誓這是真的，我才會相信你。

sweat [swɛt] 名 汗水 動 出汗

名 He rubbed off the sweat from his forehead.
　　他把前額的汗擦掉。
動 Why are you sweating in such cool weather?
　　為什麼你會在這樣涼爽的天氣裡流汗？

swell [swɛl] 動 膨脹；（河水等）上漲

The river was swollen with melted snow.
▶▶ 河水因融雪而上漲。
文法解析 swell 動詞三態變化為 swell / swelled / swollen。

swift [swɪft] 形 迅速的

The cat is too swift to catch.
▶▶ 貓跑得太快抓不到。

sword [sɔrd] 名 劍；刀

The sword glanced off the armor.
▶▶ 劍擦過盔甲。

tablet [ˋtæblɪt] 名 塊；片

The doctor told him to take two tablets of aspirin before every meal.
▶▶ 醫生告訴他每餐飯前吃兩片阿斯匹靈。

tag [tæg] 名 標籤 動 加標籤

名 The price on the tag is wrong.
標籤上的價格錯了。

動 He tagged his pens and notebooks with his name.
他在他的筆和筆記本上標上他的名字。

tailor [ˋtelɚ] 名 裁縫師 動 裁縫

名 My mother is a skilled tailor.
我媽媽是個裁縫，手藝很好。

動 Jennifer tailored some pants for her son.
珍妮佛為她兒子縫製長褲。

talent [ˋtælənt] 名 天賦；才能

Grace has a talent for writing.
▶▶ 葛瑞絲有寫作的天賦。

talkative [ˋtɔkətɪv] 形 健談的

A talkative person makes new friends quickly.
▶▶ 健談的人容易結識他人。

tame [tem] 形 溫順的；馴服的 動 馴服

形 Animals in the zoo are tame.
動物園裡的動物都已被馴服。

動 Walter is an expert in taming animals.
瓦爾特是個馴獸專家。

1 Level 基礎單字
2 Level 必備單字
3 Level 中級單字
4 Level 進階單字
5 Level 高手單字
6 Level 滿級單字

tangerine [`tændʒəˌrin] 名柑橘；橘子

You need to peel tangerines before eating them.
▶▶ 吃橘子要先剝皮。

tank [tæŋk] 名坦克

We had destroyed all the tanks of our enemy.
▶▶ 我們已經摧毀敵人所有的坦克車。

tap [tæp] 名輕拍聲 動輕打

名 Can you hear the tap on the door?
你聽見有人在敲門嗎？
動 My teacher tapped on my head to wake me up.
老師輕敲我的頭叫醒我。

tasty [`testɪ] 形好吃的

He always brings tasty snacks to treat us.
▶▶ 他總是帶好吃的甜點來款待我們。

tease [tiz] 動嘲弄 名揶揄

動 Shame on you! You tease such a little child because he is poor?
你真可恥！這麼小的孩子，你就因為他窮而嘲笑他？
名 Turn a deaf ear to the teases.
對那些揶揄充耳不聞吧。

technical [`tɛknɪkḷ] 形技術上的；技能的

For technical problems, you should turn to the person in charge of MIS.
▶▶ 這些技術問題應該問資訊系統管理人員。

technique [tɛk`nik] 名技術；技巧

My manager taught me lots of good techniques for solving problems.
▶▶ 我的經理教我很多解決問題的良好技巧。

teenage [`tinˌedʒ] 形十幾歲的

Teenage students are crazy about that jazz band.
▶▶ 十來歲的學生都為這爵士樂團瘋狂。

temper [`tɛmpɚ] 名脾氣

Mike is notorious for his ill temper.
▶▶ 麥克因壞脾氣而惡名昭彰。

temporary [`tɛmpəˏrɛrɪ] 形暫時的 同 provisional

John has got a temporary job.
▶▶ 約翰找到一份臨時的工作。

tend [tɛnd] 動傾向

Those who graduate from high school tend to enter universities.
▶▶ 高中畢業的人傾向於念大學。

tender [`tɛndə] 形溫柔的

Her tender voice comforted my sorrow.
▶▶ 她溫柔的聲音撫慰了我的憂傷。

tent [tɛnt] 名帳篷

Tents are used by campers and by soldiers in the field.
▶▶ 露營的人和戰地的士兵都會使用帳篷。

terrific [təˋrɪfɪk] 形驚人的；極好的

Everyone thought the drama was terrific.
▶▶ 大家覺得那齣戲相當驚人。

territory [`tɛrəˏtorɪ] 名領土；版圖 同 domain

A tract of level territory had been sliced out from the rainforest.
▶▶ 那片雨林被割去大塊平地。

thankful [`θæŋkfəl] 形感激的

We cannot be thankful enough to you for your timely and unselfish help.
▶▶ 我們對你們及時而無私的援助真是感激不盡。

theory [`θiərɪ] 名理論；推論 關 hypothesis 假說 / premise 假設

The theory was overthrown by a young PhD student.
▶▶ 這個理論被一個年輕的博士生推翻。

thirst [θɝst] 名口渴；渴望

The horse satisfied its thirst at the river.
▶▶ 那馬在河中喝水解渴。

Level 1 基礎單字
Level 2 必備單字
Level 3 中級單字
Level 4 進階單字
Level 5 高手單字
Level 6 滿級單字

thread [θrɛd] 名線 動穿線

名 The thread broke while the woman was sewing clothes.
當那女子在縫衣服時，線斷了。

動 The waiters threaded between the crowded tables.
服務員穿行在擁擠的餐桌之間。

threat [θrɛt] 名威脅；恐嚇

I will not surrender to your threat.
▶▶ 我不會屈服於你的威脅。

threaten [`θrɛtn̩] 動威脅

The robber threatened to hurt me if I didn't hand over my money.
▶▶ 如果我不把錢交出，搶匪威脅要傷我。

thumb [θʌm] 名拇指

The girl bit the tip of her right thumb, looking at me.
▶▶ 那女孩一邊咬著右手拇指指尖，一邊看著我。

tide [taɪd] 名潮；趨勢

Time and tide wait for no man.
▶▶ 時間不等人。

tight [taɪt] 形緊的 副緊緊地

形 The tight shoes hurt my feet.
這雙鞋子太緊，弄痛了我的腳。

副 I held the rope tight to prevent it from slipping.
我緊緊地抓住繩子，以防止它滑落。

tighten [`taɪtn̩] 動勒緊；使堅固

Raymond tightened the knot so that it wouldn't loosen.
▶▶ 雷蒙德勒緊繩結以免鬆掉。

timber [`tɪmbɚ] 名木材；樹林

The timber has been dry enough to use.
▶▶ 這木材現在已乾燥可用了。

tobacco [tə`bæko] 名菸草

The old man filled his pipe with tobacco.
▶▶ 老人用菸草填滿他的菸斗。

ton [tʌn] 名噸

Tons of coal was extracted.
▶▶ 成噸的煤礦被挖出。

toss [tɔs] 動拋；投 名拋；投

動 Let's toss a coin to decide where to go.
拋硬幣決定要去哪裡吧。
名 The rider was injured by the toss from a horse.
騎士因被馬拋下而受傷。

tough [tʌf] 形困難的

I want a challenge, so I like to do tough work.
▶▶ 我想要挑戰，所以我喜歡艱困的工作。

tourism [ˋturɪzm̩] 名觀光；遊覽

Tourism generates new job opportunities.
▶▶ 旅遊業會帶來新的就業機會。

tourist [ˋturɪst] 名觀光客

Tourists represent their nations overseas through their behavior.
▶▶ 在國外，觀光客的舉止都代表著他們的國家。

tow [to] 動拖曳 名拖曳

動 If you park your car here, the police may tow it away.
你要是把車停在這裡，警察就會把它拖走。
名 My car broke down; can you give me a tow with your big truck?
我的車拋錨了，你能讓我把車掛在你的車後面拖行嗎？

tower [ˋtauɚ] 名塔 動高聳

名 Next to the shopping mall stands a tower.
購物中心旁豎著一座高塔。
動 The skyscraper towers into the sky.
摩天大樓高聳入雲。

trace [tres] 動追溯 名蹤跡

動 The vase can be traced back to one thousand years ago.
這個花瓶的歷史可以追溯到一千年前。
名 Luckily, the thief left traces.
所幸，小偷留下了蛛絲馬跡。

Level 1 基礎單字
Level 2 必備單字
Level 3 中級單字
Level 4 進階單字
Level 5 高手單字
Level 6 滿級單字

trader [`tredɚ] 名 商人

The trader went bankrupt due to a major fall in business.
▶▶ 這個商人經商失敗而破產。

trail [trel] 名 痕跡 動 跟蹤；追獵

名 The trail of ink on the paper reminds me of something.
紙上的墨痕讓我想起某些事情。
動 The police trailed the thief.
警察追蹤小偷。

transport [træns`port ] / [ `trænsport] 動 運輸 名 輸送

動 Most of our luggage was transported by sea.
我們的大部分行李都是海運的。
名 How much does the luggage transport cost?
行李運輸要多少錢？

traveler [`trævlɚ] 名 旅行者

Strangers and travelers were welcome in the couple's home anytime.
▶▶ 那對夫婦的家隨時歡迎陌生人與旅客。

tray [tre] 名 托盤

The flight attendant held a tray with glasses and dishes.
▶▶ 空姐端了一個滿是杯盤的托盤。

trend [trɛnd] 名 趨勢；傾向

She always follows the latest trends in fashion.
▶▶ 她總是追隨最新的流行趨勢。

tribe [traɪb] 名 部落；種族

The warriors of this tribe enjoy a privileged status.
▶▶ 這個部落的戰士享有特權地位。

tricky [`trɪkɪ] 形 （事情、問題等）難對付的；狡猾的；奸詐的

The tricky person is planning to deceive you.
▶▶ 那個奸詐的人一定打算要騙你。

troop [trup] 名 軍隊

The enemy troops withdrew.
▶▶ 敵軍撤退了。

tropical [`trɑpɪkḷ] 形 熱帶的 關 tropic 回歸線

Tropical fruits include banana, papaya and coconut.
▶▶ 熱帶水果包括香蕉、木瓜和椰子。

trumpet [`trʌmpɪt] 名 喇叭；小號 動 吹喇叭

名 He plays the trumpet in the orchestra.
他在交響樂團裡吹小號。
動 Robin's neighbors complained about his trumpeting at night.
羅賓因夜裡吹喇叭被鄰居抱怨。

trunk [trʌŋk] 名 樹幹

The fallen tree trunk blocked the road.
▶▶ 倒下的樹幹堵住了路。

truthful [`truθfəl] 形 誠實的；如實的 關 truth 事實

You can count on him for a truthful report of the accident.
▶▶ 你放心，他會對事故做出如實的報導。

tub [tʌb] 名 桶；盆

Ophelia washed the clothes in the tub.
▶▶ 奧菲莉亞洗了洗盆子裡的衣服。

tug [tʌg] 動 用力拉 名 拖拉

動 The interviewee nervously tugged at his shirt.
受訪者緊張地拉了拉襯衫。
名 In spite of a tug on his arm from his mother, the boy didn't move.
不管母親怎麼拉，小男孩就是不動。

tune [tjun] 名 調子 動 調整音調

名 The tune of the song is familiar to me.
這首歌的音調對我而言很熟悉。
動 The violinist tuned his violin before he started playing.
小提琴家在演出前先替小提琴調音。

tunnel [`tʌnḷ] 名 隧道

The train entered the tunnel.
▶▶ 火車進了隧道。

1 Level 基礎單字

2 Level 必備單字

3 Level 中級單字

4 Level 進階單字

5 Level 高手單字

6 Level 滿級單字

tutor [`tjutɚ] 名家庭教師 動輔導

(名) Many parents only hire female tutors for their children.
很多家長為小孩找家教時都限女性。
(動) The man is tutoring children in arithmetic.
這人教小孩算數。

twin [twɪn] 名雙胞胎

The twin sisters are very much alike in appearance.
▶▶ 這對雙胞胎姐妹在外表上十分相像。

twist [twɪst] 動扭曲

I twisted my ankle last night.
▶▶ 我昨晚扭傷了腳踝。

UNIT 21 **U 字頭中級單字**

MP3 069

underwear [`ʌndɚ͵wɛr] 名內衣

He has many colors and styles of underwear.
▶▶ 他有各種顏色和款式的內衣。

union [`junjən] 名聯合；組織

Aaron joined the labor union to protect himself in the workplace.
▶▶ 亞倫加入工會以在職場上自保。

unique [ju`nik] 形唯一的；獨特的

Although my husband looks ordinary, he is unique in my mind.
▶▶ 雖然我老公看起來很平凡，但在我心裡是獨一無二的。

unite [ju`naɪt] 動聯合；合併

The United Nations has its own troops.
▶▶ 聯合國有自己的軍隊。

unity [`junətɪ] 名聯合；統一

The main idea of this article is to call for national unity.
▶▶ 這篇文章的主旨是呼籲民族團結。

urban [`ɝbən] 形 都市的

A hermit usually prefers rural life to urban living.
▶▶ 隱士通常喜歡鄉村生活勝於都市生活。

V 字頭中級單字

MP3 070

vacant [`vekənt] 形 空的

I feel lonely when I saw the vacant house.
▶▶ 我看著空蕩蕩的房子感到寂寞。

van [væn] 名 貨車

The wooden bridge is not strong enough to allow the passage of vans.
▶▶ 這座木橋不夠堅固，載重貨車不能通行。

vanish [`vænɪʃ] 動 消失

She vanished without saying goodbye to us.
▶▶ 她沒向我們說再見就消失了。

variety [və`raɪətɪ] 名 多樣性

There is a wide variety of patterns to choose from.
▶▶ 有種類繁多的圖案可供選擇。

various [`vɛrɪəs] 形 多種的 關 miscellaneous 混雜的

The various choices are dazzling.
▶▶ 這麼多的選擇使人眼花撩亂。

vary [`vɛrɪ] 動 使變化；改變

The temperature varies depending on location.
▶▶ 溫度隨著地點而變化。

vase [ves] 名 花瓶

The girl broke the vase accidentally.
▶▶ 小女孩無意間打破了花瓶。

vehicle [`viəkl̩] 名 交通工具；車輛

The road was just wide enough for two vehicles to pass.
▶▶ 這條路的寬度正好能容兩輛車開過。

Level 1 基礎單字
Level 2 必備單字
Level 3 中級單字
Level 4 進階單字
Level 5 高手單字
Level 6 滿級單字

verse [vɝs] 名詩；韻文

The professor was very familiar with the verses from Shakespeare.
▶▶ 那位教授對莎士比亞的詩很熟悉。

vest [vɛst] 名背心；馬甲 動授給

名 The policeman survived because of his bulletproof vest.
警察因為穿了防彈背心而倖免於難。
動 He was vested with a large house after his father's death.
在他父親過世後，他就得到一棟大房子。

victim [`vɪktɪm] 名受害者

There were over 100 victims in the fire.
▶▶ 火災的受害者超過一百位。

violence [`vaɪələns] 名暴力

The cycle of violence in this troubled part of the world seemed endless.
▶▶ 發生在這一動亂地區的暴力事件似乎永無休止。

violent [`vaɪələnt] 形暴力的；猛烈的

The violent storm caused great damage to the village.
▶▶ 猛烈的暴風雨對村莊造成巨大破壞。

violet [`vaɪəlɪt] 名紫羅蘭；藍紫色 形藍紫色的

名 A secret admirer put a bunch of violets on Elyssa's desk.
神祕愛慕者在艾莉莎桌上放了一束紫羅蘭。
形 The violet blouse is very attractive.
那件藍紫色上衣很美。

visible [`vɪzəbḷ] 形可看見的

The sea was plainly visible in the distance.
▶▶ 那片海在遠處清晰可見。

vision [`vɪʒən] 名視力；視野

Our CEO has great vision regarding market trends.
▶▶ 我們的執行長對於市場趨勢很有遠見。

vitamin [`vaɪtəmɪn] 名維生素；維他命

Vitamin C is generally used in whitening products.
▶▶ 維他命 C 廣泛被使用於美白產品。

vivid [`vɪvɪd] 形 生動的

The leopard in the painting is so vivid that it almost seems as if it is alive.
▶▶ 畫中的豹栩栩如生，好像活的一樣。

vocabulary [vo`kæbjə‚lɛrɪ] 名 單字；字彙

Memorize new vocabulary to improve your writing.
▶▶ 多背些單字來增強寫作能力。

volleyball [`vɑlɪ‚bɔl] 名 排球

Beach volleyball is fun.
▶▶ 沙灘排球很好玩。

volume [`vɑljum] 名 容量；體積；總量；音量；卷

Turn down the volume, please. It is already midnight.
▶▶ 請把音量關小，現在已經午夜了。

voter [votɚ] 名 選民 關 vote 投票

Voters usually vote for a candidate according to his or her party.
▶▶ 選民常依候選人所屬的政黨來投票。

 **W 字頭中級單字**

MP3 071

wage [wedʒ] 名 週薪；工資

The labor group protested against the unreasonable minimum wage.
▶▶ 勞工團體抗議不合理的最低工資。

wagon [`wægən] 名 四輪馬車；貨車

I prefer a station wagon to a smaller car.
▶▶ 我喜歡旅行車勝於小車。

wander [`wɑndɚ] 動 徘徊；漫步

During the storm, the ship wandered from its course.
▶▶ 船在風暴中偏離了航向。

warmth [wɔrmθ] 名 暖和

John was touched by the warmth of their welcome.
▶▶ 約翰被他們熱烈的歡迎所感動。

1 Level 基礎單字
2 Level 必備單字
3 Level 中級單字
4 Level 進階單字
5 Level 高手單字
6 Level 滿級單字

warn [wɔrn] 動警告

My father warned me not to go out at night.
▶▶ 我父親警告我夜裡不要出門。

waterfall [`wɑtəˌfɔl] 名瀑布

The river came pouring down in a waterfall off the hill.
▶▶ 河水從山上傾瀉而下形成瀑布。

wax [wæks] 名蠟

The delicate artwork was made of wax.
▶▶ 這件精美的藝術品由蠟製成。

weaken [`wikən] 動使變弱 關 weak 虛弱的

None of these setbacks could weaken her resolve to become a doctor.
▶▶ 這些挫折一點也動搖不了她當醫生的決心。

wealthy [`wɛlθɪ] 形富裕的 反 poor

Most students in this university are from wealthy families.
▶▶ 這間大學大部分學生來自富裕的家庭。

weapon [`wɛpən] 名武器

A gun is a more dangerous weapon than a knife.
▶▶ 槍是比刀子還危險的武器。

weave [wiv] 動編織 名織法

This sort of wool is mostly woven into fabric of coats.
▶▶ 這種羊毛大多用於織成大衣的毛料。

web [wɛb] 名網

Some web addicts often exhaust themselves by surfing the Internet for days.
▶▶ 一些網路沉迷者經常持續幾天上網，把自己搞得筋疲力盡。

wed [wɛd] 動結婚

Francis wedded a famous Ukrainian model.
▶▶ 法蘭西斯娶了一位烏克蘭名模。

weed [wid] 名野草；雜草

If you don't root out the weeds, they will soon grow.
▶▶ 斬草不除根，豈不後患無窮。

weekly [`wiklɪ] 形每週的 副每週地 名週刊

形 This is a weekly English paper.
這是一份英文週報。
副 My aunt visits us weekly.
阿姨每週拜訪我們一次。

weep [wip] 動哭泣；哀悼

動 She wept for days after breaking up with him.
和他分手後她哭了好幾天。
動 We weep for the deceased every year on the date of the tragedy.
每年在悲劇發生的日子，我們會為死者哀悼。
文法解析 weep動詞三態變化為 weep / wept / wept。

wheat [hwit] 名小麥；麥子

The golden wheat under the sun is a wonderful scene.
▶▶ 陽光下金黃色的麥穗真是一番美景。

whip [hwɪp] 名鞭子 動鞭打

名 The horseman cracked his whip and the horse leaped forward.
騎手甩了個響鞭，馬兒就奮蹄向前奔去。
動 The cruel man whipped the slave until his back was bloody.
那殘忍的人鞭打奴隸，直至他的背鮮血淋漓。

whistle [`hwɪsḷ] 名口哨 動吹口哨

名 On hearing his whistle, I knew he had arrived.
聽見他的口哨聲，我就知道他來了。
動 The young boy whistled to catch her attention.
年輕男孩吹口哨引起她的注意。

wicked [`wɪkɪd] 形邪惡的 同 evil

It is wicked of you to play such a prank!
▶▶ 你這樣惡作劇真的很壞！

Level 1 基礎單字
Level 2 必備單字
Level 3 中級單字
Level 4 進階單字
Level 5 高手單字
Level 6 滿級單字

widen [`waɪdən] 動變寬

As the road gradually widened, we finally saw our destination.
▶▶ 隨著路逐漸變寬,我們終於看見了目的地。

wipe [waɪp] 動擦 名擦

動 Karen wiped off the words on the whiteboard in anger.
凱倫憤怒地擦掉白板上的字。
名 Give the table a careful wipe.
仔細擦拭桌子。

wisdom [`wɪzdəm] 名智慧 形 wise 明智的

The wisdom of our ancestors is our treasure.
▶▶ 前人的智慧是我們的寶藏。

wrap [ræp] 動包裝 名包裝紙

動 She wrapped up the present and sent it out.
她把禮物包好然後寄出。
名 The colorful wrap is unsuitable for the music box.
那張色彩斑斕的包裝紙不適合這個音樂盒。

wrist [rɪst] 名腕關節;手腕

Joseph held me by the wrist and dragged me away.
▶▶ 約瑟夫抓住我的手腕把我拖走。

UNIT 24 Y、Z字頭中級單字

MP3 072

yearly [`jɪrlɪ] 形每年的 副每年地 同 annually

形 Rainfall this year exceeded the yearly average.
今年的雨量高於往年的平均降雨量。
副 We celebrate Olivia's birthday yearly.
我們每年都替奧莉薇亞慶祝生日。

yell [jɛl] 動大叫 同 shout

Ingrid yelled in pain.
▶▶ 英格麗痛得大叫。

yolk [jok] 名 蛋黃

Separate the whites from the yolks.
▶▶ 將蛋白和蛋黃分開。

youngster [`jʌŋstə] 名 年輕人 反 elder

It is hard for an old man to walk for as long as a youngster can.
▶▶ 老年人要走得和年輕人一樣久是很困難的。

zipper [`zɪpə] 名 拉鏈

The zipper of this jacket is broken.
▶▶ 這件夾克的拉鍊壞了。

zone [zon] 名 地區；地帶 動 劃分地區 同 area

名 We live in the subtropical zone.
　　我們住在亞熱帶地區。
動 The downtown area is zoned for commercial use.
　　市中心被劃為商業用地。

Level 1 基礎單字
Level 2 必備單字
Level 3 中級單字
Level 4 進階單字
Level 5 高手單字
Level 6 滿級單字

7000 Essential
Vocabulary for
High School Students

LEVEL

4

進階單字

Advanced Vocabulary

單字難易度 ★★★☆☆

文法難易度 ★★☆☆☆

生活出現頻率 ★★★★★

考題出題頻率 ★★★☆☆

名 名詞　動 動詞　形 形容詞　副 副詞　介 介係詞　連 連接詞
關 相關單字/片語　同 同義詞　反 反義詞

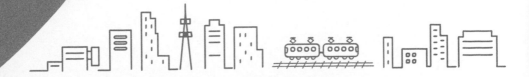

abandon [ə`bændən] 動 放棄

I have abandoned the notion that higher education is essential to either success or happiness.
▶▶ 我早已拋棄了高等教育對成功或幸福至關重要的觀念。

absolute [`æbsə‚lut] 形 絕對的 同 unconditional

There is no absolute truth in the social sciences.
▶▶ 社會科學中沒有絕對的真理。

absorb [əb`sɔrb] 動 吸收

The plants absorb water from the soil.
▶▶ 植物從土壤吸收水分。

abstract [`æbstrækt] 形 抽象的

Don't write abstract and general descriptions in your autobiography.
▶▶ 不要在自傳中寫些抽象又籠統的描述。

academic [‚ækə`dɛmɪk] 形 學院的；學術的

What were your academic records at college like?
▶▶ 你在大學時的成績怎樣？

accent [`æksənt] 名 口音；腔調

Our French teacher speaks grammatical English, but has a French accent.
▶▶ 我們的法語老師講的英文是合乎文法的，但是帶有法國腔。

acceptance [ək`sɛptəns] 名 接受

His ready acceptance of the offer surprised me.
▶▶ 他那麼快就接受提議，真令我感到意外。

access [`æksɛs] 名（接近某物或某人的）機會；使用權；通道 動 進入；存取；使用

名 Do I have access to the executive?
　　我有機會見到執行長嗎？
動 Visitors without the permission cannot access the restricted areas.
　　未經許可的遊客無法進入管制區域。

376

accidental [ˌæksəˈdɛntl̩] 形 偶然的；意外的

The accidental encounter in the rain was romantic.
▶▶ 那場雨中的意外邂逅真浪漫。

accompany [əˈkʌmpənɪ] 動 隨行；陪伴

You had better accompany your mother to the market, or she might lose her way.
▶▶ 你最好陪你媽媽去市場，否則她會迷路。

accomplish [əˈkɑmplɪʃ] 動 達成；完成 關 accomplishment 達成；成就

Is this what you intended to accomplish in your career?
▶▶ 你們的事業就是為了達到這樣的結果嗎？

accountant [əˈkaʊntənt] 名 會計師

The accountants are always overworked in the taxation period.
▶▶ 會計師在報稅時節經常超時工作。

accuracy [ˈækjərəsɪ] 名 正確 關 accurate 精準的

Accuracy is more important than speed in his new job.
▶▶ 對他的新工作而言，準確比速度更重要。

accuse [əˈkjuz] 動 控告 關 accusation 控訴

They were accused of murder.
▶▶ 他們被控謀殺。
(焦點句型) be accused of sth 被指控…

acid [ˈæsɪd] 名 酸 形 酸的；刻薄的

名 Acids harm teeth.
酸性物質會腐蝕牙齒。
形 Ruby favored food with an acid flavor when she was pregnant.
露比懷孕時喜歡酸性食物。

acquaintance [əˈkwentəns] 名 認識的人

Janice has many acquaintances in various business circles.
▶▶ 珍妮絲在各個商業圈都有很多熟人。

Level 1 基礎單字
Level 2 必備單字
Level 3 中級單字
Level 4 進階單字
Level 5 高手單字
Level 6 滿級單字

acquire [ə`kwaɪr] 動 取得

We can acquire a lot of resources from the library.
▶▶ 我們可以從圖書館取得大量資源。

adapt [ə`dæpt] 動 適應

The kid adapted soon to the new environment.
▶▶ 那孩子很快就適應了新環境。

addict [ə`dɪkt] 動 上癮

Ann is addicted to sleeping pills, and she needs to take at least two of them every night.
▶▶ 安對安眠藥上癮了，每晚她必須至少吃兩顆。

adequate [`ædəkwɪt] 形 適當的；足夠的

The manager sought an adequate solution to the problem.
▶▶ 經理尋找解決這個問題適當的辦法。

adjust [ə`dʒʌst] 動 調節 關 adjustment 調整

Daniel adjusted his watch to the right time.
▶▶ 丹尼爾把手錶調成正確的時間。

admirable [`ædmərəbl̩] 形 令人欽佩的

His perseverance in gaining admission to the university is admirable.
▶▶ 他努力考取這所大學的毅力令人欽佩。

admiration [ˌædmə`reʃən] 名 欽佩

I have great admiration for what he's done.
▶▶ 我非常欽佩他所做的事。

admission [əd`mɪʃən] 名 准許進入；承認；入場費 關 admit 容許…進入

You cannot enter the hall without paying admission.
▶▶ 未付入場費不得進入大廳。

adopt [ə`dɑpt] 動 收養

The millionaire adopted the poor orphan as his own son.
▶▶ 那名百萬富翁將那可憐的孤兒收養為自己的兒子。

agency [`edʒənsɪ] 名代理機構

The travel agency suffered a loss this month.
▶▶ 旅行社這個月虧損。

agent [`edʒənt] 名代理人

If you want more information, consult my agent first.
▶▶ 如果你想要更多資訊,先洽詢我的代理人。

aggressive [ə`grɛsɪv] 形侵略的

Raccoons seem adorable; however, they are very aggressive.
▶▶ 浣熊看起來很可愛,但牠們事實上非常兇猛。

agreeable [ə`griəbl̩] 形令人愉快的

The agreeable decorations here are to my liking.
▶▶ 這裡討喜的裝飾正合我的口味。

alcohol [`ælkə,hɔl] 名酒精

Keep fire away from the alcohol.
▶▶ 嚴禁明火接近酒精。

alert [ə`lɝt] 名警報 動警告

名 She is always on the alert.
她總是保持警覺。
動 The doctor alerted John to the dangers of smoking.
醫生警告約翰抽煙的危險。

(焦點句型) on the alert (for sth.) (對…)保持警惕

allowance [ə`lauəns] 名津貼;零用錢 同 subsidy 補貼;補助金

The child has a weekly allowance of five dollars.
▶▶ 這孩子每星期有五元零用錢。

alternative [ɔl`tɝnətɪv] 名可供選擇的事物;替代品 形可替代的

I'm afraid you have no alternative but to tell all the truth.
▶▶ 恐怕你別無選擇,只能交代實情。

amateur [`æmə,tʃuə] 名業餘愛好者 形業餘的

名 Our actors were all enthusiastic amateurs.
我們的演員都是熱情的業餘愛好者。

Level 1 基礎單字
Level 2 必備單字
Level 3 中級單字
Level 4 進階單字
Level 5 高手單字
Level 6 滿級單字

形 No professionals can participate in the amateur tennis tournament.
職業選手不得參加業餘網球賽。

ambiguous [æm`bɪgjuəs] 形 含糊不清的；模稜兩可的

Gilbert's ambiguous words made me misunderstand the meaning.
▶▶ 基爾伯特含糊的詞語讓我誤會他的意思。

ambitious [æm`bɪʃəs] 形 有野心的

Lawrence is ambitious for promotion.
▶▶ 勞倫斯對升遷很有野心。

amuse [ə`mjuz] 動 娛樂；消遣 圖 amusement 娛樂；有趣

My brother amused me by telling jokes.
▶▶ 我哥講笑話逗我開心。

analysis [ə`næləsɪs] 名 分析

We can tell you the results after a complete analysis.
▶▶ 我們要經過完整的分析才能告訴你結果。

analyze [`ænə,laɪz] 動 分析

He has analyzed the advantages of offering physical education courses to high school students.
▶▶ 他對高中體育課的優點進行了分析。

ancestor [`ænsɛstə] 名 祖先；祖宗

We worship our ancestors on Tomb Sweeping Day.
▶▶ 我們在清明節祭拜祖先。

anniversary [,ænə`vɜsərɪ] 名 周年紀念日

Today is our wedding anniversary.
▶▶ 今天是我們結婚周年紀念日。

annoy [ə`nɔɪ] 動 使惱怒

Anne was fond of Tom, though he often annoyed her.
▶▶ 安妮喜歡湯姆，雖然他經常惹她生氣。

annual [`ænjuəl] 形 一年的；年度的

My boss' annual income is more than one million dollars.
▶▶ 我老闆的年收入超過一百萬。

anxiety [æŋˋzaɪətɪ] 名不安

Some hospital patients experience high levels of anxiety.
▶▶ 有些住院病人十分焦慮不安。

apology [əˋpɑlədʒɪ] 名道歉

Please accept our apologies for the delay.
▶▶ 我們延誤了，請接受我們的道歉。

apparent [əˋpærənt] 形明顯的；外表的 關 apparently 顯然地

It was apparent that they fell in love with each other.
▶▶ 很明顯他們倆已陷入愛河。

applicant [ˋæplɪkənt] 名申請人；應徵者

The number of the applicants for the position is beyond anticipation.
▶▶ 這個職位的應徵人數超乎預期。

application [͵æpləˋkeʃən] 名應用；申請

Applications for the job should be made to the human resources manager.
▶▶ 求職申請應向人事部經理提出。

appoint [əˋpɔɪnt] 動任命；約定 關 appointment 約定（會面）

Friday has been appointed as the day for our conference.
▶▶ 我們預定於週五舉行會議。

appreciation [ə͵priʃɪˋeʃən] 名感激

Trevor showed appreciation for Amanda's help by buying her a present.
▶▶ 崔佛買了禮物，以向阿曼達的幫助表示謝意。

appropriate [əˋproprɪ͵ət] 形適當的

The matter will be dealt with by the appropriate authorities.
▶▶ 此事將由相關當局來處理。

approval [əˋpruvl] 名承認；同意

If the couple receives the girl's parents' approval, they can marry.
▶▶ 如果女方父母同意，這對情侶就能結婚了。

Level 1 基礎單字
Level 2 必備單字
Level 3 中級單字
Level 4 進階單字
Level 5 高手單字
Level 6 滿級單字

aquarium [ə`kwɛrɪəm] 名水族館

Have you been to the most famous aquarium downtown?
>> 你去過市中心最有名的那家水族館嗎？

arch [ɑrtʃ] 名拱門 動變成弓形

名 They performed the dance under the arch.
他們在拱門下表演舞蹈。
動 He arched the straw and threw it into the trash can.
他彎折吸管後扔入垃圾桶。

arise [ə`raɪz] 動出現；發生

Try to control your impatience when any unexpected problem arises.
>> 任何意外發生時，都要儘量控制住你的急躁情緒。
文法解析 arise 動詞三態變化為 arise / arose / arisen。

arms [ɑrmz] 名兵器

The policemen forced the criminals to give up their arms.
>> 員警迫使罪犯放下武器。

artificial [ˌɑrtə`fɪʃəl] 形人工的

I prefer artificial flowers to natural ones because they will not fade over time.
>> 我喜歡人造花勝過真花，因為它們不會凋謝。

artistic [ɑr`tɪstɪk] 形藝術的；美術的 相 aesthetic 美學的

Architecture features both artistic qualities and practical designs.
>> 建築要兼顧藝術品質和實用設計。

ashamed [ə`ʃemd] 形引以為恥的

The football riots made me ashamed to be British.
>> 足球騷亂事件使身為英國人的我感到羞恥。

aspect [`æspɛkt] 名方面

We have to consider the various aspects of the issue.
>> 我們必須從多方面考量一個議題。

aspirin [`æspərɪn] 名阿斯匹靈

People take aspirin to relieve their headaches.
>> 人們服用阿斯匹靈以減輕頭痛。

assemble [ə`sɛmbl̩] 動集合 同convene

Assemble on the playground with your bags.
▶▶ 帶著背包到操場集合。

assembly [ə`sɛmblɪ] 名集合；會議

For an absolute majority in the National Assembly, 280 seats are needed.
▶▶ 要在國民會議中獲得絕對多數，需要二百八十個席次。

assign [ə`saɪn] 動指定 關assignment（分派的）任務

We have assigned 20% of our budget to the project.
▶▶ 我們已將預算的百分之二十分配給該項目。

assistance [ə`sɪstəns] 名幫助

I would not have won the prize without your assistance.
▶▶ 沒有你的幫忙，我將無法獲獎。

associate [ə`soʃɪˏet ] / [ ə`soʃɪɪt] 動聯想 名同事 形夥伴的

動 We associate Egypt with the Nile River.
　我們想到埃及就聯想到尼羅河。
名 She is one of my associates at the firm.
　她是我公司裡的一位同事。

(焦點句型) associate sth. with sth. 將…和…聯想在一起

association [əˏsosɪ`eʃən] 名協會；聯合會

We planned to organize a community association.
▶▶ 我們計劃組成一個社區協會。

assurance [ə`ʃurəns] 名保證

They gave me an assurance that the goods would be delivered by Friday.
▶▶ 他們向我保證貨物會在周五前送達。

assure [ə`ʃur] 動保證；使確信 關reassure 使安心；安慰；使打消疑慮

Percy assured me that he would finish the work before the deadline.
▶▶ 波西向我保證會他在最後期限前把工作完成。

athletic [æθ`lɛtɪk] 形強壯的；擅長運動的；運動員的 關athletics 體育運動

Abby has an athletic figure.
▶▶ 艾比有運動選手的身材。

1 Level 基礎單字
2 Level 必備單字
3 Level 中級單字
4 Level 進階單字
5 Level 高手單字
6 Level 滿級單字

atmosphere [`ætməs,fɪr] 名 大氣；氣氛

The atmosphere turned lively when Jane arrived.
▶▶ 珍來了以後氣氛變得活躍。

atom [`ætəm] 名 原子

Small as an atom is, an electron is still smaller.
▶▶ 原子雖小，但電子更小。

atomic [ə`tɑmɪk] 形 原子的

The atomic bomb is the offspring of 20th century physics.
▶▶ 原子彈是二十世紀物理的產物。

attach [ə`tætʃ] 動 貼上 關 attachment 附件；依戀

You have to attach a stamp to the envelope.
▶▶ 你必須在信封上貼郵票。

attraction [ə`trækʃən] 名 魅力 關 attract 吸引

Although she is not beautiful, she holds a special attraction for me.
▶▶ 雖然她不漂亮，但對我卻有特殊的吸引力。

audio [`ɔdɪ,o] 名 聲音

Audio books are great, especially for people with poor vision.
▶▶ 有聲書很好，特別是對於視力差的人們。

authentic [ɔ`θɛntɪk] 形 真實的；可靠的

The report is authentic.
▶▶ 這個報告是可靠的。

authority [ə`θɔrətɪ] 名 權威；權力；當局

The president gave me the authority to be in charge of the department.
▶▶ 總經理授權讓我負責這個部門。

autobiography [,ɔtəbaɪ`ɑgrəfɪ] 名 自傳

Stanley read an interesting autobiography written by a famous businessman.
▶▶ 史丹利在讀一位知名商人寫的自傳。

autograph [`ɔtəˌɡræf] 名 親筆簽名 動 在⋯上親筆簽名

名 The superstar put his autograph on the photos.
這個巨星在照片上親筆簽名。

動 The author autographed my book. It made me very cheerful.
作者在我的書上親筆簽名。這讓我十分雀躍。

await [ə`wet] 動 等待

The boys sat down to await the arrival of the guests.
▶▶ 男孩們坐下來等客人到。

 **B字頭進階單字** UNIT 02

MP3 074

bald [bɔld] 形 禿頭的 關 toupee 男用假髮

The bald man bought a toupee.
▶▶ 那個禿頭男子買了一頂假髮。

ballet [bæ`le] 名 芭蕾

She started learning ballet when she was six years old.
▶▶ 她六歲開始學芭蕾。

bandage [`bændɪdʒ] 名 繃帶

The nurse eased the bandage off.
▶▶ 護士輕輕地把繃帶取下來。

bankrupt [`bæŋkrʌpt] 形 破產的 名 破產者

形 The company went bankrupt because it couldn't sell its products.
那家公司因產品滯銷而破產。

名 The poor businessman was declared a bankrupt at the end of the year.
那個可憐的商人在年底宣告破產。

(焦點句型) go bankrupt 破產

bargain [`bɑrɡɪn] 名 便宜貨；協議 動 討價還價

名 I picked up a few good bargains at the sale.
我在特價期間買了幾樣挺不錯的便宜貨。

動 Do not bargain anymore. The price is fixed.
別再殺價了，這是不二價。

Level 1 基礎單字
Level 2 必備單字
Level 3 中級單字
Level 4 進階單字
Level 5 高手單字
Level 6 滿級單字

barrier [`bærɪr] 名障礙；界線

There was no real barrier between reality and fantasy in his mind.
▷▷ 在他的頭腦中，現實與幻想之間沒有真正的界線。

basin [`besn̩] 名盆

Henry filled the basin with water.
▷▷ 亨利把盆子盛滿了水。

battery [`bætərɪ] 名電池

Our bus won't start because the battery is dead.
▷▷ 我們的公車因為電池沒電而發動不了。

beggar [`bɛgɚ] 名乞丐

The starving beggar begged me for money.
▷▷ 那飢餓的乞丐向我討錢。

behavior [bɪ`hevjɚ] 名舉止；行為

A person's behavior will be influenced by the environment.
▷▷ 人的行為會受到環境影響。

biography [baɪ`ɑgrəfɪ] 名傳記

The biography of Albert Einstein was interesting.
▷▷ 阿爾伯特‧愛因斯坦的傳記很有趣。

biology [baɪ`ɑlədʒɪ] 名生物學

He is a biology professor.
▷▷ 他是生物學教授。

blade [bled] 名刀鋒

The winds in early spring are as sharp as the blade of a pair of scissors.
▷▷ 早春的風如剪刀般凜冽。

blend [blɛnd] 名混合 動使混合

名 The blend of the two kinds of wine is popular here.
　　這裡很流行混合這兩種酒。
動 The recipe calls for blending butter with sugar.
　　食譜上說把奶油和糖混合在一起。

blessing [`blɛsɪŋ] 名恩典；祝福

My parents gave their sincere blessings to my marriage.
▶▶ 父母對我的婚姻給予誠摯祝福。

blink [blɪŋk] 動眨眼；閃爍 名眨眼

動 The stars blinked in the sky.
星星在空中閃爍。
名 He disappeared in the blink of an eye.
一眨眼他就消失了。

bloom [blum] 動開花；繁榮 名花

動 This type of cactus only blooms at night.
這種仙人掌的花只在晚間綻放。
名 All kinds of flowers are in full bloom.
百花盛開。

blossom [`blɑsəm] 名花；花簇 動開花；（人）變得更有魅力

名 Flora is happy to see the blossoms in spring.
春天時看到這些花朵盛開，芙蘿拉覺得很開心。
動 The jasmine blossoms brightly.
茉莉花生氣勃勃地盛開。

boast [bost] 名誇耀 動吹噓

名 Do not take his boast seriously.
別把他的自誇當真。
動 John boasted that he is the most handsome guy in his class.
約翰自誇是班上最英俊的人。

bond [bɑnd] 名聯繫；關係；契約；債券 動黏合；聯合；建立關係

名 The bonds can be changed into ordinary shares.
債券可兌換為普通股。
動 The manager wants to bond the whole department into a closely knit team.
主管想讓整個部門緊密團結在一起。

bounce [baʊns] 動彈 名彈

動 Colin bounced out of the door when he heard the news.
一聽到這消息，柯林立刻奪門而出。
名 You can mount here with a single bounce.
你只要一跳就可以登上這裡。

Level 1 基礎單字
Level 2 必備單字
Level 3 中級單字
Level 4 進階單字
Level 5 高手單字
Level 6 滿級單字

bracelet [`breslət] 名手鐲;手鏈

Madeline wears a huge bracelet on her wrist.
▶▶ 瑪德琳手腕上戴著大手鐲。

breed [brid] 動生育 名品種

動 Dirty hands can help germs breed.
不乾淨的手會滋生病菌。
名 This particular breed of cattle matures early.
這一特殊品種的牛發育很快。

bridegroom / groom [`braɪd͵grum] / [grum] 名新郎

The bridegroom led the bride by the hand.
▶▶ 新郎牽著新娘的手。

broke [brok] 形一無所有的;破產的

He was broke and unemployed.
▶▶ 他既破產又失業。

broom [brum] 名掃帚

The housekeeper drove the stray dog away by waving a broom.
▶▶ 管家揮動掃把驅趕流浪狗。

brutal [`brutl̩] 形野蠻的;殘暴的

With brutal honesty, Stacy told him she did not love him.
▶▶ 史黛西殘忍地直接告訴他,她不愛他。

bulletin [`bulətɪn] 名公告

Please read the latest bulletin.
▶▶ 請閱讀最新公告。

burglar [`bɝglɚ] 名入室竊賊

The burglar got in through the window.
▶▶ 竊賊是從窗戶進來的。

cabinet [`kæbɪnət] 名櫥櫃；內閣

The president will announce the Cabinet tomorrow.
▶▶ 總統明天將公布內閣人事。

calculate [`kælkjə‚let] 動計算

She is calculating the total cost of the dinner.
▶▶ 她正在計算晚餐的總額。

calculation [‚kælkjə`leʃən] 名計算

Perhaps you have made a mistake in your calculation.
▶▶ 你可能計算錯誤。

calorie [`kælərɪ] 名卡路里

You should absorb at least 2,000 calories daily.
▶▶ 你一天至少應該攝取兩千卡的熱量。

campaign [kæm`pen] 名活動 動從事（社會）運動 關 workplace 工作場所

名 They started a campaign against ageism in the workplace.
他們展開一場反對工作場所年齡歧視的運動。
動 The party campaigned vigorously in the north of the country.
該黨在本國北部展開了強而有力的競選活動。

candidate [`kændədet] 名候選人

My father is a candidate for village head.
▶▶ 我爸爸是村長候選人。

cane [ken] 名手杖

A cane is important for the blind.
▶▶ 手杖對失明者而言十分重要。

canoe [kə`nu] 名獨木舟

The whirlpool sucked down the canoe.
▶▶ 漩渦把獨木舟捲了進去。

基礎單字 Level 1

必備單字 Level 2

中級單字 Level 3

進階單字 Level 4

高手單字 Level 5

滿級單字 Level 6

389

capacity [kə`pæsətɪ] 名容積；能力

The capacity of the box is not enough for all the gadgets.
▶▶ 這個盒子的容量放不進這些零件。

capitalism [`kæpɪtəlɪzəm] 名資本主義

Capitalism is the dominant economic system in most countries.
▶▶ 資本主義是許多國家的主要經濟體系。

capitalist [`kæpətəlɪst] 名資本家

His father worked under the capitalist for a small wage.
▶▶ 他的父親為賺取微薄工資，在資本家手下做事。

cargo [`kɑrgo] 名貨物

We sailed from Japan with a cargo of coal.
▶▶ 我們載滿一船煤從日本啟航。

carrier [`kærɪɚ] 名運送者

The letter carrier was bitten by a dog.
▶▶ 信差被一隻狗咬。

carve [kɑrv] 動切成薄片

He carved the meat into pieces.
▶▶ 他把肉切成薄片。

catalogue [`kætəlɔg] 名目錄 動編輯目錄

名 An illustrated catalogue can be found at the entrance to the exhibition.
展覽會的入口有插圖目錄。
動 We catalogued the items on display.
我們為參展的項目編輯目錄。

category [`kætə͵gorɪ] 名分類；種類

These books are divided into categories according to subjects.
▶▶ 這些書按照科目分類。

cease [sis] 動停止；中止 名停息

動 After the negotiation, the two countries finally agreed to cease hostilities.
經過談判，這兩國終於停火了。
名 Justin kept studying without cease.
賈斯汀不斷讀書，從不休息。

celebration [ˌsɛləˈbreʃən] 名慶祝

Her triumph was a cause for celebration.
▶▶ 她的勝利是慶祝的理由。

chamber [ˈtʃembɚ] 名房間；寢室

No one is allowed in the judge's chamber without permission.
▶▶ 未經允許不可進入法官辦公室。

championship [ˈtʃæmpɪənˌʃɪp] 名冠軍賽

The team's efforts culminated in victory in the championships.
▶▶ 這支隊伍透過努力終於在錦標賽中取得勝利。

characteristic [ˌkærəktəˈrɪstɪk] 名特徵 形有特色的

名 Can you list some of the robber's characteristics?
　　你可以列出搶匪的幾個特徵嗎？
形 Speaking aloud is characteristic of him.
　　說話大聲是他的特色。

charity [ˈtʃærətɪ] 名慈善

He donated a lot of money to the school out of charity.
▶▶ 出於善心，他捐了一大筆錢給學校。

chemistry [ˈkɛmɪstrɪ] 名化學

Chemistry is one of the basic requirements for this major.
▶▶ 化學是本科系基本的必修課程之一。

cherish [ˈtʃɛrɪʃ] 動珍惜

I cherished the moments when you were around me.
▶▶ 我珍惜你在我身邊的那段光陰。

chew [tʃu] 動咀嚼

The dog was chewing on a bone.
▶▶ 那狗在啃骨頭。

choke [tʃok] 動窒息；堵塞

The sewer is choked up with rubbish.
▶▶ 下水道被垃圾堵住了。

chorus [`korəs] 名 合唱團

Heather sang in a chorus when she was a sophomore.
▶▶ 海瑟大學二年級時加入了合唱團。

circular [`sɜkjələ] 形 圓形的

The full moon has a circular shape.
▶▶ 滿月呈圓形。

circulate [`sɜkjə,let] 動 循環

Blood circulates in our body from head to toe.
▶▶ 血液在我們體內從頭到腳地循環著。

circulation [,sɜkjə`leʃən] 名 循環；流通；發行量

Regular exercise will improve blood circulation.
▶▶ 定期運動會促進血液循環。

circumstance [`sɜkəm,stæns] 名 情況

In such circumstances, all I can do is wait.
▶▶ 在這種情況下，我能做的只有等待。

civilian [sə`vɪljən] 名 平民；一般人 形 平民的

名 He left the army and became a civilian once again.
　　他離開軍隊，再次成為平民。
形 The former soldier adapted himself to civilian life very well.
　　這個退伍軍人很能適應平民生活。

civilization [,sɪvḷə`zeʃən] 名 文明

We don't know whether there are civilizations on distant planets that are invisible to the naked eye.
▶▶ 在肉眼看不到的遙遠星球上，是否存在未知的文明，我們不得而知。

clarify [`klærə,faɪ] 動 澄清

Sam clarified that he didn't steal the money, but nobody trusted him.
▶▶ 山姆澄清他沒有偷錢，但沒有人相信他。

clash [klæʃ] 名 衝突；猛撞 動 衝突；猛撞

名 It is reported that twenty men were killed in the clash.
　　據報導，這次衝突中有二十人死亡。

Level 1 基礎單字

Level 2 必備單字

Level 3 中級單字

Level 4 進階單字

Level 5 高手單字

Level 6 滿級單字

動 The protestors clashed with police during the demonstration.
抗議人士在示威遊行時與警方爆發衝突。

焦點句型 clash with sb./sth. 與…發生衝突；相牴觸

classification [ˌklæsəfə`keʃən] 名分類

These all belong to different classifications.
▶▶ 這些全都屬於不同的類別。

classify [`klæsəˌfaɪ] 動分類

Librarians classify books according to their subjects.
▶▶ 圖書館員將這些書依其主題歸類。

claw [klɔ] 名爪 動抓

Bears have sharp claws.
▶▶ 熊有銳利的爪子。

cliff [klɪf] 名斷崖

Ching-Shui Cliff is a famous spectacle in eastern Taiwan.
▶▶ 清水斷崖是東臺灣的著名奇觀。

clumsy [`klʌmzɪ] 形笨拙的

Natasha is clumsy in cooking.
▶▶ 娜塔莎在烹飪方面十分笨拙。

coarse [kɔrs] 形粗糙的

The peasant's clothes were made of coarse cloth.
▶▶ 那農民的衣服是粗布製的。

code [kod] 名代號

Every employee knows the code to open the main door of the company.
▶▶ 每個員工都知道打開公司大門的密碼。

collapse [kə`læps] 動倒塌

The tower collapsed in the earthquake.
▶▶ 這座塔在地震中倒塌。

colleague [`kɑlig] 名同事

My colleagues are all the same sex as me.
▶ 我的同事皆和我同性別。

combination [ˌkɑmbəˋneʃən] 名結合 關 combine 結合

The team manager still hasn't found the right combination of players.
▶ 領隊仍未找出合適的選手搭配。

comedy [`kɑmədɪ] 名喜劇

Joseph became a comedy actor after he graduated.
▶ 約瑟夫畢業後就成為一個喜劇演員。

commander [kəˋmændə] 名指揮官

The commander showed mercy to the prisoners.
▶ 司令官對囚犯十分慈悲。

comment [`kɑmɛnt] 名評論 動評論

名 We have no comment about the scandal.
　我們對這個醜聞不予置評。
動 Please comment on the essays and correct the mistakes.
　請評論他人的文章並訂正錯誤。
(焦點句型) no comment 不予置評；拒絕評論

commerce [`kɑmɝs] 名商業；貿易 關 commercial 商業的

Our country has grown rich because of its commerce with other nations.
▶ 因為與他國進行貿易，我國已變得富裕起來。

commit [kəˋmɪt] 動犯（罪、錯）；承諾

He committed that he would propose to me someday.
▶ 他承諾將來有一天會向我求婚。

communication [kəˌmjunəˋkeʃən] 名溝通 關 telecommunications 電信

The Internet provides a convenient and instant form of communication.
▶ 網際網路提供了一種便利且即時的溝通方式。

community [kəˋmjunətɪ] 名社區

We have a weekly assembly in our community.
▶ 我們社區每週有一次集會。

companion [kəm`pænjən] 名 同伴

Chester waved desperately to his companion.
▶▶ 查斯特絕望地向他的夥伴揮了揮手。

competition [ˌkɑmpə`tɪʃən] 名 競爭 關 compete 競爭

There was intense competition for the position.
▶▶ 這個職位競爭激烈。

competitive [kəm`pɛtətɪv] 形 競爭的；好勝的；有競爭力的

We all have to know the competitive advantages of our company's products.
▶▶ 我們都必須清楚自家公司產品的競爭優勢。

competitor [kəm`pɛtətə] 名 競爭者

They are not only friends but also competitors.
▶▶ 他們不只是朋友，也是對手。

complicate [`kɑmpləˌket] 動 使複雜

Her involvement complicated the problem.
▶▶ 她的介入使整個問題更加複雜。

compose [kəm`poz] 動 組成；作曲

The popular singer enjoys composing with her guitar.
▶▶ 那位當紅歌手喜歡用吉他譜曲。

composer [kəm`pozə] 名 作曲家

Mozart was a talented composer.
▶▶ 莫札特是個天才作曲家。

composition [ˌkɑmpə`zɪʃən] 名 作品；構圖；作文；成分

This piano concerto is one of the most incredible compositions of Beethoven.
▶▶ 這首鋼琴協奏曲是貝多芬最傑出的作品之一。

concentrate [`kɑnsənˌtret] 動 集中

Concentrate on your studies. Don't be absent-minded.
▶▶ 專心念書，別心不在焉。
(焦點句型) concentrate on sth./sb. 專注於…

Level 1 基礎單字
Level 2 必備單字
Level 3 中級單字
Level 4 進階單字
Level 5 高手單字
Level 6 滿級單字

concentration [ˌkɑnsən`trɛʃən] 名 集中；專心

This type of work requires total concentration.
▶▶ 做這種工作需要全神貫注。

concept [`kɑnsɛpt] 名 概念

The concept is easy to understand.
▶▶ 這個概念簡單易懂。

concerning [kən`sɜnɪŋ] 介 關於

I heard the rumor concerning her scandals.
▶▶ 我聽到關於她緋聞的謠言。

concrete [`kɑnkrit] 名 水泥；混凝土 形 具體的

名 The building is made of concrete.
這棟建築由混凝土製成。
形 Can you give me a concrete example of what you mean?
能否舉個具體例子說明你的意思？

conductor [kən`dʌktə] 名 指揮

He is the conductor of the orchestra.
▶▶ 他是這個管弦樂團的指揮。

conference [`kɑnfərəns] 名 會議 關 forum 討論會；論壇

We invited experts from every country to the conference.
▶▶ 我們邀請各國專家參加這場會議。

confess [kən`fɛs] 動 承認

Nelson confessed to cheating on the exam.
▶▶ 尼爾森承認考試作弊。
(焦點句型) confess to N./Ving 承認…（也可用 confess + that 子句）

confidence [`kɑnfədəns] 名 信心 關 confident 有信心的

I have confidence that I will pass the exam.
▶▶ 我有信心通過考試。

confusion [kən`fjuʒən] 名 迷惑 關 confuse 使困惑

Davis was in great confusion, not knowing what to do.
▶▶ 戴維斯非常困惑，不知所措。

congratulate [kənˋgrætʃəˌlet] 動 恭喜 關 congratulation 恭喜

They congratulated him on his marriage.
▶ 他們恭喜他成婚。

(焦點句型) congratulate sb. on sth. 恭喜某人某事

congress [ˋkɑŋgrɛs] 名 國會；代表大會

The president has lost the support of Congress.
▶ 總統已經失去了國會的支持。

conquer [ˋkɑŋkə] 動 征服

I finally conquered my stage fright and gave a wonderful performance.
▶ 我終於克服了怯場，並且完美演出。

conscience [ˋkɑnʃəns] 名 良心

His conscience bothered him after he lied to his friend.
▶ 對朋友說謊後，他時常受到良心的譴責。

consequence [ˋkɑnsəˌkwəns] 名 結果；影響

I am quite willing to accept the consequences.
▶ 我完全願意承擔後果。

consequent [ˋkɑnsəˌkwənt] 形 隨之而來的；由此引起的

The famine was consequent to climate change.
▶ 饑荒是由於氣候變遷引起的。

conservative [kənˋsɜvətɪv] 形 保守的 名 保守主義者

形 Gina is conservative when it comes to marriage.
吉娜對婚姻的態度很保守。
名 Conservatives disapprove of gay and lesbian marriage.
保守主義者不贊成同志婚姻。

consist [kənˋsɪst] 動 組成

The team consists of five people.
▶ 五個人組成一小隊。

(焦點句型) consist of sth. 由…組成

Level 1 基礎單字
Level 2 必備單字
Level 3 中級單字
Level 4 進階單字
Level 5 高手單字
Level 6 滿級單字

consistent [kən`sɪstənt] 形 一致的

His viewpoint is consistent with mine.
▶▶ 他的觀點和我一致。

(焦點句型) be consistent with sth. 和…一致

constitute [`kɑnstə, tjut] 動 構成

The committee had been improperly constituted, and therefore had no legal power.
▶▶ 該委員會的建立不合規定，因而沒有法律權力。

constitution [,kɑnstə`tjuʃən] 名 構造；憲法

The constitution of the building was of great quality.
▶▶ 這棟建築的構造品質非常好。

construct [kən`strʌkt] 動 建構

They constructed a new theory.
▶▶ 他們建構了一個新的理論。

construction [kən`strʌkʃən] 名 建築；結構

The Mass Rapid Transit system is still under construction here.
▶▶ 這裡的捷運系統還在蓋。

constructive [kən`strʌktɪv] 形 建設性的

Give me constructive suggestions rather than mere criticism.
▶▶ 給我建設性的建議而非僅有批評。

consult [kən`sʌlt] 動 請教；諮詢

Consult the dictionary if you don't know the meaning of words.
▶▶ 不知道字的意思時就查字典。

consultant [kən`sʌltənt] 名 顧問；諮詢師

Of all the consultants, only Mr. Wang gave us some useful proposals.
▶▶ 所有的顧問當中，只有王先生提了一些中肯的建議。

consume [kəm`sjum] 動 消耗；耗費 同 deplete 用盡

Most of Leo's time was consumed in playing computer games.
▶▶ 利奧花了大部分的時間玩電腦遊戲。

(焦點句型) be consumed by/with sth. 充滿（某種強烈的情感）

consumer [kən`sjumə] 名 消費者

The consumers crowded the supermarket for the discount.
▶▶ 大批消費者為了折扣擠滿超市。

container [kən`tenə] 名 容器

A reactor is a container for chemical reactions.
▶▶ 反應器是進行化學反應的容器。

content [`kɑntɛnt ] / [ kən`tɛnt] 名 內容；目錄 形 滿足的

名 The contents are on the first and second pages of the book.
目錄在這本書的第一和第二頁。
形 She feels content to live in the remote village.
她覺得住在這個僻靜的村落很滿足。

contentment [kən`tɛntmənt] 名 滿足

Adele gave me a smile of contentment after the nice date.
▶▶ 在這個美好的約會後，愛黛兒給我一個滿足的微笑。

contest [`kɑntɛst] 名 比賽 動 與…競爭

名 I decided to take part in the contest.
我決定參賽。
動 They are contesting for the girl's heart.
他們在爭奪這女孩的芳心。

context [`kɑntɛkst] 名 上下文；文章脈絡

You cannot quote people out of context.
▶▶ 你不能斷章取義。

continual [kən`tɪnjʊəl] 形 連續的 關 continue

The noisy traffic is a continual annoyance to the citizens.
▶▶ 城裡吵雜的交通總是使城市居民煩惱。

continuous [kən`tɪnjʊəs] 形 連續的

The continuous rain spoiled our holiday.
▶▶ 連綿陰雨破壞了我們的假期。

contrary [`kɑntrɛrɪ] 形 相反的；對立的 名 相反；反面；對立面

形 Contrary to what he said, Toronto is not the capital of Canada.
他說反了，多倫多並非加拿大的首都。

Level 1 基礎單字
Level 2 必備單字
Level 3 中級單字
Level 4 進階單字
Level 5 高手單字
Level 6 滿級單字

(名) The authority does not reject the project; on the contrary, they encourage this kind of proposals.

當局並沒有拒絕該項目，相反地，他們鼓勵這類提案。

(焦點句型) contrary to sth. 與…相反；與…不同 / on the contrary 相反地

contrast [`kɑntræst ] / [ kən`træst] (名)對比 (動)對照

(名) Gary's dark hair is in sharp contrast to his pale skin.

蓋瑞深色的頭髮與他白皙的膚色形成鮮明對比。

(動) They contrasted the two proposals and chose the better one.

他們對照一下這兩個提案，然後選擇其中較好的一個。

(焦點句型) in contrast to sb./sth. 與…形成對比

contribute [kən`tribjut] (動)貢獻

Everyone should contribute what he or she can afford.

▶▶ 人人都應該盡自己的能力作貢獻。

contribution [,kɑntrə`bjuʃən] (名)貢獻

The one who makes the greatest contribution to our company will get a bonus.

▶▶ 對公司貢獻最大的人將獲得獎金。

convenience [kən`viniəns] (名)便利 (關) convenient 方便的

We enjoy the convenience of cities, but envy the leisure of the countryside.

▶▶ 我們享受都市的便利，卻羨慕鄉村的悠閒。

convention [kən`vɛnʃən] (名)會議；傳統；社會習俗

Please brief me on the conclusions made at the convention.

▶▶ 請跟我簡報一下會議的結論。

conventional [kən`vɛnʃənl̩] (形)傳統的

Their marriage will be held in a conventional way.

▶▶ 他們的婚禮會以傳統形式舉辦。

converse [kən`vɜs] (動)談話

They conversed for three hours on the phone.

▶▶ 他們用電話談了三個小時。

convey [kən`ve] (動)傳達；運送

This train conveys over three hundred passengers every day.

▶▶ 這列火車每天運送三百多名乘客。

convince [kən`vɪns] 動說服

My student tried to convince me of her honesty.
▶▶ 我的學生試圖讓我相信她的誠實。

(焦點句型) convince sb. of sth. 說服某人相信某事

cooperate [ko`ɑpə‚ret] 動合作

The two groups agreed to cooperate with each other.
▶▶ 這兩組同意相互合作。

(焦點句型) cooperate with sb. 與…合作

cooperation [ko‚ɑpə`reʃən] 名合作 同 collaboration

Both cooperation and competition can benefit a firm.
▶▶ 合作和競爭都對公司有利。

cooperative [ko`ɑpərətɪv] 名合作社 形合作的

名 An agricultural cooperative system benefits the farmers.
農業合作社制度有利於農人。
形 Cooperative activity is essential to effective community work.
要把社區工作做好，合作活動是必不可少的。

cope [kop] 動處理

I am clumsy at coping with such problems.
▶▶ 我對處理這類事務很笨拙。

(焦點句型) cope with sth./sb. 處理…

copper [`kɑpə] 名銅；銅幣；紅棕色 形銅製的

名 I only paid a few coppers for it.
我只花了幾個銅板買下這東西。
形 The copper kettle rusted more slowly than the iron one.
這個銅水壺生鏽的速度比鐵水壺慢。

cord [kɔrd] 名電線

Jane stumbled on the long cord.
▶▶ 珍被長電線絆倒了。

correspond [‚kɔrɪ`spɑnd] 動符合；相當

Fulfillment seldom corresponds to anticipation.
▶▶ 成果很少與預期相符。

Level 1 基礎單字
Level 2 必備單字
Level 3 中級單字
Level 4 進階單字
Level 5 高手單字
Level 6 滿級單字

costume [`kɑstjum] 名服裝

The bride changed several costumes during the banquet.
>> 新娘在婚宴上換了很多套服裝。

cottage [`kɑtɪdʒ] 名小屋；別墅

The cottage is located near a lake.
>> 這座別墅座落在湖邊。

council [`kaʊnsḷ] 名議會

Michelle's on the local council.
>> 米歇爾是地方議會的議員。

counter [`kaʊntɚ] 名櫃檯 動反抗

名 The girl stood still beside the counter.
女孩站在櫃檯邊不動。
動 He countered his father, offering a different view regarding the matter.
他因為對一件事的看法不同，而反駁爸爸。

courageous [kə`redʒəs] 形勇敢的

Achilles is such a courageous man that he does not fear death at all.
>> 阿基里斯是一個非常勇敢的人，一點也不怕死。

courtesy [`kɜtəsɪ] 名禮貌

Courtesy costs nothing.
>> 禮多人不怪。

coward [`kaʊɚd] 名懦夫

Never be a coward despite any difficulty in front of you.
>> 即使面對任何險阻，也不要當個懦夫。

crack [kræk] 名裂縫；瑕疵 動砸開；使破裂

名 I returned the goods because of the crack.
我因為物品瑕疵而退貨。
動 Can you get the nut cracked?
你能把這硬果敲開嗎？

craft [kræft] 名手工藝 關 apprentice 學徒

Martin went to the factory as an apprentice to learn the craft.
>> 馬丁到工廠當學徒學習技藝。

creation [krɪ`eʃən] 名 創造；創世

The designer was proud of her latest creations.
▶▶ 這名設計師為她的最新創作頗為自豪。

creativity [ˌkrie`tɪvətɪ] 名 創造力

Do not prevent the children from doing whatever they like. That will limit their creativity.
▶▶ 不要限制孩子們做他們想做的事，那會限制他們的創造力。

creep [krip] 動 爬

Ivy creeps along the fence.
▶▶ 常春藤沿著籬笆生長。
文法解析 creep 動詞三態變化為 creep / crept / crept。

critic [`krɪtɪk] 名 批評家

The critic is known for his critical reviews.
▶▶ 這名批評家因言辭犀利而聞名。

critical [`krɪtɪkl̩] 形 評論的

The report was sharply critical of the police.
▶▶ 報導猛烈地抨擊警方。

criticism [`krɪtəˌsɪzm] 名 評論；批評

Jenny turned a deaf ear to his criticism.
▶▶ 珍妮不理睬他的批評。

criticize [`krɪtɪˌsaɪz] 動 批評

Please propose constructive suggestions while criticizing my composition.
▶▶ 在批評完我的作文之後，請給予建設性的建議。

cruelty [`kruəltɪ] 名 殘酷

The deliberate cruelty of his words cut her like a knife.
▶▶ 他故意說的那些殘酷無情的話，讓她心如刀割。

crunchy [krʌntʃɪ] 形 鬆脆的；易裂的

Crunchy and fresh vegetables are tasty.
▶▶ 爽脆而新鮮的蔬菜是很美味的。

Level 1 基礎單字
Level 2 必備單字
Level 3 中級單字
Level 4 進階單字
Level 5 高手單字
Level 6 滿級單字

crush [krʌʃ] 名毀壞 動壓碎

名 Luckily, no one was injured, although the car was left in a crush of metal.
雖然車子被撞爛了，但幸運的是沒有人受傷。

動 The cement truck crushed the fruits that had fallen onto the road.
水泥車把落在路面的水果壓爛了。

cube [kjub] 名立方體；立方

The cube of five is one hundred and twenty-five.
▶▶ 五的立方等於一百二十五。

cue [kju] 名暗示

The director gave the actor a cue to help him remember his lines.
▶▶ 導演給了演員一個暗示，以幫助他記臺詞。

cunning [`kʌnɪŋ] 名精明的；狡猾的

George was as cunning as a fox, so he was able to deceive all his friends.
▶▶ 喬治像狐狸一樣狡猾，騙過他所有的朋友。

curiosity [ˌkjʊrɪ`ɑsətɪ] 名好奇心 關 curious 好奇的

Out of curiosity, I asked him whether he had been to the temple.
▶▶ 出於好奇，我問他以前是否來過這座廟。

curl [kɝl] 名捲髮 動使捲曲 關 curly 蜷曲的

名 The curl of her hair was one of her characteristics.
捲髮是她的特徵之一。

動 Hazel twisted her hair around her fingers to make it curl.
海柔爾把頭髮繞在手指上使之捲曲。

curse [kɝs] 動詛咒；咒罵

Douglas cursed the one who stole his umbrella.
▶▶ 道格拉斯詛咒偷走他雨傘的人。

curve [kɝv] 名曲線 動彎曲

名 The curve ball is also called "arc line ball".
曲球打法又叫弧線球。

動 The road curves to the west.
這條路向西彎曲。

cushion [`kuʃən] 名 墊子 動 緩和…衝擊

名 Tina put a cushion in front of the door.
蒂娜在門前放了一個墊子。

動 The water cushioned my fall.
水減緩了我落下的衝擊力道。

 **D 字頭進階單字**

 MP3 076

damp [dæmp] 名 濕氣 動 使潮濕

名 The damp and heat were almost suffocating.
潮濕高溫令人感到窒息。

動 He damped his towel to rub his body.
他把毛巾弄濕後擦拭身體。

deadline [`dɛd.laɪn] 名 限期

You have to turn in the report before the deadline.
▶▶ 你必須在期限前繳交報告。

declare [dɪ`klɛr] 動 宣告；公告

The boss declares who gets promoted.
▶▶ 老闆公布升遷的人選。

decoration [ˌdɛkə`reʃən] 名 裝飾

I know something about decoration.
▶▶ 關於裝潢，我懂一些。

defeat [dɪ`fit] 名 擊敗 動 擊敗

名 The defeat was a bitter pill to swallow.
戰敗是顆難吞的苦藥。

動 John defeated his rival in the competition.
約翰在競賽中擊敗了他的對手。

defend [dɪ`fɛnd] 動 保衛；防禦

It's our duty to defend our country.
▶▶ 保衛祖國是我們的義務。

Level 1 基礎單字
Level 2 必備單字
Level 3 中級單字
Level 4 進階單字
Level 5 高手單字
Level 6 滿級單字

defense [dɪ`fɛns] 名保衛；防禦

The magazine's disclosure of defense secrets drew great attention.
>> 該雜誌對國防機密的披露引起了極大的關注。

defensible [dɪ`fɛnsəbḷ] 形可防禦的

Since Tim's argument was not defensible, he easily lost the debate.
>> 提姆的論點不夠有力，所以在辯論賽中，他很快就被擊敗了。

defensive [dɪ`fɛnsɪv] 形防禦的

They were very defensive about the issue.
>> 在這個問題上，他們的辯解非常激烈。

definite [`dɛfənɪt] 形確定的 關 definitely 明確地

It is definite that the star will hold a concert in August.
>> 這個明星確定會在八月舉行演唱會。

delicate [`dɛləkət] 形精細的；精巧的

Tom gave her a delicate music box on Christmas Day.
>> 湯姆在聖誕節送她一個精巧的音樂盒。

delight [dɪ`laɪt] 名欣喜 動使高興

名 She exclaimed in delight at the scene.
　看到這情景，她高興得大叫起來。
動 They delighted the crying girl by giving her a lollipop.
　他們用棒棒糖逗哭泣中的小女孩開心。

delightful [dɪ`laɪtfəl] 形令人欣喜的

I must tell mom the delightful news that you have been admitted to Harvard!
>> 我得告訴媽媽這個令人高興的好消息，你被哈佛大學錄取了！

demand [dɪ`mænd] 名要求 動要求

名 The negotiator rejected the demands from the other party.
　那位談判者拒絕了其他黨派的要求。
動 The teacher demanded everyone put the homework on their desks.
　老師要求每個人把回家作業放在桌上。

demonstrate [`dɛmən͵stret] 動展現；表明

The crew demonstrated the use of lifejackets just after take-off.
>> 空服員在飛機起飛後示範救生衣的使用方法。

demonstration [ˌdɛmən`streʃən] 名 證明；示範

After the teacher's demonstration, we understood gravity better.
▶▶ 經由老師的示範，我們對重力的了解更深入了。

dense [dɛns] 形 密集的；稠密的

Taipei is a dense city full of people, cars, and buildings.
▶▶ 台北是個稠密的城市，充滿了人、車和建築物。

depart [dɪ`pɑrt] 動 離開；走開

The flight departs at midnight.
▶▶ 班機於午夜時飛走。

departure [dɪ`pɑrtʃ] 名 離去；出發

It has only been thirty minutes since their departure. They haven't arrived at their destination yet.
▶▶ 他們出發才過了三十分鐘，尚未抵達目的地。

dependent [dɪ`pɛndənt] 名 從屬者 形 依賴的

名 The man had many dependents and, therefore, needed to earn a big salary .
這人以前有許多隨從，所以得賺進大筆薪資。
形 You cannot be dependent on your parents after you come of age.
你成年後就不能再依賴雙親。

depression [dɪ`prɛʃən] 名 憂鬱；經濟蕭條；凹陷；淺坑

Water filled the depressions in the ground.
▶▶ 水填滿了地上的坑洞。

deserve [dɪ`zɜv] 動 應得；值得

You deserve this glory.
▶▶ 這項榮譽是你應得的。

desperate [`dɛspərət] 形 絕望的 副 desperately 絕望地

Nancy felt desperate when she heard of her father's death.
▶▶ 當南西得知父親的死訊時，感到徹底絕望。

despite [dɪ`spaɪt] 介 不管；不顧

Despite the disapproval of her mother, Laura decided to study abroad.
▶▶ 蘿拉決定不顧母親的反對出國留學。

1 Level 基礎單字

2 Level 必備單字

3 Level 中級單字

4 Level 進階單字

5 Level 高手單字

6 Level 滿級單字

destruction [dɪˋstrʌkʃən] 名 破壞

The war brought death and destruction to the city.
▶▶ 戰爭給這城市帶來死亡和破壞。

detective [dɪˋtɛktɪv] 名 偵探 形 偵探的

名 The detectives hid themselves carefully.
偵探們小心地藏匿自身。
形 I enjoy reading detective fiction.
我喜歡閱讀偵探小說。

determination [dɪˌtɝməˋneʃən] 名 決心 關 determine 下定決心

You need great determination to succeed in business.
▶▶ 你需要很大的決心才能在商界取得成功。

device [dɪˋvaɪs] 名 裝置；設計

The device has been set up for a medical experiment.
▶▶ 這個裝置是作為醫學實驗之用。

devise [dɪˋvaɪz] 動 設計；想出

They've devised a plan for keeping traffic out the city center.
▶▶ 他們已經想出一個讓車流遠離市中心的計畫。

devote [dɪˋvot] 動 貢獻

The women devoted themselves to the charity.
▶▶ 這些婦女獻身於慈善事業。

dew [dju] 名 露水

I saw some drops of dew on the roses.
▶▶ 我看見玫瑰上有幾滴露水。

diagram [ˋdaɪəˌgræm] 名 圖表；圖樣 動 圖解

名 Selina gave me a diagram of the railway network.
賽琳娜給我一張鐵路網示意圖。
動 Kyle diagramed the location of his apartment.
凱爾畫圖表示他公寓的位置。

differ [ˋdɪfɚ] 動 不同；相異

Ideas on childcare may differ considerably from parent to parent.
▶▶ 不同父母間的育兒理念可能截然不同。

digest [daɪ`dʒɛst ] / [ `daɪdʒɛst] 動瞭解；消化 名摘要；簡報
動 I'm not going to go swimming until I've digested my lunch.
我要等中飯消化以後再去游泳。
名 The weekly news digests are sold here.
這裡出售每週新聞摘要。

digital [`dɪdʒɪtl̩] 形數字的；數位的
Digital cameras are now widespread in Taiwan.
▶▶ 現在數位相機在台灣已十分普及。

dignity [`dɪgnətɪ] 名威嚴；尊嚴
The real dignity of a man lies in what he is, not in what he has.
▶▶ 一個人的真正尊嚴在於他是什麼樣的人，而非他擁有什麼。

diligence [`dɪlədʒəns] 名勤勉；勤奮
I was touched by his diligence.
▶▶ 我被他的勤奮感動。

diligent [`dɪlədʒənt] 形勤勉的
I'm very diligent in preparing for exams.
▶▶ 我非常勤奮地準備考試。
(焦點句型) be diligent in N./Ving 勤於…

diploma [dɪ`plomə] 名文憑；畢業證書
We enter universities for knowledge instead of diplomas.
▶▶ 我們進大學是為了知識，而不是為了文憑。

diplomat [`dɪplə͵mæt] 名外交官
Nina's father is a diplomat who has lived overseas for years.
▶▶ 妮娜爸爸是個外交官，長年居於海外。

disability [͵dɪsə`bɪlətɪ] 名失能；無力
Eli qualifies for help on the grounds of his disability.
▶▶ 伊萊有資格因殘疾而獲得幫助。

disadvantage [͵dɪsəd`væntɪdʒ] 名缺點；不利
Your main disadvantage is your impatience.
▶▶ 你主要的缺點就是缺乏耐心。

1 Level 基礎單字
2 Level 必備單字
3 Level 中級單字
4 Level 進階單字
5 Level 高手單字
6 Level 滿級單字

disappoint [ˌdɪsə`pɔɪnt] 動 使失望 關 disappointment 失望

I'm sorry to disappoint you, but I'm afraid you didn't win the prize.
>> 很抱歉讓你失望，但你恐怕沒有得獎。

disaster [dɪ`zæstɚ] 名 災難

Losing your job is unpleasant, but it's not a disaster.
>> 失業是令人不愉快的，但還算不上災難。

discipline [`dɪsəplɪn] 名 紀律；訓練 動 懲戒

名 A good teacher must be able to maintain discipline in the classroom.
好的老師必須能維持課堂的紀律。
動 He disciplined those who violated the rules.
他懲處違反規定的那些人。

discourage [dɪs`kɝɪdʒ] 動 阻止；妨礙 關 discouragement 心灰意冷

Andrew's father discouraged him from seeing her.
>> 安德魯爸爸打消了他去見她的念頭。

disguise [dɪs`gaɪz] 名 掩飾 動 喬裝；假扮

名 A setback may turn out to be a blessing in disguise.
塞翁失馬，焉知非福。
動 The movie star disguised himself, hoping to avoid public attention.
這位電影明星喬裝自己，希望避免公眾注意。
(焦點句型) in disguise 偽裝的

disgust [dɪs`gʌst] 名 厭惡 動 使厭惡

名 The man has an intense disgust of children.
這個男人很厭惡小孩。
動 The level of violence in the film really disgusted me.
影片中的暴力程度實在讓我反感。

dismiss [dɪs`mɪs] 動 摒除；解散

The teacher dismissed the students early because of the upcoming holiday.
>> 因為快放假了，老師提早讓學生放學。

disorder [dɪs`ɔrdɚ] 名 無序

Nick's financial affairs are in complete disorder.
>> 尼克的財務狀況十分混亂。

dispute [dɪˋspjut] 名 爭論 動 爭論
- 名 Their dispute has not been settled yet.
  他們之間的爭端尚未徹底解決。
- 動 The two brothers disputed the proposed division of family property.
  這兩兄弟為了分家產的事而爭吵。

distinct [dɪˋstɪŋkt] 形 個別的；獨特的 同 striking

This region, which is distinct from other parts of the country, relies heavily on tourism.
▶ 這一地區與該國的其他地方明顯不同，十分依賴旅遊業。

distinguish [dɪˋstɪŋgwɪʃ] 動 分辨

The main symptom of color blindness is being unable to distinguish one color from another.
▶ 色盲的症狀就是無法分辨顏色。

distinguished [dɪˋstɪŋgwɪʃt] 形 卓越的

I think grey hair makes you look very distinguished.
▶ 我認為灰白的頭髮使你看起來很有威嚴。

distribute [dɪˋstrɪbjut] 動 分配；分發

The girl is distributing the flyers to the people passing by.
▶ 女孩正在分發傳單給路人。

distribution [ˌdɪstrəˋbjuʃən] 名 分配 關 distributor 發行人；經銷商

The map shows the distribution of this species around the world.
▶ 地圖上標明了這一物種在全世界的分布情況。

district [ˋdɪstrɪkt] 名 區域

Here is the district with the most serious pollution.
▶ 這裡是汙染最嚴重的地區。

disturb [dɪsˋtɜb] 動 干擾；打斷

Please do not disturb me while I am studying.
▶ 請不要在我念書時打擾我。

diverse [daɪˋvɜs] 形 互異的；不同的

There are diverse choices in the restaurant.
▶ 在這間餐廳你擁有多樣選擇。

Level 1 基礎單字
Level 2 必備單字
Level 3 中級單字
Level 4 進階單字
Level 5 高手單字
Level 6 滿級單字

411

diversity [daɪˋvɝsətɪ] 名 多樣性

Taiwan is known for its biological diversity.
▶▶ 台灣以生物多樣性聞名。

divine [dəˋvaɪn] 形 神聖的；超凡的

This deity holds a divine place in many local cultures.
▶▶ 在許多當地文化中，這位神靈都具有神聖的地位。

divorce [dɪˋvɔrs] 名 離婚 動 離婚

名 The child was reared by his mother after his parents' divorce.
這個小孩的父母離婚後，交由母親撫養。
動 They decided to divorce because of disharmony.
因為感情不和，他們決定離婚。

dodge [dɑdʒ] 動 閃開

I had to dodge between the cars to cross the road.
▶▶ 我在車流中東躲西閃才過了馬路。

dominant [ˋdɑmənənt] 形 支配的

She is the dominant child in the group.
▶▶ 她是這一群孩子中的孩子王。

dominate [ˋdɑməˏnet] 動 支配

The manager dominated all affairs in his department.
▶▶ 經理支配他部門裡的一切事務。

draft [dræft] 名 草稿 動 撰寫；草擬 同 draught

名 The draft of the design was missing.
這件設計的草稿不見了。
動 I'll draft a letter and show it to you before I type it.
我來起草一封信，你看了之後我再把它打出來。

dread [drɛd] 名 害怕 動 敬畏；恐怖

名 Sharon didn't want to go out because of her dread of meeting new people.
雪倫不想走出去，因為她怕遇到新面孔。
動 I dread to think what my father will say.
爸爸會說些什麼，我想也不敢想。

drift [drɪft] 動漂移;漂流;飄 名漂流物

動 Jeff watched the boat drifting away.
傑夫看著船漂走。
名 What is the drift floating on the river?
河上漂浮的那是什麼？

drill [drɪl] 名鑽;錐 動鑽孔

名 The worker worked with a drill.
工人帶著鑽具工作。
動 My brother is drilling in the wall.
我哥哥正在牆上打孔。

drowsy [`draʊzɪ] 形昏昏欲睡的

The heat made me feel drowsy.
▶▶ 天氣炎熱，我覺得昏昏欲睡。

durable [`djʊrəb]] 形耐穿的;耐磨的

This pair of shoes is durable.
▶▶ 這雙鞋很耐磨。

dusty [`dʌstɪ] 形覆著灰塵的 關 dust 灰塵

She found a dusty doll under the bed.
▶▶ 她在床底下發現一個滿是灰塵的洋娃娃。

dye [daɪ] 名染料 動染;著色

名 Ivy put the cloth into the purple dye.
艾薇把布料放進紫色染料裡。
動 Jessie had her hair dyed.
潔西染了頭髮。

dynamic [daɪ`næmɪk] 形動能的;動力的

Lewis knew I was energetic and dynamic and would get things done.
▶▶ 路易斯知道我精力充沛、生氣勃勃，會把事情辦成的。

dynasty [`daɪnəstɪ] 名王朝;朝代

The Qing Dynasty is the last dynasty of China.
▶▶ 清朝是中國最後一個王朝。

Level 1 基礎單字
Level 2 必備單字
Level 3 中級單字
Level 4 進階單字
Level 5 高手單字
Level 6 滿級單字

earnest [`ɜnɪst] 形 認真的

The minister is always earnest.
▶▶ 這個部長總是很認真。

earphone [`ɪr͵fon] 名 耳機

Felix cannot hear your calling because he is wearing earphones.
▶▶ 菲利克斯正戴著耳機,所以無法聽見你的呼喚。

economic [͵ikə`nɑmɪk] 形 經濟上的

The economic growth on the island is still low.
▶▶ 這個小島的經濟成長仍然低落。

economical [͵ikə`nɑmɪkḷ] 形 節儉的;節約的

It's economical to ride a motorcycle.
▶▶ 騎摩托車可以節省時間。

economics [͵ikə`nɑmɪks] 名 經濟學

She went abroad to study economics.
▶▶ 她出國攻讀經濟學。

economist [ɪ`kɑnəmɪst] 名 經濟學家

The economists said the depression would last for at least a month.
▶▶ 經濟學家表示,經濟不景氣至少會持續一個月。

economy [ɪ`kɑnəmɪ] 名 經濟

In the global economy rankings, Norway jumped from ninth to third place.
▶▶ 在全球經濟排名中,挪威由第九位躍升至第三位。

efficiency [ɪ`fɪʃənsɪ] 名 效率

Levi got a bonus due to the high efficiency of his work.
▶▶ 李維因工作效率高而獲得獎金。

elastic [ɪ`læstɪk] 形 有彈性的 名 橡皮筋

形 Our rules are quite elastic.
我們的規定很有彈性。

Level 1 基礎單字
Level 2 必備單字
Level 3 中級單字
Level 4 進階單字
Level 5 高手單字
Level 6 滿級單字

名 I use a piece of elastic to tie my hair.
我用橡皮筋綁頭髮。

electronics [ɪ‚lɛk`trɑnɪks] 名 電子學

The Department of Electronics is a popular major in this university.
▶▶ 電子系是這所大學的熱門科系。

elegant [`ɛləgənt] 形 優雅的

Claire looks extremely elegant in that dress.
▶▶ 克萊爾穿著那件洋裝看起來非常優雅。

elementary [‚ɛlə`mɛntərɪ] 形 基本的

She'll start elementary school next fall.
▶▶ 明年秋天她就要上小學了。

eliminate [ɪ`lɪmə‚net] 動 消除

The policemen want to eliminate the crime in this area.
▶▶ 警察想要消滅這個地區的犯罪活動。

elsewhere [`ɛls‚hwɛr] 副 在別處

The answer to the problem must be sought elsewhere.
▶▶ 這個問題的答案必須在別處尋找。

embarrass [ɪm`bærəs] 動 使困窘 關 embarrassment 尷尬

Her questions about my private life embarrassed me.
▶▶ 她詢問我的私生活使我感到很尷尬。

embassy [`ɛmbəsɪ] 名 大使館

The ambassadors lived in the embassy.
▶▶ 外交官住在大使館裡。

emerge [ɪ`mɝdʒ] 動 浮現

Several international events in the early 1990s weakened the trends that had emerged in the 1980s.
▶▶ 九十年代初的幾個國際事件，削弱了八十年代呈現的趨勢。

emphasis [`ɛmfəsɪs] 名 重點；強調

The teacher put emphasis on this chapter.
▶▶ 老師強調這個章節的重要性。

焦點句型 put emphasis on sth. 強調某事

415

empire [`ɛmpaɪr] 名帝國

More than two hundred years ago, the United States broke away from the British Empire.
▶▶ 兩百多年前，美國從大英帝國脫離出來。

enclose [ɪn`kloz] 動包圍

The troops enclosed the village.
▶▶ 軍隊圍住村莊。

encounter [ɪn`kaʊntɚ] 動遭遇 名遭遇

動 On encountering the scene, I was astonished and ran away.
一撞見這情景，我便驚愕地跑開。
名 A romantic encounter brought us together.
一次浪漫的邂逅讓我們兩個在一起。

endanger [ɪn`dendʒɚ] 動使陷入危險

The decision to run the red light endangered his life.
▶▶ 闖紅燈的決定讓他的生命陷入危險。

endure [ɪn`djʊr] 動忍受

Wendy endured the pain without uttering a sound.
▶▶ 溫蒂忍著痛苦，一聲不吭。

enforce [ɪn`fors] 動強制執行；使服從 名 enforcement 執法

It's the job of the police to enforce the law.
▶▶ 員警的工作就是執法。

engineering [ˌɛndʒɚ`nɪrɪŋ] 名工程學

The bridge is a triumph of modern engineering.
▶▶ 這座橋是現代工程的一大成就。

enlarge [ɪn`lardʒ] 動擴大 名 enlargement 擴張

I need to enlarge my room. It's too narrow.
▶▶ 我必須擴大我的房間，它太窄了。

enormous [ɪ`nɔrməs] 形巨大的

An enormous tree stands beside my house.
▶▶ 這棵巨樹矗立在我家旁邊。

ensure [ɪnˋʃʊr] 動 確保；保護

I can't ensure his being on time.
▶▶ 我不能保證他會準時。

entertain [ˏɛntɚˋten] 動 招待；娛樂 關 entertainment 娛樂；娛樂表演

Ann sang a song to entertain the guests.
▶▶ 安唱歌娛樂來賓。

enthusiasm [ɪnˋθjuzɪˏæzəm] 名 熱衷；熱情

He shows great enthusiasm for her.
▶▶ 他展現出對她的狂熱。

equality [ɪˋkwɑlətɪ] 名 平等

The most essential element of gender equality is respect.
▶▶ 性別平等最重要的就是尊重。

equip [ɪˋkwɪp] 動 裝備 關 equipment 裝備；設備

Please equip yourself with a sharp pencil and an eraser for the exam.
▶▶ 請準備一支削尖的鉛筆和一塊橡皮擦參加考試。
(焦點句型) equip sb. with sth. 配備；使有準備；訓練

era [ˋɪrə] 名 時代

We are in the Internet era, a time when almost everything can be done online.
▶▶ 這是個科技時代，幾乎什麼事都可以在網路上完成。

essential [ɪˋsɛnʃəl] 形 必要的；基本的 名 基本要素

形 It is essential for you to study. The exam is just around the corner.
你現在最重要的就是念書，考試快要到了。
名 The essentials of management are listed on page 10.
管理的基本要點都列在第十頁。

establish [əsˋtæblɪʃ] 動 建立 關 establishment 組織；建立

The personality of a child is well established at a young age.
▶▶ 孩子的個性在小時候已大致確定。

estimate [ˋɛstəˏmet] 動 評估 名 評估

動 I estimate the total to be 1,000 articles.
我估計總數有一千件。

1 Level 基礎單字

2 Level 必備單字

3 Level 中級單字

4 Level 進階單字

5 Level 高手單字

6 Level 滿級單字

名 This bill does not agree with your original estimate.
這張帳單與你當初的估計不符。

ethnic [`εθnɪk] 形 民族的

We should respect ethnic minorities.
▶▶ 我們應該尊重少數民族。

evaluate [ɪ`vælju͵et] 動 估計；評價

We evaluated the situation very carefully before we made our decision.
▶▶ 在做決定前，我們要先審慎評估形勢。

evaluation [ɪ͵vælju`eʃən] 名 評價

He gave a great evaluation of her dissertation.
▶▶ 他對她的論文給予高度評價。

eventual [ɪ`vɛntʃʊəl] 形 最後的

The eventual conclusion will be declared next Monday.
▶▶ 最後的結論會在下禮拜一公布。

evidence [`ɛvədəns] 名 證據 動 證明

名 In order to prove that Mike was the murderer, Ellen tried hard to find evidence against him.
為了證明麥克是兇手，艾倫努力試著找出證據。
動 As evidenced by the quality of work produced, the carpenter was highly skilled.
從作品的品質可以看出，這位木匠技藝精湛。

evident [`ɛvədənt] 形 明顯的

Isn't it evident that Manfred has something to tell you?
▶▶ 很明顯曼弗雷德有事情要告訴你不是嗎？

exaggerate [ɪg`zædʒ͵ret] 動 誇大

The effects of this policy have been greatly exaggerated by its opponents.
▶▶ 反對者過分誇大了這項政策的影響。

exception [ɪk`sɛpʃən] 名 反對；例外

Everyone supports him, and I am no exception.
▶▶ 大家都支持他，我也不例外。

exhaust [ɪɡˋzɔst] 動 使精疲力盡 名 排氣管

動 I was exhausted after running for such a long distance.
跑了那麼長的距離讓我精疲力盡。
名 Something has gone wrong with the car's exhaust system.
汽車的排氣系統出了故障。

exhibit [ɪɡˋzɪbɪt] 動 展示 名 展示器；展覽

動 Michael exhibited the antiques he treasured.
麥可把他珍藏的古董拿出來展示。
名 The exhibit of his paintings attracted many people.
他的畫展吸引了很多人潮。

expand [ɪkˋspænd] 動 擴大；延長

Mandy expanded her editorial staff.
▶▶ 曼蒂擴大了她的編輯部。

expansion [ɪkˋspænʃən] 名 擴張

It is well known that knowledge is the most important condition for expansion of mind.
▶▶ 眾所周知，知識是開闊思路不可缺少的條件。

experimental [ɪkˌspɛrəˋmɛntḷ] 形 實驗性的

The director is fond of experimental movies.
▶▶ 這個導演喜愛實驗電影。

explanation [ˌɛkspləˋneʃən] 名 說明；解釋

The doctor's explanation relieved me of my fears.
▶▶ 醫生的解釋打消了我的擔心。

explosion [ɪkˋsploʒən] 名 爆炸

The explosion was caused by chemical reactions.
▶▶ 那起爆炸是由化學反應引起的。

explosive [ɪkˋsplosɪv] 形 爆炸的 名 爆炸物；炸藥

形 The situation is explosive. We must try our best to calm people down.
形勢一觸即發，我們要儘量使人們冷靜。
名 The firemen tried to remove the explosive.
消防人員試圖移除爆裂物。

Level 1 基礎單字
Level 2 必備單字
Level 3 中級單字
Level 4 進階單字
Level 5 高手單字
Level 6 滿級單字

expose [ɪkˋspoz] 動暴露；揭發

He exposed the truth that the candidate had been in prison.
▶▶ 他透露了那位候選人曾坐過牢的事實。

exposure [ɪkˋspoʒɚ] 名顯露

There is a direct correlation between exposure to sun and skin cancer.
▶▶ 皮膚暴露在太陽下與皮膚癌直接相關。

extend [ɪkˋstɛnd] 動延長

Please do whatever you can to extend my mother's life.
▶▶ 請盡你所能延長我媽媽的壽命。

extent [ɪkˋstɛnt] 名範圍；程度 關 to some extent 某種程度上；部分

I was amazed at the extent of his knowledge.
▶▶ 他學問的廣博使我驚嘆。

 **F字頭進階單字**

MP3 078

facial [ˋfeʃəl] 形面部的；表面的

At first, Julie was given a facial massage.
▶▶ 首先，他們替朱莉做了臉部按摩。

facility [fəˋsɪlətɪ] 名場所；天資；功能

Aldrich has an amazing facility for drawing.
▶▶ 奧爾德里奇擁有驚人的繪畫天賦。

faithful [ˋfeθfəl] 形忠實的；可靠的 關 faith 信心

The faithful dog will not leave its master in times of trouble.
▶▶ 這隻忠實的狗不會在困難時離開牠的主人。

fame [fem] 名名聲

What he did was not out of charity but fishing for fame.
▶▶ 他所做的不是出於善心，而是為了沽名釣譽。

fantastic [fænˋtæstɪk] 形極好的；幻想的；怪誕的

The car cost a fantastic amount of money.
▶▶ 這輛車的價錢貴得嚇人。

fantasy [`fæntəsɪ] 名空想；幻想

The little girl always indulged herself in fantasy.
▶▶ 這個小女孩總是沉浸在幻想中。

farewell [,fɛr`wɛl] 名告別；歡送會

They held a farewell for the friend who planned to leave for America.
▶▶ 他們為那名計劃要去美國的朋友舉行歡送會。

fasten [`fæsn̩] 動繫緊

Remember to fasten your seat belt before driving.
▶▶ 開車前記得繫好安全帶。

fatal [`fetl̩] 形致命的；決定性的 同 lethal

The wound will be fatal to her.
▶▶ 這傷口將是她的致命傷。

favorable [`fevərəbl̩] 形有利的；討人喜歡的

Courtesy is favorable everywhere.
▶▶ 有禮貌在哪裡都受歡迎。

fax [fæks] 名傳真

My fax number is 2233-1568.
▶▶ 我的傳真號碼是 2233-1568。

feast [fist] 名宴會；享受 動宴請；大吃大喝

名 The evening was a real feast for music lovers.
這個晚會對音樂愛好者來說是場盛宴。
動 Adolf feasted friends to celebrate his promotion.
因為獲得升遷，阿道夫設宴款待朋友。

feedback [`fid,bæk] 名回饋

I need your feedback to improve my performance.
▶▶ 我需要你的回饋來改進我的表現。

ferry [`fɛrɪ] 名渡輪；渡船 動渡運；運送

名 We caught the ferry at Ostend.
我們在奧斯坦德及時趕上了渡船。
動 The children need to be ferried to and from school.
孩子們需要接送上下學。

Level 1 基礎單字
Level 2 必備單字
Level 3 中級單字
Level 4 進階單字
Level 5 高手單字
Level 6 滿級單字

fertile [`fɜtl̩] 形 肥沃的；豐富的

We have irrigated the desert area to make it fertile.
▶▶ 我們灌溉了沙漠地區，使其變得肥沃。

fetch [fɛtʃ] 動 取得；接來

The teacher asked one of the students to fetch the globe.
▶▶ 老師要其中一位學生拿地球儀過來。

fiction [`fɪkʃən] 名 小說；虛構

What kind of fiction do you like the most?
▶▶ 你最喜歡哪種小說？

fierce [fɪrs] 形 猛烈的；粗暴的

The fierce tiger tore its prey up.
▶▶ 這隻兇猛的老虎把牠的獵物撕碎。

finance [`faɪ,næns] 名 財務 動 供資金給…；融資 闆 deficit 赤字

名 Elsa is in charge of managing the finances of the company.
愛爾莎負責公司的財務。
動 They financed the project in return for promises of profit.
他們為該方案提供資金，以換取盈利承諾。

financial [faɪ`nænʃəl] 形 金融的；財政的 同 fiscal / monetary

New York is a great financial center.
▶▶ 紐約是一個重要的金融中心。

fireplace [`faɪr,ples] 名 壁爐；火爐

Most Japanese households have fireplaces in their living rooms.
▶▶ 大部分的日本家戶在客廳都有暖爐。

flatter [`flætɚ] 動 諂媚；奉承

David's praise flattered me.
▶▶ 大衛的讚美取悅了我。

flea [fli] 名 跳蚤

Fleas are tiny insects.
▶▶ 跳蚤是很小的昆蟲。

flee [fli] 動逃走；逃避

The mouse fled immediately when the man came into the room.
▶▶ 當那男人進房時，老鼠立刻逃走了。

flexible [`flɛksəbḷ] 形有彈性的 關 flexibility 彈性

This tube is flexible but tough.
▶▶ 這管子柔韌但很堅固。

fluent [`fluənt] 形流利的

His fluent English impressed the interviewer.
▶▶ 他流利的英文讓面試官留下深刻印象。

flush [flʌʃ] 名臉紅 動沖洗；臉紅

名 Herman's compliment left a flush on her cheeks.
赫曼的恭維使她臉紅。
動 Remember to flush the toilet before you leave the restroom.
離開廁所前記得沖水。

foam [fom] 名泡沫 動起泡沫

名 Foam rubber provides good insulation.
泡沫橡膠隔絕性能良好。
動 When the water begins to foam, it is boiling.
當水開始起泡，表示它沸騰了。

forbid [fɚ`bɪd] 動禁止

You are forbidden to enter the mansion without an ID card.
▶▶ 沒有識別證，你不能進入這棟大廈。
文法解析 forbid 動詞三態變化為 forbid / forbade / forbidden。

forecast [`for͵kæst] 名預測

According to the forecast, tomorrow will be a sunny day.
▶▶ 根據預報，明天會是好天氣。

formation [fɔr`meʃən] 名形成；成立

Do you know the physical processes of rock formation?
▶▶ 你知道岩石形成的物理過程嗎？

Level 1 基礎單字
Level 2 必備單字
Level 3 中級單字
Level 4 進階單字
Level 5 高手單字
Level 6 滿級單字

formula [`fɔrmjələ] 名 公式；法則

What is the formula for converting miles to kilometers?
▶▶ 用什麼公式把英里換算成公里？

fort [fort] 名 堡壘；炮臺

The forts exhibited here were set up one hundred years ago.
▶▶ 這些展示於此的炮臺都是一百年前所設。

fortunate [`fɔrtʃənɪt] 形 幸運的

Betty is such a fortunate person to have won the lottery.
▶▶ 貝蒂真是個幸運兒，竟然中了樂透。

fossil [`fɑsḷ] 名 化石；舊事物 形 守舊的；陳腐的

名 The professor of anthropology is a fossil collector.
這個人類學教授是個化石收藏家。
形 Irene's fossil thinking won't allow her to accept new ways of doing things.
艾琳的想法很陳腐，以致無法接受新的做事方法。

foundation [faun`deʃən] 名 基礎；根基

The society was established on a shaky foundation of natural resources.
▶▶ 這個社會建立在一個並不牢固的自然資源基礎之上。

founder [`faundɚ] 名 創立者；捐出基金者

Mr. Chuang is the founder of the charity.
▶▶ 莊先生是這個慈善機構的創辦人。

fragile [`frædʒəl] 形 脆的；易碎的

Be careful when holding this fragile porcelain.
▶▶ 拿著這些易碎瓷器時要小心。

frame [frem] 名 骨架；框架 動 構築；框架

名 The bed has an iron frame.
床架是鐵製的。
動 The team framed the building plan.
這個團隊構想建築計劃。

frequency [`frikwənsɪ] 名 頻率

The high frequency of his absence has caught the attention of the teacher.
▶▶ 他頻繁的缺席已引起老師注意。

freshman [`frɛʃmən] 名新生;大一生

Those freshmen are listening to the seniors introducing the department.
▶▶ 這些新生正在聽學長姐們介紹系所。

frost [frɑst] 名霜;冷淡 動結霜

名 The frost covered the window, so I could not see you.
窗上結了一層霜,所以我看不見你。
動 The glass was frosted.
玻璃上結了霜。

frown [fraʊn] 名不悅之色 動皺眉;表示不滿

名 After he said the truth, she glanced at him with a frown.
他說出實話後,她不悅地朝他瞥了一眼。
動 My father frowned at my score.
爸爸對我的成績不滿意。

焦點句型 frown on/upon sth. 不贊成;不允許

frustrate [`frʌs͵tret] 動挫敗

The lack of money frustrated Jonathan.
▶▶ 缺乏資金使喬納森灰心。

frustration [͵frʌs`treʃən] 名挫折;失敗

Kevin felt great frustration because the girl turned him down.
▶▶ 凱文感到十分挫敗,因為那女孩拒絕了他。

fulfill [fʊl`fɪl] 動實現 關 fulfillment 實現;符合條件

I will fulfill my dream someday.
▶▶ 有朝一日我將實現我的夢想。

functional [`fʌŋkʃən̩] 形實用的;功能性的

Bathrooms don't have to be purely functional.
▶▶ 浴室不必完全只為了實用。

fundamental [͵fʌndə`mɛnt̩] 名基礎;原則 形基礎的 同 underlying

名 You can study the fundamentals of computers on your own.
你可以自學電腦基礎原理。
形 Honesty is the fundamental element of a relationship.
誠實是建立關係的基本要素。

1 Level 基礎單字
2 Level 必備單字
3 Level 中級單字
4 Level 進階單字
5 Level 高手單字
6 Level 滿級單字

funeral [`fjunərəl] 名 葬禮；告別式

We were all in black to attend the funeral.
▶▶ 我們穿著一身黑衣去參加告別式。

furious [`fjʊrɪəs] 形 狂怒的

Dad was furious at the liar.
▶▶ 爸爸被這個騙子氣瘋了。

(焦點句型) be furious at N./Ving 對…感到憤怒

furnish [`fɜnɪʃ] 動 布置；配備（家具）

I bought some furniture to furnish my apartment.
▶▶ 我買了些家具以裝潢我的公寓。

furthermore [`fɜðə͵mor] 副 再者

You had better not bother her. Furthermore, she is sad now.
▶▶ 你最好別打擾她。而且，她現在心情正低落。

UNIT 07 G 字頭進階單字

MP3 079

gallery [`gælərɪ] 名 畫廊；美術館

They went to the gallery to see the world-famous paintings.
▶▶ 他們去畫廊看那幾幅舉世聞名的畫作。

gaze [gez] 名 注視；凝視 動 注視；凝視

名 Despite the gaze of her boss, Martha was still at ease.
儘管在她主管的注目之下，瑪莎仍然感到自在。
動 Why does the stranger gaze at me?
為什麼那個陌生人盯著我看？

(焦點句型) gaze at sb./sth. 凝視

gear [gɪr] 名 排檔；裝備 動 開動；使適應

名 Susan is not used to driving a car without automatic gears.
蘇珊不習慣開沒有自動排檔的車。
動 Education should be geared to society's needs.
教育應適應社會的需要。

gender [`dʒɛndɚ] 名性別

Over the years, gender roles have changed.
▶▶ 過了幾年，性別角色已經改變了。

gene [dʒin] 名基因；遺傳因子

They discovered that the cancer-causing genes were inactive in normal cells.
▶▶ 他們發現致癌基因在正常的細胞中並不活躍。

generation [ˌdʒɛnəˋreʃən] 名世代

There is no generation gap between my grandma and me.
▶▶ 我外婆和我之間沒有代溝。

generosity [ˌdʒɛnəˋrɑsətɪ] 名慷慨；寬宏大量

Thanks to your generosity, I am able to afford to go on a trip.
▶▶ 謝謝你的慷慨，我可以負擔這次的旅費了。

genius [`dʒinjəs] 名天才

Tim is a musical genius. He started to compose when he was only 10 years old.
▶▶ 提姆是個音樂天才。當他還只有十歲時，他就開始作曲了。

genuine [`dʒɛnjʊɪn] 形真正的

A genuine pearl costs a lot of money.
▶▶ 一顆真正的珍珠要價昂貴。

germ [dʒɝm] 名細菌

Germs can lead to diseases.
▶▶ 細菌會導致疾病。

gifted [`gɪftɪd] 形有天賦的 關 gift 禮物

The child is gifted with drawing skills.
▶▶ 這孩子有畫畫的天份。

gigantic [dʒaɪˋgæntɪk] 形巨大的

The new airplane looked like a gigantic bird.
▶▶ 這架新飛機看起來像一隻巨大的鳥。

Level 1 基礎單字
Level 2 必備單字
Level 3 中級單字
Level 4 進階單字
Level 5 高手單字
Level 6 滿級單字

giggle [`gɪg!̩] 名 咯咯笑 動 咯咯笑

名 Do you hear a strange giggle behind the wall?
你有聽到牆後傳來的奇怪笑聲嗎？

動 The students giggled when the teacher slipped.
當老師滑倒時，學生們咯咯地笑起來。

ginger [`dʒɪndʒɚ] 名 薑 形 薑黃色的；赤黃色的

名 I love drinking ginger soup in the winter.
我喜歡在冬天喝薑湯。

動 Darren has a ginger hair, and that's where he got his nickname.
達倫有一頭薑黃色的頭髮，這也是他外號的由來。

glimpse [glɪmps] 名 瞥見 動 瞥見

名 One glimpse at himself in the mirror was enough.
讓他照鏡子看自己一眼就夠了。

動 She glimpsed the newspaper headlines quickly.
她匆匆看了一遍報紙的大標題。

globe [glob] 名 地球；球

There is a population of about eight billion on the globe.
▶▶ 地球上有大約八十億的人口。

glorious [`glorɪəs] 形 輝煌的；榮耀的 關 glory 榮耀 / glorify 使…榮耀

They had three weeks of glorious sunshine.
▶▶ 他們度過了三週陽光燦爛的日子。

goods [gʊdz] 名 商品；貨物

The goods they sold were fakes.
▶▶ 他們賣的那些貨都是假貨。

gown [gaʊn] 名 女式禮服；長袍

Sherry looks gorgeous in the yellow gown.
▶▶ 雪莉穿那件黃禮服看起來真迷人。

grace [gres] 名 優雅

Mary behaved with grace.
▶▶ 瑪莉舉手投足都很優雅。

graceful [`gresfəl] 形 優雅的

The dancers were all tall and graceful.
▶▶ 這些舞蹈家的個子都很高，動作十分優雅。

gracious [`greʃəs] 形 親切的；溫和有禮的

The waitresses in the restaurant are very gracious and patient.
▶▶ 這間餐廳的女服務生都很親切有耐心。

graduation [ˌgrædʒʊ`eʃən] 名 畢業 關 graduate 畢業

My classmates and I cried during the graduation ceremony.
▶▶ 同學們和我在畢業典禮上都哭了。

grammar [`græmɚ] 名 文法

Not only grammar but also pronunciation are important in learning English.
▶▶ 學英文時，文法和發音都很重要。

grammatical [grə`mætɪkḷ] 形 文法上的

Correct all the grammatical errors in this essay.
▶▶ 把這篇文章的文法錯誤全部訂正過來。

graph [græf] 名 圖；圖表 動 用圖表說明

名 The graph shows the tendency of growth.
這個圖表呈現出成長的趨勢。
動 I graphed the math question for my brother.
我向弟弟用圖表解釋這題數學。

grateful [`gretfəl] 形 感激的

I am very grateful for your help.
▶▶ 我非常感激你的幫忙。

gratitude [`grætəˌtjud] 名 感激

I would like to express my gratitude to everyone for their hard work.
▶▶ 我要對所有辛勤工作的人表示感謝。

grave [grev] 名 墳墓 形 嚴重的

名 Here is the grave of the renowned author.
這裡就是那位知名作家之墓。
形 The country faces grave threats to peace.
這個國家正面臨重大的安全威脅。

Level 1 基礎單字
Level 2 必備單字
Level 3 中級單字
Level 4 進階單字
Level 5 高手單字
Level 6 滿級單字

greasy [`grizɪ] 形油膩的

Greasy food is not proper for patients.
▶▶ 油膩的食物不適合病人。

greeting [`gritɪŋ] 名問候；問候語

My mother sends her greetings to you all.
▶▶ 我母親向你們大家問好。

grief [grif] 名悲傷

Nicole suffered from grief after her dog died.
▶▶ 妮可自她的狗死後就忍受著悲傷之苦。

grind [graɪnd] 動研磨；碾

The coffee beans were ground several times.
▶▶ 這些咖啡豆歷經多次研磨。
文法解析 grind 動詞三態變化為 grind / ground / ground。

guarantee [͵gærən`ti] 名保證；擔保 動擔保；確保

名 This air-conditioner comes with a three-year guarantee.
這台空調保修期為三年。
動 I guarantee you that I will complete all the tasks tomorrow.
我向你保證我明天就會完成所有的任務。

guardian [`gɑrdɪən] 名守護者

My boyfriend vowed to be my guardian forever.
▶▶ 我男朋友發誓當我永遠的守護者。

guilt [gɪlt] 名罪；內疚

Many survivors were left with a sense of guilt.
▶▶ 許多倖存者都有內疚感。

guilty [`gɪltɪ] 形有罪的；內疚的

I feel guilty about being late.
▶▶ 我為遲到感到內疚。

gulf [gʌlf] 名灣；海灣

The quarrel left a gulf between the old friends.
▶▶ 那場爭吵在那對老朋友間造成極深的隔閡。

habitual [hə`bɪtʃuəl] 形 習慣性的

His habitual snoring disturbed his family very much.
▶▶ 他習慣性的打鼾讓家人十分困擾。

halt [hɔlt] 名 休止 動 停止；使停止

名 Emily works earnestly without a halt.
艾蜜莉認真地工作，毫不停歇。
動 Gavin halted his steps and looked at the flower.
蓋文停下腳步看花。

handwriting [`hænd,raɪtɪŋ] 名 手寫

The handwriting on the paper cannot be recognized.
▶▶ 這張紙上的手寫筆跡無法辨識。

hardship [`hɑrdʃɪp] 名 艱難；辛苦

We have to keep trying hard in spite of hardship.
▶▶ 儘管艱難，但我們必須堅持下去。

hardware [`hɑrdwɛr] 名 （電腦）硬體；五金用品

I am interested in your hardware.
▶▶ 我對你們的硬體感興趣。

harmony [`hɑrmənɪ] 名 一致；和諧

The five dogs live in harmony.
▶▶ 這五隻狗和平共處。

harsh [hɑrʃ] 形 嚴厲的；令人不快的

The minister received some harsh criticism.
▶▶ 部長受到一些嚴厲的批評。

haste [hest] 名 急忙；急速

More haste, less speed.
▶▶ 欲速則不達。

431

hasten [`hesn̩] 動 趕忙

She overslept and hastened to her school.

▶▶ 她睡過頭了，趕緊衝去學校。

hatred [`hetrɪd] 名 怨恨；憎惡

Hatred is a negative feeling.

▶▶ 怨恨是一種負面情感。

hawk [hɔk] 名 鷹

Bill watched her like a hawk.

▶▶ 比爾用老鷹一樣銳利的目光緊盯著她。

helicopter [`hɛlɪkɑptɚ] 名 直升機

They rescued the victims by helicopter.

▶▶ 他們用直升機搶救受難者。

herd [hɜd] 名 獸群；成群 動 放牧；使成群

名 If you feel so strongly, why do you follow the herd?
　既然你有堅定的立場，為什麼還隨波逐流？

動 The shepherd herded the sheep on the hill.
　牧羊人在山丘上放羊。

hesitation [ˌhɛzə`teʃən] 名 遲疑；躊躇 題 hesitate 猶豫

The client agreed without hesitation.

▶▶ 客戶毫不猶豫地答應了。

hive [haɪv] 名 蜂巢

Watch out! There is a hive of bees beside you.

▶▶ 小心！你旁邊有個蜂巢。

homeland [`homlænd] 名 祖國；本國

He missed his homeland but could not return because of war.

▶▶ 他很想念他的祖國，卻因戰亂無法回去。

honeymoon [`hʌnɪˌmun] 名 蜜月 動 度蜜月

名 The challenges for a couple are following the honeymoon.
　度完蜜月之後，新婚夫妻的種種挑戰才真正開始。

動 My sister honeymooned in Rome.
　我的姐姐在羅馬度蜜月。

hook [huk] 名鉤 動用鉤子鉤住

名 Do not hang your coat on the hook. It will break.
別把你的大衣掛在鉤子上，它會斷掉。

動 Hook the painting on the wall.
把畫鉤在牆上。

horizon [hə`raɪzn̩] 名地平線；視野

Experiencing foreign cultures can broaden your horizons.
▶▶ 體驗異國文化可以拓展視野。

horrify [`hɔrə,faɪ] 動使害怕

The sudden shout horrified me.
▶▶ 那陣突然的咆哮嚇到我了。

hose [hoz] 名水管 動用水管澆洗

名 The hose was turned on the fire.
消防水管對準火苗。

動 The gardener is hosing the garden.
園丁正在用水管澆洗花園。

household [`haʊs,hold] 形家用的

The household appliance that everyone must have is a refrigerator.
▶▶ 人人必備的家電為冰箱。

housework [`haʊsw3k] 名家事

Everyone in the house is responsible for the housework.
▶▶ 每個家裡的人都有責任做家事。

humanity [hju`mænətɪ] 名人類；人道

Humanity is still in its youth.
▶▶ 人道主義的發展尚未成熟。

humidity [hju`mɪdətɪ] 名濕度

Forecasters predicted that the humidity in the air tomorrow would be 60%.
▶▶ 據預報說明天的空氣濕度會是百分之六十。

hurricane [`h3ɪ,ken] 名颶風

The hurricane practically destroyed New Orleans.
▶▶ 颶風幾乎毀了紐奧良。

Level 1 基礎單字
Level 2 必備單字
Level 3 中級單字
Level 4 進階單字
Level 5 高手單字
Level 6 滿級單字

hush [hʌʃ] 動 使靜寂 名 寂靜

動 A critic claimed that the whole affair had been hushed up by the council.
一名評論家聲稱整個事件都被議會一手掩蓋住了。
名 A shout broke the hush of the night.
一聲咆哮劃破了夜的寂靜。

hydrogen [`haɪdrədʒən] 名 氫

The balloons were filled with hydrogen.
▶▶ 這些氣球裡都灌滿了氫氣。

 **I 字頭進階單字**

identical [aɪ`dɛntɪkl̩] 形 相同的

Her dress is almost identical to mine.
▶▶ 她的洋裝和我的幾乎一模一樣。

identification [aɪˌdɛntəfə`keʃən] 名 身分證

Show your identification to prove who you are.
▶▶ 亮出身分證來證明你是誰。

identify [aɪ`dɛntəˌfaɪ] 動 認出；識別

Studies show that infants are able to identify their mother by her voice.
▶▶ 研究顯示嬰兒能依靠聲音分辨出自己的母親。

idiom [`ɪdɪəm] 名 成語；慣用語

Some idioms in English such as "Pigs might fly" are very interesting.
▶▶ 有些英文慣用語很有趣，比如說「無稽之談」。

idle [`aɪdl̩] 形 閒置的 動 閒混

形 The machine is idle now. Nobody is using it.
這張椅子現在是閒置狀態，沒有人在使用。
動 Jacky idled away all day, not knowing what to do.
傑克整天閒晃，無所事事。

idol [`aɪdl̩] 名 偶像 關 icon 畫像；聖像；偶像

The fans screamed excitedly when their idol appeared.
▶▶ 當偶像出現時，歌迷們激動地尖叫。

ignorance [`ɪgnərəns] 名 無知

Ignorance of the law is no excuse.
▶▶ 不懂法律不是申辯的理由。

ignorant [`ɪgnərənt] 形 無知的

An intelligent enemy is better than an ignorant friend.
▶▶ 聰明的敵人勝於無知的朋友。

illustrate [ɪ`lʌstret] 動 舉例說明；給…畫插圖

Can you illustrate the lesson with pictures?
▶▶ 你可以用圖片來闡釋這一課嗎？

illustration [ɪ,lʌs`treʃən] 名 說明；插圖

The statistics are a clear illustration of the point I am trying to make.
▶▶ 這組統計數字清楚地闡明了我要陳述的要點。

imaginary [ɪ`mædʒə,nɛrɪ] 形 想像中的；虛構的

The little girl had an imaginary friend.
▶▶ 小女孩有一位想像的朋友。

imaginative [ɪ`mædʒə,netɪv] 形 有想像力的

Sarah is so imaginative that she can think of several possibilities.
▶▶ 莎拉很有想像力，她可以想出很多種可能性。

imitate [`ɪmə,tet] 動 仿效 關 forge 偽造

Kids imitate the behavior of adults.
▶▶ 小孩會模仿大人的行為。

imitation [,ɪmə`teʃən] 名 模仿；仿造品

The sculpture is just an imitation of the masterpiece by Ju Ming.
▶▶ 這座雕塑只是朱銘傑作的仿造品。

immigrant [`ɪməgrənt] 名 （外來）移民者

More and more immigrants from Southeast Asia are coming to Taiwan.
▶▶ 有越來越多的東南亞移民來到台灣。

Level 1 基礎單字
Level 2 必備單字
Level 3 中級單字
Level 4 進階單字
Level 5 高手單字
Level 6 滿級單字

immigrate [`ɪmə‚gret] 動遷移；移入

Dick immigrated to America 10 years ago.
▶▶ 迪克十年前移民至美國。

immigration [‚ɪmə`greʃən] 名（從外地）移居入境

The immigration numbers included many people from Hungary.
▶▶ 入境的移民中有許多匈牙利人。

impact [`ɪmpækt] 名撞擊；影響 動衝擊；影響

名 The news that Margaret got married had a mighty impact on him.
瑪格麗特結婚的消息對他造成很大的影響。
動 The cost of energy impacts heavily on family budgets.
能源費用嚴重影響到家庭預算中的開支。
(焦點句型) have an impact on sb./sth. 對⋯有影響

imply [ɪm`plaɪ] 動暗示；含有 關 implication 暗示

Gordon implied that I had to work overtime tonight.
▶▶ 戈登暗示我今晚要加班。

impose [ɪm`poz] 動徵收；強加於 同 inflict

The government imposed a heavy tax on overseas goods.
▶▶ 政府對外來品課以重稅。

impression [ɪm`prɛʃən] 名印象

My cousin made a good impression on the girl.
▶▶ 我表弟給這位女孩留下了好印象。
(焦點句型) make an impression on sb. 給某人留下印象

incident [`ɪnsədənt] 名事件

The premier promised that such an incident would not happen again.
▶▶ 總理保證這類事件不會再重演。

including [ɪn`kludɪŋ] 介包含；包括

I have many reliable friends, including you.
▶▶ 我有很多可信賴的朋友，也包括你。

indication [‚ɪndə`keʃən] 名指示；表示

They gave no indication of how the work should be done.
▶▶ 他們根本沒說這項工作該怎樣做。

infant [`ɪnfənt] 名 嬰兒；幼兒

The infant had no hair or teeth yet.
▶▶ 這個嬰兒還沒有長頭髮和牙齒。

infection [ɪn`fɛkʃən] 名 感染；傳染病

Wash your hands frequently to avoid infection.
▶▶ 經常洗手可以避免傳染病。

inflation [ɪn`fleʃən] 名 膨脹；脹大；通貨膨脹

In the past two months, inflation has been running at an annual rate of about 4 percent.
▶▶ 前兩個月通貨膨脹的速度已達到年增長率的百分之四左右。

influential [ˏɪnflu`ɛnʃəl] 形 有影響力的

Helen is the most influential student in her class.
▶▶ 海倫是她們班上最有影響力的學生。

informative [ɪn`fɔrmətɪv] 形 提供資訊的

The talk was both informative and entertaining.
▶▶ 這次談話既長見識又饒有趣味。

ingredient [ɪn`gridɪənt] 名 成份；原料

The ingredients of the bread are just flour, water, salt and butter.
▶▶ 這個麵包的原料是麵粉、水、鹽和奶油。

initial [ɪ`nɪʃəl] 形 開始的；最初的 名 姓名的首字母

形 Her initial reaction was shock, but she accepted it later.
她起初的反應是震驚，但後來還是接受了。
名 George Bernard Shaw was well known by his initials GBS.
人們對蕭伯納姓名的首字母 GBS 非常熟悉。

injure [`ɪndʒə] 動 傷害

Eric got injured in the car accident.
▶▶ 艾瑞克在車禍中受傷。

innocence [`ɪnəsn̩s] 名 清白；天真；無辜

The children laughed with innocence.
▶▶ 孩子們笑得天真無邪。

1 Level 基礎單字
2 Level 必備單字
3 Level 中級單字
4 Level 進階單字
5 Level 高手單字
6 Level 滿級單字

input [`ɪn͵pʊt] 名輸入 動輸入 反 output

名 The keyboard is an input device for computers.
鍵盤是電腦的輸入裝置。

動 Input the command into the window.
在視窗輸入指令。

insert [ɪn`sɜt] 名插入物 動插入

名 The paper contains an insert that offers discounts.
報紙裡有一張提供優惠的插頁。

動 The ATM screen displays "insert card" at the beginning.
自動提款機的螢幕一開始會顯示「插入卡片」。

inspection [ɪn`spɛkʃən] 名檢查；調查

Stephen gave the car a thorough inspection before buying it.
▶▶ 史蒂芬在買那部車之前已仔細檢查過。

(焦點句型) give sth. an inspection 檢查某物

inspiration [͵ɪnspə`reʃən] 名鼓舞；激勵

Lena's presence is the best inspiration for him.
▶▶ 麗娜的出現是他最好的鼓舞。

inspire [ɪn`spaɪr] 動啟發；鼓舞

My mother inspired me by telling the failures she experienced in her youth.
▶▶ 我媽媽用她年輕時的失敗經歷來鼓勵我。

install [ɪn`stɔl] 動安裝；裝置

We're installing a new heating system.
▶▶ 我們正在安裝新的暖氣系統。

instinct [`ɪnstɪŋkt] 名本能；直覺 形 instinctive 本能的

She was suspicious of him by instinct.
▶▶ 她出於直覺而對他起疑。

instruct [ɪn`strʌkt] 動教導；指令

Children must be instructed in road safety before they are allowed to ride a bike on the road.
▶▶ 必須先教導兒童道路安全知識，才可以讓他們在路上騎自行車。

instructor [ɪn`strʌktə] 名 教師；指導者

I attributed the honor to my instructor.
▶▶ 我將這份榮耀歸於我的導師。

insult [ɪn`sʌlt ] / [ `ɪnsʌlt] 動 侮辱 名 侮辱

動 I never meant to insult you.
我不是有意要侮辱你。
名 Julian's comments were seen as an insult to the president.
朱利安的評論被看成是對主席的冒犯。

insurance [ɪn`ʃurəns] 名 保險

Charlie has a life insurance policy, which benefits his wife when he dies.
▶▶ 查理有買一份壽險，如果他去世，他的妻子會得到一筆錢。

intellectual [ˌɪntəl`ɛktʃuəl] 名 知識份子 形 智力的

名 We intellectuals have the duty to devote ourselves to public issues.
我們知識份子有義務投身於公共議題。
形 This game stimulated the development of children's intellectual powers.
這個遊戲促進孩子的智力發展。

intelligence [ɪn`tɛlədʒəns] 名 智能

Her intelligence quotient is as high as 180.
▶▶ 她的智商高達一百八十。

intend [ɪn`tɛnd] 動 計畫；打算

They intended to skip the class tomorrow.
▶▶ 他們打算蹺明天的課了。

intense [ɪn`tɛns] 形 極度的；緊張的

The intense competition stressed Parker very much.
▶▶ 競爭的激烈讓帕克壓力很大。

intensity [ɪn`tɛnsətɪ] 名 強度；強烈

The poem showed the great intensity of the poet's feelings.
▶▶ 這首詩表現出詩人強烈的情感。

intensive [ɪn`tɛnsɪv] 形 強烈的；密集的

The patient was sent to the intensive care unit.
▶▶ 那名病患被送進加護病房。

Level 1 基礎單字
Level 2 必備單字
Level 3 中級單字
Level 4 進階單字
Level 5 高手單字
Level 6 滿級單字

intention [ɪn`tɛnʃən] 名 意圖；意向

We don't know his real intention.
▶▶ 我們不知道他真正的意圖。

interact [ˌɪntə`rækt] 動 交互作用；互動

Colleagues have many opportunities to interact and collaborate.
▶▶ 同事之間有很多互動與合作的機會。

interaction [ˌɪntə`ækʃən] 名 交互影響；互動

There is a need for greater interaction between the two departments.
▶▶ 這兩個部門需要更好的相互配合。

interfere [ˌɪntə`fɪr] 動 妨礙

The noise outside interfered with my studies.
▶▶ 窗外的噪音妨礙我念書。
焦點句型 interfere with sth./sb. 妨礙⋯；干擾⋯

intermediate [ˌɪntə`midɪət] 形 中間的

I've passed the intermediate level of Japanese exam .
▶▶ 我已經通過了日語的中級考試。

interpret [ɪn`tɜprɪt] 動 說明；解讀；口譯

Patrick interpreted the woman's words into English.
▶▶ 派翠克把那女子的話翻成英文。

interruption [ˌɪntə`rʌpʃən] 名 中斷；妨礙

They continued to talk after the interruption.
▶▶ 干擾結束後，他們又繼續說起話來。

intimate [`ɪntəmət] 形 親密的 名 知己

形 They have an intimate relationship, and there are no secrets between them.
他們關係十分親密，彼此之間沒有秘密。
名 My husband is not only my lover but also my intimate.
我丈夫不只是我的愛人，也是我的知己。

intuition [ˌɪntju`ɪʃən] 名 直覺

She knew about his illness by intuition, although he never mentioned it.
▶▶ 雖然他從未提及，可是她憑直覺就知道他的病況。

invade [ɪn`ved] 動 侵略；入侵

The nation will combat with those who invade.
▶▶ 這個國家將和所有侵略者戰鬥。

invasion [ɪn`veʒən] 名 侵犯；侵害

The man apologized for his invasion into her privacy.
▶▶ 這男人為侵犯她的隱私而道歉。

invention [ɪn`vɛnʃən] 名 發明；創造

What invention do you consider the most important in this century?
▶▶ 你認為本世紀最偉大的發明是什麼？

invest [ɪn`vɛst] 動 投資 關 investment 投資額；投資

The banker invited some of his friends to invest in real estate.
▶▶ 銀行家邀請一些朋友來投資房地產。

investigation [ɪn,vɛstə`geʃən] 名 調查 關 investigate 調查

The experts have completed their investigations in the area.
▶▶ 專家們已完成了對這個地區的調查。

involve [ɪn`vɑlv] 動 牽涉；包括 關 involvement 捲入；連累

I was involved in the accident because I was one of the drivers.
▶▶ 我捲入了那場意外，因為我是其中一位駕駛。

isolate [`aɪsḷ,et] 動 孤立；隔離

The mysterious warehouse was isolated from the house.
▶▶ 那間神祕的庫房與房屋彼此隔離。
(焦點句型) be isolated from sth./sb. 與…隔離

isolation [,aɪsḷ`eʃən] 名 分離；孤獨

His isolation from the other members of his family bothered him very much.
▶▶ 與家人分離讓他十分苦惱。

issue [`ɪʃju] 名 議題 動 發出；發行

名 We will handle this issue in accordance with international laws and practices.
我們將根據國際法和國際訴訟程序處理這個議題。
動 The magazine issued last week is very popular.
上禮拜發行的雜誌很受歡迎。

Level 1 基礎單字
Level 2 必備單字
Level 3 中級單字
Level 4 進階單字
Level 5 高手單字
Level 6 滿級單字

UNIT 10　J、K字頭進階單字　MP3 082

jealousy [`dʒɛləsɪ] 名 嫉妒

Jealousy displeases you.
▶▶ 嫉妒使你不快。

keen [kin] 形 熱心的；敏銳的

I am very keen on helping the poor.
▶▶ 我對救濟窮人很熱心。
(焦點句型) be keen on N./Ving 對…有熱忱；熱衷於…

kettle [`kɛtḷ] 名 水壺

To prepare water for his tea, Rupert put the kettle on the stove.
▶▶ 為了準備泡茶用的水，魯普特把水壺放在爐子上。

kneel [nil] 動 下跪

She knelt down to beg her father.
▶▶ 她下跪懇求父親。
(文法解析) kneel動詞三態變化為kneel / knelt / knelt。

knob [nɑb] 名 圓形把手

Jeremy turned the knob and opened the door.
▶▶ 傑瑞米轉動把手開門。

UNIT 11　L字頭進階單字　MP3 083

labor [`lebɚ] 名 勞動 動 勞動

名 Labor is a fundamental element of the economy.
　勞動乃經濟的基礎要素。
動 My mother labored in the factory for forty years.
　我媽媽在工廠裡工作了四十年。

laboratory / lab [`læbrəˌtorɪ] / [læb] 名 實驗室

Charles works at a laboratory doing tests.
▶▶ 查爾斯在一間實驗室裡工作，負責測試。

lag [læg] 名 延遲 動 延緩；掉隊

名 There was a long lag between the mailing and delivery of my letter.
我的信晚了很久才送到。

動 Elderly people and children always lag behind when we go for a walk.
我們出門散步時，年紀大的人和孩子們總是落在後頭。

landmark [`lænd,mɑrk] 名 陸標；地標

The tallest building in the city is a landmark.
▶▶ 那棟最高的建築在這座城市裡是地標。

landscape [`lænd,skep] 名 風景

The landscape around the lake is very beautiful.
▶▶ 這個湖面的景色真的很美。

largely [`lɑrdʒlɪ] 副 大部分地

The island is populated largely by sheep.
▶▶ 這個島嶼的主要生物是綿羊。

launch [lɔntʃ] 名 開始 動 發射

名 At the launch of the rocket, everyone clapped.
火箭一發射，大夥便開始拍手喝采。

動 They have launched a man-made satellite successfully.
他們成功地發射了一顆人造衛星。

lawful [`lɔfəl] 形 合法的

You have to distinguish lawful behavior and unlawful actions.
▶▶ 你必須要能分辨合法和不合法的行為。

lean [lin] 動 傾斜

Frank stood leaning against the sofa.
▶▶ 弗蘭克斜靠著沙發站著。
文法解析 lean 動詞三態變化為 lean / leant / leant。

learned [`lɜnɪd] 形 學術性的；博學的

He is a learned person. He knows everything I do not understand.
▶▶ 他是個博學的人。他知道所有我不知道的事物。

1 Level 基礎單字
2 Level 必備單字
3 Level 中級單字
4 Level 進階單字
5 Level 高手單字
6 Level 滿級單字

lecture [`lɛktʃ»] 名演講 動對…演講

名 Nearly one hundred students crowded into the hall for the professor's lecture.
將近一百名學生擠進講堂聽教授的演講。

動 The newly appointed president lectured for 20 minutes.
新任主席發表了二十分鐘的演講。

lecturer [`lɛktʃərə] 名演講者；（大學中的）講師

We call him professor though his title is actually a lecturer.
>> 儘管他的頭銜其實是講師，但我們都稱呼他教授。

legend [`lɛdʒənd] 名傳奇

The character is the hero of an old legend.
>> 這個角色是一個古老傳說中的英雄。

leisurely [`liʒəlɪ] 形悠閒的 副悠閒地

形 Kant had a leisurely walk after lunch.
午飯後康德悠閒地散步。

副 He works leisurely.
他從容不迫地工作著。

lengthen [`lɛŋθən] 動加長

You have to lengthen the belt. It's not long enough.
>> 你必須加長這條帶子，它不夠長。

liar [`laɪ»] 名說謊者

Luther is considered a liar.
>> 路德被認為是個說謊者。

librarian [laɪ`brɛrɪən] 名圖書館員

The librarian is busy dealing with the lending and returning of books.
>> 圖書館員忙於處理圖書借還事宜。

license [`laɪsɳs] 名執照 動許可

名 Take your driver license with you when you drive.
當你開車時，隨身攜帶駕照。

動 Jenny is licensed to be a pharmacist.
珍妮通過藥師檢定。

lifeguard [`laɪf͵gɑrd] 名 救生員

The lifeguard saved the little child from drowning.
▶▶ 救生員救起差點淹死的小孩。

limitation [͵lɪmə`teʃən] 名 限制

With all its advantages, a computer is by no means without its limitations.
▶▶ 儘管電腦有許多優點，但絕非沒有侷限。

linen [`lɪnɪn] 名 亞麻製品

This linen cleans well.
▶▶ 這亞麻布已經洗過。

lipstick [`lɪpstɪk] 名 口紅；唇膏

I gave her some lipstick as a birthday present.
▶▶ 我送她一條唇膏作為生日禮物。

liquor [`lɪkɚ] 名 烈酒

She drinks wine and beer, but no hard liquor.
▶▶ 她喝葡萄酒和啤酒，但不沾烈酒。

literary [`lɪtə͵rɛrɪ] 形 文學的

Fiona loves literary magazines.
▶▶ 費歐娜熱愛文學雜誌。

literature [`lɪtərətʃɚ] 名 文學

The foreign language department focuses on British and American literature.
▶▶ 外國語文學系著重在英美文學。

loan [lon] 名 借貸 動 借；貸 關 mortgage 抵押

名 Roy came to see me with a request for a loan.
羅伊來找我借錢。
動 Mr. Dorian loaned his collection of pictures to the public gallery.
多里安先生把他收藏的畫借給了公共美術館。

lobster [`lɑbstɚ] 名 龍蝦

Lobster is a popular dish in wedding banquets.
▶▶ 龍蝦是婚宴中很受歡迎的一道菜。

1 Level 基礎單字
2 Level 必備單字
3 Level 中級單字
4 Level 進階單字
5 Level 高手單字
6 Level 滿級單字

logic [`lɑdʒɪk] 名 邏輯

I cannot understand Renata's logic.
▶▶ 我無法理解蕾娜塔的邏輯。

logical [`lɑdʒɪkḷ] 形 邏輯上的

It is not logical to accuse someone without any evidence.
▶▶ 毫無證據地指控他人是不合邏輯的。

loosen [`lusṇ] 動 放鬆

Loosen his coat right now. He's out of breath.
▶▶ 立刻鬆開他的外衣，他快喘不過氣了。

lousy [`laʊzɪ] 形 糟糕的；差勁的

Scott has a lousy attitude towards work because he's so lazy.
▶▶ 由於懶惰，斯考特的工作態度很糟糕。

loyal [`lɔɪəl] 形 忠實的

She has always remained loyal to her political principles.
▶▶ 她總是信守自己的政治原則。

loyalty [`lɔɪəltɪ] 名 忠誠

The employees' loyalty to the boss is obvious.
▶▶ 員工們對老闆的忠誠顯而易見。

luxurious [lʌg`ʒʊrɪəs] 形 奢侈的

The lady appeared with a luxurious fur coat.
▶▶ 那位夫人穿著豪華的毛皮外套出現了。

luxury [`lʌkʃərɪ] 名 奢侈品

Ben spent most of his salary on luxuries.
▶▶ 班將大部分的薪水花在奢侈品之上。

 **M 字頭進階單字**

MP3 084

machinery [mə`ʃinərɪ] 名 機械；體系

There is no machinery for resolving disputes.
▶▶ 根本沒有解決紛爭的機制。

magnetic [mæg`nɛtɪk] 形 磁性的 關 magnet 磁鐵

Magnetic stones are rare nowadays.
▶▶ 磁石現在已經很稀少了。

magnificent [mæg`nɪfəsṇt] 形 壯觀的；華麗的

The magnificent landscape took my breath away.
▶▶ 這壯麗的景色使我嘆為觀止。

makeup [`mek͵ʌp] 名 化妝

It takes her 10 minutes to put on makeup.
▶▶ 化妝花了她十分鐘的時間。

(焦點句型) put on makeup 化妝

manual [`mænjʊəl] 名 手冊 形 手工的

名 The manual contains detailed instructions.
　　這本手冊有詳細的指南。
形 Trevor has done manual work for most of his life.
　　崔佛花費大半人生製作手工藝品。

manufacture [͵mænjə`fæktʃɚ] 名 製造業 動 大量製造

名 The bikes were manufactured in Taiwan.
　　這些自行車是台灣製造的。
動 Most electronic devices of this kind, which are manufactured for such
　　purposes, are tightly packed.
　　大多數這種用途的電子設備都被包裝得很扎實。

manufacturer [͵mænjə`fæktʃərɚ] 名 製造者

Our company is the prime manufacturer of makeup in Taiwan.
▶▶ 我們公司是台灣主要的化妝品製造商。

marathon [`mærəθɑn] 名 馬拉松

A contestant fainted during the marathon.
▶▶ 一名選手在馬拉松賽跑的過程昏倒了。

margin [`mɑrdʒɪn] 名 邊緣

He won by a narrow margin.
▶▶ 他以些微的差距獲勝。

Level 1 基礎單字
Level 2 必備單字
Level 3 中級單字
Level 4 進階單字
Level 5 高手單字
Level 6 滿級單字

maturity [mə`tjʊrətɪ] 名成熟

He has maturity beyond his years.
▶▶ 他過於老成。

maximum [`mæksəməm] 名最大量 形最大的

名 The maximum capacity of this tank is 100 liters.
這個水槽的容量上限是一百公升。
形 We will endeavor to reach the maximum output.
我們應該努力達到最高產量。

measurable [`mɛʒərəbḷ] 形可測量的；可預估的

The loss of our company is measurable.
▶▶ 我們公司的損失是可預見的。

measure [`mɛʒɚ] 名度量單位；尺寸

What is the measure of the box's length?
▶▶ 這個箱子的長度單位是什麼？

mechanic [mə`kænɪk] 名機械工

My father is a mechanic in the plant.
▶▶ 我爸爸是這間工廠的機械工人。

mechanical [mə`kænɪkḷ] 形機械的

The mechanical problems must be solved immediately.
▶▶ 這些機械問題必須立即解決。

memorable [`mɛmərəbḷ] 形值得紀念的

She is an earnest and memorable teacher.
▶▶ 她是個認真且令人難忘的老師。

memorial [mə`morɪəl] 名紀念品；紀念碑 形紀念的

名 The historic event was engraved on the memorial.
這件史上著名的事件刻寫在紀念碑上。
形 There will be a war memorial event next week.
下週會有戰爭紀念活動。

memorize [`mɛmə,raɪz] 動記憶 關 memory 記憶；回憶

Did you memorize your lines for the play?
▶▶ 你記住你在劇中的台詞了嗎？

mercy [`mɝsɪ] 名 慈悲

I was appreciative of her mercy.
▶▶ 我很感激她的慈悲。

mere [mɪr] 形 僅僅的

All he did was offer a mere apology.
▶▶ 他做的只不過是道歉。

merit [`mɛrɪt] 名 價值

You can be more confident if you discover your merits.
▶▶ 如果你發現自己的價值，就會變得更有自信。

messenger [`mɛsn̩dʒɚ] 名 使者；信差

He sent the order by messenger.
▶▶ 他透過郵遞員發出訂單。

messy [`mɛsɪ] 名 髒亂的

The one who made it messy has to clean it up.
▶▶ 誰把它弄亂，就要負責清理。

microscope [`maɪkrə͵skop] 名 顯微鏡

The germs became visible to us through the microscope.
▶▶ 我們能用顯微鏡來看到細菌。

mild [maɪld] 形 溫和的

He has too mild a nature to get angry, even if he has good cause.
▶▶ 他的性情太溫和了，即使有充分的理由，他也不會動怒。

mill [mɪl] 名 磨坊 動 研磨

名 The farmer took his corn to the mill.
　　農夫把他的玉米拿到磨坊去。
動 He milled the grain into flour.
　　他把穀物磨成麵粉。

millionaire [͵mɪljən`ɛr] 名 百萬富翁

He became a millionaire overnight.
▶▶ 他一夕之間成了百萬富翁。

1 Level 基礎單字
2 Level 必備單字
3 Level 中級單字
4 Level 進階單字
5 Level 高手單字
6 Level 滿級單字

miner [`maɪnɚ] 名礦工

His father worked as a miner for low pay.
▶▶ 他爸爸是個低薪礦工。

mineral [`mɪnərəl] 形礦物的

Mineral water is sold in bottles here.
▶▶ 礦泉水在此以瓶裝出售。

minimum [`mɪnəməm] 名最小量 形最小的

名 The minimum of his allowance is one hundred dollars.
他的零用錢最少也有一百元。
形 They argued that the minimum wage should be raised.
他們爭論最低工資應該要提高。

minister [`mɪnɪstɚ] 名部長

The new prime minister is generally acknowledged as a great statesman.
▶▶ 新首相是一位公認的有遠見的政治家。

ministry [`mɪnɪstrɪ] 名部長；部

He was appointed to the Ministry of Finance.
▶▶ 他被指派到財政部。

mischief [`mɪstʃɪf] 名胡鬧；危害

The children are always getting into mischief.
▶▶ 這些孩子老是惡作劇。

miserable [`mɪzərəbl̩] 形不幸的

I shed tears after hearing about her miserable experiences.
▶▶ 聽了她厄運的遭遇後我開始垂淚。

misfortune [mɪs`fɔrtʃən] 名不幸

Fortune knocks once, but misfortune has much more patience.
▶▶ 好運只會敲一次門，而災難卻有更多的耐心。

mislead [mɪs`lid] 動誤導

William misled me with his words.
▶▶ 威廉說的話誤導我。

misunderstand [ˌmɪsʌndə`stænd] 動 誤解

You misunderstood my meaning. Let me explain it, OK?
▶▶ 你誤解我的意思了，讓我解釋好嗎？

moderate [`madərɪt] 形 適度的；溫和的

The increase in tax was moderate.
▶▶ 稅收成長適中。

modest [`madɪst] 形 謙虛的

In contrast to John, Mary is much more modest.
▶▶ 和約翰相比，瑪莉謙虛多了。

modesty [`madɪstɪ] 名 謙虛；有禮

He accepted the award with characteristic modesty.
▶▶ 他以他一貫的謙遜態度接受了獎勵。

monitor [`manətə] 名 監視器 動 監視

名 The thief's face was recorded by the monitor.
小偷的臉部被監視器錄下來了。
動 Each student's progress is closely monitored.
每一位同學的學習情況都受到密切的關注。

monument [`manjəmənt] 名 紀念碑

The inscription on the monument is hardly visible.
▶▶ 紀念碑上的銘文幾乎看不見了。

moreover [mor`ovə] 副 並且；此外

These officials were riddled with corruption. Moreover, they abused their power to oppress people.
▶▶ 這些官員貪污腐敗。而且，他們還濫用權力欺壓人民。

motivate [`motə,vet] 動 刺激；激發

His encouragement motivated me to work harder.
▶▶ 他的鼓勵激勵了我，讓我工作得更努力。

motivation [ˌmotə`veʃən] 名 動機

I wonder what his motivation to commit the crime was.
▶▶ 我想知道他的犯罪動機。

mountainous [`maʊntənəs] 形多山的 關 mountain 山

Taiwan is a mountainous country.
▶▶ 台灣是個多山的國家。

muddy [`mʌdɪ] 形泥濘的 關 mud 土

When it rains, the ground becomes very muddy.
▶▶ 下雨時，地面變得很泥濘。

mule [mjul] 名騾

Mules come from male donkeys and female horses.
▶▶ 騾子是公驢和母馬的後代。

multiple [`mʌltəpl̩] 形複數的；多數的 關 multiply 乘以

Three drivers died in a multiple pile-up on the freeway.
▶▶ 三名駕駛因高速公路上的連環相撞而死亡。

murderer [`mɝdərɚ] 名兇手 關 murder 謀殺

I will find the murderer by all means.
▶▶ 不管用任何手段，我一定會找到兇手。

murmur [`mɝmɚ] 名低語 動細語；抱怨

名 Mandy gave a murmur of complaints.
曼蒂小聲地抱怨。
動 She murmured as if she was unsatisfied.
她似乎不滿地低語著。

mutual [`mjutʃʊəl] 形相互的

Mutual understanding is very important to friendship.
▶▶ 相互了解對友誼相當重要。

mysterious [mɪs`tɪrɪəs] 形神祕的

I'm eager for an adventure in the mysterious forest.
▶▶ 我渴望到那座神祕叢林裡探險。

namely [`nemlɪ] 副即；就是

The railroad connects two cities, namely, New York and Chicago.
▶▶ 這鐵路連接兩個城市，即紐約和芝加哥。

nationality [ˌnæʃən`ælətɪ] 名國籍；國民 關 national 國家的

The nationality of the largest minority group in that country is still at issue.
▶▶ 國籍問題在那個國家第一大的少數民族身上仍有爭論。

needy [`nidɪ] 形貧窮的；貧困的

They contributed a large amount of money to help the needy.
▶▶ 他們捐了一筆鉅款幫助窮人。

neglect [nɪg`lɛkt] 名不注意；不顧 動忽視

The garden was in a state of total neglect.
▶▶ 那花園完全無人管理。

negotiate [nɪ`goʃɪˌet] 名商議；談判 關 negotiation 協商

The government will not negotiate with terrorists.
▶▶ 政府不會和恐怖分子談判。

nevertheless [ˌnɛvəðə`lɛs] 連儘管如此；然而

She went abroad last week. Nevertheless, we keep in contact with each other.
▶▶ 她上禮拜出國了。儘管如此，我們仍然保持聯絡。

nightmare [`naɪtmɛr] 名惡夢

Vicky woke up in a cold sweat because of a nightmare.
▶▶ 薇琪因做惡夢而全身冷汗地醒來。

noble [`nobḷ] 形高貴的 名貴族

形 He died for a noble cause.
　　他為了高尚的理由而犧牲。
名 The nobles were rich and powerful and had a big influence over everyone.
　　貴族有錢又有權力，對眾人有著強大的影響力。

Level 1 基礎單字
Level 2 必備單字
Level 3 中級單字
Level 4 進階單字
Level 5 高手單字
Level 6 滿級單字

nonsense [`nɑnsɛns] 名 廢話；無意義的話

It's nonsense to say they don't care.
▶▶ 說他們不在意那是瞎扯。

nowadays [`naʊə,dez] 副 當今；現在

Nowadays, we can talk to our friends anytime because of cell phones.
▶▶ 現在因為有手機，我們可以在任何時候和朋友說話。

nuclear [`njuklɪə] 形 核子的

They decided to establish a nuclear power plant.
▶▶ 他們決定修建一座核電廠。

numerous [`njumərəs] 形 為數眾多的

The company was surrounded by numerous angry customers.
▶▶ 這間公司被眾多憤怒的消費者包圍。

nursery [`nɜsərɪ] 名 托兒所

Some couples send their children to nurseries since both of them have jobs.
▶▶ 有些夫妻把小孩送到托兒所，因為兩人都有工作。

UNIT 14 O字頭進階單字

MP3 086

obedience [ə`bidjəns] 名 服從；遵從 同 compliance

Obedience is very important in an army.
▶▶ 服從命令在軍隊中是很重要的。

obedient [ə`bidjənt] 形 服從的

The boy is too obedient to reject any unreasonable demands.
▶▶ 這個小男孩太過順從，無法拒絕任何不合理的要求。

objection [əb`dʒɛkʃən] 名 反對

Despite his objection, she decided to go out.
▶▶ 儘管他反對，她還是決定出門。

objective [əb`dʒɛktɪv] 形 實體的；客觀的 名 目標

形 We should be more objective about it.
我們應該更客觀地看待此事。

名 My objective is to win the prize.
我的目標是贏得獎項。

observation [ˌɑbzɚˋveʃən] 名 觀察

Observations were made of the children at the beginning and at the end of pre-school and first grade.
▶▶ 這個觀察是針對學齡前兒童，以及小學一年級開始與結束時的孩子所做的。

obstacle [ˋɑbstəkḷ] 名 障礙物；妨礙

The obstacles did not prevent her from reaching her goal.
▶▶ 這些障礙並沒有妨礙她達到目標。

obtain [əbˋten] 動 獲得

He failed to obtain a scholarship.
▶▶ 他沒有獲得獎學金。

occasional [əˋkeʒənḷ] 形 偶爾的；應景的

She likes an occasional glass of wine.
▶▶ 她喜歡偶爾喝杯酒。

occupation [ˌɑkjəˋpeʃən] 名 職業

Alex changed occupations and became a public servant.
▶▶ 艾力克斯換了工作並成為一名公務員。

occupy [ˋɑkjəˌpaɪ] 動 佔有；花費

Accompanying his girlfriend occupied most of his time.
▶▶ 陪女朋友佔據他大多數的時間。

offend [əˋfɛnd] 動 冒犯

The boy's rude words offended his mother.
▶▶ 男孩粗魯的言語冒犯了他母親。

offense [əˋfɛns] 名 冒犯

I apologize if there was any offense.
▶▶ 如有冒犯的話我道歉。

offensive [əˋfɛnsɪv] 形 令人不快的

You will find it difficult to explain away your use of such offensive language.
▶▶ 你使用這樣無禮的語言是很難說得過去的。

opera [`ɑpərə] 名 歌劇

The musical "The Lion King" was very popular. Do you think it would make a good opera?

▶▶ 獅子王這部音樂劇以前很受歡迎。你覺得它會是部好歌劇嗎？

oppose [ə`poz] 動 反對 關 opposition 相反

Why do you always oppose my proposals?

▶▶ 為什麼你總是反對我的提議？

option [`ɑpʃən] 名 選擇

Some people are afraid of flying, which limits their options when traveling.

▶▶ 有些人很害怕坐飛機，這也就限制了他們旅行的選擇。

orbit [`ɔrbɪt] 名 軌道 動 繞軌道運行

名 He is interested in studying planetary orbits.
他對於研究行星軌道很感興趣。

動 The spacecraft orbited Mars three times.
太空船在火星外繞行了三圈。

orchestra [`ɔrkɪstrə] 名 樂隊；樂團

He took part in the school orchestra last week.

▶▶ 他上星期加入學校樂隊。

orphan [`ɔrfən] 名 孤兒 動 使…成為孤兒

名 They adopted the poor orphan.
他們領養了那個可憐的孤兒。

動 She became homeless after she was orphaned.
她成為孤兒之後變得無家可歸。

otherwise [`ʌðɚ.waɪz] 副 否則；要不然

Accept your mother's advice. Otherwise, you will regret it.

▶▶ 接受你母親的建議，不然你會後悔。

outcome [`aʊtkʌm] 名 結果；成果

The outcome of the meeting was that the budget was reduced.

▶▶ 會議的結果是要減少預算。

outstanding [aʊt`stændɪŋ] 形 傑出的

An outstanding person bears more burdens.
▶▶ 能者多勞。

oval [`ovl̩] 名 橢圓形 形 橢圓形的

名 He drew an oval on the map to represent our position.
他在地圖上畫了一個橢圓形，表示我們的位置。
形 Comets move around the sun like planets, but in a long, oval pattern.
彗星像行星一樣圍繞太陽運轉，但其軌道是長長的橢圓形。

overcoat [`ovɚ,kot] 名 大衣

Put on an overcoat or you'll catch a cold.
▶▶ 穿上大衣以免著涼。

overcome [,ovɚ`kʌm] 動 擊敗；克服

They had overcome one tough problem after another before the design was finalized.
▶▶ 在設計完成之前，他們克服一個又一個難題。

overlook [,ovɚ`luk] 動 俯瞰；忽略

My apartment overlooked the city on the tenth floor.
▶▶ 我的公寓在十樓俯瞰這個城市。

overnight [,ovɚ`naɪt] 形 徹夜的 副 整夜地 關 revelry 狂歡

形 The overnight revelry exhausted everyone.
徹夜狂歡累癱了所有人。
副 He was sleepless overnight.
他徹夜難眠。

overthrow [,ovɚ`θro] 動 推翻；瓦解

The rebels tried to overthrow the government.
▶▶ 叛亂者企圖推翻政府。
文法解析 overthrow 動詞三態變化為 overthrow / overthrew / overthrown。

oxygen [`ɑksɪdʒən] 名 氧

Without oxygen, humans could not survive.
▶▶ 沒有氧氣，人類就無法存活。

Level 1 基礎單字
Level 2 必備單字
Level 3 中級單字
Level 4 進階單字
Level 5 高手單字
Level 6 滿級單字

P 字頭進階單字

MP3 087

pace [pes] 名 一步；步調 動 踱步

名 They set off at a brisk pace.
他們邁著輕快的步伐出發。

動 He paced back and forth in anxiety.
他來回焦急地踱步。

panel [`pænḷ] 名 方格；平板

The walls of the dining room featured oak panels.
▶▶ 餐廳牆壁的特點是由橡木板製成。

parachute [`pærə͵ʃut] 名 降落傘 動 空投

名 The airman boldly jumped from the airplane with his parachute.
那名空軍士兵帶著降落傘勇敢地跳下飛機。

動 They parachuted the aid to the victims.
他們空投救援物資給災民。

paragraph [`pærə͵græf] 名 段落

The third paragraph of this essay can be omitted. It's unnecessary.
▶▶ 這篇文章的第三段可以省略，它太多餘了。

partial [`pɑrʃəl] 形 部分的

The partial success should be attributed to my brother.
▶▶ 部分的功勞應該歸於我哥哥。

participation [pɑrtɪsə`peʃən] 名 參加

I'd like to be excused from further participation in this project; it takes up too much of my time.
▶▶ 我請求退出這項計畫，它佔用了我太多時間。

partnership [`pɑrtnəʃɪp] 名 合夥

We are building a constructive partnership.
▶▶ 我們正在建立一種積極的夥伴關係。

passive [`pæsɪv] 形 被動的

You cannot be so passive in looking for a job.
▶▶ 你找工作不能如此被動。

pasta [`pɑstə] 名義大利麵

We ate pasta for dinner at the restaurant.
▶▶ 我們晚餐在餐廳吃義大利麵。

paw [pɔ] 名爪子 動用爪子抓

名 The dog caught the duck in its paws.
狗用爪子抓住了鴨子。
動 The cat pawed the mouse it had caught.
貓用爪子撥弄抓到的老鼠。

peculiar [pɪ`kjuljɚ] 形奇怪的；古怪的

The fish has a peculiar taste. You really think it is all right?
▶▶ 這魚有股怪味，你真的認為牠能吃嗎？

peep [pip] 動窺視

The man peeped at her through the window.
▶▶ 那個男人從窗戶偷窺她。
(焦點句型) peep at sb./sth. 偷看…

peer [pɪr] 名同輩 動凝視

名 Peer pressure can have a powerful influence on people.
同儕壓力對個人的影響很大。
動 Mother peered at me but said nothing.
媽媽凝視著我，什麼也不說。

penalty [`pɛnl̩tɪ] 名懲罰

You'd better obey the law, or you'll be hit with a penalty.
▶▶ 你最好守法，否則你將遭受處罰。

percent [pɚ`sɛnt] 名百分比

Eighty percent of the students passed the exam.
▶▶ 百分之八十的學生通過了考試。

percentage [pɚ`sɛntɪdʒ] 名百分率

The percentage of the population in Croatia that is Serbian amounts to five percent.
▶▶ 塞爾維亞人佔克羅埃西亞總人口數的百分之五。

Level 1 基礎單字
Level 2 必備單字
Level 3 中級單字
Level 4 進階單字
Level 5 高手單字
Level 6 滿級單字

perfection [pɚˋfɛkʃən] 名完美

The fish was cooked to perfection.
▶▶ 這魚烹煮得恰到好處。

perfume [ˋpɚfjum] / [pɚˋfjum] 名香水

The perfume was made in France.
▶▶ 這種香水在法國製造。

permanent [ˋpɝmənənt] 形永久的

Although he is dead, his spirit is permanent.
▶▶ 雖然他死了，但他的精神永存。

persuasion [pɚˋsweʒən] 名說服

Defeated by Lisa's powers of persuasion, I accepted.
▶▶ 麗莎的勸說很有力，我完全接受了。

persuasive [pɚˋswesɪv] 形有說服力的

The reasons she proposed were persuasive, so I was convinced.
▶▶ 她提出的理由都很有說服力，所以我被說服了。

pessimistic [͵pɛsəˋmɪstɪk] 形悲觀的

Wendy is very pessimistic about everything.
▶▶ 溫蒂對任何事都很悲觀。

pest [pɛst] 名害蟲；令人討厭的人

That child is being a real pest.
▶▶ 那個孩子真討厭。

phenomenon [fəˋnɑmə͵nɑn] 名現象 關 phenomena（複數形）

International terrorism is not a recent phenomenon.
▶▶ 國際恐怖主義並不是近年才有的現象。

philosopher [fəˋlɑsəfɚ] 名哲學家

Aristotle was an influential philosopher.
▶▶ 亞里斯多德是個有影響力的哲學家。

philosophical [ˌfɪlə`sɑfɪkl̩] 形 哲學的

He always meditates on philosophical questions.
▶▶ 他經常沉思哲學問題。

philosophy [fə`lɑsəfɪ] 名 哲學

Her philosophy is to take every opportunity that is presented.
▶▶ 她的處世態度是，善用任何眼前的機會。

photography [fə`tɑgrəfɪ] 名 攝影學

The contrast of light and shade is important in photography.
▶▶ 在攝影中，明暗對比是很重要的。

physical [`fɪzɪkl̩] 形 身體的

His physical condition has worsened.
▶▶ 他的身體情況又惡化了。

physician [fɪ`zɪʃən] 名 內科醫師

The physician told me not to stay up too late.
▶▶ 醫師叫我不要熬夜。

physicist [`fɪzɪsɪst] 名 物理學家

The meeting of physicists is held annually.
▶▶ 這個物理學家的聚會一年舉辦一次。

physics [`fɪzɪks] 名 物理學

Mechanics is an essential part of physics.
▶▶ 力學是物理學中的重要部分。

pickle [`pɪkl̩] 名 醃菜 動 醃製

名 They have made pickles since last year.
　　他們從去年起開始製作醃菜。
動 My mother knows how to pickle plums.
　　我媽媽會醃梅子。

pioneer [ˌpaɪə`nɪr] 名 先鋒；開拓者 動 開拓

名 What happened to the pioneer spirit?
　　開拓者的精神到哪兒去了呢？

1 Level 基礎單字

2 Level 必備單字

3 Level 中級單字

4 Level 進階單字

5 Level 高手單字

6 Level 滿級單字

動 They pioneered in e-learning.
他們是數位學習的先鋒。

焦點句型 pioneer in N./Ving 開拓…（領域）；是…（領域）的先驅

plentiful [`plɛntɪfəl] 形 豐富的

Our library has a plentiful amount of books.
▶▶ 我們的圖書館有豐富的藏書。

plot [plɑt] 名 陰謀；情節 動 圖謀 同 intrigue

名 The book is well organized in terms of plot.
這本書的故事布局十分嚴謹。
動 The criminals were plotting to rob the bank.
那些罪犯當時正在謀劃搶劫銀行。

plum [plʌm] 名 李子

A black plum is as sweet as a white one.
▶▶ 烏梅和白梅一樣甘甜。

plumber [`plʌmɚ] 名 水管工人

The plumber is ringing the bell.
▶▶ 水管工人來按電鈴了。

poisonous [`pɔɪzənəs] 形 有毒的

A scorpion has a poisonous sting in its long, jointed tail.
▶▶ 蠍子的長尾巴上長著一個有毒的螫針。

polish [`pɑlɪʃ] 名 磨光 動 擦亮

名 You should give your shoes a polish.
你應該擦擦你的鞋。
動 He polished his leather shoes.
他擦亮他的皮鞋。

焦點句型 give sth. a polish 擦亮…

popularity [ˌpɑpjəˈlærətɪ] 名 流行

The reasons for the music's popularity are its fast tempo and rhythmic beat.
▶▶ 這音樂深受歡迎的原因在於它輕快的節奏與富有韻律感的節拍。

portable [`portəbḷ] 形 可攜帶的

I need a portable computer to work from home.
▶▶ 我需要可攜型電腦才能居家辦公。

portray [por`tre] 動 描繪

Teresa portrayed her experience in Greece as amazing.
▶▶ 泰瑞莎將她在希臘的經歷描繪得驚心動魄。

possess [pə`zɛs] 動 擁有

She possesses a terrible temper, so many people don't want to talk with her.
▶▶ 她脾氣很差，所以很多人都不想跟她講話。

possession [pə`zɛʃən] 名 擁有物

All the things in my room are my possessions.
▶▶ 我房內的所有東西都是我的財產。

postage [`postɪdʒ] 名 郵資

How much was the postage on that letter?
▶▶ 寄那封信要多少錢？

potential [pə`tɛnʃəl] 名 潛力 形 潛在的

名 I think she has the potential to be a good singer.
　　我認為她有成為好歌手的潛力。
形 The company is being actively considered as a potential partner.
　　正在積極考慮將該公司作為潛在的合作夥伴。

precise [prɪ`saɪs] 形 明確的

I should ask my teacher for the precise answer.
▶▶ 我應該向老師問出明確的答案。

predict [prɪ`dɪkt] 動 預測

The police officer predicted that the robber would hide himself in the woods.
▶▶ 警察預測歹徒會藏身於密林之中。

prediction [prɪ`dɪkʃən] 名 預言；預報

I don't believe the prediction of fortune-tellers.
▶▶ 我不相信算命師的預言。

Level 1 基礎單字
Level 2 必備單字
Level 3 中級單字
Level 4 進階單字
Level 5 高手單字
Level 6 滿級單字

pregnancy [`prɛgnənsɪ] 名懷孕

You are advised not to smoke during pregnancy.
▶▶ 懷孕期間你最好不要吸菸。

pregnant [`prɛgnənt] 形懷孕的

Please yield your seat to the pregnant woman.
▶▶ 請讓座給孕婦。

presentation [ˌprɛzn̩`teʃən] 名贈送；呈現

Before the presentation, I felt butterflies in my stomach.
▶▶ 在上台報告之前，我覺得很緊張。

preservation [ˌprɛzɚ`veʃən] 名保存

The preservation efforts have paid off.
▶▶ 保存工作已做得相當成功。

preserve [prɪ`zɝv] 動保存；維護

Environmentalists were able to preserve the rare bears and keep them from extinction.
▶▶ 環保人士能保育這種稀有熊類，讓牠們免於絕種。

prevention [prɪ`vɛnʃən] 名預防

Prevention is better than compensation.
▶▶ 預防勝於彌補。

prime [praɪm] 名初期 形首要的

名 In her prime, she was the best actress of her generation.
　　在早年，她是那一代最棒的女演員。
形 The prime task is to inform our clients.
　　首要工作是通知我們的客戶。

primitive [`prɪmətɪv] 形原始的

Living conditions in the camp were pretty primitive.
▶▶ 營地的生活條件非常簡陋。

priority [praɪ`ɔrətɪ] 名優先權

Complete the tasks by priority.
▶▶ 依優先順序完成這些工作。

privacy [`praɪvəsɪ] 名隱私

I prefer living in my home rather than the dormitory, because I value my privacy.
▶▶ 我喜歡住在家裡而非宿舍，因為我重視隱私。

privilege [`prɪvəlɪdʒ] 名特權 動優待

名 It is not fair that the rich have privileges in the community.
有錢人在社區中享有特權是不公平的。
動 You students are privileged to see the movie.
你們這些學生有幸看到了這部電影。

procedure [prə`sidʒɚ] 名手續、程序 關fire drill 消防演習

Do you know the correct procedures to follow during a fire drill?
▶▶ 你知道消防演習要遵守哪些正確步驟嗎？

proceed [prə`sid] 動進行

He proceeded to repair his motorcycle after answering the phone.
▶▶ 接過電話後他繼續修車。

productive [prə`dʌktɪv] 形生產的；多產的 關produce 生產

Bobby is a productive and efficient worker.
▶▶ 巴比是個多產且高效率的工人。

profession [prə`fɛʃən] 名專業

He entered the legal profession at the age of 26.
▶▶ 他在 26 歲時踏入法律界。

professional [prə`fɛʃənḷ] 名專家 形專業的

名 They hired two professionals as consultants on environmental policies.
他們雇用兩位專家作為環境政策的顧問。
形 Many of the performers were professional and had high standards.
許多表演者都相當專業，水準很高。

profitable [`prafɪtəbḷ] 形有利的 同lucrative

Good looks are more profitable in Hollywood than talent and hard work.
▶▶ 在好萊塢，美貌是一件比資質和努力更有用的東西。

prominent [`pramənənt] 形突出的；著名的；重要的

The prominent runner won the prize.
▶▶ 那名突出的跑者得獎了。

1 Level 基礎單字

2 Level 必備單字

3 Level 中級單字

4 Level 進階單字

5 Level 高手單字

6 Level 滿級單字

promising [`prɑmɪsɪŋ] 形 有可能的；有希望的

My boyfriend said we would have a promising future.
▶▶ 我的男朋友說我們將擁有充滿希望的未來。

promotion [prə`moʃən] 名 增進；促銷；升遷

The promotion of the beverage worked well.
▶▶ 這種飲品的促銷相當成功。

prompt [prɑmpt] 形 及時的 動 提詞；引起

Today, with prompt treatment, many diseases are curable.
▶▶ 如今，若有得到及時的治療，許多疾病都是可醫治的。

pronunciation [prə͵nʌnsɪ`eʃən] 名 發音

He does not qualify as a good teacher of English as his pronunciation is terrible.
▶▶ 他不是一個好的英文老師，因為他的發音糟透了。

proposal [prə`pozl̩] 名 提議

His proposal was ignored by his boss.
▶▶ 他的提議被主管忽略。

prosper [`prɑspɚ] 動 興盛 關 advent 出現；來臨

With the advent of the new chairman, the company began to prosper.
▶▶ 隨著新主席的到來，公司也開始興旺起來了。

prosperity [prɑs`pɛrətɪ] 名 繁盛

Thanks to the popularity of its products, the company enjoys great prosperity.
▶▶ 由於產品甚受歡迎，公司生意昌盛。

prosperous [`prɑspərəs] 形 繁榮的

At no time has the country been more prosperous than at present.
▶▶ 這個國家如今空前繁榮。

protein [`protiɪn] 名 蛋白質

Beans contain rich protein.
▶▶ 豆類含有豐富的蛋白質。

protest [`protɛst ] / [ prə`tɛst] 图抗議 動反對；抗議

图 Most people view protests as disorderly, but they don't try to understand the causes.
大多數人都視抗議為騷亂，卻不試圖理解原因。

動 The group of students protested the university's policies.
一群學生抗議學校政策。

psychological [ˌsaɪkə`lɑdʒɪkl̩] 形心理學的

The old man suffered from a psychological problem.
▶▶ 這位老人苦於心理問題。

psychologist [saɪ`kɑlədʒɪst] 图心理學家

The id, ego, and superego are concepts that the well-known psychologist Sigmund Freud defined.
▶▶ 本我、自我與超我是著名心理學家西格蒙德 · 佛洛伊德定義的概念。

psychology [saɪ`kɑlədʒɪ] 图心理學 關 psychiatry 精神病學

Many senior high school students are interested in psychology.
▶▶ 很多高中生對心理學有興趣。

publication [ˌpʌblɪ`keʃən] 图發表；出版

The newspaper continues to defend its publication of the photographs.
▶▶ 這家報紙繼續為刊登這些照片辯護。

publicity [pʌb`lɪsətɪ] 图宣傳；出風頭

There has been a great deal of publicity surrounding his disappearance.
▶▶ 他的失蹤已有傳媒廣泛報導。

publish [`pʌblɪʃ] 動出版

The book will be published next month.
▶▶ 這本書將於下個月出版。

publisher [`pʌblɪʃə] 图出版者；出版社

I am an editor, not the publisher.
▶▶ 我是編輯，而非出版者。

pursue [pə`su] 動追趕；追求

Three policemen pursued the thief.
▶▶ 三個警察在小偷身後緊追不捨。

1 Level 基礎單字
2 Level 必備單字
3 Level 中級單字
4 Level 進階單字
5 Level 高手單字
6 Level 滿級單字

pursuit [pɚˋsut] 名 追求；追擊

The pursuit of the murderer covered three provinces.

▶▶ 對殺人犯的追捕已跨越了三個省。

Q 字頭進階單字 MP3 088

quarrel [ˋkwɔrəl] 名 爭吵 動 爭吵

名 The harmonious couple hasn't had any quarrels in their five-year marriage.
這對夫妻感情十分和睦，在婚後的五年裡都沒吵過架。

動 They quarreled so loudly that all the roommates were awakened.
他們吵得很大聲，室友全被吵醒了。

quilt [kwɪlt] 名 棉被

He woke to find that his quilt had slipped off the bed.

▶▶ 他醒來後發現棉被從床上滑下來了。

quotation [kwoˋteʃən] 名 引用

This paragraph contains a famous quotation.

▶▶ 這個段落引用了一句名言。

R 字頭進階單字 MP3 089

radar [ˋredɑr] 名 雷達

They located the ship by radar.

▶▶ 他們通過雷達確定了船隻的位置。

rage [redʒ] 名 狂怒 動 暴怒

名 He shouted out of rage.
他狂怒地咆哮。

動 My father raged and threw down the glasses.
爸爸暴怒並摔破玻璃杯。

rainfall [ˋrenˌfɔl] 名 降雨量

The rainfall from the typhoon was record-breaking.

▶▶ 這次颱風的降雨量創新紀錄。

raisin [`rezn̩] 名 葡萄乾

The ingredients for these cookies are raisins, sugar, almonds and flour.
▶▶ 這種餅乾所需的材料有葡萄乾、糖、杏仁和麵粉。

realistic [ˌrɪə`lɪstɪk] 形 現實的

The special effects were quite realistic.
▶▶ 這些特效很真實。

rebel [`rɛbl̩ ] / [ rɪ`bɛl] 名 造反者 動 叛亂；謀反

名 The rebels attacked the presidential palace.
　　造反者攻擊總統府。
動 When the proclamation was announced, they rebelled.
　　當這個公告一發布，他們就造反了。

recall [rɪ`kɔl] 動 回憶起 名 記憶力；收回 關 reminiscent 回憶往事的

動 I can't recall meeting her before.
　　我想不起來以前曾經見過她。
名 I was not informed of the recall of the product.
　　我沒有接到產品收回的通知。
文法解析 recall 後面可接 Ving、名詞與 that 子句，表示「回想起某事」。

reception [rɪ`sɛpʃən] 名 反應；迎接；接收效果

The reception of the movie was poor.
▶▶ 這部電影評價很差。

recipe [`rɛsəpɪ] 名 食譜；祕訣

His plans are a recipe for disaster.
▶▶ 他的計畫是解決這場災難的秘訣。

recognition [ˌrɛkəg`nɪʃən] 名 認知

She strove for recognition as an artist.
▶▶ 她努力以藝術家的身分得到認可。

recovery [rɪ`kʌvərɪ] 名 恢復

The medicine will help you in your recovery.
▶▶ 這些藥對你康復有所幫助。

Level 1 基礎單字
Level 2 必備單字
Level 3 中級單字
Level 4 進階單字
Level 5 高手單字
Level 6 滿級單字

recreation [ˌrɛkrɪˋeʃən] 名娛樂

What type of recreation do you like?
▶▶ 你閒暇時的娛樂是什麼呢？

recycle [rɪˋsaɪkḷ] 動循環利用

We must recycle the cardboard boxes.
▶▶ 我們必須將紙盒子回收。

reduction [rɪˋdʌkʃən] 名減少 關 reduce 減少

The reduction of plastic waste looked promising.
▶▶ 減少塑膠用量看起來有望。

refer [rɪˋfɝ] 動提及

The speaker referred to many famous books in his speech.
▶▶ 那位講者在他的演講裡提及許多有名的書。
(焦點句型) refer to sb./sth. 提及…；談到…

reference [ˋrɛfərəns] 名參考

The answers are for your reference.
▶▶ 這些解答給你參考。

reflect [rɪˋflɛkt] 動反射

The calm lake reflected the trees on the shore.
▶▶ 平靜的湖面倒映出岸邊的樹木。

reflection [rɪˋflɛkʃən] 名反射；反省

After long reflection, I finally admitted it was my fault.
▶▶ 經過長時間的反省，我終於承認這是我的錯。

reform [ˌrɪˋfɔrm] 動改進；改造；使懊悔 名改進

動 People should try to reform criminals rather than punish them.
人們應試圖去改造罪犯，而不是去懲罰他們。
名 The reform of the system made things much easier.
系統的改良讓事情簡單多了。

refugee [ˌrɛfjʊˋdʒi] 名難民

The refugees came to the US because of the war in their country.
▶▶ 這些難民逃至美國，因他們的祖國正在打仗。

refund [`rɪˌfʌnd ] / [ rɪ`fʌnd] 名退款 動償還

名 She demanded a refund on the flawed vase.
她要求對這有瑕疵的花瓶退款。

動 We can't refund the price difference.
我們無法退還差價。

refusal [rɪ`fjuzl̩] 名拒絕

I tried very hard to persuade him to join our group but I met with a flat refusal.
▶▶ 我盡最大努力勸他參加我們團隊，但遭到了斷然拒絕。

regarding [rɪ`gɑrdɪŋ] 介關於

She is totally ignorant regarding the case.
▶▶ 她對這件案子全然不知。

register [`rɛdʒɪstə] 名名單；註冊 動登記；註冊

名 The class register contains the names of all the boys and girls.
班級名冊包括班上所有男孩和女孩的姓名。

動 You'd better register this parcel.
這個包裹你還是掛號郵寄比較好。

registration [ˌrɛdʒɪ`streʃən] 名註冊

The registration process on the website is troublesome.
▶▶ 這個網站的註冊過程很麻煩。

regulate [`rɛgjəˌlet] 動調節；管理

It is strictly regulated that access to confidential documents is denied to all but a few.
▶▶ 除了少數人外，其他人嚴格規定不得接觸機密文件。

regulation [ˌrɛgjə`leʃən] 名調整；法規

Under the new regulations, spending on office equipment will be strictly controlled.
▶▶ 根據新的規定，辦公設備的開支將受到嚴格控制。

rejection [rɪ`dʒɛkʃən] 名廢棄；拒絕 關 reject 拒絕

I was frustrated after continual rejection.
▶▶ 不斷遭到拒絕後，我感到挫敗。

1 Level 基礎單字
2 Level 必備單字
3 Level 中級單字
4 Level 進階單字
5 Level 高手單字
6 Level 滿級單字

relaxation [ˌrilæk`seʃən] 名放鬆

Bowling is his favorite form of relaxation.
▶▶ 他最喜愛的消遣是打保齡球。

relevant [`rɛləvənt] 形相關的

The artist seems displeased because the reporter keeps bringing up questions not relevant to her art.
▶▶ 這名藝術家看起來很不悅，因為記者一直提出和她作品無關的問題。

relieve [rɪ`liv] 動減緩

This lotion relieves itching.
▶▶ 這種乳膏可以止癢。

reluctant [rɪ`lʌktənt] 形勉強的

Danny is reluctant to pay the money.
▶▶ 丹尼不願意付錢。

remark [rɪ`mɑrk] 名注意；評論 動注意；評論

名 He needled her with his sarcastic remarks.
他用諷刺的評論刺激她。
動 They will resent an outsider remarking on their private matters.
一個局外人對他們的私事說三道四會令他們反感。

remarkable [rɪ`mɑrkəbl̩] 形值得注意的；卓越的

Katherine is the most remarkable student in the class.
▶▶ 凱瑟琳是這個班級最優秀的學生。

remedy [`rɛmədɪ] 名補救 動治療；補救

名 The mistake is beyond remedy.
這個錯誤是無法補救的。
動 If Tom made a mistake, he would try to remedy it.
如果湯姆有錯的話，他會去改正的。

renew [rɪ`nju] 動更新；恢復；補充

I renewed my room with brilliant decorations.
▶▶ 我用鮮豔的擺設讓房間煥然一新。

repetition [ˌrɛpə`tɪʃən] 名 重複

We do not want to see a repetition of last year's tragic events.
▶▶ 我們不想看到去年的悲劇重演。

representation [ˌrɛprɪzɛn`teʃən] 名 代表；表示；表現

The snake swallowing its tail is a representation of infinity.
▶▶ 銜尾蛇象徵著無限。

reputation [ˌrɛpjə`teʃən] 名 名譽；聲望

He has a reputation for generosity.
▶▶ 他以慷慨大方聞名。

rescue [`rɛskju] 名 搭救 動 援救

名 The rescue was forced to halt because of heavy rain.
因為大雨，搜救行動被迫中斷。
動 The firemen rescued the dog.
消防隊員救出小狗。

research [`rɪsɝtʃ] 名 研究；調查

Her research is breaking new ground in biochemistry.
▶▶ 她的研究正在開闢生物化學的新領域。

researcher [`rɪsɝtʃɚ] 名 調查員

Privately funded researchers will respond positively to the appeal.
▶▶ 私人資助的研究人員將積極響應呼籲。

resemble [rɪ`zɛmb]] 動 類似

The baby resembles his father.
▶▶ 寶寶長得像爸爸。

reservation [ˌrɛzɚ`veʃən] 名 保留；預訂

I made a reservation at the hotel.
▶▶ 我在這間飯店有訂房。

resign [rɪ`zaɪn] 動 辭職

She resigned due to sexual harassment.
▶▶ 她因性騷擾而離職。

Level 1 基礎單字
Level 2 必備單字
Level 3 中級單字
Level 4 進階單字
Level 5 高手單字
Level 6 滿級單字

resignation [ˌrɛzɪɡˋneʃən] 名 辭職；讓位

We find no one suitable for the position after Lily's resignation.
▶▶ 莉莉離職後，我們找不到該職位適合的人選。

resistance [rɪˋzɪstəns] 名 抵抗 同 defiance

Tiredness lowers your resistance to illness.
▶▶ 疲勞會降低你的抵抗力。

resolution [ˌrɛzəˋluʃən] 名 果斷；決心

His resolution never sways.
▶▶ 他的決心從不動搖。

resolve [rɪˋzɑlv] 名 決心 動 解決；分解

名 Her resolve to quit smoking is firm.
她戒菸的決心很堅定。
動 The math problem was finally resolved.
這個數學題終於解開了。

respectable [rɪˋspɛktəb!] 形 可尊敬的

Mr. Chen is a respectable scholar.
▶▶ 陳先生是個值得尊敬的學者。

respectful [rɪˋspɛktfəl] 形 有禮的 關 respect 尊敬

The onlookers stood at a respectful distance.
▶▶ 旁觀者們都站在遠處，敬而遠之。

restore [rɪˋstor] 動 恢復 同 rehabilitate

The monument was restored again and again.
▶▶ 這座紀念碑不斷在修復。

restriction [rɪˋstrɪkʃən] 名 限制 關 restrict 限制 同 constraint

The revised program would carry fewer restrictions on spending.
▶▶ 修改後的方案將減少對支出的限制。

retain [rɪˋten] 動 保持

He forgets what he did yesterday, but he still retains clear memories of decades ago.
▶▶ 他會忘記昨天做了什麼，卻不會忘記幾十年前的回憶。

retire [rɪ`taɪr] 動退休；隱退 關 retirement 退休

My grandfather retired at the age of sixty-five.
▶▶ 我的祖父在六十五歲時退休。

retreat [rɪ`trit] 名撤退 動撤退 關 retreatment 再處理

名 In case of a shortage, retreat is inevitable.
若遭遇物資短缺的情形，撤退將無可避免。
動 She watched him retreat out of the door.
她看著他退出門外。

reunion [ri`junjən] 名重聚；團圓

We had a warm reunion on Moon Festival.
▶▶ 我們在中秋節溫馨團圓。

revenge [rɪ`vɛndʒ] 名復仇；報復

I must take revenge on him for the deceitfulness.
▶▶ 我一定會報復他的詐騙。
(焦點句型) take revenge on sb. 報復某人

revise [rɪ`vaɪz] 動修正；校訂

The manuscripts have been revised three times.
▶▶ 這些手稿已經修改過三次了。

revision [rɪ`vɪʒən] 名修訂

He made some minor revisions to the report before printing it out.
▶▶ 在將報告列印出來之前，他作了一些小小的修改。

revolution [ˌrɛvə`luʃən] 名革命；改革

Revolutions often don't succeed, at least at first.
▶▶ 革命通常不會成功，至少在一開始是這樣。

revolutionary [ˌrɛvə`luʃənˌɛrɪ] 形革命的

The revolutionary invention is history-making.
▶▶ 這個革命性的發明具有劃時代的意義。

reward [rɪ`wɔrd] 名報酬；獎勵 動酬賞

名 The rewards of the contest attracted many people.
這個競賽的獎勵吸引了許多人。

Level 1 基礎單字
Level 2 必備單字
Level 3 中級單字
Level 4 進階單字
Level 5 高手單字
Level 6 滿級單字

（動）Mom rewarded me for my honesty.
媽媽因我的誠實而犒賞我。

rhyme [raɪm] 名 韻；韻腳 動 押韻

（名）Rhymes are easier to memorize.
押韻的詞比較好記。

（動）"Take" rhymes with "make".
「take」和「make」押韻。

rhythm [`rɪðəm] 名 節奏；韻律

The rhythm of the dance music is fast.
▶▶ 舞曲的節奏很快。

riddle [`rɪdḷ] 名 謎語

Lantern riddles are particular in our culture.
▶▶ 燈謎是我們的特有文化。

robber [`rɑbə] 名 強盜

The robber broke into his house and stole a lot of money.
▶▶ 強盜闖進他的家裡，並偷了許多錢。

romance [`romæns] 名 戀情；戀愛關係；愛情故事 關 romantic 浪漫的

The romances are unrealistic to me.
▶▶ 愛情故事對我來說不切實際。

route [rut] 名 路線

The route of the parade goes through the downtown area.
▶▶ 遊行隊伍的路線經過市中心。

ruin [`ruɪn] 名 破壞 動 毀滅

（名）The ruin of the environment may bring about terrible results.
環境破壞會造成可怕的影響。

（動）That one mistake ruined his chances of getting the job.
就那一個錯誤，斷送了他得到那份工作的機會。

rural [`rʊrəl] 形 農村的

I enjoyed the rural life for its intimacy with nature.
▶▶ 因為能與大自然親近，我很喜歡農村生活。

rusty [`rʌstɪ] 形生鏽的；生疏的

The wheels are rusty.
▶▶ 輪子生鏽了。

sacrifice [`sækrə,faɪs] 名獻祭 動供奉；犧牲

名 Pigs were common sacrifices.
　　豬是常見的牲禮。
動 Don't you know what your parents have sacrificed for you?
　　你不知道你父母為你犧牲了些什麼嗎？
(焦點句型) saceifice sth. for sb./sth. 為了…犧牲…

satellite [`sætḷ,aɪt] 名衛星

The broadcast came from America via satellite.
▶▶ 廣播節目從美國通過人造衛星轉播過來。

satisfaction [,sætɪs`fækʃən] 名滿足

The girl accepted the gift and smiled in satisfaction.
▶▶ 女孩接受了禮物，滿足地微笑。

scarcely [`skɛrslɪ] 副勉強地；幾乎不

Christine and her sister scarcely do any housework.
▶▶ 克麗絲汀和她姐姐幾乎不做家事。

scenery [`sinərɪ] 名風景；景色

The scenery on the beach was very impressive.
▶▶ 海灘風光令人印象深刻。

scold [skold] 動責罵

The boss scolded him in everybody's presence.
▶▶ 老闆當著大家的面責罵他。

scoop [skup] 名勺子 動鏟；舀取

名 She refilled the soup bowl using a scoop.
　　她用勺子再舀一碗湯。

Level 1 基礎單字
Level 2 必備單字
Level 3 中級單字
Level 4 進階單字
Level 5 高手單字
Level 6 滿級單字

（動）He quickly scooped the money up from the desk.
他把桌上的錢一把抓起來。

scratch [skrætʃ]（動）抓

That cat will scratch you with its claws.
▶▶ 那貓會用爪子抓你的。

sculpture [`skʌlptʃɚ]（名）雕刻；雕塑（動）雕刻

（名）I went to the gallery to see the sculpture exhibition.
我去美術館看雕塑展。
（動）She sculptured the artwork.
她雕刻出那件藝術品。

secure [sə`kjʊr]（動）保護（形）安全的

（動）The guard secured the building by locking it.
警衛替大樓上鎖，以確保安全性。
（形）I feel secure in your company.
有你的陪伴，讓我感到安全。

seize [siz]（動）抓住

Seize the days when you are alive.
▶▶ 把握活著的每一天。

settler [`sɛtlɚ]（名）殖民者；居留者

The first settlers in the Bohemian region were Czech nationals.
▶▶ 波西米亞地區的第一批居留者為捷克民族。

severe [sə`vɪr]（形）嚴厲的

My uncle is severe with my cousin but gentle with me.
▶▶ 叔叔對表哥嚴厲，但對我很溫柔。

sew [so]（動）縫；縫上

My mother sewed my ragged shirts.
▶▶ 媽媽替我縫補破襯衫。

shade [ʃed]（名）陰涼處；陰影（動）遮住；使陰暗

（名）She took a rest in the shade.
她在樹蔭下休息。

(動) Anthony shaded me with the umbrella.
安東尼用陽傘替我遮蔭。

shady [`ʃedɪ] (形) 陰涼的；陰暗的

This shady place is suitable for playing.
▶▶ 這塊陰涼之地很適合玩耍。

shameful [`ʃemfəl] (形) 恥辱的

I will never forget the shameful experience.
▶▶ 我永遠不會忘記這可恥的經驗。

shave [ʃev] (動) 刮鬍子；剃

He shaved his beard and looked much better.
▶▶ 他剃了鬍子之後看起來好多了。

shelter [`ʃɛltɚ] (名) 避難所；庇護所 (動) 保護；掩護

(名) We all dashed for shelter when it started to rain.
開始下雨時，我們全都衝向躲雨的地方。
(動) The hen sheltered her chicks with its wings.
母雞用翅膀保護小雞。

shift [ʃɪft] (名) 變換 (動) 變換

(名) She made a shift in her hairstyle.
她改變髮型。
(動) The candidate was constantly shifting his position on the issues.
這位候選人在那些爭議問題上不斷改變立場。

sightseeing [`saɪt,siɪŋ] (名) 觀光；遊覽

Our family went sightseeing on Yang-Ming Mountain.
▶▶ 我們全家到陽明山觀光。

signature [`sɪgnətʃɚ] (名) 簽名

They forged their manager's signature on the check.
▶▶ 他們在支票上偽造了經理的簽名。

significance [sɪg`nɪfəkəns] (名) 重要性

You have to let him know the significance of the case.
▶▶ 你必須讓他知道這個案子的重要性。

Level 1 基礎單字
Level 2 必備單字
Level 3 中級單字
Level 4 進階單字
Level 5 高手單字
Level 6 滿級單字

sincerity [sɪn`sɛrətɪ] 名誠懇；真摯

What I said was out of sincerity.
▶▶ 我所言句句出自肺腑。

singular [`sɪŋgjələ] 形單一的；個別的 名單數

形 A singular sock is of no use.
只有一隻襪子沒有用。
名 Bacterium is the singular of bacteria.
bacterium 是 bacteria 的單數形。

site [saɪt] 名地點；位置 動設置

名 Samuel is looking for a site to take a rest.
塞繆爾在找地方休息一下。
動 The building was sited in a good location.
這棟建築位在一個好地點。

sketch [skɛtʃ] 名素描；草圖 動描述；素描

名 The sketch needs some revision.
這草圖尚須修改。
動 It's his task to sketch out proposals for a new road.
他的任務是簡要地敘述一下開闢新路的建議。

skyscraper [`skaɪ‚skrepə] 名摩天大樓

There are many skyscrapers in Singapore nowadays.
▶▶ 現今在新加坡有許多棟摩天大樓。

slight [slaɪt] 形輕微的 動輕視 副 slightly 稍微地

形 They paid slight attention to it.
他們對此事僅略有關注。
動 He was criticized for slighting the masses as ignorant.
他因認為群眾無知而受到批評。

slogan [`slogən] 名標語；口號

The slogan of the parade is "No discrimination".
▶▶ 這場遊行的口號是「反歧視」。

socket [`sɑkɪt] 名凹處；插座

His eyes bulged in their sockets.
▶▶ 他的兩眼從眼窩裡鼓出來。

software [`sɔft,wɛr] 名軟體

You have to pay for copyrighted software.
▶▶ 你必須付費使用版權軟體。

solar [`solɚ] 形太陽的

This car is fueled by solar batteries.
▶▶ 這部車以太陽能電池為能源。

spade [sped] 名鏟子

The children took their buckets and spades to the beach.
▶▶ 孩子們帶上桶子和鏟子到海灘去了。

spare [spɛr] 形剩餘的 動饒恕；騰出

形 I must make the best use of my spare time.
我必須將剩餘時間做最好的利用。
動 Would you please spare some of your time?
可不可以請你撥出一些時間？

spark [spɑrk] 名火花 動冒火花

名 The spark from the wire scared all of us.
電線上的火花把我們都嚇到了。
動 The lighter does not spark.
這支打火機點不起來（不會冒火花）。

spear [spɪr] 名矛；魚叉 動用矛刺

名 Spears were necessary for ancient hunters.
在古代，矛對獵人而言是不可或缺的。
動 The fishermen speared the fish in the sea.
漁夫用矛刺海裡的魚。

species [`spiʃiz] 名物種

There are various species of butterflies in Taiwan.
▶▶ 台灣有很多品種的蝴蝶。

spiritual [`spɪrɪtʃuəl] 形精神的；崇高的 同 psychic

The sermon was full of spiritual inspiration.
▶▶ 那場佈道充滿了精神鼓舞。

Level 1 基礎單字
Level 2 必備單字
Level 3 中級單字
Level 4 進階單字
Level 5 高手單字
Level 6 滿級單字

splendid [`splɛndɪd] 形 極好的；華麗的；壯麗的

He earned a splendid victory.
▶▶ 他獲得了輝煌的勝利。

split [splɪt] 名 裂口 動 劈開

名 The split in the pocket allowed my keys to drop.
口袋裡的裂縫讓我的鑰匙掉出來。
動 We split the wood into long thin pieces.
我們把木頭劈成長長的薄片。
文法解析 split 動詞三態同形，皆為 split。

sprinkle [`sprɪŋkḷ] 動 灑；噴淋

She sprinkled sugar on the cake.
▶▶ 她把糖撒在蛋糕上。

stab [stæb] 動 刺；戳 名 刺傷；刺痛

動 He was stabbed to death in a racist attack.
他遭到種族主義者刺死。
名 Jill felt a sudden stab of pain in the chest.
吉兒的胸部突然感到一陣刺痛。

statistics [stə`tɪstɪks] 名 統計；統計資料；統計學

The statistics show that it was a hollow warning.
▶▶ 統計資料表明此項警告不合常理。
文法解析 表示「統計數據；統計資料」時，恆為複數形；表示「統計學」時，則為不可數名詞

status [`stetəs] 名 地位；身分；狀況

Could you tell me the status of the project?
▶▶ 你可以告訴我這項計畫的狀況嗎？

stem [stɛm] 名 莖幹 動 阻止；堵住

名 The stems of the flowers were bent by the wind.
花莖被風吹彎。
動 The present strike stems from discontent among the low-paid workers.
當前的罷工浪潮起因於低薪工人的不滿情緒。
焦點句型 stem from sth. 源於…

stereo [`stɛrɪo] 名立體音響

This program is being broadcast in stereo.
▶▶ 這個節目用立體音響播放。

stingy [`stɪndʒɪ] 形吝嗇的；有刺的

Don't be so stingy with the cream!
▶▶ 別那麼捨不得放奶油！

stocking [`stɑkɪŋ] 名長襪

Mary's going to buy a new pair of stockings.
▶▶ 瑪莉要買一雙新的長襪子。

strengthen [`strɛŋθən] 動加強；增強

She learned Spanish to strengthen her chances of getting a good job.
▶▶ 她學習西班牙文來增強得到好工作的機會。

stripe [straɪp] 名條紋

The stripes on the shirt are vivid.
▶▶ 這件襯衫上的條紋很鮮豔。

strive [straɪv] 動苦幹；努力

He strove to overcome his speech defect.
▶▶ 他努力克服演講上的缺陷。
文法解析 strive 動詞三態變化為 strive / strove / striven。

stroke [strok] 名打擊；一撞 動撫摸

名 Flunking the course felt like a stroke from a club to him.
　　對他來說，不及格就像被棍子打了一下。
動 I stroked the violin gently.
　　我輕輕地撫摸著小提琴。

submarine [`sʌbmə͵rin] 名潛水艇 形海底的；水下的

Submarines can submerge very quickly.
▶▶ 潛水艇的下潛速度非常快。

sue [su] 動控告

The thief made a promise by paying her USD 2,000, so she intended not to sue him.
▶▶ 小偷答應付她兩千美元，所以她決定不告他了。

基礎單字 Level 1
必備單字 Level 2
中級單字 Level 3
進階單字 Level 4
高手單字 Level 5
滿級單字 Level 6

suggestion [sə`dʒɛstʃən] 名 建議 關 suggest 建議

Thanks for your suggestion, it will improve my English ability.
▶▶ 謝謝你的建議，這會使我的英文有所進步。

summarize [`sʌmə,raɪz] 動 總結；概述

It is time to summarize the points.
▶▶ 現在是總結論點的時候了。

surgeon [`sɜdʒən] 名 外科醫生

The surgeon probed for the bullet in the man's back.
▶▶ 外科醫生探查這人背上的子彈。

surgery [`sɜdʒərɪ] 名 外科手術

Cancer usually requires surgery.
▶▶ 癌症通常需要外科手術。

surrender [sə`rɛndə] 名 投降 動 投降

名 Surrender is the last choice for us.
　　我們絕不投降。
動 No matter how you threaten us, we will never surrender.
　　不管你怎麼威脅，我們都不會屈服。

surroundings [sə`raʊndɪŋs] 名 環境；周圍

The house is located in beautiful surroundings.
▶▶ 這座房屋四周的環境優美。

suspicious [sə`spɪʃəs] 形 可疑的

I am always suspicious of anyone who wants to sell me something at cheap prices.
▶▶ 我總是懷疑那些向我推銷廉價商品或服務的人。
(焦點句型) be suspicious of sb./sth. 懷疑…

sway [swe] 名 搖擺；支配 動 搖擺；支配

名 The sway of the glass made some of the milk spill out.
　　搖晃使杯中的牛奶濺了一些出來。
動 My determination never sways.
　　我的決心從未動搖。

syllable [`sɪləbl] 名音節

"Hat" has only one syllable.
▶▶「hat」只有一個音節。

sympathetic [ˌsɪmpə`θɛtɪk] 形同情的

When I told her why I was worried, she was very sympathetic.
▶▶ 我告訴她我擔心的原因時，她很同情我。

sympathy [`sɪmpəθɪ] 名同情

She has no sympathy for drug addicts.
▶▶ 她不同情有毒癮的人。
焦點句型 have sympathy for sb. 同情…

systematic [ˌsɪstə`mætɪk] 形有系統的；有組織的

He's very systematic in all he does.
▶▶ 他做一切事情都很有條理。

UNIT 19 T 字頭進階單字

MP3 091

technician [tɛk`nɪʃən] 名技師；技術員

As a pianist, she's a brilliant technician, but she lacks passion.
▶▶ 以鋼琴家來說，她技藝熟練，但缺乏熱情。

technological [ˌtɛknə`lɑdʒɪkəl] 形工業技術的

The leakage of technological secrets is reaching alarming proportions.
▶▶ 技術秘密的洩露已達到驚人的程度。

telegraph [`tɛləˌgræf] 名電報機 動打電報

名 The telegraph was an important invention in the 19th century.
電報機是十九世紀的重要發明。
動 The intelligence agent telegraphed the information to the friendly country.
情報人員向友邦打電報。

telescope [`tɛləˌskop] 名望遠鏡

Astronomers observe the planets with telescopes.
▶▶ 天文學家用望遠鏡觀察行星。

Level 1 基礎單字
Level 2 必備單字
Level 3 中級單字
Level 4 進階單字
Level 5 高手單字
Level 6 滿級單字

tendency [`tɛndənsɪ] 名傾向；趨向

She has the tendency to accept his proposal.
▶▶ 她有可能會接受他的求婚。

tense [tɛns] 動繃緊肌肉；僵直 形緊張的

動 Zoe tensed when the audience focused on her.
觀眾目光集中在佐伊身上時，她渾身肌肉都有些緊繃了。
形 She sounded tense and angry.
她的聲音聽起來又氣又急。

tension [`tɛnʃən] 名緊張

There is often tension between the aims of the company and the wishes of the employees.
▶▶ 公司的目標和雇員的願望之間經常存在衝突。

terror [`tɛrɚ] 名駭懼；恐怖

Her eyes were filled with terror.
▶▶ 她的眼睛裡充滿了恐懼。

theme [θim] 名主題；題目

The theme of the speech is time management.
▶▶ 這場演講的主題是時間管理。

thorough [`θɝo] 形徹底的；仔細的

The police carried out a thorough investigation.
▶▶ 警方展開了全面的調查。

thoughtful [`θɔtfəl] 形深思的；考慮周到的；體貼的

He was thoughtful regarding the difficulty he faced.
▶▶ 面對眼前的這個難題，他陷入了深思。

tickle [`tɪkḷ] 動搔癢 名搔癢

動 The bigger girls used to chase me and tickle me.
那個大一點的女孩以前總是追趕著要搔我癢。
名 The tickle made the baby laugh.
搔癢逗得小寶寶笑了。

timid [`tɪmɪd] 形 羞怯的

Cindy is too timid to talk to strangers.
▶▶ 辛蒂太羞怯，不敢和陌生人說話。

tolerable [`tɑlərəbḷ] 形 可容忍的

The heat was tolerable at night but suffocating during the day.
▶▶ 這種炎熱的天氣在夜晚尚能忍受，但白天就太過悶熱。

tolerance [`tɑlərəns] 名 容忍；忍耐力

Her tolerance is amazing! She wears only a light jacket in the winter.
▶▶ 她的忍耐力真是驚人！她在冬天只穿一件薄夾克。

tolerant [`tɑlərənt] 形 忍耐的

As time goes by, more and more people hold a tolerant attitude towards homosexuality.
▶▶ 隨著時間演進，越來越多人對同性戀持寬容的態度。

tolerate [`tɑlə,ret] 動 忍受

I can't tolerate your bad manners any longer.
▶▶ 我再也不能容忍你無禮的行為。

tomb [tum] 名 墳墓

The Tomb Sweeping Festival is on April 5.
▶▶ 清明節是四月五日。

tortoise [`tɔrtəs] 名 烏龜 關 hare 野兔

"The Tortoise and the Hare" is a well-known fable.
▶▶ 龜兔賽跑是個知名寓言故事。

torture [`tɔrtʃɚ] 名 折磨；拷打 動 使…受折磨；拷打

名 Henry suffered torture from his headaches.
　亨利忍受著頭痛的折磨。
動 The cruel father tortured the child to tell the truth.
　那個殘忍的父親拷打孩子，逼他說實話。

tragedy [`trædʒədɪ] 名 悲劇

"Romeo and Juliet" is a tragedy written by Shakespeare.
▶▶ 《羅密歐和茱麗葉》是莎士比亞所寫的著名悲劇。

Level 1 基礎單字
Level 2 必備單字
Level 3 中級單字
Level 4 進階單字
Level 5 高手單字
Level 6 滿級單字

tragic [`trædʒɪk] 形 悲劇的

The tragic outcome was predictable.
▶▶ 這個悲劇性的結果是意料之中的。

transfer [træns`fɝ ] / [ `trænsfɝ] 動 轉移 名 遷移；調職

動 He has transferred from the army to the navy.
他從陸軍調到海軍。
名 In the past, Manchester United reached an agreement with Real Madrid over the transfer of Beckham.
過去，曼聯與皇家馬德里就貝克漢的調動達成了協定。

transform [træns`fɔrm] 動 改變

Jessica transformed the living room into a garage.
▶▶ 潔西卡把客廳改成車庫。

translate [træns`let] 動 翻譯

Please help me translate Korean into Chinese.
▶▶ 請幫我把韓文翻成中文。

translation [træns`leʃən] 名 翻譯；譯文

The translation is unreadable.
▶▶ 這篇譯文很難讀懂。

translator [træns`letɚ] 名 譯者

Pan became a translator after graduating from the Department of Foreign Languages.
▶▶ 潘從外國語文學系畢業後就成了譯者。

transportation [ˌtrænspɚ`teʃən] 名 輸送；運輸工具 關 transport 運輸

The city is providing free transportation to the stadium from downtown.
▶▶ 這城市現在提供從市中心到體育場的免費交通服務。

tremble [`trɛmbl̩] 名 顫抖 動 顫抖

名 I can see the tremble in your hands; what's wrong?
我看到你的雙手在顫抖，怎麼了嗎？
動 She trembles whenever she thinks of him.
她每回想起他都會發抖。

Level 1 基礎單字
Level 2 必備單字
Level 3 中級單字
Level 4 進階單字
Level 5 高手單字
Level 6 滿級單字

tremendous [trɪˋmɛndəs] 形非常的；巨大的

The destruction was caused by a tremendous typhoon.
▶▶ 這些損害是一場強烈颱風造成的。

tribal [ˋtraɪbəl] 形宗族的；部落的

The renowned eight-voice singing is the tribal culture of the Bunun Tribe.
▶▶ 知名的八部合音是布農族的部落文化。

triumph [ˋtraɪəmf] 名勝利 動獲得勝利

名 Don't be proud of triumph; don't be frustrated by failure.
　 勝不驕，敗不餒。
動 Justice will triumph in the end.
　 正義終將獲勝。

troublesome [ˋtrʌbḷsəm] 形麻煩的；困難的

A troublesome situation has developed.
▶▶ 這個麻煩的局勢已變本加厲。

tumble [ˋtʌmbḷ] 名摔跤 動跌倒

His tumble on the stage embarrassed him all day.
▶▶ 在舞台上摔倒讓他羞愧一整天。

twig [twɪg] 名小枝；嫩枝

The twigs were quickly consumed by the flames.
▶▶ 樹枝很快就被火焰吞噬殆盡。

typewriter [ˋtaɪpˏraɪtɚ] 名打字機

A typewriter is out of date. Now we use computers instead.
▶▶ 打字機過時了，現在我們都改用電腦。

 UNIT 20 U字頭進階單字 MP3 092

universal [ˏjunəˋvɝsḷ] 形普遍的；世界性的

Smiling is a universal language.
▶▶ 微笑是世界共通的語言。

urge [ɝdʒ] 動 驅策；勸告 名 衝動；慾望

My mother urged me to register immediately.

▶▶ 媽媽催我立刻去註冊。

urgent [`ɝdʒənt] 形 緊急的

Hurry up! It is an urgent situation.

▶▶ 快點！這是緊急情況。

usage [`jusɪdʒ] 名 習慣；使用

The usage of the phrase was confusing to Marvin.

▶▶ 這個片語的用法讓馬維感到疑惑。

V 字頭進階單字　　MP3 093

vacancy [`vekənsɪ] 名 空缺；空白

I'm sorry that we have no vacancies.

▶▶ 對不起，我們這裡客滿。

vain [ven] 形 徒然的

They made vain efforts to rescue the cat.

▶▶ 他們想救貓咪卻徒勞無功。

vast [væst] 形 巨大的；廣大的

There are vast fields of sugarcane in Queensland, Australia.

▶▶ 在澳大利亞昆士蘭州有大片甘蔗田。

vegetarian [ˌvɛdʒəˋtɛrɪən] 名 素食主義者

My father is a vegetarian. He avoids meat.

▶▶ 我爸爸是素食主義者，他不吃肉。

vessel [`vɛsḷ] 名 容器；碗

The vessels were made of porcelain.

▶▶ 這些容器是瓷製品。

violate [`vaɪəˌlet] 動 妨害；違反

He paid a fine for violating the traffic rules.

▶▶ 他因違反交通規則被處以罰金。

violation [ˌvaɪə`leʃən] 名 違反；侵害

The number of traffic violations has increased.
▶▶ 違反交通規則的案例有所增加。

virtue [`vɜtʃu] 名 美德

They say that patience is a virtue.
▶▶ 他們說忍耐是種美德。

virus [`vaɪrəs] 名 病毒

Viruses cannot live for long periods outside bodies.
▶▶ 病毒在人體外無法存活太久。

visual [`vɪʒuəl] 形 視覺的 關 vision 視力；視覺

I have a very good visual memory.
▶▶ 我有很好的視覺記憶能力。

vital [`vaɪtḷ] 形 極其重要的

It is vital to plan before a trip.
▶▶ 旅行前做好規劃很重要。

voluntary [`vɑlənˌtɛrɪ] 形 自願的

Participation in the military is voluntary in Canada.
▶▶ 加拿大採用的是志願役的兵役制度。

volunteer [ˌvɑlən`tɪr] 名 義工 動 自願做…

名 Volunteers provide service for no pay.
義工無償提供服務。
動 He volunteered to drive me home.
他自願送我回家。

voyage [`vɔɪɪdʒ] 名 旅行；航海 動 航行

名 Bon voyage!
一路順風！
動 They voyaged to Penghu and had a good time.
他們航行到澎湖，玩得很開心。

Level 1 基礎單字
Level 2 必備單字
Level 3 中級單字
Level 4 進階單字
Level 5 高手單字
Level 6 滿級單字

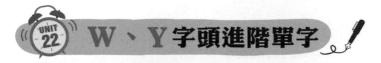

MEMORIZE 7000 VOCABULARIES ONCE AND FOR ALL !

waken [`wekn̩] 動 喚醒

She is wakened at six o'clock every morning.
▶▶ 她每天早上六點都被叫醒。

website [`wɛb,saɪt] 名 網站

Type the keywords into the search engine, and you can find the websites you want.
▶▶ 在搜尋引擎輸入關鍵字，你就可以得到你所需的網站了。

welfare [`wɛl,fɛr] 名 健康；幸福；福利

We're concerned about your spiritual welfare.
▶▶ 我們擔心你精神上的健康。

wink [wɪŋk] 動 眨眼 名 眨眼

動 He winked at me as a sign.
他向我眨眼示意。
名 You stand here as a lookout. If anyone approaches, give me a wink.
你站在這裡把風。如果有人靠近，就跟我眨眼睛。

wit [wɪt] 名 機智；幽默風趣 關 witty 機智的

Ken is a man of intelligence and wit.
▶▶ 肯頭腦聰明，說話又幽默風趣。

witch / wizard [wɪtʃ] / [`wɪzəd] 名 女巫；巫師

Burning witches in Europe was a cruel tradition.
▶▶ 歐洲曾有焚燒女巫的殘酷傳統。

withdraw [wɪð`drɔ] 動 收回；撤出

The general refused to withdraw his troops.
▶▶ 那個將軍拒絕撤回部隊。
文法解析 withdraw 動詞三態變化為 withdraw / withdrew / withdrawn。

witness [`wɪtnɪs] 名 目擊者 動 目擊 關 defendant 被告人 / testify 作證

名 The witness refused to testify for the defendant.
目擊者拒絕為被告作證。

（動）I witnessed the car crash.
我目擊車禍。

wreck [rɛk]（名）沉船；殘骸（動）摧毀（同）debris

（名）The man tried to save the crew from the wreck.
這個人試圖拯救遭遇船難的船員。
（動）The storm wrecked the ship.
風暴摧毀了那艘船。

yawn [jɔn]（動）打呵欠（名）打呵欠

（動）Laura didn't sleep well last night, so she yawned frequently in the office this morning.
蘿拉昨晚沒睡好，所以今早在辦公室呵欠連連。
（名）He stretched himself with a yawn.
他伸了伸懶腰，打了個呵欠。

youthful [`juθful]（形）年輕的

Exercise will keep you youthful.
▶▶ 運動會使你保持青春活力。

Level 1 基礎單字
Level 2 必備單字
Level 3 中級單字
Level 4 進階單字
Level 5 高手單字
Level 6 滿級單字

7000 Essential
Vocabulary for
High School Students

LEVEL
5
高手單字

Veteran Vocabulary

單字難易度 ★★★☆☆
文法難易度 ★★☆☆☆
生活出現頻率 ★★★★☆
考題出題頻率 ★★★★☆

名 名詞　動 動詞　形 形容詞　副 副詞　介 介係詞　連 連接詞
關 相關單字 / 片語　同 同義詞　反 反義詞

abnormal [æb`nɔrml̩] 形反常的 反 normal

We don't think such an abnormal phenomenon will last a long time.
▶▶ 我們不認為這樣反常的現象會持續很久。

abolish [ə`bɑlɪʃ] 動廢止；革除 關 abolishment 廢除

The unreasonable law was abolished.
▶▶ 那條不合理的法律遭到廢止。

abortion [ə`bɔrʃən] 名墮胎

The issue whether women have abortion rights is still controversial.
▶▶ 婦女是否擁有墮胎權的議題仍然有爭議。

abrupt [ə`brʌpt] 形突然的

His abrupt appearance surprised me.
▶▶ 他的突然現身使我驚訝。

absurd [əb`sɜd] 形荒謬的；不合理的

I oppose such an absurd regulation.
▶▶ 我反對這種荒謬的規定。

abundant [ə`bʌndənt] 形豐富的；充足的 同 lavish

She has abundant time to prepare for the oral exam.
▶▶ 她有充裕的時間準備口試。

abuse [ə`bjuz] 名濫用；虐待 動濫用；虐待 關 cocaine 古柯鹼

名 Alcohol abuse does harm to health.
酗酒有害健康。
動 The father who abused his daughter was arrested.
虐待女兒的父親被逮捕了。

accelerate [æk`sɛlə,ret] 動促進；加速

He accelerated the car to get to the airport on time for her flight.
▶▶ 他加速行駛汽車，以準時抵達機場，趕上她的航班。

MEMORIZE 7000 VOCABULARIES ONCE AND FOR ALL！

accessible [æk`sɛsəbl̩] 形 可取得的

The resources in the library are accessible to every student.
▶▶ 每個學生都可以使用圖書館的資源。

accommodation [ə,kɑmə`deʃən] 名 適應；和解 關 accommodate 能容納

They reached an accommodation in the end.
▶▶ 他們最後和解收場。

accord [ə`kɔrd] 動 一致；和諧；和⋯一致

Your account of the incident accords with mine.
▶▶ 你對這個事件的描述與我的描述一致。
(焦點句型) accord with sth. 和⋯一致

accounting [ə`kauntɪŋ] 名 會計學 關 account 帳目；帳戶

Camilla majors in accounting.
▶▶ 卡蜜拉主修會計。

acknowledge [ək`nɑlɪdʒ] 動 承認；供認 關 acknowledgement 承認；坦白

She acknowledged that she had made a mistake.
▶▶ 她承認自己犯了錯誤。

acquaint [ə`kwent] 動 使熟悉

You have to acquaint yourself with the intense training.
▶▶ 你必須適應高強度的訓練。
(焦點句型) acquaint someone/yourself with sth. 使（某人）熟悉⋯

acquisition [,ækwə`zɪʃən] 名 獲得

This sculpture is the latest acquisition of the museum.
▶▶ 這雕刻是博物館最新收購的。

activist [`æktɪvɪst] 名 行動主義者；激進主義份子

Environmental activists demonstrated in front of the Presidential Palace.
▶▶ 環保人士在總統府前示威。

acute [ə`kjut] 形 敏銳的；劇烈的

The report contains some acute observations on the situation.
▶▶ 報告中有些地方對情況的觀察很敏銳。

Level 1 基礎單字
Level 2 必備單字
Level 3 中級單字
Level 4 進階單字
Level 5 高手單字
Level 6 滿級單字

administration [əd͵mɪnə`streʃən] 名行政；管理

They work in administration, so they have no direct contact with customers.
>> 他們在管理部門工作，所以他們沒有與客戶直接聯絡的方式。

administrative [əd`mɪnə͵stretɪv] 形行政上的；管理上的

Sally applied for an administrative position.
>> 莎莉應徵一個行政工作。

administrator [əd`mɪnə͵stretə] 名管理者

The administrator should take most of the responsibility.
>> 管理人要負最重的責任。

adolescent [͵ædḷ`ɛsṇt] 形青春期的；青少年的

Parents should understand adolescent desires.
>> 父母應該去了解青少年內心渴望的是什麼。

adore [ə`dor] 動崇拜；敬愛

Tom adores his elder sister.
>> 湯姆敬愛他的姐姐。

advocate [`ædvəkət ] / [ `ædvə͵ket] 名提倡者 動提倡

名 Henry is a strong advocate of human rights.
　亨利是個強烈的人權提倡者。
動 Do you advocate the banning of cars in the city center?
　你主張禁止汽車進入市中心嗎？

affection [ə`fɛkʃən] 名情感；情愛

I have a great affection for my family.
>> 我對家人有著深厚的情感。

agenda [ə`dʒɛndə] 名議程；節目單

The first item on the agenda is the president's speech.
>> 第一項議程是總統演講。

aggression [ə`grɛʃən] 名侵略；進攻 關 aggressive 侵略性的

They were afraid that their neighbor's aggression could lead to war.
>> 他們害怕鄰國的侵略行動會引爆戰爭。

agony [`ægənɪ] 名痛苦；折磨

He was in an agony of remorse.
▶▶ 他處於後悔的痛苦之中。

agricultural [ˌægrɪ`kʌltʃərəl] 形農業的

We are proud of our agricultural skills.
▶▶ 我們以我們的農業技術自豪。

aisle [aɪl] 名通道

The aisle is too narrow for people to stand shoulder to shoulder.
▶▶ 這個通道窄得無法讓人並肩而行。

alcoholic [ˌælkə`hɑlɪk] 名酗酒者 形含酒精的

名 James is an alcoholic who can't control his drinking.
詹姆斯是個無法控制飲酒量的酒鬼。
形 He stays away from alcoholic beverages.
他不喝含酒精的飲料。

alien [`elɪən] 形外星的；陌生的；外國的 名外星人

形 Could it be that there are alien cultures on other planets?
有沒有可能在其他星球上有外星人的文明呢？
名 Do you believe the existence of aliens?
你相信外星人的存在嗎？

allergic [ə`lɝdʒɪk] 形過敏的；厭惡的

I am allergic to wool.
▶▶ 我對羊毛過敏。

allergy [`ælədʒɪ] 名過敏；反感

I have allergy to penicillin.
▶▶ 我對青黴素過敏。

alliance [ə`laɪəns] 名聯盟 同 coalition

We endeavor to join the alliance.
▶▶ 我們力圖加入聯盟。

allocate [`ælə͵ket] 動分配 關 allocation 分派

He allocated one-third of his salary to his wife.
▶▶ 他把三分之一的薪水交給他的太太。

Level 1 基礎單字
Level 2 必備單字
Level 3 中級單字
Level 4 進階單字
Level 5 高手單字
Level 6 滿級單字

ally [`ælaɪ] 名 同盟者 動 使結盟

名 Germany and Japan were allies in World War II.
德國和日本在二次世界大戰時是同盟國。
動 The small country allied itself to the stronger one.
這個小國和一個較強的國家結盟。

alongside [ə`lɔŋ͵saɪd] 副 沿著；並排地 介 在…旁邊

副 Two teams of the company worked alongside in this project.
在這個專案裡，公司的兩個團隊攜手合作。
介 Park a vehicle alongside another.
把車停放在另一輛的旁邊。

alter [`ɔltɚ] 動 更改；改變

I should alter some of my principles.
▶▶ 我應該改變我的某些原則。

alternate [`ɔltɚ͵net ] / [ `ɔltɚnət] 動 輪流；交替 形 交替的；間隔的

動 Mary and her sister will alternate in setting the table.
瑪莉和她妹妹輪流擺放餐桌。
形 The magazine is published on alternate weeks.
這份雜誌每隔一個禮拜發行一次。

ample [`æmpl̩] 形 充分的；大量的

I have ample time to get my things ready.
▶▶ 我有充裕的時間準備東西。

analyst [`ænəlɪst] 名 分析者；分析家

The analyst was good at explaining the complicated data.
▶▶ 這位分析家善於解釋複雜的數據。

anonymous [ə`nɑnəməs] 形 匿名的

She received an anonymous love letter.
▶▶ 她收到一封匿名情書。

anticipate [æn`tɪsə͵pet] 動 預期；期待 related anticipation 預期

I anticipate that Roger will come back on Friday.
▶▶ 我預期羅傑會在禮拜五回來。

antique [æn`tik] 名 古董 形 古董的

名 The antique is worth more than one million dollars.
這件古董價值超過一百萬。

形 The antique vase is cracked in some places.
這個古董花瓶某些地方快破了。

applause [ə`plɔz] 名 喝采

Amid warm applause, the honored guests mounted the stage.
▶▶ 在熱烈的掌聲中，貴賓們登上了主席台。

appliance [ə`plaɪəns] 名 器具；家電用品

There were no appliances for they have just moved in.
▶▶ 他們剛搬進來，所以完全沒有任何器具設備。

apt [æpt] 形 貼切的；適當的

It is apt for him to say that.
▶▶ 他那樣說很恰當。

architect [`ɑrkə,tɛkt] 名 建築師

The house was built under the careful supervision of an architect.
▶▶ 這棟房子是在一位建築師的細心監督下建造的。

architecture [`ɑrkə,tɛktʃə] 名 建築物

The architecture in Rome is exotic.
▶▶ 羅馬的建築很有異國風情。

arena [ə`rinə] 名 競技場；競爭場所

A member of Joe's family works in the political arena.
▶▶ 喬的一位親人在政界活動。

arouse [ə`rauz] 動 喚醒 同 evoke

The drama aroused a distant memory from my childhood.
▶▶ 這齣戲喚起了我童年時代的遙遠回憶。

arrogant [`ærəgənt] 形 自大的；傲慢的

He is arrogant because of his wealth.
▶▶ 他因財富而自傲。

1 Level 基礎單字

2 Level 必備單字

3 Level 中級單字

4 Level 進階單字

5 Level 高手單字

6 Level 滿級單字

articulate [ɑrˋtɪkjəlet] / [ˋɑrtɪkjəlɪt] 働清晰地講話 形清晰的

働 The Korean teacher articulated the lesson to the students.
韓文老師向學生闡明了課程內容。

形 Articulate speech is essential for a teacher.
身為老師一定要口齒清晰。

ass [æs] 名驢子；笨蛋

They called him an ass behind his back.
▶ 他們在他背後叫他笨蛋。

assault [əˋsɔlt] 名攻擊 働攻擊

名 We are ready to meet the enemy's assault on our fort.
我們準備反抗敵人對堡壘的攻擊。

働 They planned to assault the enemy at night.
他們計劃對敵人進行夜襲。

assert [əˋsɜt] 働斷言；主張

Some people assert that nothing is impossible.
▶ 有些人斷言沒有什麼事是不可能的。

assess [əˋsɛs] 働評估 關 assessment 評估；估價

It's too early to assess the effects of the price rises.
▶ 現在對物價上漲的影響做評估未免言之過早。

asset [ˋæsɛt] 名財產；資產；人才

She's a great asset to the organization.
▶ 她是組織的寶貴人才。

assumption [əˋsʌmpʃən] 名設想；假定

Her assumption that Christy would ask for leave was proven to be wrong.
▶ 她認為克莉斯提會請假的推測最後證實是錯誤的。

astonish [əˋstɑnɪʃ] 働使吃驚 關 astonishment 吃驚

Her unusual response astonished us.
▶ 她不尋常的反應使我們吃驚。

attendance [əˋtɛndəns] 働出席；參加

Attendance in the program is purely voluntary.
▶ 參加該計畫純屬自願。

attic [ˋætɪk] 名閣樓；頂樓

Alice lives in the attic, and she only goes downstairs for meals.
▶▶ 艾莉絲住在閣樓房間裡，只有吃飯時才會下樓。

auction [ˋɔkʃən] 名拍賣 動拍賣

名 The house was sold at auction.
那棟房子以拍賣方式售出。
動 They auctioned the fruits which were out of season at low prices.
他們把過季的水果以低價售出。

authorize [ˋɔθəˌraɪz] 動授權；全權委託

My boss authorized me to attend the meeting on his behalf.
▶▶ 老闆授權我在會議上代表他。

autonomy [ɔˋtɑnəmɪ] 名自治；自治權

The universities' autonomy is enshrined in their charters.
▶▶ 大學的自治權已寫入其章程中。

awe [ɔ] 名敬畏；驚奇 動使敬畏

名 As a young boy, he was very in awe of his uncle.
小時候，他十分敬畏他的叔叔。
動 I am awed by his solemnity.
他的莊嚴使我敬畏。
(焦點句型) in awe of sb. 敬畏某人

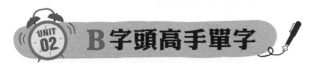

UNIT 02 B 字頭高手單字

MP3 096

backyard [ˋbækjɑrd] 名後院

They will have a barbecue in the backyard tomorrow.
▶▶ 他們明天會在後院烤肉。

ballot [ˋbælət] 名投票；選票 動投票

名 The union will hold a ballot on the new pay offer.
工會將就提出的新工資舉行不記名投票。
動 We balloted for the new chairperson.
我們投票選舉新主席。

Level 1 基礎單字
Level 2 必備單字
Level 3 中級單字
Level 4 進階單字
Level 5 高手單字
Level 6 滿級單字

ban [bæn] 動禁止 名禁令

動 The policemen banned him from passing through.
警察阻止他穿越。

名 The new ban will be enforced soon.
新禁令很快會開始執行。

banner [`bænɚ] 名旗幟；橫幅

The color of the banner is too similar to the background.
▶▶ 橫幅廣告的顏色和背景太相像了。

barren [`bærən] 形荒蕪的；貧瘠的

There are no plants here because of the barren soil.
▶▶ 因為土壤貧瘠，這裡沒有任何植物。

batch [bætʃ] 名一批；一群；一組

A batch of dancers went on the stage to prepare for the show.
▶▶ 一群舞者上台準備表演。

behalf [bɪ`hæf] 名代表

She attended the conference on behalf of her company.
▶▶ 她代表她的公司參加會議。

焦點句型 on behalf of sb. 代表某人

belongings [bə`lɔŋɪŋz] 名所有物；財產

She packed a few belongings in a bag and left on her trip.
▶▶ 她把她的幾件物品裝進提袋裡便踏上旅途了。

beloved [bɪ`lʌvd] 形鍾愛的；心愛的

I hugged my beloved doll in my sleep.
▶▶ 我抱著心愛的娃娃睡覺。

beneficial [,bɛnə`fɪʃəl] 形有益的 關 benefit 利益

A good diet is beneficial to health.
▶▶ 良好的飲食有益健康。

焦點句型 be beneficial to sth. 對…有利

betray [bɪ`tre] 動 背叛；出賣 關 betrayer 背叛者 / betrayal 背叛

He betrayed me for the reward.
▶▶ 他為了賞金而背叛我。

beware [bɪ`wɛr] 動 當心

Beware of the traps on the road.
▶▶ 小心路上的陷阱。

(焦點句型) beware of sb. 小心；注意某人

bias [`baɪəs] 名 偏心；偏見 動 使存偏見

名 Some people have a bias against foreigners.
　　有些人對外國人有偏見。
動 His background biases him against businessmen.
　　他出生的家庭背景使他對商人存有偏見。

文法解析 bias 搭配的介係詞為 against

bid [bɪd] 名 投標價 動 投標

名 The final bid for the oil painting was 500 dollars.
　　這幅油畫的投標價是五百元。
動 A syndicate of local businessmen is bidding for the contract.
　　當地一家企業聯合組織投標手取這份合約。

biological [ˌbaɪə`lɑdʒɪkḷ] 形 生物學的 關 biology 生物學

The school has a large biological laboratory.
▶▶ 這所學校有一個很大的生物學實驗室。

bizarre [bɪ`zɑr] 形 古怪的

She has some bizarre habits, such as singing loudly in class.
▶▶ 她有些古怪的習慣，例如在課堂上大聲唱歌。

blast [blæst] 名 爆炸；強風 動 炸毀；爆破

名 Her hat was blown off by a blast of wind.
　　她的帽子被強風吹走。
動 The typhoon blasted the crops.
　　颱風損害農作物。

blur [blɝ] 名 模糊；朦朧 動 變得模糊

名 Due to the blur of her eyesight, she decided to change glasses.
　　因為視線模糊，她決定換眼鏡。

Level 1 基礎單字
Level 2 必備單字
Level 3 中級單字
Level 4 進階單字
Level 5 高手單字
Level 6 滿級單字

(動) My tears blurred my eyes.
眼淚模糊了我的視線。

blush [blʌʃ] (名)臉紅 (動)臉紅

(名) A blush on his cheek implied his embarrassment.
他臉上的紅暈暗示了他的尷尬。
(動) She blushed at the sight of him.
她一見他就臉紅。

bodyguard [`bɑdɪˌgɑrd] (名)保鏢；護衛隊

The President's bodyguard is armed.
>> 總統的護衛人員攜帶著武器。

bolt [bolt] (名)門閂 (動)奔跑；閂上（門或窗）

(名) The bolt was cut by the burglar.
門閂被盜賊破壞了。
(動) She entered her room and bolted the door.
她進房然後把門閂上。

bonus [`bonəs] (名)分紅；獎金；額外的好處

All our employees receive an annual bonus.
>> 我們全體員工獲得一年一度的分紅。

boom [bum] (名)隆隆聲 (動)發出隆隆聲

(名) After the boom of thunder, it started to rain.
一陣隆隆雷聲過後就開始下雨。
(動) The guns boomed in the distance.
遠處槍聲隆隆作響。

boost [bust] (動)提高；推動

The price of gas boosted two times in a year.
>> 石油的價格一年內漲了兩倍。

booth [buθ] (名)棚子；攤子 (關) brisk 輕快的；生氣勃勃的

The stalls and booths were doing brisk trades.
>> 那些攤販的生意興隆。

boredom [`bor,dəm] 名乏味；無聊 關 bore 使無聊

She found her task an entire boredom.
▶▶ 她覺得她的工作索然無味。

bound [baʊnd] 形肯定的；註定的；受約束的 名跳躍 動跳躍

形 Most teachers are bound to suffer from vocal cord injuries since they often need to speak loudly.
大多數老師由於經常需要大聲說話，因此很容易聲帶受損。
名 The dog jumped over the gate in one bound.
這隻狗一跳就越過了柵門。
動 He bounded up on the bed.
他跳上了床。

boundary [`baʊndərɪ] 名邊界

During war, defending boundaries is of great importance.
▶▶ 戰爭期間，守住邊界相當重要。

boxer [`bɑksɚ] 名拳擊手

He rates as one of the best heavyweight boxers of the past fifty years.
▶▶ 他被列為過去五十年來最優秀的重量級拳擊手之一。

breakthrough [`brek,θru] 名突破

His invention was a breakthrough in physics.
▶▶ 他的發明是物理學界的大突破。

briefcase [`brif,kes] 名公事包

My father goes to work with his briefcase.
▶▶ 爸爸帶著公事包去上班。

bronze [brɑnz] 名青銅 形青銅製的

名 The kettle was made of bronze.
這個茶壺以青銅製成。
形 The bronze jar has bright hues.
這個青銅罐有明亮的色澤。

browse [braʊz] 名瀏覽 動瀏覽；翻閱

名 I had a browse through the exhibited items.
我瀏覽了一下展示的項目。

Level 1 基礎單字
Level 2 必備單字
Level 3 中級單字
Level 4 進階單字
Level 5 高手單字
Level 6 滿級單字

動 The public can browse through the council's homepage for the latest information.
民眾可以瀏覽地方議會的網頁以取得最新的資料。

bruise [bruz] 名瘀傷 動使瘀傷；撞傷

名 The bruise on his knee is obvious.
他膝蓋的瘀傷很明顯。

動 I bruised my arm by hitting it against the wall.
我手臂因撞到牆壁而瘀青了。

bulk [bʌlk] 名巨大的東西；大塊；大量

The cabinet of larger bulk costs more.
▶▶ 容量越大的櫃子越貴。

bully [`bulɪ] 名恃強凌弱者 動脅迫；欺負 關 bullying 霸凌

名 The bullies made the younger boys cry.
那些惡霸把年幼的男孩們弄哭了。

動 Don't try to bully me into making a decision.
不要脅迫我做決定。

bureau [`bjʊro] 名政府機關；事務處

Peter is now working at an information bureau.
▶▶ 彼得在情報局工作。

bureaucracy [bjʊ`rɑkrəsɪ] 名官僚體制；官僚主義 關 bureaucrat 官員

Getting a visa involves going through a lot of unnecessary bureaucracy.
▶▶ 申請簽證要辦理很多不必要的官僚程序。

burial [`bɛrɪəl] 名埋葬；下葬 關 bury 埋

I attended his burial with my sister.
▶▶ 我和姊姊一起參加他的葬禮。

butcher [`bʊtʃɚ] 名屠夫；肉販 動屠殺

名 Sam is a butcher in the market.
山姆是市場裡的肉販。

動 I dare not see the chicken getting butchered.
我不敢看公雞被屠宰的畫面。

calcium [`kælsɪəm] 名鈣

To grow healthy bones and teeth, calcium and magnesium are needed in your food.
▶▶ 為了讓骨頭和牙齒長得健康，你需要攝取鈣與鎂。

canal [kə`næl] 名運河；人工渠道

This canal was built a century ago.
▶▶ 這條運河是一百年前開鑿的。

canvas [`kænvəs] 名帆布

The canvas covering on it was peeled back.
▶▶ 蓋在上面的帆布被揭開了。

capability [ˌkepə`bɪlətɪ] 名能力

Linda has the capability to do simultaneous interpretation.
▶▶ 琳達有同步口譯的能力。

carbon [`kɑrbən] 名碳；碳棒

There is no steel that does not contain carbon.
▶▶ 沒有不含碳的鋼。

carnival [`kɑrnəvl̩] 名嘉年華

Our community organization puts on a carnival every year.
▶▶ 我們這個社區機構每年都會舉行一次狂歡會。

casino [kə`sino] 名賭場

Bingo is his favorite game in a casino.
▶▶ 賓果是他在賭場裡最喜歡的遊戲。

cathedral [kə`θidrəl] 名大教堂 關 cardinal 樞機主教；重要的

Shall we look around the cathedral this afternoon?
▶▶ 我們今天下午參觀大教堂好嗎？

caution [`kɔʃən] 名謹慎 動告誡；使小心

名 Walk along the street with caution.
要小心地沿著那條街走。

Level 1 基礎單字
Level 2 必備單字
Level 3 中級單字
Level 4 進階單字
Level 5 高手單字
Level 6 滿級單字

（動）The guardian cautioned me not to go into the garage alone.
管理員告誡我不要一個人進入車庫。

cautious [`kɔʃəs] （形）小心的

A cautious man always fits his standard of living to his budget.
▶▶ 謹慎的人總是使他的生活水準符合他的收支預算。

celebrity [sə`lɛbrətɪ] （名）名人 （關）celebration 慶祝

The movie star's birthday party was full of celebrities.
▶▶ 這個電影明星的生日派對充滿了名人。

cemetery [`sɛmə͵tɛrɪ] （名）公墓

The children were frightened to walk through the cemetery at night.
▶▶ 孩子們晚上害怕從墓地走過。

ceremony [`sɛrə͵monɪ] （名）典禮

What the old headmaster said at the graduation ceremony still dwells in my mind.
▶▶ 老校長在畢業典禮上講的話一直留在我的腦海裡。

certainty [`sɜtəntɪ] （名）確定；確定的情況

There is no certainty about the conclusion.
▶▶ 尚無明確的結論。

certificate [sə`tɪfəkət ] / [ sə`tɪfəket] （名）證書 （動）發證書

（名）I have not received my certificate yet.
我還沒有領到證書。
（動）The principal certificated the class leader during the ceremony.
在典禮上，校長頒發證書給班長。

chaos [`keɑs] （名）混亂；無序

After the party last night, the living room was in chaos.
▶▶ 昨夜的派對過後，客廳一片混亂。
（焦點句型）in chaos 一片混亂

chapel [`tʃæpḷ] （名）小教堂

Beside the entry to the chapel, you will see the monument.
▶▶ 在小教堂的入口旁邊，你會看到紀念碑。

characterize [`kærəktəˌraɪz] 動 是…的特徵 關 character 特質；角色

The city is characterized by tall modern buildings made of steel and glass.
▶▶ 這座城市的特點是鋼鐵和玻璃建造的高樓大廈林立。

chef [ʃɛf] 名 廚師

I'll return your chicken and ask the chef to prepare a new dish for you.
▶▶ 我會把你點的雞肉餐退回去，並請主廚重新為你煮一份。

choir [`kwaɪr] 名 唱詩班

The teacher selected you and me to be in the choir.
▶▶ 老師把我和你選進唱詩班。

chord [kɔrd] 名 和弦；和音

Wendy's speech struck a chord with the professors.
▶▶ 溫蒂的演講得到了教授們的贊同。

焦點句型 strike a chord (with sb.) 引起…共鳴；得到…贊同

chore [tʃor] 名 家庭雜務

She doesn't like doing chores everyday.
▶▶ 她不喜歡每天處理家務。

chronic [`krɑnɪk] 形 長期的；持續的

The chronic melancholy brought about his suicide.
▶▶ 長期憂鬱導致他的自殺。

chubby [`tʃʌbɪ] 形 圓胖的；豐滿的

He prefers chubby girls to skinny ones.
▶▶ 和骨感女孩相比，他更喜歡豐滿一點的。

chunk [tʃʌnk] 名 厚塊；大部分

I've already written a good chunk of the article.
▶▶ 我已寫出文章的大部分。

circuit [`sɜkɪt] 名 電路；線路；環行

The earth takes a year to make a circuit of the sun.
▶▶ 地球繞太陽運行一周需要一年的時間。

Level 1 基礎單字
Level 2 必備單字
Level 3 中級單字
Level 4 進階單字
Level 5 高手單字
Level 6 滿級單字

cite [saɪt] 動 例證；引用；舉出

They often cited the attractive but false claims to cheat consumers.
▶▶ 他們經常引用誘人但有誤的說法來欺騙顧客。

civic [`sɪvɪk] 形 城市的；公民的

People are more civic-minded than before.
▶▶ 現在的人更加熱心公益。

clarity [`klærətɪ] 名 清楚；透明

Clarity of thinking is of the greatest importance in a debate.
▶▶ 辯論中具有清晰的思維是最重要的。

clause [klɔz] 名 子句

The clause should be set off by a comma.
▶▶ 這個子句應該用逗號隔開。

cling [klɪŋ] 動 抓牢；附著

She clung to the rope with all her strength.
▶▶ 她使盡全力抓住繩子不放。
文法解析 cling 動詞三態變化為 cling / clung / clung。

clinical [`klɪnɪkḷ] 形 門診的；臨床的

Mr. Wang is a clinical psychologist.
▶▶ 王先生是一名臨床心理師。

cluster [`klʌstɚ] 名 簇；串 動 群集；使生長；使成串

名 I bought a cluster of grapes.
　　我買了一串葡萄。
動 The participants clustered in the square.
　　參加者聚集在廣場。

coffin [`kɔfɪn] 名 棺材 關 drape 把（衣物、布料等）蓋在某物上

They draped the flag over the soldier's coffin.
▶▶ 他們把國旗蓋在那個士兵的棺木上。

coherent [ko`hɪrənt] 形 連貫的；有條理的

She gave a coherent and persuasive argument to convince the clients.
▶▶ 她以連貫而有說服力的論點取信於客戶。

coincidence [ko`ɪnsədəns] 名 巧合

What a coincidence it is that we are wearing the same T-shirt!
▶▶ 真巧啊！我們穿同一件 T 恤！

collective [kə`lɛktɪv] 形 共同的；集體的

History is the collective memory of a nation.
▶▶ 歷史是一個民族的集體記憶。

collector [kə`lɛktɚ] 名 收藏家

He obtained the rare book through a collector.
▶▶ 他透過一個收藏家得到了這個珍本。

colonial [kə`lonɪəl] 形 殖民地的 名 殖民地的居民

形 The colonial laws are different from national laws.
　　殖民地法律與本國不同。
名 The colonials suffered from the tyranny of their rulers.
　　殖民地居民受統治者的暴政所苦。

columnist [`kɑləmnɪst] 名 專欄作家

Professor Li is a popular columnist, and people have learned a lot from his articles.
▶▶ 李教授是個受歡迎的專欄作家，他的文章使人們受益良多。

combat [`kɑmbæt] 名 戰鬥 動 戰鬥

名 After the intense combat, the two boxers were exhausted.
　　經歷一場激烈戰鬥，兩名拳擊手都精疲力盡。
動 Hugh has to combat the constant desire to sing.
　　休必須克制住一直想唱歌的慾望。

comedian [kə`midɪən] 名 喜劇演員

She made up her mind to be a comedian.
▶▶ 她立志當一個喜劇演員。

commentator [`kɑmən͵tetɚ] 名 評論家

The paper added a new column for the commentator.
▶▶ 報紙為這名時事評論家開了新專欄。

Level 1 基礎單字
Level 2 必備單字
Level 3 中級單字
Level 4 進階單字
Level 5 高手單字
Level 6 滿級單字

commission [kə`mɪʃən] 名委託；佣金 動委託

名 She gets 10% commission on her sales.
她賣出東西可得百分之十的回扣。

動 I was commissioned to deal with the dispute.
我受託處理紛爭。

commitment [kə`mɪtmənt] 名承諾

He made a commitment that he would pay his debt.
▶▶ 他承諾會還債。

commodity [kə`madətɪ] 名商品；物產

Air conditioners are one of the many commodities imported from Japan.
▶▶ 空調是眾多從日本進口的商品中的一種。

communism [`kamju͵nɪzm̩] 名共產主義

Communism opposes individual possession of wealth.
▶▶ 共產主義反對私有財產。

communist [`kamjunɪst] 名共產主義者

Karl is considered an outstanding communist.
▶▶ 卡爾被認為是優秀的共產主義者。

commute [kə`mjut] 動變換；通勤

She commutes between Taipei and Hsinchu every day.
▶▶ 她每天在台北和新竹之間通勤。

commuter [kə`mjutɚ] 名通勤者

As a commuter, I find traffic jams very annoying.
▶▶ 身為一個通勤族，我認為塞車真的很惱人。

compact [kəm`pækt ] / [ `kampækt] 形密實的；小巧的 名小型汽車

形 The article is compact and carefully constructed.
這篇文章精煉簡潔且結構嚴謹。

名 We rented a compact on our trip to get around.
在旅途中，我們一輛小汽車四處兜風。

comparable [`kampərəbl̩] 形相當的；類似的；可比較的

His poetry is hardly comparable to Shakespeare's.
▶▶ 他的詩很難與莎士比亞的相比。

compassion [kəm`pæʃən] 名同情；憐憫
You should distinguish compassion from love.
>> 你應該要能分辨同情和愛情。

compassionate [kəm`pæʃənət] 形憐憫的
The compassionate judge gave the young offender a light sentence.
>> 慈悲的法官對那個年輕的罪犯從輕量刑。

compatible [kəm`pætəbḷ] 形相容的；協調的
The battery is compatible with the machine.
>> 這種電池和這台機器相容。

compel [kəm`pɛl] 動驅使；迫使
The police compelled the protesters to leave.
>> 警方強制驅離抗議者。

compensate [`kɑmpən,set] 動彌補；補償
I am willing to do everything to compensate you.
>> 我願意做所有事情來補償你。

compensation [,kɑmpən`seʃən] 名賠償；補償 關 layoff 解雇
The workers asked for compensation for the layoff.
>> 工人要求臨時解雇的賠償。

competence [`kɑmpətəns] 名能力；才能
He looked down on her competence.
>> 他看輕她的能力。

competent [`kɑmpətənt] 形能幹的；有能力的
I model myself after my competent colleagues.
>> 我以我能幹的同事為榜樣。

complexity [kəm`plɛksətɪ] 名複雜
The new president has to confront many political problems of great complexity.
>> 新上任的總統必須面臨許多複雜的政治問題。

Level 1 基礎單字
Level 2 必備單字
Level 3 中級單字
Level 4 進階單字
Level 5 高手單字
Level 6 滿級單字

complication [ˌkɑmpləˈkeʃən] 名混亂;複雜化

The complication of this matter delayed the scheduled progress.
▶▶ 事情的混亂使預定進度延遲了。

compliment [ˈkɑmpləmənt] 名讚美;恭維

Your presence at my party is a great compliment.
▶▶ 你能來參加我的派對,真是讓我備感榮幸。

component [kəmˈponənt] 名成分 形合成的;構成的

名 Some components of the machine are wearing down.
機器的某些部件正在磨損。
形 You cannot lose any of the component parts.
你不能搞丟任何一個零組件。

compound [ˈkɑmpaʊnd] / [kɑmˈpaʊnd] 名合成物;混合物 動使混合

名 Water is a compound of hydrogen and oxygen.
水是一種由氫和氧結合而成的化合物。
動 A pharmacist compounds drugs from prescribed ingredients.
藥劑師按規定的成分混合藥物。

comprehend [ˌkɑmprɪˈhɛnd] 動理解

I can comprehend what the professor said.
▶▶ 我可以理解教授所言。

comprehension [ˌkɑmprɪˈhɛnʃən] 名理解

The horror of war is beyond comprehension.
▶▶ 戰爭的恐怖令人難以理解。

comprise [kəmˈpraɪz] 動構成;包含

The alliance is comprised of fifty countries.
▶▶ 這個聯盟由五十個國家組成。
焦點句型 be comprised of sb./sth. 由…構成

compromise [ˈkɑmprəˌmaɪz] 名和解 動妥協

名 The couple finally came to a compromise.
這對夫婦最後終於和解了。
動 They were obliged to compromise to reach an agreement.
他們被迫妥協以達成協議。

conceal [kənˋsil] 動 隱藏

He concealed the photo in the drawer.
▶▶ 他把照片藏在抽屜裡。

concede [kənˋsid] 動 承認

When it was clear that he would lose the election, he conceded defeat.
▶▶ 他明白自己在選舉中大勢已去，於是承認失敗。

conceive [kənˋsiv] 動 構想；構思；懷孕

He conceived the idea for the novel during his journey through India.
▶▶ 他在印度的旅途中，有了寫這部小說的構想。

conception [kənˋsɛpʃən] 名 概念；計劃 關 concept 概念

I have no conception of what you mean.
▶▶ 我完全不懂你的意思。

condemn [kənˋdɛm] 動 譴責；責難

I condemn fascism and all it stands for.
▶▶ 我譴責法西斯主義及其代表的一切。

conduct [kənˋdʌkt] / [ˋkɑndʌkt] 動 處理；進行；指揮 名 行為；舉止

動 The priest conducted the church service.
這位牧師指揮教堂的禮拜儀式。
名 He got drunk and embarrassed himself with his conduct.
他喝醉了，並因他的行為感到尷尬。

confession [kənˋfɛʃən] 名 承認；招供 關 confess 坦白

The minister's confession implicated numerous officials in the bribery scandal.
▶▶ 那位部長的招供使很多官員牽連到受賄醜聞中。

confidential [ˏkɑnfəˋdɛnʃəl] 形 機密的 關 confident 有信心的

The spy leaked the confidential information to our enemy.
▶▶ 間諜把機密情報洩露給我們的敵人。

confine [kənˋfaɪn] 動 限制

Do not confine yourself to your major.
▶▶ 不要被自己的主修科系限制住。

Level 1 基礎單字
Level 2 必備單字
Level 3 中級單字
Level 4 進階單字
Level 5 高手單字
Level 6 滿級單字

conform [kən`fɔrm] 動順從；遵從；順應習俗

He doesn't conform to the usual stereotype of the city businessman with a dark suit and rolled umbrella.

▶▶ 他不像典型的城市商人那樣，穿一身深色的西裝、 帶一把收好的雨傘。

confront [kən`frʌnt] 動面對；面臨

When I was confronted by difficulties, I never gave up.

▶▶ 當我面臨困難時，我從未放棄。

confrontation [ˌkɑnfrən`teʃən] 名對抗；對峙

She wanted to avoid another confrontation with her father.

▶▶ 她想避免和父親再次發生衝突。

consensus [kən`sɛnsəs] 名共識；一致的意見

There is a consensus among experts about the causes of global warming.

▶▶ 關於全球暖化的起因，專家們意見一致。

consent [kən`sɛnt] 名贊同 動同意

名 His silence signaled consent.
他的沉默表示同意。

動 Did your mother consent to you traveling to New Zealand?
你媽媽同意你去紐西蘭旅遊嗎？

conservation [ˌkɑnsɚ`veʃən] 名保育；保護；保存

Conservation groups are protesting against the plan to build a road through the forest.

▶▶ 自然保護組織反對興建道路穿越森林的計畫。

considerate [kən`sɪdərət] 形體貼的

Nicole is a considerate girl that always thinks of others.

▶▶ 妮可是個體貼的女孩，總是為他人著想。

constitutional [ˌkɑnstə`tjuʃənḷ] 形符合憲法的；體質的 名健身散步

形 We doubt whether the Parade and Assembly Law is constitutional.
我們懷疑集會遊行法違憲。

名 He takes a constitutional in the park every morning.
他每天早上都在公園健身運動。

consultation [ˌkɑnsʌl`teʃən] 名諮詢 關 consultant 顧問；諮商師

I turned to my teacher for consultation.
▶▶ 我找老師進行諮詢。

consumption [kən`sʌmpʃən] 名消費；消耗量 關 consume 消耗

The consumption of tissues is high.
▶▶ 衛生紙的消耗量很高。

contagious [kən`tedʒəs] 形傳染的

Smallpox is a highly contagious disease.
▶▶ 天花是一種很容易接觸傳染的疾病。

contaminate [kən`tæməˌnet] 動汙染 關 contamination 汙染

The waste from this factory contaminated the clean river.
▶▶ 來自這家工廠的廢棄物污染了乾淨的河水。

contemplate [`kɑntɛmˌplet] 動沉思 關 contemplation 深思熟慮

He didn't contemplate on these things for too long.
▶▶ 他對這些事情沒有考慮過久。

焦點句型 contemplate on sth. 深思…

contemporary [kən`tɛmpəˌrɛrɪ] 形同時期的；當代的 名同時代的人

形 Tien-Wen Chu is one of the contemporary writers.
朱天文是當代作家之一。
名 He stands out among his contemporaries.
他在同時代的人當中非常地傑出。

contempt [kən`tɛmpt] 名輕蔑；鄙視

This marketing strategy has earned the contempt of many web users.
▶▶ 這種行銷策略受到了很多網路用戶的蔑視。

contend [kən`tɛnd] 動競爭；爭奪

He is contending with the math questions.
▶▶ 他正在與數學問題奮戰。

焦點句型 contend with sth. 必須處理；必須應對（困境或難題等）

Level 1 基礎單字
Level 2 必備單字
Level 3 中級單字
Level 4 進階單字
Level 5 高手單字
Level 6 滿級單字

continental [ˌkɑntəˈnɛntḷ] 形 大陸的；洲的 關 continent 大陸；陸地

The shutters and the balconies give the street a continental ambiance.
▶▶ 百葉窗和陽臺使這條街充滿歐洲大陸風情。

contractor [ˈkɑntræktɚ] 名 立契約者 關 contract 契約

If the contractors from both sides agree, then the documents will be executed.
▶▶ 如果契約雙方都同意，那這份文件就生效了。

contradiction [ˌkɑntrəˈdɪkʃən] 名 否定；矛盾

There were a number of contradictions in what he told the police.
▶▶ 他對警方說的話有若干矛盾之處。

controversial [ˌkɑntrəˈvɝʃəl] 形 有爭議的；引起爭議的

The two legislators from different parties debated the controversial issue.
▶▶ 兩個不同黨籍的立委為這個爭議性的議題發生爭執。

controversy [ˈkɑntrəˌvɝsɪ] 名 爭議；爭論

The plans for renovating the city center caused a great deal of controversy.
▶▶ 市中心的改造計畫引起極大的爭議。

convert [kənˈvɝt] 動 變換；轉換

You can convert dollars into yen at the counter.
▶▶ 你可以在櫃檯把美金兌換成日圓。

convict [ˈkɑnvɪkt] / [kənˈvɪkt] 名 被判罪的人 動 判定有罪

名 The convicts thought of a plan to escape from the jail.
囚犯們想到一個逃獄的計畫。
動 He was convicted of fraud.
他被判詐欺罪。

conviction [kənˈvɪkʃən] 名 定罪；說服力；堅定的信念

Her words carried conviction.
▶▶ 她的話充滿說服力。

coordinate [koˈɔrdɪnet] / [koˈɔrdənɪt] 動 協調；使相配合 形 同等的

動 Mother tried to coordinate everything for her three children.
母親努力協調三個孩子的所有事務。

Level 1 基礎單字
Level 2 必備單字
Level 3 中級單字
Level 4 進階單字
Level 5 高手單字
Level 6 滿級單字

形 The Army, Navy and Air force are coordinate branches of the Armed Services.
陸、海、空軍是同等的三個軍種。

copyright [`kɑpɪˌraɪt] 名 版權；著作權 動 為…取得版權

名 The publisher licensed the copyright to the novel to a movie producer.
出版商將這本小說的版權賣給了電影製造商。
動 The software was copyrighted by Microsoft.
這套軟體的版權歸屬微軟公司。

core [kor] 名 果核；核心

Concern for the environment is at the core of our policies.
▶▶ 對環境的關注是我們政策的核心。

corporate [`kɔrpərət] 形 團體的；公司的

The law applies to both individuals and corporate bodies.
▶▶ 本條法律既適用於個人也適用於法人團體。

corporation [ˌkɔrpəˋreʃən] 名 公司；企業

John works for a large American chemical corporation.
▶▶ 約翰為美國一家大型化學公司工作。

correspondent [ˌkɔrəˋspɑndənt] 名 通訊記者；特派員

We have many correspondents around the world.
▶▶ 我們在世界各地有很多特派記者。

corridor [`kɔrədə] 名 走廊；通道

The lovers strolled hand in hand along the corridor.
▶▶ 這對情人沿著走廊牽手散步。

corrupt [kəˋrʌpt] 動 使墮落；腐蝕 形 腐敗的 關 corruption 貪汙；腐敗

動 You have sold your souls, but must you also corrupt our nation and threaten our children as well?
你們已經出賣了自己的靈魂，難道你們還要腐蝕我們的民族，威脅我們的孩子嗎？
形 The critic suggested that the whole system was corrupt.
名嘴表示整個體系都腐敗了。

counsel [`kaʊnsəl] 名忠告；法律顧問 動勸告；建議

名 The legal counsel gave me some constructive suggestions.
這名法律顧問給我一些建設性的建議。
動 A healthy man can counsel the sick.
健康的人可以為病人提供建議。

counselor [`kaʊnsələ] 名顧問；參事 關 consultation 諮詢

I was approached by the President to serve as his counselor in foreign matters.
▶▶ 我以外交顧問的身分與總統打交道。

courteous [`kɜtɪəs] 形有禮貌的

The hotel staff are friendly and courteous.
▶▶ 旅館服務人員親切又有禮貌。

coverage [`kʌvərɪdʒ] 名覆蓋範圍

I stand in the coverage of the tree to avoid a sunburn.
▶▶ 我站在樹蔭的範圍之中，以免曬黑。

credibility [ˌkrɛdə`bɪlətɪ] 名可信度；確實性 關 tabloid 通俗小報

The reports in the tabloids are often of low credibility.
▶▶ 小報的報導往往可信度不高。

creek [krik] 名小溪

Factory waste has stunk up the creek.
▶▶ 工廠的廢料使這條小河臭氣沖天。

cripple [`krɪpl̩] 名瘸子；殘疾人

Use "people with special needs" instead of "cripples" to be politically correct.
▶▶ 政治正確的說法是「特殊需求的人士」而非「殘廢」。

criterion / criteria [kraɪ`tɪrɪən ] / [ kraɪ`tɪrɪə] 名標準

Maisie is a girl with high moral criterion.
▶▶ 梅西是個有著高道德標準的女孩。
文法解析 criterion 為單數，criteria 為複數。

crucial [`kruʃəl] 形關係重大的

Whether he attends the reception is crucial.
▶▶ 他是否出席接待會事關重大。

crude [krud] 形 粗糙的；粗俗的

He made some crude jokes.
▶▶ 他講了一些粗俗的笑話。

cruise [kruz] 動 航行；巡航 名 航行；巡航

動 The captain cruised along the coast.
船長在沿海巡航。
名 They're planning to go on a cruise.
他們打算乘船出遊。

crystal [`krɪstḷ] 名 水晶 形 水晶的；清澈的；透明的

名 He wore a yellow crystal produced from Brazil.
他戴著一塊巴西出產的黃水晶。
形 The witch is holding a crystal ball in her hands.
巫婆手裡拿著一個水晶球。

cuisine [kwɪ`zin] 名 烹調；菜餚

I like Sichuan and Guangdong cuisine very much.
▶▶ 我非常喜歡川菜和粵菜。

currency [`kɝənsɪ] 名 貨幣

You'll need some cash in the local currency; however, you can also use your credit card.
▶▶ 你將需要一些當地的貨幣現金，但也可使用信用卡。

curriculum [kə`rɪkjələm] 名 課程

Latin is not in the curriculum at our school.
▶▶ 我們學校裡的課程沒有拉丁文。

customs [`kʌstəmz] 名 海關

The customs officers of Hong Kong have established themselves as an outstanding disciplinary force.
▶▶ 香港海關人員已成為傑出的紀律部隊。

Level 1 基礎單字
Level 2 必備單字
Level 3 中級單字
Level 4 進階單字
Level 5 高手單字
Level 6 滿級單字

deadly [`dɛdlɪ] 形 致命的 副 極度地

形 The deadly poison caused her to fall into a coma.
這種致命毒物使她陷入昏迷。

副 It was deadly cold in winter.
冬天非常寒冷。

decay [dɪ`ke] 名 衰敗；衰弱 動 衰敗；衰弱

名 The elder sighed that the industry has been in decay for years.
老者感嘆這行業已沒落多年了。

動 The fruit decayed due to the exposure to air.
因暴露在空氣之中，水果腐爛了。

deceive [dɪ`siv] 動 欺詐；詐騙

He deceived his mother into believing that he had earned the money, not stolen it.
>> 他欺騙母親使她相信，他的錢是賺來的，不是偷來的。

decent [`disn̩t] 形 體面的；正經的

All she wants is a decent job with reasonable wages.
>> 她所要的只是一份有合理工資的體面工作。

declaration [ˌdɛklə`reʃən] 名 聲明；宣告 動 declare 聲明

Richard is the newly appointed manager according to the declaration.
>> 根據聲明，理察是新任經理。

decline [dɪ`klaɪn] 名 下降；衰敗 動 下降；衰敗

名 The decline of wages caused a strike.
工資的下降引發罷工。

動 The standard of education has declined in this country.
這個國家的教育水準下降了。

dedicate [`dɛdəˌket] 動 奉獻；獻出 動 dedication 奉獻

The artist dedicated his life to the pure aesthetic pursuit.
>> 這位藝術家畢生致力於純粹的美學追求。

MEMORIZE 7000 VOCABULARIES ONCE AND FOR ALL！

delegate [`dɛlə͵get] 名代表;使節 動派遣

名 He is an official delegate of the U.S.
他是美國官方代表。
動 You can't do everything yourself. You must learn how to delegate things to others.
你不可能事必躬親,你一定要學會委派他人。

delegation [͵dɛlə`geʃən] 名委派;代表團

The British delegation walked out of the meeting in protest.
▶▶ 英國代表團在會議中離席以示抗議。

deliberate [dɪ`lɪbəret ] / [ dɪ`lɪbərɪt] 形慎重的;故意的 動仔細考慮

形 Was it an accident or was it deliberate?
那是偶然的還是故意的?
動 I deliberate before every purchase.
我買東西前都會慎重考慮。

democrat [`dɛmə͵kræt] 名民主主義者 關 democracy 民主

His father is an influential democrat.
▶▶ 他父親是位有影響力的民主主義者。

denial [dɪ`naɪəl] 名否認 關 deny 否認

No one trusts him in spite of his denial.
▶▶ 即使他否認,也沒有人相信他。

density [`dɛnsətɪ] 名稠密;濃密

There is a high density of wildlife in this area.
▶▶ 這地區的野生生物密度很高。

depict [dɪ`pɪkt] 動描述

The novel depicts rural life a century ago.
▶▶ 這本小說描述一個世紀以前的鄉村生活。

depress [dɪ`prɛs] 動使憂鬱;壓下;降低

Wet weather always depresses me.
▶▶ 潮濕的天氣總使我心情抑鬱。

Level 1 基礎單字
Level 2 必備單字
Level 3 中級單字
Level 4 進階單字
Level 5 高手單字
Level 6 滿級單字

deputy [`dɛpjətɪ] 名代表；代理人

Who has she designated to be her deputy?
▶▶ 她委派誰作為代表？

derive [dɪ`raɪv] 動引出；源自

The story is derived from Andersen's Fairy Tales.
▶▶ 這個故事出自《安徒生童話》。
(焦點句型) derive from sth. 來自於；源自

descend [dɪ`sɛnd] 動下降；突擊

The plane started to descend, and several minutes later we landed.
▶▶ 飛機開始下降，幾分鐘後我們就著陸了。

descriptive [dɪ`skrɪptɪv] 形描述的

He wrote a book which is descriptive of the frontier provinces.
▶▶ 他寫了一本描述邊疆各省的書。

despair [dɪ`spɛr] 名絕望 動絕望

名 She was in despair after being flunked.
她被當掉之後陷入絕望。
動 You should not despair anyhow.
無論如何你都不該絕望。

destination [ˌdɛstə`neʃən] 名目的地；終點

When the runner arrived at his destination, everyone clapped loudly.
▶▶ 當選手抵達終點，眾人拍手喝采。

destiny [`dɛstənɪ] 名命運

That was a critical moment for the nation's destiny.
▶▶ 那是涉及國家命運的一個關鍵時刻。

destructive [dɪ`strʌktɪv] 形破壞的；毀滅性的 關 destruction 破壞

It was the most destructive storm in 30 years.
▶▶ 這是三十年來最具毀滅性的暴風雨。

devotion [dɪ`voʃən] 名摯愛；奉獻 關 devote 將⋯奉獻給

We admired his devotion to the charity.
▶▶ 我們崇敬他對慈善事業的奉獻。

diagnose [`daɪəgnoz] 動 診斷

His illness was diagnosed as bronchitis.
▶▶ 他的病診斷出為氣管炎。

diagnosis [ˌdaɪəg`nosɪs] 名 診斷

I wait for the diagnosis of my disease anxiously.
▶▶ 我焦急地等待疾病診斷報告。

dialect [`daɪəlɛkt] 名 方言

The dialects are widely used in the county.
▶▶ 這個縣裡廣泛使用方言。

diameter [daɪ`æmətə] 名 直徑

Diameter is the double of the radius.
▶▶ 直徑是半徑的兩倍。

diaper [`daɪpə] 名 尿布

I just nursed him and changed his diaper, and he's crying again!
▶▶ 我剛餵完奶，換了尿布，他又哭了！

digestion [daɪ`dʒɛstʃən] 名 消化；領悟

She has problems with digestion.
▶▶ 她有消化不良的問題。

dilemma [də`lɛmə] 名 兩難

Linda is really in a dilemma because both of her admirers are great.
▶▶ 兩位愛慕者都很優秀，真讓琳達左右為難。

dimension [dɪ`mɛnʃən ] / [ daɪ`mɛnʃən] 名 尺寸；空間；維度

Time is sometimes called the fourth dimension.
▶▶ 時間有時被稱為第四維度。

diminish [dɪ`mɪnɪʃ] 動 縮小；減少

The bad news did nothing to diminish her enthusiasm for the plan.
▶▶ 那個壞消息絲毫沒有減少她對這個計畫的興致。

Level 1 基礎單字
Level 2 必備單字
Level 3 中級單字
Level 4 進階單字
Level 5 高手單字
Level 6 滿級單字

diplomatic [ˌdɪpləˈmætɪk] 形 外交的；外交官的；圓滑的

He searched for a diplomatic reply so as not to offend her.
>> 他想找一個得體的答覆以免冒犯她。

directory [dɪˈrɛktərɪ] 名 名錄；指南

I found your telephone number in the directory.
>> 我在名簿上找到你的電話。

disapprove [ˌdɪsəˈpruv] 動 反對；不贊成

He disapproves of my plans, so I have to find some arguments to persuade him.
>> 他不贊成我的計劃，所以我得找些論點說服他。

disclose [dɪsˈkloz] 動 揭露；露出

Her accent disclosed where she came from.
>> 她的口音洩露了她是哪裡人。

disconnect [ˌdɪskəˈnɛkt] 動 斷絕；打斷

If you don't pay your gas bill, your supply will be disconnected.
>> 如果你不交瓦斯費，瓦斯供應會被切斷。

discriminate [dɪˈskrɪməˌnet] 動 辨別；差別對待

It is illegal to discriminate against any ethnic or religious group.
>> 歧視任何族群或宗教團體都是違法的。

discrimination [dɪˌskrɪməˈneʃən] 名 歧視；區別對待；辨別能力

Racial discrimination has been a serious problem for such a long time in the USA.
>> 種族歧視在美國長期以來一直是嚴重的問題。

dissolve [dɪˈzɑlv] 動 (使)溶解

She dissolved the salt in hot water.
>> 她用熱水溶解鹽。

distinction [dɪˈstɪŋkʃən] 名 區別

I know the distinctions between the twin brothers.
>> 我知道這對雙胞胎兄弟有什麼區別。

distinctive [dɪˋstɪŋktɪv] 形 區別的；特殊的

The soldiers were wearing their distinctive red berets.
▶▶ 這些士兵戴著特別的紅色貝雷帽。

distract [dɪˋstrækt] 動 分散

I was distracted during the lecture, and the teacher noticed it.
▶▶ 我在課堂上分心了，老師也有注意到。

doctrine [ˋdɑktrɪn] 名 教義

Christian and Muslim doctrines are very different.
▶▶ 基督教和伊斯蘭教的教義極為不同。

document [ˋdɑkjəmənt] 名 文件 動 記載；提供證據 關 solicitor 事務律師

名 Her solicitor asked her to read and sign a number of documents.
　　律師要求她讀幾份文件，然後請她簽字。
動 I documented my argument to prove my innocence.
　　我用證據佐證我的論點，證實我的清白。

documentary [ˏdɑkjəˋmɛntərɪ] 名 紀實性節目；紀錄片 形 文件的；紀錄的

名 The director has made a series of documentaries.
　　導演拍了一系列的紀錄片。
形 I love documentary films that reveal social reality.
　　我喜歡揭露社會真實的紀錄片。

dome [dom] 名 穹頂；圓頂；半球形 動 覆以圓頂

名 The dome of St. Paul Cathedral is well known.
　　聖保羅教堂的圓頂聞名於世。
動 The architect decided to dome the tower.
　　這位建築家決定在塔上加蓋圓頂。

donate [ˋdonet] 動 捐贈

This computer was donated to us by a local firm.
▶▶ 這台電腦是當地一家公司捐贈給我們的。

donation [doˋneʃən] 名 捐款；捐贈物 同 endowment

The warehouse is full of donations to the victims.
▶▶ 倉庫裡裝滿了給災民的捐贈。

1 Level 基礎單字
2 Level 必備單字
3 Level 中級單字
4 Level 進階單字
5 Level 高手單字
6 Level 滿級單字

donor [ˋdonɚ] 名 捐贈人

The anonymous donor donated one million dollars to the school.
▶▶ 這個匿名捐贈者捐了一百萬給學校。

doorway [ˋdor͵we] 名 門口；出入口

He stood in the doorway and watched me.
▶▶ 他站在門口看我。

dough [do] 名 生麵糰

The way to make dough is very simple; you only need to mix flour with water.
▶▶ 和麵糰的方法很簡單，只要把水混合在麵粉裡就行了。

dreadful [ˋdrɛdfəl] 形 可怕的

The dreadful nightmare was still in my memory.
▶▶ 那個可怕的惡夢我仍然記得。

driveway [ˋdraɪv͵we] 名 車道

There was a car parked in the driveway.
▶▶ 有一輛汽車停在車道上。

drought [draʊt] 名 乾旱；旱災

The drought had worsened their chances of survival.
▶▶ 發生乾旱後他們就更難活命了。

UNIT 05 E字頭高手單字　　MP3 099

ecology [rˋkɑlədʒɪ] 名 生態學 關 ecological 生態的 / ecosystem 生態環境

Ecology is worthy of more emphasis.
▶▶ 生態學值得更多重視。

ego [ˋigo] 名 自我

The greatest of them have the smallest egos.
▶▶ 他們之中最偉大的人物是最不竭力表現自我的。

elaborate [rˋlæbərɪt] / [rˋlæbə͵ret] 形 精心的 動 詳述

形 They made elaborate costumes for the play.
　　他們為這齣戲精心製作戲服。

(動) Please elaborate on what you see at the scene.
請詳述你在現場看到了什麼。

eligible [`ɛlɪdʒəbl] 形 合格的；合適的
Emily is eligible for the subsidies.
▶▶ 艾蜜莉擁有獲得津貼的資格。

eloquent [`ɛləkwənt] 形 雄辯的；有說服力的
He addressed the audience in an eloquent speech.
▶▶ 他向聽眾發表了富有說服力的演說。

embrace [ɪm`bres] 動 包圍；擁抱 名 擁抱
(動) He embraced me tightly.
他緊緊擁抱我。
(名) Give him an embrace, and forget about the misunderstandings.
給他一個擁抱，盡釋前嫌吧。

enterprise [`ɛntɚ͵praɪz] 名 企業 關 entrepreneur 企業家
He started an enterprise after graduation.
▶▶ 他畢業後就創業。

enthusiastic [ɪn͵θjuzɪ`æstɪk] 形 熱心的；熱情的
Sally is enthusiastic about dancing.
▶▶ 莎莉熱衷於跳舞。
(焦點句型) be enthusiastic about N./Ving 熱衷於…

entitle [ɪn`taɪtl] 動 給…定名；賦予權力
He entitled the book "Savage Love".
▶▶ 他為這本書取名為《野性的愛》。

envious [`ɛnvɪəs] 形 羨慕的；妒忌的
She is envious of her roommate for her beauty.
▶▶ 她嫉妒她室友的美麗。
(焦點句型) be envious of sb. 嫉妒某人

epidemic [͵ɛpɪ`dɛmɪk] 名 傳染病 形 流行的
(名) The reports of the flu epidemic were not accurate.
關於流行性感冒的報導不準確。

Level 1 基礎單字
Level 2 必備單字
Level 3 中級單字
Level 4 進階單字
Level 5 高手單字
Level 6 滿級單字

形 Fake news has become epidemic these years.
假新聞近年變得很流行。

episode [`ɛpə͵sod] 名 一集；一節；插曲

The first episode runs next Friday evening at 8 p.m.
▶▶ 下星期五晚上八點播出第一集。

equation [ɪˋkweʃən] 名 方程式

2x + 5 = 11 is an equation.
▶▶ 2x + 5 = 11 是一項方程式。

equity [`ɛkwətɪ] 名 股本；股票；公正

Equity is an abstract principle.
▶▶ 公正是個抽象的原則。

equivalent [ɪˋkwɪvələnt] 名 相等物 形 相當的

名 One US dollar is the equivalent of 33 New Taiwan dollars.
一美金相當於三十三新台幣。
形 A one carat diamond, depending on the quality, is roughly equivalent to two hundred thousand NT dollars.
根據品質不同，一克拉的鑽石大約相當於新台幣二十萬。

erect [ɪˋrɛkt] 動 豎立 形 直立的

動 They erected the building in record speed.
他們以創下紀錄的速度蓋完了房子。
形 There is an erect tree beside my house.
我的房子旁邊有棵直立的樹。

errand [`ɛrənd] 名 差事；跑腿

Her husband went on an errand.
▶▶ 她丈夫出差去了。

erupt [ɪˋrʌpt] 動 爆發

They are anxious that the volcanoes will erupt someday.
▶▶ 他們擔憂火山有一天會爆發。

escalate [`ɛskə͵let] 動 擴大；延長

Their quarrel has escalated recently.
▶▶ 他們的爭執這幾天延燒得越來越烈。

essence [`ɛsəns] 名 本質

The essence of his religious teaching is love for all men.
▶▶ 他所宣揚的宗教教義要旨是愛天下人。

estate [ɪ`stet] 名 財產；莊園

He owns a large estate in Scotland.
▶▶ 他在蘇格蘭有個大莊園。

eternal [ɪ`tɜnḷ] 形 永恆的

My love for my mother is eternal.
▶▶ 我對媽媽的愛永遠不變。

ethical [`ɛθɪkḷ] 形 道德的

It is not ethical for the enterprise to conceal the toxins in their products.
▶▶ 這家企業隱瞞產品含毒是不道德的。

ethics [`ɛθɪks] 名 道德規範；行為準則；倫理

Our professional ethics require us to stay uncommitted and report the facts only.
▶▶ 我們的職業道德要求我們要保持中立，報導事實真相。

evolution [ˌɛvə`luʃən] 名 發展

Political evolution is a slow process.
▶▶ 政治發展是一個緩慢的過程。

evolve [ɪ`vɑlv] 動 演化

The small company evolved into a well-known enterprise.
▶▶ 這間小公司發展成一間知名企業。

exaggeration [ɪgˌzædʒə`reʃən] 名 誇張

The reports were full of exaggeration.
▶▶ 那些報導誇大不實。

exceed [ɪk`sid] 動 超過

His earnings exceed mine.
▶▶ 他的收入比我高。

Level 1 基礎單字
Level 2 必備單字
Level 3 中級單字
Level 4 進階單字
Level 5 高手單字
Level 6 滿級單字

exceptional [ɪkˋsɛpʃənḷ] 形 優秀的

The employer hired the most exceptional applicant.
▶▶ 這位雇主雇用最優秀的應徵者。

excessive [ɪkˋsɛsɪv] 形 過度的

Excessive passion can lead to problems.
▶▶ 過度熱情會造成問題。

exclaim [ɪkˋsklem] 動 驚叫

She exclaimed out of fear.
▶▶ 她害怕地驚叫。

exclude [ɪkˋsklud] 動 拒絕；不包含 關 exclusion 排斥

They planned to go on a trip, but I was excluded.
▶▶ 他們計劃去旅行，但我被排除在外。

exclusive [ɪkˋsklusɪv] 形 唯一的；排外的；獨家的

To gain an audience's exclusive attention can be difficult.
▶▶ 獲得觀眾的全部注意力是很困難的。

execute [ˋɛksə͵kjut] 動 執行；處決

The nurse executed the doctor's orders.
▶▶ 護士執行醫生的命令。

execution [͵ɛksəˋkjuʃən] 名 執行；處決

The execution of the plan has been postponed for three years.
▶▶ 這個計畫的執行已經耽擱了三年。

executive [ɪgˋzɛkjutɪv] 名 行政主管；領導階層 形 決策的；管理的

名 She's a senior executive in a computer company.
　　她是一家電腦公司的高級執行長。
形 The president holds the highest executive power.
　　總統握有最高行政權。

exile [ˋɛksaɪl] 名 流亡 動 放逐

名 Those days in exile were beyond description.
　　那些流亡的日子難以描述。
動 They have been exiled to the isle for many years.
　　他們被放逐到這個小島許多年了。

exotic [εgˋzɑtɪk] 形 外來的;異國的

I like the exotic atmosphere of the restaurant.
▶▶ 我喜歡這間餐廳的異國風情。

expedition [ˌεkspəˋdɪʃən] 名 探險;遠征

The scientists planned an expedition to the Arctic.
▶▶ 這些科學家計劃前往北極探險。

expertise [ˌεkspəˋtiz] 名 專門知識

Customers will be impressed by the expertise of our highly trained employees.
▶▶ 我們的員工受過專業訓練,保證讓顧客印象深刻。

explicit [ɪkˋsplɪsɪt] 形 明確的

She gave me an explicit explanation about the incident.
▶▶ 她明確地跟我解說此次事件。

exploit [ɪkˋsplɔɪt] 動 利用;剝削 名 功績 同 commend 讚揚

動 The employer exploited workers by paying extremely low wages.
這名雇主給付極低的薪資來剝削勞工。
名 The king commended him for his exploits.
國王因他的功績而讚賞他。

exploration [ˌεkspləˋreʃən] 名 探測

They decided to make a full exploration of the area.
▶▶ 他們決定對這塊區域進行全面的探勘。

extension [ɪkˋstεnʃən] 名 擴大;延長

We built an extension to the school, so now we have two more classrooms.
▶▶ 我們把學校擴建了一些,因此現在我們又多了兩間教室。

extensive [ɪkˋstεnsɪv] 形 廣泛的;廣大的

My father promised us an extensive house.
▶▶ 爸爸承諾要給我們一棟大房子。

exterior [ɪkˋstɪrɪə] 形 外部的 名 外面

形 We cannot judge things by their exterior appearance.
我們不能從外觀評判事物。
名 The exterior of the apple is ugly.
這顆蘋果外觀很難看。

Level 1 基礎單字
Level 2 必備單字
Level 3 中級單字
Level 4 進階單字
Level 5 高手單字
Level 6 滿級單字

external [ɪk`stɜnl̩] 形外在的 名外表

形 The cream is for external use only.
此軟膏只供外用。
名 He endeavored to improve the external of the buildings.
他努力改善建築物外觀。

extinct [ɪk`stɪŋkt] 形滅絕的

Polar bears could become extinct one day.
▶▶ 北極熊面臨絕種危機。

extraordinary [ɪk`strɔrdn̩ˌɛrɪ] 形特別的 同 unprecedented

She is an extraordinary lady; this includes her beauty, elegance, and wisdom.
▶▶ 她是個出眾的女子，容貌出色、氣質優雅又智慧過人。

MP3 100

fabric [`fæbrɪk] 名紡織品；布料

Chiffon is a kind of thin, almost transparent fabric.
▶▶ 雪紡綢是一種輕薄且幾乎透明的紡織物。

fabulous [`fæbjələs] 形極好的

It was a fabulous concert, and everyone enjoyed it.
▶▶ 這是一場出色的音樂會，所有人都很享受。

facilitate [fə`sɪləˌtet] 動促進；使便利

Equipping an office or plant with new computers to facilitate procedures is a good idea.
▶▶ 為辦公室或工廠配備新電腦以加速作業流程是個好主意。

faculty [`fækəltɪ] 名全體教員；系所

The university's faculty members are renowned for their expertise.
▶▶ 該大學的教職員以他們的專業知識聞名。

fascinate [`fæsəˌnet] 動迷住

Chinese culture has always fascinated me.
▶▶ 中國文化向來使我著迷。

fatigue [fə`tig] 名 疲勞 動 使…疲勞

名 My legs jerked from fatigue.
我的腿因疲勞過度而痙攣。

動 Carrying a lot of goods fatigued me greatly.
搬運一大堆貨物讓我疲勞極了。

federal [`fɛdərəl] 形 聯邦的 關 federation 聯邦 / confederation 同盟；聯盟

The United States has a federal government.
▶▶ 美國有聯邦政府。

fiber [`faɪbə] 名 纖維

Vegetables and fruit are rich in fiber.
▶▶ 蔬菜和水果含有豐富的纖維。

filter [`fɪltə] 名 過濾器 動 過濾

名 I bought some coffee filters.
我買了一些咖啡濾紙。

動 Do you filter your water?
你把水過濾了嗎？

fleet [flit] 名 船隊；艦隊

Have you ever seen the national fleet?
▶▶ 你有沒有看過國家艦隊？

flip [flɪp] 名 跳動 動 輕拍；翻轉

名 He was shocked by the fish's sudden flip.
他被魚的突然跳動嚇到了。

動 They flipped a coin to see where to go.
他們丟錢幣決定要去哪裡。

fluency [`fluənsɪ] 名 流暢；流利 關 fluently 流利地

He speaks English with fluency.
▶▶ 他的英語很流利。

fluid [`fluɪd] 名 流體 形 流質的

名 The doctor told her to drink plenty of fluids.
醫生吩咐她多喝水。

形 As a very ill patient, you had better eat fluid food.
你這個病人最好吃流質食物。

Level 1 基礎單字
Level 2 必備單字
Level 3 中級單字
Level 4 進階單字
Level 5 高手單字
Level 6 滿級單字

format [ˋfɔrmæt] 名 格式;版式 動 格式化

名 Please do as the format indicates.
請按照這種格式做。

動 If you format your hard discs, all data will be removed.
如果你格式化硬碟,所有資料都會被移除。

foster [ˋfɑstɚ] 動 收養;促進;培養 形 收養的

The parents are trying to foster an interest in traditional art in their children.
▶▶ 這對父母正試著培養孩子們對傳統藝術的興趣。

foul [faʊl] 動 汙染;弄髒 形 惡劣的;令人不快的;粗魯的

動 The naughty girl fouled the water by pouring in sand.
這個頑皮的女孩將沙子倒進水裡,使水變髒。

形 The foul air made me sick.
汙濁的空氣使我難受。

fraction [ˋfrækʃən] 名 分數;部分

I only got a fraction of the cake.
▶▶ 我只拿到蛋糕的一小部分。

fragment [ˋfrægmənt] 名 碎片 動 裂成碎片

名 The builders found fragments of Roman pottery on the site.
建築工人在工地撿到了一些古羅馬陶器的碎片。

動 My glasses were fragmented from a hit.
我的眼鏡一撞就裂成碎片。

framework [ˋfrem͵wɝk] 名 架構;框架;體制

The report provides a framework for further research.
▶▶ 這份報告為進一步的研究提供架構。

fraud [frɔd] 名 欺詐

Beware of fraud when you are shopping online.
▶▶ 在網路上購物時要小心詐騙。

freight [fret] 名 貨物;貨運 動 運輸

名 Highway freight transport reached 300 billion tons.
公路的貨運運輸量達每公里三千億噸。

動 I chose to freight the commodities by air.
我選擇用空運送貨。

frontier [frʌn`tɪr] 名邊境；國境

There was continual trouble on the frontier; fighting broke out every six months.
▶▶ 邊境紛擾頻仍，每六個月就爆發一次戰爭。

UNIT 07　G字頭高手單字

MP3 101

galaxy [`gæləksɪ] 名星雲；星系

The sun is merely a fixed star in the galaxy.
▶▶ 太陽只是銀河系裡的一顆恆星。

gasp [gæsp] 名喘息 動喘息；倒抽一口氣

名 I assured the rider was still alive from his gasp.
從他的喘息，我確信這名騎士還活著。
動 They gasped in astonishment to see the sight.
他們看到這景象驚訝得倒抽一口氣。

gathering [`gæðərɪŋ] 名集會；聚集

We went to the park for a gathering.
▶▶ 我們到公園集合。

generate [`dʒɛnə,ret] 動產生；引起

This hatred was generated by racial prejudice.
▶▶ 這種仇恨是由種族偏見引起的。

generator [`dʒɛnə,retə] 名產生者；發電機

There was a sudden black-out because the generator was out of order.
▶▶ 因為發電機故障，突然就停電了。

genetic [dʒə`nɛtɪk] 形遺傳學的

Hemophilia is a genetic disease.
▶▶ 血友病是一種遺傳性疾病。

genetics [dʒə`nɛtɪks] 名遺傳學

Genetics is beyond my scope.
▶▶ 遺傳學不是我的領域。

Level 1 基礎單字
Level 2 必備單字
Level 3 中級單字
Level 4 進階單字
Level 5 高手單字
Level 6 滿級單字

glare [glɛr] 名 怒視；刺眼的光 動 怒視；發出刺眼的光

名 She gave a glare to the man who harassed her.
   她對騷擾她的男人投以怒視。
動 He glared at his brother and then they brawled.
   他怒視他的哥哥，然後他們就爭吵起來。

(焦點句型) give a glare to sb. / glare at sb. 怒視某人

gloomy [`glumɪ] 形 陰暗的；憂鬱的 同 moody

This room is a little bit gloomy. Please turn on the lights.
▶▶ 這房間有點暗。請開燈。

gorgeous [`gɔrdʒəs] 形 極其漂亮的；美麗動人的

The bride looks gorgeous in the pink gown.
▶▶ 新娘穿著粉紅禮服看起來美麗動人。

grant [grænt] 名 撥款；補助金 動 答應；允許；承認

名 Maisie is an excellent student. She receives a grant from the government monthly.
   梅西是個優秀的學生。她每個月都領政府發的獎學金。
動 I grant the genius of your plan, but you still will not find backers.
   我承認你的計畫有創意，但你還是不會找到贊助人。

graphic [`græfɪk] 形 生動的；繪畫的；圖表的

Tony likes to read graphic novels.
▶▶ 東尼喜歡閱讀圖像小說。

gravity [`grævətɪ] 名 重力；嚴重性；地心引力

He discoursed impressively on Newton's theory of gravity.
▶▶ 他講述了牛頓的地心引力定律，給人深刻的印象。

greed [grid] 名 貪心

Nothing would satisfy her greed for power.
▶▶ 她對權力貪得無厭。

grieve [griv] 動 悲傷；使悲傷

It's no use grieving about past errors.
▶▶ 為過去的錯誤悲傷不已是無濟於事的。

grill [grɪl] 名烤架 動烤

名 He put the vegetables and sliced meat on the grill.
他把蔬菜和肉片放到烤架上。

動 The fish was grilled on the barbeque.
這條魚是在燒烤架上烤的。

grim [grɪm] 形嚴格的；嚴厲的

I finally completed the grim training.
▶▶ 我終於通過了嚴格的訓練。

grip [grɪp] 名緊握；抓住 動緊握；抓住

名 She showed her determination with a grip of my hand.
她緊握我的手表現她的堅決。

動 Grip the rope, or you will fall.
抓緊繩子，不然你會掉下去。

gross [gros] 形總共的；毛利的；令人噁心的 動總收入為

形 What I want to know is net profit, not gross profit.
我想知道的是淨利，不是毛利。

動 They grossed more than 100 thousand dollars a month by selling costumes.
他們靠著賣衣服，每月獲得超過十萬的收入。

guideline [`gaɪd͵laɪn] 名指導方針；準則

The manual contains guidelines for weaving.
▶▶ 這本手冊涵蓋了編織的指導方針。

gut [gʌt] 名內臟；魄力；膽量

The picture reminds us of the positions of the guts in the human body.
▶▶ 這張剖面圖讓我們知道內臟在人體內的位置。

UNIT 08　H 字頭的高手單字

MP3 102

habitat [`hæbə͵tæt] 名棲息地

Much of the habitat is polluted, and the creatures there are on the verge of extinction.
▶▶ 這裡大部分的棲地都遭到汙染，這裡的生物也即將滅絕。

Level 1 基礎單字
Level 2 必備單字
Level 3 中級單字
Level 4 進階單字
Level 5 高手單字
Level 6 滿級單字

haul [hɔl] 動拖；拉 名拖；拉

動 The fishermen hauled the fish onto the boat.
漁民把魚拖上船。

名 It does not move despite repetitive hauls.
不管怎麼拉它都不動。

hazard [`hæzəd] 名危險 動冒險；使遭受危險

名 Smoking is a serious health hazard.
吸煙會嚴重危害健康。

動 I will hazard my life to jump over the stream.
我會冒著生命危險躍過這條小溪。

heir [ɛr] 名繼承人

Richard was his father's only heir, since he had no brothers or sisters.
▶▶ 理查是他父親的唯一繼承人，因為他沒有兄弟姐妹。

hence [hɛns] 副因此

She lost her way; hence, she turned to the police.
▶▶ 她迷路了，所以求助於警察。

herb [ɜb] 名藥草；香草

A large range of herbs and spices are used in Indian cookery.
▶▶ 印度的烹調中使用各種藥草和香料。

heritage [`hɛrətɪdʒ] 名遺產 同 legacy

She knows only a bit about her heritage.
▶▶ 她對自己的遺產所知甚少。

highlight [`haɪlaɪt] 名精彩場面 動使顯著；強調

名 Mandy's performance was the highlight of the show.
曼蒂的表演是那場演出中最精彩的部分。

動 My teacher highlighted the equation during the class.
課堂上，我們老師非常強調這條方程式。

hockey [`hɑkɪ] 名曲棍球

We slaughtered them at hockey.
▶▶ 我們在曲棍球賽中把他們打得一敗塗地。

honorable [`ɑnərəbl] 形 體面的；可敬的

She lived an honorable and virtuous life.
▶ 她一生品行端正。

horizontal [ˌhɔrɪ`zɑntl] 名 水平線 形 水平的

名 The contrast between the horizontal and vertical is the feature of this composition.
這個構圖的特色就是縱向和橫向之間的對比。
形 The horizontal line is the X axis.
這條水平線是 X 軸。

hormone [`hɔrmon] 名 荷爾蒙

The transsexual was injected female hormones.
▶ 這名變性者注射了女性荷爾蒙。

hostage [`hɑstɪdʒ] 名 人質

They are calling for the release of the hostages on humanitarian grounds.
▶ 他們站在人道主義立場要求釋放人質。

hostile [`hɑstl] 形 敵對的；不友善的

He seems hostile to newcomers.
▶ 他對新人似乎不友善。

hostility [hɑs`tɪlətɪ] 名 敵意

Ron is showing hostility towards Ken.
▶ 榮恩對肯表現出敵意。

housing [`hauzɪŋ] 名 住宅

The demand for housing construction is declining.
▶ 住宅建設的需求下降了。

howl [haul] 動 嚎叫；哀號；呼嘯 名 嚎叫聲；呼嘯聲 關 ghastly 可怕的

動 The wind is howling outside.
風在外頭呼嘯。
名 The howl of dogs at night sounds ghastly.
夜裡的狗吠聲聽起來很可怕。

Level 1 基礎單字
Level 2 必備單字
Level 3 中級單字
Level 4 進階單字
Level 5 高手單字
Level 6 滿級單字

idiot [`ɪdɪət] 名 傻瓜；笨蛋

I know he is not an idiot. He is just absent-minded.
▶▶ 我知道他不是笨蛋，他只是心不在焉。

illusion [ɪ`luʒən] 名 幻覺

A mirage is an optical illusion.
▶▶ 海市蜃樓是一種視覺上的錯覺。

immense [ɪ`mɛns] 形 巨大的

The new airplane looked like an immense bird.
▶▶ 這架新飛機看起來像一隻巨大的鳥。

immune [ɪ`mjun] 形 免疫的

Most adults are immune to chicken pox.
▶▶ 大多數成年人都對水痘有免疫力。

implement [`ɪmplə͵mɛnt] / [ `ɪmpləmənt] 動 施行 名 工具

動 We need money to implement the program.
我們需要錢來實行這個計劃。
名 Perfect implements make your work perfect.
完善的工具讓你的工作完美。

implication [͵ɪmplə`keʃən] 名 暗示

His implication that he didn't like me was hurtful.
▶▶ 他不喜歡我的暗示非常令我受傷。

impulse [`ɪmpʌls] 名 衝動

She had a terrible impulse to rush out of the house and never come back.
▶▶ 她心裡有個衝動，恨不得衝出屋去再也不回來。

incentive [ɪn`sɛntɪv] 名 刺激；激勵；誘因

The girl has no incentive to study.
▶▶ 這個女孩缺乏學習的誘因。

MEMORIZE 7000 VOCABULARIES ONCE AND FOR ALL !

index [`ɪndɛks] 名 指數；索引 動 編索引

名 According to the consumer price index, the price of food doubled in 1980s.
從消費者物價指數來看，一九八〇年代食品價格增加了一倍。
動 They indexed all the items for future reference.
他們把所有項目都做了索引，以供將來參考之用。

indifferent [ɪn`dɪfərənt] 形 冷漠的；不關心的

Although I treat him with sincerity, he is still indifferent to me.
▶ 雖然我誠心待他，他對我卻仍然很冷淡。

indispensable [ˌɪndɪ`spɛnsəbl̩] 形 不可缺少的

Friendship is indispensable for me.
▶ 友情對我而言不可或缺。

indulge [ɪn`dʌldʒ] 動 沉溺

The man indulged himself in luxury, and finally went bankrupt.
▶ 那個男人奢靡無度，最後終至破產。
(焦點句型) indulge (oneself) in sth. 沉迷於…

inevitable [ɪn`ɛvətəbl̩] 形 不可避免的；必然發生的

The agent said: "The revolution is inevitable, merely a matter of time."
▶ 特工說道：「革命終將到來，只是時間早晚罷了。」

infect [ɪn`fɛkt] 動 感染

The laboratory animals had been infected with the virus.
▶ 實驗室的動物已受到這種病毒的感染。

infinite [`ɪnfənɪt] 形 無限的

Many scientists believe that life is common in the infinite universe.
▶ 許多科學家相信，在無限的宇宙中，生命是普遍存在的。

inherent [ɪn`hɪrənt] 形 固有的；內在的

Competition is an inherent part of free market.
▶ 競爭是自由貿易市場的本質。

inherit [ɪn`hɛrɪt] 動 繼承；接受

She inherited one million dollars after her father passed away.
▶ 她父親過世後，她繼承了一百萬元。

1 Level 基礎單字
2 Level 必備單字
3 Level 中級單字
4 Level 進階單字
5 Level 高手單字
6 Level 滿級單字

initiate [ɪˋnɪʃɪˌet] 動開始；創始 名新成員

動 They initiated the cook course last year.
去年他們開創烹飪課。
名 For initiates, making errors is a commonplace.
對初學者來說，犯錯是司空見慣的事。

initiative [ɪˋnɪʃətɪv] 名倡議；主動性；主動權

The enemy forces have lost the initiative.
▶▶ 敵軍喪失了主動權。

inject [ɪnˋdʒɛkt] 動注入

The nurse injected the drug into my arm.
▶▶ 護士把藥注入我手臂。

injection [ɪnˋdʒɛkʃən] 名注射

The drug addict had three injections every day.
▶▶ 這個毒癮者每天注射三次。

innovation [ˌɪnəˋveʃən] 名革新

Apple is known for its innovation in consumer electronic products.
▶▶ 蘋果公司以消費性電子產品的創新聞名。

innovative [ˋɪnəˌvetɪv] 形創新的

The innovative products were sold out in only three days.
▶▶ 這些創新產品三天內就銷售一空。

inquiry [ˋɪnˌkwəi] 名詢問；調查

The police are making inquiries about the crime.
▶▶ 警方正在調查這起案件。

insight [ˋɪnˌsaɪt] 名洞察力；洞悉

My best friend has deep insight into my personality.
▶▶ 我最好的朋友對我的性格有深刻了解。

installation [ˌɪnstəˋleʃən] 名安裝；就任 關 infrastructure 基礎建設

Installation of the new system will take several days.
▶▶ 新系統的安裝需要幾天時間。

institute [`ɪnstətjut] 名 協會；機構；學院 動 設立；授職

名 The Massachusetts Institute of Technology is a prestigious institution.
麻省理工學院是一間有名的學院。
動 They instituted a club for singles.
他們創立了一個單身協會。

institution [ˌɪnstə`tjuʃən] 名 團體；機構 關 affiliate 附屬機構

Mr. Hu is the founder of the social institution.
▶▶ 胡先生是這個社會機構的創辦者。

intact [ɪn`tækt] 形 完好無缺的；未受損傷的

After the earthquake, very few of the buildings remained intact.
▶▶ 地震之後，只有少數的樓房保持完好無損。

integrate [`ɪntəˌgret] 動 整合

The two small schools were integrated into the large one.
▶▶ 這兩所規模小的學校合併成為一所規模大的學校。

integration [ˌɪntə`greʃən] 名 融合；整合

They saved a great amount of expense following the integration.
▶▶ 整併之後他們省下一筆很大的開銷。

integrity [ɪn`tɛgrətɪ] 名 正直

His integrity drove him to tell the truth.
▶▶ 他的正直驅使他說出真話。

intensify [ɪn`tɛnsəˌfaɪ] 動 加強；增強

Her position in the party has intensified in recent weeks.
▶▶ 最近幾個星期以來，她在黨內的地位有所提升。

intent [ɪn`tɛnt] 形 專心的 名 意圖；目的

形 The manager is intent on following the old method despite all the persuasion.
儘管有人勸說，但主管還是一意孤行，堅持採用過時的做法。
名 The revised edition is to all intents and purposes a new book.
修訂本實際上是一本新書。

(焦點句型) be intent on N./Ving 執意要做… / to all intents and purposes 實際上

Level 1 基礎單字
Level 2 必備單字
Level 3 中級單字
Level 4 進階單字
Level 5 高手單字
Level 6 滿級單字

interference [ˌɪntɚˈfɪrəns] 名 妨礙；干擾

I left home because I couldn't stand my parents' interference in my affairs.
▶▶ 我離家是因為受不了父母干涉我的事情。

interior [ɪnˈtɪrɪɚ] 名 內部；內務 形 內部的

名 It cost a lot to redecorate the interior of the house.
重新裝潢房子的內部花了很多錢。
形 The interior decoration is luxurious.
室內裝潢非常豪華。

interpretation [ɪnˌtɝprɪˈteʃən] 名 解釋；說明

It seems your interpretation of events is unclear.
▶▶ 你對這活動的說明似乎不夠清楚。

interval [ˈɪntɚvl̩] 名 間隔；時間

She phoned her boyfriend at intervals between classes.
▶▶ 她在課堂休息時間打電話給她的男朋友。

intervention [ˌɪntɚˈvɛnʃən] 名 介入；調停

His intervention will make the situation worse.
▶▶ 他的介入會使情況更糟。

investigator [ɪnˈvɛstəˌgetɚ] 名 調查者；研究者

The investigators will be divided into three groups.
▶▶ 所有的調查員將被分為三個小組。

irony [ˈaɪrənɪ] 名 反諷

Didn't you think his praise was done out of irony?
▶▶ 難道你不覺得他的讚美是出於反諷嗎？

 **UNIT 10　J、K 字頭高手單字** 　MP3 104

journalism [ˈdʒɝnl̩ˌɪzm̩] 名 新聞學

She majors in journalism.
▶▶ 她主修新聞學。

journalist [`dʒɜnlɪst] 名新聞工作者;記者

She earns her living as a freelance journalist.
▶▶ 她靠當自由撰稿記者來維持生計。

jug [dʒʌg] 名帶柄的壺

My mother gave me a jug of ice tea.
▶▶ 我媽媽給我一壺冰茶。

jury [`dʒʊrɪ] 名陪審團

The jury was prohibited from reading newspapers to keep objective.
▶▶ 陪審團被禁止閱讀報紙以保持客觀。

justify [`dʒʌstə‚faɪ] 動證明…有理;為…辯護

Can you justify your decision?
▶▶ 你能證明你的決定是對的嗎?

juvenile [`dʒuvənaɪl] 形青少年的;未成熟的 名青少年

形 He's twenty but he is still quite juvenile.
　　他都二十歲了,但還是相當幼稚。
名 The singer is popular among juveniles.
　　這名歌手很受青少年歡迎。

kidnap [`kɪdnæp] 動綁架;勒索

After criminals kidnapped the rich man's daughter, they demanded a large sum of money for her return.
▶▶ 罪犯團夥勒索富翁的女兒後,要求一大筆贖金。

UNIT 11　L 字頭高手單字

MP3 105

landlord [`lænd‚lɔrd] 名房東;地主

The landlord has put the rent up again.
▶▶ 房東又提高房租了。

laser [`lezɚ] 名雷射

Does laser surgery have any risks?
▶▶ 雷射手術有風險嗎?

Level 1 基礎單字
Level 2 必備單字
Level 3 中級單字
Level 4 進階單字
Level 5 高手單字
Level 6 滿級單字

lawmaker [lɔ`mekə] 名 立法者

I think lawmakers should know what people really need.

▶▶ 我認為立法者應該知道人民真正需要什麼。

lawsuit [`lɔˌsut] 名 訴訟

Their company filed a patent lawsuit against the manufacturer.

▶▶ 他們公司對這家製造商提出專利權訴訟。

layer [`leə] 名 層 動 分層 關 compost 混合肥料

名 A thin layer of dust covered everything.
所有的物品上都積了一層薄薄的灰塵。

動 The gardener layered lime and leaves to make compost.
園丁把石灰和樹葉分層堆成肥料。

league [lig] 名 聯盟 動 同盟

名 Which team is top of the league at the moment?
現在哪一隊名列聯盟榜首？

動 They leagued together to fight against their enemies.
他們結盟對抗敵人。

legendary [`lɛdʒəndˌɛrɪ] 形 傳說的

I firmly believed the legendary stories of my childhood.

▶▶ 我對孩童時代聽過的的傳說故事堅信不移。

legislation [ˌlɛdʒɪs`leʃən] 名 立法；法規

The committee proposed that new legislation should be drafted.

▶▶ 委員會建議著手起草新法規。

legislative [`lɛdʒɪsˌletɪv] 形 立法的

A legislative assembly is being held.

▶▶ 正在召開立法會議。

legitimate [lɪ`dʒɪtəmət] 形 合法的；合理的

How could he earn so much from legitimate business activities in such a short time?

▶▶ 他要是做正當生意，哪能在短時間內賺得了這麼多錢？

Level 1 基礎單字

Level 2 必備單字

Level 3 中級單字

Level 4 進階單字

Level 5 高手單字

Level 6 滿級單字

lest [lɛst] 連 以免

You had better go to bed earlier lest you oversleep tomorrow.
▸▸ 你應該早點睡覺，以免明天睡過頭。

likelihood [`laɪklɪ͵hʊd] 名 可能性；可能的事物

Is there any likelihood that she will come?
▸▸ 她有沒有可能來？

likewise [`laɪk͵waɪz] 副 同樣地

He spoke to me impolitely. Likewise, I did not treat him well.
▸▸ 他對我說話很不禮貌，同樣地，我也對他不好。

lounge [laʊndʒ] 名 休息室；等候室；交誼廳 動 （舒適或懶散地）站或坐著

名 She is waiting for me in the departure lounge.
　　她在候機室等我。
動 The tweny-four-year-old student is lounging on the sofa.
　　那位二十四歲的學生舒適地坐在沙發上。

lump [lʌmp] 名 塊 動 結塊；笨重地移動

名 The artist started with a big lump of clay.
　　藝術家用一大塊黏土開始雕塑。
動 The elephant lumped from here to there.
　　大象笨重地從這裡走到那裡。

UNIT 12　M 字頭高手單字

MP3 106

mainstream [`men͵strim] 名 主流

We don't have to follow the mainstream.
▸▸ 我們不需跟隨主流。

maintenance [`mentənəns] 名 維護；保養；保持

The organization raised funds for its maintenance.
▸▸ 這一組織為了維持運轉而籌集資金。

mammal [`mæml̩] 名 哺乳動物

Whales are the biggest mammals.
▸▸ 鯨魚是最大的哺乳動物。

manifest [`mænə͵fɛst] 動顯示 形明顯的

動 His expression manifested his reluctance.
他的表情顯得很不情願。

形 It is manifest that I don't fit the job.
顯然我不適合這份工作。

manipulate [mə`nɪpjə͵let] 動操縱

Do you know how to manipulate this machine?
▶▶ 你會操作這台機器嗎？

mansion [`mænʃən] 名大廈 關 stately 宏偉的；莊嚴的

The stately mansion crested the hill.
▶▶ 這棟宏偉的大廈位於小山上。

marine [mə`rin] 形海洋的 名海軍陸戰隊

形 The marine life along the coast is endangered by the chemical waste.
化學廢料危及沿岸的海洋生物。

名 He was assigned to the marines.
他被指派為海軍陸戰隊。

masculine [`mæskjəlɪn] 名男性 形男性的

She bought masculine perfume for her husband.
▶▶ 她買了男性香水給她丈夫。

massage [mə`saʒ] 名按摩 動按摩

名 A thorough massage will make you feel good when you are tired.
在你疲勞時，一次徹底的按摩會讓你感覺很舒服。

動 Massaging the neck can ease your fatigue.
按摩頸部可以消除疲勞。

massive [`mæsɪv] 形巨大的；大量的 關 mass 大眾；大量

Doctors discourage massive doses of painkillers.
▶▶ 醫生不贊成大量服用止痛藥。

masterpiece [`mæstə͵pis] 名傑作

He turned out to be a celebrity because of his masterpiece.
▶▶ 他因為一個傑作而成了名人。

mattress [`mætrɪs] 名床墊

It is better to put the mattress on a solid bed base.
▶▶ 把床墊放在結實的床架上較好。

meantime [`min,taɪm] 名期間；同時 副同時

名 My brother works as an engineer. In the meantime, I am a college student.
我哥哥在當工程師，同時，我則是個大學生。
副 They will come here to support us, and meantime you can take a rest.
他們會來此幫助我們，同時你就可以休息一會。

mechanism [`mɛkə,nɪzəm] 名機械裝置；機制；體制

This watch made in Switzerland works well and the mechanism rarely fails.
▶▶ 這支瑞士生產的手錶運行良好，它的裝置很少出毛病。

medication [,mɛdɪ`keʃən] 名藥物治療

Her mental illness is being treated with medication.
▶▶ 她的心智疾病已接受藥物治療。

merge [mɜdʒ] 動合併

Our company merged with theirs.
▶▶ 我們的公司與他們的合併了。
(焦點句型) merge with sth. 和…合併

metaphor [`mɛtəfə] 名隱喻；象徵

Eileen Chang utilized subtle metaphors to a splendid level.
▶▶ 張愛玲將精妙的比喻運用得出神入化。

metropolitan [,mɛtrə`pɑlətn̩] 形大都市的 名都市人

形 There is a wide variety of metropolitan newspapers.
大都市的報刊非常多樣。
名 Caroline is truly a metropolitan. She has never experienced the rural life.
凱洛琳真的是個都市人。她從未體驗過鄉村生活。

midst [mɪdst] 名中間

The hunters camped in the midst of the thick forest.
▶▶ 獵人們在密林深處宿營。

Level 1 基礎單字
Level 2 必備單字
Level 3 中級單字
Level 4 進階單字
Level 5 高手單字
Level 6 滿級單字

migration [maɪˋgreʃən] 名 遷移

The annual migration of birds is around the corner.
▶▶ 候鳥的遷徙即將來臨。

milestone [ˋmaɪl͵ston] 名 里程碑

It is an essential milestone that I graduate from university.
▶▶ 大學畢業是我人生一個重要的里程碑。

miniature [ˋmɪnɪətʃə] 名 縮圖；縮影 形 小型的

名 The miniature of the library lets you know the layout clearly.
這個圖書館的縮樣能讓你更清楚它的布局。
形 The child was playing with his miniature toy railway.
這孩子正在玩他的小型玩具鐵路。

minimal [ˋmɪnɪml̩] 形 最小的

The work was carried out at minimal cost.
▶▶ 這項工作是以最少的花費完成的。

minimize [ˋmɪnə͵maɪz] 動 減到最小

The explorers tried their best to minimize the dangers of their trip.
▶▶ 探險家們極力把探險途中的危險減到最低。

mint [mɪnt] 名 薄荷；薄荷糖

Mints are good refreshments.
▶▶ 薄荷糖是很好的提神用品。

missionary [ˋmɪʃən͵ɛrɪ] 名 傳教士 形 傳教的

名 The missionary invited me to go to church.
傳教士邀請我上教會。
形 She went to a missionary school to study theology.
她去一所教會學校念神學。

moan [mon] 動 呻吟 名 呻吟聲；悲嘆

動 I moaned when he touched my wound.
當他碰到我的傷口，我就發出呻吟。
名 Each time she moved her leg, she let out a moan.
每次她一移動腿就發出呻吟。

mock [mɑk] 動嘲笑 名嘲弄 形模擬的

動 The children mocked their ugly classmates.
這些孩子嘲笑長得醜的同學。
名 She shed tears because of his mock.
她因他的嘲弄而落淚。
形 I did a good job in the mock exams.
我模擬考考得很好。

mode [mod] 名模式;方式

The mode of his success is worth learning.
▶▶ 他的成功模式值得學習。

modify [`mɑdə‚faɪ] 動修改

We have to modify our plan a little bit.
▶▶ 我們得將計劃稍加修改。

molecule [`mɑlɪ‚kjul] 名分子

Molecules are tiny and are composed of just one or more atoms.
▶▶ 分子很微小,是由一個或多原子組成的。

monopoly [mə`nɑpl̩ɪ] 名壟斷

The company has a monopoly on the broadcasting rights for international football.
▶▶ 這家公司享有國際足球賽事的獨家轉播權。

morality [mə`rælətɪ] 名道德;德行

Standards of morality seem to be dropping.
▶▶ 道德標準似乎在下降。

motive [`motɪv] 名動機

The motive for the murder is still a puzzle.
▶▶ 他謀殺的動機仍然是個謎。

mount [maʊnt] 動增加;上升;登上 名(用於山名)山;峰

動 My siblings and I mounted the hill in an hour.
我和兄弟姊妹們一小時內就登上這座小山。
名 It is of great danger to climb Mount Everest.
攀登聖母峰非常危險。

Level 1 基礎單字
Level 2 必備單字
Level 3 中級單字
Level 4 進階單字
Level 5 高手單字
Level 6 滿級單字

mumble [`mʌmbḷ] 動含糊地說 名含糊不清的話

動 He mumbled unconsciously.
他無意識地咕噥著。
名 I cannot understand her mumbles.
我聽不懂她含糊的言語。

municipal [mju`nɪsəpḷ] 形市政的；自治區的

Can you describe the municipal system common in ancient Rome?
▶▶ 你可以描述一下古羅馬常見的市政系統嗎？

muscular [`mʌskjələ] 形肌肉的

He admires muscular men.
▶▶ 他欣賞肌肉發達的男性。

mustard [`mʌstəd] 名芥末

This meat should be seasoned with salt and mustard.
▶▶ 這肉應該加些鹽和芥末調味。

myth [mɪθ] 名神話；傳說；迷思 關 mythology 神話

When you are dealing with myths, it is hard to be either proper, or scientific.
▶▶ 對於神話，很難將其合理化或是科學化。

MP3 107

naive [naɪ`iv] 形天真的；幼稚的

I can't believe you were so naive to trust him!
▶▶ 我真是難以相信你會這麼天真地信任他！

narrative [`nærətɪv] 名敘述 形敘事的

名 We applauded her enthralling narrative.
我們為她精彩的描述鼓掌。
形 Writing narrative essays is her specialty.
寫記敘文是她的專長。

nasty [`næstɪ] 形糟糕的；讓人討厭的

This room has a very nasty smell.
▶▶ 這房間有一股很難聞的氣味。

negotiation [nɪˌgoʃɪˋeʃən] 名 協商 關 negotiate 協商

In all the delicate negotiations, the diplomat never made a wrong move.
▶▶ 在棘手的談判中，這位外交官從未出過差錯。

neutral [ˋnjutrəl] 形 中立的 名 中立者

形 He remained neutral during the debate.
他在辯論中保持中立。
名 Switzerland was a neutral in World War II.
瑞士在二次大戰時是中立國。

nominate [ˋnɑməˌnet] 動 提名；指定

You may nominate a representative to speak for you.
▶▶ 你可以派一位代表代替你發言。

nomination [ˌnɑməˋneʃən] 名 任命

His nomination as chief executive was approved by the board.
▶▶ 董事會批准了將他任命為行政總裁。

nominee [ˌnɑməˋni] 名 被提名的人

He's the party leader's nominee for the post.
▶▶ 他是黨魁提名的候選人。

norm [nɔrm] 名 行為準則；規範 關 normal 正常的

Every employee should follow the norms.
▶▶ 每位員工都應該遵守規範。

noticeable [ˋnotɪsəb!] 形 顯眼的 關 notice 注意

Her shining earrings are noticeable.
▶▶ 她閃亮的耳環很顯眼。

notify [ˋnotəˌfaɪ] 動 通知；報告 關 notification 通知

He notified us that he was going to leave.
▶▶ 他通知我們他將要離開。

notion [ˋnoʃən] 名 觀念；意見

I have to reject the notion that greed can be a good thing.
▶▶ 我必須反駁貪婪是件好事的這種想法。

Level 1 基礎單字
Level 2 必備單字
Level 3 中級單字
Level 4 進階單字
Level 5 高手單字
Level 6 滿級單字

nowhere [`no͵hwɛr] 副 無處；任何地方都不…；任何地方

I'm going nowhere after this bankruptcy.
▶▶ 破產後我已走投無路。

nutrient [`njutrɪənt] 名 營養物 形 滋養的

名 This soil contains valuable nutrients.
這種土壤含有寶貴的養分。
形 I rub nutrient cream on my face.
我在臉上擦滋養霜。

nutrition [nju`trɪʃən] 名 營養物；滋養

Good nutrition is essential for children's growth.
▶▶ 良好的營養對兒童成長至關重要。

nutritious [nju`trɪʃəs] 形 有養分的

Vegetables and fruits are nutritious.
▶▶ 蔬菜水果富含營養。

UNIT 14 O字頭高手單字

MP3 108

obligation [͵ɑblə`geʃən] 名 義務；責任 關 obligate 使負義務

You are under no obligation to buy anything.
▶▶ 你不必非買什麼東西不可。

obscure [əb`skjur] 形 陰暗的；模糊的；無名的 動 遮蔽；隱藏

形 Is the meaning still obscure to you?
你覺得意思仍然不清楚嗎？
動 His stammer obscured what he said.
口吃掩蓋了他所說的話。

observer [əb`zɝvɚ] 名 觀察者 關 observation 觀察

He was sent abroad as an observer.
▶▶ 他被派出國作觀察員。

odds [ɑdz] 名 可能性；機率

I wonder about the odds of winning the contest.
▶▶ 我想知道這次比賽的勝算。

offering [`ɔfərɪŋ] 名 禮物;供品;祭品 關 offer 提供

The offerings from the followers are considerable.
▶▶ 信眾的捐獻相當可觀。

olive [`alɪv] 名 橄欖樹;橄欖 形 橄欖的;橄欖色的

名 I love to eat olives after dinner.
晚飯後我喜歡吃橄欖。
形 He put some olive oil on his temples.
他在太陽穴抹上橄欖油。

operational [͵apə`reʃənḷ] 形 操作的

The new airport should be fully operational by the end of the year.
▶▶ 新機場應在年底前全面投入營運。

opponent [ə`ponənt] 名 對手

He overwhelmed his opponent with his superb technique.
▶▶ 他以高超的技術戰勝了對手。

opposition [͵apə`zɪʃən] 名 反對

Despite my opposition, she still left with him.
▶▶ 儘管我反對,她還是跟他走了。

optimism [`aptə͵mɪzəm] 名 樂觀主義 關 optimistic 樂觀的

He is a person of optimism.
▶▶ 他是個樂觀的人。

optional [`apʃənḷ] 形 可選的;非強制的

Some items are optional on the form.
▶▶ 表格上的某些項目非必填。

orchard [`ɔrtʃəd] 名 果園

Three thieves stole fruit from his orchard.
▶▶ 三個小偷從他的果園裡偷拿水果。

organism [`ɔrgən͵ɪzəm] 名 有機體;生物體 關 organ 器官 / decompose 腐爛

Organisms decompose after death.
▶▶ 有機體死後會腐爛。

1 Level 基礎單字
2 Level 必備單字
3 Level 中級單字
4 Level 進階單字
5 Level 高手單字
6 Level 滿級單字

originality [ə͵rɪdʒə`næləti] 名 獨創性；創造性 關 original 原創的

She has a striking originality in her design.
▶▶ 她的設計具出眾的獨創性。

outfit [`aut͵fɪt] 名 裝束 動 配備

名 The celebrity was wearing an expensive new outfit.
那位名人穿著一身昂貴的新衣裳。
動 Hank was outfitted with the latest equipment before mountain-climbing.
漢克在登山前準備了最新的裝備。

outlet [`autlɛt] 名 出口；發洩途徑

She needed to find an outlet for her many talents and interests.
▶▶ 她需要為自己的多才多藝和眾多興趣找到一個出口。

output [`autput] 名 輸出；產量 動 生產；輸出

名 The output of this machine are cans.
這台機器的產品是罐頭。
動 Input your order, and the computer will output the correct data automatically.
輸入你的命令，電腦將會自動輸出正確資料。

outsider [͵aut`saɪdə] 名 局外人；外來者

As an outsider, I do not comment on anything.
▶▶ 身為局外人，我不作任何評論。

overall [`ovə͵ɔl] 形 全部的 副 整體而言

形 Under certain conditions, guerrilla warfare helps secure an overall victory better than trench warfare does.
在特定狀況下，游擊戰比起陣地戰更能確保全局勝利
副 Overall, I think you should apologize to him.
整體來說，我覺得你該向他道歉。

overhead [`ovə͵hɛd] 形 頭頂上的；在空中的 副 在上方地；在頭頂上地

形 The overhead light was broken.
吸頂燈壞了。
副 A flock of wild geese flew overhead.
一群野雁從空中飛過。

overtake [͵ovə`tek] 動 大於；超過；趕上

A gigantic truck overtook us.
▶▶ 一輛巨型卡車超過了我們。

overturn [ˌovəˋtɝn] 動打翻;傾覆 名打翻;傾覆

動 The wave overturned the boat.
海浪傾覆了小船。

名 The glass was empty because of the accidental overturn.
玻璃杯因意外翻倒而變成空的。

overwhelm [ˌovəˋhwɛlm] 動壓倒;征服

The rebels were overwhelmed by the empire.
▶▶ 帝國已經制服了叛亂者。

 **UNIT 15 P 字頭焦點單字**

 MP3 109

parallel [ˋpærəˌlɛl] 形平行的 名平行線 動與⋯平行

形 The road and the canal are parallel to each other.
這條道路與運河平行。

名 Parallels do not cross, at least in plane geometry, or Euclidean geometry.
至少在平面幾何,或者說歐氏幾何中,平行線不會相交。

動 The street paralleled the railroad.
這條街道與鐵路平行。

participant [parˋtɪsəpənt] 名參與者 關 participate 參與

All the participants are elites of their school.
▶▶ 所有參與者都是他們學校的菁英。

particle [ˋpartɪkḷ] 名微粒;極小量

There is not a particle of truth in the statement.
▶▶ 這篇陳述沒有一句真話。

partly [ˋpartlɪ] 副部分地

I believe what he just said is partly true.
▶▶ 我相信他剛才說的話有一部分是真實的。

passionate [ˋpæʃənɪt] 形熱情的 關 passion 熱情

Diana is very passionate about singing.
▶▶ 黛安娜對唱歌極具熱情。

(焦點句型) be passionate about sth. 對⋯有熱情

pastry [`pestrɪ] 名糕點

My mother treated my friends with pastries.
▶▶ 我媽媽以糕點招待我朋友。

patch [pætʃ] 名補丁 動縫補；修補

名 I sewed patches on the knees of my jeans.
我在牛仔褲的膝部縫了幾個補丁。
動 He patched the hole with a new cloth.
他用一塊新布修補裂縫。

patent [`pætənt] 名專利權 形顯然的；專利的

名 The company had the patents of many new inventions.
這家公司擁有許多新發明的專利權。
形 You can take the patent medicine.
你可以使用這種專利藥物。

pathetic [pə`θɛtɪk] 形悲慘的

The girl whose mother passed away looked so pathetic.
▶▶ 那個母親去世的女孩看起來很可憐。

patrol [pə`trol] 名巡邏者 動巡邏

名 We chanced upon an enemy patrol.
我們碰巧遇上敵方的巡邏兵。
動 We've been patrolling for days but have seen nothing.
我們已巡邏了好幾天，但什麼也沒有發現。

patron [`petrən] 名贊助者；資助人

Mr. Belvedere is a strong patron of the arts.
▶▶ 貝維德爾先生是藝術的堅定支持者。

peasant [`pɛzn̩t] 名農夫

I prayed for the peasants, hoping they would have a plentiful harvest.
▶▶ 我為農民祈禱，希望他們豐收。

pedal [`pɛdl̩] 名踏板；踩踏板

The pedals of the bicycle are broken.
▶▶ 腳踏車的踏板壞了。

pedestrian [pəˋdɛstrɪən] 名行人 形單調的；行人的

名 The drivers have to give the right of way to pedestrians.
駕駛者應該讓行人先行。
形 Since retiring, Gordon's life has been pretty pedestrian.
自從退休後，高登的生活已變得很單調。

penetrate [ˋpɛnə͵tret] 動刺入

The crazy man penetrated her chest with a knife.
▶▶ 那個瘋狂的男人用刀刺進她胸膛。

pension [ˋpɛnʃən] 名退休金 動給退休金

名 The veteran got a considerable pension.
那名退伍老兵得到一筆可觀的退休金。
動 Corporations must pension their employees.
公司必須發放退休金給員工。

perceive [pəˋsiv] 動察覺

I perceived that she hadn't told the truth.
▶▶ 我察覺她並沒有說實話。

perception [pəˋsɛpʃən] 名見解；知覺；感知能力

What is your perception of the situation?
▶▶ 你對這個情況有什麼看法？

performer [pəˋfɔrmə] 名表演者；執行者

He was a poor performer at school and dropped out without a diploma.
▶▶ 他在學校成績很差，沒拿到文憑就輟學了。

persist [pəˋsɪst] 動堅持

In spite of the fact that Professor White's initial experiments had failed, he still persisted in his research.
▶▶ 儘管懷特教授的初次實驗失敗了，他仍然堅持他的研究。

personnel [͵pəsṇˋɛl] 名人員；人事部門

There was a lack of well-trained personnel in the company.
▶▶ 公司缺乏訓練良好的人員。

Level 1 基礎單字
Level 2 必備單字
Level 3 中級單字
Level 4 進階單字
Level 5 高手單字
Level 6 滿級單字

pessimism [`pɛsə͵mɪzəm] 名 悲觀；悲觀主義 關 pessimistic 悲觀的

A person of optimism is apt to succeed more than a person of pessimism.
>> 一個樂觀的人比悲觀的人更容易成功。

petty [`pɛtɪ] 形 瑣碎的；小的

Our difficulties seem petty when compared to those who never get enough to eat.
>> 跟那些吃都吃不飽的人相比，我們的困難看起來微不足道。

phase [fez] 名 階段 動 分段實行

名 It was just a confused, transitional phase anyway.
反正那只是一個迷茫的過渡階段。
動 They will begin to phase in the withdrawal in one month.
他們會在一個月內逐步撤軍。

photographic [͵fotə`græfɪk] 形 攝影的

The equipment of the photographic studio was expensive.
>> 這個攝影室的裝備花費龐大。

pier [pɪr] 名 碼頭

A woman stood still at the pier silently .
>> 有個女人在碼頭邊靜靜佇立。

pillar [`pɪlə] 名 樑柱

She felt dizzy, and leaned against the pillar.
>> 她感到頭暈便倚靠在柱子上。

pipeline [`paɪp͵laɪn] 名 管線

They have laid an underground pipeline.
>> 他們鋪設了一條地下管道。

pirate [`paɪrət] 名 海盜 動 盜印

名 The sailor suddenly saw a pirate jumping onto the deck.
那水手忽然看到一名海盜跳上了甲板。
動 There are individuals pirating our books recently.
近來有些個人非法複印我們的書籍。

pitcher [`pɪtʃɚ] 名投手

The senior pitcher injured his arm.
▶▶ 這名資深投手弄傷了手臂。

plea [pli] 名懇求；申訴

Her plea for help went unnoticed.
▶▶ 沒人注意到她的求救。

plead [plid] 動懇求

The little girl pleaded with the policeman for help.
▶▶ 這名小女孩向警察請求幫助。
(焦點句型) plead with sb. for sth. 向某人請求某事

pledge [plɛdʒ] 名誓言 動發誓

名 He gave me his pledge that he had tried his best.
　他向我發誓他已經盡力了。
動 I pledged to fulfill my dream.
　我立誓要實現夢想。

plunge [plʌndʒ] 名跳入 動驟然移動；暴跌

名 He took a plunge into the river.
　他躍入河中。
動 I encouraged my dog to plunge into the water.
　我揮手示意我的狗跳入水中。
(焦點句型) take the plunge 打定主意；決心行動

plural [`plʊrəl] 名複數 形複數的

名 The verb should be in the plural.
　這個動詞應該用複數形式。
形 Media is the plural form of medium.
　media 是 medium 的複數形。

poetic [po`ɛtɪk] 形詩意的

There is poetic quality in her performance.
▶▶ 她的表演富有詩意。

poke [pok] 動戳；插 名戳

動 He poked a toothpick into the cake.
　他在蛋糕上插了根牙籤。

Level 1 基礎單字
Level 2 必備單字
Level 3 中級單字
Level 4 進階單字
Level 5 高手單字
Level 6 滿級單字

(名) She gave her sister a poke on the temple.
她朝她妹妹的太陽穴戳了一下。

porch [portʃ] (名)玄關；門廊；走廊

He took off his shoes on the porch.
▶▶ 他在玄關脫掉鞋子。

precaution [prɪˋkɔʃən] (名)預防措施；警惕

We have taken every possible precaution against thieves.
▶▶ 我們已採取各種可能的防盜措施。
(焦點句型) precaution against sth. 針對⋯的預防措施

preference [ˋprɛfərəns] (名)偏好

She has a great preference for spicy food.
▶▶ 她很喜歡吃辣的食物。
(焦點句型) have a preference for sth. 喜歡⋯

prejudice [ˋprɛdʒədɪs] (名)偏見 (動)使存有偏見

(名) His prejudice against gays annoys me.
他對男同志的偏見惹惱了我。
(動) One unfortunate experience prejudiced him against all lawyers.
一次不幸的經驗讓他對所有律師產生偏見。
(焦點句型) prejudice against sb. 對⋯的偏見

preliminary [prɪˋlɪməˌnɛrɪ] (形)初步的 (名)初步行動

(形) We have included some of the preliminary findings.
我們的報告包括了一些初步的發現。
(名) He spent a long time on polite preliminaries.
他花了許多時間在剛開始的客套上。

premature [ˌprimǝˋtjur] (形)過早的；未熟的

The premature bananas taste terrible.
▶▶ 還沒成熟的香蕉嘗起來很糟糕。

premier [ˋprimɪǝ] (名)總理；首相 (形)首要的

(名) He was elected as the premier.
他被選為首相。
(形) Kaohsiung port is the premier port in Taiwan.
高雄港是台灣第一大港。

prescribe [prɪ`skraɪb] 動 開藥；規定

Can you prescribe something for my cough please, doctor?
▶▶ 醫生，請你給我開一些咳嗽藥，可以嗎？

prescription [prɪ`skrɪpʃən] 名 處方；藥方

With the doctor's prescription, I came to the pharmacy to get the medicine.
▶▶ 拿著醫生的處方，我到藥房取藥。

presidency [`prɛzədənsɪ] 名 總統職位

The two candidates competed for the presidency.
▶▶ 兩名候選人角逐總統職位。

presidential [`prɛzədɛnʃəl] 形 總統的

An American presidential campaign lasts for eighteen months.
▶▶ 美國總統競選歷時十八個月。

presume [prɪ`zum] 動 假設 關 presumably 可能

We presume the shipment has been stolen.
▶▶ 我們假設裝運的貨物已被竊。

prevail [prɪ`vel] 動 流行；戰勝

"Truth is mighty and will prevail" is an old maxim.
▶▶ 「真理強大，且必將獲勝」是一句古老的箴言。

prey [pre] 名 獵物 動 捕食

名 That miserable orphan once fell prey to domestic violence.
　　那可憐的孤兒曾深受家暴所折磨。
動 Snakes prey on mice.
　　蛇捕食老鼠。
(焦點句型) be/fall prey to sth. 成為⋯的犧牲品；深受⋯之害；被⋯欺騙

prior [`praɪɚ] 形 在前的；優先的

He had no prior knowledge of information technology before taking the course.
▶▶ 在上課之前，他對資訊科技不甚了解。
(焦點句型) prior to sth. 在⋯之前

Level 1 基礎單字
Level 2 必備單字
Level 3 中級單字
Level 4 進階單字
Level 5 高手單字
Level 6 滿級單字

productivity [ˌprodək`tɪvətɪ] 名生產力

A worker with higher productivity is worthy of a better salary.
▸▸ 生產力較高的工人應該值得更好的薪水。

profile [`profaɪl] 名簡介；個人資料；大眾關注 動描繪…輪廓；簡略描述

The agent is asked to keep a low profile.
▸▸ 特工被要求保持低調。

profound [prə`faʊnd] 形深奧的

I fathomed the profound meaning in his words.
▸▸ 我揣摩他話裡的深意。

progressive [prə`grɛsɪv] 形進步的 關 progress 進步

The approach taken by US courts has been more progressive than those of some other nations.
▸▸ 美國法庭的辦案方式比其他國家的先進。

prohibit [prə`hɪbɪt] 動禁止 關 prohibition 禁止

Eating is prohibited in the station.
▸▸ 車站內禁止進食。

projection [prə`dʒɛkʃən] 名推測；預估 關 project 方案

Sales have exceeded our projections.
▸▸ 銷量超過我們的預測。

prolong [prə`lɑŋ] 動延長

This medicine can prolong the lifespans of some cancer patients.
▸▸ 這種藥可以延長一些癌症患者的壽命。

prone [pron] 形易於

Wendy is prone to believing others.
▸▸ 溫蒂容易相信別人。

(焦點句型) be prone to N./Ving 容易受（負面事物）影響的；有（消極）傾向的

propaganda [ˌprɑpə`gændə] 名宣傳活動

Art may be used as a vehicle for propaganda.
▸▸ 藝術可用作宣傳工具。

prophet [`prɑfɪt] 名先知

He was so good at predicting stock performance that he was almost a stock market prophet.

▶ 他擅長預測股市行情，根本是股市先知。

proportion [prə`pɔrʃən] 名比例 動平均分配；調整比例 關 quota 配額

名 We must increase the proportion of consumption in gross domestic product.
我們必須提高國內生產總值中的消費比重。

動 He proportioned the total cost to every participant.
他把總開銷平均分攤給每位參與者。

prosecution [ˌprɑsə`kjuʃən] 名起訴；檢舉

They bribed the official into giving up the prosecution.

▶ 他們向官員行賄，要他放棄告發。

prospect [`prɑspɛkt] 名期望；前景 動勘察

名 The man said that his prospects were ruined by gambling.
這個男人說他的前途被賭博給毀了。

動 They are prospecting for coal in the area.
他們在這一區探勘煤礦。

province [`prɑvɪns] 名省

The government of China says Taiwan is one its provinces.

▶ 中國政府表示台灣是他們國家的一個省份。

provoke [prə`vok] 動激起

His glare provoked a severe fight.

▶ 他的瞪視引起一場激烈的打鬥。

pulse [pʌls] 名脈搏 動搏動

名 Fear sent her pulse racing.
恐懼使她的脈搏急速跳動。

動 A rush of joy pulsed through his body.
一陣喜悅的感覺振動他的全身。

purchase [`pɝtʃəs] 動購買 名購買

動 I went to the department store to purchase new clothes.
我到百貨公司買新衣服。

Level 1 基礎單字
Level 2 必備單字
Level 3 中級單字
Level 4 進階單字
Level 5 高手單字
Level 6 滿級單字

名 She spent all of her salary on the purchase of luxuries.
她因購買奢侈品而把薪水花光了。

pyramid [`pırəmɪd] 名金字塔；三角錐

The Pyramids of Egypt were among the Seven Wonders of the World.
▶▶ 埃及金字塔是世界七大奇觀之一。

MP3 110

qualify [`kwɑlə,faɪ] 動使合格

She is qualified to be a doctor.
▶▶ 她有醫師資格。

quest [kwɛst] 名探索；探求

Never stop the quest for knowledge.
▶▶ 永遠不要停止對知識的探求。

questionnaire [,kwɛstʃə`nɛr] 名問卷

I asked my friends to fill out the questionnaire.
▶▶ 我請朋友填寫這份問卷。

quiver [`kwɪvə] 名顫抖 動顫抖；抖動

名 Trissy's lips are quivering out of excitement.
特莉絲的嘴唇因激動而顫抖著。
動 The moth quivered its wings.
蛾抖動翅膀。

MP3 111

racism [`resɪzəm] 名種族主義 關 boycott 抵制；杯葛

The students held a one-week boycott of classes to oppose racism.
▶▶ 黑人學生罷課一週來抗議種族歧視。

rack [ræk] 名架子 動折磨

名 I looked all the racks of clothes in the back of the shop.
我看了商店後面所有架子的衣服。

動 He was racked by jealousy.
他因嫉妒而飽受折磨。

radiation [ˌredɪˋeʃən] 名放射；發光 同 emission 關 apparatus 儀器；設備

This apparatus produces harmful radiation.
▶▶ 這儀器散發有害的輻射物。

radical [ˋrædɪkl̩] 形激進的；根本的 名激進分子

形 His shortsighted proposal does not take radical problems into consideration.
他短視近利的提案，沒有把根本的問題納入考量。
名 Don't listen to that guy; he's a radical.
別聽這傢伙的話，他是個激進分子。

ragged [ˋrægɪd] 形破爛的

He looks dirty in those ragged clothes.
▶▶ 他穿著那些破爛的衣服，看起來很骯髒。

raid [red] 名突擊 動襲擊

名 The correspondence stopped after the enemy's air raid.
敵人空襲後通信中斷了。
動 Our troops raided the enemy beyond their expectation.
我們的軍隊出乎其所料地襲擊了敵人。

rail [rel] 名鐵路交通；鐵軌；欄杆

He leaned against the rail to overlook the valley.
▶▶ 他倚著欄杆俯瞰山谷。

rally [ˋrælɪ] 名集會；大會 動集合

名 Thousands of people held a rally against abolition of the capital punishment.
數千人舉行了反對廢除死刑的集會。
動 The officer rallied his men.
軍官把士兵集合起來。

ranch [ræntʃ] 名大農場 動經營農場

名 Life on a ranch has always centered on the cowboys.
牧場的生活總是以牛仔為中心。
動 The man of wealth ranched in the countryside.
這名有錢人在郊區經營農場。

Level 1 基礎單字
Level 2 必備單字
Level 3 中級單字
Level 4 進階單字
Level 5 高手單字
Level 6 滿級單字

random [`rændəm] 形 隨機的

I chose a random student to answer the question.
▶▶ 我抽一個學生回答問題。

ratio [`reʃio] 名 比率；比例

The ratio of females in Congress is growing.
▶▶ 國會中的女性比例正在提升。

rational [`ræʃənḷ] 形 理性的

Man is a rational animal.
▶▶ 人是有理性的動物。

rattle [`rætḷ] 名 嘎嘎聲；波浪鼓 動 煩擾；發出嘎嘎聲

名 The infant played with a rattle.
　　那嬰兒在玩波浪鼓。
動 The ox cart rattled along the road.
　　這輛牛車嘎嘎地駛過道路。

realism [`rɪəl͵ɪzəm] 名 現實性；現實主義 關 realistic 現實的 / reality 現實

The realism of the artificial fruit on the coffee table was incredible.
▶▶ 咖啡桌上的假水果栩栩如生

realm [rɛlm] 名 領域；範圍；王國

After the continual invasion from enemies, the king expanded his realm.
▶▶ 在外敵不斷入侵後，國王擴張了王國領土。

rear [rɪr] 形 後面的 名 後面

形 I guess the rear tire is punctured.
　　我猜後輪被戳破了。
名 He sat in the rear of the classroom.
　　他坐在教室後面。

rebellion [rɪ`bɛljən] 名 叛亂 同 uprising

When a lot of people rebel, there is a rebellion.
▶▶ 當許多人造反時，就有了叛亂。

recession [rɪ`sɛʃən] 名 衰退

The economy is in deep recession.
▶▶ 經濟正處於嚴重的衰退之中。

recipient [rɪˋsɪpɪənt] 名接受者 形接受的

名 She is one of the recipients of the prizes.
她是獲獎者之一。

形 All of the recipient customers felt lucky to receive the prizes.
所有獲獎的顧客都對得獎感到幸運。

recite [rɪˋsaɪt] 動背誦

The girl recited three poems to her mother after dinner.
▶▶ 這名小女孩晚餐後背了三首詩給她媽媽聽。

recommend [ˌrɛkəˋmɛnd] 動推薦

The movie was recommended by all of my friends.
▶▶ 我的朋友一致推薦這部電影。

recommendation [ˌrɛkəmɛnˋdeʃən] 名推薦

The committee made recommendations to the board on teachers' pay and working conditions.
▶▶ 委員會就教師的工資和工作條件問題向董事會提出建議。

（焦點句型）make recommendation 建議

recruit [rɪˋkrut] 動徵募 名新兵

動 The enterprise is recruiting three engineers.
這家企業正在招募三名工程師。

名 New recruits are trained at the boot camp.
新兵在新兵訓練營接受訓練。

refuge [ˋrɛfjudʒ] 名避難（所）；庇護（所）

They rushed into the refuge upon hearing the explosions.
▶▶ 聽到爆炸聲時，他們迅速趕入避難所。

regardless [rɪˋgardləs] 副無論如何；不管

She went out alone regardless of danger.
▶▶ 她不顧危險地單獨出門。

（焦點句型）regardless of sth. 儘管…

Level 1 基礎單字
Level 2 必備單字
Level 3 中級單字
Level 4 進階單字
Level 5 高手單字
Level 6 滿級單字

regime [re`ʒim] 名政權

Things will change under the new regime.
>> 在新政權下，事情將會發生變化。

rehearsal [rɪ`hɜsl̩] 名排演

The orchestra did a rehearsal before putting on a performance.
>> 這個交響樂團在演出之前進行彩排。

reinforce [ˌriɪn`fɔrs] 動加固；強化

Our defences must be reinforced against attack.
>> 我們必須加強防禦設施以抵禦進攻。

reminder [rɪ`maɪndə] 名提醒（物） 關 remind 提醒

He put a note on his desk as reminder of the meeting.
>> 他在桌上放了筆記，作為開會的提醒。

removal [rɪ`muvl̩] 名移除 關 remove 移除

Clearance of the site required the removal of a number of trees.
>> 清理此地需要移走不少樹。

render [`rɛndə] 動給予；提供；翻譯

The young boy rendered his seat to the old man.
>> 這個年輕男孩把位子讓給老人。

rental [`rɛntl̩] 名租金 關 rent 出租

He makes his living through the rental of cars.
>> 他以出租汽車維生。

repay [rɪ`pe] 動償還；報答

I forgot to repay her the money that I borrowed from her last week.
>> 我忘了還我上週跟她借的錢。

republican [rɪ`pʌblɪkən] 名共和主義者 形共和主義的 關 republic 共和國

名 Republicans opposed the monarchy's power.
　　共和黨人反對君權。
形 He is a member of the Republican Party.
　　他是共和黨黨員。

resemblance [rɪ`zɛmbləns] 名類似

Jimmy bears a strong resemblance to his father.
▶▶ 吉米長得很像他爸爸。

reservoir [`rɛzə͵vwɑr] 名蓄水池；儲備

This reservoir is used to store water for our town.
▶▶ 這個水庫是用來為我們小鎮儲水的。

residence [`rɛzədəns] 名住家

Susan wants to insure her residence.
▶▶ 蘇珊想為自己的住宅保險。

resident [`rɛzədənt] 名居民 形居留的

名 Kelly is not a resident here. She is just a tourist.
　凱莉不是這裡的居民，她只是個旅客。
形 Resident students need to pay for their own utilities.
　寄宿學生需要向學校繳交水電費。

residential [͵rɛzə`dɛnʃəl] 形居住的

Gradually the surrounding farmland turned residential.
▶▶ 周圍的農田漸漸變成了住宅區。

resort [rɪ`zɔrt] 名休閒勝地 動求助；訴諸

名 Brighton is a leading south coast resort.
　布萊頓是南部地區最著名的海濱勝地。
動 Beaten by her husband, she resorted to violence herself.
　遭到丈夫毆打，她選擇訴諸暴力。

resume [͵rɛzə`me ] / [ rɪ`zjum] 名履歷表 動重新開始；繼續

名 The strong resume impressed the interviewer.
　這份強而有力的履歷讓面試官印象深刻。
動 He resumed his work after a nap.
　他小睡過後繼續工作。

retail [`ritel] 名零售 動零售 形零售的 副以零售的方式

名 They planned to open a retail store.
　他們計劃開一間零售店。
動 He retailed umbrellas to earn a living in his youth.
　他年輕時零售雨傘維生。

1 Level 基礎單字
2 Level 必備單字
3 Level 中級單字
4 Level 進階單字
5 Level 高手單字
6 Level 滿級單字

形 The retail price of the candies is cheap.
這種糖果的零售價很便宜。

revenue [`rɛvə,nju] 名收入

Tax revenues increased last year.
▶▶ 去年的稅收增加了。

reverse [rɪ`vɜs] 動反轉 名相反的情況；背面 形相反的

動 He reversed the paper to see what was written on the other side.
他把紙翻過來看上面寫了什麼。
名 Tom said he is smarter than his brother, but the reverse is true.
湯姆說他比他哥哥聰明，但事實正好相反。

rhetoric [`rɛtərɪk] 名修辭；修辭學

It really does not matter if he is a little confused about points of rhetoric and grammar.
▶▶ 如果他對於修辭或文法的問題有點困惑也沒關係。

rib [rɪb] 名肋骨

He broke a rib in the accident.
▶▶ 他在意外中斷了一根肋骨。

ridge [rɪdʒ] 名山脊

They were inching their way along the slippery ridge.
▶▶ 他們沿著易滑的山脊慢慢前進。

ridiculous [rɪ`dɪkjələs] 形荒謬的

His excuse is ridiculous.
▶▶ 他的藉口相當荒謬。

rifle [`raɪfl̩] 名來福槍；步槍 動迅速翻查；洗劫

名 His rifle has jammed.
他的來福槍卡住了。
動 The thief rifled everything in the apartment.
竊賊將公寓內洗劫一空。

rigid [`rɪdʒɪd] 形嚴格的

He is a rigid military disciplinarian.
▶▶ 他是個嚴格執行軍紀的領導。

rim [rɪm] 名 邊緣 動 加邊於

名 An ant is crawling on the rim of his glass.
一隻螞蟻在他的杯緣爬行。
動 Trees rimmed the square.
樹環繞在廣場四周。

riot [`raɪət] 名 暴動 動 騷動

名 In May 1968, there was a massive wave of student riots.
一九六八年的五月曾發生過大規模的學生暴動。
動 The workers were rioting due to unemployment.
工人因失業而暴動。

rip [rɪp] 名 裂口 動 扯裂

名 I noticed the rip on her sleeve.
我注意到她袖子上的裂口。
動 He ripped the envelope at the sight of the sender.
他一看到寄件人就將信封撕掉。

ritual [`rɪtʃʊəl] 名 儀式 形 儀式的 關 denomination （宗教）分支；派別

名 Some of the differences between Protestant denominations have to do with ritual.
新教各教派之間的一些差異與宗教儀式有關。
形 Some of those ritual dances look scary.
那些儀式性舞蹈中，有些看起來很可怕。

rival [`raɪvl] 名 對手 動 競爭

名 He viewed Edison as his rival.
他將艾迪森視為他的對手。
動 They rival in courting the girl.
他們競爭追求那個女生。

rod [rɑd] 名 竿；棒；教鞭

In the past, some teachers hit students with rods.
▶▶ 過去有些老師用教鞭打小孩。

Level 1 基礎單字
Level 2 必備單字
Level 3 中級單字
Level 4 進階單字
Level 5 高手單字
Level 6 滿級單字

MEMORIZE 7000 VOCABULARIES ONCE AND FOR ALL !

sacred [`sekrɪd] 形 神聖的 關 decease 去世

She considered it a sacred duty to fulfill her deceased father's wishes.
▶▶ 她認為完成已故父親的遺願，是她神聖的職責。

saddle [`sædl] 名 鞍 動 套以馬鞍

名 Three weeks after the accident, he was back in the saddle again.
出事的三個星期後，他又重新掌權了。

動 He caught the horse and saddled it up.
他牽住馬並套上馬鞍。

焦點句型 in the saddle 騎馬；掌權

saint [sent] 名 聖人；聖徒

The children were all named after saints.
▶▶ 這些孩子都以聖人的名字命名。

salmon [`sæmən] 名 鮭魚 形 鮭肉色的；淺粉橙色的

名 The salmon sold here is fresh.
這裡賣的鮭魚很新鮮。

形 I love the salmon pink dress.
我喜歡這件粉橙色的洋裝。

sandal [`sændl] 名 涼鞋

It is improper to enter a library with sandals.
▶▶ 穿涼鞋進圖書館是不合宜的。

scan [skæn] 動 掃描；瀏覽 名 掃描；瀏覽

動 I scanned the list quickly to find my name.
我很快瀏覽了一下名單，看有沒有我的名字。

名 The scan showed there was a tumor in one of his lungs.
掃描結果顯示他的肺裡有顆腫瘤。

scandal [`skændl] 名 醜聞；恥辱

The star was involved in a scandal that hurt her reputation.
▶▶ 這位明星捲入一樁有害名譽的醜聞。

基礎單字 Level 1
必備單字 Level 2
中級單字 Level 3
進階單字 Level 4
高手單字 Level 5
滿級單字 Level 6

scar [skɑr] 名傷痕 動使留下疤痕

名 His years in prison have left deep scars on him.
他在獄中的歲月讓他留下很深的創傷。

動 Cindy was scarred in the car accident.
辛蒂在那場車禍中留下了疤痕。

焦點句型 leave a scar 留下傷痕

scent [sɛnt] 名氣味；痕跡 動聞；嗅 關waft （在空氣中）飄蕩

名 The scent of lemon wafted up from the garden below.
從下面的花園裡飄來一陣檸檬香。

動 The dog is scenting the trash can.
狗正在聞垃圾桶。

scheme [skim] 名計畫；陰謀 動計劃；密謀

名 Only successful schools will be given extra funding under the new scheme.
在新體制下，辦得好的學校才可獲得額外經費。

動 They are scheming out a substitute method.
他們正在計劃一個替代方法。

scope [skop] 名範圍；領域

What you asked is not included in the agreed scope of discussion.
▶▶ 你剛才問的不在我們討論範圍之內。

scramble [`skræmbl̩] 動攀爬；爭奪 名攀爬；爭奪

動 I scrambled up the enclosure.
我攀爬圍牆。

名 The scramble between them was fierce.
他們之間的爭奪相當激烈。

scrap [skræp] 名碎片；少許 動丟棄

名 I tore a scrap of paper and used it as notepaper.
我撕下一小張紙作為便條。

動 Jenny scrapped the ragged doll.
珍妮丟掉那個破舊的娃娃。

script [skrɪpt] 名劇本；原稿 動為…寫稿

名 The script plays an important role in the success of a movie.
劇本是一部電影成功的重要因素。

動 She scripted the novel for a movie.
她把這本小說改編為電影劇本。

sector [`sɛktɚ] 名部分

Owing to the conservation of the forest, tourists are forbidden to go into this sector.
▶▶ 由於森林保育，旅客禁止進入這個地段。

segment [`sɛgmənt] 名部分；片段 動分割；劃分

名 This product is designed for some specific market segments.
這一個產品是專特為某一特定的市場部分設計。
動 In that country, universities are segmented into three kinds.
在那個國家，大學劃分成三種。

seminar [`sɛmənɑr] 名研討會

They discussed globalization in the seminar.
▶▶ 他們在研討會裡討論全球化的問題。

senator [`sɛnətɚ] 名參議員；上議員

Senators are not elected but nominated in Canada.
▶▶ 加拿大的參議員不是民選，而是任命的。

sensation [sɛn`seʃən] 名感覺；知覺

The patient has very little sensation left in the right leg.
▶▶ 病人的右腿幾乎沒有知覺。

sensitivity [,sɛnsə`tɪvətɪ] 名敏感度；靈敏度 關 sensor 感應器

Michelle has great sensitivity to others' feelings.
▶▶ 蜜雪兒對他人的感受非常敏感。

sentiment [`sɛntəmənt] 名情緒；感傷

I don't like this novel. There's too much sentiment in it.
▶▶ 我不喜歡這本小說，它太傷感了。

sentimental [,sɛntə`mɛntl̩] 形多愁善感的

Hank is so sentimental that he is always moved to tears on hearing love songs.
▶▶ 漢克非常多愁善感，一聽到情歌就會感動得掉淚。

sequence [`sikwəns] 名順序；連續

He described the sequence of events leading up to the robbery.
▶▶ 他描述了搶劫案發生前的一連串相關事件。

series [`sɪrɪz] 名連續 形 serial 連續的

A series of robberies were finally taken seriously by the police.
▶▶ 一連串的搶劫案終於引起警方的注意。

server [`sɝvɚ] 名伺服器；上菜用具；侍者

The server of the social media crashed, which caused millions of users to complain.
▶▶ 社群媒體的伺服器崩潰了，讓數以百萬計的用戶抱怨連連。

session [`sɛʃən] 名會議；（活動的）一段時間；一場；學期

Following this session, we shall formulate a series of laws.
▶▶ 這次會議以後，要接著制定一系列的法律。

setting [`sɛtɪŋ] 名位置；情節背景；布景

What did you think of the stage setting?
▶▶ 你覺得舞臺布景怎麼樣？

shatter [`ʃætɚ] 動粉碎；砸破

The glass was shattered to pieces.
▶▶ 玻璃被砸得粉碎。

shed [ʃɛd] 動流出

She shed crocodile tears over his failure.
▶▶ 她對他的失敗流下了虛偽的淚水。
文法解析 shed 動詞三態同形，皆為 shed。

sheer [ʃɪr] 形完全的；徹底的 動急轉向

形 Our army was beaten by sheer weight of numbers.
我軍是因敵軍徹底的人數優勢而戰敗。
動 He sheered away to avoid the cat.
他急速轉彎以免撞上那隻貓。

sheriff [`ʃɛrɪf] 名警長

The sheriff ordered the suspicious-looking stranger to hit the road.
▶▶ 警察局長命令模樣可疑的陌生人立刻上路。

Level 1 基礎單字
Level 2 必備單字
Level 3 中級單字
Level 4 進階單字
Level 5 高手單字
Level 6 滿級單字

shield [ʃild] 名盾 動遮蔽；保護

名 Police officers hold shields when dealing with riots.
警察拿著盾牌站在示威者面前。

動 The sunglasses shield your eyes from the sun.
太陽眼鏡可以遮住太陽光以保護眼睛。

shiver [ˋʃɪvɚ] 名顫抖 動顫抖

名 I gave a shiver when I thought of him.
我一想到他就發抖。

動 He shivered in the cold wind.
他在冷風中直打哆嗦。

(焦點句型) give a shiver 發抖

shortage [ˋʃɔrtɪdʒ] 名不足；短缺

There is an obvious shortage of money for our daughter's education.
▶▶ 顯然我們缺乏女兒的教育經費。

shove [ʃʌv] 動推；推擠 名推；推擠

動 I don't like having the sorrowful state of the world shoved at me in every news broadcast.
我不喜歡每條新聞廣播都將這個世界的悲慘局面推到我面前。

名 The rude person gave me a shove, and I fell down.
那個粗魯的人推我一把，讓我跌倒了。

(焦點句型) give sb. a shove 推某人

shrug [ʃrʌg] 動聳肩

He shrugged, indicating he didn't know.
▶▶ 他聳聳肩，表示自己不知道。

shuttle [ˋʃʌtl̩] 名穿梭的車輛；接駁車；梭子 動往返

名 There are free shuttle buses available now due to the partial closure of the MRT.
由於捷運部分停擺，現在有免費的接駁公車服務。

動 He shuttled from Taipei to Kaohsiung every day.
他每天往返台北與高雄。

siege [sidʒ] 名包圍；圍攻

The castle is provisioned for a siege.
▶▶ 城堡已為圍攻做好準備。

skeleton [`skɛlətn̩] 名骨骼；骨架；概要

I've written the skeleton of my report, but I have to fill in the details.
▶ 我已經寫好報告的概要，不過我還要把細節補足。

skull [skʌl] 名頭骨

The anthropologists discovered a skull in the valley.
▶ 人類學家在山谷裡發現一塊頭骨。

slam [slæm] 動砰地關上；重重撞上 名突然發出的巨大聲響

動 The angry girl slammed the door.
這個氣憤的女孩砰然一聲把門關上。
名 A wind blew the door closed with a slam.
一陣風把門吹得砰然關上。

slap [slæp] 名掌擊 動掌擊

名 The angry father gave his daughter a slap in the face.
這個憤怒的父親給了女兒一個耳光。
動 She slapped his face hard.
她狠狠打了他一個耳光。

焦點句型 a slap in the face 一記耳光；侮辱；打擊

slavery [`slevərɪ] 名奴隸制度；蓄奴；奴隸身分

At one time, slavery was common in the United States.
▶ 奴隸制度曾在美國盛行一時。

slot [slɑt] 名狹縫；凹槽

Insert the card to the slot.
▶ 把卡插入插槽。

smash [smæʃ] 名粉碎；碰撞 動粉碎；碰撞

名 The teapot fell from the table with a smash.
茶壺從桌上掉下來摔個粉碎。
動 The plate dropped on the floor and smashed into pieces.
盤子掉在地板上，摔成了碎片。

smog [smɑg] 名霧霾；煙霧

The smog in some cities is terrible.
▶ 有些城市的霾害問題十分嚴重。

Level 1 基礎單字
Level 2 必備單字
Level 3 中級單字
Level 4 進階單字
Level 5 高手單字
Level 6 滿級單字

snatch [snætʃ] 動奪取；抓住 名奪取

動 He snatched the book from my hands.
他從我的手裡把書搶走。
名 The thief made a snatch at the woman's purse.
小偷搶奪那婦女的錢包。

焦點句型 make a snatch at sth. 奪取某物

sneak [snik] 動潛行；偷偷地走

He sneaked in and stole a sausage.
▶▶ 他潛進去偷了一根香腸。

sniff [snɪf] 名聞；嗅 動聞；吸氣

名 She took a sniff at the unknown liquid.
她聞了一下這不知名的液體。
動 She was sniffing and wiping her tears with a tissue.
她邊抽泣邊用面紙擦眼淚。

焦點句型 take a sniff at sth. 聞某物

soak [sok] 名浸泡 動浸泡

名 Only a soak of bleach can remove the stain.
只要浸泡一下漂白劑就可以去除髒污。
動 Wet the cloth by soaking it in the bucket.
把布浸到水桶裡弄濕。

soar [sor] 動驟升；翱翔；高達

Apartment rents soared, and many tenants had to relocate.
▶▶ 公寓的房租飛漲，許多房客不得不搬到別處去。

sob [sɑb] 動嗚咽；啜泣 名啜泣

動 I saw my mother sobbing in her room.
我看到媽媽在房裡啜泣。
名 She broke into uncontrolled sobs.
她一下子失控地啜泣起來。

sober [`sobɚ] 形清醒的；沒喝醉的 動使清醒

形 I promised him that I'd stay sober tonight.
我答應過他，今晚我不會喝醉。
動 She sobered him up by splashing water on his face.
她朝他臉上潑水讓他清醒。

焦點句型 sober sb. up 使某人清醒

soften [`sɑfən] 動 使柔軟

The rain softened the earth.
▶▶ 雨水使土壤變鬆軟。

sole [sol] 形 唯一的

Maggie is the sole female in our company.
▶▶ 瑪姬是公司裡唯一的女性。

solo [`solo] 名 獨唱；獨奏 形 單獨的

Love is a chord in life, not a solo.
▶▶ 愛是人生的和絃，而不是獨奏曲。

sophisticated [sə`fɪstə‚ketɪd] 形 精於世故的；見多識廣的

She is very sophisticated with plenty of working experiences.
▶▶ 工作經驗豐富的她非常懂得人情世故。

sophomore [`sɑfə‚mor] 名 （大學的）二年級學生

I am a sophomore at First University.
▶▶ 我是第一大學的二年級學生。

souvenir [‚suvə`nɪr] 名 紀念品；特產

Remember to bring us souvenirs from Japan!
▶▶ 記得帶日本的特產回來給我們！

sovereignty [`sɑvrəntɪ] 名 主權

The sovereignty of the island is under negotiation.
▶▶ 這座小島的主權正在協商之中。

sow [so] 動 播種

The girl sowed the seeds then sprinkled water on them.
▶▶ 小女孩播下種子，然後在上面澆水。

spacious [`speʃəs] 形 寬敞的；寬廣的

The house has spacious grounds.
▶▶ 這棟房子有寬敞的庭院。

1 Level 基礎單字

2 Level 必備單字

3 Level 中級單字

4 Level 進階單字

5 Level 高手單字

6 Level 滿級單字

sparkle [`spɑrkl̩] 名閃耀；閃爍 動閃爍；使閃耀

名 We lay on the ground, seeing the sparkle of the stars.
我們躺在地上，望著星星閃耀。

動 Drops of water sparkled under the sun.
水滴在陽光下閃閃發光。

specialist [`spɛʃəlɪst] 名專家

They consulted the specialists about climate change.
▶▶ 他們詢問專家關於氣候變遷的問題。

specialize [`spɛʃəl‚aɪz] 動專長於

Edward specializes in computer engineering.
▶▶ 愛德華專精電腦工程。

(焦點句型) specialize in sth. 專精於⋯

specialty [`spɛʃəltɪ] 名專業

Mathematics is her specialty.
▶▶ 數學是她的專業。

specify [`spɛsə‚faɪ] 動明確說明

The doctor specified that the patient should reduce the amount of sugar he ate.
▶▶ 醫生向病人明確說明，他該減少糖份的攝取。

specimen [`spɛsəmən] 名樣本；樣品

He has collected more than five hundred kinds of insect specimens.
▶▶ 他已經蒐集超過五百種昆蟲標本。

spectacular [spɛk`tækjələ] 形壯觀的；壯麗的 名壯觀場面；盛大演出

形 They are going to hold a spectacular fashion show.
他們準備舉辦一次壯觀的時裝秀。

名 Everyone is amazed by the spectacular.
每個人都因這奇觀而吃驚。

spectator [spɛk`tetə] 名旁觀者

The spectators ignored the robbed woman and just passed by hastily.
▶▶ 旁觀者無視遭搶的婦人，只是匆匆經過。

spectrum [`spεktrəm] 名光譜

We owe the discovery of prismatic spectrum to Isaac Newton.
▶▶ 稜鏡光譜的發現得歸功於艾薩克‧牛頓。

sphere [sfɪr] 名球；天體

Our Earth is a sphere.
▶▶ 我們的地球是一個球體。

spicy [`spaɪsɪ] 形辛辣的；加香料的

I dare not eat spicy food.
▶▶ 我不敢吃辣。

spine [spaɪn] 名脊椎

My spine has curved slightly.
▶▶ 我的脊椎有輕微彎曲。

sponge [spʌndʒ] 名海綿 動用海綿吸收

名 A sponge can absorb water.
海綿可以吸水。
動 Tina sponged the spilt milk.
提娜用海棉吸乾濺出的牛奶。

sponsor [`spɑnsɚ] 名贊助者 動贊助 關 sponsorship 資助

名 The sponsors of a television program pay the costs of making the program.
電視節目贊助人出資承擔編製節目的費用。
動 The firm is sponsoring an engineering student for the training.
這家公司正資助一名工科學生參加培訓。

spouse [spauz] 名配偶；夫妻

His spouse deserved the compensation after he died.
▶▶ 他死後，他的配偶應該得到賠償金。

squad [skwɑd] 名小隊；班

The besieged squad battled on.
▶▶ 被圍困的小隊繼續進行戰鬥。

squash [skwɑʃ] 動壓扁 名擠壓

動 The fruit at the bottom of the box had been squashed.
箱底的水果已經被壓爛了。

Level 1 基礎單字
Level 2 必備單字
Level 3 中級單字
Level 4 進階單字
Level 5 高手單字
Level 6 滿級單字

squat [skwɑt] 動 蹲 名 蹲；深蹲 形 低矮的；矮胖的

動 She squatted to see the ladybug on the leaf.
她蹲下來看樹葉上的瓢蟲。

名 With no chairs available, they sat in a squat.
沒椅子可坐了，他們就蹲下來。

stability [stə`bɪlətɪ] 名 穩定；穩固

Political stability is essential to economic prosperity.
▶▶ 經濟想要繁榮，政治必須穩定。

stack [stæk] 名 一堆 動 堆疊

名 There's a stack of unopened mail waiting for you at home.
家裡有一大堆信等著你拆。

動 I stacked the old books in the corner of my room.
我把舊書堆在房間的角落。

stain [sten] 動 弄髒 名 汙點

動 My white shirt was stained by ketchup.
我的白襯衫被番茄醬弄髒了。

名 Use a stain remover to clean the clothing.
用去污劑來清潔衣服。

stake [stek] 名 股本；股份；樁 動 把…綁在樁上

Wayne holds a ten percent stake of the company.
▶▶ 韋恩持有公司百分之十的股份。

stall [stɔl] 名 攤位；貨攤

The objects displayed at the stall are all handmade.
▶▶ 這些攤位展覽的物品都是手工製成的。

startle [`stɑrtl̩] 動 使驚嚇

Rita was startled by the sudden blackout.
▶▶ 瑞塔被突然的停電嚇到。

statistical [stə`tɪstɪkl̩] 形 統計的；統計學的

The statistical techniques are useful in analyzing data.
▶▶ 統計方法在分析資料時很實用。

steer [stɪr] 動 駕駛；掌舵 名 建議

動 He steered the ship carefully between the rocks.
他小心地在礁石間駕駛船。

名 Maybe a professional can give you a steer in the right direction.
也許專業人士可以在正確的方向上給你建議。

(焦點句型) give (sb.) a steer 給予…建議

stereotype [`stɛrɪə,taɪp] 名 刻板印象 動 對…有成見

名 Stereotypes result in prejudice.
刻板印象造成偏見。

動 The manager is accused of stereotyping sexual minorities.
經理被指控為對性少數族群抱有成見。

stew [stju] 名 燉菜 動 燉；燜

名 The stews my mother made were wonderful.
我媽媽煮的燉菜非常棒。

動 She stewed the soup for lunch.
她燉湯當午餐。

stimulate [`stɪmjə,let] 動 刺激

It can stimulate appetite.
▶ 它能刺激食欲。

stimulus [`stɪmjələs] 名 刺激；刺激物

Her praise is his best stimulus.
▶ 她的讚美是他最好的激勵。

stink [stɪŋk] 動 散發異味；發臭 名 惡臭

動 The waste from the factory stinks up the small town.
工廠的廢棄物使這個小鎮臭氣沖天。

名 The stink from the trash can is disgusting.
垃圾桶傳來的惡臭令人作嘔。

(文法解析) stink 動詞三態變化為 stink / stunk / stunk。

stock [stɑk] 名 庫存；股票 關 shareholder 股東

The book is not in stock now.
▶ 這本書已經沒有庫存了。

(焦點句型) be in stock 有庫存

storage [`storɪdʒ] 名 儲存；倉庫

The area is being used as a storage for weapons.
▶▶ 那地區正被用作武器儲藏地。

straighten [`stretn] 動 弄直；整頓

She tugged the corner of the rug to straighten it.
▶▶ 她拉了小地毯的一角，把它擺正。

straightforward [`stret.forwəd] 形 直接的；正直的

Give me a straightforward response.
▶▶ 給我一個直接的回應。

strain [stren] 名 張力；緊張 動 拉緊；盡全力

名 The rope broke under the strain.
繩子耐不住張力而斷裂。

動 They strained the rope to pull the boat in.
他們拉緊繩子使船靠岸。

(焦點句型) under the strain 在壓力下

strand [strænd] 名（線、繩的）一縷；濱；岸 動 擱淺；處於困境

名 The children are playing on the strand.
孩子在海灘上玩耍。

動 When the blizzard forced closure of the airport, stranded travelers were put up in local schools.
機場因暴風雪而停擺時，受困的旅客在當地學校過夜。

strap [stræp] 名 皮帶；帶子 動 約束；用帶子綑

名 A strap is fastened under the chin to keep the helmet in place.
頭盔帶子被繫在下巴上以固定頭盔。

動 She strapped the two packages together.
她把兩個包裹綁在一起。

strategic [strə`tidʒɪk] 形 戰略的

We made a strategic withdrawal, so that we could build up our forces for a renewed attack.
▶▶ 我們實施了戰略性撤退，以便集結兵力再次進攻。

structural [`strʌktʃərəl] 形 構造上的；結構上的

Storms have caused structural damage to hundreds of houses.
▶▶ 幾場暴風雨造成了成千上百所住宅結構的損壞。

stumble [`stʌmbl̩] 動 跌倒 名 絆倒

動 I stumbled over a tree root.
我被樹根絆了一跤。
名 Jessie was injured by a stumble.
潔西因絆倒而受傷。

sturdy [`stɜdɪ] 形 強健的；穩固的

The child has sturdy legs.
▶▶ 這個孩子有健壯的雙腿。

submit [səb`mɪt] 動 提交；屈服；服從

I hope you can submit your term paper before the deadline.
▶▶ 我希望你們能在限期之前繳交學期報告。

subsequent [`sʌbsɪˏkwɛnt] 形 隨後發生的

They made plans for a visit, but subsequent difficulties with the car prevented it.
▶▶ 他們原計劃去遊覽，但後來車子出問題，只好作罷。

substantial [səb`stænʃəl] 形 實際的；重大的 關 substance 物質

The growing unemployment rate is a substantial problem.
▶▶ 失業率攀升是個重大的問題。

substitute [`sʌbstəˏtjut] 動 代替 名 代替者

動 Mary substituted for Joy in the game.
瑪莉代替喬伊玩遊戲。
名 Beach volleyball does not allow substitutes.
沙灘排球不允許替補。

subtle [`sʌtl̩] 形 微妙的

The message of this novel is so subtle that most readers cannot understand.
▶▶ 這本小說的內涵非常隱晦，大部分讀者都難以理解。

Level 1 基礎單字
Level 2 必備單字
Level 3 中級單字
Level 4 進階單字
Level 5 高手單字
Level 6 滿級單字

suburban [sə`bɜbən] 形 郊外的

Since housing prices downtown are so expensive, Mark could only afford to be a suburban resident.
▶▶ 因為市中心的房價太貴，所以馬克只能住在郊區。

successor [sək`sɛsə] 名 繼承人；繼承者

This car is the successor to the popular Ford Mondeo.
▶▶ 這款車是很受歡迎的福特蒙地歐小轎車的下一代產品。

suite [swit] 名 套房

The university student rents a suite near her school.
▶▶ 這名大學生在學校附近租了一間套房。

superb [su`pɜb] 形 極好的；超群的

The actor gave a superb performance.
▶▶ 這演員演得好極了。

superstition [ˌsupə`stɪʃən] 名 迷信

It's a common superstition that crows are unlucky.
▶▶ 認為烏鴉不吉利是一種普遍的迷信思想。

supervise [`supəvaɪz] 動 監督；管理 同 oversee

He is responsible for supervising my work.
▶▶ 他負責監督我的工作。

supervision [ˌsupə`vɪʒən] 名 監督；管理 同 surveillance

There are more than 200 workers under his supervision.
▶▶ 他管理的員工超過兩百位。
(焦點句型) under the supervision 在管理下

supervisor [`supəˌvaɪzə] 名 監督者；管理人；指導者 同 superintendent

The university students handed in their essays to their supervisor.
▶▶ 大學生們把論文交給指導教授。

supreme [sə`prim] 形 至高無上的

The Supreme Court has the final say in the United States.
▶▶ 美國最高法院擁有最終解釋權。

surplus [`sɜpləs] 名盈餘 形額外的；過多的 關 prune 修剪；刪除

名 How should we deal with the surplus of donations?
　我們應該如何處理這些多餘的捐款？

形 We must prune away some of our surplus staff.
　我們必須精簡多餘的人力。

suspend [sə`spɛnd] 動暫停；中止；停職；懸掛

The oil price was given another push up this week when Russia suspended oil exports.

▶▶ 俄羅斯暫停石油出口後，本週油價再度上漲。

sustain [sə`sten] 動保持；維持 關 sustainable 可持續的；能長期維持的

He sustains himself by selling flowers.
▶▶ 他靠賣花維生。

symbolic [sɪm`bɑlɪk] 形象徵的

The dove is symbolic of peace.
▶▶ 鴿子是和平的象徵。

(焦點句型) be symbolic of sth. 象徵…；是…的象徵

symptom [`sɪmptəm] 名症狀；徵兆 關 syndrome 併發症；症候群

Headache is a symptom of influenza.
▶▶ 頭痛是流行性感冒的一個症狀。

 **T 字頭高手單字**

MP3 113

tackle [`tækḷ] 動處理；對付

They don't know how to tackle the problem.
▶▶ 他們不知如何處理這件麻煩。

tactic [`tæktɪk] 名戰術；策略

Different circumstances involve adopting different tactics.
▶▶ 不同的形勢需採取不同的策略。

tangle [`tæŋgḷ] 名糾結；混亂 動使混亂；使糾結

名 What he said put my thoughts in a tangle.
　他說的話讓我心亂如麻。

Level 1 基礎單字
Level 2 必備單字
Level 3 中級單字
Level 4 進階單字
Level 5 高手單字
Level 6 滿級單字

動 The little cat tangled the wool.
小貓把毛線糾結成一團。

tempt [tɛmpt] 動誘惑；引起

I was tempted to do him a favor, but I thought he should do it himself.
▶ 我很想幫他的忙，但我覺得他應該自己做。

temptation [tɛmp`teʃən] 名誘惑

The temptation for me to steal is greater than ever before now since I am unemployed.
▶ 我失業了，現在偷竊對我來說前所未有地誘人。

terminal [`tɝmənḷ] 形晚期的；末期的 名航廈；月台

形 I stayed up late last night preparing for the terminal examination of the semester.
我昨晚熬夜準備期末考。
名 The train reached its terminal.
火車抵達終站。

terrify [`tɛrə͵faɪ] 動使恐懼；使驚嚇 關 terrorist 恐怖分子 / terrorism 恐怖主義

He terrified his sister with an ugly mask.
▶ 他用一個醜陋的面具嚇他妹妹。

texture [`tɛkstʃɚ] 名質地；質感

The texture of the cloth is soft and smooth.
▶ 這塊布料的質地軟又滑。

theft [θɛft] 名竊盜

The man was accused of theft.
▶ 這個男人被控偷竊。

theoretical [͵θiə`rɛtɪkḷ] 形理論上的 關 thesis 論文

It's a theoretical possibility, but I don't suppose it will happen.
▶ 這是一種理論上的可能性，但我認為這種情況不會發生。

therapist [`θɛrəpɪst] 名治療師

When teens are going through a rough time, they might feel more supported if they talk to a therapist.
▶ 當年輕人遇到困境時，和治療師談話會讓他們感受到更多支持。

therapy [`θɛrəpɪ] 名 療法;治療 關 psychotherapy 精神療法

Physical therapy alternates with chemical therapy at that hospital.
▶▶ 在那間醫院裡,物理治療和化療交替進行。

thereby [ðɛr`baɪ] 副 藉以;因此

He found her unfaithful and thereby left as vengeance.
▶▶ 他發現她的不忠,因此離開作為報復。

thigh [θaɪ] 名 大腿

The muscles in my thighs are sore after climbing that hill.
▶▶ 爬過那座山後我的大腿肌肉酸痛。

threshold [`θrɛʃold] 名 門檻;界限;閾值

Please take off your shoes at the threshold.
▶▶ 請在入口處脫鞋。

thrill [θrɪl] 名 戰慄;激動;興奮 動 使激動

名 I felt a thrill when I knew I had passed the examination.
　 當我得知考試及格後非常興奮。
動 He was thrilled by the conversation with her.
　 與她談話使他很激動。

thriller [`θrɪlə] 名 驚悚作品(小說、電影等)

Bob was sleepless after reading the thrillers.
▶▶ 鮑伯看完驚悚小說後就失眠了。

thrive [θraɪv] 動 繁茂

This industry once thrived before the outbreak of war.
▶▶ 在戰爭爆發之前,這個產業一度繁榮興旺。

throne [θron] 名 王位;寶座

The prince rose to the throne as everyone had expected.
▶▶ 王子如眾人期待地登基了。

thrust [θrʌst] 動 推;塞;插入 名 要點;猛推

動 He thrust the baby into my arms and ran off.
　 他把嬰兒往我懷裡一塞就跑了。
名 The students fail to understand the main thrust of the author's argument.
　 學生無法理解作者論述的主旨。

Level 1 基礎單字
Level 2 必備單字
Level 3 中級單字
Level 4 進階單字
Level 5 高手單字
Level 6 滿級單字

tick [tɪk] 名 滴答聲 動 發出滴答聲

名 He counted the ticks of the clock during his sleepless night.
他數著鬧鐘的滴答聲度過失眠的夜。

動 The clock ticks loudly.
鬧鐘的滴答聲很大。

tile [taɪl] 名 瓷磚 動 鋪以磚瓦

名 The bathroom is decorated with tiles.
浴室鋪著瓷磚。

動 The tiled floor looks smooth and bright.
瓷磚地板看起來平滑又明亮。

tin [tɪn] 名 錫 動 鍍錫

名 Tin is not easily oxidized, and it is resistant to corrosion.
錫不易氧化與腐蝕。

動 The cover of the box was tinned.
這個盒蓋鍍了一層錫。

toll [tol] 名 通行費 動 徵收費用

名 Tolls are collected at the gateway.
在進出口處收過路費。

動 We will be tolled when passing on the highway.
我們經過高速公路會被徵收費用。

torch [tɔrtʃ] 名 火炬

They held torches to light the way in the cave.
▶▶ 他們舉著火炬照亮洞穴裡的路。

torment [`tɔrmɛnt ] / [ tɔr`mɛnt] 名 折磨；痛苦 動 折磨

名 Love brings delight and torment.
愛情帶來喜悅和痛苦。

動 I was tormented by a one-sided love.
我深受單戀所苦。

tournament [`tɝnəmənt] 名 錦標賽

We did a great job in the tournament.
▶▶ 我們在比賽中表現傑出。

toxic [`tɑksɪk] 形 有毒的

The milk powder of the brand produced in China was proven to be toxic.
▶▶ 這個品牌在中國製造的奶粉已證實含有毒性。

trait [tret] 名 特色；特性

She has several pleasant personality traits.
▶▶ 她有些許討人喜愛的特質。

traitor [`tretɚ] 名 叛徒

The traitor spilled the beans to our enemy.
▶▶ 這個叛徒向我們的敵人洩露消息。
(焦點句型) spill the beans 洩漏秘密

transformation [ˌtrænsfɚ`meʃən] 名 變形；轉變

What a transformation! You look so much better than before.
▶▶ 你看起來好多了，和以前簡直是判若兩人！

transit [`trænsɪt] 名 運輸 動 通過

名 The cost includes transit.
　　成本中包括運費。
動 They transited the narrow path.
　　他們經過那條窄徑。

transition [træn`zɪʃən] 名 轉變；過渡 關 seamless 無縫的

A transition is seldom seamless.
▶▶ 轉變往往需要一陣過渡期。

transmission [træns`mɪʃən] 名 傳達

We now interrupt our normal transmission to bring you a special news flash.
▶▶ 我們現在中斷正常節目，插播一則特別新聞。

transparent [træns`pɛrənt] 形 透明的

What is transparent underwear for? It can conceal nothing.
▶▶ 透明內衣是做什麼用的？它什麼也遮不住。

trauma [`trɑmə] 名 心理創傷；損傷

The trauma of breaking up with her boyfriend caused her great heartache.
▶▶ 和男友分手的創傷讓她心很痛。

1 Level 基礎單字

2 Level 必備單字

3 Level 中級單字

4 Level 進階單字

5 Level 高手單字

6 Level 滿級單字

treaty [`tritɪ] 名條約 關 ratify 正式批准

The treaty was ratified by Congress.
▶▶ 國會批准了該條約。

tribute [`trɪbjut] 名致敬

Let's give tribute to the working class.
▶▶ 讓我們向勞動階層致敬。

trigger [`trɪgə] 動觸發 名扳機

動 What triggered the rebellion?
是什麼原因觸發了這次叛變？
名 He pulled the trigger accidentally.
他意外扣下了扳機。

trim [trɪm] 動修剪 形整齊的；端莊的 名修整

動 The gardener trimmed the flowers and trees carefully.
園丁小心翼翼地修剪花木。
形 Her trim look makes her popular.
她整齊端莊的樣子讓她很受歡迎。
名 The trees need a trim.
這些樹木該修剪了。

triple [`trɪpl̩] 形三倍的 動變成三倍 名三倍

形 She does triple the work of her coworkers because of her high efficiency.
因為她工作效率很高，所以工作量是同事的三倍。
動 I will triple your pay if you turn in the blueprint tomorrow.
如果你明天交出藍圖，我給你三倍的薪酬。

trivial [`trɪvɪəl] 形平凡的；淺薄的；瑣碎的

What he asked were trivial questions.
▶▶ 他問的都是些淺薄的問題。

trophy [`trofɪ] 名戰利品

The hunter kept the lion's skin and head as trophies.
▶▶ 獵人把獅子的毛皮和頭顱作為戰利品保存起來。

tuition [tju`ɪʃən] 名教學；學費

The tuition of national universities is cheaper than that of private ones.
▶▶ 國立大學的學費比私立大學便宜。

tumor [`tumə] 名 腫瘤

The doctor said the tumor in his brain must be removed.
▶▶ 醫師說他腦裡的腫瘤必須要切除。

tuna [`tunə] 名 鮪魚

She likes tuna sandwiches.
▶▶ 她喜歡鮪魚三明治。

MP3 114

ultimate [`ʌltəmət] 形 終極的；極端的；最終的 名 終極；極致

形 After many defeats, the war ended for us in ultimate victory.
　　經過多次失敗，戰爭以我們的最終勝利而結束。
名 Rolls-Royce is the ultimate in luxury transportation.
　　勞斯萊斯是極致奢華的交通工具。

焦點句型 the ultimate in sth. …中的極品；…中的極致

uncover [ʌn`kʌvə] 動 掀開；揭露 同 unveil

The reporter uncovered his lie publicly.
▶▶ 這名記者公開揭穿他的謊言。

undergo [ˌʌndə`go] 動 度過；經歷 關 underway 進行中的

I just underwent an amazing adventure.
▶▶ 我剛剛經歷了一場驚奇的冒險。

undergraduate [ˌʌndə`grædʒuət] 名 大學生

Many undergraduates worry about their futures.
▶▶ 很多大學生擔心他們的未來。

underline [ˌʌndə`laɪn] 動 劃底線；強調 名 底線

動 I underlined the key sentences of the paragraph.
　　我把這個段落的關鍵句子劃底線。
名 She drew an underline as an emphasis.
　　她劃底線作為重點。

Level 1 基礎單字
Level 2 必備單字
Level 3 中級單字
Level 4 進階單字
Level 5 高手單字
Level 6 滿級單字

undermine [ˌʌndəˈmaɪn] 動 （逐漸地）削弱；損害

Streams had undermined the rocks.
▶▶ 流水侵蝕岩石的基部。

undertake [ˌʌndəˈtek] 動 承擔；保證

He undertook to pay the money back within six months.
▶▶ 他保證六個月內還錢。

undo [ʌnˈdu] 動 消除；取消

He undid what he just entered and then keyed in his correct password.
▶▶ 他把剛剛輸入的取消，然後輸入正確的密碼。

undoubtedly [ʌnˈdaʊtɪdlɪ] 副 無庸置疑地

Undoubtedly, the man in the yellow T-shirt is handsome.
▶▶ 不用懷疑，那個穿黃色 T 恤的男人相當英俊。

unemployment [ˌʌnɪmˈplɔɪmənt] 名 失業 同 redundancy

The unemployment rate this month is higher than last month's.
▶▶ 這個月的失業率比上個月還高。

unfold [ʌnˈfold] 動 攤開；打開

I unfolded and read the letter.
▶▶ 我展信而讀。

unlock [ʌnˈlɑk] 動 開鎖；揭開

He unlocked his safety deposit box and showed me his treasure.
▶▶ 他把保險箱打開，展示他的寶貝給我看。

update [ʌpˈdet] / [ˈʌpdet] 動 更新 名 最新資訊

動 You have to update the information frequently.
你必須時常更新訊息。
名 Please inform me if there is any update.
如果有任何新消息請告知我。

upgrade [ʌpˈgred] 動 升級；提升 名 升級

動 Organizations may suddenly need to upgrade servers.
各單位可能突然會需要升級伺服器。
名 Your virus protection needs an upgrade.
你的防毒軟體需要升級。

utility [ju`tɪlətɪ] 名（公共）設施；實用性

The store deals in objects of domestic utility.
▶▶ 那家商店出售家庭用品。

utilize [`jutḷˌaɪz] 動 利用

He utilized all the handy reference books to complete his report.
▶▶ 他使用手邊所有的參考書完成他的報告。

 V字頭高手單字

MP3 115

vacuum [`vækjum] 名 真空 動 以吸塵器打掃

名 We could not pull apart the two plates which enclosed a vacuum.
　　如果兩個盤子間是真空，我們就無法將它們分開。
動 I vacuum the floor on Sundays.
　　我每個禮拜天都用吸塵器吸地板。

vague [veg] 形 不明確的；模糊的

He gave me a vague answer about his scores.
▶▶ 他對於他的分數含糊其辭。

valid [`vælɪd] 形 有效的 反 invalid

This method is not valid to me.
▶▶ 這個方法對我無效。

variable [`vɛrɪəbḷ] 形 不定的；易變的 名 變數 關 vary 使多樣化

Michelle has a variable temper.
▶▶ 蜜雪兒的脾氣多變。

variation [ˌvɛrɪ`eʃən] 名 變動

The variation in temperature from day to night is great.
▶▶ 日夜溫差變化劇烈。

vein [ven] 名 靜脈 關 deplete 消耗

Veins are blood vessels that carry oxygen-depleted blood towards the heart.
▶▶ 靜脈是將缺氧的血液輸送到心臟的血管。

1 Level 基礎單字

2 Level 必備單字

3 Level 中級單字

4 Level 進階單字

5 Level 高手單字

6 Level 滿級單字

vendor [`vɛndə] 名攤販

I bought fried chicken from that vendor.
▶▶ 我和那個攤販買了炸雞。

venture [`vɛntʃə] 名冒險 動冒險

名 They were the first astronauts on the venture to the moon.
他們是首批冒險登陸月球的太空人。
動 He's never ventured abroad in his life.
他一生中從來不敢冒險出國。

verbal [`vɝbḷ] 形口頭的；言詞上的

She was angry about his verbal offense.
▶▶ 她因他的言語冒犯而發怒。

version [`vɝʒən] 名版本

The latest version has some new material in it.
▶▶ 最新的版本有一些新素材。

versus [`vɝsəs] 介對抗

The game tonight is China versus South Korea.
▶▶ 今晚的比賽是中國對南韓。

vertical [`vɝtɪkḷ] 名垂直線；垂直面 形垂直的 副 vertically 垂直地

名 The vertical on the graph represents revenue in millions of dollars.
圖表上的這條直線代表收入，單位是百萬元。
形 The northern side of the mountain is almost vertical.
這座山的北側幾乎與地面垂直。

veteran [`vɛtərən] 名老手；老練者

Some corporations hire only veterans.
▶▶ 有些公司只雇用有經驗的人。

via [vaɪə] 介經由 副 viable 可行的

He knew me via Vivian.
▶▶ 他經由薇薇安認識我。

vicious [`vɪʃəs] 形邪惡的；惡毒的

Going to bed late and getting up late becomes a vicious circle.
▶▶ 晚睡和晚起形成一個惡性循環。

viewer [`vjuɚ] 名觀眾 關 view 觀看 / viewpoint 觀點

The viewers were touched by the characters' friendship.
▶▶ 觀眾都被人物之間的友情感動。

vinegar [`vɪnəgɚ] 名醋

Vinegar contains a type of acid.
▶▶ 醋含有一種酸類。

virtual [`vɝtʃʊəl] 形實質上的；虛擬的 關 virtually 事實上

Our deputy manager is the virtual head of the business.
▶▶ 我們的副理是公司的實際負責人。

visa [`vizə] 名簽證

You need a visa to visit some countries.
▶▶ 入境某些國家必須要有簽證。

vocal [`vokl] 形發聲的；直言不諱的 名演唱部分

形 We were very vocal about our rights.
我們直言不諱地談到了我們應有的權利。
名 I love the vocals in that song.
我喜歡這首歌的歌聲。

volcano [vɑl`keno] 名火山

Six other volcanos were still erupting.
▶▶ 還有六個火山仍在爆發。

vomit [`vɑmɪt] 動嘔吐 名嘔吐物

動 The boy vomited after eating the bad meat.
這男孩吃了變質的肉之後就吐了。
名 The vomit on the sidewalk had a disgusting smell.
人行道上的嘔吐物散發著噁心的惡臭。

vow [vaʊ] 動發誓 名誓言

動 Wallace vowed that he would never cheat anyone.
華萊士發誓他不會欺騙任何人。
名 Nuns take a vow of chastity.
修女發誓要貞潔。
焦點句型 take a vow (to V.) 發誓（要⋯）

1 Level 基礎單字
2 Level 必備單字
3 Level 中級單字
4 Level 進階單字
5 Level 高手單字
6 Level 滿級單字

vulnerable [`vʌlnərəb!] 形 易受傷的；易受影響的；脆弱的

I'm very vulnerable to ridicule.
▶▶ 我對嘲弄非常敏感。
焦點句型 be vulnerable to sth. 易受…所傷；易受…影響

UNIT 22 W、Y 字頭高手單字

warehouse [`wɛr,haʊs] 名 倉庫 動 把…存放於倉庫 關 infest 大批出沒；騷擾

名 The warehouse is infested with rats.
　倉庫裡老鼠橫行。
動 My father warehoused the old newspapers and books.
　爸爸把舊報紙和舊書放進倉庫。

warrior [`wɔrɪɚ] 名 武士；戰士

The warrior struck his opponent with a sword.
▶▶ 戰士用劍刺穿了對手。

wary [`wɛrɪ] 形 注意的

Be wary of strangers.
▶▶ 小心陌生人。
焦點句型 be wary of sth. 小心…

weird [wɪrd] 形 怪異的

The old man is not as weird as people believe.
▶▶ 那個老人並沒有人們想得那麼怪異。

whatsoever [,wɑtso`ɛvɚ] 副 無論怎樣；絲毫；任何 形 任何的

Mary has no interest in the project whatsoever.
▶▶ 瑪莉對這個項目完全沒有興趣。
文法解析 whatsoever通常用於否定句後表示強調。

wheelchair [`hwil,tʃɛr] 名 輪椅

He's been confined to a wheelchair since the car accident.
▶▶ 他從車禍以後就離不開輪椅了。

whereabouts [ˌwɛrəˋbauts] 名所在；下落 副在何處

名 Do you know her whereabouts?
你知道她的下落嗎？

副 Whereabouts on earth can you be?
你到底在哪裡？

whereas [wɛrˋæz] 連雖然；卻；儘管

Some people are highly educated, whereas others are too poor to receive a good education.
▶▶ 有些人受過高等教育，然而其他人卻因太窮而無法接受良好的教育。

whine [waɪn] 名哀泣聲 動哀鳴；泣訴；抱怨

名 I heard my dog's whines and went out to see what had happened.
我聽見狗的哀鳴，便出外看看發生了什麼事。

動 My cousin keeps whining about how harsh his mother was.
表弟一直在抱怨他媽媽有多嚴厲。

widespread [ˋwaɪdˌsprɛd] 形廣為流傳的

The widespread news turned out to be a rumor.
▶▶ 結果那個流傳很廣的消息是個謠言。

wig [wɪg] 名假髮

The woman's wig was blown off in the violent storm.
▶▶ 這個女人的假髮被強風吹掉了。

wilderness [ˋwɪldənəs] 名荒野

Antarctica is the world's last great wilderness.
▶▶ 南極洲是世界上最晚發現的大荒原。

wildlife [ˋwaɪldˌlaɪf] 名野生生物

Some wildlife is fierce.
▶▶ 某些野生生物很兇猛。

windshield [ˋwɪndˌʃild] 名擋風玻璃

A rock struck the windshield and cracked it.
▶▶ 石頭砸破了擋風玻璃。

Level 1 基礎單字
Level 2 必備單字
Level 3 中級單字
Level 4 進階單字
Level 5 高手單字
Level 6 滿級單字

wither [`wɪðɚ] 動 枯萎，衰弱

This type of industry will wither away in the years to come.
▶▶ 這種工業幾年以後就會衰退。

witty [`wɪtɪ] 形 機智的

The witty host made every guest laugh happily.
▶▶ 機智的主持人讓每位來賓開懷大笑。

workshop [`wɜkʃɑp] 名 工作坊；研討會

A workshop will take place next Wednesday.
▶▶ 下禮拜三將舉行一場研討會。

worship [`wɜʃɪp] 動 崇拜 名 （對神的）敬奉；崇尚

動 Venus was a goddess worshiped by the Romans.
維納斯是羅馬人所崇拜的女神。
名 I went to the famous temple for worship.
我去那間知名廟宇拜拜。

worthwhile [`wɜθˌhwaɪl] 形 值得的

Traveling is worthwhile, even though it can be expensive.
▶▶ 儘管可能所費不貲，但旅行往往是值得的。

worthy [`wɜðɪ] 形 有價值的；值得的

Mandy is worthy of your love for she is such a nice girl.
▶▶ 曼蒂是個好女孩，值得你去愛。
(焦點句型) be worthy of sth. 值得…

yacht [jɑt] 名 遊艇 動 駕駛遊艇

名 We sailed on our new yacht today.
我們今天讓新遊艇下水。
動 My brother yachted to that island.
我哥哥駕著遊艇到那座島去。

yield [jild] 動 讓出；生產 名 產量

動 Please yield your seats to the elderly.
請將位子讓給年長者。
名 The yield this year is terrible.
今年的產值很糟糕。

7000 Essential
Vocabulary for
High School Students

Expert Vocabulary

LEVEL
6
滿級單字

單字難易度 ★★★★☆

文法難易度 ★★☆☆☆

生活出現頻率 ★★★★☆

考題出題頻率 ★★★★☆

名 名詞 動 動詞 形 形容詞 副 副詞 介 介係詞 連 連接詞
關 相關單字 / 片語 同 同義詞 反 反義詞

abbreviate [əˋbrivɪˏet] 動縮寫 關 abbreviation 縮寫

"The United Nations" is usually abbreviated to "the UN".

▶▶ 「聯合國」通常縮寫成「UN」。

abide [əˋbaɪd] 動容忍；忍耐

Californians and New Englanders speak the same language and abide by the same federal laws.

▶▶ 加利福尼亞人和新英格蘭人說同樣的語言，遵守同樣的聯邦法律。

文法解析 abide動詞三態變化為 abide / abode / abode。

焦點句型 abide by sth. 遵守，遵循（協議、規章等）

aboriginal [ˏæbəˋrɪdʒənḷ] 名原住民 形原始的

名 The Atayal are one tribe of Taiwanese aboriginals.
泰雅族是台灣原住民的一個族群。

形 We should cherish the aboriginal culture.
我們應該珍惜原住民文化。

abound [əˋbaʊnd] 動大量存在

The mountain abounds in mines.

▶▶ 這座山富含礦藏。

焦點句型 abound in/with sth. 富含…

abstraction [æbˋstrækʃən] 名抽象 關 abstract 抽象的

There are many abstractions in philosophy.

▶▶ 哲學中有許多抽象概念。

abundance [əˋbʌndəns] 名充足；豐富

There is an abundance of wildlife in the forest.

▶▶ 森林裡有很多野生動植物。

academy [əˋkædəmɪ] 名學院；專科院校 關 acdemic 學術的

Plato's Academy continued for several hundred years after he died.

▶▶ 在柏拉圖死後，柏拉圖學院延續了幾百年。

accessory [æk`sɛsərɪ] 名附件；配件 形附加的

名 The car has accessories such as an electronic alarm.
這輛車子裝有電子警鈴之類的附加設備。
形 The accessory battery is very useful for me.
這顆附加的電池對我而言非常實用。

accordance [ə`kɔrdəns] 名根據；依照

We have to deal with the problem in accordance with the rules.
▶▶ 我們必須按照規定處理這個問題。
(焦點句型)in accordance with sth. 依照…

accordingly [ə`kɔrdɪŋlɪ] 副因此；於是

He fainted in class. Accordingly, we took him home.
▶▶ 他在課堂上昏倒了，於是我們送他回家。

accountable [ə`kaʊntəbḷ] 形應負責的

She is too young to be accountable for what she did.
▶▶ 她太年輕，以至於她無法對自己所做的事負責。
(焦點句型)be accountable for sth. 對…負責

accumulate [ə`kjumjə‚let] 動累積

The shelf holding the accumulated books is about to collapse.
▶▶ 架上的書堆快要倒塌了。

accumulation [ə‚kjumjə`leʃən] 名累積

An accumulation of work is waiting for you to be done.
▶▶ 成堆的工作等著你做。

accusation [‚ækjə`zeʃən] 名控告

The accusation against Mark is murder.
▶▶ 馬克受到的指控是謀殺。
文法解析 accusation搭配介系詞 against。

accustom [ə`kʌstəm] 動使習慣

I was accustomed to his company.
▶▶ 我習慣於他的陪伴。
(焦點句型)be accustomed to sth. 習慣於…

Level 1 基礎單字
Level 2 必備單字
Level 3 中級單字
Level 4 進階單字
Level 5 高手單字
Level 6 滿級單字

acne [`ækni] 名粉刺；面皰

Young girls worry about the acne on their faces.
▶▶ 年輕女孩煩惱臉上的痘痘。

acre [`ekɚ] 名英畝

He has bought a 250-acre farm.
▶▶ 他買了一個占地二百五十英畝的農場。

adaptation [ˌædəp`teʃən] 名適應；改編 同 adaption 關 adapt 適應

I made a quick adaptation to the new house.
▶▶ 我很快地適應新居。

(焦點句型) make an adaptation to sth. 適應…

addiction [ə`dɪkʃən] 名上癮；熱衷

He finally mastered his addiction to drugs.
▶▶ 他最終戰勝了毒癮。

(焦點句型) addiction to sth. 對…上癮

administer / administrate [əd`mɪnəstɚ ] / [ əd`mɪnəˌstret] 動管理

She administered our department well.
▶▶ 她把我們部門管理得很好。

admiral [`ædmərəl] 名海軍上將

The admiral ordered all the warships to open fire.
▶▶ 海軍上將命令所有戰艦開火。

adolescence [ˌædl̩`ɛsn̩s] 名青春期；青春

Teenagers are curious about love in adolescence.
▶▶ 青少年在青春期對愛情感到好奇。

affectionate [ə`fɛkʃənət] 形深情的；充滿感情的

I am very affectionate with my mother.
▶▶ 我很愛我媽媽。

(焦點句型) be affectionate with sb./sth. 愛…

affirm [ə`fɝm] 動斷言；證實 關 affirmation 斷言

He is really a nice person. I can affirm his honesty and friendliness.
▶▶ 他真的是個好人，我能證實他的誠實與友善。

airtight [`ɛr,taɪt] 形 密閉的

Please make the jar of jam airtight.
▶▶ 請把果醬密封。

airway [`ɛr,we] 名 航線

The airway of the flight is from Taiwan to Japan.
▶▶ 這架班機的航線是從台灣到日本。

algebra [`ældʒəbrə] 名 代數學；代數

For Mark, algebra is a difficult subject.
▶▶ 對馬克而言，代數是個困難的科目。

alienate [`eljən,et] 動 使疏遠

Long distance alienated Jack from his girlfriend.
▶▶ 遠距離戀愛讓馬克和女友的感情日漸冷淡。
(焦點句型) alienate sb. from sb. 使疏遠…

alligator [`ælə,getə] 名 鱷魚

Keep away from the alligators. They are fierce.
▶▶ 不要靠近鱷魚，牠們很兇猛。

altitude [`æltə,tjud] 名 高度；海拔

Some species only survive at high altitudes.
▶▶ 有些物種在高海拔才能生存。

aluminum [ə`lumɪnəm] 名 鋁

Nowhere in nature is aluminum found free, owing to the fact that it's always combined with other elements.
▶▶ 在自然界很難找到純淨的鋁，這是因為它總會和其他元素相結合。

ambiguity [,æmbɪ`gjuətɪ] 名 模稜兩可 關 ambiguous 含糊的

The officials tend to answer in ambiguity.
▶▶ 官員在回答時經常含糊其辭。
(焦點句型) in ambiguity 模稜兩可地

amid / amidst [ə`mɪd ] / [ ə`mɪdst] 介 在…之中

An old house stands amid the rubble.
▶▶ 一棟破舊的房子聳立在殘垣斷壁之中。

Level 1 基礎單字
Level 2 必備單字
Level 3 中級單字
Level 4 進階單字
Level 5 高手單字
Level 6 滿級單字

amplify [`æmplə,faɪ] 動擴大；放大 關 amplification 擴大

He amplified his voice to let everyone hear the news.
▶▶ 他提高音量，讓大家都知道這則消息。

analogy [ə`nælədʒɪ] 名類似；類比

You could make an analogy between the human body and a car engine.
▶▶ 你可以將人的身體和汽車引擎作類比。

(焦點句型) make an analogy between sth. and sth. 類比某兩件事物

analytical [,ænə`lɪtɪkḷ] 形分析的

Over time, they should commit themselves to developing a broader and deeper analytical capacity.
▶▶ 隨著時間的過去，他們應該投身於開發更廣更深的分析能力。

anchor [`æŋkə] 動停泊；使穩固 名錨；精神支柱；主播

動 The ship anchored off shore.
船停泊在離岸不遠的地方。
名 Anchors should have both good looks and wisdom.
主播應兼具美貌與智慧。

animate [`ænə,met] 動賦予生命；使有活力 形活的；有活力的

動 Linda animated the party with her humor and eloquence.
琳達用她的幽默和口才炒熱了宴會的氣氛。
形 Do any animate creatures exist on other planets?
其他星球上有任何生物存在嗎？

annoyance [ə`nɔɪəns] 名煩惱 關 annoy 惹惱

She breathed a deep sigh to show her annoyance.
▶▶ 她長嘆以示厭煩。

anthem [`ænθəm] 名讚美詩；聖歌

They sang religious anthems in the church.
▶▶ 他們在教堂裡唱聖歌。

antibiotic [,æntɪbaɪ`ɑtɪk] 名抗生素 形抗生素的

名 Antibiotics can be used against infections.
抗生素可以用來防止感染。
形 The medicine is composed of some antibiotic ingredients.
這種藥含有一些抗生素成分。

anticipation [æn͵tɪsə`peʃən] 名預期；期待 關 anticipate 期待

I wait for her with eager anticipation.
▶▶ 我懷著強烈的期待等著她。

antonym [`æntə͵nɪm] 名反義字

"Same" is the antonym of "different".
▶▶ 「相同」的反義字是「不同」。

applaud [ə`plɔd] 動鼓掌；喝采

The audience applauded enthusiastically after the excellent speech.
▶▶ 聽眾在精采的演講過後熱情地鼓掌。

applicable [`æplɪkəbl̩] 形適用的；適當的 關 application 應用

This part of the form is only applicable to married women.
▶▶ 表格的這部分只適用於已婚女性。

apprentice [ə`prɛntɪs] 名學徒 動使…做學徒

名 He agreed to my request to be his apprentice.
他同意了我當他學徒的要求。
動 The sculptor was apprenticed to one of the most famous artist in his time.
這位雕塑家師從當代最知名的藝術家之一。

approximate [ə`prɑksə͵mət ] / [ ə`prɑksə͵met] 形大約的 動接近

形 The approximate distance between the two cities is five miles.
這兩座城市之間的距離大約是五英哩。
動 The number of the books approximates three thousand.
這些書的數量將近三千本。

arithmetic [ə`rɪθmə͵tɪk] 名算術 形算術的

名 I'm not good at mental arithmetic.
我不太善於心算。
形 He is good at arithmetic questions.
他擅長於算術的題目。

ascend [ə`sɛnd] 動上升；登高 關 ascendant 上升的

He watched the airplane ascending higher and higher.
▶▶ 他看到飛機越飛越高。

Level 1 基礎單字
Level 2 必備單字
Level 3 中級單字
Level 4 進階單字
Level 5 高手單字
Level 6 滿級單字

assassinate [ə`sæsn͵et] 動 行刺

President Kennedy was assassinated.
▶▶ 甘迺迪總統遭到暗殺。

asthma [`æzmə] 名 氣喘

She was born with asthma.
▶▶ 她天生就有氣喘。

astray [ə`stre] 副 迷路的；誤入歧途的

He went astray for one hour.
▶▶ 他迷路了一個小時。

astronaut [`æstrə͵nɔt] 名 太空人

The astronauts brought back rock specimens from the moon.
▶▶ 太空人從月球帶回了岩石標本。

astronomer [ə`strɑnəmɚ] 名 天文學家

Astronomers used to wonder whether there were any creatures on Mars.
▶▶ 天文學家曾想知道火星上是否有生物。

astronomy [əs`trɑnəmɪ] 名 天文學 關 astrology 占星術；占星學

Astronomy is the study of stars and the universe.
▶▶ 天文學是關於天體和宇宙的學問。

attain [ə`ten] 動 實現；獲得 關 attainment 到達

I have finally attained my goals, and I am now searching for new challenges.
▶▶ 我終於達成目標，現在正尋找新的挑戰。

attendant [ə`tɛndənt] 名 侍者 形 陪從的；護理的

名 The flight attendant is well-dressed and polite.
這個空服員穿著得體又有禮。
形 She asked the attendant nurse to take care of her mother.
她拜託隨侍護士照顧她母親。

auditorium [͵ɔdə`tɔrɪəm] 名 禮堂；觀眾席

All students gathered in the auditorium for the weekly assembly.
▶▶ 所有學生都到禮堂參加週會。

aviation [ˌevɪˋeʃən] 名 航空；飛行

They pioneered in early aviation.
▶▶ 他們是早期航空業界的先驅。

awesome [ˋɔsəm] 形 很好的；令人敬畏的

The students obeyed the awesome teacher.
▶▶ 學生們服從威嚴的老師。

awhile [əˋwaɪl] 副 暫時；片刻

Please wait for me awhile.
▶▶ 請等我一下。

 **B字頭滿級單字**

MP3 118

bachelor [ˋbætʃələ] 名 單身漢；學士

After four years, she finally got a bachelor's degree from Cambridge University.
▶▶ 過了四年，她終於得到劍橋大學的學士學位。

backbone [ˋbækˌbon] 名 脊柱；支柱

My mother is the economic backbone of my family.
▶▶ 媽媽是我們家的經濟支柱。

badge [bædʒ] 名 徽章

Our school badge was designed by a well-known alumnus.
▶▶ 我們的校徽是由一位知名校友設計的。

banquet [ˋbæŋkwɪt] 名 宴會 動 宴請

名 Everyone dressed in formal attire to attend her wedding banquet.
每個人都盛裝出席她的婚宴。
動 My cousin banqueted all the relatives.
我表姐設宴款待所有的親戚。

barbarian [barˋbɛrɪən] 名 野蠻人 形 野蠻的

名 To call aboriginal people "barbarians" is not only ignorant but also discriminatory.
稱原住民為「野蠻人」不僅無禮，也是歧視。
形 He is so barbarian to thrash her like that!
他竟如此野蠻，把她打成這樣！

Level 1 基礎單字
Level 2 必備單字
Level 3 中級單字
Level 4 進階單字
Level 5 高手單字
Level 6 滿級單字

bass [bes] 名低音樂器；男低音歌手 形低音的；低沉的

名 The famous bass player will hold concerts in July.
這個知名貝斯手將於七月舉行演奏會。

形 His voice is bass but moving.
他的聲音低沉但動人。

batter [`bætɚ] 名連擊；重擊

The wind battered against the window.
▶▶ 風敲打著窗戶。

焦點句型 batter against sth. 敲打…

beautify [`bjutə͵faɪ] 動美化

The movie and TV stars you see are beautified by beauticians.
▶▶ 你看到的電視和電影明星都是有美容師打扮過的。

beep [bip] 名嘟嘟聲；滴滴聲 動發出嘟嘟聲或滴滴聲

名 The thief ran away on hearing the beep.
小偷一聽到警笛聲就跑了。

動 The policeman beeped to stop the rider.
警察鳴笛要騎士停下。

beforehand [bɪ`for͵hænd] 副事前；預先

Think carefully beforehand, or you might regret your decision.
▶▶ 事前慎重考慮，不然你可能會為你的決定後悔。

beverage [`bɛvərɪdʒ] 名飲料

I prefer sugar-free beverages.
▶▶ 我偏好無糖飲料。

blaze [blez] 名火焰；爆發

The firefighters spent four hours trying to put out the blaze.
▶▶ 消防員花了四個小時撲滅那場大火。

焦點句型 put out the blaze 滅火

bleach [blitʃ] 名漂白劑 動漂白

名 My father used bleach on the stain.
爸爸在髒污上使用漂白劑。

動 Do not bleach the colored shirts; they will fade.
不要漂白有色襯衫，它們會褪色。

blonde / blond [blɑnd] 名金髮女郎 形金髮的

名 I thought she would be a small blonde but she's the complete opposite.
我原以為她是一位身材嬌小的金髮女郎，但她恰好相反。
形 The man never took his eyes off the blonde girl.
這個男人目不轉睛地看著金髮女孩。

blot [`blɑt] 名汙漬 動弄髒

名 The blot on the dress is hard to remove.
這件洋裝上的汙漬很難清除。
動 My skirt was blotted by sauce.
我的裙子被醬汁弄髒了。

blunt [blʌnt] 動使遲鈍 形遲鈍的

動 Taking the cold medicine blunted my thinking.
感冒藥使我的思考變得遲鈍。
形 She is so blunt that she often offends people.
她很遲鈍，以至於她時常冒犯人。

bodily [`bodəlɪ] 形身體上的

The bodily pain of children is the mental suffering of parents.
▶▶ 孩子身上的痛楚，是父母心裡的折磨。

bosom [`buzəm] 名胸懷；懷中

She clutched the child to her bosom.
▶▶ 她把小孩摟在懷裡。

boulevard [`bulə,vɑrd] 名林蔭大道

On Sunday evening, people stroll along the boulevard.
▶▶ 星期日的傍晚，人人都沿著林蔭大道散步。

boxing [`bɑksɪŋ] 名拳擊

Some boxing terms puzzle me.
▶▶ 有些拳擊術語我不懂。

boycott [`bɔɪ,kɑt] 名抵制；杯葛 動抵制；杯葛

名 Due to the boycott of the congress, the plan was aborted.
因為國會的杯葛，這個計劃中途失敗了。
動 Several countries boycotted the Olympic Games in protest.
幾個國家抵制這一屆奧林匹克運動會，以示抗議。

Level 1 基礎單字
Level 2 必備單字
Level 3 中級單字
Level 4 進階單字
Level 5 高手單字
Level 6 滿級單字

619

brace [bres] 名 支架 動 支撐；準備

名 He's in a neck brace for a dislocated jaw.
他下巴脫臼了，戴著頸托。

動 He braced himself for the shock.
他做好了準備面對衝擊。

brassiere [brəˋzɪr] 名 胸罩；內衣

An undergarment is a combination of a light corset and a brassiere.
▶▶ 內衣結合了輕馬甲和胸罩的功能。

breadth [brɛdθ] 名 寬度；幅度

He measured the length and breadth of the table.
▶▶ 他測量桌子的長寬。

breakdown [ˋbrek͵daʊn] 名 故障；崩潰

I hope we don't have a breakdown on the freeway.
▶▶ 希望我們的車子不要在高速公路上拋錨。

breakup [ˋbrek͵ʌp] 名 分散；分離

The couple decided on a breakup after a three-year marriage.
▶▶ 這對夫妻歷經三年的婚姻，最後還是分開了。

bribe [braɪb] 名 賄賂 動 行賄

名 By taking bribes, the judge made a mockery of his high office.
法官收受賄賂，使其崇高的職務淪為笑柄。

動 If the candidates try to bribe you, you can report them to the police.
如果候選人試圖向你行賄，你可以向警察檢舉。

(焦點句型) take bribes 收取賄賂

brink [brɪŋk] 名 邊緣

The rare tree grew on the brink of the cliff.
▶▶ 那棵稀有的樹長在懸崖邊緣。

broaden [ˋbrɑdn̩] 動 加寬 關 broad 寬的

My mom broadened the sleeves of the coat to fit me.
▶▶ 媽媽把大衣的袖子加寬，讓我穿得更合身。

brochure [bro`ʃur] 名小冊子 同 booklet

If you want more information, you can read the brochure.
▶▶ 如果你需要更多資訊，可以看這本小手冊。

broil [brɔɪl] 動烤；炙

Please broil a medium steak.
▶▶ 請烤一塊五分熟的牛排。

brook [bruk] 名川；小河；溪流

The brook ran through the meadow.
▶▶ 這條溪流曲折地流過草地。

broth [brɔθ] 名肉湯

It is very comfortable to have a hot broth in such a cool weather.
▶▶ 在這樣的涼天裡喝碗熱湯，真的非常舒服。

brotherhood [`brʌðə,hud] 名兄弟關係；手足之情；兄弟會

There is profound brotherhood between them.
▶▶ 他們之間有深刻的手足之情。

bulky [`bʌlkɪ] 形龐大的

What is inside the bulky package?
▶▶ 這個龐大的包裹裡裝著什麼？

C 字頭滿級單字

MP3 119

caffeine [`kæfin] 名咖啡因

Caffeine can lead to sleeplessness.
▶▶ 咖啡因會導致失眠。

calculator [`kælkjə,letə] 名計算機

Using a calculator is allowed in the statistics examination.
▶▶ 統計學考試可以用計算機。

calligraphy [kə`lɪgrəfɪ] 名書法

He is a master of calligraphy.
▶▶ 他精通書法。

1 Level 基礎單字
2 Level 必備單字
3 Level 中級單字
4 Level 進階單字
5 Level 高手單字
6 Level 滿級單字

cape [kep] 名峽；海角；披風；斗篷

"Cape No.7" broke box office records for Taiwanese movies.
▶▶ 「海角七號」破了台灣電影的票房紀錄。

capsule [`kæps!]] 名膠囊

Swallow the capsule with cold water.
▶▶ 吞膠囊要配冷水。

caption [`kæpʃən] 名標題；說明文字；字幕 動下標題；以文字說明

名 Can you think up a caption that exactly covers the whole idea?
你能想出一個概括全部內容的標題嗎？
動 It is difficult for me to caption the photo.
為這張照片下標題對我來說很難。

captive [`kæptɪv] 名俘虜 形被俘的

名 They made efforts to rescue the captive from the enemy.
他們努力從敵人那裡營救俘虜。
形 These captive animals will be set free.
這些被捕獲的動物將被放生。

captivity [kæp`tɪvətɪ] 名監禁；囚禁

Wild animals are often unhappy in captivity.
▶▶ 關在籠中的野生動物通常都不開心。

cardboard [`kɑrdbɔrd] 動卡紙、硬紙板

I used cardboard to make a birthday card.
▶▶ 我用卡紙做生日卡片。

carefree [`kɛr,fri] 形無憂無慮的

On a fine spring day like this, I felt quite carefree.
▶▶ 在這樣春光明媚的日子裡，我感到無憂無慮。

caretaker [`kɛr,tekɚ] 名看管人；照顧者

They employed a caretaker to look after their baby.
▶▶ 他們請了個看管人照顧嬰兒。

carton [`kɑrtn̩] 名紙盒；紙板箱

He put a carton under his lunch box.
▶▶ 他在便當下放了個紙盒。

cashier [kæˋʃɪr] 名收銀員；出納員 關cash 現金

The cashier invoiced me.
▸▸ 出納員開發票給我。

casualty [ˋkæʒuəltɪ] 名（事故或戰爭的）傷亡人員；受害者 關casual 偶然的

In war, there are many casualties.
▸▸ 戰爭中有許多人員傷亡。

catastrophe [kəˋtæstrəfɪ] 名大災難

The natural catastrophe dealt a blow to this country's economy.
▸▸ 自然災害給這個國家的經濟帶來了嚴重打擊。

cater [ˋketɚ] 動提供食物；承辦宴席

The menu caters to all tastes.
▸▸ 這菜單迎合所有人的口味。

(焦點句型) cater to sb./sth. 滿足或迎合需求

caterpillar [ˋkætɚˏpɪlɚ] 名毛毛蟲

Most people scream on seeing caterpillars.
▸▸ 大多數人看到毛毛蟲都會尖叫。

cavity [ˋkævətɪ] 名洞；穴

The dog gave birth to the puppies in the cavity in the ground.
▸▸ 這隻狗在地洞裡生小狗。

celery [ˋsɛlərɪ] 名芹菜

I love celery soup.
▸▸ 我喜歡喝芹菜湯。

cement [səˋmɛnt] 名水泥 動用水泥砌合

名 The cement has already set.
那水泥已經凝固了。
動 The workers cemented the wall and began to paint it.
工人們在牆上砌好水泥，開始粉刷。

ceramic [səˋræmɪk] 形陶瓷的

You may buy some similar plates at the ceramic shop.
▸▸ 你可以在陶器店買到類似的碟子。

1 Level 基礎單字

2 Level 必備單字

3 Level 中級單字

4 Level 進階單字

5 Level 高手單字

6 Level 滿級單字

certify [`sɝtəˌfaɪ] 動 證明 關 certificate 證書

The accused is confident the evidence will certify his innocence.
▶▶ 被告有信心證據將會證明他的清白。

chairperson / chairman / chairwoman / chair

[`tʃɛrˌpɝsn̩ ] / [ `tʃɛrmən] / [`tʃɛrˌwʊmən] / [tʃɛr] 名 主席；女主席

When the chairperson began her speech, everyone stopped talking.
▶▶ 當主席開始演講，每個人都停止了交談。

champagne [ʃæm`pen] 名 香檳

We always celebrate our wedding anniversary with a bottle of champagne.
▶▶ 我們總是用一瓶香檳來慶祝我們的結婚紀念日。

chant [tʃænt] 動 吟唱 名 讚美詩歌

動 The choir chanted in the background.
唱詩班在後面唱歌。
名 The minister taught us to sing the chant.
牧師教我們唱讚美歌。

charitable [`tʃærətəbl̩] 形 溫和的；仁慈的 關 charity 慈善

The charitable woman donates money to the orphanage every month.
▶▶ 這個仁慈的女人每個月都捐錢到孤兒院。

checkup [`tʃɛkˌʌp] 名 核對

The doctor gave Jim a clean bill of health during the checkup.
▶▶ 吉姆體檢之後，醫生給他開了一份身體健康證明。

chemist [`kɛmɪst] 名 化學家；藥劑師 關 chemistry 化學

Paul is acknowledged as the best chemist in the nation.
▶▶ 保羅被公認為本國最傑出的化學家。

chestnut [`tʃɛsnʌt] 名 栗子 形 紅棕栗色的

名 Squirrels eat chestnuts.
松鼠吃栗子。
形 She dyed her hair chestnut.
她把頭髮染成栗子色。

chill [`tʃɪl] 動 使變冷 名 寒冷 形 寒冷的；令人放鬆的

動 I chilled the soup with an electric fan.
我用電扇把湯弄冷。

名 The chill in winter is unbearable for me.
我很受不了冬天的寒冷。

形 The chill wind made me tremble.
冷風使我顫抖。

chimpanzee [ˌtʃɪmpæn`zi] 名 黑猩猩

People take photos of the chimpanzees in the zoo.
▶▶ 人們為動物園裡的黑猩猩拍照。

chirp [tʃɝp] 名 蟲鳴鳥叫聲 動 蟲鳴鳥叫

名 The chirps outside the window present a beautiful melody.
窗外的蟲鳴鳥叫是段美麗的旋律。

動 Birds are chirping among the trees.
鳥兒在樹叢間啁啾。

cholesterol [kə`lɛstəˌrɑl] 名 膽固醇

Too much cholesterol is thought to be a cause of heart disease.
▶▶ 膽固醇過多會導致心臟病。

cigar [sə`gɑr] 名 雪茄

He lit a cigar.
▶▶ 他點了一枝雪茄煙。

civilize [`sɪvəˌlaɪz] 動 使開化 衍 civilization 文明

The Romans hoped to civilize all the tribes of ancient Europe.
▶▶ 羅馬人曾希望教化古代歐洲各部落。

clam [klæm] 名 蛤；蚌

I am as happy as a clam every day.
▶▶ 我每天都笑口常開。

clasp [klæsp] 名 釦子；緊抱；緊抓 動 抱緊；抓緊

名 The clasp on her necklace is open.
她項鍊上的釦子開了。

動 The mother is clasping her son tightly in her arms.
那位母親把兒子緊緊抱在懷裡。

Level 1 基礎單字
Level 2 必備單字
Level 3 中級單字
Level 4 進階單字
Level 5 高手單字
Level 6 滿級單字

clearance [`klɪrəns] 名清潔；清掃 關 clear 清晰的

Jack made a complete clearance of his room.
▶▶ 傑克把他的房間做了全面清潔。

climax [`klaɪmæks] 名頂點 動達到頂點

名 The climax of the film is a brilliant car chase.
這部電影的高潮是一場精彩的汽車追逐戲。
動 The party climaxed when the host started dancing.
當主持人開始跳舞時，這場派對達到高潮。

clockwise [`klɑk͵waɪz] 形順時針方向的 副順時針方向地

形 Put some sugar in and make a clockwise stir.
放一些糖，然後順時針方向攪拌。
副 They take turns clockwise.
他們依順時針方向輪流進行。

clone [klon] 名複製

It is not easy for me to differentiate the clone from the original.
▶▶ 我無法輕易分辨出複製品和真品。

closure [`kloʒɚ] 名關閉；結束

The closure of the factory was a devastating blow to the workers.
▶▶ 工廠的關閉對工人來說是個重大的打擊。

coastline [`kost͵laɪn] 名海岸線

As evening came, the coastline faded away in the darkness.
▶▶ 夜晚降臨時，海岸線在黑暗中逐漸消失。

collision [kə`lɪʒən] 名碰撞

She apologized to me for the careless collision.
▶▶ 她因不小心的碰撞向我道歉。

colloquial [kə`lokwɪəl] 形白話的；通俗的

Many colloquial expressions have acquired literary currency by magazines.
▶▶ 許多口語用法是先由雜誌採用之後才得以在文學中使用。

comet [`kɑmɪt] 名彗星

The comet will split during its close approach to the sun.
▶▶ 這顆彗星在接近太陽時將會分裂。

commonplace [`kɑmən‚ples] 名 寒暄客套；老生常談 形 平凡的

名 Foreign travel has become a commonplace.
最近幾年到國外旅遊已是司空見慣的事。

形 His commonplace comment showed how little interested he was in the conversation.
他敷衍的評論顯示出他對此對話多不感興趣。

communicative [kə`mjunə‚ketɪv] 形 愛說話的；口無遮攔的

The outgoing girl is beautiful and communicative.
▶▶ 這個活潑的女孩既漂亮又健談。

comparative [kəm`pærətɪv] 形 比較上的；相對的

He was living in comparative comfort.
▶▶ 他那時生活比較舒適。

compass [`kʌmpəs] 名 羅盤

Compasses are indispensable in sailing.
▶▶ 航海時不可缺少羅盤。

compile [kəm`paɪl] 動 收集；資料彙編

The police have compiled a list of suspects.
▶▶ 警方已經收集了涉嫌者的名單。

complement [`kɑmpləmənt ] / [ `kɑmplə‚mɛnt] 名 補充物 動 補充

名 Travel can be an excellent complement to one's education.
旅遊是教育的極佳補充。

動 A flaming dessert complemented the dinner.
熱騰騰的點心使晚飯更加豐盛。

complexion [kəm`plɛkʃən] 名 氣色；血色

Makeup makes her complexion look better.
▶▶ 化妝讓她氣色更好。

comprehensive [‚kɑmprɪ`hɛnsɪv] 形 綜合的；全面的；包羅萬象的

The state government gave a very comprehensive explanation of its development plans.
▶▶ 州政府對電子工業發展的規劃作了詳盡的解釋。

Level 1 基礎單字
Level 2 必備單字
Level 3 中級單字
Level 4 進階單字
Level 5 高手單字
Level 6 滿級單字

compute [kəm`pjut] 動 計算

Can you compute the total cost, please?

▶▶ 可以請你計算全部的花費嗎？

computerize [kəm`pjutə͵raɪz] 動 用電腦處理

She computerized all the data collected from questionnaires.

▶▶ 她把從問卷蒐集來的資料全用電腦處理。

comrade [`kɑmræd] 名 同伴

I feel content with so many comrades nearby.

▶▶ 身邊有這麼多夥伴，我感到滿足。

concession [kən`sɛʃən] 名 讓步；妥協

Neither of them wants to make a concession.

▶▶ 他們雙方都不願讓步。

(焦點句型) make a concession 讓步

concise [kən`saɪs] 形 簡潔的；簡明的

Her concise conclusion made a perfect ending to the speech.

▶▶ 她簡潔的結論為這場演講做了完美的結尾。

condense [kən`dɛns] 動 縮小；凝結

Steam condenses into water when it touches a cold surface.

▶▶ 水蒸氣接觸寒冷的表面即凝結成水珠。

(焦點句型) condense into sth. 凝結成…

congressman / congresswoman

[`kɑŋgrɛs͵mən ] / [ `kɑŋgrɛs͵wumən] 名 男國會議員；女眾議員

She pleaded with the congressman for help.

▶▶ 她向眾議員求助。

conquest [`kɑŋkwɛst] 名 征服

I succeeded in the conquest of the high mountain.

▶▶ 我成功征服這座高山。

conscientious [͵kɑnʃɪ`ɛnʃəs] 形 認真的

Students are conscientious about their studies.

▶▶ 學生們認真念書。

conserve [kən`sɝv] 動 保存；保護；節約

Conserving the natural resources is our duty.
▶▶ 節省自然資源是我們的責任。

consolation [,kɑnsə`leʃən] 名 撫恤；安慰

I felt better after Lisa's consolation.
▶▶ 麗莎的安慰使我好多了。

console [kən`sol ] / [ `kɑnsol] 動 安慰；慰問 名 控制臺

動 We tried to console her when her mother passed away, but it was very difficult.
她母親去世時我們設法安慰她，但很難奏效。

名 Several objects were positioned on the console.
很多雜物堆在控制臺上。

consonant [`kɑnsənənt] 名 子音 形 和諧的

名 There are more consonants than vowels in most languages.
子音在大部分語言裡都比母音多。

形 His habit is consonant with mine, so we are harmonious roommates.
他的習慣和我很一致，所以我們能成為和諧的室友。

焦點句型 be consonant with sth. 和…一致

conspiracy [kən`spɪrəsɪ] 名 陰謀

His conspiracy of laundering money was revealed.
▶▶ 他洗錢的陰謀被揭穿了。

contestant [kən`tɛstənt] 名 競爭者

All contestants assembled in the hall.
▶▶ 所有參賽者在這座大廳裡集合。

continuity [,kɑntə`njuətɪ] 名 連續性

Due to the continuity of rain, we cannot go on a picnic.
▶▶ 因為連日下雨，我們不能去野餐了。

contradict [,kɑntrə`dɪkt] 動 反駁；矛盾

Eddie contradicted his own points.
▶▶ 艾迪與他自己的論點相矛盾。

1 Level 基礎單字

2 Level 必備單字

3 Level 中級單字

4 Level 進階單字

5 Level 高手單字

6 Level 滿級單字

coral [`kɔrəl] 名 珊瑚 形 珊瑚製的

名 Coral is often used to make jewelry.
珊瑚常用來做成首飾。
形 She wore a coral ornament in her hair.
她在頭髮上戴了一個珊瑚飾品。

corpse [kɔrps] 名 屍體

The rescue team found the corpses of the mother and son.
▶▶ 救援隊找到了那對母子的屍體。

correspondence [ˌkɔrəˋspɑndəns] 名 符合

What he said has little correspondence with her words.
▶▶ 他說的跟她大相逕庭。
(焦點句型) have correspondence with sth. 和…符合

cosmetic [kɑzˋmɛtɪk] 形 化妝用的

She put on some powder with a cosmetic brush.
▶▶ 她用化妝刷撲了點粉。

cosmetics [kɑzˋmɛtɪks] 名 化妝品

She always applies cosmetics before going out.
▶▶ 她出門前都會化妝。
(焦點句型) apply cosmetics 化妝

counterpart [`kaʊntəˌpɑrt] 名 相對應者；作用相同者

I racked my brain in vain for its counterpart in literature.
▶▶ 我絞盡腦汁也想不出它在文學中的對應。

coupon [`kupɑn] 名 優待券 同 voucher

Show the coupon when you pay the bill, and you can get a 10% discount.
▶▶ 付帳時出示優待券，可以打九折。

courtyard [`kortˌjɑrd] 名 庭院；井

The hotel is built around a courtyard, with a fountain and palm trees.
▶▶ 這家飯店圍繞一座庭院而建，有著噴泉和棕櫚樹。

cowardly [`kauədlɪ] 形怯懦的

He is too cowardly to ask questions.
▶▶ 他太怯懦以至於不敢發問。

cozy [`kozɪ] 形舒適的

I rent a cozy suite near school.
▶▶ 我在學校附近租了一間舒適的套房。

cracker [`krækə] 名薄脆餅乾

She distributed some crackers to the children.
▶▶ 她發了一些餅乾給孩子們。

cram [kræm] 動把…塞進；狼吞虎嚥地吃東西

He crammed eight people into his car.
▶▶ 他往他的車裡硬塞進八個人。

cramp [kræmp] 名抽筋 動痙攣

名 I suddenly got a cramp in my right leg.
　我的右腿突然抽筋了。
動 Bill's stomach felt badly cramped, and he was taken to the hospital.
　比爾的胃發生嚴重痙攣，被送到了醫院。

(焦點句型) get a cramp in sth. …抽筋

crater [`kretə] 名火山口

You can see the crater in this photograph.
▶▶ 你可以在這張照片裡看見火山口。

credible [`krɛdəbl̩] 形可信的；可靠的

The mistake makes people wonder how credible the report is.
▶▶ 這錯誤讓人們好奇這報導有多可信。

crocodile [`krɑkə͵daɪl] 名鱷魚；鱷魚皮

Her purse is made of crocodile skin.
▶▶ 她的皮包由鱷魚皮製成。

crossing [`krɔsɪŋ] 名橫越；交叉點；十字路口

The child was killed when a car failed to stop at the crossing.
▶▶ 汽車在十字路口剎車不及，將孩童撞死了。

Level 1 基礎單字
Level 2 必備單字
Level 3 中級單字
Level 4 進階單字
Level 5 高手單字
Level 6 滿級單字

crutch [krʌtʃ] 名支架；拐杖

One of his legs was amputated; therefore, he needed to walk on crutches.
▶▶ 他的一隻腳被截肢了，所以現在必須靠拐杖走路。

(焦點句型) walk on crutches 靠拐杖走路

cub [kʌb] 名幼獸

They found a two-month-old leopard cub.
▶▶ 他們發現一隻年僅兩個月的幼豹。

cucumber [`kjukʌmbɚ] 名小黃瓜

Mother sliced the cucumber and threw the pieces into the boiling water.
▶▶ 媽媽把小黃瓜切片後扔進滾水。

cultivate [`kʌltə͵vet] 動耕種 衍 cultivation 培養

Farmers start cultivating their crops in spring.
▶▶ 農人在春天開始耕種農作。

cumulative [`kjumju͵lətɪv] 形累積的；累加的

Cumulative voting is a multiple-winner voting system intended to promote proportional representation.
▶▶ 累計票數是促進比例代表制的一種多位獲勝者的表決系統。

curb [kɝb] 名抑制 動遏止

名 I need a curb of passion for her.
　　我必須抑制對她的感情。
動 The government did nothing to curb inflation.
　　政府沒有採取措施來控制通貨膨脹。

curry [`kɝɪ] 名咖哩粉 動用咖哩調味

名 He added curry to his rice.
　　他在飯裡加了咖哩。
動 The curried chicken smells great.
　　咖哩雞聞起來真棒。

customary [`kʌstə͵mɛrɪ] 形慣例的；習慣上的

He arrived with his customary promptness.
▶▶ 他像平常那樣迅速到達。

dazzle [`dæzl̩] 名炫目;燦爛 動炫目

名 The dazzle of the gown fascinated her.
那件禮服耀眼的光芒把她迷住了。

動 He was dazzled by the glamor of the movie star.
電影明星的魅力使他感到炫目。

deafen [`dɛfn̩] 動使耳聾

The noise of the siren deafened her.
▶▶ 汽笛聲震得她耳朵都快聾了。

decisive [dɪ`saɪsɪv] 形有決斷力的 關 definitive 最終的;決定性的

A decisive person will not hesitate.
▶▶ 一個果斷的人不會猶豫不決。

dedication [ˌdɛdə`keʃən] 名奉獻

His dedication to education is worth commendation.
▶▶ 他對教育的奉獻值得表揚。

deem [dim] 動認為;視為

He is always deemed to be my twin brother.
▶▶ 他總是被當作我的孿生兄弟。

defect [`dɪfɛkt ] / [ dɪ`fɛkt] 名缺陷;缺點 動脫逃;脫離

名 She thinks she has a lot of defects but no merits.
她認為她有一大堆缺點,卻沒有半個優點。

動 I chose to defect from my violent father.
我選擇逃離暴力的父親。

dental [`dɛntl̩] 形牙齒的 關 dentist 牙醫

She turned to the dentist for her dental disease.
▶▶ 她因牙齒病變而求助牙醫。

deprive [dɪ`praɪv] 動剝奪;使…喪失

The slaves are deprived of freedom.
▶▶ 奴隸的自由遭到剝奪。

(焦點句型) deprive sb. of sth. 剝奪某人的…

633

descent [dɪˋsɛnt] 名 下降

The pilot informed us that we were about to begin our descent.
▸▸ 機長通知我們說快要開始降落。

despise [dɪˋspaɪz] 動 鄙視

He despised me for my poverty.
▸▸ 他鄙視我的貧窮。
(焦點句型) despise sb. for sth. 因…鄙視某人

destined [ˋdɛstɪnd] 形 命中注定的 關 destiny 命運

She feels she is destined to be unhappy for the rest of her life.
▸▸ 她認為自己注定失去餘生的快樂。

detach [dɪˋtætʃ] 動 分開 關 detachment 分離

Detach the form at the bottom of the page and send it to this address.
▸▸ 撕下本頁底下的表格，寄往這個地址。

detain [dɪˋten] 動 留住；耽擱 關 detention 滯留

The boy burst into tears to detain his mother from leaving.
▸▸ 小男孩突然大哭來留住他媽媽。

deter [dɪˋtɝ] 動 威懾；阻撓

Your threat will not deter me from continuing.
▸▸ 你的威脅不會讓我罷休。
(焦點句型) deter sb. from Ving 嚇得某人不敢做某事

detergent [dɪˋtɝdʒənt] 名 清潔劑

Be careful to rinse the detergent from these dishes.
▸▸ 注意務必沖洗掉這些盤子上的清潔劑。

devour [dɪˋvaʊr] 動 狼吞虎嚥；吞食

He sat by the fire, devouring beef and onions.
▸▸ 他坐在火爐旁，狼吞虎嚥地吃著牛肉和洋蔥。

diabetes [ˌdaɪəˋbitɪz] 名 糖尿病

Diabetes is often passed on from generation to generation.
▸▸ 糖尿病會代代遺傳。

dictate [`dɪktet] 動命令；決定；口授

Parents can't dictate to their children how they should run their lives.
▶▶ 父母不能強行規定子女應該怎樣生活。

dictation [dɪk`teʃən] 名命令；口述

He put down his teacher's entire dictation.
▶▶ 他把老師的口述原封不動地抄下來。

dictator [`dɪktetɚ] 名獨裁者 關 dictatorship 獨裁統治

Hitler was a notorious dictator.
▶▶ 希特勒是一個惡名昭彰的獨裁者。

differentiate [dɪfə`rɛnʃɪˌet] 動辨別；區分

Helen can differentiate among various butterflies.
▶▶ 海倫可以分辨各式各樣的蝴蝶。

diplomacy [dɪ`pləməsɪ] 名外交；外交手腕

The eminent envoy was a master of diplomacy.
▶▶ 這位出色的特使是一位外交大師。

disable [dɪs`ebḷ] 動使傷殘；使喪失能力；使故障

My arm was disabled in the car accident.
▶▶ 我的手臂在車禍中殘廢了。

disastrous [dɪz`æstrəs] 形災害的；悲慘的

She was unwilling to recall the disastrous experience.
▶▶ 她不願再回想那個慘痛經驗。

disbelief [ˌdɪsbə`lif] 名不信任；懷疑

We show our disbelief in his words.
▶▶ 我們對他的話表示懷疑。
焦點句型 disbelief in sth. 不信任…

discard [dɪs`kɑrd] 動拋棄；丟掉 名被拋棄者

動 The furniture was discarded.
這些家具被丟棄了。
名 How can we help the discards of society?
我們該如何幫助被社會遺棄的人？

Level 1 基礎單字
Level 2 必備單字
Level 3 中級單字
Level 4 進階單字
Level 5 高手單字
Level 6 滿級單字

discharge [dɪs`tʃɑrdʒ] 名離開；排放 動允許…離開；排放

名 I should do something to stop the discharge of blood.
我得做些什麼來止血。

動 She had discharged herself against medical advice.
她不聽醫生囑咐擅自離開了醫院。

disciple [dɪ`saɪpl̩] 名信徒；門徒；追隨者

We are disciples of the grand master.
▶▶ 我們是那位宗師的追隨者。

disciplinary [`dɪsəplɪˌnɛrɪ] 形訓練上的；紀律的

He leads a disciplinary team, and he has also put much effort into training the members.
▶▶ 他領導一支紀律良好的隊伍，而且他也費了不少心思訓練成員。

disclosure [dɪs`kloʒɚ] 名透露；揭發

He resigned after the disclosure about his private life.
▶▶ 他的私生活曝光後就辭職了。

discomfort [dɪs`kʌmfɚt] 名不安；不適 動使不安

名 His obscene expression brought about my discomfort.
他淫猥的表情讓我感到不舒服。

動 Polly was discomforted by her delay.
她的遲到令波利感到不安。

discreet [dɪ`skrit] 形謹慎的；慎重的

I don't want anyone to find out about our agreement, so please be discreet.
▶▶ 我不想讓任何人知道我們的協議，因此請你謹慎行事。

disgrace [dɪs`gres] 名恥辱 動使蒙羞

名 She left the company in disgrace after admitting stealing from colleagues.
她承認偷了同事的東西，不光彩地離開了公司。

動 You really disgraced yourself by cheating on the exam!
考試作弊是在丟你自己的臉！

(焦點句型) in disgrace 羞辱地

dismay [dɪs`me] 名沮喪 動使沮喪

名 He was my only supporter when I was in dismay.
我沮喪時，他是我唯一的支持者。

動 The failure dismayed him very much.
這次失敗讓他非常沮喪。

焦點句型 in dismay 沮喪地

dispensable [dɪˋspɛnsəbḷ] 形 非必要的

Do not put many dispensable objects in your bag.
▶▶ 不要在背包裡放一大堆非必要的東西。

dispense [dɪˋspɛns] 動 分送；分配

He dispensed handouts to the students.
▶▶ 他把講義發給學生。

disposable [dɪˋspozəbḷ] 形 用完即丟的

Disposable tableware leads to a large amount of garbage.
▶▶ 免洗餐具造成了大量的垃圾。

disposal [dɪˋspozḷ] 名 處理；清理；拋棄 關 dispose 清理；處理

His disposal of the difficulty pleased everybody.
▶▶ 他對困境的處理使大家都感到滿意。

distraction [dɪˋstrækʃən] 名 分心；不安 關 distract 使分心

The television and the internet are distractions to those working from home.
▶▶ 電視與網路會讓在家工作者分心。

distress [dɪˋstrɛs] 名 憂慮；苦惱 動 使悲痛

名 Can I share your distress?
我可以為你分憂嗎？
動 It distressed her very much that her father died.
她父親的死讓她非常悲痛。

disturbance [dɪsˋtɜbəns] 名 干擾；騷亂

We can work here without disturbance.
▶▶ 我們可以在這裡不受干擾地工作。

diversify [daɪˋvɜsəˏfaɪ] 動 使…多樣化

He intended to diversify the company's products.
▶▶ 他打算讓公司的商品多樣化。

Level 1 基礎單字
Level 2 必備單字
Level 3 中級單字
Level 4 進階單字
Level 5 高手單字
Level 6 滿級單字

diversion [daɪ`vɝʒən] 名轉向；改變用途；分心的事物；消遣

The magician's talk created a diversion of attention.
▶▶ 魔術師的談話分散了人們的注意力。

divert [dɪ`vɝt] 動使轉向

They diverted from left to right according to the instruction of the commander.
▶▶ 他們依照指揮官的指示由左轉向右。

doom [dum] 名厄運；死亡；毀滅 動注定

名 She's always full of doom and gloom.
她老是滿臉愁雲慘霧的。
動 Do you believe we are doomed to fail?
你相信我們命中注定要失敗嗎？

(焦點句型) be doomed to V. 注定要…（不好的事情）

dormitory / dorm [`dɔrmə,torɪ] / [dɔrm] 名學校宿舍

Living in dormitories is much cheaper than renting apartments.
▶▶ 住學校宿舍比租公寓便宜多了。

downward [`daʊnwəd] 形下降的

The molten lava got into every nook and cranny on its downward path.
▶▶ 熔岩在向下流淌的過程中鑽進每一個角落。

downwards / downward [`daʊnwədz ] / [ `daʊnwəd] 副下降地

He took the elevator downwards.
▶▶ 他搭電梯下樓。

doze [doz] 名打瞌睡 動打瞌睡

名 She drank coffee to avoid dozing.
她喝咖啡防止打瞌睡。
動 He dozed off in front of the television.
他坐在電視機前打起瞌睡來了。

drastic [`dræstɪk] 形激烈的；猛烈的

The government is threatening to take drastic action.
▶▶ 政府警告說要採取激烈措施。

dresser [`drɛsɚ] 名 梳妝臺

Her dresser contained various types of makeup.
▶▶ 她的梳妝臺擺了各式各樣的化妝品。

dressing [`drɛsɪŋ] 名 佐料；（包紮傷口的）敷料；穿著

Her strange dressing attracted the attention of the passersby.
▶▶ 她古怪的服飾引起了路人的注意。

dual [`djuəl] 形 成雙的；雙重的

His dual role as a composer and a conductor made him very busy.
▶▶ 作曲家和指揮家的雙重身份使他非常忙碌。

dubious [`djubɪəs] 形 可疑的；不確定的；懷疑的

His dubious reply really made me impatient.
▶▶ 他含糊的回應讓我很不耐煩。

duration [dju`reʃən] 名 持久；持續

Please remain seated during the duration of the flight.
▶▶ 飛行途中請勿離座。

dusk [dʌsk] 名 黃昏

We watched the sunset at dusk.
▶▶ 我們在黃昏時欣賞日落。

dwarf [dwɔrf] 名 矮人 動 萎縮；使矮小

名 The dwarfs in fairy tales always live in the deep forests.
童話故事裡的小矮人通常都住在森林深處。
動 Your height may dwarf when you are elderly.
你老了以後身高會萎縮。

dwell [dwɛl] 動 居住

I have dwelled in Taipei for over twenty years.
▶▶ 我在台北居住超過二十年了。

dwelling [`dwɛlɪŋ] 名 住宅；住處

These dwellings have been put to good use.
▶▶ 這些住宅已得到妥善的利用。

Level 1 基礎單字
Level 2 必備單字
Level 3 中級單字
Level 4 進階單字
Level 5 高手單字
Level 6 滿級單字

eccentric [ɪk`sɛntrɪk] 形 古怪的 名 古怪的人

形 People said he was mad, but I think he was just slightly eccentric.
人們都說他瘋了，但我認為他只是有點古怪。

名 Tom is said to be an eccentric, but I don't think so.
湯姆被稱為怪人，但我不這麼認為。

eclipse [ɪ`klɪps] 名 蝕 動 遮蔽；使失色

名 We observed the lunar eclipse by telescope.
我們用望遠鏡觀察月蝕。

動 Her beauty eclipses everyone else's.
她的美麗使眾人失色。

edible [`ɛdəbḷ] 形 食用的

This kind of mushroom is not edible.
▶▶ 這種菇類不能食用。

editorial [ˌɛdə`torɪəl] 名 社論 形 編輯的

名 The editorial he wrote is partial towards the ruling party.
他寫的這篇社論偏袒執政黨。

形 He intends to expand the editorial department.
他打算擴充編輯部門。

electrician [ɪˌlɛk`trɪʃən] 名 電機工程師

David worked as an electrician in the company.
▶▶ 大衛在這間公司擔任電機工程師。

elevate [`ɛləˌvet] 動 舉起；提高 關 elevation 高度

The teacher hoped to elevate the minds of her young pupils by reading them religious stories.
▶▶ 這位老師希望藉由讀宗教故事來提升學生的心靈境界。

emigrant [`ɛməgrənt] 名 移民者 形 移民的

名 Those emigrants live mainly in this district.
那些移民者主要居住在這一區。

形 I think we should put emphasis on the rights of emigrant labors.
我認為我們應該重視移民勞工的權利。

emigrate [`ɛmə,gret] 動 移居

Ted emigrated from Germany to America.
▶▶ 泰德從德國移居到美國。

emigration [,ɛmə`greʃən] 名 移民

Her family moved to Canada at the height of emigration to that country.
▶▶ 在移民潮的高峰時她們舉家遷往加拿大。

encyclopedia [ɪn,saɪklə`pidɪə] 名 百科全書

You can check the details of the incident in the encyclopedia.
▶▶ 你可以在百科全書中確認這個事件的詳盡敘述。

endeavor [ɪn`dɛvə] 名 努力 動 盡力

名 The endeavor to win the prize was in vain.
　　獲獎的努力都白費了。
動 I endeavored to understand his meaning.
　　我努力瞭解他的意思。

endurance [ɪn`djurəns] 名 耐力 關 endure 忍耐

He showed remarkable endurance throughout his illness.
▶▶ 他在整個生病期間表現出非凡的忍耐力。

enhance [ɪn`hæns] 動 提高；增強 關 enhancement 增進

I'd like to enhance the magazine by adding some illustrations.
▶▶ 我想藉由增加插圖來加強這本雜誌。

enlighten [ɪn`laɪtn] 動 啟發 關 enlightenment 啟發

His story enlightened me and reminded that I should never give up.
▶▶ 他的故事啟發我永遠不要放棄。

enrich [ɪn`rɪtʃ] 動 使富有 關 enrichment 豐富

Reading books enrich your spirit.
▶▶ 閱讀使你的心靈富足。

enroll [ɪn`rol] 動 登記；註冊 關 enrollment 註冊；登記

We enrolled him as a member of our club.
▶▶ 我們登記他為本俱樂部的會員。

Level 1 基礎單字
Level 2 必備單字
Level 3 中級單字
Level 4 進階單字
Level 5 高手單字
Level 6 滿級單字

equate [ɪˋkwet] 動使相等 關 equal 相等的

The chef equated the two meals.
▶▶ 廚師使這兩份餐點的份量相等。

escort [ˋɛskɔrt] 動護送 名護衛者；護送

(動) He escorted his sister home.
他護送妹妹回家。
(名) He arrived under the escort of police.
他在警方護送下到達。

esteem [əˋstim] 名尊重 動尊敬

(名) I have great esteem for my benefactor.
我很尊敬我的恩人。
(動) Please esteem every person on the platform.
請尊敬講臺上的每個人。

eternity [ɪˋtɜnətɪ] 名永遠；永恆 關 eternal 永恆的

Nobody can live for all eternity.
▶▶ 沒有人能活到永遠。

evacuate [ɪˋvækjʊˏet] 動撤離 關 evacuation 撤離

The residents here were evacuated due to the coming flood.
▶▶ 因為洪水將至，這裡的居民被強制撤離。

evergreen [ˋɛvəˏgrin] 名常綠植物 形常綠的

(名) My neighbors planted evergreens in the yard.
我的鄰居在後院種植常青樹。
(形) Pines, firs, and hollies are evergreen trees.
松樹、杉樹以及冬青是常綠樹。

examinee [ɪɡˏzæməˋni] 名應試者

Thirty examinees waited in the conference room.
▶▶ 三十位應試者在會議室等待。

examiner [ɪɡˋzæmɪnə] 名主考官；審查員

Sometimes the examiner pretends to be solemn, observing the responses of examinees.
▶▶ 有時主考官會裝得很嚴肅，藉此觀察受試者的反應。

excel [ɪk`sɛl] 勔勝過

I excelled others in the math exam.
▸▸ 我在這次數學考試中勝過其他人。

excerpt [`ɛks3pt ] / [ ɛk`s3pt] 名摘錄 勔引用

名 The excerpts of the newly published book are fascinating.
這本剛出版的新書摘錄很吸引人。

勔 I excerpted some sentences I liked from the book.
我從書裡摘錄一些我喜歡的句子。

excess [`ɛksɛs] 名超過 形過量的

名 Her debts are in excess of 1,000 dollars.
她欠債超過一千美金。

形 Taking an excess dosage can be fatal.
服藥過量可能會致命。

(焦點句型) in excess of sth. 超過…

exert [ɪg`z3t] 勔運用；盡力

He exerts himself in everything he does.
▸▸ 他做任何事都盡心盡力。

expiration [ˏɛkspə`reʃən] 名到期；結束

The expiration date of the milk is today.
▸▸ 這瓶牛奶的保存期限到今天。

expire [ɪk`spaɪr] 勔到期；期滿；結束

He is planning another tour abroad, yet his passport will expire at the end of this month.
▸▸ 他打算再出國一次，但是這個月底他的護照就要到期了。

extract [`ɛkstrækt ] / [ ɪk`strækt] 名摘錄；提取物 勔拔出；提取

名 The main ingredient of the beverage is ginkgo extract.
這種飲料的主要原料是銀杏萃取物。

勔 I think this tooth will have to be extracted.
看來我得把這顆牙拔掉。

extracurricular [ˏɛkstrəkə`rɪkjələ] 形課外的

She is enthusiastic about extracurricular activities.
▸▸ 她對課外活動很熱衷。

Level 1 基礎單字
Level 2 必備單字
Level 3 中級單字
Level 4 進階單字
Level 5 高手單字
Level 6 滿級單字

eyelash / lash [`aɪ,læʃ] / [læʃ] 名睫毛 關 eyebrow 眉毛

Long and curly eyelashes are her characteristics.
▶▶ 纖長捲翹的睫毛是她的特色。

eyelid [`aɪ,lɪd] 名眼皮

He heard the bad news without batting an eyelid.
▶▶ 他聽到這個壞消息時面不改色。

eyesight [`aɪ,saɪt] 名視力

His eyesight was exceedingly defective.
▶▶ 他的視力有很大的缺陷。

F字頭滿級單字

MP3 122

fable [`febl̩] 名寓言

Cinderella is the fable little Johnny loves the most.
▶▶ 灰姑娘是小強尼最愛的寓言故事。

faction [`fækʃən] 名派系

The party split into petty factions.
▶▶ 這個黨內分割成許多派系。

Fahrenheit [`færən,haɪt] 名華氏溫度

Fahrenheit is a widely-used measure in America.
▶▶ 華氏溫度在美國廣為使用。

falter [`fɑltɚ] 動動搖；畏縮

His voice faltered when he told us he hadn't finished school.
▶▶ 他結巴地說他尚未完成學業。

familiarity [fə,mɪlɪ`ærətɪ] 名熟悉；親密 關 familiar 熟悉的

Her familiarity with English is her best advantage.
▶▶ 精通英語是她的最佳優勢。
(焦點句型) familiarity with sth. 熟悉…

fascination [ˌfæsəˋneʃən] 名魅力；迷惑 關 fascinate 使著迷

The topic seemed to have a fascination for her.
▶▶ 這個題目似乎對她很有吸引力。

(焦點句型) **have a fascination for sb.** 對…有吸引力

feasible [ˋfizəbḷ] 形可行的

We have no feasible scheme to put the theory into practice.
▶▶ 我們沒有可行的方案可以實踐這個理論。

feeble [ˋfibḷ] 形虛弱的；無力的

Grandmother has been feeble from illness lately.
▶▶ 祖母近來因病而變得虛弱。

feminine [ˋfɛmənɪn] 形女性的 名女性

形 He has feminine personality characteristics although he has a masculine body.
雖然他擁有男性身體，卻有著女性特質。
名 Feminine is the opposite of masculine.
女性的相反是男性。

fertility [fɝˋtɪlətɪ] 名肥沃 關 fertile 肥沃的

The fertility of the soil has been greatly improved through modern agricultural methods
▶▶ 土壤的肥沃度透過現代農業方法大大地改善。

fertilizer [ˋfɝtḷˌaɪzɚ] 名肥料

Crushed animal bones make one of the best fertilizers.
▶▶ 碎骨是最好的肥料之一。

fiancee [ˌfiənˋse] 名未婚妻 關 fiancé 未婚夫

Terry and his fiancee will marry next month.
▶▶ 泰瑞和他的未婚妻將於下個月結婚。

fin [fɪn] 名鰭

On seeing the fin of a shark, you should escape right away.
▶▶ 看到鯊魚鰭的時候，你應該立刻逃跑。

Level 1 基礎單字
Level 2 必備單字
Level 3 中級單字
Level 4 進階單字
Level 5 高手單字
Level 6 滿級單字

finite [`faɪnaɪt] 形 有限的

We must accept finite disappointment, but never lose infinite hope.
▶▶ 我們必須接受有限的失望,但是千萬不可失去無限的希望。

firecracker [`faɪr͵krækɚ] 名 鞭炮

We set off firecrackers to celebrate Chinese New Year.
▶▶ 我們放鞭炮慶祝中國新年。

fireproof [`faɪr͵pruf] 形 防火的;耐火的

The building is made of fireproof material.
▶▶ 這棟建築以防火材料製成。

fishery [`fɪʃərɪ] 名 漁業;水產業

The fishery in Taiwan is on the wane.
▶▶ 台灣的漁業日漸蕭條。

flake [flek] 名 雪花;小薄片 動 剝落;雪片般地降落

名 The boy stuck his tongue out to catch some flakes of snow.
那男孩伸出舌頭來接一些雪花。
動 The paint on the wall flaked off.
牆上的油漆剝落了。

flaw [flɔ] 名 瑕疵;缺陷 動 弄破;破裂;糟蹋

名 One flaw can ruin a product.
一點瑕疵可以毀掉一個產品。
動 Mark flawed the glass by chipping it.
馬克把玻璃杯打破了。

flourish [`flɝɪʃ] 名 繁榮 動 繁盛

名 Their business turned into a flourish.
他們的生意變好了。
動 I hope your business flourishes.
祝你生意興隆。

flunk [flʌŋk] 動 失敗;不及格 名 失敗

動 Gary flunked the English test.
喬治英文考試不及格。
名 Do not despair because of the flunk.
不要因為失敗而絕望。

foe [fo] 名敵人；敵軍

The knights prevailed against their foes.
▶▶ 那些騎士戰勝了他們的敵人。

folklore [`fok.lor] 名民俗；民間傳說

The story rapidly became a part of family folklore.
▶▶ 這個故事很快就成為家族傳說的一部分。

formidable [for`mɪdəbəl] 形可怕的；難應付的 副 formidably 可怕地

In her work as a scientist, Mary confronts formidable problems every day.
▶▶ 身為一位科學家，瑪莉每天都面對一些難以應付的問題。

formulate [`fɔrmjə.let] 動制定；規劃；構想 關 formula 公式；慣例

The company is going to formulate a new plan.
▶▶ 公司將要制定新的計畫。

forsake [fə`sek] 動拋棄；放棄

She forsook her wealth and became a volunteer in India.
▶▶ 她放棄財富，到印度去當志工。
文法解析 forsake動詞三態變化為forsake / forsook / forsaken。

forthcoming [.forθ`kʌmɪŋ] 形即將到來的 同 pending

Everyone is anticipating the forthcoming holidays.
▶▶ 每個人都很期待即將到來的假日。

fortify [`fɔrtə.faɪ] 動加固；強化工事

The tragedy was caused by not fortifying the bridge enough.
▶▶ 這次悲劇是因為橋梁工事加固程度不足所導致。

fowl [faul] 名鳥；家禽

Chickens and ducks are two types of fowl.
▶▶ 雞和鴨是兩種類型的家禽。

fracture [`fræktʃə] 名破碎；骨折 動破碎；挫傷

名 The fracture caused him intense pain.
骨折對他造成了劇烈的疼痛。
動 He fractured his ankle.
他的腳踝骨折了。

Level 1 基礎單字
Level 2 必備單字
Level 3 中級單字
Level 4 進階單字
Level 5 高手單字
Level 6 滿級單字

fragrance [`fregrəns] 名芳香

The fragrance of this perfume is wonderful.
▶▶ 這瓶香水的香氣真是迷人。

fragrant [`fregrənt] 形芳香的；愉快的

The flowers gave off a fragrant odor.
▶▶ 花發出一陣芳香的味道。

frantic [`fræntɪk] 形狂暴的；發狂的

A drug addict will get frantic without drugs.
▶▶ 毒癮者沒有毒品就會發狂。

freak [frik] 名怪胎 形怪異的

名 People often call those who are different from them freaks.
　人們常把跟自己不一樣的人稱為怪胎。
形 His freak behavior is suspicious.
　他怪異的舉止有些可疑。

freeway [`frɪˌwe] 名高速公路

His new car certainly can drive fast on the freeway.
▶▶ 他的新車在高速公路上確實開得快極了。

friction [`frɪkʃən] 名摩擦；衝突

Friction causes a rolling ball to stop eventually.
▶▶ 摩擦力使一顆滾動的球最終會停下來。

fume [fjum] 動發怒；生悶氣 名煙；蒸氣

動 He was fuming at my delay.
　他對於我遲到感到生氣。
名 The fumes emitted from the gas container.
　蒸氣從氣體容器中冒出。
焦點句型 fume at sth. 對…生氣

fury [`fjʊrɪ] 名憤怒；狂怒 關 furious 憤怒的

She was speechless with fury.
▶▶ 她氣得說不出話來。
焦點句型 with fury 憤怒地

fuse [fjuz] 名保險絲 動熔合；（保險絲）熔斷

名 The lights went off, because the system was overloaded with electrical appliances, which blew the fuse.
電燈熄滅了，因為電器用品使系統超過負荷量，而把保險絲燒斷了。

動 We fused the two metals.
我們熔合兩種金屬。

fuss [fʌs] 名大驚小怪 動焦急；使焦急

名 I am used to her fuss over everything.
我已經習慣她對每件事大驚小怪。

動 She fussed about the loss of her purse.
她因皮包不見了而焦急。

(焦點句型) fuss about sth. 因…而焦急

 G字頭滿級單字

MP3 123

gallop [ˋgæləp] 名（馬的）疾馳；飛奔 動（馬的）疾馳

名 My horse suddenly broke into a gallop.
我的馬突然飛奔起來。

動 The horse galloped away at full speed.
這匹馬全力奔馳而去。

gangster [ˋgæŋstɚ] 名歹徒；匪徒

The gangster ended up in prison.
▶▶ 那個歹徒最後死在獄中。

garment [ˋgɑrmənt] 名衣服

Why did you leave these garments on the floor?
▶▶ 你為什麼把這些衣服放在地板上？

gay [ge] 名（男）同性戀 關 lesbian 女同性戀

Gay, lesbian, bisexual, and transgender issues are the common topics in the gender studies.
▶▶ 男同性戀、女同性戀、雙性戀和跨性別是性別研究中常見的主題。

geometry [dʒɪˋɑmətrɪ] 名幾何學

Archimedes made a significant contribution to the study of geometry.
▶▶ 阿基米德對幾何學有重大貢獻。

Level 1 基礎單字
Level 2 必備單字
Level 3 中級單字
Level 4 進階單字
Level 5 高手單字
Level 6 滿級單字

glacier [`gleʃɚ] 名 冰河

The glacier washed the rocks into a canyon.
▶▶ 冰河把岩石沖挖成一座峽谷。

glamour [`glæmɚ] 名 魅力 關 glamorous 迷人的

Young people are often attracted by the glamour of city life.
▶▶ 年輕人常常被城市生活的魅力所吸引。

gleam [glim] 名 一絲光線 動 閃爍

名 A few gleams of sunshine lit up the gloomy afternoon.
幾道陽光使陰暗的下午亮了起來。
動 Her eyes gleamed in the dark.
她的眼睛在黑暗中閃閃發亮。

glide [glaɪd] 名 滑動；滑走 動 滑行

名 The glide of the plane was gentle and smooth.
那架飛機滑行得平穩而緩和。
動 The snake glided smoothly towards its prey.
那條蛇動作流暢地向獵物滑行過去。

glitter [`glɪtɚ] 名 光輝；閃光；小發光物 動 閃爍

名 Her dress looked pretty with all the glitter.
她洋裝上的亮片看起來很漂亮。
動 An ornate temple glittered in the distance.
一座華麗的廟宇在遠處閃閃發光。

gloom [glum] 名 陰暗；昏暗 動 變幽暗；悶悶不樂

名 Do not put yourself in gloom.
不要讓你自己沉浸於黑暗裡。
動 He gloomed the whole night and refused to eat anything.
他整晚都悶悶不樂，也拒絕吃任何東西。

gorilla [gə`rɪlə] 名 大猩猩

The gorilla gobbled up the bananas.
▶▶ 大猩猩狼吞虎嚥地吃著香蕉。

gospel [`gɑspl̩] 名 福音；真理

You mustn't take his words as gospel.
▶▶ 你不要把他的話當作真理。

grapefruit [`grep,frut] 名 葡萄柚

Small jars of grapefruit jam are on the breakfast table.
▶▶ 早餐桌上有幾小罐葡萄柚果醬。

graze [grez] 動 吃草；放牧

You can graze your sheep on the field on the other side of the stream.
▶▶ 你可以在小溪對面的田地上放羊。

grease [gris] 名 油脂 動 塗油

名 See the grease left on the dish.
　　看看盤子裡殘留的油脂。
動 You may grease the machine to make it work more smoothly.
　　你可以在機器上塗點油，讓它運作得更順暢。

groan [gron] 名 呻吟 動 呻吟

名 I heard groans coming from the ward.
　　我聽見病房傳出呻吟。
動 He groaned in pain.
　　他痛苦地呻吟。

growl [graul] 名 咆哮聲 動 咆哮

名 The noisy growl made me sleepless yesterday.
　　吵鬧的咆哮聲讓我昨晚失眠。
動 He growled at me without reason.
　　他莫名其妙對我咆哮。

(焦點句型) growl at sb. 對某人咆哮

grumble [`grʌmbḷ] 名 牢騷 動 抱怨

名 I am fed up with her frequent grumbles.
　　我對她經常發牢騷感到厭倦。
動 The students were always grumbling about the poor quality of the food.
　　學生老是抱怨伙食差。

(焦點句型) grumble about sth. 抱怨…

1 Level 基礎單字
2 Level 必備單字
3 Level 中級單字
4 Level 進階單字
5 Level 高手單字
6 Level 滿級單字

MEMORIZE 7000 VOCABULARIES ONCE AND FOR ALL！

hacker [`hækɚ] 名 駭客

The hacker stole a lot of money from a bank.
▶▶ 駭客從銀行偷了許多錢。

hail [hel] 名 冰雹 動 歡呼

名 Many of the crops are damaged by the hail.
許多農作物被冰雹砸壞了。

動 The conference was hailed as a great success.
這個會議被稱頌為一次巨大的成功。

handicap [`hændɪ͵kæp] 名 障礙；殘疾 動 妨礙；使不利

名 Losing our best player was a handicap to the team.
失去最好的運動員對我隊不利。

動 I was handicapped by nearsightedness.
近視對我不利。

(焦點句型) sb. be handicapped by sth. 某事對某人不利

handicraft [`hændɪ͵kræft] 名 手工藝品

They sold the handicrafts in the shop.
▶▶ 他們在商店販售手工藝品。

harass [hə`ræs] 動 騷擾 關 harassment 騷擾

The middle-aged man keeps harassing her.
▶▶ 那個中年男子一直騷擾她。

harden [`hɑrdən] 動 使硬化

Their suspicions hardened into certainty.
▶▶ 他們由懷疑變成肯定。

harmonica [hɑr`monɪkə] 名 口琴

He performed a melody on his harmonica.
▶▶ 他用口琴表演了一段曲子。

harness [`hɑrnəs] 名 輓具；繫帶 動 裝上輓具；控制

名 You have to prepare a harness before riding on the horse.
騎馬前你必須準備馬具。

1 Level 基礎單字

2 Level 必備單字

3 Level 中級單字

4 Level 進階單字

5 Level 高手單字

6 Level 滿級單字

(動) The farmer harnessed the horse to the cart.
農夫把馬套到馬車上。

haunt [hɔnt] (動)不斷困擾；（鬼魂）經常出沒 (名)常到的場所

(動) It seems that the war would haunt him for the rest of his life.
看來那場戰爭給他留下了餘生都揮之不去的陰影。
(名) The pub is one of my haunts. I come here every night.
這間酒吧是我常去的場所之一，我每晚都會來。

headphone [`hɛdfon] (名)頭戴式耳機

He wore the headphones and enjoyed the music.
▶▶ 他掛著頭戴式耳機享受音樂。

healthful [`hɛlθfəl] (形)有益健康的

Vegetables are healthful for you.
▶▶ 蔬菜對你有益健康。

hearty [`hɑrtɪ] (形)熱誠的；衷心的

He nodded his head in hearty agreement.
▶▶ 他點點頭，表示由衷的贊成。

hedge [hɛdʒ] (名)樹籬；籬笆 (動)設籬笆；圍起；設障礙於…

(名) He wriggled through the thick hedge.
他穿過濃密的樹籬蜿蜒而行。
(動) We are hedged about by special regulations.
我們受到特殊法規所限制。

heighten [`haɪtṇ] (動)增高 (開) height 高度

She heightened the table by adding three bricks below.
▶▶ 她在下面墊了三塊磚頭把桌子增高。

hemisphere [`hɛməsˌfɪr] (名)半球

Taiwan is located in the Northern Hemisphere.
▶▶ 台灣位於北半球。

heroic [hɪ`roɪk] (形)英雄的；英勇的

The epics portrayed heroic deeds.
▶▶ 這些史詩描繪英雄事蹟。

heroin [`hɛroɪn] 名 海洛因

He is addicted to heroin.
▶▶ 他是海洛因成癮者。

heterosexual [ˌhɛtəro`sɛkʃuəl] 名 異性戀者 形 異性戀的

名 Peter is a heterosexual and has a wife and two kids.
　彼得是個異性戀者，他有老婆跟兩個小孩。
形 Heterosexual culture is different from homosexual culture.
　異性戀文化和同性戀文化有所不同。

hijack [`haɪˌdʒæk] 名 劫持 動 劫持

名 The hijack was organized by a group of opponents to the government.
　劫機事件是由一個反對政府的小集團策劃的。
動 Five terrorists hijacked the bus.
　五個恐怖份子劫持巴士。

hoarse [hɔrs] 形 嘶啞的

We shouted ourselves hoarse at the football match.
▶▶ 我們在足球比賽時把嗓子都喊啞了。

homosexual [ˌhomo`sɛkʃuəl] 名 同性戀者 形 同性戀的

名 As a homosexual, Wayne has a different lifestyle from that of his brother's.
　身為一名同性戀者，韋恩和他弟弟有不同的生活方式。
形 Homosexual literature is blooming now.
　同性戀文學正當盛行。

honorary [`ɑnəˌrɛrɪ] 形 榮譽的 關 honor 榮譽

Daisy got an honorary degree from the college.
▶▶ 黛西獲得那所大學的榮譽學位。

hospitable [`hɑspɪtəbl̩] 形 善於待客的

The Mongolians were very hospitable and treated us to a delicious meal.
▶▶ 這些蒙古人很好客，還招待我們豐盛的一餐。

hospitality [ˌhɑspɪ`tælətɪ] 名 好客

Thank you for your kind hospitality.
▶▶ 謝謝你的盛情款待。

hospitalize [`hɑspɪtəˌlaɪz] 動 送…住院治療 關 hospital 醫院

They hospitalized their insane mother for three months.
▶▶ 他們將患有精神疾病的母親送院治療三個月。

hostel [`hɑstḷ] 名（免費或廉價的）旅社；收容所

I stayed at a hostel last night.
▶▶ 我昨夜住在青年旅舍。

hover [`hʌvɚ] 動 盤旋；徘徊 名 徘徊

動 The shark was still hovering around.
　鯊魚仍在附近徘徊。
名 I dare not go out due to the hover of the bees.
　我不敢出門，因為蜜蜂徘徊不去。

humiliate [hju`mɪlɪˌet] 動 侮辱 關 humiliation 侮辱

He was accused of humiliating the president publicly.
▶▶ 他被指控公然辱罵元首。

hunch [hʌntʃ] 名 直覺；預感 動 突出；弓起背部

名 Evans had a hunch that he was in serious trouble.
　直覺告訴伊文斯，他麻煩大了。
動 She hunched down on the ground.
　她弓著身坐在地上。

hurdle [`hɝdḷ] 名 障礙物；跨欄 動 跳過障礙

名 The horse jumped over the hurdles lightly.
　這匹馬輕鬆地跳過跨欄。
動 My dog failed to hurdle the fence.
　我的狗無法跨過柵欄。

hygiene [`haɪdʒin] 名 衛生學；衛生

High standards of hygiene are essential when you are preparing food.
▶▶ 預備食物的過程要嚴格講求衛生。

hypocrite [`hɪpəkrɪt] 名 偽君子

He is a complete hypocrite because he never practices what he advises.
▶▶ 他是個徹底的偽君子，他所說的從來沒做到。

1 Level 基礎單字

2 Level 必備單字

3 Level 中級單字

4 Level 進階單字

5 Level 高手單字

6 Level 滿級單字

iceberg [`aɪs͵bɝg] 名冰山

The Titanic hit an iceberg and sank.
▶▶ 鐵達尼號撞到冰山而沉沒。

illuminate [ɪ`lumə͵net] 動照明；點亮 關 illumination 照明

The light of candles illuminated the house.
▶▶ 燭光照亮了屋子。

imperative [ɪm`pɛrətɪv] 名極重要；緊急 形極重要的；迫切的

名 Job creation has become an imperative for the government.
創造工作機會是政府必做的事。
形 The boss issued an imperative command.
老闆宣布了一個重要的命令。

imperial [ɪm`pɪrɪəl] 形帝國的；至高的

He has the imperial power in the country.
▶▶ 他在這個國家擁有至高權力。

implicit [ɪm`plɪsɪt] 形含蓄的；不明確的

She corrected my composition with implicit language.
▶▶ 她措辭含蓄地糾正我的作文。

imposing [ɪm`pozɪŋ] 形壯觀的；宏偉的 關 impose 把…強加於

The imposing view of the mountain really impressed me.
▶▶ 這座山雄偉的風景讓我印象深刻。

imprison [ɪm`prɪzn̩] 動禁閉 關 imprisonment 坐牢

He was imprisoned for theft.
▶▶ 他因竊盜罪被關。

incline [ɪn`klaɪn ] / [ `ɪnklaɪn] 動傾向 名傾斜面 關 inclination 傾向

動 Allen was inclined to change his job.
艾倫有換工作的想法。
名 She tried hard to climb the steep incline.
她努力試著爬上那座陡坡。
(焦點句型) beV inclined to V 傾向於…

inclusive [ɪn`klusɪv] 形包含在內的

He bought a lot of goods, inclusive of food and daily necessities.
▶▶ 他買了一堆東西，包括食物和日用品。

indifference [ɪn`dɪfərəns] 名不關心；不在乎 關 indifferent 冷漠的

Their father treated them with indifference.
▶▶ 他們的父親對他們漠不關心。

indignant [ɪn`dɪgnənt] 形憤怒的

They were indignant that they had to pay more for worse services.
▶▶ 他們對於要花更多錢，服務卻變得更糟相當氣憤。

induce [ɪn`djus] 動引誘；引起

Nothing in the world would induce me to do that.
▶▶ 什麼也不能引誘我做那種事。

industrialize [ɪn`dʌstrɪə,laɪz] 動工業化

The southern part of the country was slow to industrialize.
▶▶ 這個國家的南部工業化進程緩慢。

infectious [ɪn`fɛkʃəs] 形傳染的 關 infect 傳染

Influenza is a highly infectious disease.
▶▶ 流行性感冒是一種高傳染性的疾病。

infer [ɪn`fɝ] 動推斷；推理 關 inference 推理

I inferred from your letter that you have not made up your mind yet.
▶▶ 從你的信中推測，你還沒有下定決心。

inhabit [ɪn`hæbɪt] 動居住

Johnson and his family inhabited the suburbs.
▶▶ 強森和家人住在郊區。

inhabitant [ɪn`hæbətənt] 名居民

He is an inhabitant of Croatia.
▶▶ 他是克羅埃西亞人。

1 Level 基礎單字

2 Level 必備單字

3 Level 中級單字

4 Level 進階單字

5 Level 高手單字

6 Level 滿級單字

inland [`ɪnlənd] 形 內陸的 副 在內陸 名 內地

形 Tax incomes of inland provinces have risen this year.
內陸省份今年的稅收有所增加。

副 This kind of flower can only be found inland.
這種花只有在內陸才能找到。

innumerable [ɪn`njumərəbl̩] 形 數不盡的

The little boy tried to count the innumerable stars.
▶▶ 小男孩努力數著數不盡的星星。

inquire [ɪn`kwaɪr] 動 詢問；打聽

I inquired about their work.
▶▶ 我向他詢問他們的工作。

(焦點句型) inquire about sth. 詢問…

insistence [ɪn`sɪstəns] 名 堅持

Vicky's insistence on taking part in social movements never sways.
▶▶ 薇琪參與社會運動的堅持從未動搖。

intellect [`ɪntə,lɛkt] 名 理解力；智力

Sally is a person of great intellect who can understand almost anything in no time.
▶▶ 莎莉是個聰慧的人，幾乎所有事情她都可以立刻理解。

interpreter [ɪn`tɜprɪtə] 名 口譯員；解釋者

An interpreter must be very quick-witted.
▶▶ 口譯員必須非常機靈。

intersection [,ɪntə`sɛkʃən] 名 相交；十字路口

Turn left at the next intersection.
▶▶ 在下一個十字路口左轉。

intervene [,ɪntə`vin] 動 介入

She would have died if the neighbors hadn't intervened.
▶▶ 要不是鄰居出面介入，她早就沒命了。

intimacy [`ɪntəməsɪ] 名親密

An intimacy grew between us.
▶▶ 我們之間的關係日漸親密。

intimidate [ɪn`tɪmə,det] 動恐嚇

The reporter was intimidated to keep the secret.
▶▶ 這名記者被恐嚇要保守祕密。

intonation [,ɪntə`neʃən] 名語調;聲調

In English, some questions have a rising intonation.
▶▶ 英語中有些疑問句會提高語調。

intrude [ɪn`trud] 動侵入;打擾 衍 intrusion 入侵

I'm sorry to intrude during your Sunday lunch.
▶▶ 抱歉打擾你們的星期天午飯。

intruder [ɪn`trudə] 名侵入者

She spared no effort to resist the intruder.
▶▶ 她奮力抵抗入侵者。

invaluable [ɪn`væljəbḷ] 形無價的

My benefactor is invaluable to me.
▶▶ 我的恩人對我的價值難以估計。

inventory [`ɪnvən,tɔrɪ] 名存貨;物品清單 動盤點;清點存貨

名 He checked the inventory to see if large paper clips were available.
他查看了一下清單,看看是否有大迴紋針可用。
動 His work is to inventory the stock in the warehouse.
他的工作就是清點倉庫裡的存貨。

ironic [aɪ`rɑnɪk] 形諷刺的 同 cynical 衍 irony 諷刺

She congratulated my success in an ironic way.
▶▶ 她語帶諷刺地祝賀我成功。

irritable [`ɪrətəbḷ] 形暴躁的;易怒的

He's always in an irritable mood on Mondays.
▶▶ 他在星期一的情緒總是很煩躁。

1 Level 基礎單字

2 Level 必備單字

3 Level 中級單字

4 Level 進階單字

5 Level 高手單字

6 Level 滿級單字

irritate [`ɪrəˌtet] 動 使生氣 關 irritation 煩躁

He irritated his mother by disobeying her.
▶ 他因不服從母親而惹她生氣。

isle [aɪl] 名 小島 關 island 島嶼

The ownership details of the isle are kept confidential.
▶ 這個小島所有權的細節仍是機密。

itch [ɪtʃ] 名 癢 動 發癢

名 Kenny thinks the itch is tolerable.
　肯尼認為癢可以忍受。
動 My nose is itching.
　我鼻子發癢。

ivy [`aɪvɪ] 名 常春藤

The ivy entwined the column.
▶ 常春藤纏繞著柱子。

UNIT 10　J、K 字頭滿級單字　　MP3 126

jade [dʒed] 名 玉；翡翠

The jade bead necklace looks elegant. How much does it cost?
▶ 這條翡翠珠項鍊看起來很雅緻，要多少錢？

janitor [`dʒænətə] 名 管理員；看門者

The janitor checked the furnace because the pressure was too high.
▶ 由於壓力過高，火爐看管者檢查了一下熔爐。

jasmine [`dʒæsmɪn] 名 茉莉

Jasmine is her favorite flower.
▶ 茉莉是她最喜歡的花。

jingle [`dʒɪŋgl̩] 名 叮噹聲 動 使發出叮噹聲

名 I knew there were many coins in his pocket by the jingle.
　我從叮噹聲知道他的口袋裡有很多錢幣。
動 He jingled the bell to wake up the baby.
　他搖鈴叫醒嬰兒。

jolly [`dʒɑlɪ] 形 愉快的 副 非常地 動 哄；說好話

形 In jolly spirits, they urged the donkeys to go.
他們以愉快的心情趕著驢子前進。

副 It will be a jolly tough competition.
這將會是一場非常艱難的競賽。

動 The girl jollied her father into buying her the earrings.
女孩哄她爸爸幫她買下耳環。

joyous [`dʒɔɪəs] 形 歡喜的；高興的

I really cherished the memory of my joyous school life.
▶▶ 我很珍惜學校生活的快樂回憶。

kin [kɪn] 名 親戚 形 有親戚關係的

名 She is no kin of mine.
她和我沒有親戚關係。

形 When he found he was kin to his lover, he went bananas.
當他發現他和情人有親戚關係，他便發瘋了。

kindle [`kɪndḷ] 動 生火；點燃

We kindled a fire to warm up.
▶▶ 我們生火取暖。

knowledgeable [`nɑlɪdʒəbḷ] 形 博學的

My mother is knowledgeable, knowing a lot in every field.
▶▶ 我媽媽很博學，在每個領域都懂很多。

 L 字頭滿級單字

 MP3 127

lad [lad] 名 （口語）小夥子；少年

My lad, how have you been recently?
▶▶ 老弟，近來可好？

landlady [`lænd͵ledɪ] 名 女房東

The landlady rents a room to me at an acceptable price.
▶▶ 女房東以我可接受的價錢將房間租給我。

landslide [`lænd͵slaɪd] 名山崩

The continuous rain caused the landslide.
▶▶ 連日大雨造成山崩。

latitude [`lætə͵tjud] 名緯度

The two cities are at approximately the same latitude.
▶▶ 這兩個城市差不多位於同一緯度上。

layman [`lemən] 名門外漢

As a layman, you need a primer on this subject.
▶▶ 身為一名門外漢，你需要一本這個學科的入門書。

layout [`le͵aut] 名規劃；布局

The book designer will have to redo the page layout.
▶▶ 書籍設計者得重新編排版面。

legislator [`lɛdʒɪs͵letɚ] 名立法者

These legislators are debating whether to abolish the old law.
▶▶ 這些立法委員正在辯論是否廢除這個舊法條。

lengthy [`lɛŋθɪ] 形漫長的

He just idled away on his lengthy vacation.
▶▶ 漫長的假期中，他整天無所事事。

lessen [`lɛsn̩] 動減少

The heat will lessen during the evening.
▶▶ 晚間氣溫會降低。

liable [`laɪəbl̩] 形可能的 關 liability 傾向；責任

Steven is liable to be admitted to the university.
▶▶ 史提芬可能會錄取那所大學。
(焦點句型) be liable to V. 很可能…

liberate [`lɪbə͵ret] 動使自由

All the prisoners were liberated from the jail.
▶▶ 所有囚犯都被釋放了。

liberation [ˌlɪbəˋreʃən] 名解放

The 70s were the summit of women liberation.
▶▶ 七〇年代是婦女解放運動的高峰期。

lieutenant [luˋtɛnənt] 名中尉

A young lieutenant was given an award.
▶▶ 一名年輕的中尉獲獎。

lifelong [ˋlaɪflɔŋ] 形終身的

Lifelong learning is a philosophy of life, which is fired by curiosity and passion.
▶▶ 終生學習是一種由好奇心和熱情激發的生活哲學。

lighten [ˋlaɪtn̩] 動變亮；減輕

She lightened up the room with a candle.
▶▶ 她用一根蠟燭照亮了房間。

limp [lɪmp] 動跛行

She had twisted her ankle and was limping.
▶▶ 她把腳踝扭傷了，一瘸一拐地走著。

liner [ˋlaɪnɚ] 名郵輪；大型客輪

In the old days, cruise ships were known as ocean liners.
▶▶ 在過去，郵輪被被稱為遠洋客輪。

linger [ˋlɪŋgɚ] 動徘徊

He lingered in front of her home.
▶▶ 他在她家門前徘徊。

liter [ˋlitɚ] 名公升

She drinks two liters of water every day.
▶▶ 她每天喝兩公升的水。

literacy [ˋlɪtərəsɪ] 名識字能力；知識；能力

We are planning to make a national survey of economic literacy.
▶▶ 我們計畫做一個經濟能力的全國性普查。

1 Level 基礎單字

2 Level 必備單字

3 Level 中級單字

4 Level 進階單字

5 Level 高手單字

6 Level 滿級單字

literal [`lɪtərəl] 形字面的；根本的

Quite often, literal translations of idioms into other languages are confusing.
▶▶ 慣用語的字面翻譯經常令人感到困惑。

literate [`lɪtərət] 形識字的 名識字的人

形 The literate population is rising every year.
識字人口逐年上升。
名 He likes to make acquaintances with literates only.
他只喜歡結交識字的人。

livestock [`laɪv,stɑk] 名家畜

In the severe winter of 1947, farmers had to dig their livestock out of huge snowdrifts.
▶▶ 在一九四七年嚴峻的冬天，農民們必須挖開大雪堆把他們的家畜救出來。

lizard [`lɪzəd] 名蜥蜴

Lizards and snakes are cold-blooded animals.
▶▶ 蜥蜴和蛇是冷血動物。

locker [`lɑkə] 名有鎖的收納櫃；寄物櫃

Put your bag into the locker before you enter the multimedia classroom.
▶▶ 進入視聽教室前，把你的包包放進置物櫃。

lodge [lɑdʒ] 名小屋 動寄宿；存放

名 He is the master of the lodge.
他是這間小屋的主人。
動 This cabinet lodges our oldest wines.
這個櫃子裡存放著我們年代最久的酒。

lofty [`lɔftɪ] 形非常高的；高聳的

The lofty building is astonishing.
▶▶ 那座高聳的建築很驚人。

logo [`logo] 名商標

He designed the logo for our corporation.
▶▶ 他替我們公司設計商標。

lonesome [`lonsəm] 形 孤獨的

I feel lonesome in the new environment.
▶▶ 在新環境裡我感到孤獨。

longevity [lɑn`dʒɛvətɪ] 名 長壽

Longevity is a main concern for everyone.
▶▶ 長壽為每個人所關注。

longitude [`lɑndʒə,tjud] 名 經度

The captain determined the latitude and longitude of his ship's position.
▶▶ 船長測定船所在位置的經緯度。

lotion [`loʃən] 名 洗潔劑；乳液

I use the lotion to make my hands softer.
▶▶ 我用乳液讓我的手更柔嫩。

lottery [`lɑtərɪ] 名 彩券；樂透

He told everyone that he won a lottery.
▶▶ 他告訴大家他中獎了。

lotus [`lotəs] 名 蓮花

The lotus leaves are unfolding.
▶▶ 荷葉正舒展著。

loudspeaker [`laʊd`spikɚ] 名 擴音器

The anxious mother called her daughter over a loudspeaker to find her.
▶▶ 這位焦急的媽媽用擴音器喊她女兒的名字尋找她。

lullaby [`lʌlə,baɪ] 名 搖籃曲 動 唱催眠曲

名 She hummed a lullaby for the infant.
　　她哼搖籃曲給嬰兒聽。
動 The caring father lullabied his baby.
　　慈祥的父親唱催眠曲哄嬰兒入睡。

lunar [`lunɚ] 形 月亮的；陰曆的

When is your lunar birthday?
▶▶ 你的農曆生日是幾月幾號？

Level 1 基礎單字
Level 2 必備單字
Level 3 中級單字
Level 4 進階單字
Level 5 高手單字
Level 6 滿級單字

lure [lur] 名誘惑力；誘餌 動誘惑

名 Money is a great lure for greedy people.
錢對貪婪的人來說是很大的誘惑。

動 Those who had lost their homes and livelihoods were lured westward by advertisements for work.
失去家和生計的人們被廣告所誘惑來到西部工作。

lush [lʌʃ] 形青翠的

I lay down in the lush grass.
▸▸ 我躺在青翠的草坪上。

M 字頭滿級單字 MP3 128

madam / ma'am [`mædəm] / [mæm] 名夫人；女士

May I help you, madam?
▸▸ 需要我的協助嗎，女士？

magnify [`mægnə‚faɪ] 動擴大

The microscope magnified the object 100 times.
▸▸ 這台顯微鏡將物體放大了一百倍。

maiden [`medn̩] 名處女；少女 形（女性）未婚的；首次的

名 The prince fell under the spell of a beautiful maiden.
王子被一名美麗的少女迷住了。

形 Her maiden name is Wood.
她的婚前姓氏是伍德。

mainland [`menlænd] 名大陸

The Hebrides are to the west of the Scottish mainland.
▸▸ 赫布里底群島位於蘇格蘭大陸的西邊。

majestic [mə`dʒɛstɪk] 形雄偉的；壯麗的

Gazing at that majestic painting was an transcendental experience for me.
▸▸ 凝視那幅莊嚴的畫，對我是一種堪稱超凡的體驗。

majesty [`mædʒəstɪ] 名威嚴

I was astonished by his majesty at first sight.
▸▸ 初次見面時我就被他的威嚴震懾。

manuscript [`mænjə͵skrɪpt] 名手稿；原稿

The manuscript of the famous book sold for a lot of money.
▶▶ 這本知名書籍的手稿以高價賣出。

maple [`mepl̩] 名楓樹

Maples were planted along the street.
▶▶ 楓樹沿著街道種植。

mar [mɑr] 動毀損

My notebook was marred by my one-year-old sister.
▶▶ 我的筆記本被一歲的妹妹弄壞。

marginal [`mɑrdʒɪnl̩] 形邊緣的

I made some marginal notes on the textbook.
▶▶ 我在課本上做了一些旁註。

martial [`mɑrʃəl] 形軍事的

Many foreigners come to Taiwan to learn martial arts.
▶▶ 很多外國人來台灣習武。

marvel [`mɑrvl̩] 名令人驚奇的事物 動驚嘆

名 It was indeed a marvel that he recovered.
　他能康復實在是太令人驚奇了。
動 I marveled at his changes.
　我驚訝於他的轉變。

焦點句型 marvel at sth. 驚訝…；感嘆…

mastery [`mæstərɪ] 名精通；掌握

Her mastery of Japanese helped her get the promotion.
▶▶ 精通日語有助於她的升遷。

mediate [`midɪ͵et] 動調解

He tried to mediate between them.
▶▶ 他試圖在他們之間居中調解。

medieval [͵mɪdɪ`ivəl] 形中世紀的

He doesn't like studying medieval history.
▶▶ 他不喜歡學習中古歷史。

Level 1 基礎單字
Level 2 必備單字
Level 3 中級單字
Level 4 進階單字
Level 5 高手單字
Level 6 滿級單字

meditate [`mɛdə,tet] 動沉思

I'm meditating on the meaning of life.
▶ 我在沉思生命的意義。

(焦點句型) meditate on sth. 沉思⋯

meditation [,mɛdə`teʃən] 名沉思；冥想

During the yoga session, everyone engaged in meditation.
▶ 在瑜伽課上，每個人都在冥想。

melancholy [`mɛlən,kɑlɪ] 名憂鬱 形憂鬱的

名 There is a vein of melancholy in his character.
他性格中帶有一點兒憂鬱的氣質。
形 I made efforts to cheer up the melancholy guy.
我努力要讓那個憂傷的人開心。

mentality [mɛn`tælətɪ] 名心態；心性

I just can't understand his mentality!
▶ 我真沒辦法理解他的心態！

merchandise [`mɜtʃən,daɪz] 名商品 動買賣

名 The merchandise in this department store is very expensive.
百貨公司的商品都很昂貴。
動 He started merchandising at the age of twenty.
他二十歲就開始做買賣。

mermaid [`mɜ,med] 名美人魚

A mermaid only exists in tales.
▶ 美人魚只存在於傳說中。

migrant [`maɪgrənt] 名候鳥；移民

Those migrants flew to the south.
▶ 那些候鳥飛向南方。

mimic [`mɪmɪk] 動模仿 名善於模仿者

動 The artist is adept at mimicking other stars.
這位藝人很會模仿其它明星。
名 Observing is the basic skill for a mimic.
對模仿者而言，觀察是基本技巧。

mingle [`mɪŋgl̩] 動 混合

She mingled the two liquids to see what would happen.
▶▶ 她把兩種液體混合，看會發生什麼事。

miraculous [mə`rækjələs] 形 奇蹟的

His appearance was miraculous for me.
▶▶ 他的出現對我宛如奇蹟。

mischievous [`mɪstʃɪvəs] 形 淘氣的；頑皮的

The mischievous tricks will do no harm to you.
▶▶ 這種惡作劇不會傷害到你。

mistress [`mɪstrəs] 名 女主人；女教師

All the girls like their new English mistress.
▶▶ 所有的女孩子都喜歡她們新來的英語女教師。

mobilize [`mobə͵laɪz] 動 動員

Our country is in great danger; we must mobilize the whole nation.
▶▶ 我們的國家正處於極度的危險之中，必須把全國人民動員起來。

modernization [͵mɑdənə`zeʃən] 名 現代化

Modernization brings about convenience and alienation.
▶▶ 現代化帶來了便利，也帶來了疏離。

modernize [`mɑdən͵aɪz] 動 現代化

The company is investing nine million dollars to modernize its factories.
▶▶ 這家公司正投資九百萬元將其工廠現代化。

monarch [`mɑnək] 名 君主；國王

They attempted to overthrow the monarch.
▶▶ 他們企圖推翻國王。

momentum [mə`mɛntəm] 名 【物】動量；動力

The environmental movement is gathering momentum.
▶▶ 環境保護運動的聲勢日益壯大。

monotony [məˋnɑtənɪ] 名 單調

The Internet relieves the monotony of our everyday life.
▶▶ 網路緩解了我們日常生活的單調。

monstrous [ˋmɑnstrəs] 形 醜惡的；駭人的；像怪物的

The monstrous creature in my dream does not exist in the real world.
▶▶ 我夢裡那個巨大的怪物不存在於真實世界上。

morale [məˋræl] 名 士氣

Our team members have great morale.
▶▶ 我們的隊員士氣高昂。

mortal [ˋmɔrtḷ] 形 終有一死的；致命的 名 凡人 關 mortality 死亡率

形 The disease proved to be mortal.
　　這種疾病證明是致命的。
名 We are all mortals, but we can endeavor to be uncommon.
　　我們都是凡人，但是我們可以努力讓自己不平凡。

motherhood [ˋmʌðəhud] 名 母性；母親的身分

Motherhood suits her.
▶▶ 她很適合作母親。

motto [ˋmɑto] 名 座右銘

Never put off what you can do today is his motto.
▶▶ 今日事今日畢是他的座右銘。

mound [maund] 名 小丘 動 堆積

名 The wind swept the sand into a mound.
　　風把沙子吹成一座小丘。
動 They mounded the rubbish at the corner.
　　他們把垃圾堆在角落。

mourn [mɔrn] 動 哀悼

She is still mourning her child's death.
▶▶ 她仍然為她孩子的死感到哀痛。

mournful [ˋmɔrnfəl] 形 令人悲痛的

I shed tears over the mournful story.
▶▶ 這個悲傷的故事讓我掉淚。

Level 1 基礎單字
Level 2 必備單字
Level 3 中級單字
Level 4 進階單字
Level 5 高手單字
Level 6 滿級單字

mow [mo] 動 收割

We have to mow the lawn twice a week.
▶▶ 我們每週得修剪草坪兩次。

muse [mjuz] 動 深思

He sat alone, musing about his future.
▶▶ 他獨自坐著，思考未來的人生。

mustache [`mʌstæʃ] 名 髭；八字鬍

The name of Chaplin conjures up the image of a little tramp with a brush mustache.
▶▶ 卓別林的名字會使人在腦海中勾勒出一個身材矮小、蓄著一撇小鬍子的流浪漢形象。

mute [mjut] 名 啞巴 形 沉默的

名 Raymond was born a mute. He can hear but not talk.
雷蒙德生來就是啞巴，他可以聽但不能說。
形 She kept mute during the discussion.
她整個討論會都沉默不語。

 **N 字頭滿級單字**

MP3 129

nag [næg] 名 嘮叨的人 動 嘮叨

名 My father is a nag, but I know he loves me very much.
我爸爸很嘮叨，但我知道他很愛我。
動 Martha constantly nags her daughter about getting a boyfriend.
瑪莎一直嘮叨著要她女兒交個男朋友。

narrate [næ`ret ] / [ `nɛret] 動 敘述故事

Shall I narrate a strange experience of mine?
▶▶ 我該把我的奇遇敘述一下嗎？

narrator [næ`retɚ] 名 敘述者

The narrator explained the meaning of the pictures.
▶▶ 解說員講解這些圖畫的含義。

nationalism [`næʃənəlɪzəm] 名 國家主義；民族主義

Nationalism today has also evolved into a new form.
▶▶ 民族主義已發展成一種新的形式。

671

navigate [`nævə͵get] 動 駕駛；導航

He navigated the ship to a safe port.
▶ 他將船駛進一個安全的港口。

navigation [͵nævə`geʃən] 名 導航（術）；航海

Navigation is fundamental for the island country.
▶ 海運對這個島國來說很重要。

nearsighted [͵nɪr`saɪtɪd] 形 近視的

I became nearsighted because of the overuse of my eyes.
▶ 我因為過度用眼而得到近視。

nickel [`nɪkl̩] 名 鎳；鎳幣 動 鍍鎳於…

名 Rick found a nickel in his pocket.
　　瑞克在口袋發現一枚鎳幣。
動 He nickeled the plate.
　　他在盤上鍍鎳。

nostril [`nɑstrəl] 名 鼻孔

A strange smell assaulted the nostrils.
▶ 一股奇怪的味道撲鼻而來。

notable [`notəbl̩] 形 顯著的；值得注意的 名 名人；顯要人物

形 Danny is a notable writer that nobody is unfamiliar with him.
　　丹尼是個知名作家，沒有人不知道他。
名 Many notables attended the press conference.
　　很多名人出席記者會。

notorious [no`tɔrɪəs] 形 聲名狼藉的

The playboy is notorious.
▶ 這個花心男孩惡名昭彰。

nourish [`nɝɪʃ] 動 滋養 關 nourishment 營養

Milk is all we need to nourish a small baby.
▶ 供給嬰兒營養只需餵奶就夠了。

novice [`nɑvɪs] 名 初學者

Trial and error are what novices should do.
▶ 試錯是新手的必修課。

nucleus [`njuklɪəs] 名 原子核；細胞核

These 1,000 books will form the nucleus of the new school library.
▶▶ 這一千本書將構成學校新圖書館的核心。
(焦點句型) (form) the nucleus of sth. （成為）…的核心

nude [njud] 形 裸體的 名 裸體；畫

A nude man is sunbathing on the balcony.
▶▶ 一名裸體男子正在陽台上享受日光浴。

nurture [`nɜtʃə] 名 養育；培育 動 養育；培育

名 The early nurture of infants is very important.
嬰兒的早期養育是很重要的。
動 It's the parents' duty to nurture their children.
養育孩子是父母的責任。

UNIT 14 O字頭滿級單字

MP3 130

oasis [o`esɪs] 名 綠洲；樂土

We rode on the camels and reached the oasis at sunset.
▶▶ 我們騎著駱駝並在太陽下山時到達了綠洲。

oath [oθ] 名 誓約；宣誓

Government employees take an oath not to reveal official secrets.
▶▶ 政府雇員宣誓不洩露官方機密。
(焦點句型) take an oath 發誓…

oatmeal [`ot,mil] 名 燕麥片；燕麥粥

I had oatmeal for breakfast.
▶▶ 我早餐吃燕麥粥。

oblige [ə`blaɪdʒ] 動 強迫；迫使；幫助

I was obliged to attend my brother's wedding.
▶▶ 我不得不出席哥哥的婚禮。

obstinate [`abstənət] 形 固執的；頑固的

He is too obstinate to accept others' advice.
▶▶ 他很頑固，無法接受他人的忠告。

Level 1 基礎單字
Level 2 必備單字
Level 3 中級單字
Level 4 進階單字
Level 5 高手單字
Level 6 滿級單字

occurrence [ə`kɝəns] 名出現;發生

Satellites have extended the power of communications to report events on the instant of occurrence.

▶▶ 衛星擴大了報導即時發生事件的通訊能力。

octopus [`ɑktəpəs] 名章魚

Snails and octopuses are molluscs.

▶▶ 蝸牛和章魚是軟體動物。

odor [`odɚ] 名氣味

A strange odor emitted from the kitchen.

▶▶ 一股奇怪的氣味由廚房傳出。

offspring [`ɔfsprɪŋ] 名子孫;後裔

His offspring are as successful as he.

▶▶ 他的後代都和他一樣有成就。

oppress [ə`prɛs] 動壓迫

Those who are oppressed are worth more attention.

▶▶ 受壓迫的人值得更多關注。

oppression [ə`prɛʃən] 名壓迫;壓制

We are under the oppression of tyranny.

▶▶ 我們在暴政的壓迫之下。

ordeal [ɔr`diəl] 名磨難;嚴峻考驗

After going through the ordeal, I really made remarkable progress.

▶▶ 經歷那場嚴酷的考驗後,我確實有了驚人的進步。

orderly [`ɔrdəlɪ] 名勤務兵;護工 形整齊的

名 Call the orderly if you need help.
需要幫忙的時候呼叫護理人員。

形 She always keeps her room clean and orderly.
她總是把房間維持得乾淨整齊。

organizer [`ɔrgən͵aɪzɚ] 名組織者

Elaine is the organizer of the association.

▶▶ 伊蓮是那個協會的組織者。

orient [`ɔrɪənt] 名東方;東方國家 動使適應 相 orientation 定位 / oriental 東方的

名 Many decades ago, Asia was often called the Orient.
好幾十年前,亞洲常被稱為東方。

動 Jessica spent a long time to orient herself.
潔西卡花了好長一段時間才找到自己的位置。

(焦點句型) orient oneself 確定自己的位置;辨別方向

originate [əˋrɪdʒəˌnet] 動起源於

The film originated from a short story.
▶▶ 這部電影取材於一篇短篇小說。

ornament [`ɔrnəmənt] 名裝飾品 動裝飾;美化

名 She put several ornaments on the Christmas tree.
她在聖誕樹上放了幾個裝飾品。

動 They ornamented the cake with cream.
他們用奶油裝飾蛋糕。

orphanage [`ɔrfənɪdʒ] 名孤兒院

I founded an orphanage for the orphans last year.
▶▶ 去年我為孤兒們創辦了一所孤兒院。

ounce [aʊns] 名盎司

Three ounces of sugar are needed to make the cookies.
▶▶ 做這種餅乾需要三盎司的糖。

outbreak [`aʊtˌbrek] 名爆發

The outbreak of plague astonished everyone.
▶▶ 瘟疫的爆發震驚了所有人。

outgoing [`aʊtˌgoɪŋ] 形外向的

Cathy has many friends because of her outgoing personality.
▶▶ 凱西因個性外向而有很多朋友。

outing [`aʊtɪŋ] 名郊遊;遠足

I am planning an outing with my family.
▶▶ 我正在計劃和家人一同郊遊。

Level 1 基礎單字
Level 2 必備單字
Level 3 中級單字
Level 4 進階單字
Level 5 高手單字
Level 6 滿級單字

outlaw [`aʊt‚lɔ] 名不法之徒 動禁止；取締

名 The outlaw had no alternative but to surrender himself to police.
這名逃犯走投無路，只好向警方自首。

動 In some places, gay relationships are still outlawed? Really?
某些地方仍然禁止同性戀？真的嗎？

outlook [`aʊt‚lʊk] 名觀點；前景；景色

The hotel room, which faced the ocean, had a wonderful outlook.
▶▶ 面對海洋的旅館房間，可見美麗的風景。

outnumber [aʊt`nʌmbɚ] 動數目勝過

The demonstrators were heavily outnumbered by the police.
▶▶ 示威者人數遠不及員警人數。

outrage [`aʊt‚redʒ] 名憤慨；暴行 動激怒

名 The residents' outrage was due to the fact that a sex offender was living nearby.
居民們因附近住著性犯罪者而感到憤怒。

動 Many people were outraged by the government's policy.
很多人都被政府的政策激怒了。

outrageous [aʊt`redʒəs] 形駭人的；無法接受的

The price of eggs at that time was once outrageous.
▶▶ 當時雞蛋價格一度高得離譜。

outright [`aʊt‚raɪt] 形完全的；徹底的 副完全地；徹底地

形 She was the outright winner.
毫無疑問她是優勝者。

副 The smuggler told me the truth outright.
走私販毫無保留地告訴我真相。

outset [`aʊt‚sɛt] 名開始；開頭

From the outset, they loved each other.
▶▶ 一開始，他們就彼此相愛了。

outskirts [`aʊt‚skɝts] 名郊區

They live on the outskirts of Athens.
▶▶ 他們住在雅典郊區。

outward / outwards [`autwəd ] / [ `autwədz] 形 向外的；外面的 副 向外

形 From his outward appearance, Terry looked calm, but he was actually quite nervous.

泰瑞表面上來看很冷靜，但實際上他很緊張。

副 He ran outward to see who was calling him.

他衝向外面看是誰在叫他。

overdo [ˌovə`du] 動 做得過火

She really overdid the sympathy.

▶▶ 她真是同情得過火了。

overflow [ˌovə`flo ] / [ `ovəflo] 動 溢出 名 滿溢

動 The water is overflowing from the sink.

水從水槽溢出來了。

名 He was annoyed by the overflow of soup.

他因溢出來的湯感到惱怒。

overhear [ˌovə`hɪr] 動 無意中聽到

I overheard that she is pregnant.

▶▶ 我無意間聽到她懷孕了。

overlap [ˌovə`læp ] / [ `ovəlæp] 動 重疊 名 重疊的部份

動 One feather overlaps another on a bird's wing.

鳥的翅膀上的羽毛互相交疊著。

名 Please calculate the square measure of the overlap between the two circles.

請計算這兩個圓之間重疊部分的面積。

overwork [ˌovə`wɜk] 動 工作過度 名 過度工作

動 Sally overworks every day. I'm anxious about her health.

莎莉每天都超時工作，我很擔心她的健康。

名 He got sick owing to overwork.

他因過度工作而病倒。

oyster [`ɔɪstə] 名 牡蠣

Oyster beds on the mudflats are a form of fish farming.

▶▶ 淤泥灘上的牡蠣養殖場是一種水產養殖業的形式。

ozone [`ozon] 名 臭氧

The ozone layer is becoming thinner and thinner.

▶▶ 臭氧層變得越來越薄。

Level 1 基礎單字

Level 2 必備單字

Level 3 中級單字

Level 4 進階單字

Level 5 高手單字

Level 6 滿級單字

packet [`pækɪt] 名小包；包裹

The packet weighs twenty-five grams.
▶▶ 這個包裹重二十五公克。

paddle [`pædl] 名划槳 動以槳划動

名 We cannot move the boat without paddles.
沒有槳，我們無法使船移動。
動 They paddled the canoe to the village.
他們划獨木舟到那個村落去。

paradox [`pærə‚dɑks] 名悖論；似是而非的說法

The clue seemed to be a paradox.
▶▶ 這條線索看起來自相矛盾。

paralyze [`pærə‚laɪz] 動麻痺

Nancy is paralyzed from the waist down.
▶▶ 南西下半身癱瘓。

parliament [`pɑrləmənt] 名議會

The parliament decided to impeach the president.
▶▶ 國會決定彈劾總統。

pastime [`pæs‚taɪm] 名消遣

My pastimes include reading, listening to music and writing.
▶▶ 我的消遣包括了閱讀、聽音樂和寫作。

patriot [`petrɪət] 名愛國者

Those patriots fought for their country.
▶▶ 那些愛國者為國家而戰。

patriotic [‚petrɪ`ɑtɪk] 形愛國的

The patriotic soldier refused to surrender to the enemy.
▶▶ 這名愛國的士兵拒絕向敵人投降。

MEMORIZE 7000 VOCABULARIES ONCE AND FOR ALL!

peacock [`pikɑk] 名孔雀

A crowd of people wanted to see the peacocks in the zoo.
▶▶ 成群的人想看動物園裡的孔雀。

pebble [`pɛbḷ] 名小圓石

The sidewalk was paved with pebbles.
▶▶ 這條路用小圓石鋪成。

peek [pik] 名偷看 動窺視

名 He took a peek at her.
他偷看了她一眼。
動 I couldn't resist peeking in the drawer.
我忍不住偷看了一下抽屜裡面。
(焦點句型) take a peek at sb. 偷看某人

peninsula [pə`nɪnsələ] 名半島

His house is located at the top of the peninsula.
▶▶ 他的房子位於半島的頂端。

perch [pɝtʃ] 動棲息 名（鳥的）棲息處

動 The sparrow perched on a branch.
麻雀在樹枝上歇息。
名 The nightingale shuffled along its perch.
夜鶯在棲息地來回踱步。

peril [`pɛrəl] 名危險 動使…有危險

名 The country's economy is now in grave peril.
這個國家的經濟現在陷入了嚴重危機。
動 She felt periled by the situation.
她覺得這種情況很危險。

perish [`pɛrɪʃ] 動喪生；死去

Five people perished in the accident.
▶▶ 五個人死於這次意外。

permissible [pə`mɪsəbḷ] 形可允許的

You should ask your mother whether it is permissible to do that.
▶▶ 你應該問你媽媽是否允許這樣做。

Level 1 基礎單字
Level 2 必備單字
Level 3 中級單字
Level 4 進階單字
Level 5 高手單字
Level 6 滿級單字

persevere [ˌpɝsəˋvɪr] 動 堅持

They persevered in helping the poor.
▶▶ 他們堅持幫助窮人。

(焦點句型) persevere in N./Ving 堅持…

persistence [pəˋsɪstəns] 名 固執；堅持

Her persistence in getting what she wanted was astounding.
▶▶ 她對得到她所想要的事物的堅持程度，令人震驚。

(焦點句型) persistence in N./Ving 對…的堅持

persistent [pəˋsɪstənt] 形 固執的 ；堅持地

How do you deal with persistent salesmen who won't take no for an answer?
▶▶ 你怎麼對付那些不輕言放棄的推銷員？

petroleum [pəˋtrolɪəm] 名 石油

The price of petroleum is decreasing.
▶▶ 油價下跌了。

pharmacist [ˋfɑrməsɪst] 名 藥師

Ken is a pharmacist in the clinic.
▶▶ 肯是這間診所的藥師。

pharmacy [ˋfɑrməsɪ] 名 藥劑學；藥房

Please pick up your medication at the pharmacy.
▶▶ 請到藥房取藥。

pianist [pɪˋænɪst] 名 鋼琴師

The pianist accompanied her singing.
▶▶ 這位鋼琴家為她的歌伴奏。

pickpocket [ˋpɪkˌpɑkɪt] 名 扒手

The pickpocket made his way into the crowd.
▶▶ 扒手鑽進了人群。

pilgrim [ˋpɪlgrɪm] 名 朝聖者

We met many pilgrims on their way to Mecca.
▶▶ 我們遇到許多去麥加朝聖的人。

pimple [`pɪmpḷ] 名面皰

If you squeeze pimples, you may make them worse.
▶▶ 如果你擠痘痘，可能會使情況惡化。

pinch [pɪntʃ] 動掐；捏 名掐；捏；少量

動 My sister always pinches me.
我姐姐總是捏我。
名 He gave her a pinch on the cheek.
他在她臉頰上捏了一下。

(焦點句型) give sb. a pinch 捏某人一下

plague [pleg] 名瘟疫

A plague came in the wake of the earthquake.
▶▶ 地震之後，瘟疫緊接而來。

plantation [plæn`teʃən] 名農場

The plantation was deserted after the farmer died.
▶▶ 農夫死後，這座農場就廢棄了。

playwright [`ple,raɪt] 名劇作家

The playwright is adept at comedies.
▶▶ 這名劇作家擅長寫喜劇。

plow [plau] 名犁 動耕作

名 He put the plow on the ox.
他把犁套在牛上。
動 They plowed sweatily under the sun.
他們在太陽下汗流浹背地耕作。

pneumonia [nju`monjə] 名肺炎

He was indebted to her for nursing him through pneumonia.
▶▶ 他對於她照顧自己度過肺炎十分感激。

polar [`polɚ] 形極地的

The habitats of polar bears are disappearing because of greenhouse effect.
▶▶ 因為溫室效應，北極熊的棲息地減少了。

Level 1 基礎單字
Level 2 必備單字
Level 3 中級單字
Level 4 進階單字
Level 5 高手單字
Level 6 滿級單字

ponder [`pɑndɚ] 動仔細考慮

I'm pondering whether to go with him.
▶▶ 我考慮著要不要跟他去。

pony [`ponɪ] 名小馬

The children rode their ponies all over the farm.
▶▶ 孩子們騎著小馬在農場四處跑。

populate [`pɑpjə‚let] 動居住

New York City is populated by people of many different ethnicities.
▶▶ 許多不同種族的人居住於紐約市。

porter [`pɔrtɚ] 名搬運工；門房

The hotel porter will get you a taxi.
▶▶ 旅館的門廳服務員會替你叫計程車。

posture [`pɑstʃɚ] 名姿勢 動擺姿勢

名 He took off his coat and assumed a fighting posture.
　　他脫掉上衣，擺出一副想打架的姿勢。
動 The model postured as the photographer asked.
　　模特兒照攝影師的要求擺姿勢。

焦點句型 adopt/assume a posture 擺出姿勢

poultry [`poltrɪ] 名家禽

He ate plenty of fish and poultry.
▶▶ 他吃很多魚和禽肉。

preach [pritʃ] 動傳教；說教；鼓吹

She preached economy as the best means of solving the crisis.
▶▶ 她鼓吹節約是解決危機最好的方法。

precede [pri`sid] 動在前

He preceded his lecture with a practical demonstration.
▶▶ 他在講課之前做了實際演示。

precedent [`prɛsədnt] 名前例

The prince was not allowed to break with precedent and marry a divorced woman.
▶▶ 王子未能獲准打破先例娶離婚的女子為妻。

precision [prɪˋsɪʒən] 名 精確；準確

She can predict the weather with great precision.
▶▶ 她可以準確地預測天氣。

(焦點句型) with precision 準確地

predecessor [ˋprɛdəˌsɛsɚ] 名 祖先；前輩

What he had done shamed his predecessors.
▶▶ 他的作為讓祖先蒙羞。

prehistoric [ˌprihɪsˋtɔrɪk] 形 史前的

We depicted the prehistoric culture according to the found remains.
▶▶ 我們根據尋獲的遺跡，描繪史前的文化。

preside [prɪˋzaɪd] 動 主持

The hostess presided at the table with tact.
▶▶ 女主人招待客人進餐時得體又風雅。

prestige [prɛsˋtidʒ] 名 聲望

The speech attracted a lot of people because of speaker's prestige.
▶▶ 因為講者的聲望，這場演講吸引了很多人。

preventive [prɪˋvɛntɪv] 名 預防物 形 預防的

名 Condoms are preventives of pregnancy.
保險套預防懷孕。
形 She took preventive measures to avoid thievery.
她採取預防措施來避免盜竊。

preview [ˋpriˌvju] / [priˋvju] 名 預習；預覽 動 預習

名 Turn to page 12 for a preview of next week's program.
請翻到第十二頁，來預習下週課程。
動 I previewed the lesson before class.
我在上課前先預習這一課。

priceless [ˋpraɪsləs] 形 無價的

The necklace my mother gave me is priceless.
▶▶ 媽媽送我的這條項鍊是無價的。

Level 1 基礎單字
Level 2 必備單字
Level 3 中級單字
Level 4 進階單字
Level 5 高手單字
Level 6 滿級單字

procession [prəˋsɛʃən] 名 隊伍；行列

Thousands of people joined the funeral procession.
▶▶ 數千名工人加入了送葬行列。

proficiency [prəˋfɪʃənsɪ] 名 精通

My father has proficiency in playing the piano.
▶▶ 我爸爸是彈鋼琴的行家。

prohibition [ˌproɪˋbɪʃən] 名 禁止

There is a prohibition against smoking.
▶▶ 這兒禁止吸菸。

propel [prəˋpɛl] 動 推動

We should energetically promote IT application and use IT to propel and accelerate industrialization.
▶▶ 我們應該積極地推進資訊化來帶動工業化，加速工業化進程。

prose [proz] 名 散文

She writes prose most of the time, but sometimes she also composes poetry.
▶▶ 她大部分時間都寫散文，但有時她也會作詩。

prosecute [ˋprɑsɪˌkjut] 動 檢舉；告發

He vowed that he would prosecute them for fraud.
▶▶ 他鄭重宣布將起訴他們犯有詐欺罪。

prospective [prəˋspɛktɪv] 形 潛在的

They want to sell their car, and already have several prospective buyers.
▶▶ 他們想賣掉他們的車，並且已有幾位可能的買主。

proverb [ˋprɑvɝb] 名 諺語

As the proverb says, "When in Rome, do as the Romans do."
▶▶ 有句諺語說：「入境隨俗」。

provincial [prəˋvɪnʃəl] 名 省民 形 省的

名 Most provincials moved out after the outbreak of the plague.
瘟疫爆發後，大部分的省民都搬離了。
形 Do you feel satisfied with the provincial government?
你對省政府滿意嗎？

publicize [`pʌblɪˌsaɪz] 動 公布;宣傳

We are trying to publicize our products through advertisements on buses.
▶▶ 我們正試圖在公車上作廣告來宣傳我們的產品。

puff [pʌf] 名 噴;吹 動 噴出

名 He extinguished the candle with a puff.
他吹氣把燭火熄滅。

動 The smoke is puffing from the chimney.
煙從煙囪中噴出。

punctual [`pʌŋktʃʊəl] 形 準時的

Being late is impolite to the punctual members.
▶▶ 遲到對準時的成員很失禮。

purify [`pjʊrəˌfaɪ] 動 淨化

The water you drank was purified.
▶▶ 你剛剛喝下的水已經過淨化。

purity [`pjʊrətɪ] 名 純粹

A lily symbolizes purity.
▶▶ 百合花象徵純潔。

 Q、R字頭滿級單字

MP3 132

quake [kwek] 名 地震;震動 動 搖動;震動

名 His sudden quake shocked me.
他突然的震動嚇我一跳。

動 The ground quaked as the bomb exploded.
炸彈爆炸時,地面都震動了。

qualification [ˌkwɑləfəˋkeʃən] 名 資格

What qualifications have you got to apply for this job?
▶▶ 申請這個工作你所具有的條件是什麼?

radiant [`redjənt] 名 發光體 形 發光的

名 What is the radiant in the sky? Is it UFO?
天上那個發光體是什麼?是幽浮嗎?

1 Level 基礎單字
2 Level 必備單字
3 Level 中級單字
4 Level 進階單字
5 Level 高手單字
6 Level 滿級單字

(形) Her radiant costume caught everyone's eye.
她明豔的穿著抓住了每個人的目光。

radiate [`redɪˌet] (動) 放射 (形) 放射狀的 (關) radioactive 放射性的

(動) All the roads radiate from the center of the town.
所有道路都是從市中心向四面八方伸展出去。
(形) Radiate railways are very convenient to commuters.
放射狀的鐵路網對通勤者來說很方便。

radish [`rædɪʃ] (名) 小蘿蔔

He cooked radish soup for dinner.
▶▶ 他煮蘿蔔湯當晚餐。

radius [`redɪəs] (名) 半徑

The radius of the circle is 3 cm, so the circumference is about 19 cm.
▶▶ 這個圓的半徑是三公分,所以圓周長大約是十九公分。

rash [ræʃ] (名) 疹子 (形) 輕率的

(名) The rash on her back made her very itchy.
背上的疹子讓她覺得很癢。
(形) The rash policy of the president evoked fierce opposition.
總統的草率政策引發了強烈反彈。

realization [ˌriələˋzeʃən] (名) 領悟

I finally came to realization that I had been cheated.
▶▶ 我終於明白我被騙了。

reap [rip] (動) 收割

As you sow, so shall you reap.
▶▶ 要怎麼收穫,先怎麼栽。

reckless [`rɛkləs] (形) 魯莽的;不顧後果的

His brother is a reckless gambler.
▶▶ 他的弟弟是個不計後果的賭徒。

reckon [`rɛkən] (動) 計算;認為

He reckoned that there were more than 100 people at the event.
▶▶ 他認為那活動超過百人參加。

reconcile [`rɛkən͵saɪl] 動調停；和解

I can't reconcile those two different opinions.
▶▶ 我無法調和那兩種不同的主張。

recreational [͵rɛkrɪ`eʃənḷ] 形娛樂的

The recreational facilities in the community are excellent.
▶▶ 這個社區的娛樂設施非常棒。

reef [rif] 名暗礁

Oil pollution could damage the ecology of the coral reefs.
▶▶ 石油汙染可能破壞珊瑚礁的生態環境。

referee [͵rɛfə`ri] 名裁判 動擔任裁判

名 A referee should be very just and objective.
　　裁判必須公正客觀。
動 Dylan was appointed to referee the game.
　　迪倫被指派擔任這場比賽的裁判。

refine [rɪ`faɪn] 動精煉 關 refinement 精良

Reading good books helps to refine one's speech and behavior.
▶▶ 閱讀優質書籍有助於讓一個人的言行舉止變得更好。

reflective [rɪ`flɛktɪv] 形反射的；反映的

The grades are not actually reflective of your performance.
▶▶ 成績並不能完全反映你的表現。

refresh [rɪ`frɛʃ] 動提神

A cup of coffee refreshed me.
▶▶ 一杯咖啡使我恢復精神。

refreshment [rɪ`frɛʃmənt] 名清爽；提神物

I drink a cup of coffee every morning as a refreshment.
▶▶ 我每天早上喝一杯咖啡作為提神物。

refute [rɪ`fjut] 動反駁

Nothing could refute her testimony that the driver was drunk.
▶▶ 她關於司機醉酒的證詞是無可辯駁的。

Level 1 基礎單字
Level 2 必備單字
Level 3 中級單字
Level 4 進階單字
Level 5 高手單字
Level 6 滿級單字

rehearse [rɪ`hɝs] 動排練；排演

As the presentation is around the corner, dancers rehearse frequently.
▶▶ 隨著上演將近，舞者們勤於排練。

reign [ren] 名統治 動統治

名 The country is under a reign of terror.
這個國家籠罩於恐怖統治之中。
動 The young president reigned over the country for only three months.
這個年輕的總統只統治了這個國家三個月。

rejoice [rɪ`dʒɔɪs] 動歡喜

People rejoiced at the good news.
▶▶ 人們為這個好消息感到高興。
焦點句型 rejoice at sth. 為…而高興

relay [`rɪle ] / [ rɪ`le] 名接力（賽） 動傳達

名 He ran one hundred meters in the relay.
他在接力賽跑中跑一百公尺。
動 He relayed the news to me.
他把消息傳達給我。

reliance [rɪ`laɪəns] 名信賴；依賴 關 reliant 依賴的

Don't place too much reliance on others. You should stand on your own two legs.
▶▶ 不要太依賴別人，你應該自立。
焦點句型 place reliance on sb./sth. 依賴…

relic [`rɛlɪk] 名遺物

The site is considered holy because a religious relic was found there.
▶▶ 因為在那裡發現宗教遺物，人們認為那裡是聖地。

remainder [rɪ`mendɚ] 名剩餘

Charlie ate the remainder of the cake that had been left in the fridge.
▶▶ 查理吃了冰箱裡剩下的蛋糕。

renowned [rɪ`naund] 形著名的

It is incredible that you don't know the renowned actor.
▶▶ 你不知道那個著名演員，真讓人不敢置信。

reproduce [ˌriprəˋdjus] 動 複製；再生；繁殖

It is illegal to reproduce these worksheets without permission from the publishers.
▶▶ 未經出版商許可翻印這些習題是違法的。

reptile [ˋrɛptaɪl] 名 爬蟲類 形 爬蟲類的

名 Lizards are reptiles.
蜥蜴是爬蟲類。
形 Snakes are kept in the reptile section of the zoo.
蛇被放在動物園裡的爬蟲類動物區。

resent [rɪˋzɛnt] 動 憤恨 關 resentment 憤慨

He resented the person who stole his wallet.
▶▶ 他痛恨偷了他錢包的人。

reside [rɪˋzaɪd] 動 居住

People residing in the community are friendly to each other.
▶▶ 這個社區的居民對彼此都相當友好。

resistant [rɪˋzɪstənt] 形 抵抗的

These insects have become resistant to pesticides.
▶▶ 這些昆蟲對殺蟲劑已經有抵抗力了。
（焦點句型）be resistant to sth. 對⋯有抵抗力；抗拒⋯

respective [rɪˋspɛktɪv] 形 各自的；分別的 關 respectively 分別

They are each recognized as specialists in their respective fields.
▶▶ 他們在各自的領域都被視為專家。

restoration [ˌrɛstəˋreʃən] 名 恢復

The restoration of the lighthouse took a long time .
▶▶ 燈塔的修復花了很長一段時間。

restrain [rɪˋstren] 動 抑制

At that time, the government must restrain prices and profits.
▶▶ 在那時，政府必須限制物價和利潤。

restraint [rɪˋstrent] 名 抑制 同 hamper

Her anger was beyond restraint.
▶▶ 她怒不可遏。

Level 1 基礎單字
Level 2 必備單字
Level 3 中級單字
Level 4 進階單字
Level 5 高手單字
Level 6 滿級單字

retort [rɪˋtɔrt] 名反駁 動反駁；回嘴

名 His retort annoyed his teacher.
他的反駁惹惱了老師。

動 Johnny retorted that my faults were as many as his.
強尼反駁說我的錯誤和他的一樣多。

retrieve [rɪˋtriv] 動取回

Remember to retrieve your manuscript after copying it on the photocopier.
▶▶ 影印後記得取回原稿。

revelation [ˌrɛvəˋleʃən] 名揭發

He disappeared after the revelation of the scandal.
▶▶ 醜聞爆發後他就消失了。

revival [rɪˋvaɪvl̩] 名復甦

Revival is impossible for a dead person.
▶▶ 人死不能復生。

revive [rɪˋvaɪv] 動復甦；復原

He revived while being given medical treatment.
▶▶ 當他在接受治療時，他就康復了。

revolt [rɪˋvolt] 名反叛 動叛變

名 The people living underneath the tyranny rose in open revolt.
生活在暴政下的人民公開反叛了。

動 The farmers started to revolt out of anger.
農民們出於憤怒開始叛變。

revolve [rɪˋvɑlv] 動旋轉；轉動

The wheel is revolving about its axis.
▶▶ 輪子正繞著軸轉動。

(焦點句型) revolve about/around sth. 繞⋯旋轉

rigorous [ˋrɪgərəs] 形嚴密的

Planes have to undergo rigorous safety checks.
▶▶ 飛機必須接受嚴密的安全檢查。

ripple [`rɪpḷ] 名 波動；漣漪 動 起漣漪

名 There were ripples on the surface of the pool as the wind grew stronger.
當風變大時，池塘表面起了漣漪。
動 The water rippled after I threw a stone into it.
我把石頭丟入水裡後，水起了漣漪。

rivalry [`raɪvəlrɪ] 名 競爭

Historically, there has always been a great deal of rivalry between the two families.
▶▶ 在歷史上，這兩個家族世世代代對立鬥爭。

roam [rom] 名 漫步 動 徘徊；漫遊

名 The professor took a leisurely roam on the street.
教授在街上悠閒地漫步。
動 The sheep are allowed to roam freely on this land.
綿羊可以在這片地上自由走動。
(焦點句型) take a roam 散步

robust [ro`bʌst] 形 強健的

He looks quite robust because he goes to the gym five times a week.
▶▶ 他看起相當健壯，因為他一週去健身房五次。

rotate [`rotet] 動 旋轉

The top is rotating on the ground.
▶▶ 陀螺正在地上旋轉。

rotation [ro`teʃən] 名 旋轉

This switch controls the number of rotations per minute.
▶▶ 這個開關控制著每分鐘的轉數。

royalty [`rɔɪəltɪ] 名 王權；貴族

With the passage of time, royalty was replaced with civil rights.
▶▶ 隨著時間進展，王權被民權取代了。

rubbish [`rʌbɪʃ] 名 垃圾

The waterway is clogged with rubbish.
▶▶ 下水道被垃圾堵住了。

Level 1 基礎單字
Level 2 必備單字
Level 3 中級單字
Level 4 進階單字
Level 5 高手單字
Level 6 滿級單字

rugged [`rʌgɪd] 形 粗糙的；高低不平的

The countryside around here is very rugged.
▶▶ 這裡的鄉村地勢起伏很大。

salute [sə`lut] 名 招呼；敬禮 動 致意；致敬

名 They gave salutes to each other.
他們相互敬禮。
動 The soldier saluted the national flag.
這位軍人向國旗敬禮。

焦點句型 give salute to sb. 向…敬禮

sanitation [ˌsænə`teʃən] 名 公共衛生

With no education, all Barney could find was sanitation work.
▶▶ 因為沒受過教育，巴尼能找的工作只剩清潔工。

savage [`sævɪdʒ] 名 野蠻的人 形 荒涼的；粗魯的

名 He is such a savage that nobody can reason with him.
他真是個野蠻的人，沒有人能跟他講道理。
形 Do not use savage words with your seniors.
別對長輩講粗魯的話。

scenic [`sinɪk] 形 風景優美的

I walked along the scenic route, whistling my favorite song.
▶▶ 我沿著風景美麗的小道走著，用口哨吹著我最喜歡的歌。

scorn [skɔrn] 名 輕蔑 動 輕蔑；不屑做

名 The noblewoman looked at her with scorn.
這個貴婦輕蔑地看著她。
動 You have no right to scorn the poor girl.
你無權輕蔑這個可憐的女孩。

焦點句型 with scorn 輕蔑地

scrape [skrep] 名 摩擦 動 刮；擦

名 He got a scrape on his knee when he fell to the ground.
他因跌倒而擦傷了膝蓋。

動 She is scraping the path clear of snow.

她正在把路上的積雪鏟掉。

screwdriver [`skru͵draɪvɚ] **名** 螺絲起子

Turn the screws round and round with a screwdriver.

▶▶ 用螺絲起子把螺絲轉幾圈。

sculptor [`skʌlptɚ] **名** 雕刻家

Ju Ming is a famous sculptor.

▶▶ 朱銘是個知名雕刻家。

seagull / gull [`sigʌl] / [gʌl] **名** 海鷗

Many seagulls flew across the sky.

▶▶ 許多海鷗飛過天際。

seduce [sə`djus] **動** 勾引；誘惑

He was seduced to commit a crime.

▶▶ 他被引誘犯罪。

selective [sə`lɛktɪv] **形** 有選擇性的

About 3,000 boys turned up for the selective trials.

▶▶ 有三千個男孩子參加了選拔賽。

serene [sə`rin] **形** 寧靜的；安詳的

The baby feels serene when it is full.

▶▶ 嬰兒吃飽時就非常安靜。

sergeant [`sɑrdʒənt] **名** 士官

The sergeant trained the recruits.

▶▶ 那名士官訓練新兵。

sermon [`sɜmən] **名** 布道；講道

The sermon predicated the perfectibility of humankind.

▶▶ 這篇布道文斷言了人類的完美性。

serving [`sɜvɪŋ] **名** 一份

Ron had three servings of spicy pork beans.

▶▶ 榮恩吃了三份辣味肉豆。

Level 1 基礎單字
Level 2 必備單字
Level 3 中級單字
Level 4 進階單字
Level 5 高手單字
Level 6 滿級單字

setback [`sɛt,bæk] 名 逆轉；挫折

Tina was frustrated by the setback.
>> 蒂娜因挫敗感到喪氣。

shabby [`ʃæbɪ] 形 衣衫襤褸的

An old man in shabby clothes knocked on the door.
>> 一名衣衫襤褸的老人來敲門。

sharpen [`ʃɑrpn̩] 動 使銳利

She sharpened the pencil with a sharpener.
>> 她用一把小刀把鉛筆削尖。

shaver [`ʃevɚ] 名 刮鬍刀

Melody used a shaver on her legs.
>> 美樂蒂用刮鬍刀刮腿毛。

shortcoming [`ʃɔrt,kʌmɪŋ] 名 短處；缺點

Human beings all have shortcomings.
>> 人皆有缺點。

shortsighted [,ʃɔrt`saɪtɪd] 形 近視的

I became shortsighted when I was in elementary school.
>> 我小學時就近視了。

shred [ʃrɛd] 名 碎片 動 撕成碎片

名 The shredder made the paper into shreds.
碎紙機把紙割成碎片。
動 He shredded the confidential document.
他把密件撕毀。

shriek [ʃrik] 名 尖叫 動 尖叫

名 The crowd of people let out continual shrieks of excitement while watching the acrobatics.
這群人一面看雜技表演，一面不斷發出尖叫。
動 The boy shrieked on seeing the wolfhound.
這個小男孩一看到狼犬就尖叫。

shrub [ʃrʌb] 名灌木

Plant these shrubs in full sun.
▶▶ 把這些灌木種在陽光充足的地方。

shutter [`ʃʌtɚ] 名百葉窗

There are shutters on the windows in the office.
▶▶ 辦公室的窗戶上裝了百葉窗。

simplicity [sɪm`plɪsətɪ] 名單純；簡單

The advantage of the proposal is simplicity.
▶▶ 這個提案的優點在於簡單明瞭。

simplify [`sɪmplə͵faɪ] 動使單純

Her explanation simplified the question.
▶▶ 她的解釋把問題變簡單了。

simultaneous [͵saɪml̩`tenɪəs] 形同時發生的

This event was almost simultaneous with that one.
▶▶ 這件事幾乎是與那件事同時發生的。

skeptical [`skɛptɪkl̩] 形懷疑的

I am skeptical about his real intentions.
▶▶ 我懷疑他真正的企圖。
(焦點句型) be skeptical about sth. 懷疑…

skim [skɪm] 動掠過；略讀

I skimmed this chapter because of limited time.
▶▶ 我大致看了一遍這個章節，因時間有限。

slang [slæŋ] 名俚語

There are many interesting slangs in English.
▶▶ 英文中有許多有趣的俚語。

slash [slæʃ] 動劈砍 名砍傷

動 We had to slash our way through the undergrowth with sticks.
　　我們揮舞著木棍一路劈砍，才在密林裡開出一條路。
名 He got a slash on the thigh.
　　他的大腿被砍傷了。

slaughter [`slɑtɚ] 名屠殺 動屠殺

名 Wholesale slaughter is awful.
大批的屠殺十分嚇人。
動 The Nazis slaughtered the Jews in World War II.
納粹黨在二次世界大戰時屠殺猶太人。

slay [sle] 動殺害

No one knew why the young man slew the girl.
▶▶ 沒人知道為什麼這個年輕人要殺害那個女孩。
文法解析 slay 動詞三態變化為 slay / slew / slain。

sloppy [`slɑpɪ] 形不整潔的

A sloppy person is hardly popular.
▶▶ 邋遢的人很難受人歡迎。

slum [slʌm] 名貧民區 動進入貧民區

名 Slums are the poor parts of towns.
貧民區是城鎮裡貧窮的區域。
動 The mayor went slumming.
市長去探訪貧民窟。

slump [slʌmp] 名下跌；不景氣 動下跌

名 I think it's just a slump.
我想這只是不景氣而已。
動 The prices slumped amid a fall in demand.
需求減少，價格就會下跌。

sly [slaɪ] 形狡猾的

He is so sly that he stole my design and claimed that it was his!
▶▶ 他真的很狡猾，偷了我的設計說是他的！

smuggle [`smʌgl] 動走私

He was caught smuggling drugs into the country.
▶▶ 他向這個國家走私毒品被抓。

sneaker [`snikɚ] 名運動鞋

His mother bought him a pair of sneakers as a reward.
▶▶ 他媽媽送他一雙運動鞋作為獎賞。

sneaky [`snikɪ] 形 鬼祟的

This sneaky girl is disliked by the rest of the class.
▶▶ 全班同學都不喜歡這個行為鬼祟的女同學。

sneeze [sniz] 名 噴嚏 動 輕視；打噴嚏

名 His loud sneeze shocked me.
他大聲的噴嚏嚇著了我。
動 You have been sneezing for minutes. Maybe you've caught a cold.
你打了好一陣子的噴嚏，也許你感冒了。

snore [snor] 名 鼾聲 動 打鼾

名 His snore makes me sleepless every night.
他的鼾聲讓我夜夜失眠。
動 He fell asleep and started to snore.
他睡著後開始打呼。

sociable [`soʃəbl̩] 形 愛交際的

Ivan is sociable and outgoing, so he has many friends.
▶▶ 伊凡喜好交際又個性活潑，所以有很多朋友。

socialism [`soʃəl͵ɪzəm] 名 社會主義

Socialism hopes to eliminate poverty.
▶▶ 社會主義主張消滅貧窮。

socialist [`soʃəlɪst] 名 社會主義者

He was seen as a traitor to the socialist cause.
▶▶ 他被視為社會主義事業的叛徒。

socialize [`soʃə͵laɪz] 動 使社會化

We become socialized as we grow, so we can live more harmoniously with others.
▶▶ 我們在成長的過程中社會化，以便與他人更和諧地相處。

sociology [͵sosɪ`ɑlədʒɪ] 名 社會學

Interaction, construction, and networks are important concepts in sociology.
▶▶ 互動、建構和網絡是社會學中的重要概念。

Level 1 基礎單字
Level 2 必備單字
Level 3 中級單字
Level 4 進階單字
Level 5 高手單字
Level 6 滿級單字

solemn [`sɑləm] 形 鄭重的；莊嚴的

Her face grew solemn.
▶▶ 她的臉嚴肅起來。

solidarity [ˌsɑlə`dærətɪ] 名 團結

"We must show solidarity with the strikers," declared the student leaders.
▶▶ 學生領袖聲稱「我們要與罷工工人團結一致」。

solitary [`sɑləˌtɛrɪ] 形 單獨的；孤獨的 名 獨居者

形 The old man leads a solitary life.
　老人過著孤單的生活。
名 The solitary lives alone in the cottage by the river.
　這名獨居者孤身住在河邊小屋裡。

solitude [`sɑləˌtjud] 名 孤獨；寂寞

I enjoy living in solitude.
▶▶ 我喜歡獨居。

soothe [suð] 動 安慰；撫慰

This should soothe the pain.
▶▶ 這個應該能緩解疼痛。

sorrowful [`sɑrəfəl] 形 哀痛的；悲傷的

She felt sorrowful on seeing these photos.
▶▶ 看到這些照片使她感到哀傷。

sovereign [`sɑvrɪn] 名 最高統治者 形 擁有主權的

名 The sovereign ruled over the land for nearly 50 years.
　這位統治者治理這塊土地跡近五十年了。
形 Whether Taiwan is a sovereign nation is still controversial.
　台灣是否為主權國家仍然飽受爭議。

spacecraft / spaceship [`spesˌkræft ] / [ `spesˌʃɪp] 名 太空船

How many spacecraft are orbiting the moon?
▶▶ 有多少太空船繞月球軌道飛行？

span [spæn] 名 一段時間；跨度 動 持續；橫跨

名 He has lived here for a long span of time.
　他居住在這裡已有很長的一段時間了。

(動) Many bridges span the River Thames.
許多橋橫跨泰晤士河。

sparrow [`spæro] 名麻雀

A sparrow may be small, but its body has every organ it needs.
▶▶ 麻雀雖小，五臟俱全。

spectacle [`spɛktəkl̩] 名奇觀

The canyon is indeed a spectacle.
▶▶ 這座峽谷著實是個奇觀。

spiral [`spaɪrəl] 名螺旋 動急遽上升 形螺旋的

(名) The spiral of silence is a mass communication theory.
沉默螺旋理論是一種大眾傳播理論。
(動) Military budgets continued to spiral.
軍事預算持續增加。
(形) A spiral staircase can save a lot of space.
螺旋狀樓梯可以節省很多空間。

splendor [`splɛndə] 名燦爛；輝煌

The mansion is shorn of its splendor.
▶▶ 這棟大廈已失去輝煌景象。

spokesperson / spokesman / spokeswoman

[`spoks͵pɝsn̩] / [ `spoksmən] / [`spoks͵wumən] 名發言人

The spokesperson for the president answered the journalist's question.
▶▶ 總統的發言人回答了記者的問題。

spontaneous [spɑn`tenɪəs] 形自發的

The eruption of a volcano is spontaneous.
▶▶ 火山爆發是自發的。

sportsman / sportswoman

[`sportsmən ] / [ `sports͵wumən] 名男運動員/女運動員

The sportsmen and sportswomen gathered on the field.
▶▶ 男女運動員在這場競賽中齊聚一堂。

Level 1 基礎單字
Level 2 必備單字
Level 3 中級單字
Level 4 進階單字
Level 5 高手單字
Level 6 滿級單字

sportsmanship [`spɔrtsmən,ʃɪp] 名運動家精神

Perseverance is an element of sportsmanship.
▶▶ 堅持不懈是運動家精神的一種。

spotlight [`spɑt,laɪt] 名聚光燈 動用聚光燈照

名 Spotlights are widely-used in stage dramas.
　　聚光燈在舞台劇中廣泛使用。
動 Spotlight the lead actor.
　　把聚光燈打向主角。

spur [spɝ] 名馬刺 動策馬飛奔

名 It is the bridle and spur that make a good horse.
　　要造就一匹好馬，韁繩和靴刺是少不了的。
動 She spurred her horse on.
　　她策馬飛奔。

stabilize [`stebə,laɪz] 動保持穩定

The old man leans on a stick to stabilize himself.
▶▶ 老人家拄著拐杖來保持穩定。

stagger [`stæɡɚ] 名搖晃；蹣跚 動搖晃；蹣跚

名 She decided to drive me home on seeing my stagger.
　　她看到我蹣跚的模樣後，決定載我回家。
動 I staggered to the restroom after getting up.
　　我起床後搖搖晃晃地到廁所去。

staple [`stepl̩] 名訂書針 動用訂書針訂

名 The stapler has run out of staples.
　　訂書機的針用完了。
動 He stapled the pile of handouts.
　　他把這疊講義訂起來。

starvation [stɑr`veʃən] 名飢餓

He stole the bread out of starvation.
▶▶ 他出於飢餓偷了麵包。

stationary [`steʃən,ɛrɪ] 形不動的

While the car was stationary, another vehicle ran into the back of it.
▶▶ 當車子不動時，另一輛車從後面撞了上來。

700

stationery [`steʃənˌɛrɪ] 名 文具

Stationery is indispensable for students.
▶▶ 文具對學生來說必不可少。

stature [`stætʃə] 名 聲譽；身高

People care about their stature very much in their adolescence.
▶▶ 人們青春期的時候非常在乎身高。

stepchild [`stɛpˌtʃaɪld] 名 繼子；繼女

After her mother died, his father remarried and she is now a stepchild to her stepmother.
▶▶ 在她母親過世後，父親再婚，現在對她的繼母而言是繼女。

stepfather [`stɛpˌfɑðə] 名 繼父；後父

The news that Sara's stepfather beat her badly startled all of us.
▶▶ 莎拉被繼父嚴重毆打的消息震驚了我們所有人。

stepmother [`stɛpˌmʌðə] 名 繼母；後母

Why is the boy often scolded by his stepmother?
▶▶ 為什麼這小男孩經常挨他繼母罵？

stimulation [ˌstɪmjə`leʃən] 名 刺激；興奮

He who has no motive to work needs stimulation.
▶▶ 沒有動力工作的人需要刺激。

strait [stret] 名 海峽

Taiwan and China are divided by a strait.
▶▶ 台灣和中國被一道海峽隔開。

strangle [`stræŋgl] 動 勒死；絞死

The man who killed his parents strangled them to death.
▶▶ 殺害他雙親的人是用勒死的方式行兇。

stray [stre] 名 流浪者 動 迷路；漂泊 形 迷途的

名 The poor strays are starving.
可憐的遊民們餓壞了。
動 He strayed into the path of an oncoming car.
他迷路走到有一輛汽車迎面駛來的車道上。

Level 1 基礎單字
Level 2 必備單字
Level 3 中級單字
Level 4 進階單字
Level 5 高手單字
Level 6 滿級單字

形 A stray dog lingered on the street.
有隻流浪狗在街上徘徊。

stride [straɪd] 名跨步；大步 動大步走；跨過

名 There have been great strides of progress in this field.
在這塊領域有很大的進展。
動 Can you stride the brook?
你能一步跨過這條小溪嗎？
文法解析 stride動詞三態變化為 stride / strode / stridden。

stroll [strol] 名漫步；閒晃 動漫步

名 He invited her to take a stroll but she refused.
他邀請她出去散步，但遭到拒絕。
動 The couple strolled in the park after lunch.
飯後這對夫婦在公園散步。
焦點句型 take a stroll 散步

stun [stʌn] 動大吃一驚

I was stunned by the thunder.
▶▶ 我被雷聲嚇得大吃一驚。

stutter [`stʌtɚ] 名結巴；口吃 動結巴地說

名 He is very intelligent, but he cannot express himself well because of his stutter.
他非常聰明，但是口吃使他無法好好表達自己。
動 She stuttered that it was her fault.
她結巴地說這是她的錯。

stylish [`staɪlɪʃ] 形時髦的；漂亮的

Her new hairstyle is stylish.
▶▶ 她的新髮型非常時髦。

subjective [səb`dʒɛktɪv] 形主觀的

Our perception of things is often influenced by subjective factors.
▶▶ 我們對事物的感知能力常受到主觀因素的影響。

subordinate [sə`bɔrdənet] 名下屬；部下 形從屬的；下級的

名 I am not your subordinate, so I do not have to report everything to you.
我不是你的部下，所以我沒有必要向你報告每件事。

Level 1 基礎單字

Level 2 必備單字

Level 3 中級單字

Level 4 進階單字

Level 5 高手單字

Level 6 滿級單字

形 Pleasure should be subordinate to work.
娛樂應置於工作之下。

subscribe [səb`skraɪb] 動 訂閱；捐款；簽署

The newspaper is worth subscribing to.
▶▶ 這份報紙值得訂閱。

subscription [səb`skrɪpʃən] 名 訂閱；捐款；簽署

I got a subscription to the electronic publication.
▶▶ 我訂了那份電子報。

焦點句型 get a subscription (to sth.) 訂閱（⋯）

succession [sək`sɛʃən] 名 連續

He's been hit by a succession of injuries since he joined the team.
▶▶ 自入隊以來他一再受傷。

successive [sək`sɛsɪv] 形 連續的 同 consecutive

They won the successive championship.
▶▶ 他們蟬連冠軍。

suffocate [`sʌfə͵ket] 動 使窒息

The fireman was suffocated by the fumes.
▶▶ 那個消防隊員因濃煙而窒息死了。

suitcase [`sut͵kes] 名 手提箱 同 portfolio

One suitcase is enough to carry all your clothes with you on a short holiday.
▶▶ 一個手提箱裝得下短期渡假時的衣服。

summon [`sʌmən] 動 召集

He was summoned to appear in court as a witness.
▶▶ 他以目擊者的身分被傳喚出庭。

superficial [supə`fɪʃəl] 形 表面的；外表的

He was fooled by her superficial friendliness.
▶▶ 他被她表面的友好給騙了。

superiority [sə͵pɪrɪˋɔrətɪ] 名優越；卓越

The plan is merely designed to maintain their nuclear superiority.
▶▶ 制定這個計畫只是為了保持他們的核武優勢。

superstitious [͵supəˋstɪʃəs] 形迷信的

He is superstitious and believes that black cats are unlucky.
▶▶ 他很迷信，相信黑貓不吉祥。

supplement [ˋsʌpləmənt] / [ˋsʌplə͵mɛnt] 名補充 動補充

名 He doesn't eat enough fruit and vegetables, so he takes vitamin supplements.
他蔬果攝取不足，所以吃維他命補充。
動 Please supplement the kettle with water.
請補充水到茶壺裡。

suppress [səˋprɛs] 動壓抑；制止 關 crackdown 壓迫

The army suppressed the rebels violently.
▶▶ 軍隊暴力鎮壓反抗者。

surge [sɝdʒ] 名大浪 動湧動 關 surgical 外科的

名 The sea was rolling in immense surges.
大海上浪濤洶湧。
動 Watch out! The tides are surging now.
小心！浪潮正洶湧。

surpass [sɚˋpæs] 動越過；超過

He tried hard to surpass me in his career.
▶▶ 他努力嘗試在事業上超越我。

suspense [səˋspɛns] 名懸念；焦慮；擔心

I try to add an element of suspense and mystery to my novel.
▶▶ 我試圖為我的小說增加一點懸疑和神祕的元素。

suspension [səˋspɛnʃən] 名暫停；懸掛

I think her suspension from the team is a harsh punishment.
▶▶ 我認為她被暫停參加團隊的比賽是很嚴厲的處罰。
(焦點句型) suspension from sth. 暫停…

swamp [swɑmp] 名 沼澤 動 陷入

名 The swamp is home to various kinds of animals.
這片沼澤是許多物種的家。

動 Ted's boat was swamped and sank.
泰德陷在小溪裡。

swarm [swɔrm] 名 群；群集 動 群集

名 A swarm of mosquitoes are flying around the rubbish.
成群的蚊子在垃圾堆旁飛來飛去。

動 The students swarmed to see the superstar.
這些學生蜂擁著要看巨星。

symbolize [`sɪmbə,laɪz] 動 作為…的象徵

The national flag symbolizes our country.
▶▶ 國旗是我國的象徵。

symmetry [`sɪmətrɪ] 名 對稱；相稱 關 bilateral 雙邊的

I love the delicate symmetry of a leaf.
▶▶ 我喜歡一片樹葉完美的對稱性。

sympathize [`sɪmpə,θaɪz] 動 同情

We deeply sympathized with our classmate whose mother was very ill.
▶▶ 我們十分同情那個母親得了重病的同學。

焦點句型 sympathize with sb. 同情…

symphony [`sɪmfənɪ] 名 交響樂；交響曲

His latest symphony is better than anything he has ever written before.
▶▶ 他最新的交響曲勝過他過去的所有作品。

synonym [`sɪnə,nɪm] 名 同義字

There are many synonyms for happy, such as joyful, delightful, and glad.
▶▶ happy 有很多同義字，像是 joyful、delightful 和 glad。

synthetic [sɪn`θɛtɪk] 形 人造的

The room was decorated with synthetic flowers.
▶▶ 房間用人造花裝飾。

Level 1 基礎單字
Level 2 必備單字
Level 3 中級單字
Level 4 進階單字
Level 5 高手單字
Level 6 滿級單字

syrup [`sɪrəp] 名糖漿

She put some syrup on the pancakes.
▶▶ 她在鬆餅上抹了點糖漿。

tan [tæn] 名日曬後的棕褐膚色 形棕褐色的

名 I got a dark tan after swimming in the ocean.
在海裡游完泳後我曬黑了。
形 Her tan skin makes her look more beautiful.
她小麥般的膚色讓她看起來更美了。

tedious [`tidɪəs] 形沉悶的 關 dozy 想睡的

His tedious tone made me dozy.
▶▶ 他沉悶的語調讓我想睡。

teller [`tɛlɚ] 名講話者；敘述者 關 eloquence 流利的口才

The teller of the story has great eloquence.
▶▶ 說這個故事的人有著卓越的口才。

tempo [`tɛmpo] 名速度；拍子

They danced to the tempo.
▶▶ 他們隨著節拍起舞。

tenant [`tɛnənt] 名房客；租戶 動租賃（房屋）

名 The tenant was dissatisfied with the apartment he rented.
這位房客對他租的公寓不滿意。
動 The apartment was tenanted by a young lady.
這間公寓由一名年輕的小姐承租。

tentative [`tɛntətɪv] 形暫時的

We made a tentative arrangement to meet again next Friday.
▶▶ 我們暫定下星期五再相聚。

terrace [`tɛrəs] 名梯田 動使成梯形地

名 In China, hill farmers grow rice on terraces.
在中國，山區農民在梯田上種稻米。

textile [`tɛkstaɪl] 名織布 形紡織的

名 Their main exports are textiles, especially silk and cotton.
他們的主要出口貨物是紡織品，特別是絲綢和棉布。
形 Sue has worked in the textile industry for forty years.
蘇在紡織業工作四十年了。

thereafter [ðɛr`æftɚ] 副此後；以後

They have had no contact thereafter.
▶▶ 他們自此後再也沒有聯絡。

thermometer [θɚ`mɑmətɚ] 名溫度計

The thermometer lets us know what the temperature is.
▶▶ 溫度計讓我們知道溫度是多少。

tilt [tɪlt] 名傾斜 動傾斜

名 The water spilled out because of a careless tilt.
因為粗心的傾斜使水溢了出來。
動 During a conversation, he likes to tilt his head forward to show he is very attentive.
和人談話的時候，他喜歡把頭向前傾，表明他很專注。

tiptoe [`tɪp͵to] 名腳尖 動用腳尖走路

名 She walked to the balcony on tiptoes.
她踮著腳尖走到陽台。
動 He tiptoed to his room so that he wouldn't wake up his parents.
他踮起腳尖進房，以免吵醒父母。
焦點句型 on tiptoe(s) 踮著腳尖

tiresome [`taɪrsəm] 形無聊的；可厭的

The tiresome routine annoyed him.
▶▶ 這些惹人厭的例行公事惹惱了他。

token [`tokən] 名表徵；標誌

The birthmark on her face has become her token.
▶▶ 她臉上的胎記成了她的標誌。

Level 1 基礎單字
Level 2 必備單字
Level 3 中級單字
Level 4 進階單字
Level 5 高手單字
Level 6 滿級單字

tornado [tɔr`nedo] 名龍捲風

A tornado is a violent, rotating column of air.
▶▶ 龍捲風是一種暴烈迴旋的縱柱狀氣流。

torrent [`tɔrənt] 名洪流；急流

The river was a torrent after the storm.
▶▶ 暴風雨過後，河水暴漲成了急流。

trademark [`tred,mɑrk] 名標記；商標

The trademark symbol of our company is a sunflower.
▶▶ 我們公司的商標是一朵向日葵。

transcript [`træn,skrɪpt] 名副本

He produced a transcript from the conversation.
▶▶ 他把對話抄寫成副本。

transmit [træns`mɪt] 動傳播；寄送

Transmit him the message as soon as possible.
▶▶ 儘快把這訊息傳達給他。

transplant [træns`plænt ] / [ `træns,plænt] 動移植 名（器官）移植

動 A piece of skin was transplanted on her face.
一小部分的皮膚被移植到她的臉上。
名 Ted is going to receive a heart transplant.
泰德將要接受心臟移植手術。

treasury [`trɛʒərɪ] 名國庫；金庫

Gordon had a long career with the Treasury Department.
▶▶ 高登在財政部工作許久。

trek [trɛk] 名長途跋涉 動長途跋涉

名 The tribe made a trek to a faraway valley.
這個部落翻山越嶺來到遠方的山谷。
動 Our ancestors trekked from China to Taiwan.
我們的祖先從中國長途跋涉到台灣。

trifle [`traɪfl̩] 名瑣事 動疏忽；輕視

名 He told her not to pester him with trifles.
他告訴她別拿些瑣事來煩他。

Level 1 基礎單字
Level 2 必備單字
Level 3 中級單字
Level 4 進階單字
Level 5 高手單字
Level 6 滿級單字

動 He trifled with his mother's advice.
他輕忽了他母親的勸告。

tropic [`trɑpɪk] 名回歸線

The Tropic of Cancer passes through the town.
▶▶ 北回歸線穿越這座市鎮。

trout [traʊt] 名鱒魚

This trout in the bucket is my harvest today.
▶▶ 水桶裡的鱒魚是我今天的漁獲。

tuck [tʌk] 名打褶 動把（布料等的末端）塞進；把…舒服地裹好

名 The dress was too big, so my mother put a tuck in it.
洋裝太大，所以媽媽在裡面打褶。
動 He fell asleep before I tucked him in bed.
在我幫他蓋好毯子之前，他就睡著了。

turmoil [`tɝmɔɪl] 名騷動

Since the outbreak of the war, the city has been in turmoil.
▶▶ 戰爭爆發後，這個城市現在一片混亂。

twilight [`twaɪ͵laɪt] 名黃昏；薄暮

I promised to meet her at twilight near the bridge.
▶▶ 我答應她傍晚時在橋附近碰面。

twinkle [`twɪŋkḷ] 名閃爍 動閃爍

名 The twinkle of the fireflies is very pretty.
螢火蟲的閃爍非常耀眼。
動 Her eyes twinkled with amusement.
她含著笑意，雙眸閃閃發亮。

UNIT 19 **U 字頭滿級單字**

MP3 135

unanimous [juˋnænəməs] 形一致的；和諧的

The resolution got an unanimous reception.
▶▶ 該項決議得到了一致的認可。

underestimate [ˌʌndɚˋɛstəˌmet] 動 低估 名 低估

動 Those who underestimate the intelligence of their rivals will come to grief.
低估對手智慧的人會大吃苦頭。

名 He made an underestimate of the degree of difficulty.
他低估了難度。

underneath [ˌʌndɚˋniθ] 介 在…下面

The coin rolled underneath the piano.
▶ 硬幣滾到了鋼琴底下。

underpass [ˋʌndɚˌpæs] 名 地下道

We used the underpass to cross the street.
▶ 我們使用地下道過馬路。

unify [ˋjunəˌfaɪ] 動 使一致，聯合 關 unification 統一

In my opinion, Abraham Lincoln was honored in the US mostly because he unified the country.
▶ 在我看來，美國人敬重林肯，主要是因為他保持了美國的統一。

upright [ˋʌpˌraɪt] 名 直立的東西；柱 形 直立的 副 直立地

名 He replaced the broken upright on the fence.
他更換了圍欄上損壞的直柱。

形 I sat under an upright tree.
我坐在一棵挺直的大樹下。

副 The model stood upright with a confident expression.
模特兒一臉自信、筆直地站著。

upward / upwards [ˋʌpwəd] / [ˋʌpwədz] 形 向上的 副 向上地

形 She is already upward of sixty.
她已年過六十。

副 They went upward to the summit.
他們向上走到山頂。

urgency [ˋɝdʒənsɪ] 名 迫切 關 adrenalin 腎上腺素

We gain strength in urgency because of adrenalin.
▶ 腎上腺素讓我們的力氣在危急時增加。

(焦點句型) in urgency 迫切地

usher [`ʌʃɚ] 名引導員 動引導；引領

名 She asked the usher where she should sit.
她向引導員詢問她該坐哪裡。
動 The secretary ushered me into his office.
秘書把我引進他的辦公室。

utensil [ju`tɛnsḷ] 名用具；器皿

This store sells cooking utensils.
▶▶ 這商店出售炊具。

utter [`ʌtɚ] 形完全的 動出聲；說

形 To my utter amazement, she agreed.
令我大感意外的是，她同意了。
動 She uttered a sigh when she heard about the failure.
當她得知失敗時，嘆了一口氣。

MP3 136

vaccine [`væksin] 名疫苗

The Salk, or polio, vaccine is a "killed" vaccine.
▶▶ 沙克疫苗（或稱為小兒麻痺疫苗）是一種不會傳染的疫苗。

vanilla [və`nɪlə] 名香草

Pure vanilla is expensive.
▶▶ 純種香草十分昂貴。

vanity [`vænətɪ] 名虛榮心；自負

He bought luxuries to satisfy his own vanity.
▶▶ 他購買奢侈品來滿足自己的虛榮心。

vapor [`vepɚ] 名蒸氣；水氣

A cloud is a mass of vapor in the sky.
▶▶ 雲是天空中的一團水氣。

veil [vel] 名面紗 動遮蓋

名 Muslim women have to cover their faces in veils when going out.
穆斯林婦女外出時必須戴面紗遮蓋臉孔。
動 The robber had veiled his face.
那名強盜蒙住了臉。

Level 1 基礎單字
Level 2 必備單字
Level 3 中級單字
Level 4 進階單字
Level 5 高手單字
Level 6 滿級單字

velvet [`vɛlvɪt] 名天鵝絨 形柔軟的；平滑的

名 The coat was covered with velvet.
這件外套鋪了一層天鵝絨。

形 The princess has velvet hands.
這位公主擁有柔嫩光滑的雙手。

versatile [`vɜsətəl] 形多才多藝的；多種用途的

The versatile girl is adept in music, dancing, painting and calligraphy.
▶▶ 這個多才多藝的女孩擅長音樂、舞蹈、繪畫和書法。

veterinarian / vet [,vɛtərə`nɛrɪən] / [vɛt] 名獸醫

The veterinarian diagnosed the dog's illness.
▶▶ 獸醫替小狗診斷病情。

veto [`vito] 名否決 動否決

名 The President threatened to use his veto over the bill.
總統威脅要對這個議案行使否決權。

動 The majority vetoed the proposal.
多數人否決了這個提議。

vibrate [`vaɪbret] 動振動

When he called me, my cellphone started to vibrate.
▶▶ 當他打電話給我時，我的手機就開始震動。

vibration [vaɪ`breʃən] 名振動

Your finger can feel the vibration on the violin string.
▶▶ 你的手能感覺小提琴琴弦的振動。

vice [vaɪs] 名不道德的行為；邪惡

Cheating is a vice.
▶▶ 欺騙是不道德的行為。

victor [`vɪktə] 名勝利者；戰勝者

We won't know who the victor will be until the final game is over.
▶▶ 不到最後一場比賽結束，我們無法知道誰是贏家。

vigor [`vɪgə] 名精力；活力

The leader of the expedition must be a man of great vigor.
▶▶ 探險隊的領導者必須是有活力的人。

vigorous [ˋvɪgərəs] 形 有活力的

A vigorous person can encourage his or her peers.
▶▶ 一個有活力的人可以激勵夥伴。

villa [ˋvɪlə] 名 別墅

His villa was located in the suburbs.
▶▶ 他的別墅位於近郊。

villain [ˋvɪlən] 名 惡棍

He often plays a villain in films.
▶▶ 他經常扮演電影裡的反派角色。

vine [vaɪn] 名 葡萄藤

A snail was crawling up the vine.
▶▶ 一隻蝸牛正往葡萄藤上爬。

vineyard [ˋvɪnjəd] 名 葡萄園

Soon we came to the beautiful vineyard.
▶▶ 一會兒我們就來到美麗的的葡萄園。

violinist [ˏvaɪəˋlɪnɪst] 名 小提琴手

He is one of the violinists in the orchestra.
▶▶ 他是管弦樂隊中的小提琴手之一。

virgin [ˋvɝdʒɪn] 名 處女 形 純淨的

名 Before she got married, Louise was a virgin.
　　路易絲在嫁人前是個處女。
形 There were no footmarks on the virgin snow.
　　潔白的雪上沒有腳印。

vitality [vaɪˋtælətɪ] 名 生命力

I feel a strong vitality in his drawing.
▶▶ 他的畫讓我感到強烈的生命力。

vocation [voˋkeʃən] 名 職業

No vocation is inferior to another.
▶▶ 職業無貴賤。

Level 1 基礎單字
Level 2 必備單字
Level 3 中級單字
Level 4 進階單字
Level 5 高手單字
Level 6 滿級單字

vocational [voˋkeʃənḷ] 形職業的

My brother went to a vocational school to learn automotive mechanics.
▶▶ 我弟弟進入職業學校，學習汽車機械。

vowel [ˋvauəl] 名母音

A vowel can form a syllable by itself.
▶▶ 母音能單獨構成音節。

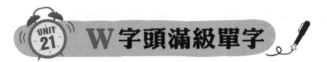

UNIT 21 **W 字頭滿級單字**

MP3 137

wag [wæg] 動搖擺 名搖擺

動 She wagged her finger in response.
她晃晃手指以示回應。
名 The wag of a dog's tail represents friendliness.
狗搖尾巴是友好的意思。

walnut [ˋwɔlnət] 名胡桃樹；胡桃

Try to crack the walnut with this device.
▶▶ 試試用這個裝置敲開核桃。

ward [wɔrd] 名行政區；保護；病房 動保護；避開

How many wards is the city divided into?
▶▶ 這座城市分成幾個行政區？
(焦點句型) ward off 避開；擋開

wardrobe [ˋwɔrd͵rob] 名衣櫃

There were several expensive suits hanging in the wardrobe.
▶▶ 衣櫃裡掛著幾套昂貴的西裝。

warranty [ˋwɔrəntɪ] 名依據；保證書 同 warrant 擔保 關 lapse 失效

The warranty lapsed two months ago.
▶▶ 那保證書兩個月前就已經失效了。

waterproof [ˋwɔtɚˋpruf] 形防水的

My waterproof watch kept working after dropping into the pool.
▶▶ 我的防水手錶掉進池子之後還是持續運作。

weary [`wɪrɪ] 形 疲倦的；厭煩的 動 疲倦；厭煩

形 Pan grew weary of the noise.
潘對噪音感到厭煩。

動 I wearied of the daily routine.
我對每日的例行公事感到厭煩。

(焦點句型) weary of sth. 對…厭煩

wharf [hwɔrf] 名 碼頭

We walked her to the wharf and put her aboard the ship.
▶▶ 我們陪她走到碼頭，將她安頓到船上。

whiskey / whisky [`hwɪskɪ] 名 威士忌

Whiskey is a kind of liquor.
▶▶ 威士忌是一種酒。

wholesale [`hol͵sel] 名 批發 動 批發 形 成批的 副 成批地

名 Retailers buy at wholesale.
零售商按批發價採購。

動 My uncle wholesales clothes to merchants.
我叔叔批發衣服給商人。

形 Wholesale goods are cheaper than those bought in stores.
批發貨比在零售商店買的便宜。

wholesome [`holsəm] 形 有益健康的

Exercising every day is wholesome.
▶▶ 天天運動有益健康。

widow / widower [`wɪdo ] / [ `wɪdoɚ] 名 寡婦 / 鰥夫

The widow reared her son on her own.
▶▶ 這名寡婦獨自撫養兒子。

woe [wo] 名 悲痛

His woes were too many to mention.
▶▶ 他的苦難太多，不勝枚舉。

woodpecker [`wud͵pɛkɚ] 名 啄木鳥

Woodpeckers are said to be the doctors of trees.
▶▶ 啄木鳥被稱為樹木的醫生。

Level 1 基礎單字
Level 2 必備單字
Level 3 中級單字
Level 4 進階單字
Level 5 高手單字
Level 6 滿級單字

wrestle [`rɛsḷ] 名 角力；搏鬥

He got injured in the wrestle with a robber.
▶▶ 跟搶匪搏鬥間他受傷了。

wrinkle [`rɪŋkḷ] 名 皺紋 動 皺起

名 The wrinkles on her face show her age.
她臉上的皺紋說明了她的年紀。
動 She wrinkled her nose at the bad smell.
聞到臭氣，她皺起了鼻子。

UNIT 22 Y、Z字頭滿級單字

MP3 138

yearn [jɜn] 動 渴望

The people yearned for peace.
▶▶ 人民渴望和平。
(焦點句型) yearn for sth. 渴望…

yoga [`jogə] 名 瑜伽

My mother goes to yoga classes after work.
▶▶ 我媽媽下班後去上瑜珈課。

yogurt [`jogət] 名 優酪乳

Yogurt is good for digestion.
▶▶ 優酪乳利於消化。

zoom [zum] 動 將畫面拉近（或拉遠）；快速移動；猛漲

He zoomed in to see the object clearly.
▶▶ 他把畫面拉近以看清楚物體。

more =>

7000 Essential
Vocabulary for
High School Students

實力測驗

單字難易度 ★★★☆☆
文法難易度 ★★☆☆☆
生活出現頻率 ★★★★★
考題出題頻率 ★★★★☆

名 名詞　動 動詞　形 形容詞　副 副詞　介 介係詞　連 連接詞
關 相關單字 / 片語　同 同義詞　反 反義詞

1. Bobby cared a lot about his _____ at home and asked his parents not to go through his things without his permission.
   (A) discipline　(B) facility　(C) privacy　(D) representation

2. The new manager is a real gentleman. He is kind and humble, totally different from the former manager, who was _____ and bossy.
   (A) eager　(B) liberal　(C) mean　(D) inferior

3. The weather bureau _____ that the typhoon would bring strong winds and heavy rains, and warned everyone of the possible danger.
   (A) conveyed　(B) associated　(C) interpreted　(D) predicted

4. Different airlines have different _____ for carry-on luggage, but many international airlines limit a carry-on piece to 7 kilograms.
   (A) landmarks　(B) restrictions　(C) percentages　(D) circumstances

5. Many people were happy that the government had finally _____ Children's Day as a national holiday.
   (A) appointed　(B) declared　(C) performed　(D) involved

6. To reach the goal of making her company a market leader, Michelle _____ a plan to open ten new stores around the country this year.
   (A) advised　(B) occupied　(C) proposed　(D) recognized

7. Silence in some way is as _____ as speech. It can be used to show, for example, disagreement or lack of interest.
   (A) sociable　(B) expressive　(C) reasonable　(D) objective

8. This TV program is designed for children, _____ for those under five. It contains no violence or strong language.
   (A) particularly　(B) sensibly　(C) moderately　(D) considerably

9. Tommy, please put away the toys in the box, or you might _____ on them and hurt yourself.
   (A) stumble　(B) graze　(C) navigate　(D) dwell

10. The _____ costume party, held every September, is one of the biggest events of the school year.
    (A) initial　(B) annual　(C) evident　(D) occasional

11. In a job interview, attitude and personality are usually important _____ that influence the decision of the interviewers.

（A）factors　（B）outcomes　（C）missions　（D）identities

12. The snow-capped mountain is described so _____ in the book that the scene seems to come alive in front of the reader's eyes.

（A）distantly　（B）meaningfully　（C）cheerfully　（D）vividly

13. Surrounded by flowers blooming and birds _____ merrily, the Wangs had a good time hiking in the national park.

（A）napping　（B）scooping　（C）flipping　（D）chirping

14. It is essential for us to maintain constant _____ with our friends to ensure that we have someone to talk to in times of need.

（A）benefit　（B）contact　（C）gesture　（D）favor

15. The young generation in this country has shown less interest in factory work and other _____ labor jobs, such as house construction and fruit picking.

（A）causal　（B）durable　（C）manual　（D）violent

實力測驗第一回 答案&解析

解答 CCDBB CBAAB ADDBC

1. 鮑比很注重他在家裡的隱私，要求父母沒經過允許不要翻看他的東西。

（A）紀律　（B）設施　（C）隱私　（D）代表

補充詞彙 go through 經歷（苦難等）；仔細查看

2. 新任經理真是位紳士，為人親切又謙虛，和惡毒又跋扈的前任經理完全不同。

（A）熱切的　（B）自由的　（C）惡毒的　（D）低等的

3. 氣象局預測颱風將會帶來強風和豪雨，提醒大家注意可能出現的危險。

（A）傳達　（B）聯想　（C）詮釋　（D）預測

4. 各家航空公司對隨身行李設有不同的限制，但許多國際航空公司對登機行李的限重都是七公斤。

（A）地標　（B）限制　（C）百分比　（D）情況

5. 政府終於宣布兒童節是國定假日，許多人對此感到很開心。
（A）指派　（B）宣布　（C）表演　（D）牽涉

6. 為了達到讓公司成為市場龍頭的目標，蜜雪兒提議今年在國內新開十家分店。
（A）勸告　（B）佔領　（C）提議　（D）認出

7. 某方面來說，沉默和言語一樣具備表達性。比如說，沉默可以表達不同意或缺乏興趣的態度。
（A）社交的　（B）表現的　（C）合理的　（D）客觀的

8. 這個電視節目是專為兒童設計的，特別是五歲以下的兒童。節目中沒有任何暴力情節和激烈言辭。
（A）特別地　（B）明智地　（C）適度地　（D）可觀地

9. 湯米，請把盒子裡的玩具收起來，否則你可能被玩具絆倒受傷。
（A）絆倒　（B）放牧　（C）導航　（D）居住

10. 年度化裝舞會於每年九月舉行，是學年間最盛大的活動之一。
（A）起首的　（B）年度的　（C）明顯的　（D）偶爾的

11. 在求職面試中，態度與個性通常是影響面試官決定的重要因素。
（A）因素　（B）結果　（C）任務　（D）身分

12. 書中對雪山的描寫栩栩如生，彷彿活生生的場景就在讀者眼前。
（A）遙遠地　（B）有意義地　（C）雀躍地　（D）生動地

13. 在鳥語花香的環繞中，王氏一家在國家公園度過了一段美好的健行時光。
（A）打盹　（B）舀取　（C）翻轉　（D）發出啁啾聲

14. 我們必須時常和朋友保持聯繫，以確保在需要的時候有人可以傾訴。
（A）利益　（B）聯繫　（C）手勢　（D）贊同

15. 這個國家的年輕一代對工廠作業與其他體力勞動工作（如房屋建設和水果採摘）興致缺缺。
（A）因果的　（B）持久的　（C）體力的　（D）暴力的

1. After hours of discussion, our class finally reached the _____ that we would go to Hualien for our graduation trip.

   (A) balance　(B) conclusion　(C) definition　(D) harmony

2. Jane _____ her teacher by passing the exam with a nearly perfect score; she almost failed the course last semester.

   (A) bored　(B) amazed　(C) charmed　(D) informed

3. The vacuum cleaner is not working. Let's send it back to the _____ to have it inspected and repaired.

   (A) lecturer　(B) publisher　(C) researcher　(D) manufacturer

4. Due to the global financial crisis, the country's exports _____ by 40 percent last month, the largest drop since 2000.

   (A) flattered　(B) transformed　(C) relieved　(D) decreased

5. The potato chips have been left uncovered on the table for such a long time that they no longer taste fresh and _____.

   (A) solid　(B) crispy　(C) original　(D) smooth

6. The townspeople built a _____ in memory of the brave teacher who sacrificed her life to save her students from a burning bus.

   (A) monument　(B) refugee　(C) souvenir　(D) firecracker

7. The students in Professor Smith's classical Chinese class are required to _____ poems by famous Chinese poets.

   (A) construct　(B) expose　(C) recite　(D) install

8. Although Mr. Tang claims that the house belongs to him, he has not offered any proof of _____.

   (A) convention　(B) relationship　(C) insurance　(D) ownership

9. Ancient Athens, famous for its early development of the democratic system, is often said to be the _____ of democracy.

   (A) mission　(B) target　(C) cradle　(D) milestone

10. The candy can no longer be sold because it was found to contain artificial ingredients far beyond the _____ level.

    (A) abundant　(B) immense　(C) permissible　(D) descriptive

11. Jack's excellent performance in last week's game has _____ all the doubts about his ability to play on our school basketball team.

（A）erased （B）canceled （C）overlooked （D）replaced

12. It is bullying to _____ a foreign speaker's accent. No one deserves to be laughed at for their pronunciation.

（A）mock （B）sneak （C）prompt （D）glare

13. Mary lost ten kilograms in three months, so her _____ skin-tight jeans are now hanging off her hips.

（A）barely （B）evenly （C）currently （D）formerly

14. The police officer showed us pictures of drunk driving accidents to highlight the importance of staying _____ on the road.

（A）sober （B）majestic （C）vigorous （D）noticeable

15. The claim that eating chocolate can prevent heart disease is _____ because there is not enough scientific evidence to support it.

（A）creative （B）disputable （C）circular （D）magnificent

實力測驗第二回 答案&解析

解答→ BBDDB ACDCC AADAB

1. 經過幾個小時的討論，我們班最後得出的結論是我們畢業旅行要去花蓮。

（A）平衡 （B）結論 （C）定義 （D）和諧

2. 珍以接近滿分的成績通過考試，讓她的老師大吃一驚，因為她上學期差一點就不及格了。

（A）使…感到無聊 （B）使…驚訝 （C）吸引 （D）通知

3. 吸塵器壞了。把它送回製造廠商檢查維修吧。

（A）講師 （B）出版商 （C）研究者 （D）製造商

補充詞彙 vacuum cleaner 吸塵器

4. 受全球金融危機的影響，該國上個月的出口額下降了百分之四十，這是自 2000 年以來的最大降幅。

（A）奉承　　（B）轉換　　（C）緩解　　（D）減少

5. 洋芋片在桌上放了很長一段時間，都沒有包裝隔絕空氣，吃起來不再新鮮爽脆。
　　（A）固態的　　**（B）脆的**　　（C）原始的　　（D）滑順的

6. 鎮民建造了一座紀念碑，以紀念這位勇敢的教師，她犧牲自己的生命從燃燒的公車上救出學生。
　　（A）紀念碑　　（B）難民　　（C）紀念品　　（D）鞭炮

7. 在史密斯教授的古典中國文學課上，學生需要背誦中國著名詩人的詩作。
　　（A）建造　　（B）暴露　　**（C）背誦**　　（D）安裝

8. 雖然湯先生聲稱那棟房子是他的，但他還沒有提供任何所有權證明。
　　（A）常規　　（B）關係　　（C）保險　　**（D）所有權**

9. 古代雅典作為民主體制的初期發展代表為人熟知，人們常說雅典是民主的搖籃。
　　（A）任務　　（B）目標　　**（C）搖籃**　　（D）里程碑

10. 由於發現含有遠超允許標準含量的人工成分，這種糖果不能再出售了。
　　（A）豐富的　　（B）巨大的　　**（C）准許的**　　（D）描寫的

11. 傑克在上週比賽的傑出表現，打消了人們對於他是否有足夠能力加入籃球校隊的懷疑。
　　（A）消除　　（B）取消　　（C）俯瞰　　（D）取代

12. 嘲笑外國人的口音是一種霸凌。沒有人應該因為說話的發音而遭人嘲笑。
　　（A）嘲笑　　（B）偷溜　　（C）促使　　（D）怒瞪

13. 瑪莉在三個月內瘦了十公斤，所以她以前緊身的牛仔褲現在已經從臀部垂下來了。
　　（A）幾乎不　　（B）均勻地　　（C）目前　　**（D）從前**

💡**補充詞彙** hang off 鬆脫

14. 警察拿酒駕事故的照片給我們看，以強調在路上保持清醒的重要性。
　　（A）清醒的　　（B）雄偉的　　（C）有活力的　　（D）明顯的

15. 吃巧克力可預防心臟病的說法備受爭議，因為沒有足夠的科學證據支持這一點。
　　（A）有創意的　　**（B）受爭議的**　　（C）圓形的　　（D）華美的

1. Tom is really a naughty boy. He likes to _____ and play jokes on his younger sister when their parents are not around.
   (A) alert　(B) spare　(C) tease　(D) oppose

2. Elderly shoppers in this store are advised to take the elevator rather than the _____, which may move too fast for them to keep their balance.
   (A) airway　(B) operator　(C) escalator　(D) instrument

3. Upon hearing its master's call, the dog wagged its tail, and followed her out of the room _____.
   (A) obediently　(B) apparently　(C) logically　(D) thoroughly

4. Since many of our house plants are from humid jungle environments, they need _____ air to keep them green and healthy.
   (A) moist　(B) stale　(C) crisp　(D) fertile

5. The skydiver managed to land safely after jumping out of the aircraft, even though her _____ failed to open in midair.
   (A) glimpse　(B) latitude　(C) segment　(D) parachute

6. The invention of the steam engine, which was used to power heavy machines, brought about a _____ change in society.
   (A) persuasive　(B) harmonious　(C) conventional　(D) revolutionary

7. To encourage classroom _____, the teacher divided the class into groups and asked them to solve a problem together with their partners.
   (A) operation　(B) interaction　(C) adjustment　(D) explanation

8. Lisa _____ onto the ground and injured her ankle while she was playing basketball yesterday.
   (A) buried　(B) punched　(C) scattered　(D) tumbled

9. Hundreds of residents received free testing _____ from the city government to find out if their water contained any harmful chemicals.
   (A) kits　(B) trials　(C) zones　(D) proofs

10. The 2011 Nobel Peace Prize was awarded _____ to three women for the efforts they made in fighting for women's rights.
    (A) actively　(B) earnestly　(C) jointly　(D) naturally

11. The company is _____ and making great profits under the wise leadership of the chief executive officer.

（A）applauding （B）flourishing （C）circulating （D）exceeding

12. It is absolutely _____ to waste your money on an expensive car when you cannot even get a driver's license.

（A）absurd （B）cautious （C）vigorous （D）obstinate

13. The problem of illegal drug use is very complex and cannot be traced to merely one _____ reason.

（A）singular （B）countable （C）favorable （D）defensive

14. The non-profit organization has _____ $1 million over five years to finance the construction of the medical center.

（A）equipped （B）resolved （C）committed （D）associated

15. One week after the typhoon, some bridges were finally opened and bus service _____ in the country's most severely damaged areas.

（A）departed （B）resumed （C）transported （D）corresponded

實力測驗第三回 答案&解析

解答 CCAAD DBDAC BAACB

1. 湯姆真是個頑皮的男孩。他喜歡在父母不在時捉弄妹妹、開妹妹的玩笑。

(A) 使…警覺 (B) 饒恕 (C) 捉弄 (D) 反對

2. 在這間店裡年長的顧客最好搭電梯，不要搭乘電扶梯，因為電扶梯移動速度太快，可能會讓他們無法保持平衡。

(A) 航空路線 (B) 操作者 (C) 電扶梯 (D) 樂器

3. 聽到主人的呼喚，狗就搖著尾巴乖乖跟著她走出了房間。

(A) 順從地 (B) 明顯地 (C) 邏輯地 (D) 徹底地

4. 因為我們許多室內植物都來自潮濕的叢林環境，所以需要濕潤的空氣來保持青翠健康。

(A) 潮濕的 (B) 陳舊的 (C) 脆的 (D) 肥沃的

5. 跳傘運動員跳出飛機之後，雖然降落傘在半空中沒有打開，但她仍設法安全
   著陸了。

   （A）一瞥　（B）緯度　（C）部分　**（D）跳傘**

6. 由於能用於驅動笨重的機器，蒸汽機的發明給社會帶來了革命性的改變。

   （A）有說服力的　（B）和諧的　（C）習慣的　**（D）革命性的**

   💡**補充詞彙** steam engine 蒸汽機

7. 為了鼓勵課堂互動，老師把全班學生分成幾個小組，讓他們和夥伴共同解決
   問題。

   （A）操作　**（B）互動**　（C）調整　（D）解釋

8. 麗莎昨天打籃球時不慎摔倒在地，傷到了腳踝。

   （A）埋　（B）用拳猛擊　（C）分散　**（D）跌倒**

9. 數百位居民收到了市政府免費提供的檢測套組，以檢測他們的水是否含有有
   害的化學物質。

   （A）成套工具　（B）試驗　（C）區域　（D）證據

10. 2011 年的諾貝爾獎共同授予了三位女性，以表彰她們為爭取女性權利所做
    的努力。

    （A）積極地　（B）認真地　**（C）共同地**　（D）自然地

11. 在執行長的英明領導下，公司生意蒸蒸日上，賺了很多錢。

    （A）鼓掌　**（B）繁榮**　（C）循環　（D）超過

12. 連駕照都拿不到的情況下，把錢浪費在昂貴的汽車上是絕對荒謬的行徑。

    （A）荒謬的　（B）謹慎的　（C）有活力的　（D）頑固的

13. 非法使用毒品的問題非常複雜，不能僅僅歸咎於單一原因。

    （A）單一的　（B）可數的　（C）有利的　（D）防禦性的

14. 這個非營利組織承諾在五年內出資一百萬美元建造醫療中心。

    （A）使裝備　（B）解決　**（C）承諾**　（D）聯想

15. 颱風過後一週，一些橋梁終於開放通行，國內受損最嚴重地區的公車也恢復
    行駛了。

    （A）出發　**（B）恢復**　（C）運輸　（D）符合

728

1. When Jeffery doesn't feel like cooking, he often orders pizza online and has it _____ to his house.
   (A) advanced　(B) delivered　(C) offered　(D) stretched

2. Jane is the best _____ I have ever had. I cannot imagine running my office without her help.
   (A) assistant　(B) influence　(C) contribution　(D) politician

3. The temple celebrated Mazu Festival by hosting ten days of lion dances, Taiwanese operas, and traditional hand _____ shows.
   (A) chat　(B) quiz　(C) puppet　(D) variety

4. The new vaccine was banned by the Food and Drug Administration due to its _____ fatal side effects.
   (A) potentially　(B) delicately　(C) ambiguously　(D) optionally

5. _____ the photos with dates and keywords help you sort them easily in your file.
   (A) Tagging　(B) Flocking　(C) Rolling　(D) Snapping

6. An _____ person is usually pleasant and easy to get along with, but don't expect that he or she will always say "yes" to everything.
   (A) enormous　(B) intimate　(C) agreeable　(D) ultimate

7. Hidden deep in a small alley among various tiny shops, the entrance of the Michelin star restaurant is barely _____ to passersby.
   (A) identical　(B) visible　(C) available　(D) remarkable

8. The original budget for my round-island trip was NT$5,000, but the _____ cost is likely to be 50 percent higher.
   (A) moderate　(B) absolute　(C) promising　(D) eventual

9. After watching a TV program on natural history, Adam decided to go on a _____ for dinosaur fossils in South Dakota.
   (A) trial　(B) route　(C) strike　(D) quest

10. With pink cherry blossoms blooming everywhere, the valley _____ like a young bride under the bright spring sunshine.

（A）bounces　（B）blushes　（C）polishes　（D）transfers

11. After the first snow of the year, the entire grassland disappeared under a _____ of snow.

（A）flake　（B）blossom　（C）blanket　（D）flash

12. Peter likes books with wide _____, which provide him with enough space to write notes.

（A）angles　（B）margins　（C）exceptions　（D）limitations

13. At the beginning of the semester, the teacher told the students that late assignments would receive a low grade as a _____.

（A）hardship　（B）comment　（C）bargain　（D）penalty

14. Various studies have been _____ in this hospital to explore the link between a high-fat diet and cancer.

（A）conducted　（B）confirmed　（C）implied　（D）improved

15. Intense, fast-moving fires raged across much of California last week. The _____ firestorm has claimed the lives of thirty people.

（A）efficient　（B）reliable　（C）massive　（D）adequate

實力測驗第四回 答案&解析

解答 BACAA　CBDDB　CBDAC

1. 傑弗里不想做飯的時候，經常會線上訂披薩外送到家裡。
   （A）進步　（B）運送　（C）提供　（D）伸展

2. 珍是我僱用過最棒的助理。如果沒有她的幫助，我無法想像要怎麼經營公司。
   （A）助理　（B）影響　（C）貢獻　（D）政治家

3. 寺廟舉辦為期十天的舞獅、歌仔戲與傳統布袋戲來慶祝媽祖慶典。
   （A）聊天　（B）小考　（C）木偶　（D）變化

4. 新型疫苗因其潛在的致命副作用而遭食品藥物管理局禁止使用。
   （A）潛在地　（B）精緻地　（C）含糊地　（D）可選地
   補充詞彙 side effect 副作用

5. 給照片加上日期和關鍵字標籤，有助於輕鬆地在文件中對照片進行分類。

   （A）給…貼上標籤　　（B）聚集　　（C）捲動　　（D）咬

6. 隨和的人很好相處，往往讓人感到舒適，但不要期待他們對任何事情都說「好」。

   （A）巨大的　　（B）親密的　　**（C）隨和的**　　（D）最終的

7. 充斥著許多小店的巷口深處，藏著一家米其林星級餐廳的入口，路人幾乎都看不到。

   （A）相同的　　**（B）可見的**　　（C）可用的　　（D）卓越的

8. 我環島旅行原先的預算為五千元，但最終花費可能要高出百分之五十。

   （A）適度的　　（B）絕對的　　（C）有希望的　　**（D）最終的**

9. 看完自然歷史的電視節目後，亞當決定去南達科他州尋找恐龍化石。

   （A）試驗　　（B）路線　　（C）打擊　　**（D）探索**

10. 粉紅櫻花遍地盛開，山谷在明媚的春光下宛如剛出嫁的新娘一般綻放著紅暈。

    （A）彈跳　　**（B）臉紅**　　（C）擦亮　　（D）轉移

11. 今年的初雪後，整片草原消失在茫茫白雪之中。

    （A）薄片　　（B）花朵　　**（C）毯子**　　（D）閃光

12. 彼得喜歡頁面邊緣較寬的書，這樣他就有足夠的空間寫筆記。

    （A）角度　　**（B）邊緣**　　（C）例外　　（D）限制

13. 在學期初，老師告訴學生遲交作業會得到低分作為懲罰。

    （A）艱難　　（B）評論　　（C）講價　　**（D）處罰**

    💡**補充詞彙** at the beginning of sth 在…的初期

14. 這間醫院進行了多項研究，探討高脂肪飲食和癌症之間的關係。

    （A）進行　　（B）證實　　（C）暗示　　（D）改善

15. 上週猛烈又快速擴散的大火肆虐加州大部分地區。這場大火奪走了三十人的生命。

    （A）效率高的　　（B）可信賴的　　**（C）大規模的**　　（D）足夠的

    💡**補充詞彙** intense 強烈的 / claim one's life 奪去…的生命

1. The bus driver often complains about chewing gum found under passenger seats because it is _____ and very hard to remove.
   (A) sticky　(B) greasy　(C) clumsy　(D) mighty

2. Jesse is a talented model. He can easily adopt an elegant _____ for a camera shoot.
   (A) clap　(B) toss　(C) pose　(D) snap

3. In order to draw her family tree, Mary tried to trace her _____ back to their arrival in North America.
   (A) siblings　(B) commuters　(C) ancestors　(D) instructors

4. Upon the super typhoon warning, Nancy rushed to the supermarket—only to find the shelves almost _____ and the stock nearly gone.
   (A) blank　(B) bare　(C) hollow　(D) queer

5. Even though Jack said "Sorry!" to me in person, I did not feel any _____ in his apology.
   (A) liability　(B) generosity　(C) integrity　(D) sincerity

6. My grandfather has astonishing powers of _____. He can still vividly describe his first day at school as a child.
   (A) resolve　(B) fraction　(C) privilege　(D) recall

7. Recent research has found lots of evidence to _____ the drug company's claims about its "miracle" tablets for curing cancer.
   (A) provoke　(B) counter　(C) expose　(D) convert

8. Corrupt officials and misguided policies have _____ the country's economy and burdened its people with enormous foreign debts.
   (A) crippled　(B) accelerated　(C) rendered　(D) ventured

9. As a record number of fans showed up for the baseball final, the highways around the stadium were _____ with traffic all day.
   (A) choked　(B) disturbed　(C) enclosed　(D) injected

10. Studies show that the _____ unbiased media are in fact often deeply influenced by political ideology.

（A）undoubtedly （B）roughly （C）understandably （D）supposedly

11. Mangoes are a _____ fruit here in Taiwan; most of them reach their peak of sweetness in July.

（A）mature （B）usual （C）seasonal （D）particular

12. Writing term papers and giving oral reports are typical course _____ for college students.

（A）requirements （B）techniques （C）situations （D）principles

13. If we work hard to _____ our dreams when we are young, we will not feel that we missed out on something when we get old.

（A）distribute （B）fulfill （C）convince （D）monitor

14. Few people will trust you if you continue making _____ promises and never make efforts to keep them.

（A）chilly （B）liberal （C）hollow （D）definite

15. Becky _____ her ankle while she was playing tennis last week. Now it still hurts badly.

（A）slipped （B）dumped （C）twisted （D）recovered

實力測驗第五回 答案＆解析

解答 ACCBD DBAAD CABCC

1. 公車司機經常抱怨在乘客座位底下發現口香糖，因為口香糖很黏，很難清除。
   （A）黏的 （B）油膩的 （C）笨拙的 （D）強大的

2. 傑斯是個很有才華的模特兒，可以輕鬆擺出優雅的姿勢進行拍攝。
   （A）拍手 （B）拋擲 （C）擺姿勢 （D）咬

3. 為了畫出族譜，瑪莉試圖追溯她的祖先到達北美洲的歷史。
   （A）手足 （B）通勤者 （C）祖先 （D）指導者

4. 收到超強颱風警報後，南西急忙趕去超市，卻發現貨架上空空如也，存貨幾乎都沒了。
   （A）空白的 （B）空的 （C）空心的 （D）古怪的

5. 儘管傑克當面對我說了：「對不起！」但在他的道歉裡，我感受不到任何誠意。
   (A)責任　　(B)慷慨　　(C)正直　　**(D)真誠**

6. 我祖父有著驚人的記憶力，他至今仍能生動地描述自己小時候第一天上學的情景。
   (A)決心　　(B)分數　　(C)特權　　**(D)記憶力**

7. 關於那間製藥公司聲稱其「奇蹟」藥片可以治療癌症，最近的研究發現了許多證據能反駁這個說法。
   (A)挑釁　　**(B)反駁**　　(C)揭露　　(D)轉換

8. 貪官汙吏和錯誤政策嚴重損害了國家的經濟，使人民背負巨額外債。
   (A)嚴重損害　　(B)加速　　(C)提供　　(D)冒險

   💡**補充詞彙** misguided 受錯誤指導的

9. 由於前來觀看棒球決賽的球迷人數多到破紀錄，體育場周圍的高速公路整天都交通堵塞。
   (A)堵塞　　(B)干擾　　(C)封閉　　(D)注射

10. 研究顯示，本應公正的媒體實際上往往深受政治意識型態的影響。
    (A)無疑地　　(B)大致地　　(C)合乎情理地　　**(D)應該**

11. 在台灣，芒果是一種季節性的水果，大多數芒果在七月是最甜的。
    (A)成熟的　　(B)通常的　　**(C)季節的**　　(D)特別的

12. 寫學期論文和口頭報告對大學生而言是典型的課程要求。
    (A)要求　　(B)技巧　　(C)情形　　(D)原則

13. 如果我們年輕時努力工作、實現夢想，到老了就不會覺得自己錯過了什麼。
    (A)分配　　**(B)實現**　　(C)說服　　(D)監視

    💡**補充詞彙** miss out 錯失機會

14. 如果你繼續做出空洞的承諾，卻從不努力兌現，那麼很少有人會相信你。
    (A)寒冷的　　(B)自由的　　**(C)空洞的**　　(D)明確的

    💡**補充詞彙** make efforts to 努力做… / keep a promise 信守諾言

15. 貝琪上週打網球時扭傷了腳踝，現在都還很痛。
    (A)滑　　(B)傾倒　　**(C)扭**　　(D)恢復

國家圖書館出版品預行編目資料

五感學+練！7000英單過腦不忘強記術 / 張翔 著. --
初版. -- 新北市：知識工場出版 采舍國際有限公司發
行, 2024.07 面；公分. --（試在必得；05）
ISBN 978-986-271-966-4（平裝）

1.CST: 英語　　2.CST: 詞彙

805.12　　　　　　　　　　　　112003131

知識工場 · 試在必得 05

五感學＋練！
7000英單過腦不忘強記術

出 版 者／全球華文聯合出版平台‧知識工場
作　　者／張翔
出版總監／王寶玲
總 編 輯／歐綾纖

印 行 者／知識工場
英文編輯／張季元
美術編輯／May

台灣出版中心／新北市中和區中山路2段366巷10號10樓
電話／（02）2248-7896
傳真／（02）2248-7758
ISBN-13／978-986-271-966-4
出版日期／2024年7月初版

全球華文市場總代理／采舍國際
地址／新北市中和區中山路2段366巷10號3樓
電話／（02）8245-8786
傳真／（02）8245-8718

港澳地區總經銷／和平圖書
地址／香港柴灣嘉業街12號百樂門大廈17樓
電話／（852）2804-6687
傳真／（852）2804-6409

全系列書系特約展示
新絲路網路書店
地址／新北市中和區中山路2段366巷10號10樓
電話／（02）8245-9896
傳真／（02）8245-8819
網址／www.silkbook.com